Barbara Taylor Bradford was born in Leeds, and by the age of twenty was an editor and columnist on Fleet Street. Her first novel, *A Woman of Substance*, became an enduring bestseller and was followed by sixteen others, most recently, *The Triumph of Katie Byrne*. Her novels have sold more than sixty-one million copies worldwide in more than eighty-nine countries and thirty-nine languages. She lives in New York City with her husband, producer Robert Bradford.

BARBARA TAYLOR BRADFORD

Power of a Woman

*A Sudden Change
of Heart*

HarperCollins*Publishers*

This omnibus edition published in 2001 by
HarperCollins*Publishers*

HarperCollins*Publishers*
77-85 Fulham Palace Road,
Hammersmith, London W6 8JB

www.fireandwater.com

ISBN 0 00 764579 1

Printed and bound in Great Britain by
Mackays of Chatham plc, Chatham, Kent

Power of a Woman

As always for Bob,
who makes my world go round,
with all my love

CONTENTS

PART ONE

Thanksgiving

1

A FINE MIST FLOATED LIKE PALE WATER OVER THE MEADOWS, DRIFT-ing, eddying, blurring the trees, turning them into illusory shapes that loomed against the somber sky.

Beyond these meadows, the distant Litchfield hills were pur-plish in the dimming light, their bases obscured by the rising mist so that only their peaks were visible now.

And all about this wintry landscape lay an unremitting silence, as if the world had stopped; everything was washed in a vast unconsciousness. The stillness was all-pervasive; nothing moved or stirred.

In the summertime these low meadows were verdant and lush with billowing grass, and every kind of wildflower grew among the grasses. But on this cold Wednesday afternoon in November they appeared bleak and uninviting.

Stevie Jardine normally did not mind this kind of misty weather, for inevitably it brought the past back to her, and happily so, reminding her as it did of the Yorkshire moors and the lovely old farmhouse she owned. Yet now the vaporous air was chilling her through and through; it seemed to permeate her bones.

Unexpectedly, she experienced a rush of apprehension, and this startled her. Pulling her woolen cape closer to her body, she hurried faster, trying to shake off the strange feeling of foreboding that had just enveloped her. Involuntarily, Stevie shivered. Somebody walked over my grave, she thought, and she shivered again. She looked up.

The sky was remote and cold, turning color, curdling to a peculiar faded green. A bitter sky, eerie; she increased her pace, running, eager now to get home. She no longer liked it outside, regretted her decision to take a long walk. The fog had closed in, but earlier the weather had been beautiful, almost an Indian summer's afternoon, until the dankness had scuttled the day.

Her feet knew well the path across the fields, and her step was sure, did not falter as it suddenly dipped, curved down into the dell. The fog was dense on this lower ground. Shivering once more, she drew herself farther into her cape.

Soon the narrow path was rising upward as the landscape changed, became hilly; the mist was evaporating up there, where the land was higher. When she reached the crest of the hill the air grew colder, but it was much clearer.

From this vantage point Stevie could make out her house nestling cozily in the valley below, and she felt a surge of relief. Smoke curled up from its chimneys, lights glimmered brightly in the windows. It was a welcoming sight, warm and inviting in the dusk.

She was glad she was home.

The house was two hundred years old, built in 1796, and stood in a long, green valley under the shadow of Connecticut's Litchfield hills. It had been something of an eyesore when she had first seen it five years before, an unsightly hodgepodge of additions that had been built onto it over the decades. After some skillful remodeling and restoration, its former graciousness and charm were recaptured.

Stevie moved rapidly across the wet lawn and up the steps onto the covered porch, entering the house through the side door, which led directly into the cloakroom.

Once she had hung up her damp cape she went into the great hall. This was vast, with a wide staircase at one end and a dark wood floor so highly polished it gleamed like glass. A beamed ceiling, heavy oak doors, and mullioned windows bespoke the age of the house.

Stevie always thought of the great hall as the core of the house, since all the other rooms flowed around it. From the moment she moved in, the hall had been used as a family living room, where everyone congregated. Several pink-silk–shaded lamps had been turned on, and they glowed rosily, adding to the inviting atmosphere. It was a comfortable, welcoming room, with an old, faded Savonnerie rug in front of the fireplace, antique Jacobean tables and chests made of dark carved wood. Big sofas, covered in a fir-green tapestry, were grouped with several chairs around the fire.

Stevie's face instantly brightened as she crossed the hall. It was cheerful, safe, reassuring. A log fire roared in the big stone hearth and the air was redolent with the spicy scent of pine, a hint of wood smoke and ripe apples. From the kitchen there floated the fragrant aroma of bread baking.

Coming to a standstill at the fireplace, Stevie stood with her hands outstretched to the flames, warming them. Unexpectedly, laughter bubbled in her throat and she began to laugh out loud. At herself. How foolish she had been a short while ago when she was crossing the meadows. There was no reason for her to feel apprehensive. Her sense of foreboding had been irrational. She laughed again, chastising herself for her uneasiness earlier.

After a few seconds she turned away from the fireplace and crossed to the staircase, heading upstairs. She loved every corner of this lovely old house, in particular the small study that opened off her bedroom. As she pushed open the door and walked in, she could not help admiring the room. It was beautifully proportioned, with a cathedral ceiling, tall windows at one end, and a grand fireplace flanked on either side by soaring bookshelves.

Stevie had had the study decoratively painted by an artist, who had layered innumerable coats of amber-colored paint on the walls, then given them a glazed finish. This Venetian stucco treatment created a soft golden sheen, as if sunshine had been perpetually trapped within the confines of the room.

Lovely paintings, selectively chosen over the years, family photographs in silver frames, a variety of treasured mementos, and well-loved books were the things that made this room hers, and very special to her.

The fire was laid and she went and knelt in front of it. Striking a match, she brought the flame to the paper and within seconds a roaring fire was blazing up the chimney.

Rising, she walked across the floor and seated herself at the oval-shaped Georgian desk in the window area. Papers from her briefcase were neatly stacked on it, but after a quick, cursory glance at these she turned away from them, sat back in the chair. Her mind was suddenly far, far away.

She found herself gazing at various objects on her desk, an absentminded expression etched on her delicate face . . . the Art Nouveau lamp she had picked up for next to nothing in the flea market in Paris, a Georgian silver inkwell her mother had given her years before, a plethora of photographs of those she loved, her grandmother's Meissen cream jug in the Red Dragon pattern filled with small pencils, and a copy of an ancient Hindu saying displayed in a mother-of-pearl frame.

Staring intently at this, she read it again, perhaps for the thousandth time in her life: "He who buys a diamond purchases a bit of eternity."

This old saying had been written out by Ralph in handwriting so beautiful it was like calligraphy, and he had given it to her not long after they were married. As he would so often tell her, the saying summed up what he felt about diamonds. They were his business, he loved them; and it was from him that she had learned so much about them herself.

Stevie's light gray-green eyes strayed to the photograph of Ralph and her, taken on their wedding day in November 1966. Thirty years ago to this very day. Ever since early this morning, Ralph had been in and out of her thoughts, and once again she fell down into herself, for a moment contemplating him and their early years together.

He had been such a good man, the best person she had ever known, so very loving, adoring even, and devoted to her from the first moment they met. And certainly he had taken a strong stand against his parents when they had fiercely objected, and vociferously so, to the idea of their marrying.

Bruce and Alfreda Jardine had disapproved of her right from the start, because, they said, she was far too young. And also an American, not to mention a girl with no background or fortune, although her nationality and the word *money* had never crossed their lips.

Stevie had always somehow known deep within herself, had actually *understood* without ever being told, that had she been born an heiress with a great fortune to bring to the marriage, her age and her nationality would have been of little or no importance to the Jardines.

To her, Ralph's parents were as transparent as glass. They were snobs who had long harbored grand ideas for their son, formulated grand plans for him, at least where matrimony was concerned. But Ralph was not having any of that. Always his own man, he had been unshakable in his determination to make her his wife. He had openly defied them, and in so doing had ruined their elaborate schemes, thwarted their ambitions for him.

From a very long distance she heard a faint echo reverberating in her head. It was Bruce Jardine's aristocratic English voice raised harshly in a shout of rage, as he uttered the most ugly words she had ever heard, words she had never forgotten.

"For God's sake, man, you're twenty-seven! Surely by now you know enough about sex to take care of matters properly! Why didn't you have your way with her without getting her pregnant? You'd better make arrangements for her to get rid of it. Talk to Harry Axworth. He's a bit of a bounder, I'm the first to acknowledge, certainly not someone I would normally wish you to associate with. However, because of his nefarious indiscretions, he's the best chap for this purpose. He'll be able to point you in the right direction. He's bound to know a doctor down on his luck who'll no doubt do the job for fifty pounds."

She had been waiting for Ralph in the grandiose front entrance hall, sitting on the edge of a chair, a nervous wreck, her hands trembling, her heart in her mouth as Bruce Jardine's voice had echoed through the closed mahogany door.

Ralph had chosen not to dignify his father's words with a response. He had walked out of the library and straight into her arms. After holding her close for a moment, calming her, he had then led her out into the street and away from the Jardine mansion in Wilton Crescent. His face had been white with fury, and he had not said a word to her until they were safely inside his bachelor flat in Mayfair. Once there, he had told her how much he loved her, and that he wanted to spend the rest of his life with her.

They were married two weeks later in the register office in Marylebone. She had been sixteen years old, younger than Ralph by eleven years, and four months pregnant by then.

The elder Jardines, always contentious, had shown their disdain and anger by boycotting the marriage of their only son. So had Alicia, Ralph's sister.

But her mother had been present, her beautiful mother, Blair Connors, once the most famous model in the world, a supermodel before the term had even been invented.

Accompanying her mother that morning had been *her* new husband, Derek Rayner, the great English stage actor who everyone said was the heir apparent to Larry Olivier's crown.

After the wedding ceremony, Derek had taken them all to lunch at The Ivy, London's famous theatrical restaurant, which the elite of stage, film, and cafe society favored. And then they had gone to Paris for their honeymoon.

Ostracized by Ralph's parents, Stevie and Ralph had lived for each other, and the world had been well lost to them.

A wistful sigh escaped her. For a long time now she had recognized that the weekends and holidays she had spent on the Yorkshire moors had been the most happy of times for her, perhaps the happiest in her entire life. It saddened her that they could never be recaptured, that this particular kind of happiness would never be hers again.

So young, she thought, I was so young then. But already the mother of three: Nigel, born when I was just seventeen, and the twins, Gideon and Miles, when I was nineteen.

A smile animated her face as images of her children leapt into her mind unbidden. Three tow-headed little boys, each with eyes as blue as speedwells. Grown men now. And she was still young herself, only forty-six, but a grandmother for the past two years, thanks to Nigel.

Stevie laughed inwardly. How often she was mistaken for her sons' sister, much to Nigel's chagrin. He did not like it; the twins, on the other hand, gleefully encouraged this deception whenever they could. They were incorrigible, loved to pass her off as their sibling to those who were unsuspecting of the truth, and they were usually successful at their mischievous little game.

Gideon and Miles were proud of her youthful looks, slender figure, energy, and vitality. Nigel felt just the opposite. It seemed to her that everything about her was an irritant to him. A small frown furrowed her smooth brow as Nigel's presence nudged itself into her mind. Swiftly, she pushed aside the flicker of dismay that flew to the surface.

She loved her eldest son, but she had always known he had a lot of his grandfather in him. And Bruce Jardine had never been one of her favorites, although as the years had passed, he had behaved decently toward her. Most especially after Alfreda's death. But as long as her mother-in-law had been alive, that awful contention had persisted, at least as far as Alfreda was concerned.

A small sigh escaped her and she turned her head, looked toward the fire, her mind sliding back in time as she remembered Alfreda and Bruce as they were then . . .

Four years after she and Ralph had been married, his sister, Alicia, had died of leukemia. The elder Jardines had been forced to reconsider the situation and effect a compromise, in order to come to terms with them. Ralph and she were the parents of their only grandchildren, their heirs, three boys who one day would follow in their grandfather's and father's footsteps, running Jardine and Company of London, the Crown Jewellers.

Eventually she and Ralph had succumbed to his parents' conciliatory overtures, albeit somewhat reluctantly, and certainly with a great deal of trepidation. They had accepted the proffered olive branch. As it turned out, they were forever fighting off interference from the senior Jardines, who tried, without success, to take over the rearing of the boys.

Their great escape had been the trips to Yorkshire to stay at Aysgarth End, the farmhouse on the moors above the Dales, where they had fled with the children whenever they had been able to get away. Large, rambling, in constant need of repairs, it was, nevertheless, their blessed haven, a little bit of heaven on earth, the place they really called home.

They liked their apartment in Kensington; it was spacious and comfortable, ideal for rearing a growing young family. For some reason Aysgarth End meant so much more to them emotionally. Stevie had never really been able to fathom what it was *exactly* that made the farm so special, except that it was full of love and laughter. And a special kind of joy.

She still believed, as she had all those years ago, that this joy sprang from Ralph's natural goodness, his genuine spirituality. He was truly a pure man, the only one she had ever known, filled with kindness and compassion, and he had had such an understanding heart.

That absolute joy in each other and their children had flourished at Aysgarth End until the day Ralph had died. He had been only thirty-four. Too young, by far.

She had become a widow at twenty-three.

And it was then that her troubles had begun.

Of course it was her parents-in-law who were the troublemakers. Endeavoring to brush her aside, ignoring her terrible grief and the enormous sense of loss she was experiencing, they had tried to wrest the children away from her. Foolishly so. They did not have a leg to stand on. She was the perfect mother, exemplary, without blemish, and untouched by any kind of scandal or wrongdoing.

Ralph's best friend, James Allerton, had also been his solicitor, and with Ralph's death he had become Stevie's legal representative. It was to James that she had turned when her in-laws had started to make their moves.

At a meeting with the Jardines, James had almost, but not quite, laughed in their faces, and had told them to go to hell, in more polite terms, of course. Not only was the law of the land on her side, there was the matter of Ralph's will. In it he had made his feelings for her abundantly clear. He had reiterated his love and admiration of her, not to mention his confidence in her ability to rear their sons. He had left her everything he owned, and in so doing had ensured her financial security. He had also made her entirely independent of his parents.

The trusts he had inherited from his grandparents he had passed on to his three sons; he had named his wife as the administrator of the trusts and executrix of his will.

As James so succinctly pointed out to the Jardines, Stevie was holding all the cards and she had a winning hand. They slunk away, defeated; for once they had been outmaneuvered.

It was her resentment of the Jardines, and her anger at them, that had served her so well in 1973. Especially the anger. She had turned it around, made it work to her advantage; it had also fueled her determination to keep her sons close at all times.

Although she did not know it at that moment, the anger had kindled her ambition as well, and eventually it would spur her on to do things she had never dreamed possible. At the back of her mind a plan was developing, a plan that would make her indispensable to Bruce Jardine, and ensure her control of her children until they were old enough to fend for themselves. That year, beset as she was with problems and crushed by grief, the plan did not come to flower. But the seed had been sown.

Stevie was a pragmatist at heart. She never forgot that one day her sons would inherit the family business, and that they must be properly educated and prepared for this. Founded in 1787 by one Alistair Jardine, a Scottish silversmith who had made his way to London and opened a shop there, Jardine's had always been run by a Jardine.

And so in 1974, as she began to recover from Ralph's death and regain her equilibrium, she had contacted his parents. Her main purpose was to affect a rapprochement, which she eventually was able to do with the help of James Allerton; but it was an uneasy truce at best. Alfreda seemed determined to upset her, or cause trouble, and whenever her mother-in-law could make her life difficult, she did.

Nonetheless, Stevie realized that her sons must come to know their grandparents, most especially their grandfather, who was the key to their future. It would be Bruce who would train them, lead them through the labyrinths of the family business, so that when he retired they could take over.

Jardine's had been the Crown Jewellers since Queen Victoria's day. It was important that her sons understood their inheritance, the great jewelry company that would be theirs one day, and the family dynasty into which they had been born.

The ringing of the telephone made her start, and, as she reached for it, Stevie was pulled back into the present.

"Hello?"

"I'd like to speak to Mrs. Jardine, please."

"This is she."

"Hello, Stevie, it's Matt Wilson."

Taken by surprise, she exclaimed, "Hello, Matt! And where are you calling from?" She glanced at her watch; it was five-thirty. "Not Paris, surely? It's very late at night there."

He laughed, and said, "No, I'm in Los Angeles. With *Monsieur*. We arrived yesterday to see a client. He would like to speak with you. I'll put him on."

"Thank you, Matt."

A moment later André Birron was at the other end of the wire. "Stephanie, my Stephanie, *comment vas-tu?*"

"I'm wonderful, André," Stevie said, smiling with pleasure on hearing his voice. At seventy-five, André Birron was considered to be one of the greatest jewelers, perhaps even *the* greatest jeweler, in the world. Known as the *grand seigneur* of the jewelry business, he had been her lifelong friend. He had always been there for her whenever she had needed him.

"It is a pleasure to hear your voice, Stephanie," he went on, "and it will be an even greater pleasure to see you. I am coming to New York in about ten days. For the Sotheby's auction. You plan to be there, I am certain of that."

"I do. And I hope you'll have time for dinner, André. Or lunch."

"Whichever, or both, *ma chérie.*" There was a small pause before the Frenchman asked, "You are going to bid on the White Empress, are you not?"

"Yes."

"I thought you would. You have always wanted to own it." He chuckled. "You have dreamed about it, Stephanie."

"Salivated, actually," she responded, laughing with him. "And how well you know me, André. But listen, who wouldn't want to own it? I consider the White Empress to be one of the most beautiful diamonds in the world."

"You are correct; however, *I* shall not bid on it, Stephanie. Out of deference to you, really. If I bid, I would only escalate the price exorbitantly, and there will be enough people doing that. And, of course, I do not have the love for this diamond that you do, although I can admire its beauty. Yes, it is a diamond you and only you should own."

"Thank you for letting me know you're not going to participate. I expect the bidding to go sky high. Don't you agree?"

"Yes, I do. The stone has not been on the market since the fifties, and so obviously there is a great deal of interest in it. That is the reason I telephoned you, Stephanie, *ma petite*, to inform you we shall not be bidding against each other, competing. But it will be my great honor to escort you to the auction, if you will permit me to do so."

"I'd love it, André, thank you."

"And after the auction we shall dine together, and it will be a grand celebration."

She laughed a soft, light laugh. "We'll be celebrating only if I get the White Empress, my dear old friend."

"There is no doubt in my mind that you will, Stephanie."

2

ALTHOUGH SHE KNEW EVERYTHING THERE WAS TO KNOW ABOUT HER favorite diamond, Stevie could not resist taking the Sotheby's catalogue out of her briefcase after she had said good-bye to André Birron and hung up.

Flipping open the catalogue, she quickly found the page where the White Empress was featured, and gazed for a moment or two at the photograph of the gem. The picture was excellent, but even so it did not do justice to the magnificent stone.

The White Empress. Stevie repeated the name to herself. It certainly deserved to be called that. It was so named because it was graded D-flawless and was therefore perfect. And as such it was colorless—pure white, brilliantly, blindingly white—hence the first portion of its name. Because it was extremely rare and very beautiful, and also categorized as a *grand* stone, the title of Empress had been chosen to complete its name.

Automatically, Stevie's eyes shifted to the left-hand page of the catalogue, and she scanned the text. Yet again she was reminded that the White Empress had started out as a 427-carat diamond of exceptionally fine color, and that it had been found in 1954 at the Premier Mines in South Africa.

This piece of rough was subsequently sold in 1956 to Harry Winston, the renowned American jeweler, as part of an eight-million-four-hundred-thousand-dollar parcel.

The largest stone Winston cut from this piece was a 128.25-carat D-flawless pear-shaped diamond, and it was this stone that retained the original name of White Empress. Harry Winston had the stone set as a pendant on an exquisite diamond necklace, designed specially, and then he had sold it that same year to a European industrialist.

Now, after forty years in the hands of one family, it was finally back on the market. Sotheby's would put it on the auction block at their auction rooms on York Avenue in New York at the beginning of December.

Stevie's eyes lingered on the photograph for a short while longer before she finally closed the catalogue and returned it to her briefcase. Her thoughts settled on André. Though he was not bidding on the stone, there were many others who *would* be bidding, and automatically the price would be driven up, as it usually was at these big auctions for important items.

It could skyrocket, she thought, sitting back in the chair, frowning. No, it *would* skyrocket. There was no doubt in her mind about that; she made the decision to stay in the bidding no matter what, since she was determined to acquire the stone whatever it cost.

Seven-figure numbers jumped around in her head. Six million dollars, seven million dollars . . . no, too low. Eight million, she speculated, her eyes narrowed in concentration. Still too low, she decided. Suddenly she was convinced the stone would be sold in the eight-figure category. Ten million, she said under her breath. Could it go as high as that?

At this moment Stevie knew that if she had to, she would pay that amount for the stone. She craved it, not for herself, of course, but for Jardine's in New York, which she had founded.

Once she owned the stone, she would hold on to it for a year or two, displaying it at exhibitions, making it the centerpiece of the store's permanent collection. She had no intention of cleaving it—cutting it—into several stones, or disposing of it immediately. It was quite obvious to her that the White Empress was a great investment, and in a variety of ways, not the least of which was the publicity the diamond would engender for Jardine's.

Certainly it would never decrease in value; it could only increase, in fact; and she knew she would have no problem selling it whenever she wished to do so. There were many rich men and women in the world who coveted the grand stones, some of whom were already her clients, and there would always be buyers for this most spectacular of diamonds. After all, in the business it was now considered to be a *historic* stone.

Owning the White Empress would be the crowning glory of Jardine's. This thought pleased her. She had started the American company eight years earlier, and although she had done so with Bruce Jardine's consent, his accord had been grudgingly given. Even today he barely acknowledged its existence.

The store on Fifth Avenue was an enormous success and had been from the very first day it opened. And so Stevie always felt justified in pushing for it, vindicated, in a sense, because the annual earnings were enormous, the profits burgeoning on a yearly basis.

When she had told her father-in-law that she wanted to take Jardine's, the Crown Jewellers of London, to New York's Fifth Avenue, he had blanched, gaping at her in astonishment. Naturally, he had balked at the idea. Right from the beginning he had predicted nothing but failure. She had had to use a great deal of charm and persuasiveness to get him finally to agree.

Stevie had realized immediately that he fought the idea of her moving to New York because he wanted to keep her by his side at the London store. Later, he had admitted that this was indeed the case. Put simply, he could no longer do without her. As he grew older, he was becoming more and more dependent on her at work.

When he had stopped ranting at her and calmed down, Stevie had pointed out that he had a grandson who was almost twenty-two, and very capable of taking her place at his side. A young man who couldn't wait to step into her shoes, in point of fact.

"Under your supervision, Nigel will do a fine job," she had reassured her father-in-law. Bruce knew as well as she that this was the truth, but he would not admit it, and once more he scotched the idea of opening a store in New York. Stevie had bided her time, worked on him in a gentle but persistent manner, and never lost a chance to point out to him how profitable the American branch could be.

"But I'll miss you, Stephanie," Bruce had murmured one afternoon, weeks after she had first presented her plans for Jardine's of New York. Those few muttered words had told her that however reluctant he was to do it, he was, nonetheless, going to give her his support. This he did, although he never ceased to remind her that it was against his better judgment.

That had happened in 1987; one year later, in 1988, the Fifth Avenue store had opened its doors. And for the first time in more than twenty years she had found herself living in the city where she had been born. She had moved to London at the age of fourteen, after her mother had married Derek Rayner. Even though she had visited New York, it was a foreign city to her. Within the short space of a few weeks, Manhattan was under her skin, and she felt comfortable, at home.

Stevie rose and walked over to the hearth, where she threw another log onto the fire, and then sat in a chair, leaned back, and closed her eyes. It seemed to her that her mind was full of the past today, perhaps because it was November the twenty-seventh. A very special date in her memory. Her wedding day. If Ralph Jardine had lived, this would have been their thirtieth anniversary.

She had never remarried. Some of her friends thought this was odd, but she didn't, no, not at all. It was really very simple. She had never met anyone she cared about enough to marry. No, that was not strictly true, she corrected herself. After Ralph's death she *had* loved another man once, for a brief time, long ago. Marriage had never come into play, at least not from his standpoint, but it had from hers. She knew she would have married him in a flash if he had asked her. He never had. It wasn't meant to be, she told herself, as she had done over and over again for years. Some things just weren't meant to happen; and, anyway, you couldn't have everything in life.

But we believe we can when we're young, she suddenly thought. When we're young we're so certain of our invincibility, our immortality. We're full of *ourselves*, blown up with ourselves, our power, our strength. We're just so *sure* of it all, so *sure* we can mold life to our will, make it bend whichever way we want. But we can't, that's not the way it is. Life gets at us all in one way or another. It mangles us, brings us down, causes us so much pain. It's the great leveler, the ultimate equalizer.

Still, my life's not been so bad, she reminded herself, looking at the positives, as she always did. Her children had turned out relatively well; at least, none of them was drug addicted or soaked in alcohol. And she had built herself a career out of nothing. After all, she had not been gifted with some sort of creative talent to use as a springboard into success. All she had was a practical nature, a steady, levelheaded temperament, and a good head for figures and business, as it had turned out.

She had once said this to André. "But you also know the diamonds, *chérie*. Ralph taught you almost everything he knew about the stones," the French jeweler had exclaimed, looking at her in surprise. Vaguely, she heard André's voice coming to her from a long distance, from the past. "You have a good idea, Stephanie. Go to Bruce. You will see; he will listen to you. The argument you have is a strong one. *Valid.* Indeed, it is a necessity."

Her thoughts leapt backward in time, back to the year 1976, and in her mind's eye she could see Bruce Jardine as he had been then. Tall, dark, good-looking in a saturnine way. But as stubborn and rigid as always. An unbending man.

How well she remembered his scornful expression, his mirthless laugh when she had told him she wanted to work. And at Jardine's, at that.

Before he could answer her, she added in a quiet voice that she wanted him to train her to run the company.

He had stared at her speechlessly, disbelievingly, all those years ago, and then he had asked her if she had taken leave of her senses.

Twenty years ago. Yet sometimes it seemed like only yesterday. She had been a young widow of twenty-six that summer; it was exactly three years after Ralph's bungled operation for an appendicitis. Her rage about this shocking tragedy had dissipated with the passing of time, and yet, when she least expected it, she would feel a spurt of anger and dismay about her husband's unnecessary death.

As it turned out, Ralph had not had appendicitis at all, but a perforated peptic ulcer. The surgeon had not recognized the trouble on the operating table. He had performed the appendectomy, but had not made a second incision to reach and repair the perforation. Peritonitis had advanced to cause the sepsis that had killed Ralph. Everyone knew it was a death that should never have happened.

With his son Ralph gone so unexpectedly, Bruce was now the only Jardine in the family business. His older brother, Malcolm, had retired several years earlier because of ill health, and Bruce was suddenly carrying the burden of Jardine's entirely alone.

And then, without any warning, he was struck down with a heart attack in February 1976; when he finally recovered, he was debilitated, and panicked.

Stevie had instantly recognized the latter, and had understood the reason for his nervousness. Young though she was at the time, she had a great deal of insight into people, knew what made them tick, what motivated them to do the things they did. In a sudden flash, and with genuine clarity of vision, she realized what she must do, what the solution to Bruce's problem was.

She was the solution.

And so she had taken André's advice and gone to see her father-in-law on a warm Thursday afternoon in July, arriving at his office in the Bond Street store unannounced. He had been startled and put out by her unprecedented visit, but being a gentleman of the old school, and courteous, he had invited her into his inner sanctum.

"Teach me the business, train me," she had said earnestly. "I'm the only Jardine you have right now. Nigel and the twins are still little boys. What will happen to the company if you have another heart attack? Or get sick? Or die?"

Startled by the bluntness of her words, he had looked affronted. And he had stared at her askance, for a moment at a loss for words in the face of her breathtaking directness.

Swiftly she had gone on to explain. "Look, nobody wants to

think of his own mortality, or think about dying, I know that. But *you* have to, you *must*. Ralph always said you were the most intelligent man he knew. He told me you were extremely clever, a genius really, and clearheaded. So think clearly now. Think *unemotionally*. You need someone you can trust, a person who could run the company if ever you were incapacitated. And it must be someone who has your grandsons' interests at heart. Since I'm their mother, that's me. Obviously. You need *me*. Anyway, face up to it, I'm the only Jardine available."

Bruce Jardine had seen the rightness of her words. She *was* the only adult Jardine he could turn to, and therefore she was the only solution to his very real dilemma. Also, her sincerity, eagerness, and enthusiasm had convinced him that she really did want to work for him and learn the business. And so he had taken her on as his junior assistant, hoping she would not disappoint him.

"You've got to love this business if you're going to be a success at it," he would tell her repeatedly during the first years she worked at Jardine's, and Stevie quickly discovered she did love it, every facet of it.

She loved the diamonds particularly, and the other gems and the creative side of the jewelry business. Yet it was the intricacies of the financial and corporate side that fascinated her. Within the first six months of working at Jardine's, she displayed a talent for figures plus business acumen as well. Bruce had been pleasantly surprised.

It was only natural that she became indispensable to her father-in-law. Bruce Jardine, once her deadly enemy, eventually came around to making his peace with her. He recognized her considerable attributes, her talent, her genuine ability, and her willingness to work hard for long hours. As the months passed, he came to respect her. And he depended on her more and more. One day, after she had been at Jardine's for five years, the ani-

mosity and contentiousness she had come to expect simply
ceased to exist.

Alfreda never became one of her admirers. On the other
hand, Bruce's wife had apparently realized the validity of her
husband's moves; she well understood that Stevie was the one
person they could trust as the mother of their grandchildren,
their heirs. And so she had kept a civil tongue in her head and
stayed out of her daughter-in-law's way. Alfreda had died in
1982, almost fifteen years ago, but right up to the day of her
death she had disliked Stevie, had never shown her any affection
or made even the smallest friendly gesture.

Rising, walking back to the desk, Stevie bent forward, picked
up her wedding photograph, and peered at it intently for a
moment or two. How young she and Ralph had looked. But
then, they had been young, she most especially. *I was just a little
girl, only sixteen,* she thought. *A child. Why, I was younger than
Chloe is now.*

*Oh, Ralph, who would have believed it? Believed that your
father would take me into the business? Or that one day I would
be head of Jardine's on both sides of the Atlantic?* She could not
help thinking that life, the great leveler, was also so very unpredictable. *I couldn't have accomplished all that I have without
friends, good friends, and most especially André Birron.* She
knew that André had taught her as much as Bruce ever had
about the jewelry business. He had been her mentor in certain
ways, and a genuine friend, almost like a father.

André had always given her the best advice, the soundest.
When she was twenty-seven, she fell in love again, after four
years of widowhood. She discovered she was pregnant a year
later, and it was to André she had turned. She had flown to Paris
to see him, to confide in him, although, being wary by nature,
she had done so only to a degree. She had merely alluded to the

identity of her lover, the father of her unborn child. Even before she had finished her sentence, André had held up his hand as if in warning.

"Do not tell me who he is. I do not want to know. Remember this, my Stephanie. Confide a secret to one person and it is a secret no longer," the sage old Frenchman had cautioned.

And so she had kept her own counsel always, for this was her natural inclination. No one had ever known who her lover had been, or even tried to guess the man's real identity. Not even Chloe knew who her father was.

Chloe. Stevie's expression changed, became softer as she thought of her eighteen-year-old daughter. Now *she* was a D-flawless diamond. Quite perfect.

Stevie suddenly broke into a chuckle. Well, not really. Her daughter was only almost perfect, thank goodness. No one wanted a paragon of virtue. They were no fun, and usually too good to be true.

Chloe would be arriving later that afternoon, hopefully in time for dinner, and they would enjoy a cozy evening together. Tomorrow her mother and stepfather would be driving up from Manhattan to spend Thanksgiving Day with them, and the rest of the holiday weekend. She was looking forward to it, just as she knew Chloe was.

Derek Rayner had been knighted by the queen some years before, and he and her mother were now Sir Derek and Lady Rayner. As had been predicted long ago, he was now the greatest classical actor on the English stage, and at sixty-eight a living legend. He had been good to her mother and to her and her children.

Derek and her mother were childless, and so he played the role of father and grandfather to the hilt. But his love for them all was very genuine, and he adored Chloe.

Her son Miles was driving to Connecticut with the Rayners. He was her favorite son, if the truth be known, although she always tried to hide this fact from the others. She loathed playing favorites amongst her children.

Miles was a talented artist and a brilliant set designer. Currently he was living in New York, where he was designing the stage sets for a Broadway play. Unlike his brother Nigel and his twin, Gideon, he had never shown any desire to go into Jardine's, although with his artist's eye he had always appreciated the beauty of the jewels and the other objects of art Jardine's made.

Despite his lack of interest in working in the family business, his grandfather had insisted he become a director since he was a major shareholder in the company. He had done so immediately. Jardine's was his inheritance, and it had always been an important part of his life; his mother had seen to that.

It was Gideon who was the true jeweler in the family; Stevie had recognized that when he was a child. He was a talented, indeed gifted, lapidary, and he had inherited his father's love of stones, most especially diamonds. Like Ralph, he was an expert when it came to cutting stones, and as one of the chief lapidaries at Jardine's, he was involved in the creation of the exquisite jewels that the Crown Jewellers had been renowned for over the centuries.

Nigel, ever the businessman, and the spitting image of Bruce in so many different ways, ran the business end of the company, under her direction.

But Nigel wanted it all for himself.

Stevie was well aware of this these days. There were even moments when she thought her eldest son was plotting her departure from the company, planning her fall from grace.

Now she expelled a long sigh as she strolled back to the fireplace. She stood leaning against the mantelpiece, her thoughts focused on Nigel.

She had no real evidence to go on, it was just plain old gut instinct that told her that her son was against her. For a long time now she had seen Nigel for what he was . . . very much the way Bruce had been when he was a younger man—cold, calculating, controlling, and very ambitious.

There was nothing wrong with ambition as long as it was focused in the right direction. She was the first to admit this. But it was somewhat ridiculous of her son to be ambitious at her expense. After all, the business would be his one day. He would share it with his brothers equally, of course, but he would be running it as the eldest of the three and the undoubted business brain.

She wished she could shake off the worrying suspicion that Nigel wanted her to trip up in order for him to justify taking over from her in London. And indeed, New York as well.

Fat chance of that, she muttered. Bruce would never permit it. Her father-in-law was eighty-two now, and semiretired after some terrible attacks of gout, which had plagued him for years. But he was as alert as ever, not a bit senile, and very spry when he was free of his crippling ailment. She was very well aware that he cared about her, even though he did not show it very often.

Furthermore, and perhaps more to the point, he trusted her implicitly when it came to running the company. She had earned that trust, had proved to him time and again that she not only knew what she was doing but that she was brilliant at it. No, Bruce would not tolerate Nigel's machinations, what he would term "youthful insubordination." And he would be on her side.

Rousing herself from her thoughts about her eldest son, Stevie hurried out of the study and headed along the second floor landing. Of medium height and slim, Stephanie Jardine was an attractive woman, with a head of dark curls, light gray-green eyes, and a well-articulated face. High cheekbones and a slender nose gave her a look of distinction; she was elegant in an understated way, dressed in a loden-green wool pants suit and sweater that brought out the green lights in her eyes.

Stevie took the stairs at a rapid pace, realizing that she had wasted a great deal of time dwelling on the past and Ralph, living through her memories both good and bad. She had guests arriving the next day, and even though they were family, everything had to be well prepared for them nonetheless. Her mother, in particular, had very high standards and was accustomed to a great deal of luxury as the wife of a famous star of stage and screen.

As she reached the great hall, the grandfather clock standing in the corner began to strike. It was exactly six o'clock. Chloe was due to arrive in an hour, and a smile touched Stevie's eyes at this thought. She could not wait to see her daughter.

Somewhere nearby a door was banging, and she felt a rush of cold air blowing down the great hall. It seemed to be coming from the direction of the sun room, and she went through the archway that led to this area of the house.

The solarium, as it was usually called, was long with many windows; two sets of French doors led out to the covered porch that stretched the length of the back facade of the house. One of the doors had sprung open and it was swinging back and forth on its hinges, banging against a wooden chair.

She went to close it, then paused at the door and peered out. It was a dark night, with a black sky empty of stars. A corridor of bright lamplight streamed out from the solarium, illuminating the porch and its stone balustrade beyond. It diminished the darkness.

Stevie went outside, as she often did at this hour, loving the tranquility, the silence of the countryside. It was so pleasing to her after the din of New York, and especially so at nighttime.

Her eyes scanned the sky and the landscape surrounding her. She noticed then that the mist of earlier had settled in the well of the garden. It was heavier now, and it hugged the grass, swirled in thick patches, obscuring the stone benches, the fountain, and the flagged rose garden. How eerie everything looked tonight, she thought. Stevie swung around and made a swift retreat back to the house.

As she stepped inside, a strange feeling swept over her. It was a premonition really ... and it made her catch her breath. The feeling was similar to the one she had experienced that afternoon, but this time it was much stronger, more forceful.

She threw it off. And then Stevie Jardine laughed at herself again, as she had earlier, and shook her head. She, who had never believed in portents or omens and was totally unsuperstitious, was actually having presentiments of trouble. Ridiculous. She laughed again.

Some months later Stevie was to remember these strange feelings, and wonder.

3

Everyone said she was special.

Chloe herself, when she was old enough to understand such things, did not agree, although she did know she was different. She was different because she was illegitimate.

She bore the name Jardine because that was her mother's name, but she had long understood that she was not actually *of* the Jardine family.

Her mother had never hidden her illegitimacy from her, and when she was eight years old she had carefully explained the details of her birth to her. It was for this reason that Chloe had always accepted the facts in the most natural way. So did her three brothers. Even Old Bruce, as she and Miles called him, seemed to tolerate her, and obviously he did not object to her using his name. Nor did he seem to mind that she called him Grandfather; as far as they both were concerned he was exactly that, and he had always treated her the same way he did his biological grandsons.

When she was a small girl she hadn't wanted to be different or special. This only confused her, made her feel self-conscious. She just wanted to be like everyone else—ordinary.

Once, when she was about ten years old, she had asked Miles why people said she was special. He had looked at her closely through his piercing blue eyes, and smiled his warm, gentle smile. "Because you're such a happy little sprite, Pumpkin, all airiness and golden light. You remind everyone of the summer and sunshine . . . even in winter, and you're brimming with laughter, full of gaiety. That's the first reason—your effervescent personality. Secondly, you're a very pretty girl, who's beautiful inside as well as out. And finally, you're . . . well, you're an old soul, Pumpkin."

She had frowned at him, instantly picked up on this last thing. "What does that mean, Miles? What's an old soul?"

"Someone who's been here before, who seems to have a knowledge beyond her years, who is wise . . . "

"Oh." She had pondered this for a second or two and then asked, "Is that good?"

Miles had burst out laughing, his eyes crinkling at the corners, and he had rumpled her hair affectionately. "Yes, I think so, and be glad you're all the things you are, little sister. There are too few of you in this ugly world we live in."

Miles was her favorite brother. He had always been easier to be around than his twin, Gideon, and their elder brother, Nigel. Miles was never too busy for her, even though he was nine years older than she.

Despite the fact that Miles had explained why she was special, to the best of his ability anyway, she never thought of herself in that way. She was merely different, that was all, and then only because of the circumstances of her birth. There was nothing more to it than that.

Chloe had never felt embarrassed or awkward about her illegitimacy, nor had she given much thought to it when she was growing up, other than occasionally to wonder about her father. On her birth certificate his name was given as John Lane. She wasn't even sure if this was his real name, since her mother was so secretive about him.

Recently, thoughts of her father had insinuated themselves into her mind, and she had been besieged by questions, things she wanted to ask her mother but didn't dare.

Whenever she had broached the subject of her paternity in the last couple of years, her mother had simply repeated what she had always said: John Lane, her father, had been killed in a car crash.

Because her mother had always looked extremely upset, even on the verge of tears, when they had these discussions, Chloe never did probe further. Of late, she had needed to know more about her father, wanted her mother to describe him to her, tell her other things about him, give her an inkling of his personality and character. And so, on the drive up to Connecticut, she had wondered if she could question her mother at some point during the Thanksgiving weekend.

Now Chloe stood in front of the mirror on the dressing table in her bedroom, staring at herself but not really focusing. Instead, she was thinking of her mother, whom she had always adored. Chloe was absolutely certain there was no one quite like Stevie Jardine. Her mother was a true original, loving, generous spirited, and kind. She usually gave everyone the benefit of the doubt and tried always to see the best in people. Even in Old Bruce, who was such an ogre.

Her mother had brought her up well, given her all the right standards; Old Bruce had once told her that. Her mother and she were very close, pals really, and so many of her classmates at Brearley envied her. "Your mother's so cool," her best friend, Justine Seawell, was always telling her, and Justine was correct. Stevie was more like an older sister in so many ways, and yet she was a tough disciplinarian. Chloe had to abide by the rules at all times.

Chloe suddenly knew she wouldn't be able to summon up the nerve to talk to her mother during the family weekend; it would upset her if she brought up John Lane, dead more than eighteen years. It occurred to her that she could talk to her grandfather, Derek Rayner. She was close to him, and he had always treated her as an adult, even when she was a small child. Derek could enlighten her, if anyone could.

With this decision made she felt more cheerful, and the acute worry she had been feeling miraculously abated. Leaning forward, Chloe picked up a silver hairbrush and smoothed it over her shoulder-length dark hair, then adjusted the cowl neckline of her burgundy cable-knit tunic.

Stepping away from the mirror, she was able to get a better view of herself, a full-length view. She decided she liked the way she looked in the tunic with its matching leggings; she was five feet seven inches tall, and the outfit made her appear taller and more willowy than she already was. This pleased her. After spraying on a light floral scent, she put on a pair of gold-coin earrings, left her bedroom, and ran downstairs.

When she had arrived at the house half an hour earlier, her mother had been making a beeline for the kitchen, and so Chloe headed in that direction.

She found Stevie sitting at the big oak refectory table talking to Cappi Mondrell, their housekeeper and cook. Both women stopped chatting and glanced across at her as she came in.

"Hi, Chloe!" Cappi exclaimed, smiling broadly, obviously glad to see her.

"Hello, Cap!" Chloe responded, and rushed over, gave the housekeeper an affectionate hug. Cappi had been with them for eight years, and was like a member of the family; Chloe was devoted to her, and it was very clear the older woman loved the eighteen-year-old.

Wrinkling her nose, Chloe said, "Do I smell my favorite dish cooking?"

"You do indeed. Chicken in the pot for my favorite girl."

"You spoil me, Cappi."

"I know, but it gives me such pleasure," the housekeeper shot back, laughter echoing in her voice.

"You look lovely in that outfit," Stevie said with a glowing smile. She couldn't help thinking that her daughter was beginning to look so very grown-up all of a sudden. And she really was a beautiful girl with her shining dark eyes, luxuriant hair, and creamy skin.

"Thanks, Mom. You don't look bad yourself. Positively blooming, as I said when I first got here."

"Thank you, darling."

"When are the others arriving?" Chloe asked.

"Tomorrow morning, around noon."

"Is Miles bringing his girlfriend?"

Stevie was so startled, she sat back, surprised. "I don't think so," she answered. "He would have mentioned it. Anyway, I didn't know there was a girlfriend. At least, not anyone special." She stared at Chloe intently, and when her daughter didn't answer, she pressed, "Well, is there?"

Chloe shrugged, leaned against the table, and said hesitantly, "Not sure, Mom." She pursed her lips. "Maybe. He's been seeing a lot of Allison Grainger, but he's been really closemouthed about it."

"Who's Allison Grainger?" Stevie asked, a dark brow lifting quizzically.

"The costume designer who's working on the play with him. You've met her, Mom. She's got red hair and lots of freckles."

"Oh, yes, I remember her now. She's rather pretty." Stevie's eyebrows drew together in a frown. "Is it serious, do you think?"

"I doubt it," Chloe responded, and began to laugh. "I guess it will be for about another week or two. And then it'll probably be over. You know Miles and Gideon, Mom, they're very alike when it comes to women."

"What do you mean?"

"When they fall for a woman they get very intense for a few weeks, it's finally the great love at long last. But it quickly peters out. And they always like to surround themselves with extra girls, just in case. And anyway, Miles says there's safety in numbers."

Stevie smiled; how well her daughter knew her brothers. "He's coming alone apparently, so it may well be over already."

"I wouldn't be surprised," Chloe murmured, and then looked from her mother to Cappi. "Did I interrupt anything? You were very deeply engrossed."

"No, we were just planning the menus, going over a few things for the weekend. And actually we were just about finished when you came into the kitchen."

Cappi said, "I'd better set the table for —"

"Oh, don't bother," Stevie cut in. "Let's eat in the little sitting room tonight. It's much cozier. Two trays in front of the fire will do us fine, thanks, Cappi."

Later that evening they were halfway through dessert when Chloe put down her fork, looked at her mother, and said, "There's something I want to talk to you about, Mom."

"Yes, darling," Stevie said, swiftly glancing at her daughter, noting the sudden tenseness of her voice. "Tell me."

"It's about next year, Mom. I mean about going to college after I graduate from Brearley. And, you see . . ." Chloe's voice trailed off, and she gazed at her mother, biting her lip.

"What is it, Chloe?"

"I really don't want to go . . . I mean go to college."

Stevie sat up a little straighter and stared at her daughter. "Do you mean you don't want to go to college here in America? Or college anywhere?"

"Correct, Mom! I don't want to go to college."

"Not even to Oxford? You talked about that so much, and you always sounded very excited. Why, only a few months ago you said you couldn't wait to go there."

"I know. But I've changed my mind. I'd prefer to go into the jewelry business, Mom. I want to work at Jardine's."

Stevie was genuinely surprised by this announcement, even though she had always known her daughter liked the store in New York. She said cautiously, "I like the idea of you working with me at Jardine's, but I still want you to attend university. You can come into the business with me when you're twenty-one or twenty-two."

Chloe shook her head vehemently. "Honestly, Mom, I really don't want to go to college. What's the point, when I want to go to work. Surely you of all people understand that. You work like a dog and enjoy every minute of it."

"That's true, I do. And I understand everything you're saying, but nevertheless, I would like you to finish your education. It's important, Chloe."

"You didn't go to college."

"I wish I had."

"What could you have learned at college? About the jewelry business, I mean. Nothing. And look how successful you've been. You're a terrific businesswoman, you know all about diamonds and other precious stones. You're . . . well . . . Gideon says you're a legend in the business. Not going to college didn't hurt you, or stop you from becoming what you are."

"True. But then again, I learned a lot from Ralph in the early years of our marriage. And later I had Bruce to teach me. Working with him was like going to several universities. He was the greatest professor there was, and so was Uncle André. I learned a lot from him as well."

"And I can learn a lot from Gideon in London. That's where I want to go, Mom, I want to go to London and work with Gideon at the Bond Street store."

Stevie was taken aback by this statement, and for a moment she made no response. Then she said slowly, a little hesitantly, "But why wouldn't you want to work with me in New York? I don't understand . . ." She did not finish her sentence, just sat staring at her daughter through baffled eyes.

Chloe said quickly, "Oh, Mom, I'd love to work with you in New York. Eventually. But I want to start out in London because Gideon is such a great lapidary and he could teach me so much. And besides, the London workshops are much bigger than the one in New York. I just think I'd get better training there, and Old Bruce is there. I mean, I know he's semiretired and all that, but he does go to the store twice a week, and, well, I mean, he could teach me a lot, just like he taught you."

"I see."

"Are you angry, Mom?"

Stevie shook her head.

"Yes, you are, I can tell. Please don't be cross with me, Mom. Please."

"I'm not angry; really, I'm not, Chloe."

"Then what?"

"Disappointed, I suppose."

"Because I don't want to go to college?"

"Yes, there's that. But I'm also disappointed that you don't want to work with me in New York. Of course, the workshops *are* much larger in London, that's true. But ours is not so bad, you know. And we do have Marc Sylvester and several wonderful lapidaries at the Fifth Avenue store. They could teach you just as much as you'd learn in London."

"But I want to learn from Gideon."

"I know you've always been close to him."

"I'm closer to Miles actually, Mom, but I love Gideon and he's a good teacher. He's taught me a few things about jewelry already when I've gone to see him at the workshops during vacations."

"He's certainly patient and painstaking, and a bit of a perfectionist, so I have to believe you when you say he's a good teacher. Yes, I can see that aspect of him." Stevie gave her daughter a long, speculative look, and then asked quietly, "Have you discussed this with Gideon already?"

Chloe shook her head. "Oh, no, Mommy, I haven't! I wouldn't do that, not before talking to you." Chloe leaned forward, her young face expectant and eager. "Can I go, then?"

"I don't know. I'll have to think about this. It's a big step for you, going to live in London. Alone."

"But Mother, I wouldn't be alone. I've got two brothers and a sister-in-law there, plus Old Bruce. And my grandparents. Blair and Derek would keep an eye on me for you."

"*If* I agreed, and it is an *if*, I'd want someone to do much more than keep an eye on you, Chloe. You'd have to live with a member of the family."

Chloe was immediately crestfallen on hearing this, and it showed on her face. "You mean I can't live in your flat in Eaton Square?"

"Certainly not. There's no one there to look after you."

"There's Gladys."

"Gladys comes in only a few times a week to clean. No, no,

that would be out of the question, *if* I agreed to this plan of yours."

"I could live with Gideon. He'd love it."

"Nonsense. He'd hate it. A single man of twenty-seven who has legions of women friends, according to you, wouldn't want his baby sister for a roommate. It would cramp his style no end."

"Nigel would have me. He's *married,* and Tamara likes me a lot."

"Yes, I know she does. But once again, it wouldn't be suitable. They're practically newlyweds, they wouldn't want you around."

"Oh, Mom, they have two kids!"

Stevie bit back a smile, amused by Chloe's logic, then she said, "Even so, a young couple like Nigel and Tamara don't need the responsibility of looking after you. They have their hands full as it is."

"I wouldn't want to live at Old Bruce's house in Wilton Crescent, if that's what you're thinking. That place is so gloomy, it would be like being in prison. You wouldn't do that to me, would you, Mom?"

"I haven't agreed that you can go, Chloe."

"Grandma would let me live with her and Derek, and you know they love me . . . a lot," Chloe volunteered.

"Yes, they do. But you're putting the cart before the horse. I have to think about this matter, and at great length. I'm certainly not going to make any hasty decisions."

"When will you decide?"

"I don't know."

"But, Mommy —"

"No buts, darling," Stevie interrupted. "You've told me what *you'd* prefer to do, and now *I* must give it some thought. I want you to think about it as well, Chloe. Think about what you'd be missing by not going to university. Think about those three years at Oxford and all that they would mean. Not just the education you'd get, but the fun you'd have, and the people you'd meet. Friends you make at university are your friends for the rest of your life. And I must admit, Chloe, I'm a bit baffled, you were always so keen about studying at Oxford. What happened?"

"I've changed my mind, Mom."

"Promise me you'll think about this."

"Oh, all right," Chloe muttered, looking suddenly put out.

Stevie glanced at her quickly and said in a sharp tone of voice, "Don't sound so grudging about it, Chloe. It doesn't become you one little bit."

Chloe flushed at this chastisement, mild as it was, and bit her lip. Then, pushing the tray table away, she jumped up and sat next to Stevie on the sofa.

Taking hold of her mother's hand, she squeezed it, then reached up and kissed her on the cheek. "Don't be angry with me, Mommy."

Observing her daughter's worried expression and detecting the concern in her eyes, Stevie murmured softly, "I'm not angry, Chloe, but I do want to do what's best for you, and you must try to understand that. After all, *you've* obviously been thinking about this for some time, whilst *I've* just heard about it . . . so please, give me a few days to get used to the idea. And let me talk to Gideon. And my mother and Derek."

Chloe nodded and her face brightened considerably as she exclaimed, "So you're definitely not saying no?"

"No, of course not . . ." A faint smile surfaced on Stevie's face. "I'm saying . . . *maybe*."

Stevie had learned long before that when she couldn't sleep it was far better to get up and keep busy, especially if she had a problem on her mind. To her way of thinking, it was much easier to worry when she was upright and moving around than when she was lying down.

She and Chloe had both gone upstairs to bed at eleven. Stevie had fallen asleep at once, lulled into a deep slumber by the two glasses of red wine she had drunk at dinner.

Then she had awakened suddenly several hours later, at three in the morning. Sleep had proved elusive thereafter; at four o'clock she had slipped out of bed, taken a shower, dressed in a pair of blue jeans and a sweater, and gone downstairs.

After making a cup of coffee and a slice of toast, Stevie had walked around the house, collecting her many orchid plants. These she had taken to the plant room next to the laundry; carefully, methodically, she had watered them individually in the big sink, letting the water run through each one, then slowly drain away.

Everyone knew she loved orchids, and so she frequently received them as gifts. In consequence, her collection was quite large; two or three dozen were scattered throughout this house, and there were more in her New York apartment.

Mostly they were various species of the Phalaenopsis, with white or yellow blooms, plus pale, blush-pink cymbidiums. She also collected the miniature slipper orchid with pale green or dark brown blooms, and the dark brownish-wine–colored Sharry Baby with its tiny flowers and delicious chocolate scent.

But of them all her real favorites were the white and yellow Phalaenopsis, and she did very well with them, making them last for months. The house was an ideal spot for them to grow, cool, and full of soft, muted light most of the time.

Now Stevie lifted a pot containing a yellow-blooming Phalaenopsis and carried it through into the sun room, where she returned it to its place.

Stepping back, her head on one side, she admired it for a

moment, thinking how beautiful it looked, so elegant against the white walls and standing on the dark wood surface of the antique chest. This was positioned in a corner between two windows, and the orchid had the most perfect light there.

Stevie moved around the house for almost another hour, carrying the plants back to their given spots in different rooms, and then she poured herself a mug of coffee and went back to the solarium.

She stood in front of the French windows, warming her hands on the hot mug, sipping the coffee occasionally. Her eyes scanned the sky. It was cold and leaden, and she could tell already that it would be a gray day, bleak, overcast, sunless. Even the landscape had a bleak look to it, the trees bereft of leaves, the lawn covered with a sprinkling of white frost. Thanksgiving Day 1996 had not dawned very brightly.

Stevie turned away from the window. Seating herself on one of the large overstuffed sofas, she put the mug on the table in front of her and leaned back, resting her head against the soft cushion covered in a faded antique chintz.

What to do? What to do about Chloe? She was not sure. In fact, she was very uncertain, really. Her daughter had surprised and disappointed her when she had abruptly announced she did not want to go to university, most especially since she had been so gung-ho about attending Oxford. Stevie had always wanted Chloe to have a good education, to graduate with a college degree. The last thing she had expected was to hear her daughter express the desire to work at Jardine's. There had never been any real indication on Chloe's part that she was keen on the jewelry business, other than a passing interest in the New York store.

Admit it, she's hurt you badly, wanting to work in London, a small voice at the back of her head whispered. And yes, that was the truth. Chloe's words had been like a slap in the face.

Stevie knew that Chloe could learn everything in New York. There was no need for her to go to London. Jardine's was the one store left on Fifth Avenue that had its own workshop on the second floor, and it was excellent. Marc Sylvester, her top lapidary, was brilliant, and Chloe could learn as much from him as she could from her brother Gideon, or Gilbert Drexel, the chief lapidary at the London shop.

Am I being selfish, wanting to keep her with me? Stevie asked herself. Possessive? Overprotective? If she was honest with herself, she had to admit it was a little bit of all three.

But then again, what mother didn't want to keep her daughter by her side, and for as long as possible? And if not by her side, then at least in the same country. What Chloe wanted was not only to leave the nest, but fly away to distant shores.

Stevie let out a long sigh, thinking of her daughter. Chloe was only just eighteen, and she was so much younger in many different ways, more like fifteen, in fact. For one thing, she had led a very sheltered life, particularly when they had resided in London. She had been surrounded by family . . . her three brothers, and her grandparents, and had attended Lady Eden's exclusive private school for young ladies as a day girl. The harsh everyday world had hardly penetrated her consciousness.

Even in the eight years they had lived in New York, Chloe's life had been somewhat cloistered. She'll never make it on her own, Stevie thought. She'll be overwhelmed. She's too sensitive, too delicate, and just far too young to be away from home, away from me. I'm going to say no. I must. I'm not going to let her go to England. She can go a year from now only if she is enrolled at Oxford.

It seemed to Stevie at that precise moment that a load had been lifted from her shoulders. Just making the decision was a blessed relief. The tight pain in her chest, which had been like a steel band since four o'clock that morning, was beginning to ease at last.

4

No matter how busy she was, Stevie always found time at some point each day to write in her daily journal. And so that morning, while she waited for her mother, Derek, and Miles to arrive, she opened her current diary and wrote: *Thanksgiving Day 1996: Connecticut*, then sat staring at the page, lost in her thoughts.

She had kept a journal for years, most of her life, and there were volumes of them locked away in a cupboard at the other side of the upstairs study, where she now sat at the desk.

Thirty-four years had been recorded in them since her mother had presented her with her first diary when she was twelve. That had been in 1962. It seemed very far away now; so much had happened to her in the intervening years. She had lived a lifetime and then some, or so it seemed to her.

Her first diary had had its own little lock and key and it had withstood the test of time very well; she had looked at it recently and been amazed that it had weathered the years so well. The paper was a bit yellowed at the edges, the ink faded on some pages, but that was the only damage, if you could even call it that.

On the whole, a miracle of preservation, Stevie thought, and put down her pen, sat back in the chair, her thoughts turning to her mother, who had also kept a diary most of her life. They had always been close, had had a symbiotic relationship when she was a child. Her father, Jerome Anderson, had not been the right husband for Blair, nor had he been a very good father, and this had brought her and her mother even closer together.

Newspaperman, ladies' man, bon vivant, and man-about-town, Jerry had not been cut out for family life, and that was exactly what her mother had craved. Beautiful, glamorous, international supermodel Blair Connors had wanted only to be a wife and mother. She was the success she was because of her face and figure, the way she dominated the catwalk and made love to the camera. It was certainly not because of drive or ambition. Even at the height of her career she had wanted to stay at home and cook, raise children, be a housewife, a mother, and a good wife to the right man. Domesticity was her idea of bliss.

Derek Rayner, English classical actor par excellence, handsome matinee idol and movie star, had seemed such an unlikely candidate for the role Blair had cast him in all those years ago. The wrong man, as far as Blair's friends were concerned.

But as it happened, he *had* been the right man, the perfect choice, the perfect mate. Blair and Derek had been married for over thirty years and still adored each other. Their only disappointment was that they had not had any children of their own. Perhaps that was one of the reasons they were inseparable, and Derek never went anywhere without his beautiful and accomplished wife.

Stevie was relieved they were coming to spend Thanksgiving with her. On the phone yesterday her mother had sounded worn out, which was unusual for her. She had mentioned that Derek was exhausted after twelve weeks on location making a movie in

Arizona, then looping at the studio in Los Angeles. The film assignment had come right on top of his long run in the Broadway revival of *Becket*. According to her mother, it was now essential that he get a good rest.

"No more work for a while," Blair had said. "He's really looking forward to the long weekend with you, Stevie, before we fly back to London next week," her mother had added, and Stevie was determined to make it a wonderful few days. She wanted her mother and Derek to have the great luxury of peace and quiet in comfortable surroundings, with lots of good food and rest. And certainly no pressure.

She thought suddenly of Chloe. She would have to have a talk with her later, warn her not to take all of her little problems to Derek. She had a tendency to pester him at times. Stevie supposed that was understandable, in that Derek was the closest thing to a father Chloe had ever had.

Certainly Bruce Jardine had been more like a grandfather. He was much older than Derek, less active, and decidedly crotchety a good part of the time. No wonder Miles and Chloe called him Old Bruce. He *was* such an old man in many ways; he had not aged well at all.

Stevie was aware that Chloe loved him, despite her protestations to the contrary and desire to cast him in the role of ogre or tyrant. As for Bruce, there was no doubt in Stevie's mind that Bruce Jardine loved the girl in return. He had shown her daughter too much favor, displayed too much kindness to her for it to be otherwise. Whilst this baffled Stevie occasionally, it nonetheless pleased her. Bruce had treated Chloe as a Jardine all of her young life, and Stevie would always be grateful to him for that.

Bruce was not an easy man to care about or even like, but she had grown quite attached to him over the years. They had worked well together in a very temperate climate for twenty years, and there had rarely been any display of temperament or outbursts of anger on his part. Most of the years had rolled by on a very even keel, it seemed to her now.

It struck Stevie that it might be a good idea to talk to Bruce about Nigel. She and Chloe were going to spend Christmas in London, and that would be the ideal time to unburden herself. *Unburden myself,* she thought in amazement. Do I really feel that strongly about Nigel's attitude? She sighed, thinking that perhaps she did.

Not only did she love her eldest son, she admired him no end, and there *was* a lot to admire. He was a clever, indeed brilliant young man with a great deal of talent and a good head on his shoulders. But he had a flaw, and it was a flaw that was fatal. He believed he knew better than anyone else, was convinced of the rightness of his ideas and beliefs, and he never took no for an answer, would brook no argument. He was far too stubborn and opinionated for his own good. His attitude verged on arrogance. It dismayed her that he could not compromise, that he was so rigid.

He was just like his grandfather. No, he's worse, she thought, and laughed a hollow little laugh. He *was* Bruce's clone. As Bruce had been when he was a younger man. Perhaps more so.

It would be hard to speak critically to Bruce about his clone. This brought a smile to Stevie's face. She wasn't going to talk to Bruce about her son's character, rather about her suspicion that he wanted to oust her from the company. If this were the case, Bruce would surely put a stop to his manipulations.

But then, she could do that herself. She could fire Nigel.

He was, after all, her *employee.*

He worked for *her.*

She was the managing director of Jardine's of London and president of Jardine's of New York, just as Bruce was chairman of the board. Nigel was a director of the company, as were his two brothers, and they would always be directors. That was their right, their inheritance.

But she could take Nigel's job away from him at any time if she so wished. It was as easy as that, just like snapping her fingers together.

No, not so easy, she reminded herself. He's my son, my first-born, I wouldn't want to hurt him, to humiliate him, or to destroy him. Besides, he's good at his job. The very best.

I simply have to make him toe the line, curb his ambition for the moment. He has to bide his time until I retire.

Stevie laughed out loud. Easier said than done when she was on the other side of the Atlantic . . . thousands of miles away.

Her mind swung to Gideon. Now, there was a son who was not one bit ambitious, at least not when it came to possessing the company and amassing power. All he wanted was to create flaw-less diamonds from the rough . . . make beautiful things. Gideon did worry her on a personal level, and she had been worried about him for some time now. He had not looked well, had seemed distracted, fretful, and impatient when she had seen him at the London showroom in late September. She remembered how pale and gloomy he had looked. In her opinion, he hadn't been himself since he had broken up with Margot Saunders. Had he cared for that young woman more than he'd let on? She would talk to Miles about his twin during the weekend.

Her face instantly changed, took on a warm glow, and her eyes brightened. Miles was her pride and joy, she admitted it freely . . . in the privacy of her thoughts.

And Miles would help to take Chloe in hand too; she could rely on him to do that. Chloe and Miles had always had an affin-ity for each other and he was good with his little sister. Unlike Gideon, who had considered her to be a bit of a nuisance. And now Chloe wanted to learn from her brother Gideon. Stevie shook her head. People were so very strange.

She had often thought how odd it was that although Miles and Gideon were identical twins and looked alike, when it came to their personalities and characters, they were as different as chalk and cheese.

Miles was so much lighter, more carefree, gentle, well balanced, and a genuine charmer. Conversely, his twin was introverted, stubborn—more like Nigel in that way—and a perfectionist who at times seemed ridiculously persnickety, almost old-maidish. And yet he could be generous to a fault, and he truly did have the soul of an artist. He loved anything and everything that was beautiful, be it a woman, a painting, a sculpture, a tree, a seascape, a garden, a priceless gemstone, or a piece of jewelry. And he had an extraordinary eye, refined and exquisite taste.

Picking up her pen, Stevie looked down at the page and realized she had put nothing on paper so far other than the day and where she was.

Slowly she began to write, and when she had filled two pages, she screwed on the top of her fountain pen, took the diary in her hands, leaned back in the chair, and read it.

Thanksgiving Day, 1996
Connecticut

When I think of my children and the things they do, it seems to me they are like strangers. Except for Miles. But then, he is the child of my heart, so like me in so many ways. Of course, I love them all, but he has always been special to me since he was small. I wonder, are all mothers like I am? Do they favor one child more than the others? I'm sure that it is so, but it's hard to ask anyone that kind of . . . leading question. And do the children know? Do they detect it, sense it, feel it? Do they know there is one who is the real favorite of the mother?

Each of my children is different. Yet I can see traits in them that are mine. And some are Ralph's. There are traits in them that come from Bruce. Fortunately, none of them have inherited anything of their grandmother, Alfreda, and for that I can honestly say I'm thankful. She was not a nice woman; she was cold, repressed, and bitter. She never had a kind word for me or anyone she considered to be her inferior. It is their other grandmother who shows up in them. My mother. Chloe has inherited her beauty, her willowy figure, her pleasing personality, and her desire to please; Miles has inherited her sense of humor and geniality.

I love them. I love all of my children. It's the truth, I do. Maybe too much. And yet somewhere along the way I suppose I hurt them, damaged them without meaning to do so. But then we're all damaged goods, aren't we? Life damages us, people damage us, we even damage ourselves. I must have caused them pain and heartache. And hurt their feelings. We do that so often to those we love the most without even realizing it or meaning to. And perhaps I did neglect them at times when I was caught up with work and travel. But I never stopped loving them.

I think of them as my children. But, of course, they're not children, not anymore. They're adults. Grown-ups. People. Other people, not my children. They're so different in so many ways. Strangers. Sometimes, anyway. Even Chloe is grown-up all of a sudden, knowing her own mind, hell-bent on getting her own way.

Soon I'm going to stop being a mother, stop thinking of myself as such. Instead I'll be . . . ? I'll be . . . just there for them. If they need me. Is that possible? How do you stop being a mother? How do you stop worrying about them? Caring about them? Perhaps you don't. How DO you stop being a mother? Can anyone tell me that?

Will I fare better with my grandchildren? I asked myself that question in the middle of the night, when I woke up with such suddenness. I will be a good grandmother to Natalie and Arnaud. Grandmothers are better than mothers, I've been told. Less possessive. My grandchildren are so precious and Nigel is lucky to have them, to have Tamara. She's a good wife, a wonderful mother. A good young woman.

I think I'm beginning to resent the fact that Gideon teases her, calls her "the foreigner." Her father is French, her mother Russian, and Gideon wants to make an issue about it. Why, I'll never know. But it's unkind. He says it's in jest; yet I sense that's how he really perceives her. I'd hate to think he was bigoted in some way. But I am very aware that my son Gideon thinks that anything not English is inferior. I wonder why he's not learned otherwise yet? I did years ago.

Chloe. I can't let her go to London. Chloe alone there at the age of eighteen! No, never. I feel it's unwise. She's too young. And she must go to university. She can't just drop out.

Soon my family will be with me. Well, some of them, and that makes me happy. And each one of us has a lot to be thankful for this November of 1996. And I, in particular, am such a lucky woman. I have so much.

Stevie closed her diary, put it in the desk, and locked the drawer. As she pushed back her chair and rose, she heard the sound of the car on the gravel driveway outside.

Moving to the window, she pulled back the lace curtain and looked out. Her heart lifted when she saw Miles alighting.

He glanced up at the window, saw his mother, and waved.

She waved back, dropped the curtain, and hurried out, almost running down the stairs to the great hall.

5

MILES JARDINE COULDN'T HELP THINKING THAT AS HE AND HIS twin brother grew older, their mother appeared to be getting younger.

That morning she looked like a woman in her mid-thirties, and quite wonderful, as she came down the front steps to greet him and his grandparents. She was wearing a chalk-stripe gray-wool pants suit and a white silk shirt, and she was her usual elegant self.

It struck him that Gideon was correct when he said they were rapidly catching up with her, and that when they were forty-six she herself would still be forty-six, at least in her appearance anyway.

But then, she *had* been a mere nineteen-year-old when they were born, and she was blessed with youthful looks, thanks to her genes. His grandmother, who would soon be sixty-seven, didn't look her age either, nor did she seem it. Blair was as youthful as anyone he knew, had great vitality, energy, and an enormous sense of fun.

"Hello, Ma," Miles said as his mother drew to a standstill in front of him. "You look fabulous." He smiled at her hugely, dropped the two bags he was carrying, and hugged her to him.

"I'm so glad you're here, Miles darling," she responded, smiling back. "And thanks for the compliment." She drew away and went on down the steps. His eyes followed her as she embraced her mother and then Derek, who had been helping the driver unload the trunk of the car.

Suddenly Cappi and the two local young women who worked with her on weekends were greeting him. One of them grabbed his suitcases despite his protestations that he could manage perfectly well; she paid no attention, simply departed with the luggage.

Miles shrugged to himself and went on down the last few remaining steps, close on the heels of Cappi and her other helper.

But when he heard Chloe calling his name, he paused, swung around, and a second later his sister was hurtling into his arms.

"Hi, Pumpkin," he exclaimed, and gave her a big bear hug.

"I've been waiting all morning for you, Miles, you're late."

He grinned at her. "I think I'm *early* actually, kid. We weren't due until noon, and it was just eleven thirty as we turned into the gates. Anyway, how're things at Romany Hall?"

"Okay," she answered laconically. There was a slight pause, then she added softly, "But I want to—" She broke off abruptly, as if she had changed her mind.

"Come on, Pumpkin, what were you going to tell me?"

"Oh, nothing . . . it was nothing important, honestly."

Miles thought otherwise, but he made no comment, as always discreet. "Come on, then, let's help Cappi and Lola with all that stuff. When the Rayners travel, it's like old-style royalty on the move. And God only knows what they bring with them."

"The kitchen sink," Chloe chortled. "That's what Mom says

anyway. She told me earlier that they'd arrive with two dozen suitcases plus the kitchen sink."

"Not quite, but almost," Miles agreed, laughing with his sister.

They went down to the driveway holding hands. Chloe glanced at him out of the corner of her eye. "So you didn't bring Allison."

Miles threw her an odd look. "Now, why would I bring *her?*"

"Bring who?" Derek asked as he braced himself for Chloe's enthusiastic hugs and kisses.

Stevie stared at her son, waiting to hear his response to her stepfather's question.

Glancing at Derek, Miles said, "Nobody. Nobody important, that is."

Well, at least that's to the point, Stevie thought. And leaves nothing to our imagination.

"Hello, darling," Blair murmured, accepting Chloe's kisses, which were, to her relief, more restrained than those just bestowed on Derek. "And who is Allison?" she asked, casting her glance on them all.

"Don't look at me, I've no idea, my darling," Derek intoned in his mellifluous actor's voice and, hoisting two of the valises, went up the steps. Stevie and Blair followed, carrying some of the smaller bags.

After Miles had thanked the driver and tipped him, he too made his way to the front door with Chloe in tow. He said in a pointed voice, "Little pigs not only have big ears, but apparently loose tongues as well."

Chloe giggled.

"Why did you mention Allison of all people, and in front of our mother? You know she's longing for me to get married and have kids, so she can have more grandchildren. It was wrong of you, Chloe."

"Well, you have been seeing a lot of Allison, and I thought it was . . ." Her voice trailed off lamely; she looked chagrined. And she felt suddenly uncomfortable under his fixed scrutiny.

"That's my business, kid, not yours."

"I thought it was getting serious between you two."

"No. And even if I did have serious intentions, that has nothing to do with you or Mother or anyone else. It's a private matter and it's certainly not open for discussion within the family."

"Oh." There was a momentary pause, and she looked at him through worried eyes. "Are you mad at me?"

"No, but let's not discuss my personal business in front of the rest of the family. Okay?"

"Yes, Miles, and I'm sorry."

"That's all right. Just remember what I said though. You've got to learn some discretion. You're not a little kid anymore, you're eighteen, and you must start growing up, behaving like an adult."

Chloe nodded, her face suitably serious for once.

After coffee and hot buttered scones in front of the fire in the great hall, everybody dispersed in different directions. Stevie sent Cappi, Lola, and Chloe to help Blair and Derek unpack their voluminous luggage; Shana, the other young woman who worked with Cappi, took Miles's bags up to his room. And his mother hurried off to the kitchen, explaining that she had to baste the turkey that was roasting in the oven.

Left alone, Miles wandered down the great hall into the dining room, and then slowly strolled through into the living room which adjoined it. He couldn't help admiring the ambiance his mother had created in the house. It was immensely seductive, just as it was in her other homes. But he especially liked Romany Hall because it was an airy, spacious house filled with clear, crys-

talline light that poured in through the many windows upstairs
and down, a great number of which were unencumbered by
draperies.

Everything was sparkling and fresh throughout. The white
paintwork was pristine; the windows shone; the wood floors
gleamed, and there was not a speck of dust anywhere. No shabby
corners, worn fabrics, or frayed rugs here. His mother was something of a perfectionist, and she maintained the house at the
highest level. Every piece of furniture, each object and painting,
was well cared for and in its proper place.

Although it was beautifully decorated, Romany Hall was not
overdone and there was no unnecessary clutter or ostentation.
The air was fragrant with potpourri, perfumed candles, and the
unusual chocolate smell of the Sharry Baby orchids, their curva-
ceous stems laden with exotic dark blooms.

Miles did not linger very long in the living room, but continued on to the solarium, a room he generally gravitated to at least
once every day when he was staying with his mother.

He had always been taken with its simple yet effective
beauty—white walls, warm terra-cotta–tiled floor, and the eyecatching Pierre Frey fabrics patterned in reds, yellows, and blues
that his mother had used on the sofas and chairs. The solarium
had a French feeling to it, with its high-flung cathedral ceiling
and beams, stone fireplace and the French Provençal furniture
his mother had picked up at sales in the Loire Valley and the
Maritime Alps.

The many windows and French doors made the solarium
seem part of the outside, and the clarity of light was particularly
noticeable here. Although it was a sunless day, and somewhat
bleak, the cloudless sky was a soft bluish-white, almost etiolated,
and it was incandescent.

A good light for painting, he thought, and made up his mind

to bring his easel and paintbox down there tomorrow. He was suddenly in the mood to do a few watercolors.

Orchids abounded throughout the house, but there was a greater profusion of them in the solarium. His mother had always been addicted to orchids; and, even as a child, he too had been fascinated by them, by the intricacy of the flowers, the fantastical shapes of the petals, and the truly exotic colors.

He had grown up with orchids; there had always been a plethora of them in their farmhouse on the Yorkshire moors. Once a week he had helped his mother to water them, then put them in large metal bowls to drain.

"*Sissy, sissy, sissy!*" From a long way off, in the far reaches of his memory, he heard Nigel's voice echoing down through the years. His elder brother had always teased him about watering the orchids with their mother. He hadn't really cared; he had been independent even then. But his mother had cared when Nigel's taunting had become a tiresome pattern, and his older sibling had been suitably punished.

Their mother had made Nigel clean all the lavatories at Aysgarth End, six in all, and he had had the last laugh, although he hadn't dared to crack a smile. If he had, there would have been retribution of some kind. Nigel had been born a tough little bugger.

And nothing's changed, he thought coldly.

Opening the door, Miles stepped out onto the covered porch, walked over to the balustrade, and stood looking out toward the distant hills. Kent was such a beautiful part of the world, his kind of country with its rolling wooded hills and crystal lakes. It reminded him of Yorkshire and of his childhood, a good part of which was spent there.

These days it was mostly Nigel who used Aysgarth End as a weekend home when he could get away from London, and for all the national holidays when they didn't go to France to see

Tamara's parents. Certainly it was a marvelous spot to raise a family. When he went back to England he would go up there for a few days. He had long been planning to do an oil painting of Nigel's two children, and he wanted to paint them against a moorland background.

Now the view of the distant Litchfield hills reinforced this idea, was quite inspirational in a way. His fingers suddenly itched to hold a brush; he would start tomorrow, do a few sketches of Natalie and Arnaud from memory. It would be the beginning of the portrait. The prospect pleased him.

Miles shifted his stance slightly and glanced down into the garden below. It looked dank and foggy, and the mere sight of the sunken rose garden stripped of all its summer radiance and color made him conscious of the cold weather. He turned away and went inside.

Drifting back to the great hall, he sat for a few moments in front of the fire, staring into the flames, thinking unexpectedly about Allison Grainger.

He had been startled, not to mention miffed, when Chloe had brought her name up in front of the others. He was loath to give his family anything to speculate about, even his mother, whom he adored. Nonetheless, like all mothers, she wanted to see him settled for life.

He liked Allison, liked her a lot in fact. She was a really great human being and a lovely young woman, and they had had a lot of fun together these past few months. But he did not want to spend the rest of his life with her—for a very simple reason. He was not in love with her.

In any event, he had learned his lesson today, and learned it well. Young Chloe wasn't to be trusted. It was patently obvious that she was a little blabbermouth, and this disturbed him. She was always poking her nose into his business, and he was going to have to put a stop to that. He loved her, and he didn't want to hurt her feelings, but she didn't know how to edit herself. Wasn't it his fault though? He had let her into his life since he had been in New York. Oh, what the hell, he thought, no harm done, and I'd better keep my own mouth shut from now on. At least around baby sister.

Later, upstairs in his bedroom, Miles glanced around with satisfaction, noting the blazing fire, the bowl of fresh fruit, the bottled water, and the collection of magazines and newest books on a long library table behind the sofa.

His mother had always paid great attention to detail, and provided great comfort in her homes, thinking of everything. The perfect reading lamp stood close to the overstuffed armchair next to the fireside; a cashmere blanket was thrown over the back of the sofa; a plump duvet skimmed across the top of the big double bed; and naturally, orchids bloomed on tables in various corners.

She cossets, he suddenly thought, that's exactly the right word. She did the same when we were children. She's always done it, pampered us, and everyone else. "Smothers us, more like," he heard Nigel's voice say. He frowned, thinking of his brother once again. Nigel had developed a very acerbic tongue of late and could be quite vituperative. It's as if he's bitter, Miles muttered under his breath, walking over to the fireplace, standing with his back to the blazing logs. He had no clue what was wrong with Nigel; Gideon deemed him the man with everything, and this was true. He had a beautiful, intelligent wife, two marvelous kids, a successful career with a guaranteed future. And one day he would be the big cheese at Jardine and Company, the Crown Jewellers of London. But seemingly this wasn't enough. What a fool his brother was.

Miles sighed, dragged his thoughts away from Nigel, and walked into the bathroom. After washing his hands, he ran a comb through his hair and then peered at himself. He saw a reflection of his parents gazing back at him. He had his mother's dark, wavy hair, the same finely etched face, but he had inherited his father's long, straight nose and vivid blue eyes. And, of course, he was a replica of his identical twin.

Gideon. He had been very much on his mind of late. He couldn't understand what was ailing him. His brother was morose, moody, and depressed. Last week, when he was in London, he had attempted to talk to Gideon; but all he had got for his trouble was a flea in his ear. And several warning glances from his brother had finally made him back off completely. But there *was* something wrong with Gideon. As Derek, who was always quoting Shakespeare, would say: *Something is rotten in the state of Denmark.*

6

"THE ACTOR PLAYING THE HEAVY BECAME SUDDENLY ILL, AND THERE we were, in the middle of the picture and in a mess, looking for a replacement, and, of course, everyone was mentally casting," Derek explained to them, his marvelous voice echoing around the great hall.

"And," he went on, "I happened to remark to the assistant producer that who we needed was Sydney Greenstreet. I told her that he'd be great as Redner, the villain. And she asked me who his agent was so that she could be in touch and try to hire him at once."

Derek began to laugh. It was infectious. The others laughed with him, as always enjoying his anecdotes about the movies he had worked on. "Anyway, she was appallingly dense, the poor girl, and I'm afraid none of us could resist taking the mickey out of her. Most of the time too. Very young, of course. Too young for the job, as a matter of fact. Didn't know that old Sydney had gone to meet his maker long ago. Doubt if she'd ever heard of him. Or seen *The Maltese Falcon.*"

"Or *Casablanca*," Chloe volunteered. "I loved him in that."

"So did I, darling girl," Derek agreed, beaming at her.

Chloe beamed back. "*Casablanca* is my all-time-favorite movie. It's *awesome*."

"My favorite too," Miles said, and then, glancing at Derek, he remarked, "I had a similar sort of conversation the other day with one of the young women working in Wardrobe. I said that Deborah Kerr had been the greatest Anna ever, that she'd been brilliant in the part, and the girl just gaped at me, looking totally blank."

Derek nodded, moved forward in the chair slightly, sounding serious. "Look here, I'm all for youth and a great booster of this generation, but some of these kids in their late teens and early twenties who are working in the theater and movies today seem awfully uninformed to me. Not a bit knowledgeable about the past, even the recent past."

"Only too true," Miles agreed. "It's like they've landed from another planet."

"Deborah was divine in *The King and I*," Blair murmured.

"And so was Yul Brynner. They don't make stars like that anymore," Derek said quietly.

"Well, I wouldn't go as far as that!" Blair exclaimed a trifle heatedly. "What about you, my love?"

Derek merely inclined his head and smiled at his wife.

Stevie said, "Mother's right, of course, but I do know what you mean. So many of the great stars I love have retired or died."

"Very gloomy thought indeed, my dear," Derek answered. "And I must admit, I miss quite a number of them. Larry Olivier, Jack Hawkins, Duke Wayne, Bill Holden, but most especially Rich. God, we had some splendid times together. He was such an extraordinary man, an extraordinary talent. I remember when he was in *Hamlet* in the fifties. I think it was 1953, when he was with the Old Vic. Claire was in it with him, played Ophelia to his

Hamlet. They were fabulous together. I went up to Edinburgh to see it, to see them. Rich was bloody marvelous. *Miraculous*." There was a moment's pause, and then Derek added softly, "I always envied him his voice, you know."

"You did!" Miles sounded surprised, and he threw Derek a curious look. "But *your* voice is wonderful. Everybody remarks about it, Derek."

"Thank you, Miles, however, it's not as great as Burton's was. Rich had . . . well, probably the greatest voice that's ever been heard on the English stage. It was a *thrilling* voice, and it was much more sonorous and emotional than Larry's, in my opinion anyway. It was the Celt in him, the Welsh in him, we love words so, us Welsh do. And as they always say in our native valleys of Wales, he had a bell in every tooth. Usually they say that about a singing voice, but it can be applied to a speaking voice as well, you know. As far as Rich was concerned, that is. His voice literally *rang* with feeling, and I for one could listen to him for hours."

"As we all could, and did," Blair reminded him.

"I think I'd better check with Cappi about lunch," Stevie exclaimed, and rose, began to walk across the great hall. "I should find out how things are progressing. And anyway, they probably need a bit of help in the kitchen."

"I'll come with you, darling," Blair murmured, and followed her daughter.

Chloe called, "Do you need me, Mom?"

"No, darling, we can manage, I'm sure," Stevie answered over her shoulder before disappearing into the kitchen.

Derek strolled across to the tray of drinks on a large Jacobean chest, picked up the bottle of white wine, and swung to face Miles, showing him the bottle. "Need yours topped up?"

"No thanks, Gramps, I'm fine."

Derek poured himself another glass of the wine and then walked back to the fireside. He sat down on the sofa next to Chloe and, glancing across at Miles, he asked, "How're the sets coming along for *The King and I*?"

"Pretty good, actually. It's a fabulous play to work on, and I can really give my imagination free rein with this one. Temple bells and Buddhas, carved elephants, exotic fabrics, lots of gold and silver. And jewels. And vivid colors. All of those things that help to recreate the palace in Siam are really very visual, and have tremendous impact from the stage. And, I have to say, the costumes are sensational, especially Anna's . . . all those lovely floating crinolines."

"As a musical, it does take a lot of beating because it is such a fabulous play to look at, quite aside from listen to." One of Derek's brows lifted eloquently as he now asked, "How's Martine Mason faring? *How* is she as Anna?"

"She's good, Gramps, and so is Ben Tresner as the king. He may not be Yul Brynner, and Martine's certainly no Deborah Kerr, but I think we've got a winning package."

"And therefore a hit, presumably."

"From your mouth to God's ears, Gramps!" Chloe exclaimed. The two men exchanged amused looks and laughed.

Cappi appeared suddenly in the great hall and beckoned to Chloe. "Your mother wants you to come and help us, nothing too complicated. We just need another pair of hands for a few minutes."

"I don't care if it *is* complicated, you know I'm very good at complicated things," Chloe shot back, and ran across the room, exclaiming to her brother and grandfather, "Excuse me, I won't be long, and please don't talk about me while I'm gone."

Again they laughed in amusement. Derek said, "You should be so lucky."

Once they were alone, Miles rose, took a chair closer to Derek, and began. "I want to ask you something before Ma comes back from the kitchen."

Derek looked at him with alertness, wondering what this was all about. "Go ahead, Miles old chap. I'm all ears. What's troubling you? And I guess you *are* troubled, if the look on your face is anything to go by."

"Yes, I am troubled. I'm worried about Gideon."

"Oh." Derek sat up straighter, giving Miles his full attention.

"I know you saw Gideon when he came to Los Angeles on business three weeks ago, and I just wondered what you thought. I mean—" Miles paused, cleared his throat, and went on. "What I mean is . . . well, what did you think about Gideon? His demeanor? His behavior?"

Without even having to think about this, Derek answered immediately. "He seemed relatively normal to me. But what are you driving at?"

"I saw him last week, when I was in London for a few days, and . . . well . . . frankly, I thought he seemed a bit under the weather, not himself at all."

"I see. However, Miles, I can honestly say I didn't notice anything different about him. No, not quite true, actually. He *was* a bit vague the second night we saw him for dinner. I'd even go so far as to say he was remote, and now that I think about it more carefully, he was somewhat distracted."

"He was depressed when I was with him, *and* morose," Miles said.

"He's always been a bit gloomy, Miles, even as a child," Derek pointed out. "You might look alike, but your personalities are very different."

"I know. But listen, his moroseness has been more pronounced than usual. And you didn't notice it then?" Miles stared at his grandfather.

Derek shook his head. "No, and neither did your grandmother, or she would have mentioned it to me. As I just said, he appeared to be distracted, as if he were preoccupied about something, and he was a bit distant. Looking back now, I remember I thought his mind must be on business. But that's all." Derek's eyebrows furrowed. "Tell me something, why didn't you want your mother to hear this conversation?"

"You know how she worries. And about everything."

"Yes, but she's always coped, no matter what's been flung at her. And brilliantly so, I might add."

"That's true. But I didn't want to bring Gideon up today, not on Thanksgiving. You know, it's her most favorite holiday of all. I didn't want to spoil it for her, voicing my concern about my twin."

Derek was chuckling. "Oh, I know it's her favorite holiday, and none of us has escaped it. Ever. I've eaten more of your mother's turkey over the years than I care to remember, and it's not even my favorite bird. I prefer duck, pheasant, or partridge any day. But she hasn't ever listened to me, at least not about turkeys anyway."

Miles half smiled, and wondered whether to bring up his elder brother. After a moment's thought he decided he would do so, since Derek had always been his confidant, and like a father to him all his life. He said slowly, "Has Ma mentioned Nigel to you?"

"No, she hasn't, but then, Blair and I haven't seen her in New York. We've been back from Los Angeles only a few days, and she seems to have been awfully busy at Jardine's. Is there something wrong with Nigel too, in your considered opinion, Miles?"

"No, not that I know of. However, Ma's indicated to me a few times that she thinks he's ... sort of—" Cutting himself off, Miles hesitated, and then, dropping his voice an octave, he finished in a stage whisper, "Plotting against her."

"Ah, I see." There was a dramatic pause. Then, holding Miles with his eyes, Derek intoned, "Uneasy lies the head that wears a crown."

"I suppose there's truth in that. Shakespeare always got it right, didn't he? And you should know, you've been in enough of his dramas."

A thoughtful look crossed the actor's expressive face, and he was silent for a moment or two, and then he asked quietly, "Do you believe he's plotting, Miles?"

"I . . . I just don't know."

"I *know* your mother. She doesn't imagine things, she's far too pragmatic for that. Therefore, if she thinks he is, then he is. Although, to be truthful, I'm damned if I know the reason he would do such a thing. After all, the business will be his one day."

"Maybe he's in a hurry."

"I can't imagine the reason."

"Neither can I, Gramps."

Derek sighed. "Ambition. Greed. The lust for power. It's toppled many a throne, caused murder and mayhem on a grand scale. We've only got to look at the Plantagenets and the Tudors to understand that." He shook his head, and a sad, rather regretful expression settled on his handsome face. "Nigel always was something of a mystery to me, Miles, I must admit. I never really understood him when he was a child. Nor did I understand his actions when he was a teenager. But then, that's another story altogether, isn't it?"

"Yes, it is. I didn't understand all that mess either."

Derek stared off into space for a moment, lost in memories of the past, before saying eventually, "How is Nigel's marriage? Is that all right? No problems with Tamara?"

"None as far as I know, and she's a smashing girl. He's bloody lucky to have her and those two great kids."

"Ah, but does *he* know it, Miles?"

Miles shrugged, lifted his hands in a helpless gesture.

Derek averted his head, looked into the fire, lost in thought again.

After a moment Miles said, "Getting back to Gideon, I've been wondering if he's upset about Margot. But then, why would he be, when *he* broke it off with her?"

"Could he possibly have regrets?" Derek suggested, turning to face Miles, looking directly at him.

"Maybe. But it wasn't very good between them in the end. I think she was getting on his nerves. Margot always was something of a social butterfly, and you know Gideon's not very keen on partying. He's too serious, too dedicated to work." Miles exhaled heavily. "Oh, God, I don't know . . . and who knows what Gideon really thinks or feels? It beats me."

"Have you tried talking to him?"

Miles threw back his head and guffawed. "Oh, come on, Gramps, of course I have! And he bit my head off the last time I did."

"Perhaps he's just going through one of those phases all young men go through—at some time or other," Derek said, thinking out loud. "Trying to find himself, et cetera, et cetera, et cetera. But more than likely, it's woman trouble." A brow lifted knowingly. "That's usually what's ailing men when they appear troubled and despairing but without any real reason to be so afflicted."

"I suppose you're right, Derek."

A split second later, Chloe appeared in the archway of the great hall. "Coo-ee, coo-ee," she called, waving frantically, trying to gain their attention. "It's almost three-thirty and lunch is ready! Mom would like you to come to the dining room. *Now*, she says."

"Her wish is our command, my darling." Derek put down his glass and rose.

So did Miles.

Together the two men went to join her, and the three of them slowly made their way to the dining room.

1

It was a festive lunch.

Everyone talked a lot and laughed and exclaimed about the good things offered to them, since by now they were all extremely hungry.

Cappi and her two helpers had prepared a truly memorable Thanksgiving lunch. There were all manner of delicious and succulent things to eat with the large, plump turkey—sweet potatoes with a marshmallow topping, mashed potatoes as well as potatoes roasted in the oven, and parsnips, red cabbage, cranberries, a thick, fragrant-smelling gravy, and, of course, Stevie's famous, mouthwatering sage-and-onion bread stuffing.

Along with the turkey, Cappi had baked a Virginia ham and roasted a batch of quail, much to Derek's amusement. He knew that these had been made in order to tempt him; after years of complaining to Stevie about her Thanksgiving turkeys, she had apparently taken the hint. And yet hadn't he always explained to her that English turkeys were not as good as those to be found in America, an important point, since over the years most of her Thanksgiving meals had been served in London.

He had been partially teasing her; she had taken his words to heart.

"A little of everything," he told Cappi, who was hovering around the sideboard, where the turkey, ham, and quail were arrayed on large platters, alongside all the accompanying vegetables. "And only dark meat, please, if you're giving me turkey."

"And what about vegetables, Sir Derek?"

"Mashed potatoes would be lovely, and stuffing and gravy, but that's it, thanks, Cappi. Must watch the waistline, you know."

Miles moved slowly around the table, pouring the red Bordeaux, a Château Gruaud-Larose, his favorite Saint-Julien. It had been bottled in 1989, a good year, and he commented on this to Miles, who nodded and smiled. "Chosen specially for you," Miles told him with a conspiratorial wink.

Chloe followed on her brother's heels, filling their water glasses; Blair passed around the basket of homemade breads and Stevie offered cranberry sauce. Then at last they were all served, and they settled down to eat.

Derek ate slowly, savoring his food, saying a word or two occasionally. Mostly he listened, and observed everyone.

He was very content to be here today, enjoying this respite from his work, enjoying being with his family. Part of his family, at any rate. He could not help wishing Gideon were here, and Nigel and Tamara with their two children, and then they would have been complete. A true family all together under one roof for once.

This was his second family; long ago there had been his daddy and his mam, his brothers, Owen and David, and sister, Gwyneth. The family of his blood, whom he had loved so much when he was growing up in Ystradyfodwg, that little parish that was the Rhondda. *The Rhondda . . .* how he loved the sound of it, loved rolling the name around on his tongue. The place of his heart ... where all his hopes and dreams had been born ... another of the great industrial valleys of South Wales, where coal mining was the main industry.

The pit. The dreaded pit. The giver of wealth, the taker of life.

His daddy had worked in the pit all his life, from being a young boy until the day he died. Claimed by the pit. It was an explosion in the belly of the earth that took so many of their men and ravaged the town. His daddy had died with the others when the walls of the mine had collapsed and water had flooded the shafts.

His brother Owen had not been on the same shift as their daddy that day, and so, thankfully, he had been spared. Spared to become the breadwinner for them all.

It was because of his elder brother that *he* had been spared. Owen, and Gwyneth too, had seen something special in him when he was a boy. Eventually they had come to calling it "the gift," and as it turned out, it was just that, something deep within himself that he could draw on and that would eventually take him to great heights as an actor, although he had not known it then. Nor had he or they known at that time exactly what this gift was, not really. They could not define it. But, very simply, his brother and sister had discerned something in him that made him different, lifted him high above the mediocrity of the crowd.

In a sense, it was a mixture of things: his talent for acting, his genius for mimicry, his boy's soprano voice that everyone said was so beautiful—this would go, they all knew that—but they recognized these attributes in him and rejoiced. Owen, in partic- ular, appreciated his aptitude for learning and was convinced that this alone was his great chance. That rare chance to escape the fate of most boys of his age in South Wales in the 1940s: Working in the mines underground.

"He's not going down the pit, I won't let him," Owen was forever announcing to Gwyneth; his sister, mother, and brother, David, would agree that he was too good to be wasted "down there."

Owen was awed by his renditions of poetry; he had a natural talent for reciting reams of it, all learned by heart and committed to memory; equally, Owen was awed by his overwhelming ambition, his consuming desire to act. To be an actor, that was his goal.

He wanted to walk out on a stage and become someone else. Yes, *to act*, of all things, and he a poor boy from the Welsh valleys. Yet they had a rare respect for the language in those once-glorious valleys where the bright hillsides had been spoiled, seamed as they were with mine shafts, the tops of the lovely green hills scarred by pit heads.

They had immense respect for the written word, and the spoken, those Celts did. That strangely alien tribe, which, some said, was the lost tribe of Israel. This love of words was inherited from their ancestors, his ancestors, and he too loved the language, perhaps more than anything else. As a boy he had loved the music and the singing in the chapel on Sundays and the eisteddfods, those wonderful musical festivals where he had excelled whilst his voice had lasted.

His first language, as a boy, had been Welsh, and he still spoke it, loved speaking it. But he had learned that foreign tongue, *English*, when young, had conquered it, made it his own in a most singular way.

Owen and Gwyneth had saved him from going down the pit. He had been forever grateful to them for that, and he had shown his gratitude whenever he could. He was fiercely loyal to them; his brothers and sister meant the world to him. They had, after all, given him this life. Or at least given him the chance to grab this life, make it his own, just as he made a stage his own whenever he stepped onto it.

His Welsh family, his blood family. They were fortunately still intact, except for his mamgu, his mam, who had died twenty years ago. She had lived to witness his success, his triumphs, had seen him play Henry IV and Henry V. She had been thrilled by his Hamlet and had applauded his Richard III, had sat there in the theater and watched him mesmerize an audience, hold them spellbound for two and three hours at a stretch. His beloved Welsh family, to which he forever returned, as always reveling in his roots, his heritage, dragging this with him wherever he went, like a banner in the wind.

Wait. He was wrong. Surely he was wrong. Not two families in his life, but three. There had been another one long ago, a family of actors, a few young men who had gravitated to each other in the early fifties.

Rich, of course, and Stanley Baker, and himself. And a handful of other Welshmen who had eventually fallen by the wayside. But all of them of common background, come out of those great green valleys of rugby football and singing, poetry, poverty, and the pits. Working-class boys who became working-class heroes. Especially to each other.

He and Rich and Stanley had been real boyos in those days, treading the boards and boozing it up in the pubs, and wenching hard when they were lucky enough to get the chance. Boasting more than doing, as he recalled it now. And the three of them had shared a love of rugby football, playing it, watching it, and cheering on the Welsh team.

Oh, how young they had been and full of power and pride and piss and vinegar. And each of them growing more famous. Heady stuff it had been then, in the London of the fifties.

It was their Welshness, their talent, and their acting that had bonded them together, bound them as a family, and Richard Burton, his beloved Rich, had been their leader. The Welsh chieftain out of the valleys, and ready to lead them on to triumphs beyond their wildest dreams. And he had done so. Their wonderful Welsh warrior, all fire and brilliance, with his brightly burning genius, immensely powerful as a man, charismatic and compelling, and one of the greatest classical actors of his time. Of all time, in fact, with a voice one critic described as "memorably beautiful." And that voice was, in his opinion, the source of Rich's genius as an actor.

And then Rich had gone and died at the age of fifty-eight, in 1984, and how he had wept for him, just as he and Rich had wept for that other fallen friend, Stanley, when he had died so absurdly young in 1976. *Sir* Stanley Baker by then, honored by all. And he and Rich had mourned him, and they had shared their rage, their anger that he had died so young and left them so bereaved.

And it was only a short eight years later that Rich was gone himself, felled by a massive brain hemorrhage at his home in Switzerland. And that little family of actors was no more. There was only him left.

But he had *this* family. It was they who concerned him now as they all sat around Stevie's circular table in her dining room at Romany Hall in Kent, Connecticut, so far away from the valleys of South Wales and his youth.

He glanced at Miles, who caught his eye and smiled. Derek smiled back, but immediately he fell inward, thinking about *this* family, these people who had become, over the years, the mainspring of his life.

Miles. More like a son than a grandson. He had tried to help Stevie raise him after Ralph died so young, at least as much as she would allow. Fiercely independent, she had not wanted any interference with the boys, not from anyone.

He had also tried to help her bring up Gideon and Nigel, but her attitude had been the same. "I'll manage," she would say, and yes, she had always managed, there was no denying that.

Gideon had been such a moody boy, but *good* like Miles, who had been everybody's favorite because of his sweetness of disposition, easygoing nature, and steady reliability. He hadn't changed much, simply grown better, if the truth be known. Miles was the most lovely human being and certainly the peacemaker in the family.

Nigel had been too much of a Jardine to listen to anyone, not even his mother. But she had a strong will and had won the day in the end. But Nigel would not listen to *him;* after all, what did a mere actor know, and one who was his grandmother's husband to boot and not a blood relative. Nigel had gravitated to Bruce Jardine automatically, almost without having to think about it. He had allied himself with the Jardines, even standing with them against Stevie at one moment in time.

Derek had never really been able to forgive Nigel for that desertion. He had tried, even convinced himself at times that he *had* forgiven Nigel for his treachery. But he hadn't really; he had merely elected to *forget*, in order to get on with the business of fraternizing with Nigel, since he was Stevie's eldest son and an integral part of the family. Temporary amnesia, Blair called it.

Blair. The woman he adored and had from the first day he met her. When he had first set eyes on her he had forgotten everyone and everything, and in an instant he had known that he had been looking for her his whole life.

His marriage to Nina, his first wife, was already beginning to break apart, to crumble. And his falling for Blair, head over heels falling, had been like someone throwing a stick of dynamite into the marriage. All had come tumbling down in a heap around him. What's more, he hadn't really cared. Nothing mattered but her. He wanted Blair. He was going to have her. He and Nina had no children to be concerned about, and Nina was already dissatisfied with him, so *anti* him at that point in their life she had described him to an acquaintance as a drunken actor, which he wasn't, far from it. An actor, yes, but not a drunk. Many things, but not that.

And so he and Blair had eventually married and, contrary to what everyone had predicted, they lived happily ever after. She was his true love, his muse, his devoted partner, his greatest critic, and his greatest fan.

She was the one who was always there for him, cheering at the ringside; always there to bandage his wounds; to mop up the mess; assuage his pain; ease the terrible hurts of his daily life. She was everything to him. Like his mother and sister before her, she was a woman he idolized as he had idolized them, and as he still idolized his sister, Gwyneth.

He and Blair had not had children, but this did not really matter to him. After all, there was Stevie and her children, and Nigel's children. He loved them all, even Nigel, who was so difficult and hard to understand at times. But he was part of Stevie and part of Blair, and therefore he deserved to be loved despite his transgressions.

He glanced at Chloe, who was sitting next to Blair. How amazing it was . . . she looked as Blair must have looked when she was a young girl. There was no mistaking *her* genes. Chloe will be a heartbreaker one day, he decided, observing her surreptitiously. If he and Blair had had a daughter, he felt sure she would have looked like Chloe.

Chloe. So young, almost too young for eighteen in this day and age, or so it seemed to him. Children were so very grown-up now. He loved Chloe; she was his adored grandchild. And he was terribly guilty of spoiling her, but he just couldn't help himself.

She was very precious to him, this young girl, and he decided that he must talk to Stevie about Chloe going to college. To Oxford University. That was what she had always wanted. This summer, after she graduated, she must come to England and live with them and do the Oxford extrance exams. Chloe was an intelligent girl, and artistic like her twin brothers, and sharp in the way that Stevie was sharp. He was sure she would do well, go as far as her mother had gone.

Stevie. His dearest Stevie. He had always thought of her as his daughter, and she was exactly that, blood or no blood. She had been fourteen when he and Blair married, and rebellious. He had known immediately that she would be a handful, but he simply hadn't cared or worried about that. He had been ready and willing to take her on and bring her up as his own when he had married her mother. Those two came as a package, but it was a lovely, and loving, package, one he had been more than happy to accept.

As it turned out, he hadn't had much bringing up to do in the end. Just two years. And then Stevie had met Ralph Jardine and married him within the short span of a year.

He had not been sure about Ralph in the beginning, asking himself what kind of a man it was that seduced a girl of sixteen, an innocent, inexperienced girl who was eleven years his junior.

But their marriage had worked, and he knew that Ralph had truly loved Stevie. He had grown to like Ralph as time went on, and it was with sorrow that he had mourned Ralph's passing.

Derek shifted in his chair and looked across at Stevie, his eyes suddenly appraising. He was very proud of her. She had become an extraordinary woman. Powerful in so many ways. Powerful in her own business, powerful in the international world of jewelry, and yet it was the power she had within herself that impressed him the most. Her inner strength constantly amazed him. The power of a woman could be formidable.

She was the one who had held everything together after Ralph's sudden death, once her grief had begun to abate. Bruce Jardine had been hugely affected by his son's death. After his own heart attack, the man had been half useless, as far as he could ascertain at the time. As for Alfreda, she had been one of the most stupid women he had ever met, a numbskull if ever there was one. An ignorant woman totally crippled by her own ridiculous, and laughable, snobbery.

He knew that it was Stevie who had pulled the company around, kept everything running smoothly, and she a mere girl with no experience of business whatsoever then. She had inherited her mother's guts, and she had immense intelligence, not to mention an uncommon kind of bravery. For indeed it had taken a great deal of courage to go in there at the age of twenty-six and start helping Bruce to run the business. Bruce could deny her tremendous efforts and contributions as much as he wanted, until the day he died, but Derek knew what had really gone on, how much she had done. It was because of Stevie that Jardine and Company, the Crown Jewellers, still existed in London today.

Now his eyes rested on her lovingly. It saddened Derek that she had never remarried. He felt sorry that she was alone, and he frequently worried that she would be lonely in her old age without a partner by her side. For the moment she was a busy woman, of course, caught up in the daily running of Jardine's. But one day she would retire, step down, hand over to Nigel.

Nigel. His mind settled on Stevie's eldest son. There was no question that Nigel must be plotting against her, if she believed this. But why? It didn't really make sense.

8

"GRANDPA! GRANDPA! WAIT FOR ME. *WAIT FOR ME!*"

Derek swung around and saw Chloe racing after him across the lawn, and so he paused, stood waiting for her.

"What is it, Chloe? Is there something the matter?" he asked when she finally drew to a standstill next to him.

"No, Grandpa," she panted, endeavoring to catch her breath. "I just wanted you to wait for me so that I could come with you on your walk."

"And I thought there was a major disaster, the way you were screaming like a banshee."

She threw him a swift glance, saw at once that he had a teasing look in his light blue eyes. She relaxed, laughed lightly, then she said, "I *can* come with you, can't I?"

"Of course, but come along, let's not stand here. It's not that warm today. I was making for the summerhouse down by the river. It's a pleasant walk there and back."

Chloe nodded, tucked her arm through Derek's, and fell in step with him.

He said, "You mustn't shout like that, Chloe, screaming so hard, you could very easily damage your voice."

"But I'm not going to be an actress, Gramps."

"Nevertheless, you could hurt yourself, strain your larynx. I once did, and it was very painful, let me tell you."

"When did you do that?"

"Oh, a long time ago, when I was a young actor just starting out. I was shouting very loudly instead of throwing my voice. You see, I wanted it to reach the back of the theater, and I really did hurt myself in the process, quite badly too. It taught me a good lesson. I went out of my way to learn how to project my voice after that. I could pitch it quite high, but that wasn't really what was needed to reach the last row. So I worked with a voice coach, who told me that if I spoke very distinctly, I would make everyone in the theater hear me. I soon learned that volume didn't matter. It was distinctness that did. I also learned to enunciate my words very carefully, without making it seem labored."

"It must have been exciting when you first became an actor."

"It was, and it still is, Chloe. There's nothing quite like walking onto a stage for me, or saying those first lines. It's truly thrilling, if a little frightening sometimes."

"Frightening?"

"Oh, yes. Like many actors, I often suffer from stage fright. Not as much as I used to, but it still attacks me now and then."

"You?" Chloe swung her eyes, looked at him, and shook her head in wonder. "Gramps, I can't believe it! Not *you*, Sir Derek Rayner, the greatest classical actor on the English stage today."

He smiled slightly. "As I just said, many actors do have attacks of stage fright. My friend Rich did, he used to tremble excessively at times. Other actors I know experience nausea, and poor old Larry Olivier had a curious nervous laugh when he first walked onto a stage. At the beginning of his career, that is. He managed to get that laugh under control eventually, at least most of the time."

"And you, Grandpa? What happens to you?"

"I shake a bit, feel sick, think I'm going to vomit, worry that I'm going to forget my lines and make a fool of myself. I suppose that's what stage fright is about actually, the terrible *fear* that one is going to make a mess of it all and look ridiculous in front of an audience."

"I understand. It must be awful."

"It is. Fortunately, it doesn't last long for me. Once I've said my first few lines, I'm off and away, and I forget everything because I've become the character I'm playing. The drama of it sweeps me along."

"Sometimes I've thought that I would like to be an actress, and I once even talked to Grandma about it, but she sort of . . . put me off."

"Did she now." Derek's eyes twinkled. He continued. "But you should follow your star, my dear, and never listen to anyone."

"You'd better not let Mom hear you say that, she'll be mad at you," Chloe cautioned.

"You're right, she would indeed be angry. However, she's bright enough to know that I speak the truth. Shakespeare said it best when he wrote, 'To thine own self be true.' You must always remember that. If you live by this yardstick, you won't go too far wrong."

"What Shakespeare meant was that we should be true to our own beliefs. Isn't that so?"

"Indeed it is. You're eighteen now, Chloe, and growing up fast. It'll be time for university soon."

"Yes," she said quietly, and held her breath for a moment, wondering whether to confide in him.

"That's a very small yes, and not at all like you. Why, you sound like a scared little church mouse."

Chloe had to laugh. "No, I don't."

"Well, what about it? I thought it was always Oxford for you."

When she did not respond, Derek came to a sudden stop, took hold of her shoulders and turned her to face him. "Chloe, Oxford is magical . . . a city of colleges and quads, domes and shining spires, the Bodleian Library, All Souls, and the Union. This glorious place does exist, if you want it, darling."

"I don't know anymore, Gramps," she answered, as always being scrupulously honest with him because of his immense integrity and his love for her.

"I see." There was a moment's pause before he murmured, "But you were so very positive about going up to Oxford when you were old enough." He stared at her keenly, his eyes penetrating. "What's happened to make you change your mind?"

Chloe hesitated fractionally, then answered quietly, "Nothing, not really." She shrugged her shoulders lightly. "I think . . . well, to be honest, I don't want to go to college at all, Gramps. I'd like to . . . work at Jardine's."

"Good God! You can't be serious!" Not waiting for her to say anything, he rushed on. "I can see that you are *very* serious from the look on your face. Why the change of heart, darling?"

"I don't know, I can't really explain it."

"Have you told your mother this?"

Chloe nodded. "Yes, on Wednesday night, when I first got here."

"Mmmm. Is she pleased that you want to go and work with her at the store?"

Chloe bit her lip. "Mom wants me to finish my education, go to college. More specifically, she wants me to go to Oxford."

"That's perfectly understandable."

Before she could stop herself, she blurted out, "I'd like to work with Gideon at the London store."

Derek was flabbergasted when he heard this, although his expression was unreadable when he said, "I sincerely hope you didn't tell your mother that."

"Yes, I did."

"Oh, dear . . . she must have been terribly upset."

Chloe bit her lip and nodded again.

Derek took hold of her hand, tucked her arm through his, and started to walk on toward the river. A silence fell between them.

Eventually, Derek broke the silence when he murmured, "I am quite certain that it hurt her very much, Chloe, hearing this from you."

"I suppose so," she mumbled.

"I don't understand you!" he exclaimed, sudden irritation rushing to the surface. "Why London? You could learn as much in New York. And there's no one smarter than your mother. Being at the Fifth Avenue store with her would please her no end, I know that for a fact. It wouldn't do you any harm either."

"I think I would learn a lot more about stones and designing jewelry in London. The showrooms are bigger, so are the workshops, and there are many other kinds of craftsmen there, as well as lapidaries—silversmiths, goldsmiths. Anyway, Gideon would teach me better than anyone. He's one of the greatest lapidaries there is, and he's the Crown Jeweller, the only person allowed to handle the Crown Jewels of England."

"Yes, yes, I know all that," Derek exclaimed irritably. "But look here, Chloe, you could work at Jardine's, be it in London or New York, *after* you've graduated. I'm the last person to stop you from chasing your dream, didn't I just say that to you? Nevertheless, won't you consider going to university? For yourself, for your mother, and for me too, but mostly for yourself. It's so important for your future, whatever career you choose ultimately."

There was only the slightest hesitation before she said, "I'll think about it, Grandpa."

The two of them walked on quietly, without speaking, lost in their own thoughts, still heading in the direction of the river that flowed past the house at the bottom of the gardens.

Derek was truly dismayed about his conversation with Chloe, and genuinely upset for Stevie. Knowing her as well as he did, he realized how terrible she must be feeling, hurting inside. Oh, the young, how carelessly cruel they could be with their rash words, usually uttered without a single thought. And no hurt ever intended, of course. *Selfish youth.* But then, hadn't he been selfish when he was young? When he thought he knew it all, believed he had all the answers?

He was sixty-eight years old now, and in so many ways he felt as though he knew nothing, had learned nothing, in spite of the multitudinous experiences in his life. The longer he lived, the less he knew, or so it seemed to him. He was always telling Blair that nothing surprised him anymore, because he always expected the worst. Yet he was constantly being surprised. Chloe had just done that.

They arrived at the summerhouse, which stood under the willows close to the river's bank. Derek marched purposefully up the steps, saying over his shoulder, "Let's sit in here for a few minutes, it's nice to watch the wildlife on the river from here, and we're protected from the wind. Anyway, I need a rest, that was quite a long walk."

Dutifully Chloe tramped after him up the short flight of steps and joined him on the wooden bench where he had seated himself.

Slowly she unwound her scarf, pulled off her knit cap, and sighed as she ran her hands through her hair, pushing it away from her face.

"All the troubles of the world on your shoulders, eh, Chloe?"

She shook her head.

He looked at her intently and realized that she was on the verge of tears. Reaching out, Derek put his hand on her arm and murmured gently, "Now, now, what's all this?"

"Nothing, nothing, Grandpa," she said, shaking her head, and then she flicked her fingers across her eyes, swallowed hard, and tried to smile without success. Her bottom lip quivered slightly.

"There's nothing to cry about, Chloe. Was I too harsh with you, darling? I didn't mean to be."

"No, no, you weren't. Honestly, you weren't. It's just me. I'm being silly, I suppose."

"In what way?"

"I've upset my mother about not going to college, and you too, Grandpa. And I guess I've really hurt her feelings, telling her I prefer to work in London. I didn't want to cause trouble. I really didn't, and I didn't want to hurt anyone either, especially Mom."

"I know that, Chloe, and I'm quite certain that she does too. Anyway, you did say you would consider going to Oxford first, before embarking on a career, be it at Jardine's or not. If you tell her this, you will please her, make her feel so much better, I promise you."

Chloe was silent. After a split second she nodded and then, swiveling her head to Derek, she stared at him, biting her lip nervously. Quite unexpectedly, and much to her mortification, tears welled in her eyes, slowly slid down her cheeks.

"Chloe, Chloe, whatever's the matter?" Derek asked, staring at her in concern, reaching out once more, taking hold of her hand this time.

When she remained silent, he asked, "Is there something you want to tell me? Do you have some sort of problem?"

Taking a deep breath, Chloe replied, "One of the reasons I wanted to come for a walk with you was to ask you something—" She cut herself off and simply stared at him as blankly as before.

Derek nodded. "Go on, then, ask me. I'm not going to bite your head off, you silly goose."

"It's . . . it's about . . . about my father."

"What about him?" Derek asked, although he knew at once what she was going to say.

"Who was he *really*?"

Derek sighed heavily. "I don't know, truly I don't, Chloe."

"Would you tell me if you *did* know?"

"I most certainly would."

"I don't think my mother is being fair to me. I'm grown up now. Anyway, I've known about being illegitimate for years. I think I should know about my father, know about his background, who he was, what he was like."

"I agree, Chloe," Derek replied, and he meant this.

"Then help me, Gramps, please."

"How, darling?"

"Talk to Mom. She listens to you. Tell her she should tell me everything about my father."

"She won't tell you."

"Why not?"

"I've no idea." He shook his head. "She's always been very secretive about him."

"You never met him? Never knew him?"

"No, I didn't, Chloe."

"And Grandma?"

"She didn't meet him either. He was always . . . the mystery man."

"I don't even know what my father looked like," Chloe whispered, her eyes filling.

"Don't cry, sweetheart."

"Grandpa, please talk to her."

"First, let's go and talk to your grandmother."

9

Blair stood in the middle of the small sitting room that adjoined their bedroom, staring first at Derek and then at Chloe. She exclaimed, "You're both looking very conspiratorial! What is it?"

Derek said, "Ask Chloe, my dear," and walked across the room, where he positioned himself in front of the fire, stood warming his back against the flames.

"Is something wrong, Chloe?" Blair asked, searching her granddaughter's face intently, frowning as she did so.

"I want to know about my father, everything about him. Mom has never told me a thing. Please, Grandma, you tell me," Chloe said, getting straight to the heart of the matter. "*Please?*"

Blair was somewhat taken aback and showed it. Then she sat down heavily in a chair and said, "But I can't tell you anything, Chloe. For the simple reason I never knew your father. I never met him, never even spoke to him on the phone."

"But Mom must have said something about him, mentioned him to you."

"She didn't."

"But how . . . how did she tell you about *me*, Gran?"

"She came to me one day and said she was pregnant. I was very happy for her, enthusiastic, because naturally I thought there was going to be a wedding."

"But there wasn't because—" Chloe stopped with abruptness. She went and flung herself on the sofa, looking disconsolate.

Derek and Blair exchanged pointed looks, and Derek said, "Because *what*, darling?"

"Because he was *dead*. She told me my father was killed in a car crash before they could get married."

"Oh," Blair said.

"Didn't she tell you that, Grandma?"

Blair shook her head.

"Then *what* did she say?" Chloe demanded quietly.

"Nothing much, actually, Chloe," Blair told her, and explained, "When I said something about her getting married, how happy I was for her, she said, 'I'm not getting married. There won't be a wedding.' I've always remembered her words, remembered that particular day very clearly. It was a rainy day in London, and I recall walking over to the window, looking out at our garden. We lived in Hampstead in those days. Near the Heath. I just stood there, feeling numb, looking out at the sodden trees, watching the rivulets of water running down the panes. And I thought, it's like my tears, the rain is like my tears."

"So you were upset then, Gran?"

"Of course I was upset! For your mother. After all, she wasn't getting any younger, she was almost twenty-eight. I wanted her to find happiness with someone, have a second chance at life, a chance with another husband."

"Instead of another husband, she got me. The bastard."

"Chloe! Don't speak in that way! You've never been made to

feel unwanted or unloved, and certainly you've never been made to feel like a bastard. That's most *unfair* of you," Blair chastised, her voice reproving, her face stern. "We've all loved you very much, Bruce Jardine included. And you're a Jardine, don't you ever forget that. Why, nobody's given a thought to your father, or asked questions about his identity, for the past eighteen years. There's another thing you should remember—" She paused, and her voice softened as she finished. "You've given us all a great deal of joy, and you've made a difference in all of our lives. As I just said, we love you, Chloe, cherish you."

"Indeed we do!" Derek exclaimed. "And we want only the best for you. Your mother most of all wants that."

Chloe said, "On my birth certificate it says my father was John Lane. *Who* was John Lane?"

"I don't know. Your grandpa doesn't know." Blair leaned forward, an earnest look washing across her face. "Until the day your mother told me she was expecting a child, I didn't even know she had a boyfriend. She worked extremely hard, and she was bringing up your brothers, and it seemed to me she didn't have very much time left to conduct an affair, have any kind of personal life."

"She had John Lane, Gran. Ask her. Ask her about *him*. Make her tell you. *Everything*. I've a right to know."

"I understand how you feel, I really do. And I'll gladly speak to your mother. However, I can't promise I'll be successful. She's my daughter, don't forget, and I know her better than anyone. Once she's made up her mind about something, she rarely, if ever, changes it."

Chloe sighed. "If she'll tell anyone, it'll be you, Gran."

"Well, I don't know about that," Blair responded carefully, shaking her beautifully coiffed blonde head. "She's kept him a secret since before you were born, so why should she divulge anything now? Not even André Birron knows about your father, and if she'd been going to confide in anyone, it would have been André. They've always been very close."

"You've discussed this with Uncle André?"

"A long time ago, yes."

"And he had no clue?"

"No, he didn't, and he actually told me to leave it alone. He told me my prying would do no good, only antagonize Stevie, possibly even cause an estrangement if I wasn't careful, if I persisted. Since I didn't want that to happen, I took André's advice."

Derek said, "I feel for you, Chloe, and I know your grandmother does too. It's only natural for you to want to know a little more about your father. If your grandmother is in agreement with me on this, *I'll* speak to your mother this weekend. But you must leave it to me, Chloe, you mustn't pester me. I'll do it when the right opportunity presents itself."

"Oh, thank you, thank you, Gramps!" Chloe cried, and jumped up, ran across the room, hugged him tightly.

Derek held her close to him, loving her. She was so young, so vulnerable. He met Blair's eyes across the room, smiled faintly, and raised a brow. He had recognized the look on his wife's face instantly. It mirrored what he himself was thinking: Stevie would tell him nothing.

Later that afternoon, Derek put down the script he had been reading and, looking over at his wife, he said, "Do you think all families are like ours?"

"What do you mean?"

"Dysfunctional."

"How can you say that, Derek! We're not dysfunctional!"

"We're trotting along in that direction."

"I don't believe we're having this conversation."

"Believe it, darling." Derek laughed hollowly. "There's nothing new about dysfunctional families. They've been around since the Stone Age." He glanced at the script on the ottoman next to his chair. "Take the Plantagenets, for example."

Blair simply gaped at him.

Derek grinned, amused by her expression of mingled disbelief and denial. "Seriously, Blair, look at Henry Plantagenet and Eleanor of Aquitaine, their three sons, Richard, Geoffrey, and John, and Alais Capet, their French ward who was also Henry's mistress. Now, that was a dysfunctional family if ever there was one. Things haven't changed much since 1183, when Henry II was king of England and half of France."

"Are you going to do the revival of *The Lion in Winter*?" Blair asked, her eyes swinging to the script he had been reading.

"I might. It's an awfully good play and it hasn't been seen on Broadway since 1966. The dialogue is fabulous. And James Goldman really got it right, had Henry and Eleanor down pat. There's such wit, comedy, and drama in it. A lot to get my teeth in here."

"But will a revival work? Don't you think people remember the movie with Katharine Hepburn and Peter O'Toole?"

"I sincerely hope they do, and with pleasure, so that they'll want to see it again. As a play." Derek paused for a moment, and then added quietly, "But leaving the year 1183 behind, and getting back to 1996, and *our* dysfunctional family rather than the royal Plantagenets, what are we going to do about Chloe?"

"You're going to talk to Stevie."

"If you think I should."

"I do," Blair murmured. "She'll accept that kind of discussion from you more than she would from me, Derek. She'd just be very dismissive if I mentioned any of this to her. Anyway, she's always listened to you, paid attention to your words."

"She's awfully angry."

"Chloe?"

"Who else?" Derek replied, shifting slightly in the chair. "And I can understand why. Stevie should have told her all about John Lane years ago. God knows, she told the girl she was illegitimate."

Blair shook her head sadly. "Stevie had to tell her that, once she was old enough to understand. After all, there was no man around, and Stevie was a widow."

"Why all the secrecy about this John Lane?" Derek asked.

"Years ago you said that wasn't his real name. Have you changed your mind? Are you now saying that it *is* the man's name?"

"No, I'm not, Blair. I've always thought it was phony, that Stevie invented it for convenience's sake."

"In order to protect someone's identity?" Blair said softly.

Derek nodded.

"But who?" she asked, her voice full of puzzlement.

Derek raised a brow eloquently. "Who indeed? I've often thought it might be somebody we know. I've said that to you in the past, but you always pooh-poohed the idea, told me I was on the wrong track."

"I don't believe that. Not anymore, Derek. It could easily have been one of our friends, or someone she met through us. If you look back, really think about it, we were the only diversion she had in those days, working the way she did and stuck with the boys. Any social life Stevie had was with us. Perhaps she got involved with one of your actor chums. And it would have had to have been somebody famous. Otherwise, why bother to protect him?"

"Correct," Derek said, and rose. He walked across the room and stood looking out of the window for a few moments.

Blair's eyes followed him, rested on him, and admiringly so. To her he was the most extraordinary man she had ever known. Great actor, glamorous star, a man whose singular talent had won him accolades around the world.

And yet to her, perhaps the most amazing thing about him was his beginning. She had always found it incredible that at a very early age he had plucked himself up out of the Rhondda Valley and flung himself into the center of London's theatrical world, making a name for himself very quickly when he was so young, only nineteen.

What was even more astounding was that with only a ridiculously meager amount of training he had turned himself into a great classical actor, literally by an act of will. His first rendition of Hamlet in the West End was still talked about with awe.

Aside from his spectacular talent, Derek was a lovely man, very down to earth and real; he had humility, was honorable, and honest, not to mention a kind and loving human being. And he truly had an understanding heart. All were characteristics she valued, and she was certain she would have been hard pressed to find them *all* in anyone else.

Derek had loved her, and loved her well, for all those years, and she had loved him in return. They had been a good team, were still a good team. Looking back, she realized how much his astonishingly beautiful voice had cast a spell over her when she met him all those years ago. It still thrilled her, and when she sat listening to him in a theater, she was spellbound. Naturally, she had also fallen for his dark good looks, as most women did, had found herself mesmerized by those expressive, liquid eyes of a blue so light they were almost transparent.

He's sixty-eight but he doesn't look it. He's still straight as a ramrod, broad of chest, tall, and unbowed. And yet he seems tired today, Blair thought. His face was relatively unlined and youthful, except for tiny, finely etched lines around his eyes, but there were white wings at his temples now.

Suddenly Blair hoped he would not do the play. He was exhausted from his long Broadway run in *Becket* and the movie he had just finished in Arizona. She had hoped he would take a well-earned rest once they returned to London, but perhaps this wasn't possible for him.

Did he really want to play Henry II? Strut around a stage as that roaring Plantagenet king of England whom he had just portrayed in *Becket?* Probably. Henry II seemed to hold some sort of fascination for him, and anyway, Derek could be a glutton for punishment.

Derek interrupted his wife's thoughts when he swung away from the window and said, "She's eighteen, and naturally she is fascinated by her father . . . who he was, what he was like as a man. She wants to know all about him in order to know herself, understand herself better. However, Blair, I'm afraid Chloe has other problems, quite aside from the true identity of Papa."

"She does?"

"She did rather a lot of confiding on our little walk after lunch today."

"Apparently. What other bricks did she drop on you?"

Derek sighed and rubbed his hand over his face. "Chloe doesn't want to go to college."

"Now, *that* does surprise me!" Blair exclaimed. "In fact, it almost takes my breath away. Chloe has been so enthusiastic about going to Oxford, and for as long as I care to remember. In fact, she got me to drive her there last summer, then dragged me around the university and the city, if you recall. And she was excited about the whole idea of it. Look here, although she says she doesn't want to go to college now, she could easily change her mind later. The young only realize how tough it is when they get out there on their own."

"I hope Chloe will change her mind, but I have my doubts," Derek murmured, sounding regretful. "It's sad really that she intends to forgo Oxford. Those would be wonderful years for her, years she'd draw on and remember for the rest of her life. And it's upsetting for Stevie, who has wanted her to go there so badly."

"She's told her mother?"

"Yes. She's also informed Stevie that she wants to work at Jardine's."

Startled to hear this, Blair was silent for a moment. Then she said quickly, "Not my choice for her. On the other hand, perhaps it will please Stevie."

"Jardine's of London."

"*Oh, dear.* And I suppose she's announced that to her mother?" Blair looked at him questioningly.

"Yes, she did. When do the young ever hold anything back? They love to let it all hang out."

"No wonder you're talking *dysfunctional.*"

"There's more, my darling."

"No, Derek, don't say that. What else could possibly be troubling Chloe?" Blair's face filled with sudden apprehension.

"Oh, it's not Chloe I'm speaking about, but Miles."

"Miles is the sanest of us all."

"Very true. However, he's worried about Gideon. He thinks his twin has problems. Miles described him to me as being gloomy and depressed. He asked me how we thought Gideon seemed when we saw him in Los Angeles."

"Self-involved," Blair shot back.

Derek threw her a rapid glance and continued. "I told Miles that I thought Gideon appeared to be preoccupied. With business."

"Self-involved," Blair repeated in a knowing, confident voice.

Derek said, "There's more."

"Do tell. Get it over with, Derek." She sat back, waiting.

"Miles says that his mother believes Nigel is plotting against her, and that he wants to oust her from the company."

"Whatever will she think of next?"

Derek frowned. "Don't you believe it's true?"

"All joking apart, I'm afraid I do. I trust Stevie's judgment absolutely. I've never known it to be flawed. Apparently Nigel's is though." Blair's face grew thoughtful, and she sat staring into space for a second or two before continuing. "If Stevie says Nigel is working against her, then undoubtedly he is. And no wonder you bring up the Plantagenets. Shades of that bloodied family indeed, what with their plotting and double-dealing, secrets and scheming . . . their constant quarreling and hidden agendas."

He laughed. "Are *we* as bad as that, do you think?"

Blair leaned against the needlepoint cushions on the sofa and stared at him without making a comment. Suddenly she said, "Aren't all families?"

"I'm not sure. It depends on what's at stake. Let me ask you something else, Blair. Why would Nigel plot against his own mother? Especially when he will be taking over the company from her one day anyway."

"That's what is so baffling, Derek." Blair lifted her shoulders in a shrug. "I haven't got a clue. But Nigel has always been devious, that we both know." She threw him a pointed look. "Even as a child, remember? Anyway, darling, what are we going to do?"

"Do what all families do . . . work it out the best way we can, I suppose." Derek moved closer to the fire and sat down in the chair he had vacated a moment before. He picked up the script of *The Lion in Winter*, which dealt with a small segment of royal Plantagenet family life, and began to read again. After only a few minutes he closed the script, leaned back in the chair, and studied his wife.

Blair sat relaxed on the sofa, lost in thought; there was a faraway look in her eyes, and he knew she was worrying about the family, as she had been prone to do for years.

Blair was a remarkable woman—stoic, stalwart, dependable, and diplomatic. She had been blessed with an understanding of people, had enormous insight into them. He knew that being married to an actor, and a famous one at that, was no easy ride on a merry-go-round for a woman. Quite the opposite. You had to be strong, tenacious yet flexible, and willing to compromise. It

struck him that she looked more beautiful than ever today. When he had first met her, he had thought of her as the epitome of the all-American beauty, tall, long-legged, with a clear, shining skin, glossy blonde hair, passionate dark eyes, and gleaming white teeth. Blair had a truly lovely face, and Chloe, in particular, resembled her greatly.

He nodded to himself. Blair had aged well, like a really good wine, and she was as slim and elegant as ever. But it was her integrity, the joyousness of her spirit, her wit, humor, and warmth that he loved the most.

Blair said, "When should we talk to Stevie about Chloe, Derek?"

He shrugged. "I'm not sure, when we find the right moment, I suppose. Today's Saturday, and we're leaving tomorrow afternoon. I think it will have to be tonight sometime. After dinner might be best." He shook his head and exhaled. "I have a feeling she's not going to like it. You know how she hates interference."

"Maybe you should see Steve alone. She has always respected you and taken your advice into account."

"I've never discussed John Lane with her before."

"There's always a first time for everything, Derek."

10

"I WISH YOU COULD TELL CHLOE SOMETHING ABOUT HIM, STEVIE," Derek said quietly. "Believe me, anything at all would help to assuage her rampant curiosity, my darling."

Stevie returned her stepfather's steady gaze with one that was equally as steady, then walked across the study and draped herself against the mantel. She answered in a low voice, "I can't, Derek. You see, I don't know anything about him myself . . ." She let her sentence dangle, at a sudden loss for words.

Derek appeared surprised, and he gave her an odd look, his brows furrowing. "I'm not sure I'm following you."

Clearing her throat, Stevie murmured, "I hardly knew him. I think the best way to explain it is to say that it was a . . . a . . . brief encounter. We met at a cocktail party, discovered we were incredibly attracted to each other, and went off to dinner. Later that same week we met again. At a hotel. I slept with him. And that's when I got pregnant."

"And what did the gentleman in question have to say about

that? I presume you told him you were pregnant when you found out?" Derek replied carefully.

"Yes, I did tell him. Actually, he couldn't handle it, Derek."

"He didn't want to marry you?"

Stevie shook her head. "We hardly knew each other."

"So he threw you onto your own resources?"

"If you want to put it that way, yes."

"Charming."

Stevie was silent.

Derek said slowly, "He didn't really die in a car crash before Chloe was born, did he, darling?"

"No, he didn't. I told Chloe that story because it seemed to be the best explanation there was, the only thing I could come up with anyway. She had started to ask so many questions about him. I was embarrassed, to tell you the truth." Stevie cleared her throat. "But he is dead."

"Isn't there anything you could give her, Stevie?"

"Such as what?"

"A letter, a photograph, something tangible of that sort."

"Don't be silly, I hardly knew him."

"When *did* he die?" Derek asked.

"About a year after Chloe was born."

"How did he die? What of?"

"Natural causes."

"And presumably you found out about his death."

"Correct."

"How did you find out?"

Stevie gave Derek a hard stare and began to laugh. "What's this, the Spanish Inquisition? You sound like Torquemada."

"I'm sorry," Derek apologized swiftly, looking chagrined. "I'm afraid I'm a bit guilty of being curious myself. After all, we've never ever discussed this before."

"I know that and I cut off any discussion with Mom years ago. And you never asked me. Good thing you didn't too!" she exclaimed, and laughed again.

"If you didn't know this man, had no contact with him, how on earth did you know that he had died?"

"It was in the papers," she improvised.

"Ah, so he was well known, then," he asserted.

"Sort of."

"And was John Lane his real name?"

"Only partially."

"You changed the surname for convenience?"

"I thought it better, wiser to keep him totally anonymous."

"Would I recognize the name? Did I know him?"

Stevie stood staring at Derek, who had now seated himself in a chair near the fireplace.

"Was he an actor?" he asked when she did not respond.

"Listen, Derek, I don't really want to continue this conversation. It happened years ago. It's not very important who he was."

"Chloe seems to think it is," he reminded her.

Stevie let out a long, weary sigh. "I don't know why she's got a bee in her bonnet about her father all of a sudden. She's not mentioned him to me for years, now she's bothering you and God knows who else. As if it mattered in the scheme of things. Here's a girl who's had everything handed to her on a plate. Now she wants to know about her father. A man who has done nothing for her, played no role in her life. Come on, Derek, let's be fair."

"You're absolutely right, unfortunately the young are just that: *young*. She seems to think you're being unfair. And please don't kill the messenger, I'm only relating what she said."

"Derek, surely I've made it clear. It was a one-night stand! I'm embarrassed. I told you that before. The grieving widow of three years had a fling one night and got caught. It's an old, old story, and it's happened to countless women since the beginning of the world . . . sleeping with a man for the first time and getting pregnant."

"I understand."

"Unfortunately, Derek, there's nothing I can tell you or Mom or Chloe about him . . . because of the circumstances."

"I know. But listen to me for a moment. You said you met him at a cocktail party. So it was most probably at our house, wasn't it? And no doubt he was an actor. In which case, I would have known him. Tell me his real name, and I'll think of something suitable to say to Chloe."

"I didn't meet him at your house, Derek! Mother and you did not know him!" Stevie exclaimed, her voice full of exasperation, her face taut.

Derek looked at her keenly. He knew without a shadow of a doubt that she was lying.

After Derek had left, Stevie changed into her nightgown and then went back into the study adjoining her bedroom. Seating herself at her desk, she opened her daily journal and reached for the pen.

But she did not write, merely gazed blankly at the empty page, her mind awash with so many different and troubling thoughts.

A sudden knock on the door startled her, made her jump, and she sat up in the chair. "Who is it?"

"It's only me," her mother said from the doorway.

"Another nocturnal visitor, I see."

Ignoring her sarcasm, Blair glided into the room, came to a stop at the desk, and put a hand on Stevie's shoulder. "Derek thinks he's upset you."

"He hasn't. He never upsets me, and he should know that after over thirty years. Look, Mom, I know he means well, but—"

"But the road to hell is paved with good intentions."

"I didn't say that, Mother."

"That's what you meant. Come, sit with me on the sofa."

Stevie got up, followed her mother, seated herself next to her, and said, "I hope you haven't come here to rehash everything Derek and I discussed."

"Certainly not. Nor do I want to start asking questions about something that happened so very long ago. The details of your relationship with John Lane, or whatever his name was, are your business. You didn't want to tell me anything at the time. Now it's eighteen years too late."

"An intelligent comment at last."

"Derek feels the same way I do, you know, Stevie. He's rather sorry he started this tonight, but we were both concerned about Chloe. She seemed so troubled this afternoon. Full of questions about her father."

"God knows why! I've been mother and father both to her, and frankly, I thought I'd done a good job. I've nurtured her, loved her, given her understanding and guidance. Furthermore, the whole family loves her, supports her, caters to her, and actually spoils her terribly. She has everything a girl could ever possibly want. An education, money, a future. And now, suddenly, she's running around asking, 'Who's my father? Why won't she tell me about him?' That's her new cry." Stevie shook her head and gave her mother a hard stare. "I can't tell her anything because I didn't have a relationship with him. It was a one-night stand. He was a total stranger."

"Derek told me all that," Blair replied, and sighed. "I know you sacrificed a great deal for Chloe, so I'm not one bit surprised that you're feeling impatient with her now."

"I never thought of it as a sacrifice, Mother," Stevie muttered with a frown.

"Yet it was, in my opinion. You were so devoted to her, you never gave yourself a chance to meet anyone, to have a life of your own, get married again. And you could have, Stephanie. By then the boys were all away at boarding school and you had Nanny for Chloe."

Stevie made no comment; she knew that everything her mother had just said was true. But she had felt so guilty about the circumstances of Chloe's birth, she had overcompensated in so many different ways. She had denied herself the possibility of personal happiness with a man, had chosen instead her children and her work.

"The young are very selfish, Stevie dear," Blair remarked. "Well, we're all selfish, I suppose, that's the human condition. But the young are more selfish. I remember I was, and so were you when you were a girl. And then there's that awful, all-consuming self-centeredness of the young. When we're in our teens and twenties we think we're the only thing that matters in the entire world. And that's what Chloe is going through now, Stevie. She has the pressing need to know about her biological father because of her need to know about herself. In a way, it has nothing to do with you, it's not against you. I hope you realize that."

"Yes, I guess I do, Mom. I'm just a bit annoyed she dumped all of this on Derek this weekend. I wanted you both to have a rest, enjoy yourselves."

"Oh, but we did, and we've loved being here. It's been wonderful, very cozy and relaxing. You've spoiled us." Blair shifted slightly on the sofa and looked at Stevie closely. "Do you think Derek looks tired?"

Stevie shook her head. "Not at all. He seems marvelous to me. Full of vim and vigor."

Blair smiled. "I do worry about him, you know. A long run in a play is always very taxing. Are you coming to London for Christmas?"

"Don't we always? I wouldn't miss it for the world."

After the merest hesitation, Blair asked, "Is she serious about not going to college?"

"I honestly don't know, Mom. I've decided to play the waiting game . . . let's see what she says after she's graduated from Brearley next summer."

"And what about her working at Jardine's?"

"That could be a whim. She seems to be somewhat focused on Gideon at the moment. And I don't know why. She and Miles are closer."

"What *about* Gideon, Stevie? Miles seems to think his brother is depressed. He told Derek he's very gloomy."

"Gideon has always been rather gloomy . . . perhaps morose is a better word. It's funny, they're so different in temperament. Miles is positive, his cup is always half full, while Gideon is just the opposite. Anyway, as far as Gideon's present mood is concerned, I personally think he's suffering from women trouble. More precisely, Margot trouble. I've noticed this odd mood of his in the past few months whenever I've been in London, and I think he's perturbed because he broke up with her."

"Is that all! Goodness, we'll soon fix that!"

Stevie laughed. "Oh, Mom, there's no one like you. You're always so positive you can cure what ails us."

After her mother had left, Stevie went back to the desk and once more picked up her pen. Again she did not write anything in her journal. Instead, she sat back, her thoughts centering on Chloe. *I mustn't be too hard on her. My mother's right. This is not about me. It's about her. If only I could tell her something about her father, but I can't.*

Stevie thought about him for a brief moment. She closed her eyes, and his image danced around in her head, as it had so often in the past. Thinking about him was futile, she knew that, but there were moments when she couldn't help herself. Like now. How different her life, their lives, would have been if only she had had more courage . . . the courage to tell him the truth. It was all too late now. No use dwelling on the past. As her mother had said earlier, it was eighteen years too late.

Almost against her own volition, Stevie rose and went to her briefcase, where she found her keys. Crossing the floor, she unlocked the large cupboard, bent down to the safe, and punched in the code on the keypad, then turned the handle. All of her diaries were stacked in neat piles inside the safe; it took her only a split second to find the one dated 1977. She took it out and went and sat on the sofa in front of the fire.

Stevie sat staring at the diary for a while without opening it, smoothing her hands over the gold-embossed numbers on the leather front: *1977*. What a year that had been. All kinds of memories flooded her, and *he* jostled for prominence in her mind. But she shook off thoughts of him, swiftly began to flip the pages until she came to the first week of December. Here it was, that fateful day, the day she had made all of her decisions. She began to read.

December 5th, 1977
London

I've been thinking a lot about the predicament I'm in. In fact, I've thought of nothing else really for days. And tonight I made my decisions. I'm going to have the baby.

Last week, when Jennifer Easton took me to see her doctor, I was thrilled when he confirmed that I was about eight weeks pregnant, as I suspected. And then on the drive home reality took over. I began to panic. Jennifer told me about a doctor in Mayfair. A well-known doctor who was associated with a clinic. Jennifer said that all I had to do was go and see him for an examination and explain my circumstances. He would then check me into the clinic and perform a D & C. When I came out I would no longer be pregnant. But I don't want to have an abortion. I want the baby. His baby. I never thought I would love another man after Ralph, but I do. I love him. We cannot be. But I can have his child. Some people are not so lucky.

Jennifer asked me what I'm going to tell people if I go ahead and have the baby. I've decided I'm not going to tell them anything. They can't force me to, and nobody's going to put me up against a wall and shoot me because I'm silent. My mother and Derek won't be a problem. Alfreda might make trouble, but I don't care about her. And anyway, I'm holding all the cards as far as the Jardines are concerned. My three sons. Sons who are in my custody. They are Jardines. Heirs to the Jardines. As for Bruce, whatever he really thinks he'll be diplomatic, careful with me. He needs me at Jardine's. He's not a well man; sometimes he seems much older than his years. Daily he grows more dependent on me. No, I won't explain myself. Not to anyone. I cannot tell him either. What to do? I'll have to break off with him. It will be difficult because I care about him.

There was more on the page, and the page after that, but Stevie had read enough. And so she closed the diary without finishing that particular entry to the end, just sat there, absently gazing at the dying embers in the grate.

Rightly or wrongly, those had been her decisions and she had abided by them. She filled with sadness. It was an old familiar, that ache inside. She had learned to live with it long ago.

11

WHENEVER SHE WAS WITH ANDRÉ BIRRON, STEVIE FOUND HERSELF smiling. There was something about him, about his demeanor and his personality that made her feel at ease, even happy, and it seemed to her that he brought out the best in her.

André was a small, stocky, energetic man with silver hair, a round, cherubic face, and shrewd eyes that looked like shiny black buttons. He had been a friend of her husband who had described André to her as "a little leprechaun of a man," and that first description had stayed in her mind ever since.

She had met André just before Nigel was born, when she had been heavy with child and slow on her feet. André, the father of two himself, had been very solicitous of her, and caring. This kindness aside, they had taken to each other at once. Despite the difference in their ages they had become fast friends over the years.

After Ralph's unexpected, very sudden death, André had gone out of his way to stay in touch with Stevie. "I must keep a fatherly eye on you," he would say whenever he came to London. And for many years now he had been her mentor; she listened to him, took his advice, and had never regretted doing so, since he always brought to her problems an unprejudiced point of view. And he was wise in the ways of the world.

It was from André that she had learned about the international side of the jewelry business, and about such great designers as Belperron, Boivin, and the Duke of Verdura, to name only a few.

André was an expert on these renowned designers of the thirties, forties, and fifties, as well as on Jean-Baptiste Tavernier, the intrepid merchant-traveler who had moved between Paris and the Golconda mines of India in the seventeenth century, and who had first brought diamonds back to Europe from the subcontinent. Tavernier had supplied diamonds to Louis XIV, the Sun King, and those members of the French court who could afford them. One of the first big "name" diamonds was called the Grand Mazarin, named after Cardinal Mazarin, who bequeathed it to the Sun King on his death.

Ralph had already taught her a great deal about diamonds by the time she met André; the latter had been impressed that a woman so young and inexperienced had acquired so much knowledge in so short a time. As she explained to him, she was a quick study, had a photographic memory, and had always harbored a genuine desire to learn about precious stones and Ralph's business, which fascinated her.

Ralph had told her once that he had two great passions in his life. "You, my love, and diamonds. So let me share my second passion with you, my first."

And that was really how she had been given such a well-rounded education about diamonds and other gems. Ralph had impressed two things on her when teaching her about diamonds: that the rarity and value of a diamond was determined by the four Cs: carat—the weight and size—plus the clarity, color, and cut of a stone, and that only the largest, rarest, and most dazzling stone is given a name.

And tonight, for the first time in her twenty-one-year career as a jeweler, she herself was going to bid on a big "name" diamond, the famous White Empress, which would go on the auction block at Sotheby's at seven o'clock exactly.

Only a few hours away. She did not feel nervous or apprehensive. Quite to the contrary. She was relaxed, self-confident and calm. And her mood, she was quite sure, was due to some extent to André's reassuring presence.

Stevie sat with him now in the sitting room of his suite at the Carlyle Hotel, sipping a glass of carbonated water, her attention riveted on him.

"And so, *ma chérie*, it was a decision I made . . . to show you the pieces first, before disposing of them elsewhere if you are not interested."

"I'm sure I will be, André," Stevie responded, smiling at him. "As you know, I'm always looking for lovely old things for the antique jewelry department at the London store. Some of my clients are interested only in the very old pieces these days."

"They are in vogue, yes," he answered, and got up, hurried off to another room in the capacious suite. Within a few seconds he returned, explaining, "Matt is bringing them so that you can view them, Stephanie."

Once again he sat down opposite her and then instantly jumped up, as sprightly as ever at seventy-five. He exclaimed, "Let us sit over there. At the table near the window. It is the better light, I think, no?"

"Yes, it is," Stephanie agreed, adding, "And there's also a good lamp on the table." She followed him across the room, eager to see what he had brought with him from Paris.

André Birron owned one of the most elegant and prestigious jewelry shops in the world, located on the Place Vendôme near the Ritz Hotel. The business had been founded in the nineteenth century by his great-grandfather, Pierre Birron, who had made a name for himself when he had outbid other jewelers for some of the royal jewels. At an auction in Paris in 1887, the diamonds of the Crown of France had been put on the block by the Third Republic. All the great jewelers were present, including Frédéric Boucheron of Paris, Tiffany & Company of New York, and Bonynge of London. It was Pierre Birron who had won some of the more magnificent spoils by going for broke. He never looked back. Like Jardine's, Birron et Cie was family owned and run. André's two sons worked with him at the Place Vendôme shop.

Matt Wilson, André's assistant, came in carrying a briefcase, which he brought over to André.

"*Bien, bien, ouvrez-le!*" André exclaimed.

Matt opened the briefcase, took out various gray suede pouches and jewelry wallets. Opening one of the large wallets, he pushed it toward Stevie without comment, but his expression said more than any words could.

Stevie stared at the necklace Matt had revealed. It was made of two strands of stained blue chalcedony beads. She felt a little shiver run through her as she gazed at the blue-gray beads that glistened as they caught and held the light. Then she exclaimed, "It's Belperron, isn't it?" Her voice held a note of excitement as she glanced at André.

"Yes, it is most probably Belperron." He let out a small sigh and shook his head, looking regretful. "It is unfortunate that Suzanne never signed her pieces. She believed her designs were so absolutely unique and unconventional that they were easily recognizable as being hers, and no one else's. 'My signature is redundant, André,' she used to tell me."

"More's the pity she never signed her creations. May I look at this more closely?"

"*Mais naturellement.*" The Frenchman lifted the necklace out of the suede wallet and handed it to her.

Stevie held it under the lamp on the table, examined the chalcedony beads and the flowerhead clasp. This was composed of larger, carved chalcedony stones that formed the petals; the center was set with a cluster of eight cabochon sapphires and bands of brilliant-cut diamonds.

André sat back in his chair, observing her, thinking what a stylish woman she was. Tonight she wore a well-cut tailored suit of black wool with black satin lapels and cuffs, and to his seasoned eye it was obviously couture. Her only pieces of jewelry were mabe pearl earrings, a single strand of large South Sea pearls, and a platinum watch. Simple, understated, very chic. She had a refined and elegant taste in all things, and especially so in jewelry; not unnaturally, her perfect taste was reflected in her own personal style of dressing.

André Birron was very proud of Stephanie Jardine and of what she had become. He had watched her grow and change and develop; he had also watched over her for some twenty-odd years. She was like the daughter he and his wife Elise had never had, and his wife was just as fond of her as he was.

Stephanie had turned herself into a formidable business-woman, and a jeweler par excellence. This gave him great pleasure and satisfaction, since she was his protégé in a sense.

But beyond her professionalism, there was something else, a uniqueness about her that made him feel all that much better for knowing her. Frequently, he had tried to define this particular quality in her, and had eventually come to the conclusion that it was the mixture of her integrity, decency, and genuine compassion that lifted her so high above others, made her so different.

There was something fine in her that was very rare, and admirable.

André felt that at the core of her there was a repose, a calmness, and a certain kind of aloofness that had more to do with reserve than snobbery, and it was also this that set her apart.

There were times when he wondered about the lover Stephanie had taken when she was a young widow, the father of Chloe, wondered why the relationship had never flourished, gone forward, led to a permanent situation such as matrimony. He had constantly discouraged her from confiding the intimate details of her life in him or anyone else, and apparently she had always followed those guidelines he had given her so long ago.

No one knew a single thing about Stephanie Jardine's private life other than what was obvious, which was there for all to see; not even her family had an inkling about what she did. If anything at all.

He assumed there must have been other boyfriends over the years, maybe even lovers, and yet he had never seen her with a man other than a business associate. In consequence, there was not one shred of gossip about her. That in itself was an accomplishment, he believed.

It suddenly struck him, and quite forcibly, that perhaps there was no gossip because there was nothing to gossip about. There was the strong possibility that her children, Jardine's, and her career had been, and were, enough for her. Yet only part of him believed this. He was a Frenchman and a romantic, and therefore he could not envision life without love. And what a barren life that would be, and so very lonely. To be alone was not enviable. He shrank from the thought that Stephanie lived such a cold and isolated private life. Surely that could not be so? he asked himself, and discovered he had no answer. And he did not have the courage to ask her.

It took Stevie only a moment longer to examine the necklace before she glanced up at André and said in a confident voice, "It's Belperron. No question in my mind about that. She made it anywhere between 1935 and 1938, I'd say. Yes, André, only Belperron herself could have designed this—" Very abruptly Stevie cut herself off, looked at him intently, and exclaimed, "You know, we've seen something very similar, you and I. In 1987, at the Sotheby's sale of the Duchess of Windsor's jewels in Geneva. Don't you remember, there was a necklace of hers that was rather like this one? One could say it was the sister to this. I certainly raved enough about it at the time, so I'm sure you couldn't possibly have forgotten."

"I do recall the occasion. And your enthusiasm." He smiled at her warmly. "That is one of the special things about you, *ma chérie*. You are not jaded. And when I saw this necklace a few weeks ago, I realized that you would be the one to truly appreciate its beauty. Do you not recall that when we were in Geneva for the Windsor sale, I told you that the duchess had been a frequent visitor to the Herz-Belperron shop in the rue de Châteaudun in Paris in the thirties?"

"Yes, I do remember."

"It was apparent to me in Geneva that the necklace at the auction was a Belperron piece, even though it was listed as 'probably Belperron.' Unfortunately, that is the problem with an unsigned item, it can only ever be listed as *probably*. But it was real. It had to be. The duchess wore a great many of Suzanne's creations. The one you are now holding is of the same style, quality, and period, do you not think so?"

She nodded. "Where did you find it?"

"The owner is a very well-known Frenchwoman, from *le gratin*, the upper crust, in Paris. She inherited it from her mother, who inherited it from *her* mother. She insists it is Belperron, not a fake, not a copy from the thirties."

"We are all in agreement," Stevie murmured. "But surely Belperron would have made earrings to match."

"*Voila!* My clever one! You know your designers well." He laughed.

"Thanks to you," she said, smiling back at him.

"These are the ear clips that complete the set." He took them out of a pouch and placed them on a table in front of her.

Reaching for the earrings, Stevie held them in the palm of her hand and examined them carefully. They were made of the same stained blue chalcedony, each one designed as a small leaf and set with a tapered band of diamonds and surmounted by a cluster of cabochon sapphires and diamonds.

"They're exquisite, and the set is perfect. I have just the right client, an elegant woman who collects thirties jewelry. I am sure she will be interested. She's in London though, not New York."

"That does not present any problem, as you are well aware. When I return to Paris this weekend, I will have the jewelry sent to London by the usual courier, the way I have done in the past."

"How much is the set?" she asked.

"Forty-five thousand dollars."

"Expensive."

"No, I do not think so, Stephanie, not for Belperron. The Duchess of Windsor's necklace and earrings went for more than that in 1987. Nine years ago."

"But that was a glamour auction and all the world came to it, don't forget. The prices were driven sky high because of the great interest in the Windsors—to be more precise, in the Duchess of Windsor."

André chuckled admiringly. "You never forget a thing, and what you say is true. However, let me please explain this particular situation. *I* am not selling the jewels, they are *not* the property of Birron et Cie. I am merely acting as a—how do you say?—a go-between, for a client. I am doing her a favor. She had the necklace and ear clips appraised and was informed they were worth about forty thousand dollars approximately. She asked me if I could get my own appraisal, which I did, and, *mon Dieu!* My appraiser came in with an even higher figure—fifty thousand. So we decided, she and I, to set a price somewhere in the middle. I will explain everything to you later if you decide to buy the pieces. Let you know how you will pay for them."

"All right."

"You do not doubt that the jewels are by Belperron, do you?"

"Oh, no, of course I don't. They bear her inimitable stamp, signature or not. The price is not a problem. What else did you bring from Paris?" she asked, now eyeing the other gray suede pouches on the table, her curiosity getting the better of her.

"Ah, yes, I will show you. There is a diamond pin by Jeanne Boivin. *Signed.* A lovely example of her individualistic work. Perfection, I think. Here it is." He took it out, gave it to Stevie. "It is owned by the same woman in Paris, and again it is a family heirloom. *Très jolie, oui?*"

"It is indeed." Stevie held the pin out in front of her, gazing at it, and admiringly so. It was a spray of flowers, Queen Anne's lace, she thought, and beautifully executed. It was typical of Jeanne Boivin's nature-theme designs of the mid-thirties, when the renowned designer copied her favorite plants and simple flowers in diamonds and platinum.

"I like this very much, and it's perfect for another client of mine," Stevie explained, instantly thinking of Derek. Her stepfather had asked her to look for something unusual he could give her mother for Christmas. Certainly this pin would suit Blair. It was stylish without being overwhelming.

"This is extremely rare," André announced as he presented a dramatic orange-shell brooch to her next.

"It's Verdura!"

André smiled with pleasure. "It seems I taught you well, *ma chérie*. Yes, it is the duke's famous lion's paw shell pin. As you know, he made several of them in the thirties, until the shells became extinct, difficult to find anymore. It has become a much-sought-after piece of jewelry, not only because of its individuality but because it is by Verdura. When my client showed it to me, and hesitated about putting it up for sale, I convinced her to do so. She will never wear it and she is in need of money. But look, Stephanie, at this workmanship . . . at the encrustation of diamonds set in gold strips which run up the front of the paw. The work is superb, *incroyable*, do you not agree?"

"I certainly do, and it's a very unusual pin. Ideal for a brunette with a strong personality." She placed the shell pin on the table and leaned back against the chair, smiling at her old friend. She had not had to think twice about buying the antique jewelry, and so she said, "I shall take this, as well as the Boivin and the Belperron pieces. It's not very often that something by Verdura comes on the market, and the duke's jewelry has become very popular in the last few years."

"I am happy you are taking them. Each item is unique. Because they are so rare they are extremely valuable. You can almost put any price on them you want, *chérie*."

Stevie laughed. "You'd better get out your calculator and tot this up. And then I think we must leave for the auction. I want to get there early."

"*Mais oui*, the auction! I am looking forward to it. And even more than that, I am looking forward to being your escort. What a triumph it is going to be for you, Stephanie, when you win the White Empress."

Stevie stared at him but said nothing. Quite unexpectedly she felt apprehensive and at a loss for words.

André said, "Before we leave I have something for you. Excuse me." He almost ran out of the room, calling for Matt as he disappeared into the small foyer of the suite. In a moment he was back, holding a black leather box in his hands. Giving it to Stevie, he said, "This is for you, Stephanie, and it comes to you with our love."

Stevie was so completely taken aback, she gaped at him, and then she opened the box. She caught her breath when she saw the delicate diamond pin on the black velvet; it was a long, curling feather and it was extraordinary. "Oh, André, it's beautiful! But I can't accept this . . . it's far too valuable."

"No, no, you cannot refuse! You must not refuse. It is special . . . a *cadeau, ma chérie,* for your birthday."

"My birthday's not until next week."

"I will not be in America next week."

Realizing how ungracious it would be to argue with him any further, she said, "Thank you, André, it was so lovely of you and Elise to remember. I shall call her tomorrow to thank her."

"My wife adores you . . . to her you are like a daughter."

"I know. And I love her too." Stevie now began to laugh, shaking her head. "I can't believe I am going to be forty-seven next week. It doesn't seem possible."

"I cannot believe it either. What has happened to the time? It seems to me it was only the other day I met you with Ralph. You were not quite seventeen and very pregnant. Thirty years ago."

"*Please!*" she exclaimed. "Don't remind me!"

"I am proud of you, proud of what you've become. And if he were alive, Ralph would be also proud. You are only forty-seven and at the apex of your career . . . considered to be one of the world's great jewelers. And you are revered."

"Thank you for your lovely words, André," she replied, touched by what he had just said. "But it is *you* who is *revered,* not I." Rising, she walked across to the mirror hanging on a side wall and fastened the diamond feather on the lapel of her jacket. Then she turned around, her expression one of great affection. "How does it look, your beautiful feather?"

"*Superbe, ma chérie.*"

She walked across to him, bent down, and kissed him on each cheek. "Thank you again, André. I shall treasure it always."

He nodded, and patted her hand resting on his shoulder, his dark eyes twinkling. He was pleased their gift had been so well accepted, and said, "I will tell Matt we must leave for the auction at once," and got up, strode off.

Stevie sat down at the table, began to put the jewelry back in the pouches and wallet. Then she placed them in the briefcase.

Together, André and Matt came into the sitting room; they were both wearing their overcoats and Matt carried Stevie's Trigère cape of black wool lined with red silk. He helped her into it, then locked the briefcase and picked it up.

André's assistant said, "I'll take the briefcase down with us, leave it in the hotel safe."

"*Bien, bien,* but let us hurry now, Matt, we must not be late."

As the three of them went down in the elevator, Matt turned to Stevie. "The brooch is gorgeous on you. And you know what, you could wear it on that black velvet beret you favor . . . then you'll have"—he grinned at her, and finished—"a feather in your cap."

"Oh, Matt . . ." She smiled up at him, shaking her head.

André also smiled, then asked, "And how are you feeling, *chérie*? Excited, I am quite certain."

"No, nervous," Stevie answered, and gave a funny little laugh.

"No, no, you must not be nervous! You must be your usual cool self. Cool and contained. I am here. Matt is here. All will be well. You will see. And it is going to be your evening, my Stephanie."

12

STEVIE FELT THE BUZZ IN THE AIR THE MOMENT THEY ARRIVED AT Sotheby's on York Avenue. A sense of anticipation and excitement permeated the auction rooms, and to her they seemed like palpable things. People milled around, greeting each other, talking, laughing, and commenting about the auction due to take place within the next half hour.

As Stevie glanced around, she spotted a bevy of well-known New Yorkers, some of them her clients, and also recognized any number of renowned jewelers from London, Paris, Rome, and Geneva as well as from New York.

It was a smartly dressed crowd. The men wore expensive, well-tailored suits; the women were mostly in black, as they usually were in New York at night. She had lived there long enough now to know that black with diamonds or pearls was the compulsory, and very chic, uniform. She had enough black suits, dresses, and silk pumps in her wardrobe to attest to that.

"Let's not waste time out here," Stevie said, glancing from André to Matt, and headed toward the room where the auction was to be held.

As they entered, they were given catalogues and numbered paddles to use for the bidding, and then moved on into the room. Matt found three good seats in the center, where they all sat down, with Stevie positioned between the two men. After settling in her seat, she glanced around, eyeing her immediate neighbors.

"*Quelle scène*," André said, his eyes sweeping around. "*Mon Dieu!* Everyone is here!"

"Sure they are—the world and his mother," Matt remarked.

"Such quaint expressions you have, Matt," André murmured, then exclaimed, "Ah, there is my old friend, Gilberto Guantano from Brazil. It is a long time since I have seen him. I must go to him, embrace him. Excuse me, Stephanie, Matt." So saying, he slipped out of his seat and hurried down the aisle to speak to his friend.

After a moment, Matt rose, stood looking around, wondering who was there that *he* knew. He saw two notable jewelers from Paris, lifted his hand in greeting, and remained standing next to Stevie, his eyes continuing to scan the room, his curiosity running high. "André is correct, this is some turnout," he said, looking down at Stephanie. "Everyone is here, or they've sent representatives . . . I see people from Harry Winston, Cartier, and Boucheron. I've just spotted one of the directors of Van Cleef, the Garrard group, and David Morris is over there with his wife, Suzette. Quite a lot of people from London have flown in."

"Yes, I know. And I saw a couple of familiar faces from Geneva as well."

Matt finally took his seat, then went on. "But I wonder how many are actually serious bidders?"

"I'm not sure," Stevie responded, "but I have a feeling I'm going to get a run for my money."

"And my money's on you," Matt said with a wide grin.

Stevie shook her head. "I don't know, Matt . . . well, we'll see."

"Nervous?"

"A bit," she admitted, and gave him a rueful smile.

"Try not to worry," Matt advised. "You'll see, it'll be all right."

"That's what André keeps telling me. I hope he's right."

"He is. We both feel it in our bones, you're going to get the White Empress."

"By the looks of this crowd, I'm going to have to pay for it . . . *really pay.*"

"Have you set a limit on it?"

"I don't really want to go beyond ten million," she said sotto voce, not wanting anyone to overhear. "But I will if I have to. I'd go up to twelve million."

Matt nodded but made no further comment. Then he stood up again, glancing around, wondering somewhat worriedly who her *real* competitors were going to be.

Stevie shifted slightly in her chair, endeavoring to relax, but it was hard for her to do so. She was taut with nerves, strung tight like a violin string, and growing anxious all of a sudden. She wanted the auction to begin so that she could get it over with, be done with it now. The noise level was rising as more and more people flooded in; she felt far too warm, and the smell of mingled perfumes was overwhelming.

The White Empress. One of the most fabulous diamonds in the world. Her mind settled on it for a moment or two. She wanted it. She was determined to get it, but there was the real possibility that she might not. Somebody might easily outbid her. She was accustomed to being in control—of herself, her business, her life, and she was not happy when she was not. It was certainly not possible to be in control of a public auction. Only the auctioneer had that kind of control, since it was he who determined everything, at least to a certain extent.

An unexpected thought popped into her head, and she had to bite back a smile. Of course she could be in control of this auction. But only if she was prepared to pay *anything* for the White Empress, top any bid. I will, she said under her breath, I'll outbid everybody here. Somehow this idea was liberating, and she felt the tension easing out of her. If she was prepared to pay any price, then she was not only in control already, she already owned the diamond. So invigorating and exciting was this possibility, Stevie clamped her mouth shut and looked at the catalogue. She was afraid that she might blurt out her thoughts to Matt. *A still tongue and a wise head,* she heard Ralph's voice saying in the far recesses of her mind.

Focusing in on the White Empress again, Stevie asked herself what she might conceivably have to pay for it, given her decision to outbid everyone present? Twelve, thirteen even fourteen million? Possibly. Maybe more. She wasn't sure. The auction could go any which way; she knew this only too well. The reserve price, the presale price, was six million. In a way this did not mean very much. As Matt had just pointed out to her, the auction was jammed with many prominent international jewelers as well as a number of multimillionaires and billionaires whom she had recognized instantly. If they *all* bid, the price would be pushed so high, it would be ludicrous.

André came back to his seat and squeezed her hand. "Gilberto thinks a lot of people are merely here for the excitement, for the fun of it. Do not worry."

"Oh, I'm not worried, André darling," she said, and she sounded positively nonchalant. So much so that both André and Matt looked at her alertly, then glanced at each other.

Suddenly the auctioneer was stepping up to the podium.

Instantly the room fell silent.

And so it began. The auction for the White Empress.

The lights dimmed and the color slides of the diamond suspended on its superb Harry Winston necklace flashed onto the screen that stood on the left of the podium. The auctioneer made his statement, giving all the details of the great diamond and its origins. The slide show finished, the lights went up, and the auctioneer started the bids rolling.

Looking out into the crowded room, he said with undisguised enthusiasm, "I'll take the opening bid to my right. Two million dollars." His eyes swiveled to the other side of the room. "Two million two hundred and fifty thousand from the center left. Two million five hundred thousand from the back of the room."

After the opening bid of two million, the price was rising in increments of two hundred fifty thousand dollars. After years of attending auctions all over the world, Stevie was aware that the amount could change at the will of the auctioneer. It was he who made the decisions.

Finally she raised her paddle. The auctioneer acknowledged this with the merest flicker of an eyelash. "Three million from the center. Three million two hundred fifty thousand to my left. Three million five hundred thousand to the left front. Three million seven hundred fifty thousand at the back. Do I hear four million?"

Once more Stevie raised her paddle, bringing the price up to the desired four. It went on climbing after this, as others raised their paddles and made their bids. The pace was rapid, the excitement mounting.

André and Matt were on the edges of their seats, as was she. Her adrenaline was pumping hard when she plunged in once more and made her bid for five million. Yet again it did not end there, as she had known it wouldn't; the reserve price had to be met. The person who had outbid her was outbid several times by others wanting to claim the White Empress as their own.

The auction was moving at a fast and furious pace. The tension in the room was a most viable thing, and Stevie felt as though she could reach out, touch it, take it in her hand. Just as she was determined to take the diamond in her hand—for Jardine's.

Another bid came in, and another, and then another, and another after that, until the price had escalated even higher, had gone well over the presale figure of six million.

Stevie was relaxed, sat staring straight ahead, holding her paddle in her lap, making no moves at all. I must wait now, she told herself. Drop back so that the auctioneer will wonder about me, wonder if I'm dropping out altogether. She kept a poker face, but inside she was smiling.

André, watching her closely, knew what she was doing. She was biding her time, not wanting to contribute to the acceleration of the price.

Twenty minutes later Stevie sat up straighter, her attention fully directed on the auctioneer, all of her senses alerted. The bidding had reached eight million five hundred thousand even without her participation. And then it had slowed. Several people had resisted, had not bid, and to all intents and purposes they had now dropped out. Stevie waited for the auctioneer to change the amount of the increments, which he did almost immediately. He lowered them to one hundred thousand dollars.

Now that this had happened, the bidding started to move again, although not quite as rapidly or as intensely as before. The price rose accordingly as ten bids came in, bringing the price up to nine million eight hundred thousand dollars. And then once more it slowed, and, somewhat unexpectedly, came finally to a halt.

"Nine million eight hundred thousand," the auctioneer repeated, his voice rising slightly. "Do I hear nine million nine?"

Stephanie raised her paddle.

"*Nine million nine hundred thousand in the center!* I want to hear ten million. Ten million dollars for the White Empress."

A bid came from somewhere in the room, and she heard the auctioneer cry, "Ten million from the front. *Ten million!* Ten-million-one, am I getting an offer of ten million one hundred thousand for this magnificent diamond?"

To Stevie the silence in the room seemed to magnify. It became so hushed, a pin dropping would have sounded like a crash. Every person sat on the edge of his or her seat, their attention focused on the auctioneer.

Stevie held her breath.

The auctioneer repeated himself. "Do I hear ten million one? Surely I do." There was a brief pause; not one paddle was raised.

"Ten million one hundred thousand. Do I have that offer?" The auctioneer cleared his throat. "Ten million, then, to the bidder at the front, unless I hear ten million one hundred thousand."

André touched her arm.

Stevie brought her paddle up.

"*Ten million one hundred thousand!*" cried the auctioneer, sounding triumphant, full of jubilance.

Stevie's heart was pounding against her rib cage and her mouth was dry like sandpaper. She sat as though turned to stone, again hardly daring to breath, waiting for the next bid, for someone to top her. But no one did. The stone was hers. For a moment it didn't seem possible.

"Ten million one hundred thousand dollars it is. Sold to the lady in the center."

Everyone in the room brought their eyes to her. Someone

began to applaud. Others joined in. The applause became louder. A woman cried, "Bravo! Bravo!"

André hugged her to him and kissed her cheek. And so did Matt, who exclaimed, "You're as cold as ice."

Stevie shook her head. "No, I'm fine, really I am, Matt."

"I would say you are indeed fine," André murmured against her ear, smiling broadly. "As fine as you'll ever be, Stephanie. And when you are ready to leave, I shall take you to dinner at La Grenouille."

They came to speak to her then, streaming across the room, people she knew, clients and friends, and colleagues from the jewelry business. And they brought their congratulations and they wished her well.

13

STEVIE SAT IN HER OFFICE ON THE TOP FLOOR OF THE JARDINE BUILD-
ing on Fifth Avenue in the fifties.

It was Tuesday morning, a few days after the auction at
Sotheby's the week before, and the White Empress had just been
delivered a short while ago. The previous Friday the paperwork
had been completed and the money had been wired bank to
bank.

And so here it was at last, one of the most important stones
in the world, and it belonged to her, or, rather, to Jardine's.

Stevie now lifted the necklace out of the dark blue leather
Harry Winston jewelry case and held it up in front of her. The
huge pear-shaped diamond was 128.25 carats with fifty-eight
facets on the crown and pavilion and eighty-five additional
facets around the girdle. The diamond threw off a myriad of
prisms as it blazed in the sunlight pouring in through the window. The stone was D-flawless and therefore perfect, and it was
so blindingly white, so pure, it was breathtaking.

It is magnificent, heartstopping in its beauty, she thought,
examining it very closely, appreciating its perfection. The stone

hung on a single-strand necklace composed of sixty-eight round and pear-shaped diamonds, and the whole thing was a spectacular piece of jewelry.

On the spur of the moment, Stevie rose and went across to the antique French gilt mirror hanging on the wall of her office and held the necklace against her black dress. It was stunning. And she could not help wondering, in an abstract way, who would end up wearing it one day, when she finally came to sell it.

Walking back to the antique Louis XV *bureau plat* near the window, she sat down and held the necklace up toward the light again, admiring the way its facets threw off a brilliant rainbow sparkle. Then she glanced up with a start as the door burst open unexpectedly, and her son Nigel marched in. Stevie was taken aback, so startled she almost dropped the necklace. It took all of her self-possession to keep her face completely neutral.

"Nigel! This is a surprise!" she exclaimed, and placed the necklace in the jewelry case. Rising, she took a tentative step toward him, intending to greet him, as always full of warmth and love for her firstborn, despite her growing suspicion of his duplicity.

"Hello, Mother," he said coldly, and immediately sat down in a chair, making it perfectly obvious that he wanted no displays of affection from her.

This gave Stevie no alternative but to sit down herself, which she did.

Glancing at the necklace on her desk, Nigel said in a scathing voice, "Drooling, I see."

Annoyed though she was with his tone and superior manner, she ignored both. "I didn't know you were coming to New York. When did you get in?"

"Last night."

"Oh." There was a slight pause on her part, and then she said,

"I wish you'd let me know beforehand. I could have planned something . . . for us all to get together."

A brow lifted sardonically, but he said nothing.

She said, "You could have seen Chloe and Miles."

He draped himself in the chair, looking immensely bored, and she felt compelled to add, "Wouldn't you like to see your brother and sister?"

"Not particularly."

Stevie leaned back, gazing at him, filling with dismay at his manner and at his attitude. He had behaved somewhat in the same rude and churlish way when she had last been in London, and it puzzled her. After a moment, she said, "What are you doing in New York?"

Nigel hesitated, but only fractionally. "The Sultan of Kandrea wants to see me. About some stones. And since he cannot come to London at the moment, I came here."

"Is he in New York or Los Angeles?"

"New York."

"We could easily have handled it ourselves if you'd informed us. In fact, I would have been quite happy to see the sultan myself. There was really no need for you to fly all this way, Nigel."

"But he doesn't want to deal with you, Mother. He prefers to do business with me."

"That's something of a departure, since he and I have been doing business for years. Perhaps it isn't so surprising, now that I think about it. The sultan does have a reputation for being unpredictable. And fickle. Be alerted to those traits, Nigel."

"I can make my own judgments, Mother. I'm no longer a snot-nosed boy in short pants."

Biting back the sharp retort on the tip of her tongue, she said, "Quite," gave him a slight smile and asked, "What kind of stones is the sultan looking for?"

"I don't know yet. I have an appointment to see him later."

"And how long are you staying in New York?"

"I'm either leaving tonight on the evening flight or on tomorrow's Concorde."

"We have some really spectacular stones available, and some magnificent —"

"The sultan certainly wouldn't be interested in *that*," he interrupted peremptorily, nodding his head at the White Empress, his expression disdainful.

"*That's* not for sale!" she shot back, and closed the lid of the jewelry case with a small thud. "But certainly it's *big* enough for him. He has always favored big diamonds, and I'm positive he still does."

"You paid far too much for that stone, Mother. A bad buy."

"No, it wasn't, Nigel. If and when I do decide to sell it, I will make a very good profit. I've already had two offers for it since the auction, and I took delivery of it myself only half an hour ago. If I'm not careful, it'll be whisked out of here before I can even blink. Quite aside from those offers, my purchasing the White Empress has generated enormous publicity. Jardine's acquisition of the stone has been reported in every newspaper in the world."

"I wouldn't boast about that kind of vulgar publicity if I were you, Mother."

"Not vulgar publicity, Nigel. *Good publicity.*"

"Jardine's doesn't need publicity of any kind," he snapped in his most superior voice, "at least, the London branch doesn't."

"*Touché.* But you're quite wrong, Nigel. We need good publicity on both sides of the Atlantic. We've a lot of competition these days, and we've got to sell ourselves as aggressively as any other jewelry company. That's the way it is in the nineties. Ask any spin doctor."

"Really, Mother, you begin to sound more American every day."

"I *am* an American, Nigel, and you are half American. Or had you forgotten that?"

"You go too far, Mother."

She wasn't quite sure what he meant by this, but choosing not to be goaded into taking the bait, she ignored his derisive comment, continuing evenly. "As for the White Empress, it was not only a good buy, but a bargain at the price."

"Grandfather doesn't think so. He also says you paid too much."

"Bruce said that?" she exclaimed incredulously, and then started to laugh. "Did he *really* say that?"

"Yes, he did," Nigel answered. "He says you have always paid too much for stones, especially diamonds."

"And when did I start doing this? Did he tell you that?"

Nigel inclined his head and gave her a defiant stare. "When you opened the Fifth Avenue store."

"What a curious thing for him to say when Jardine's in New York is actually making a huge profit. Do you think that Bruce has gone a bit senile?"

"Certainly not, Mother."

"And when did you last see him?"

"Yesterday. Before I left. He came into the London store. He's been coming in quite a lot lately."

"How interesting." Stevie rose, stood leaning against the *bureau plat,* her shrewd eyes leveled steadily on her son. "We have a new turn of events, so it seems. When I was in London a few weeks ago, your grandfather said he did not propose to come to the store anymore."

"Perhaps he changed his mind."

"Whether he did or not is quite beside the point. *I* run

Jardine's in London, as well as here, and Bruce's opinion about what I pay for stones doesn't particularly interest me. Nor does anyone else's opinion, for that matter. But getting back to your grandfather, he has no power. He retired long ago. And his title of chairman is simply a courtesy—" She paused to let her words sink in before adding, "A courtesy on my part."

Nigel stared at her, his expression hostile, but he knew better than to make any kind of adverse remark.

Returning his stare with one equally as cold, Stevie couldn't help thinking what a good-looking young man he was at twenty-nine, with his bright blue eyes set wide apart, aquiline features, and dark blond hair. And he was tall, well dressed, elegant. What a pity it was his personality did not match his pleasant and most appealing looks.

Nigel was the first to grow uncomfortable, to blink and look away from her icy gray-green eyes, her appraising gaze. He jumped up from the chair, edged toward the door. "I'd better be going," he muttered, and strode across the room, then paused in the doorway. "Good-bye, Mother."

"Will I see you again before you go back to London, Nigel?" she asked quickly, and cursed herself under her breath for her weakness, for suddenly being his mother rather than his boss.

"I don't think so. I want to catch the night flight if I can."

"I understand. Anyway, I'll be in London in about ten days."

"You're coming for Christmas?"

"Yes. Chloe and I are leaving on the twentieth."

He nodded, opened the door.

"Give my love to Tamara, and kiss the children."

"Yes," he said, and was gone, slipping out of her office without a backward glance, closing the door softly behind him.

Stevie remained standing, staring at the door, a look of total bafflement on her face. She understood him less and less. It suddenly struck her that he had not told her why he had visited Jardine's that morning on his extremely quick trip to New York. Perhaps he didn't have a reason, had just stopped by out of habit. Or maybe he was curious to see what was going on in the store. He might even have wanted to get a glimpse of the White Empress despite his disparaging attitude about it. Or had he come in intentionally to taunt her, to pick a fight? She did not know.

Certainly he had not come in to wish her happy birthday, which is what she originally had thought when he had first burst in on her, but he had soon disabused her of that idea with his contentious manner and obvious desire to be combative. He hadn't even mentioned her birthday, in fact.

Later that same day, Tuesday, the tenth of December, Jardine and Company closed earlier than the usual time of six o'clock.

Once the main doors, which opened onto Fifth Avenue, were locked, the White Empress was put on display in an illuminated showcase in the center of the main salon. This was a medium-sized room with a high ceiling from which dropped several antique crystal chandeliers; showcases in which jewels were displayed were built in on several walls, and were cleverly and effectively illuminated. Underfoot, a luxuriously thick silver-gray wool carpet stretched the length of the floor; an antique Louis XV *bureau plat* and two antique French desks were strategically placed in different areas of the room. Normally used by the sales executives, tonight they were decorated with beautiful arrangements of flowers.

At six-thirty promptly, members of the staff gathered together in the salon to toast Stevie on her birthday, as well as celebrate her acquisition of the great diamond. Champagne and hors d'oeuvres were served to her employees and the few guests she had invited. Miles and Chloe were present, along with Matt Wilson and André Birron. André, delayed in his return to Paris, was giving a small dinner for her birthday later that evening.

The four of them surrounded her like a phalanx, wishing her a happy birthday, singing her praises. And all were impressed by the pear-shaped diamond, stood there staring at it mesmerized, bedazzled by its beauty, unable to tear their eyes away from the display case.

André finally turned to Stevie and said, "I am glad I was delayed here on business, and that I could be present tonight, *ma chérie*. To see this incomparable diamond again and to celebrate your birthday, Stephanie, that is wonderful."

"I am happy you're here, André, and I want to thank you again for being so supportive the other evening at the auction. I really was full of anxiety."

"It was nothing at all. And as for your nervousness, you did not show it."

Moving forward, Chloe clutched her mother's arm, exclaimed, "Mom, it's just awesome! *Awesome.* And it was so neat, the way you beat everybody out at the auction. *Cool.* You're the greatest, Mom."

"Thank you, Chloe," Stevie murmured, pleased that her daughter was so enthusiastic and filled with her usual natural warmth. For the first few days after Thanksgiving she had been sulky and mute, acting up in the way teenagers could, making everyone else feel uncomfortable and miserable. This recalcitrant mood had slowly diminished, and completely vanished tonight.

André said, "It is indeed awesome, Chloe. And so is your mother, *ma petite*."

"There's nobody like her, Uncle André."

"I am glad to hear that you appreciate her. She deserves it. Shall we go over to the far side of the salon and look at the other jewels? Your mother just told me that she is showing the latest collection of new designs for the first time tonight."

"Okay," she agreed, and tucked her arm through his.

"I'll join you," Matt said, following André and Chloe across the salon.

Stevie now stood alone with Miles in front of the glass show-case where the White Empress reposed, and she was intrigued by the look on her son's face. "It does knock the breath out of you, doesn't it, Miles?"

"It sure does. I'm blown away by it, actually, Ma." Miles turned to his mother and went on. "I've never seen a stone like this one. But I guess you have."

"Yes, I've seen some which were just as big, and others which were even bigger. There is something about this particular stone that is . . . *unique*. Actually, all stones are unique because no two are ever *exactly* alike. There is just something so extraordinary about this one, something that is hard to describe."

Miles nodded, turned to the display case again. "What fire and beauty there is under its icy exterior."

"It's the cut. Harry Winston had this one cleaved from a large piece of rough, but he studied it for months and months on end first before he let a lapidary get anywhere near it. He had an unerring instinct about stones, Miles, and he could look at a piece of rough and see what others couldn't see."

"I'm glad you got it, Mother, you wanted it so much. Congratulations again. And happy birthday again. By the way, your present is being delivered to the apartment later. I hope you like it."

"I'm sure I will, darling."

"André's diamond feather is beautiful, Ma."

"Isn't it just? He's so pleased he can be here tonight after all, and so am I."

"Chloe seems on top of the world," Miles remarked, then grinned. "I wouldn't want to be a teenager again. It's a bumpy ride."

Stevie agreed, and then, turning away from the showcase, she took hold of Miles's arm, led him to a corner of the salon. "Nigel came into the store today."

"Nigel! What the hell's he doing in New York?" Miles stared at his mother, flabbergasted.

"He flew in to see the Sultan of Kandrea, who is apparently looking for some stones."

"I thought the sultan was your client?"

"So did I until this morning. Apparently he prefers to deal with Nigel now."

"Who says?"

"Nigel."

"I don't believe *that*!"

"Nigel made a great point of it in our brief conversation."

"He's lying. He was always full of it. I bet he's trying to worm his way into the sultan's good graces. Maybe he told Kandrea it was your idea, that you don't want to handle his business anymore. I wouldn't put it past Nigel."

"I don't know . . ." She shook her head, took a sip of champagne.

"If you phoned the sultan I bet he'd tell you exactly that, Mother. Tell you what's what."

"I really couldn't do that, it would seem a little . . . strange. And I certainly wouldn't want the sultan to think there was something—"

"Rotten in the state of Denmark?" he cut in, giving her a pointed look and raising a dark brow.

"That's one way of putting it, I suppose. But we must show a united front, I've always told you that. Anything else is bad for business."

"Nigel's definitely up to something, Ma."

She nodded. "He baffles me, Miles."

"I get the feeling he wants to be top dog at Jardine's. But is he capable of running the company by himself?"

"He will be eventually. He has a lot to learn yet, of course. Still, to give the devil his due, he's a good businessman. Not at all creative though, not in the way that Gideon is creative. And he doesn't know a lot about stones. On the other hand, there are a lot of experts on stones at Jardine's, both here and in London, so that's not so important. Not at the moment anyway." Stevie paused, her expression regretful. "And I tend to agree with you, he'd like me to disappear."

"You're too young to retire. What on earth would you do if you didn't work?"

"God knows, Miles. I'd be at a loss. Totally bored out of my mind. However, I'm not planning to retire, not for a long time, I can assure you of that. Whatever Nigel wants, Nigel *won't* get."

Miles laughed, then gave her an intent look. "You're forty-seven today."

"Don't remind me."

"Can I ask you something?"

"Anything, darling."

"You're a young woman, and yet you've . . . you've never married again. Why?"

"For a perfectly good reason."

"Us, Ma?"

"Partially. But I've never met anyone I wanted to marry." She threw him an amused smile. "It takes two to tango, you know. Now that all my children are grown up, perhaps I'll start looking around for a husband." She chuckled, then, wishing to change the subject, she said, "Nigel was very churlish today, he didn't even wish me a happy birthday."

"Rotten sod," Miles muttered. "But then, he hasn't changed much. He was always a bit of a bugger even when he was a kid."

Stevie stared at her son, startled by the animosity in his voice. "I didn't know you so actively disliked your brother," she murmured, her eyes searching his face. "You never told me this before."

"Oh, Ma, why *would* I mention it? Anyway, I don't dislike him all the time. Only part of it. Nigel's a chameleon. One minute he's the basilisk, totally inscrutable and hard to read, the next he's turned into a romping puppy dog, licking your hand and bowling you over with his winsome personality and adorable charm."

"That's an apt way of putting it. But I must admit, I haven't seen much of Nigel's charm of late."

"He couldn't possibly have forgotten your birthday, Mother. He always made such a fuss about it when we were kids. He actually got to be a bit of a bore—" Miles cut himself off and his expression was chagrined as he added swiftly, "I didn't mean that the way it sounded."

"I know you didn't."

"I'm certainly glad you didn't invite Nigel to Uncle André's dinner for you tonight."

"I wouldn't do a thing like that!"

"Yes, you would, Ma! You've always been a bit of a softie when it comes to your family," he contradicted Stevie.

"It never crossed my mind to invite him, Miles. He was too unpleasant. Besides, he seemed hell-bent on catching the evening flight to London."

"I wonder how Tamara puts up with him?"

"Nigel can be very winning. You just said so. And Tamara is an exceptional young woman. She understands Nigel, has his number. Not only that, she's wise for her age, and she really knows how to handle him."

"I suppose she does. Is Uncle André taking us to La Grenouille?"

"Of course, it's his favorite restaurant in New York, and I like it too. But now we'd better circulate, don't you think, mingle with the other people here, otherwise they'll think we're being rude."

"Lead the way, Mother," he said, taking her arm affectionately, his pride in her much in evidence on his glowing face and in his wide smile.

PART TWO

Christmas

14

Stevie had lived in London half her life, and she was always happy when she returned.

It was not that she did not like New York, because she did. That city meant entirely different things to her, commanded another place in her heart. New York was the city of her birth, her early childhood, and teen years until she was fourteen, when her mother had married Derek and they had moved to London. New York also signified the last eight years of her life, of raising Chloe, buying and remodeling Romany Hall, starting and operating Jardine's on Fifth Avenue. She constantly thought of it as a city of new challenges and, in a certain way, of rebirth.

London represented the years of her marriage to Ralph, the birth and upbringing of her children, his untimely death, and, finally, her emergence as a businesswoman. It was the place she had spent her most formative years and where she had become a woman. And so, in a sense, London was a city of old challenges.

It was also a city rich in a multitude of memories and talismans of the past for her. Whenever she thought of it, she did so with enormous affection and nostalgia. Her mind would focus on those places that were special to her, meaningful because of their past associations, and she would be carried back in time.

As she sat at her desk in her office above the Jardine showrooms in Bond Street, she found herself suddenly thinking of those earlier days in London and her favorite spots ... Whitestone Pond in Hampstead on a spring day bright with sunlight, where she and Ralph had so often taken the boys to sail their toy boats and then taken them to tea at Briar Lodge.

This was the big old stone house on Hampstead Heath where her mother and Derek had spent half their married life, and where she had lived for two years until she had married Ralph at age sixteen.

Stevie sat gazing into the distance for a moment, remembering Briar Lodge. It had been an oasis of love overflowing with welcoming warmth and hospitality, and she had been very attached to it, loved every nook and cranny of it.

Her mother had decorated the house with charming fabrics and antiques, old faded carpets and lovely paintings. Derek's books—thousands of them—reigned supreme, filling endless shelves in the library. His acting awards and the carefully collected, much-cherished theatrical memorabilia were given pride of place in his study. Stevie always thought of Briar Lodge as a house that had known only laughter and happiness.

The boys had loved to play hide-and-seek in the attics when they were young. Just by closing her eyes she was instantly transported back to those days. She saw them as they had been then, her three sons, and their rambunctious shrieks and bloodcurdling yells reverberated in her head, carrying her back into her memories even more deeply.

The garden of the house on the Heath had been another oasis for her, particularly in the spring and summer months. In spring it was a bower of leafy trees, green and restful; in summer the herbaceous borders and many rosebushes were riotous rafts of bright color against the smooth green lawn, and they filled the air with fragrance.

Several old apple trees created a canopy of shade on sunny days, and it was there that they had so frequently picnicked. Recalling those picnics now, her mouth suddenly began to water at the thought of the delicious tiny tea sandwiches filled with smoked salmon, egg salad, sliced cucumber, and watercress and cheddar. And there were always homemade scones lathered with Devonshire cream and strawberry jam, all washed down with scalding hot tea laced with lemon and poured from the big brown teapot Derek swore by.

It had been a rather sad day for her when Derek and her mother had sold Briar Lodge seventeen years ago and moved to the apartment overlooking Regent's Park, where they still lived. She had understood the move. Even though the flat was very large with many large rooms, it was, nevertheless, easier to run than the big old house.

There were other corners of London that she treasured in her heart. Cavendish Square was one, because it was there that she had first stumbled, and quite by accident, on Jacob Epstein's extraordinary sculpture, *Madonna and Child*. She hadn't known its name then, nor had she known the name of the sculptor, but she had made a point of finding out later, and she had become a devotee of his.

She had first noticed the sculpture one spring afternoon not long after Ralph's death, when she had been walking through the square, heading in the direction of Oxford Street. It had suddenly started to rain, and pausing, she had groped around in her handbag for her scarf. As she had tied it over her head she had happened to half turn around, and it was then that she had seen the sculpture; she had caught her breath, stunned by its beauty.

It was set on the wall above an archway in Deans Mews, which opened off the square. Mounted in such a way that it stood slightly away from the wall, it appeared to be levitating, actually floating upward of its own accord.

The sculpture was life-sized and towered toward the sky, and she had walked over to it fascinated, gazing up at it in the pale spring light.

Because of the manner in which it was sited on the wall of the arch, and its slight tilt forward, the rain struck the eyes of the sculpture. It seemed to her that the Madonna was crying real tears. They were trickling down her cheeks, dripping onto the head of the child Jesus, who stood immediately in front of the Virgin, also levitating.

Now Stevie saw the sculpture in her mind's eye, the image of it crystal clear. She recalled how she had been quite oblivious to the rain that afternoon, had been awed by the sculpture, had stood transfixed in front of it for ages. Only her dripping head scarf and soaking wet coat had forced her finally to hurry away, looking for a taxi. Its poignancy had touched her deeply, and she had made a point of going back to Deans Mews for many years afterward, in order to look at Sir Jacob's remarkable sculpture.

I'll go and see it this trip, she thought, before I go back to New York in January. And then she suddenly wondered why it was that she was so deeply engrossed in the past that morning.

Perhaps it was because she did not want to deal with the present. With Nigel, to be precise. After all, it was Monday, December the twenty-third, just two days before Christmas, and the last thing she wanted was to cause family discord at this time.

In any case, he was noticeably absent from the Bond Street showrooms that day; his secretary Angela had told her he had gone to Amsterdam with Gilbert Drexel, who was one of the diamond experts at Jardine's. She could not help wondering if they were off hunting stones for the Sultan of Kandrea.

After Christmas, Stevie thought, I'll tackle Nigel after the holidays.

The antique French striking clock by Le Roy et Fils of Paris, which stood on the William and Mary inlaid chest at the other side of the room, suddenly struck the hour. Stevie glanced up, peered at it, saw that it was noon. She had a luncheon appointment with Derek in half an hour. Rising, she crossed the floor to her small bathroom to freshen up before leaving to meet him at Harry's Bar.

When she first went downstairs, Stevie stood on the doorstep of Jardine's for a moment or two, debating whether to walk or take a taxi. It was a very cold day, but the sky was blue and the sun was shining, so she decided, in the end, to brave the cold wind and walk to South Audley Street where Harry's Bar, a private club, was located.

Wrapping her heavy red-wool cape closer around her, she set off at a brisk pace down Bond Street. Within minutes she was turning onto Grosvenor Street; she continued at the same rapid speed, heading up toward Grosvenor Square which would lead her into South Audley.

Stevie enjoyed walking in cities she liked, and because of the length of time she had lived in London, she knew it well, better than any other place. In particular, she enjoyed walking through Mayfair with its grand old mansions and stately hotels, cobbled mews with quaint little houses and tree-lined squares.

When she pushed open the door of Harry's Bar some ten minutes later and went inside, she saw Derek leaning against the bar, drinking a glass of water. Instantly he put it down, came forward to greet her, and helped her off with her cape.

"And don't you look smashing today, Stevie," he exclaimed, staring across at her and smiling, once they were seated at a corner table. "Positively blooming. Very bonny indeed."

She laughed and thanked him. "You don't look so bad either, Derek."

"I'm feeling pretty terrific." Leaning closer, her stepfather confided, "I've decided to do the play—*The Lion in Winter*. It's not going on until next autumn, and we won't start rehearsals until late spring, so I'll be well rested and ready to plunge into a new project by then."

"I'm delighted, I know how easily you get bored. What does my mother think about it?"

"She wants me to do it. She's been worried that I was over-tired and run-down after *Becket* and the film, but I'm feeling great and she knows it." Derek paused as the waiter came to the table to take their drinks order. "What would you like, Stevie? A Bellini perhaps?" Derek suggested.

"Thanks, that's fine."

Once the waiter had disappeared, Derek continued. "If it's a success in the West End, I think the producers will take it to Broadway eventually."

"I'm glad it's opening here, that you're going to be in London for a while. I think my mother really misses it when she's away."

"I agree with you, and speaking of your mother, tell me about the brooch you mentioned on the phone."

"It's a lovely old piece and it was designed by Jeanne Boivin, probably in the 1930s, thereabouts anyway. I thought it would suit my mother because it's stylish without being overpowering. It's made of clusters of small diamonds set in platinum, and it's two stems of Queen Anne's lace, and it *is* very *lacy*, rather delicate-looking. Of course, it's a signed piece and quite valuable. André found it by chance."

"So you said. Is that the feather pin André gave you for your birthday?" There was an admiring look on Derek's face as he eyed the lapel of her tulip-red wool suit.

"Yes, and I've never stopped wearing it since he gave it to me. It's the kind of pin that seems to go with everything. Night or day. The Boivin brooch is the same, actually, Derek, in that it can be worn at any time and with almost everything."

"I'd like to see it. From what you say, I think it'll make a wonderful Christmas gift for Blair. Actually, I was going to walk back to Jardine's with you later. After lunch."

"Great minds think alike. The same thing crossed my mind on my way here to meet you."

He nodded and asked, "Did you like your birthday present from Miles?"

Stevie glanced at her stepfather alertly. "Oh, so you knew about it, did you?"

Derek grinned. "We did indeed, but Miles swore us to secrecy."

"It's a beautiful portrait of Chloe. And apparently he painted it rather quickly. Just dashed it off, he said. He's a really good painter, isn't he? I sometimes wonder why he settled for designing stage sets, even though he is brilliant at it."

"His painting of Chloe is spectacular in my opinion, Stevie, and why he prefers to design sets I will never know either. The main thing, though, is that he's happy doing what he's doing. And happy with his life, it seems to me." Derek peered at her closely. "Have you seen Gideon since you arrived on Friday?"

"Ah, the other side of the coin, so to speak. Yes, we had—" She cut herself off.

The waiter had arrived with their Bellinis.

After toasting each other, Stevie went on. "Chloe and I had lunch with Gideon yesterday. I'm afraid he was morose, down in the dumps. Just as Miles said he was when he last saw him."

"Did Gideon mention anything? Confide in you? Tell you what's ailing him?"

"Oh, no, Derek, and with Chloe present I didn't want to question him. After all, he *is* twenty-seven. A grown man capable of taking care of himself. And whatever it is that's troubling him, he'll snap out of it, I'm sure. The young are very resilient."

"True," Derek agreed, and deeming it wise to move on, he changed the subject, said, "I think we'd better look at the menu, order lunch, darling."

"I know what I'm having . . . the same thing I always have when I lunch here. A mixed salad, then risotto primavera."

"And I'm going to have fish and a small portion of pasta. One can't come to Harry's Bar without having a bit of pasta, now, can one?" Derek flashed her a smile and then turned his attention to the menu, concentrating on it.

When he finally looked up, Stevie said, "It's not Gideon I'm worried about, but Bruce."

"*Bruce?*" Derek threw her a questioning look, and he was unable to conceal his surprise. "What's wrong with Bruce?"

"I'm not really sure, to be honest. I spent some time with Gilbert Drexel at the showroom on Saturday, we'd quite a lot of business to go over. And he made a point of telling me that he was very worried about Bruce, and he did stress *very*. Gilbert thought he seemed frail, not agile anymore, although that could be his gout acting up again. He said Bruce kept going into the showroom, more than ever lately, which has surprised Gilbert, since Bruce had said he wouldn't be making many appearances."

"Interesting," Derek murmured. He wondered if Bruce Jardine harbored any suspicions about Nigel, but he did not say this. He asked, "Did Gilbert tell you anything else, Stevie?"

"Just that Bruce seemed very *preoccupied*." Stevie shook her head. "He was rather emphatic about that, mentioned it several times. I asked him if he meant that Bruce was senile, and Gilbert said no, not at all. He actually added that Bruce had all his marbles, and that was his exact expression."

"Mmmm." Derek looked thoughtful as he murmured, "He is in his eighties, of course. I don't suppose you've had a chance to see him yet, have you?"

"No, but I'm lunching with him tomorrow, as I have for years on Christmas Eve. It's a tradition with us."

"Bruce has always seemed so . . . *indestructible,* I think that's the best word," Derek mused out loud. "It just goes to show, none of us is that. Nor are we immortal, as we're often prone to think, as much as we'd like to be."

He sounded so rueful when he said this, Stevie couldn't help smiling, and she said, "If anybody's going to be immortal, it's you, Derek. After all, you're the one who's captured on film. You'll live forever, in a sense."

Derek smiled back at her but made no comment.

Stevie went on. "When I said I was worried about Bruce, I really wasn't referring to his health, but rather to his demeanor. I can't imagine why he continues to trail into Jardine's, there seems to be no purpose to it."

"I'm sure he'll tell you when you see him tomorrow."

"Yes, I suppose so."

"I think perhaps we ought to order lunch, don't you?" Derek said, picked up his Bellini, and took a sip. He couldn't help wondering about Bruce's behavior himself. Did that wily old bird know something no one else did?

15

"I KNOW YOU'RE GOING TO TELL ME TO MIND MY OWN BUSINESS, BUT I'm going to say this anyway." Miles paused, gave Gideon a hard stare, and added, "So please hear me out."

Gideon returned his brother's stare but made no response. Instead, he studied him for a moment. What he saw was a reflection of himself; dark brown hair, bright blue eyes, pleasant, well-defined face. A good-looking chap, Miles was. And very personable. Women went for him. Didn't he just know it. They shared the same problem. After all, he and Miles were identical twins. As their mother used to say to them, they were like two peas in a pod.

"Come on, Gideon, say something!" Miles exclaimed, leaning across the table. They were at Mark's Club in Charles Street, where they were having lunch, their first in a long time. It was obvious they were happy to be together.

Gideon permitted a small smile to slide briefly across his mouth, then he said, "I'm waiting for you to tell me what's bothering *you*. Spit it out. I won't bite your head off. Nor will I tell you to mind your own business."

"Right! It's *you*, Gideon, *you're* bothering me. Or, rather, your behavior is, and it has for the past few months. You're either morose or melancholic. Or worse, depressed and unapproachable. It's obvious you're disturbed about something. Ma's noticed it, Gid, and once she really gets on your case she's not going to give you a moment's peace. You know she can be like a dog with a bone when she gets her teeth into something."

"Thanks for the warning, Miles, but I can handle Ma. It's true, I have been a bit down for some time now. But I'm coming out of it, I promise."

"What's been wrong with you, for God's sake? I've been worried to death."

"Women. Bloody women. That's all."

"What women?"

"Not really women, but *woman*. Margot Saunders, to be precise. She's tried to create problems for me since we broke off—since I broke off with her, I should say."

"Do you mean she's been pursuing you?"

Gideon was silent for a second, then he explained in a low voice, "*Fatal Attraction* kind of pestering. You did see that film, didn't you?"

"Yes. But look here, you don't have a wife, and—"

"I know," Gideon cut in. "But she hasn't stopped harassing me, and she's been quite—" There was a pause before he finished in a mutter. "Quite pernicious, in a way."

"Odd word to use, but I know what you mean. Anyway, brother of mine, one must never forget that hell hath no fury like a woman scorned."

Miles looked at Gideon closely, his eyes narrowing, as he continued. "So, she's giving you a hard time. What can I do to help?"

"Nothing, but thanks for offering. Actually, she's going to go away like a good girl and not give me any further trouble."

"What makes you say that?"

"She promised."

"And you believe her?"

"Oh, yes." Observing the doubtful look on his brother's face, Gideon added, "Take my word for it, she won't create any more problems."

"I believe you. Mind telling me how you accomplished this feat?" Miles raised a brow, his eyes suddenly quizzical.

"I said I'd tell Jack Bellanger all about it, about her behavior . . . her following me, harassing me, virtually stalking me. And it put the fear of God into her. I mean, what socially prominent young deb wants to see her name splattered all over the *Daily Mail* and in such a way? And in the most widely read gossip column?"

"She really believed you'd do it?"

"Oh, yes, she's met Jack with me, knows we all went to Eton together, and that we're very close friends. You know Margot's pretty frightened of the Fleet Street boys, ever since that awful scandal involving her brother. She's never recovered from the press coverage. She thought it was diabolical, and her mother had a nervous breakdown."

"Very clever of you, Gid. And when did you accomplish all this?"

"Don't look so suspicious." Gideon laughed. "I've told you the truth. And I accomplished it about a week ago."

"Then why did you look so down in the dumps yesterday, when you had lunch with Ma and Chloe?"

"She told you that? Ma, I mean."

"Yep, she did."

Gideon sighed, decided not to answer his brother's question. Instead, he asked, "I wonder when the bangers and mash are coming? I'm famished."

"So am I, and any minute now, I'm sure. Bruno did say they were very busy today when I called to make the reservation. And you've only got to look around to see that the place is jammed. He did us a favor, pulled a table out of thin air for us, actually."

"I know." Gideon stared off into space for a split second, thinking of his dilemma. Then, brushing it aside, he attempted to reassure his brother. "Listen, Miles, I'm all right now, really I am. It's been a bad couple of months, I admit that. But Margot is well and truly disposed of, and I know my life's going to be easier."

"I'm glad to hear it." Miles took a swallow of his red wine, and there was a slight hesitation as he murmured, "Mind if I ask you something?"

"No, go ahead."

"Why *did* you break off with Margot? I for one thought it was the real thing at last."

"So did I. In the beginning. And for quite a while. And that's why I broke it off. Because it wasn't."

"I see." Miles leaned back against the banquette, toyed with the bread roll.

"And what about you and Allison Grainger? You haven't mentioned her lately."

"Same as you, old chap. Not the real thing. She's a lovely girl, and I still see her occasionally, but on a much more casual basis than before. I'm easing my way out of the relationship, in fact."

"Not to change the subject, Miles, but I was a bit surprised when Ma told me at lunch yesterday that Nigel showed up in New York just after the auction at Sotheby's."

"I was too. What do you make of it, Gid?"

Gideon shrugged, stared at his brother.

They exchanged long, pointed looks.

Finally Gideon said, "I don't know *what* to make of it. He

never told me he was going to New York. But on the other hand, why would he? He's a bit of a funny bugger these days. Bad tempered, more impatient than ever." Gideon shook his head and finished, "And very secretive."

"Ma thinks he's plotting against her," Miles volunteered.

"She told me."

"Were you able to confirm Ma's suspicions?"

"How could I? I don't know a damn thing, and I hardly ever see him at Jardine's. Listen, I'm sure nobody else knows anything. And in any case, Nigel's always played everything close to the vest. *If* he is plotting, then only Nigel knows he is."

"You're right," Miles agreed. "I wish I'd had a chance to see him, I might have been able to make a judgment, even found something out just chatting with him, drawing him out. But since I've been back in London I haven't had time to come over to Jardine's."

"Don't worry, you'll see him on Christmas Day with Tamara and the kids."

Miles did not hide his surprise. "He usually takes Tamara and the kids to see her parents in Paris for Christmas. Why the change of plans, do you know?"

"Her father has been ill. Very ill. He had a heart attack. Anyway, her parents decided to go to Martinique or St. Barts, somewhere like that, for the Christmas holidays, part of his recuperation, I suppose."

"So we're stuck with Nigel."

"Only too true. But there's Tamara, our beautiful little Russian."

"Oh, here's our sausage and mash," Miles said.

"About bloody time too," Gideon muttered.

Miles had to laugh. "We haven't been waiting all that long, Gid. You should have ordered something first if you were so hungry, potted shrimps or smoked salmon."

"Leave me alone," Gideon grumbled, and made a sour face. Then he winked at his twin. "I'm only kidding, you know how I like to grouse."

"Only too well."

They ate in silence for a while, but at one moment Miles glanced at his brother, his face serious. "All joking aside, Gideon, do you really think you're finished with this Margot business? Has she really gone away? And for good?"

"I'm certain of it. And it's a weight off my mind, I can tell you. It's been depressing me for ages. She really did behave in the most impossible way. Made my life miserable."

"I wish you'd told me, maybe I could have helped."

"Perhaps I should have."

"What's a twin for, if not to stand by your side and do battle with you? I'd expect it of you, you know."

Gideon smiled. "And I'd be right there for you, count on that."

Miles studied him for a moment, then said, "You don't know how happy it makes me to see you smile, Gid, to hear the lightness in your voice again."

Gideon nodded. "She really was rather a nuisance, Miles."

"It's rotten luck that you had to go through all that."

"Let's not talk about it anymore. It's over." As these words left his mouth, Gideon prayed that this was true.

Miles said, "What about Chloe? Is she going to be a nuisance to you at the store?"

"Oh, no, not at all. She's okay, you know, a good kid, and she's going to come in for only a few hours a day, until she goes back to New York with Ma in January."

"I'm glad Ma decided to let her hang around Jardine's. It was a very smart move on our mother's part, and it might make Chloe change her mind about working there after she graduates."

"I hope so, for Ma's sake. She really doesn't want this at all. In fact, she's dead set against it."

"I know, and she's being a very good sport. Do you realize how lucky we are to have a mother like Stevie Jardine?"

"I most certainly do!" Gideon exclaimed. "There's no one like Ma. She's the best there is."

Miles nodded, and, changing the subject, he said in a quiet voice, "I just want to add this to our previous conversation. Promise you'll confide in me, let me help you, if ever you're in trouble in the future."

Gideon only nodded, not trusting himself to speak. He wondered if this was the right time to unburden himself further to Miles. Don't do it, a small voice at the back of his mind warned. It's too dangerous. And so Gideon remained silent, concentrated on his food. For the next few minutes he was afraid even to look at his brother in case he gave himself away or blurted out what must be left unsaid.

Gideon Jardine sat in the study of his flat in Cadogan Square, his mind awash with troubling thoughts. It had turned seven, and he knew he ought to be dressing for the dinner he had been invited to by close friends; he was already running late. Suddenly his energy had ebbed away, and he felt an odd kind of lassitude settling over him.

Only one table lamp was turned on, and the light in the room was dim, but even this was too bright for him. Rising, he went and turned off the lamp, then lay down on the sofa under the window, stretching out his long legs, easing his back into the cushions.

The darkness soothed him. Everything was quiet in the flat. The only sounds came from the ticking of the carriage clock on the mantelpiece, the faint buzz of the traffic outside, the hiss of wheels traveling on wet roads on this damp night.

He was glad he had seen Miles for lunch today, and also relieved that he had confided in his brother. He had told Miles the truth . . . for the most part anyway.

Margot had not wanted their relationship to end, and she had striven hard to hold on to him, her demeanor growing uglier in the process. But there was no way for him to stay with a woman he did not love.

It was also true that she had begun to harass him, stalk him, phone him endlessly at work and here at home. She had made his life hell for weeks, until, as a last resort—when reasoning with her had proved to be fruitless—he had threatened her with Jack Bellanger.

Of course, it had worked. She loathed the tabloid press, the entire press corps in actuality, because, she said, they had crucified her brother and destroyed her mother. In all likelihood they probably had, but who could blame them really? They were only doing their jobs, and Julian Saunders had left himself wide open to become their target because of his extraordinary financial chicanery in the City. He felt sorry for the mother, though, an innocent victim.

Gideon knew he would never forget the expression of mingled disbelief and horror on Margot's face, and the way she had recoiled when he had said he planned to tell his good old chum Jack about the problems he was having with her.

When he had first thought of this as a means of combating her intrusive and frightening behavior, Gideon had instantly dismissed it from his mind, had backed away from it, loath to do that to her. In the end, though, he had come to realize that he had no choice. Threatening her with the press was his only weapon; he had to think of himself, defend himself.

Margot had become so obnoxious, she was verging on the deranged, and it had crossed his mind several times that she might do him bodily harm. He was only twenty-seven, and he did not want to die needlessly at the hands of a crazed young woman.

There was another thing, something Margot had seen, and which he could hardly bear to think about, because it made him vulnerable to her. On the other hand, he felt reasonably sure that with Jack Bellanger hanging over her head like the sword of Damocles, he was safe.

Gideon was unable to keep his eyes open; he felt his lids dropping, and he began to doze. Images of Margot danced in his head, and a remembrance of their last evening together seemed suddenly trapped under his lids.

Instantly, he snapped his eyes open, not wanting to think about it. Still, the memory insinuated itself into his consciousness once again, as it frequently did.

That night . . . more than three months ago now . . . they had gone out to dinner and then later in the privacy of her flat, he had realized he could not stay. He wanted to leave at once, go home to his own bed. He was not only exhausted, but worried about an old, old friendship that had spiraled out of hand and out of control in the past few weeks.

Margot had forced the issue, and, of course, it hadn't worked. Put simply, he had been unable to perform.

At first, Margot had been sweet, loving, and very understanding. And then unexpectedly, as he was dressing, she had turned on him with a vengeance, angry and vehement in her condemnation of him, which had been venomous.

"You're impotent with me because of *her!*" she had cried. "I knew you'd be unfaithful to me because of your reputation as a womanizer. But I hadn't realized that it would be quite so soon!"

Stunned by her words, by the seed of truth in them, he had stood gaping at her, cringing inside at the use of the word *impo-*

tent. And he had continued to stand there speechlessly, suddenly afraid to say a single word, knowing that somehow she would use it to her advantage and against him.

When she repeated her accusation about there being another woman in his life, he had swiftly denied that there was anyone else.

"But I saw you with her," she had shot back, dropping her bomb on him.

Aghast though he had been, he had managed to keep a poker face, and he had kept his mouth well and truly shut as well. It was as if he had known then that she was going to be trouble; he hadn't realized just how much trouble.

His silence had served only to goad her into saying more. She told him where she had seen him, and described the woman with him as "blonde, beautiful, but that goes without saying when you're concerned. She looked older than you though. That *was* surprising." Glaring at him, Margot had added, "Her face was so familiar. If only I could remember her name."

He hoped to God she wouldn't, because if she did, it would spell disaster. For himself. And others. He remembered now how he had finished dressing without saying another word to her, and he had left silently, without so much as a good-bye. But good-bye it had been for him. The next day, not wanting to waste any time, he had told her it was over, finished, kaput. She simply hadn't wanted to accept this decision on his part and that same week her harassment of him had begun.

The shrill ringing of the phone brought him upright with a start. Swinging his legs onto the floor, Gideon reached for it, glad that it had stopped the flow of his thoughts.

"Hello, darling," she said before he even spoke.

"Lenore?" Gideon gripped the phone a little tighter, knowing it was her. He knew that voice so well.

"Of course. Are you all right?"

"Sort of . . . where are you?"

"In the country. It's cold and gloomy up here in Yorkshire."

"Should you be calling me? Is it safe?"

"Oh, yes. I'm alone."

"Where are the children?"

"Here with me. What I meant was that—"

"I know what you meant," he said, cutting her off. "God I miss you, and it's been only two days."

"It's the same for me."

"I can't bear to think that he'll be there with you and—"

"Don't, Gid. Don't do this to yourself. It has to be like this . . . for the time being anyway."

"I wish you were here," he said in a low voice, picturing her in his mind's eye, seeing her sweet face, the blonde halo of hair, the misty gray eyes.

"So do I. All I want is to be in your arms, close to you, kissing you. I love it when you kiss me, darling. I always did when we were little. You were a good kisser then, but much better now that you're grown up." She laughed softly, it was a low, sexy laugh, and then she whispered, "I can feel your lips on mine, your tongue sliding into my mouth. Oh, Gideon, tell me what you want to do, how you want to make love to me."

"I can't," he answered, his voice rasping with emotion.

"Why not?" she murmured, breathing softly into the phone.

"You're exciting me too much."

"I'm excited too, Gideon. Oh, God, I do so want to be with you, darling. In the biblical sense. And with you for always for the rest of my life."

"Get a divorce, Lenore! Tell him about us. *Leave him.*"

"You're not the marrying kind, Gideon. You know it, I know. The world knows it."

"To hell with the world and what it knows. It knows nothing!" he exclaimed, and taking a deep breath, he said earnestly, "I love you. I've always loved you since we were children. I know that now."

"And so have I. And I'll love you till the day I die."

"Don't talk about dying. Let's talk about living, about you living with me. Come and live with me in the New Year. Let's start it right."

"Gideon, I have children . . . one of them is your godchild, for heaven's sake. How *could* I live with you under the circumstances?"

"Get a divorce," he said again in a voice suddenly harsh.

"Gideon, I—"

"I want to marry you, for God's sake, don't you understand that?" he interrupted in a softer tone, and then he laughed quietly. "This is a hell of a way to propose to the woman you love, I think. Over the telephone. But here goes. Eleanor Elizabeth Jane Armstrong, will you marry me? Please."

"As soon as possible, Gideon." There was a tiny pause before she went on, "If only I were there now, darling, the lovely things I would do to you. Mmmmm. Yummy. Do you know, you do taste very yummy indeed."

"Don't do this, darling, it's too much for me to bear."

"Sorry. Did you really mean it, Gid? About getting married?"

For a moment he did not respond, and then he said steadily, firmly, "Yes. I meant it, and for what it's worth, this is the first time I've ever proposed."

"That's not true."

"But it is."

"No, you've proposed before. *To me.* When I was ten and you were nine. At the back of the stables at Aysgarth End. And I said yes."

"And you're saying yes again?"

"I just did. I said as soon as possible, didn't I?"

"Will Malcolm divorce you?"

She was silent.

"Well, will he?"

"I hope so, Gideon. You know what he's like, so stubborn and uncompromising. He knows our marriage has been over for a long time, but he won't see that or accept it. And even though he doesn't really care about me anymore, he doesn't want anyone else to have me."

"I'll talk to him."

"No, no! That'd be like a red rag to a bull. He's always grumbled about you, Gid, said you had a thing about me."

"I do."

"Thank God for that, since I have one about you. Where are you going tonight?"

"The Mallinghams have asked me to their Christmas party."

"Who're you going with?"

"No one. I'm strictly stag from now on, Lenore. Until I have you on my arm, my love."

"Christmas is going to be foul without you." She sighed heavily. "Never mind, it's a time for children, and they'll make it reasonably bearable. I wish I weren't so far away, I'd drive over to see you every day, Gideon darling."

"I know you would, and Christmas is going to be lousy for me without you. When are you coming back to town?"

"Not until Sunday . . . the twenty-ninth."

"Then I'll see you the next day, won't I?"

"Absolutely. Listen, I have an idea." She lowered her tone and said in that sexy voice of hers that he loved, "Can you take the morning off?"

"Yes. But why?"

"I could come over at ten, and we could have breakfast together. An intimate little breakfast for two."

"In bed," he asserted.

She was suddenly laughing, and so was he, and they had another five minutes of conversation before they hung up, after repeating their undying love for each other umpteen times.

Gideon lay on the sofa, staring up at the ceiling in the darkened room, thinking of the things they had just said. He had asked her, no, told her, to leave her husband and get a divorce. And he had promised to marry her. And yet he did not feel nervous or panic stricken that he had made the demand and the commitment. He wanted to marry her, and what he felt now at this moment was absolute certainty . . . certainty about his emotions and about her. He had known Lenore Philips all his life; they had grown up together, and he had loved her ever since those days.

That was the reason he had been a bit of a womanizer all these years . . . because *she* was the one for him. She had married another man, had married Malcolm Armstrong when his back had been turned, and before he himself had understood how much he loved her.

Margot Saunders had gotten one thing right, he decided. He was impotent with her *because* of Lenore. She was the only woman he wanted to make love to ever again.

So, he had proposed. She had accepted. And oh, the blessed relief of it . . . of knowing at last what his life was all about. *Lenore.*

16

"I AM PERFECTLY WELL, STEVIE, VERY MUCH IMPROVED, AND THANK you for asking," Bruce Jardine said, looking across at her and smiling.

Stevie smiled back, and there was both warmth and affection in her voice when she asked, "Was it gout again? Has it been bothering you lately, Bruce?"

He nodded. "But fortunately my doctor put me on a new medication a few weeks ago, and miracle of miracles, it seems to have done the trick."

She was about to ask him about the medicine, when there was a tap on the library door, and the butler entered carrying two glasses of sherry on a small tray. He offered one to Stevie.

"Thank you, Alan," Stevie said, and once Bruce had taken his glass, she raised hers and said, "Merry Christmas, and here's to your good health."

"And yours, Stevie, and I wish *you* a very Merry Christmas, my dear."

"Thank you." Taking another sip, Stevie glanced at him surreptitiously over the rim of her glass, thinking how well he *did* look. She had been pleasantly surprised when she had arrived at the house in Wilton Crescent a few minutes before. After her conversation with Gilbert Drexel the other day, she had expected to be greeted by a wraith on the verge of expiring. Instead, Bruce looked extremely fit and healthy, and not in the least debilitated. Nor was he showing his eighty-two years. To her this was most unusual, since she had always thought he had not aged well, but perhaps she had been wrong after all.

A tall, slender man with severe,m almost ascetic features, and silver hair, Bruce looked every inch the English gentleman and a member of the establishment.

That morning he was elegantly dressed in a navy blue pinstriped suit, a pristine white shirt, and a dark blue silk tie patterned with white dots. As she continued to study him, she couldn't help thinking that he seemed to have acquired a whole new lease on life. The last time she had seen him, only a scant few weeks earlier, he had appeared to be as transparent and brittle as glass.

As if he had just managed to read her thoughts, Bruce said, "I've been going to a new physician, Stevie, and he's worked wonders for me, especially with the new medications he has prescribed for my various ailments. He also sent me to see a nutritionist, an American, and she has created a special diet for me, and put me on all kinds of vitamins and supplements." He chuckled. "I take so many tablets these days, I'm surprised I don't rattle when I walk." Again he let out a deep-throated laugh before adding, "But her methods have shown excellent results, wouldn't you say?"

"They have indeed, and I'm delighted to see you looking so much better. You seem so fit, Bruce."

The phone suddenly rang and Bruce rose, excused himself, walked over to the desk, and lifted the receiver. "Yes, Alan?"

There was a pause as he listened to the butler, then he said, "Oh, all right, put her through."

As he stood there, speaking quietly to someone on the other end of the telephone, Stevie's eyes rested on him briefly before she turned her head away and stared at the fire, thinking of all the years they had known each other. Thirty-one years, to be exact, since she was sixteen; she had grown up and matured with him and Alfreda.

It had not always been as tranquil between them as it was now. Warfare had been the order of the day for a number of years. But they had settled their differences, made their peace long ago, and she had forgiven the little cruelties and slights, the heartache he had caused her in the past. Although in her innermost self she had not forgotten every one of them; indeed, some were deeply embedded in her soul, and would be for always.

The early years of battling, being at loggerheads with each other, were but a memory now, and she was glad of that. As it had turned out, in the end Bruce had become a good friend, and she had come to trust him because, finally, she had understood that he was on her side. For her part, she had proved herself to be a Jardine through and through, and this had pleased him greatly. He trusted her, confided in her, relied on her.

Glancing around, Stevie decided that her redecoration of the library had vastly improved it, as she had known it would when she had undertaken the job for Bruce in the summer. Although she had retained the paneling that lined the walls and the bookshelves, she had had the wood stripped and refinished to a lighter tone, and this had made the room look larger. She had also disposed of the old, very worn Oriental carpet and heavy blue velvet draperies; in their place she had used an antique Aubusson rug, blue-and-yellow-striped silk draperies, and she had reupholstered the sofas and chairs in a lovely rose-colored cotton brocade. The finished effect pleased her; the library had lost its Victorian heaviness that smacked of the late Alfreda's ponderous, uncompromising taste and the gloomy aspects created by the dark colors and outdated fabrics.

As her glance swung around the room approvingly, she noticed that one of the orchids in the big planter on the console table had two wilted flowers. She made a mental note to have the planter put somewhere in the room where the light was better.

Bruce finished his phone conversation, hung up, and walked back to the fireplace. Seating himself opposite her, he said, "It's very remiss of me not to congratulate you, Stevie, on the acquisition of the White Empress. An undoubted coup on your part, and I'm very proud of you, very proud indeed, as we all are at Jardine's, in fact. I thought it was quite a feather in our cap to get it, and the interest it has created in Jardine's is most extraordinary. It's brought many new customers into the showroom. By the way, you handled the media in a most masterful way, I thought, and the press coverage has been very positive."

Startled by his words, Stevie exclaimed, "But you thought I paid too much for the diamond."

"No, of course I didn't," he said with a laugh, looking at her oddly. "Actually, I believed the White Empress would fetch much more than it did. But whoever it was in the final bidding did us a great favor when they suddenly dropped out. That was a rather nice surprise, since the price immediately stabilized . . . for you. I read the report of the auction in *The Times* with a great deal of satisfaction, I can tell you." There was a small pause, and he looked at her keenly, as he finished. "However, even if you had paid twelve million dollars for it, I would have approved."

"I see," she said in a clipped voice.

"What is it, Stevie?" Bruce leaned forward slightly, peering at her intently and in sudden puzzlement. He had noticed the way she had stiffened; he could not miss the tone of her voice. "You have a most peculiar look on your face. What's wrong?" he probed again.

"Nigel told me that you thought I'd paid too much for the White Empress, and that—"

"Absolute nonsense!" he exclaimed, interrupting her. "I don't know where he got such an idea."

"He said *you* told him that."

"But it's not true!" Bruce's eyes narrowed, and there was sudden annoyance in his voice as he added, "The young whippersnapper's lying! I'll have him on the carpet for this."

"He also told me you said I had *always* paid too much for stones."

Bruce sat up ramrod straight in the chair, and there was a faint tinge of white around his mouth, as if the skin were bleached. Stevie knew this was a sign of his anger; it was an odd physical trait she had grown accustomed to over the years. It happened whenever he was enraged, and it was something he could not fake.

After a moment, he said in a controlled voice, "I simply don't *understand.* Why would he tell you these ridiculous lies? Invent things I've never said? It's preposterous." His brows drew together, knitted in a frown. He shook his head. "I was very laudatory about your acquisition of the stone. I told Nigel that you'd done well, and I praised you."

"Perhaps that's why he concocted his lies."

Her father-in-law drew back slightly and stared at her, perplexed. "If that is so, then Nigel is not as clever as I have always believed him to be. Surely he must have realized he would be found out at some point, that his lies would catch up with him?" His eyes fastened on hers.

Stevie saw the truth in this comment, but she had no answer

for him. She simply shrugged her shoulders, shook her head in bafflement, and then leaned back against the cushions. She was quite resigned to the fact that her son was duplicitous, just as she had suspected he might be.

Bruce shifted in his chair, his expression thoughtful as he sipped the sherry.

It became very quiet in the library. There was only the tick-tick-ticking of the antique clock on the mantel and the crackle of the logs in the fireplace.

Eventually, Stevie broke the silence when she said, "I don't know whether you know this, but Nigel came to New York at the beginning of this month. He came to Jardine's on the Monday after the Sotheby's auction. It was December the ninth, actually. He didn't stay very long, and he didn't seem to have any business at the store. No one to see, as far as I've been able to ascertain. He came up to my office, chatted a few minutes, made some scathing comments about the White Empress, and then left. Apparently he was on his way to see the Sultan of Kandrea, who, he told me that morning, prefers to do business with him now, rather than with me."

"Balderdash! The sultan's always wanted to deal with you, Stevie, and no one else. We both know he dotes on you. He's made no secret of the fact that when you've gone to see him in Kandrea he'd like nothing better than for you to stay. Indefinitely."

Stevie had to laugh, despite the seriousness of the conversation about Nigel. "I'm not so sure of that, Bruce, he is a bit of a flatterer, you know. However, I am sure about one thing."

"And what is that?"

"Nigel came into the Fifth Avenue store to pick a fight with me. It was my birthday, and he knew it was, yet he didn't even mention it. And he did that on purpose. There's another thing

. . . I have the distinct feeling he's working against me. Plotting, actually."

"But with whom is he plotting, Stevie?" Bruce asked in a curious voice. His eyes did not leave her face.

"I don't know." She gazed at her father-in-law helplessly. Then she grimaced. "It's a silly thing to say, isn't it? After all, with whom *could* he plot? *No one.* What I think is this, Bruce . . . he's plotting with himself. Plotting in his head, plotting to oust me. He wants to run the whole show, you see."

Bruce grew disturbed, and this instantly showed in his face. He pushed himself up out of the chair, went and stood near the fireplace, resting one hand on the mantelshelf. For a moment he was silent, his worry showing in his eyes. Then he said slowly, "I can't believe he would be so foolish." He looked down at her sadly, and added in the quietest of voices, "He knows he's your successor, that he'll be taking over from you one day. He's the heir apparent, for God's sake. And that's something he's known all his life. He doesn't have to . . . *plot.*"

Stevie nodded her understanding, looking at him steadily. A long sigh escaped her, and she felt, for a moment, that Bruce doubted her words. Then all of a sudden it struck her that his demeanor had changed, was slightly different. His anger had abated and a resigned expression was registering on his face. As she went on staring at him silently, she noticed a knowing look enter his eyes.

And then it hit her. She nodded, as if to confirm something in her own mind, and said in a low, steady voice, "You've suspected him yourself. You just didn't want to say anything to me . . . unless I confided in you. And that's one of the reasons you've been going into the showroom more than usual. To keep an eye on him . . . and to snoop around."

When he made no response, Stevie continued. "I know I'm right, Bruce."

"Yes," he admitted at last, and sighed. "I have suspected Nigel, although to tell you the truth, I'm not sure what I've suspected him of really, Stevie."

She watched him closely as he moved away from the fireplace, came over, and sat down next to her on the big sofa. Taking hold of her hand, looking deeply into her face, he continued. "I had recently begun to realize that Nigel was courting a lot of your personal clients. I asked Gilbert Drexel about this, and he confirmed that Nigel was handling their business with us, or rather, endeavoring to do so, even though they wanted to deal with you. Gilbert didn't seem to think there was anything wrong with Nigel's taking over, since you were in New York a great deal. I sort of . . . well, actually, I took his word for this, when perhaps I shouldn't have, and therefore I never said anything to Nigel. At least, not initially."

"But you found it strange?"

"Yes, I did," he told her. "After all, when a client is going to spend five, ten, even fifteen million pounds with us, and often much, much more, I know you would take the Concorde in, which you have always done in the past. After I'd thought about this for a few days, I felt uncomfortable, so I did finally speak to Nigel. He told me he was merely trying to help, that he wished to alleviate your burdens, and that you were extremely grateful to him for doing so. I accepted this, why wouldn't I?" He emitted another long, slow sigh. "I had no reason to doubt him. I see now how wrong I was. I trusted my grandson. I believed him. I realize now that I should have spoken to you right away."

"Perhaps you should have." She averted her head, thinking that ten years ago, no even five years ago, Bruce would have been on the phone to her at once. His age *was* showing after all; he wasn't so fast on the draw anymore.

"Then again," he continued to explain, "Gilbert was totally

unconcerned. However, I began to notice a grave change in Nigel the past few weeks, and this has troubled me greatly."

"What do you mean exactly?"

"He's become extremely impatient and irritable. And he is temperamental. It's struck me numerous times he's rather sarcastic and acerbic with people when speaking to them. That's not the way to behave around the staff, nor is it the way to handle them. Or to run a business."

"I agree. But Nigel's always been a bit of a know-it-all, and he's—" she began to say, then stopped abruptly. She'd been about to say, like you were once, but had cut herself off just in time. Clearing her throat, Stevie went on quickly. "And he can be arrogant."

"Yes, that's true. And argumentative. He's had several run-ins with Gideon recently, and when Gideon was not in the least at fault."

"Run-ins about what?"

"Minor things apparently, of no real consequence. Nigel's exaggerated their importance, blown them out of all proportion."

He drew away from her, watched her quietly, waited for her to speak. He was troubled by this conversation, and he felt great empathy for her. She had grown up to be a brilliant woman; he had watched her grow, seen her become what she was today. She was steadfast, loyal, dedicated, hardworking, and a decent person. If Nigel *was* trying to oust her, then her son had made a terrible mistake. And there was no question in his mind whom he would back. If it came to that, of course.

The silence between them lengthened.

Bruce, glancing at her covertly, realized she seemed tired, and there was a stricken expression in her eyes. His heart went out to her. Stevie, aware of her father-in-law's scrutiny, drew herself up on the sofa and half smiled at him. "So, you suspected him your-self . . . "

Bruce nodded. "But of *what* I wasn't at all certain." He cleared his throat, said in a low, concerned voice, "I never thought for one moment that he wanted—" He paused, looked at her askance, and finished, "That he wanted your job, Stevie."

"I've realized that he did, does, and has for some time." Her laugh was hollow as she added, "Ah, well, uneasy lies the head that wears a crown."

"Quite so."

"It's funny, Bruce. At Thanksgiving I made up my mind to unburden myself to you. Then on the plane coming over I changed my mind. I decided all this could wait until after Christmas. I didn't want to spoil the festivities with problems. Now it's all come out in such a rush of words."

"Perhaps that's just as well, my dear. And we must talk to Nigel, don't you think?"

Stevie bit her lip. "Yes, but I believe I should be the one to do that. Not you."

"We should talk to him together, Stevie."

She shook her head vehemently. "I don't think so. It would be much better if I saw him alone. Please, Bruce, let me handle it."

"Very well," he replied in a somewhat resigned voice, having learned long ago not to argue with her when she had already made up her mind about something.

"After Christmas?" A dark brow lifted questioningly.

He nodded.

Stevie took a deep breath and continued. "He's not the only one I have problems with."

"Oh." Bruce threw her a swift glance. "Who else?"

"Chloe."

"Not Chloe! That couldn't possibly be. She's such a sweet girl," Bruce murmured, staring at Stevie aghast.

She saw his love for the girl reflected in his eyes, and so very carefully she explained. "Chloe announced at Thanksgiving that she doesn't want to go to college."

"Not even Oxford?" he asked, sounding surprised.

"Correct. She wants to drop out."

"But she must at least graduate from Brearley," Bruce murmured with a worried frown. "She must not forgo that."

"Yes, you're right, and she won't."

"And then what?"

"She wants to work at Jardine's. *In London.* Chloe would like to go into the family business, Bruce."

Bruce Jardine could not help smiling. Try though he did to keep a sober face, knowing this was a serious matter, the smile forced its way through and settled on his mouth. It wouldn't budge.

Stevie, watching him, said, "Well, I might have known *you'd* be pleased."

"I shan't deny that I am, Stevie, my dear. You know I have an extremely soft spot for Chloe, and she's such a smart, intelligent girl. There's a place for her at Jardine's whenever she wants it as far as I'm concerned. However, you're her mother, and, of course, you're the managing director at Jardine's here. You run the company. Whether you want to give her a job or not is up to you." Reaching forward, he patted her hand, and there was an air of genuine friendship and affection in his manner. "She's so young, only eighteen. Don't be too harsh on her."

"I'm not being harsh. I just want to do what's best for her."

"Naturally, and so do I. Why don't you let her come to London next summer? She can live here with me at Wilton Crescent, and go to Jardine's every day. Gideon can take her under his wing. She can get her feet wet, so to speak, and she will soon know whether she likes the family business or not."

"That had also crossed my mind. Well, we'll see." She let out a long sigh.

Bruce eyed her keenly. "What is it?"

"She's a teenager. Not an enviable age. They're full of excitement one moment, depressed the next. They go through terrible mood swings, temperamental outbursts, and are at the mercy of raging hormones." She forced a smile. "By next summer she may have changed her mind yet again."

A smile touched his dark eyes. "I hope not. I'd like to think she'll be part of Jardine's eventually. The whole idea pleases me. . . . "

Stevie was silent for a moment and then she rose, walked across the room, stood at the window looking out. After a few seconds she swung around and said, "If I do let her come next year, she'll be living with my mother, Bruce. I think that would be the best thing for her."

She saw the disappointment flash across his face and settle in his eyes. "That's understandable," he murmured, sounding sad, and looked away.

Quietly, Stevie went on. "My mother's expecting you for Christmas lunch tomorrow. You are coming, aren't you?"

"I wouldn't miss it for the world."

"Nigel's going to be there."

"He told me he wasn't taking the family to Paris this year, so I assumed they would be with us."

"Why do you think he wants me out of the company? Because he does, you know," she asked unexpectedly.

Bruce seemed to be weighing her words. "I trust your judgment implicitly. If you say he does, then he does. And to answer your question, I can't imagine why. And it would be ridiculous to speculate."

"That's true."

There was a knock on the door and the butler reappeared. "Lunch is ready, Mr. Jardine. Cook would like you to come to the table. She's afraid the cheese soufflé might fall."

"Right away, Alan, right away," Bruce replied, and stood up.

Stevie said, "I just realized how hungry I am. And I love Elsie's cheese soufflé. It's going to hit the right spot."

Bruce merely nodded, and together they left the library.

As they walked across the grand entrance foyer to the dining room, Stevie remembered the night she had sat in this vast cavernous hall and listened to Bruce's voice raised in anger. He had told Ralph she should get rid of her baby. If she had, Nigel would never have been born.

17

"I'M CERTAINLY GLAD TO SEE EVERYONE'S BEHAVING WELL TODAY," Stevie said, turning to Derek, and then once more glancing around the room. "I can't believe it."

"Neither can I," he answered, following the direction of her gaze, observing the other family members, who were sitting or standing in different parts of the room, chatting to each other. "They actually seem rather chummy, which is something of a relief. There's usually some sort of contention going on, or an undercurrent. Mmmmm." He nodded to himself, added, "And these are noticeably absent, Stevie." Grinning at her, he said sotto voce, "As far as I'm concerned, they can all go off and murder one another later, so long as they don't upset the applecart this afternoon. Blair's been working for days to make this Christmas Day a very special one."

"Yes, I know she has," Stevie murmured, settling back on the sofa, "and everything will be fine, don't worry. Why even Nigel's smiling for once."

"So I noticed. And he'd better keep on smiling. If he doesn't, or if he starts any kind of trouble, I'll have his guts for garters."

Stevie began to laugh. "I haven't heard that expression for years. Oh, Derek, look how sweet the little ones are being with Bruce ... and he's so proud, tickled to death to have great-grandchildren. I ought to take a picture, don't you think? Three generations of Jardines."

"It's a great idea. Do it after lunch, when we're opening the presents. And perhaps you'll take one of your mother and me with the babies and Tamara. That would be a nice shot to have for our family album."

"Yes, I will, and doesn't Tamara look beautiful? I don't think I've ever seen her looking lovelier than she does this afternoon."

Derek nodded in agreement. "Red suits her, it looks fabulous with her hair. She's got great style, you know, that one. It's a special kind of chic only the French seem to have. Well, at least have naturally, and without having to make a big effort. I'm glad she's part of the family, she's been such a positive influence on Nigel."

"Yes, he's generally much pleasanter when Tamara's around, that's true. It's a marriage made in heaven, thankfully. She seems to have a soothing effect on him."

"She tempers his recalcitrant attitude. And makes him smile occasionally," Derek added succinctly.

Stevie threw him a quick look. "Please don't worry, no one is going to spoil the day. I won't let anyone. I know how hard Mom's worked. Incidentally, this room looks wonderful since she redecorated it."

"Your mother's very talented when it comes to design, but then I don't have to tell *you* that."

Derek once again swung his eyes, followed Stevie's gaze, seeing the drawing room of the Regent's Park flat objectively, through her eyes. And of course it *was* beautiful and grand and impressive, with its pale silk fabrics and fine antiques, the lovely old paintings gracing the cream silk walls.

So far from the Welsh valleys of his youth, the little back-to-back house where he had grown up, so far from the poverty and grind that had been his family's lot in life for generations.

The grand leap.

That was the way he thought of it. And even today, after so long, there were moments when he would stop whatever he was doing and survey this world where he now lived—and he couldn't help marveling at himself just a little. He marveled that he had been able to make that great leap from there to here. And the fact that he *was* here with a career, fame, success, wealth, and a title to boot said something for his courage, his nerves of steel, his strength of will, his drive, energy and desire to succeed.

It was a leap out of a place and out of a class . . . out of the working class, the underclass, and the underprivileged. The poor boy from Wales . . . now the toast of the town . . . of many towns and cities and villages the world over. An impossible dream achieved. And only by looking clearly at his beginnings could he understand how far he had come, and just how high that leap had been.

"Penny for your thoughts," Stevie said, touching his arm lightly.

"They're not worth a penny, since I was thinking of nothing in particular," Derek replied, tearing himself away from his thoughts.

He stood up, glanced at the champagne flute in her hand, and asked, "How about a refill?"

"I'm fine right now, Derek, thanks."

"Back in a minute." He excused himself and strolled in the direction of the dining room, where a small bar had been set up.

Stevie sat back against the cushions, looked around the room. Her entire family was present for once—her mother and stepfather, her three sons and daughter, her daughter-in-law and two grandchildren, and her father-in-law. It was not such a big family by some standards; there were others she knew of that were much larger. For a small family, they had had their fair share of troubles over the years, and still had them.

Stevie instantly clamped down on this thought before it took hold, not wanting to spoil the day, knowing that the problems would still be there tomorrow and could be dealt with then. If they could be dealt with at all.

She lifted her glass and took a sip of Dom Pérignon. A split second later her eyes were focused on Tamara.

Her daughter-in-law was coming toward her; she looked as if she were walking on air, so graceful was she. Tamara had the longest legs Stevie had ever seen, and the slender, streamlined body of a model. Her hair was her most spectacular feature though, being neither silver nor gold but a mixture of both, and it was most arresting.

Tamara's face was narrow and elegant below her silver-gilt bangs. These stopped short of large jet-black eyes, a narrow nose, and a wide, generous mouth. She was beautiful in an offbeat way, and that was part of her charm and appeal. The red silk dress she wore swished slightly as she walked, its full short skirt fluid around those lovely long legs, the latter shown off by very high-heeled red silk shoes.

Her good looks aside, Tamara was a kind and considerate young woman who did not have a bad bone in her body, and Stevie had always adored her. Like Blair, Tamara had been a model before her marriage to Nigel, and both women shared certain characteristics, chiefly the desire to be a wife, a mother, and a homemaker more than anything else.

"Can you come to dinner tomorrow, Stevie?" Tamara asked, hovering in front of her mother-in-law. "I'd love it if you could."

"Are you sure, Tamara?" Stevie frowned. "Or perhaps I

should say does Nigel want me to come? You see, darling, he's been a bit odd with me lately."

"Of course he does! We both want you to come. And please don't pay attention to Nigel's temperamentality. He's been a bit snotty and irritable with me these last few weeks. I hope he's not sickening for something. And the Christmas rush always gets to him, you know that. Please come, Stevie, with Chloe. And perhaps Miles and Gideon will come too!"

"What's all this about Gideon?" Gideon asked, drawing to a standstill next to her.

"I want you to come to dinner tomorrow, Gid, well, supper really. A Russian supper on Boxing Day. Doesn't that tempt you?" She eyed him, laughter bubbling inside her.

"Ha! I knew *you'd* have to come up with a foreign meal at some point this Christmas," Gideon teased, looking at her fondly, putting his arm around her shoulders. "Why not a bit of good old roast lamb and Yorkshire pud for a change? Instead of all this foreign mishmosh."

Accustomed as she was to Gideon's teasing, she laughed and said, "Beluga caviar and Scottish smoked salmon a mishmosh! Goodness me, Gideon."

"How wonderful it sounds, my pet. And I'd love to come. What's the rest of the menu? Are you going to make that delicious borscht?"

"If you like. With piroshki. And what about your favorite, chicken Kiev?"

"That's great. But you're making me hungry." He turned to Stevie. "It's almost four o'clock, Ma. When's Grandma going to serve lunch, do you know?"

"In a few minutes. At four."

"All joking aside, I love your cooking," Gideon announced, turning back to Tamara. "I bet they didn't teach you how to make chicken Kiev at that snooty English boarding school you went to."

"You know they didn't, Gid. It was my Russian grandmother who taught me everything I know about cooking."

Suddenly Gideon swung around as a small boy hurtled across the room, calling, "Uncle Gid, Uncle Gid, look what Papa Bruce gave me!" As he came to a sudden stop next to Gideon, he opened his hand. "A little car!" he exclaimed, and showed it to his uncle, beaming up at him.

Gideon bent down to examine the new possession. "Aren't you the lucky boy. And it's a Jaguar, Arnaud."

The four-year-old's big blue eyes fastened on Gideon's face and he said carefully, "Jwagwar."

"Me. Look me," Natalie cried as she ran to join them, holding out her arm. "Papa give me."

"It's beautiful, sweetheart," Gideon said, smiling at her as he examined the slender silver chain with a heart, which Bruce had obviously just fastened on her wrist. That was a favorite game of his grandfather's, pulling surprises out of his pockets.

Natalie laughed and ran to Stevie. "Granma, look!"

"Oh, how lovely." Stevie put down her flute of champagne quickly as the three-year-old scrambled onto her lap unexpectedly. Natalie looked into her face and patted it. "Love you, Granma."

"I love you too, Natalie." Stevie hugged her vivacious little blonde grandchild closer and kissed the top of her head.

A moment later Blair came back into the living room and announced, "Lunch is ready at last, everyone. Shall we go into the dining room?"

Nigel suddenly appeared in front of Stevie, looking happy and lighthearted. He smiled warmly at his mother and said, "Can I relieve you of your little burden, Ma?" As he spoke he reached forward and lifted his small daughter out of Stevie's lap and placed her on the floor. Then he offered Stevie his hand. "Here, let me help you up," he said, and promptly pulled her to her feet.

Leaning into her, he smiled again, much to Stevie's astonishment, and then kissed her on the cheek. "I haven't had a chance to wish you a Merry Christmas yet."

"Thank you, Nigel," she replied. "And the same to you." She was relieved that he was in a friendlier mood than the last time she had seen him, in New York on her birthday.

Gideon said, "Let's go in, Ma, I'll escort you."

"Along with me," Miles said, joining them, taking her other arm.

Stevie laughed and allowed them to maneuver her across the floor.

Gideon said in a quiet, confiding tone, "Can I talk to you later, Ma?"

"Of course. But is there something wrong, Gideon?" she asked, quickly glancing at him.

"No, no. I just wanted to tell you something. It's nothing bad, honestly. Good, really. I'll drive you and Chloe back to Eaton Square after lunch, and we can have our little chat then."

18

"WHAT DID YOU WISH TO TALK TO ME ABOUT?" STEVIE ASKED LATER that evening, once she and Gideon were alone and settled in the small study of her flat in Eaton Square. She leaned back, crossed her legs, and focused her eyes intently on her son, who was seated opposite.

"The future, my future. Before I get to that, I just want to say something else. I know you've been concerned about me, Ma, and I'm sorry I worried you. But I am all right now. I've managed to sort out the things which were bothering me."

Stevie nodded, then asked curiously, "What was it you had to sort out, Gideon?"

"Margot Saunders. She was making a lot of trouble for me ... because I broke off with her."

"If your mood was anything to judge by, she must have really been making your life hell."

"She was harassing me, and growing more hysterical as the weeks went by."

Stevie shook her head, looking regretful. "How awful for you. I'm sorry you had to struggle through something like that. It's frightening. I know that hysteria and irrationality of that nature can often lead to violence."

Gideon stared at his mother, and it struck him again how smart she was. There was very little she didn't know about people or about life. "You're right, Ma. I had to stop her before she went too far."

"How did you manage to do that?" Stevie asked swiftly.

"I said I would tell Jack Bellanger about the way she was behaving."

"It obviously worked. But *why*?"

"Margot hates the press. Don't you remember, her brother Julian was involved in some sort of scandal in the City a few years ago. He almost went to jail. The press coverage was pretty relentless. The minute I mentioned Jack's name, you'd have thought I'd held a loaded gun to her head."

"And she's left you alone ever since?"

"Yes."

"I'm relieved to hear it. It's funny, Gideon, how little we know about people really. The last person I would have suspected of being irrational was Margot. I always thought she was so down-to-earth and levelheaded."

"So did I. But I soon found out otherwise. She's really unbalanced, Ma. Well, that's all over and done with now, thank God."

Stevie said, "You've been lucky, Gideon. She could have hurt you—physically, I mean. But let's move on. You said you wanted to talk to me about the future, your future. I suppose I am right in thinking you meant your future as far as your personal life is concerned, and not your future at Jardine's?"

He grinned. "You hit the nail on the head, Mother. I wanted you to be the first to know that I'm getting married."

This was the last thing Stevie had expected to hear, and she stared at Gideon in astonishment. "I can't believe it."

"Believe it, Ma. It's true."

"Who are you going to marry?"

He didn't immediately answer her. Rising, he walked over to the window, stood looking down into the gardens of the square, wondering how best to explain the situation. There was only one way. He must jump in at the deep end and tell her everything. His mother would understand, he was quite sure of that.

When he did not respond, Stevie probed, "Is that the reason you broke up with Margot?"

Turning around, Gideon answered quietly. "Not really. I told you, the relationship wasn't working very well. When I realized how unbalanced she was, I became alarmed. However, I was . . . well, I *was* kind of getting involved with someone else by then."

"And it's this person you want to marry?"

"Yes. It's an old friend, Ma, someone you like, so I know you're going to be pleased."

"Who is it, Gideon?"

"It's Lenore, Ma."

"*Lenore. Our* Lenore?"

He nodded.

"But she's married already! Unless she got a divorce in the last week." Stevie was thunderstruck, and this showed in the expression on her face and in her tone of voice.

"She's going to get a divorce as quickly as possible. She's not been happy with Malcolm for a long time. The marriage is on the rocks."

"Oh, Gideon, are you *sure* about your feelings? Really sure? There have been so many young women passing through your life . . ." Her voice trailed off, and she looked at her son, filling with dismay. "And is Lenore sure? There are children involved here, and they must be considered. And what about Malcolm?"

"What do you mean?"

"He might not want to give her a divorce," Stevie ventured.

"The marriage has been over for a long time, Mother. Lenore is not at all happy with him."

"When did you realize you loved her?" Stevie asked, her voice low pitched and concerned.

"Years ago, just after she'd married Malcolm. It hit me then that I'd been such a stupid fool to let her get away, let her escape. You know how close we were. All of our lives, actually."

"Yes, I do, but—" Stevie cut her sentence off, stared into the distance.

Noticing the worry deepening on her face, Gideon said, "But *what*, Ma?"

"You can't build happiness on somebody else's *unhappiness*, at least that's my opinion. You must both think very carefully about this."

"Malcolm won't be unhappy, if that's what you're getting at. He wants a divorce."

"I see. But again, I ask you, are you really sure that you love Lenore, Gideon?"

"Yes, I am. Why do you doubt me?"

"It seems to me you've been . . . a bit fickle over the years. In and out of love at the drop of a hat."

"This is different, Ma. I really and truly love Lenore, and she loves me. It's going to be all right. Trust me. This love's going to last a lifetime. We were meant to be together."

Stevie was silent.

Gideon crossed the floor, sat down next to her on the sofa. Leaning into her, he took hold of her hand and squeezed it tightly. She turned her head to look at him.

"I love her so much, Mother, honestly I do. I know what you're getting at . . . the upset of the divorce, all of the problems involved, the children, their feelings and their young lives to be taken into account. But I'm ready and willing to shoulder it all, and take the children on too. Lenore will never give them up anyway. She wants custody, obviously."

"This is a big step," she murmured.

"It's a step I want to take."

"I hope you're both doing the right thing."

"Don't throw cold water on it, Ma, *please*," he exclaimed. He searched her face, his eyes as troubled as hers. "I know I don't have a very good record as far as women are concerned, but that's easy to understand, and explain now. It was always Lenore I loved, and that is the reason I soon became disenchanted with all the women I dated. They weren't her."

Stevie looked at him thoughtfully and slowly nodded. "I know what you mean." A little sigh trickled out of her mouth, and she said softly, "I've loved Lenore Philips since she was a little girl. And I love you too. And that's why I don't want either of you to make a mistake, do the wrong thing, and get hurt in the process. I've always believed Malcolm Armstrong to be pretty tough. Whatever you say to me to the contrary, it's not going to be *quite* as easy as you think." She bit her lip and finished in a voice so low it was almost inaudible. "I don't want you to cause others pain either."

"That can't always be avoided, Ma. Everyone gets damaged in a divorce. In my considered opinion."

Stevie merely nodded, but she knew he was correct.

"Aren't you happy for me, Mother?"

"Yes, of course I am, darling, if this is what you really want." Stevie forced herself to smile. "I suppose I just wish the situation were a little less complicated." Squeezing his hand, she said as reassuringly as she could, "I'm here for you, Gideon, for both of you, if you need me. Surely you know that."

"Thanks, Ma," he said, beaming at her. Pulling her into his arms, he hugged her to him.

Later that night, from the privacy of her bedroom, Stevie phoned Derek and recounted her conversation with Gideon. When she had finished, there was a silence at the other end of the phone.

"Are you still there, Derek?" she asked after a moment.

"I am, Stevie darling. Just thinking as I sit here, and wondering what to say to you."

"There's not much you can say, I suppose. After all, he is twenty-seven, he's going to do what he wants." As she finished speaking, Stevie laughed a little hollowly.

"What is it?"

"I always thought they would marry, you know. I hoped they would, actually. You must remember how close they were when they were children and teenagers."

"How could I ever forget it, Stevie? Your mother and I were always rather anxious about them. I for one held the strong conviction that he would get her pregnant. They lived in each other's pockets and behaved as if none of us existed. I was always very curious about what they did over at Lindenhill. They were alone so much, and let's face it, Jacquetta Philips had her head in the clouds. She wasn't much of a disciplinarian. They spent an awful lot of time there without any supervision."

"Except for Miles. He was often along, over there with them. But I know what you're getting at. To tell you the truth, I was startled when Gideon and Lenore stopped seeing each other. Even more startled when Lenore married Malcolm. That was probably a huge mistake, under the circumstances, and I can see why she and Gideon got back together again. Oh, God, more complications."

"They're really serious, then?" Derek asked.

"I'm positive of it. Gideon wouldn't have made the announcement."

"Then we'd better fasten our seat belts, we're in for a bumpy ride."

19

STEVIE HAD NOT WRITTEN VERY MUCH IN HER JOURNAL OF LATE, BUT once she said good-night to Derek, she took it out and entered the date and the place at the top of the page.

Christmas Day, 1996
London

> I was startled earlier this evening when Gideon confided that he and Lenore were involved again, but only momentarily, given the circumstances of their lives. Because they were so extraordinarily close as children, and in their early teens, I'd fully expected them to marry when they were old enough to do so.
>
> Something happened between them at one point, and they drew apart. Neither of them has ever spoken to me about it, but I was aware there was a rift. How could I not be? Gideon was like a bear with a sore head and gloomier than ever, and Lenore became withdrawn and remote. She eventually vacated our lives and was absent most of the time.
>
> If only they had confided in me then, perhaps I might have

been able to help them straighten it out, whatever IT was. Certainly I would have perhaps been able to prevent all these problems now.

I always thought it was rather sudden, the way Lenore married Malcolm Armstrong. He's never been a favorite of mine, and I've never grown to like him, not one iota, even though I've known him and his family for donkey's years. Too cocksure, arrogant, and tough, to my way of thinking.

I've often thought that part of Malcolm's attraction for Lenore at that time was his age. At twenty-five, he must have appeared more sophisticated and grown-up than Gideon, who was only seventeen, two years younger than Lenore. Yes, the older man would seem much more desirable, that's quite obvious to me now.

I don't dare write here that she was too young to get married at nineteen; after all, I was much younger when I married Ralph.

Stephen, my godson and namesake, was born a scant eight months later. A premature baby, Lenore said. But I've always had my doubts about that. Still do. If Malcolm got her pregnant, this might explain the suddenness of that unfortunate marriage. I think of it as unfortunate, because Lenore and Malcolm are as different as chalk and cheese, and ill suited.

Pansy was born a year after Stephen, and then came Thomas, Gideon's godson, just eighteen months after that. Three children one after the other in just under four years. But who am I to talk? I had three myself in a short span of time before I was even twenty.

I hope these children don't become pawns in this breakup of a marriage and the ensuing divorce. All are under ten. They will be Gideon's charges one day if he gets his way and weds Lenore. Quite a responsibility, taking on a ready-made family. Is he up to it? I don't even have to think twice about that. I know he is. Gideon has a great sense of responsibility.

And Lenore is strong, and in many ways she is like me. She's very down-to-earth, practical, and independent by nature. Thankfully, she didn't lose her wonderful sense of independence after her marriage.

As I think of that now, I realize it must have been quite a battle for her. Malcolm is a male chauvinist. Obviously, though, she really made her mind up not to become an appendage, a "yes" wife walking three steps behind her husband.

As I look back, Lenore was determined to be her own woman even when she was a young girl. And I know she always considered herself to be Malcolm's equal, which, of course, she is. How fortunate it is now that she went ahead and carved out her own life and her own career.

To me she has always been a clever girl; I think it is very clever of her, using her knowledge of old paintings, art objects, and furniture to her advantage the way she has, opening her own arts and antiques consultancy firm when she did.

I remember now how we used to laugh years ago, when she would take me on guided tours of Lindenhill, where her family has lived for centuries ... one of the great stately homes of England.

Lindenhill is full of priceless objects that she knows everything about, right down to the last detail. All of this information, this knowledge, was force-fed into her by Allan, her father, before he died.

Lenore is twenty-nine now, and it has taken her ten years to come back to Gideon. Oh, dear, the trouble they are about to have. I can hardly bear to think about it. Derek was so right tonight when he said we're in for a bumpy ride. We are.

Whatever my son says, I know that Malcolm Armstrong is going to be a problem. I doubt very much that he wants a divorce. It would be inconvenient for him; in a sense, he would lose face. Lenore's aristocratic lineage was always of enormous importance to him. She was born Lady Eleanor Elizabeth Jane Philips, and her brother is the Marquess of Linden, and that is most meaningful to Malcolm, such a silly snob.

I suppose he thinks their impeccable background gives him stature, but he's wrong. He's an insignificant man and he will never be anything else. Anyway, I know he won't want to let go of her because of who she is.

Gideon asked me if I'm happy for him, for them, and I am. They are so right for each other, I know that. But I don't envy them the battle they will have to wage. I wonder how I can best help them. Just be here, I suppose, be a friend, help them however I can.

Well, looking back over this rather long day, I realize it was a day of confidences. Tamara drew me to one side after our long lunch and told me that she and Nigel are trying to have another baby. I hope it happens; she's so keen to have a third child. They want a big family, at least six, so she told me. Sweet Tamara, a mother-in-law's dream and so dear to me. I'm glad Nigel's made her happy, and vice versa; he's such a difficult man. Before he met Tamara, I thought he would never find a girl that pleased him. He's so critical.

He was much nicer to me today. That startled me too. Tamara softens him. He worships her, that's evident, and he adores the children. I'm thankful they're such a happy little family.

Everyone was so generous to me this Christmas. Bruce gave me a beautiful Nécessaire, a vanity case, made by Louis Cartier in the 1930s. It's a gorgeous little thing: black enamel decorated with tiny diamonds, rubies, and emeralds. He knows I love collecting these old signed pieces by well-known jewelers, and apparently he went to a great deal of trouble to find me a Cartier piece. This one he found in Rome, of all places. At least, someone found it for him.

My mother and Derek gave me a shagreen box; the shagreen is a lovely greenish-gray color. My mother said she thought it was meant for me, since an S made of gold decorates the lid. It will make a nice box for stationery on my desk. Chloe presented me with a lavender-colored cashmere shawl that's perfectly beautiful, and the twins gave me peridot earrings designed and made by Gideon, and paid for by the two of them. Their note said they chose peridots because they matched the color of my green eyes. They're all so loving. I'm a lucky woman.

The gift from Nigel and Tamara took me by surprise, because it's so obviously valuable, and not the kind of thing they usually give me. It's an icon, Russian of course, and exquisitely painted and intricately decorated with gold and semiprecious stones, and it's old. Very old. I'm quite certain it was Tamara's idea to get me the icon, and that she was the one who found it. But the note was loving, and Nigel seemed eager to know if I really liked it.

My adorable grandchildren gave me presents they had made themselves. Arnaud painted a picture of Natalie, not at all like her, naturally, but the intention was there. She gave me a small, fancy paper bag full of kisses, awkwardly drawn on a long sheet of paper, folded and tied with ribbon by Tamara.

All in all, it was a happy time, and there were no quarrels or disagreements for once. Everyone enjoyed the day, even Nigel, who was very amicable with us all. I hope his behavior today bodes well for the future.

On the way home from Regent's Park, Chloe started to talk about coming back to London for Easter. It's true that Brearley breaks for almost three weeks in March, and there's no reason she shouldn't come. I'm just reluctant to let her visit here on her own, and I don't really understand myself. After all, she is eighteen, *and she would be staying with my mother and Derek. But something's holding me back from saying yes to her.*

I'm so happy that Chloe has remained contented since Thanksgiving, that she hasn't gone on about working at Jardine's. She's sensible in that way. Having broached the idea to me, she's now waiting for me to make a decision.

She's so special, and in so many ways. She always was, too, from being a little girl. I'm blessed really. My lovely daughter has never given me any trouble.

Gideon didn't say too much when she said she wanted to have the Easter break in London, and spend time at Jardine's with him. His response was, "It's up to Ma." But he does love her, and he seems willing to take her under his wing. Well, we'll see. Tomorrow I'll talk to Gideon . . .

Gideon . . . Lenore . . . I understand only too well the pull between them, the overwhelming attraction that draws them back to each other. That kind of feeling is so hard to fight. I know.

On the other hand, it's wrong to build one's happiness on someone else's unhappiness. Doing that somehow always comes back to haunt you. It's like throwing out a boomerang that returns to hit you in the face.

It was a long time ago that I was faced with a similar kind of decision, and I knew I had to walk away, not look back. And, for the most part, I never have. There have been moments when a yearning for him has surfaced, the desire to see him blinding me to reason. But it was only ever for a moment or two. Sanity prevails. It always will. But how I've longed for him.

Stevie put down the pen, closed her journal, and returned it to the drawer. She had written enough.

Later, when she went to bed, she found it hard to fall asleep, she had so much on her mind. She tossed and turned for almost an hour until she finally dozed off.

And she dreamed of him.

It was a dream so vivid, it remained with her long after she awakened the next morning. As she lay in bed in her charming blue and white bedroom, watching the early light seep in through the curtained windows, she struggled through the residue of the dream. It still clung to her, enveloped her.

Stevie found it hard to shake off, so real had it been. It was as if he had actually been there with her in the room all night. She could feel his dominating presence surrounding her, could smell his cologne. Closing her eyes, she saw him again.... saw the dark, passionate eyes, the sensitive mouth, the wide and generous smile, the even teeth so white against the tan of his skin.

And she heard his voice, heard him telling her how much he loved her, and for a while she was transported back into the dream. For in it they had made love to each other, had been joined together in the perfect harmony that had once been theirs, and she longed to recapture it, just as she yearned for him at this moment.

Against her own volition she began to weep. Tears slid out from under her lids, trickled down her cheeks. She pushed her face into the pillow and she wept for the loss of him, for the life they could have had together, for all that might have been.

Eventually, when her tears had abated, Stevie got up, and after pulling on her dressing gown she went into the kitchen. As she pushed open the door, Chloe exclaimed, "Good morning, Mommy. I've made the coffee, do you want a cup? I'll—"

Chloe broke off, stared at her, then asked with a frown, "Are you all right, Mom?"

Stevie nodded. "Of course I am. Why do you ask?"

"You're so white, you look as if you've seen a ghost."

Stevie shook her head, thinking her daughter's choice of words was unfortunate. "I didn't sleep well; I'm a little tired, I guess. Too much on my mind," she improvised.

"I'm sorry. And you work too hard, Mom." Chloe stepped over to her mother, put her hand on her arm, and continued. "Sit down here, and I'll bring you a mug of coffee. Would you like some toast? I'll make it for you."

"Thanks, darling." Stevie smiled at her wanly.

Impulsively, Chloe grabbed hold of Stevie and wrapped her arms around her. "I love you, Mom." The girl hugged her tightly, clinging to her for a long moment.

"And I love you too, darling."

They finally drew apart, and Stevie, staring into her daughter's face, thought how much she resembled her father in coloring. She had his dark eyes, his hair. She was his child, even though she had a strong look of Blair.

"Let me get the coffee for you." Chloe hurried across the kitchen, suddenly filled with worry about her mother. She had dark rings under her eyes and she looked so sad this morning. Chloe wondered why, what had upset her.

A moment later, walking back to the kitchen table with the coffee, Chloe exclaimed, "I'm going to start *really* looking after you. That's going to be my New Year's resolution!"

Stevie laughed. "I'm perfectly all right, truly I am. As I said, I seem to have so many things on my mind right now. But you don't have to worry about me, Chloe. I'll be fine."

Chloe merely nodded and went back to make the toast. When it was ready, she brought it to the table along with her own mug of coffee. Sitting down opposite her mother she murmured, "You're not still angry with me, are you? I mean about wanting to work at Jardine's."

"I was never angry, Chloe. Just concerned about your education. I spoke to Bruce about it the other day, and he seemed quite tickled at the idea of you working in the company."

"He did?"

"Yes." Stevie saw the sudden excitement flashing on her daughter's face, the hope in her eyes, and on the spur of the moment she said, "You can spend the Easter break here, Chloe, if you like. It seems to mean so much to you."

"Oh, Mom, can I! Thank you, oh, thank you so much!" She jumped up and hugged Stevie, and showered her with kisses.

"But you have to stay with your grandmother and gramps in Regent's Park. You can't live here in this flat alone, you know," Stevie pointed out quickly.

"That's fine. Oh, I'm so excited; I can hardly wait."

Stevie took a sip of coffee, looking at her eighteen-year-old daughter over the rim. It gave her pleasure to see Chloe so happy. It had taken so little to bring that enthusiasm back. She fell down into herself for a few moments, her mind focusing on *him*. She had not dreamed about him for several years now, nor did her thoughts often dwell on him. But there had been so much talk about him since Thanksgiving, no wonder he was on her mind once more. The memories of him were painful. Long ago she had vowed to herself that she would not fall into the trap of wishful thinking, of dwelling on the past. And so she pushed aside thoughts of him. They were futile anyway.

Rising, walking to the door, Stevie said, "I'm going to get ready for work. Do you want to come to the store with me today, Chloe? You can spend some time with Gideon in the workshops if you want."

Chloe nodded and jumped up. "I'd love to come with you, Mom. I'll get ready too."

20

"AND WHAT EXACTLY DID THE SULTAN TELL YOU WHEN YOU WENT TO see him?" Bruce asked, leaning forward slightly, pinning his eyes on her.

Stevie was seated behind her desk in her office above the Bond Street store, and returning his steady gaze, she answered, "He said he thought I did not wish *personally* to handle his business anymore *and* that I was passing it on to my son. He had been wondering *why* this was so, *why* it had happened. He even wondered if he had offended me in some way, and this had worried him considerably. Mind you, Bruce, he couched all this in a most diplomatic way."

"I understand. How did he get this impression? Did he tell you?"

Stevie nodded. "Yes, he said his executive assistant, Gareth James, phoned me here at the beginning of December. The switchboard put him through to Nigel without any explanation. When Gareth asked for me again, Nigel told him I wasn't available, that I was abroad. Nigel then intimated he was now handling all of my clients for me. Gareth asked if I was in New York, and Nigel confirmed this. Once more he reiterated that he was looking after my clients, and he asked how he could be of assistance to the sultan. Gareth said the sultan was interested in seeing some of our newest designs. They made a date for Nigel to go over to Claridge's later in the week, to meet with the sultan. However, the next day Gareth called back and explained that the sultan had to leave unexpectedly for America. That's when Nigel suggested he could meet with the sultan in New York, at the sultan's convenience. And so they made a date."

"I see." Bruce steepled his fingers, sat staring into space, a reflective look on his face.

"It was for December the ninth," Stevie clarified.

Bruce sighed. "Nigel's being rather stupid, wouldn't you say? Playing these games. We could have lost a major client because of his manipulations."

"A mega client, as we say in New York."

"Well, we know what he's up to, don't we? First Gilbert told him he was courting your clients, and now we actually have it from the horse's mouth, so to speak. The sultan has given you all the ammunition you need. By the way, how did you straighten it out with the sultan? I'm presuming you did, since you sold him the yellow diamonds."

"I told him I'd taken some time off to recuperate from bronchitis, which, as you know, is partially true. I did take things a bit easier in late October and November, because I'd been so sick in September. I was very diplomatic. I explained that Nigel had been looking after things for me. *Temporarily.* You see, I didn't want him to think there was any problem within the family."

"Quite right too. The sultan wasn't insulted, was he? These chaps easily take offense, you know, especially if they think they're being slighted."

"No, no, he believed me. Why wouldn't he? And I told him I

was now available again, and whenever he needed me. I gave him my private number in New York, and I told Gareth James to call me there if I wasn't at the London store."

"That was a wise move."

"You don't have to worry, Bruce, the sultan understands. I think mostly he was terribly baffled, and whilst not slighted, perhaps he was a bit hurt."

"I'm relieved you've cleared it up, Stevie. When are you going to deal with Nigel?"

"I told you I would talk to him after the holidays, and since it's now the third of January, I'll have a word with him today. I have to, because I'm leaving for New York on Monday morning."

"I'm glad you're not wasting any time." Bruce rose. "I've got to go, I'm afraid. I have an appointment with my nutritionist." He paused at the door. "I wish you luck with Nigel, and don't be too soft with him, Stevie, he deserves to be on the mat for this. If he's difficult, unrepentant, do what you have to do."

Stevie got up, went around the desk, and embraced her father-in-law. "I'll phone you later."

Once she was alone, Stevie sat thinking for a short while, then finally coming to a decision, she picked up the phone and dialed Nigel's private extension.

"Hello? Nigel Jardine here," he said in his usual clipped, upper-class tone.

"Nigel, could you come to see me for a moment, please?"

"No, I can't. I'm very busy, Mother. Whatever you want to see me about will have to wait."

"It can't, I'm afraid. In any case, I think the Sultan of Kandrea is an important enough client for you to stop what it is you're doing and come in here. At once. We've rather a lot to talk about."

"Oh, all right," he mumbled, and banged the phone down.

Within the space of a few seconds he was barging into her office. From the doorway he asked, "What *about* the sultan?" His stance was angry and he glared at her, then he pushed the door closed with his foot.

It struck Stevie that his insouciant mood of a few days ago had completely vanished. She said slowly, "I just wanted you to know that I sold the sultan the yellow diamond necklace, with the matching earrings, bracelet, and ring."

"The set Peter designed and Gideon made?" he asked, looking slightly taken aback.

"Yes."

"When?"

"Yesterday."

"The sultan's in London?" His brows drew together in a frown.

"Oh, yes, Nigel, he is. And he sent me a handwritten note, inviting me to have coffee with him. You see, he was somewhat baffled at my behavior. He couldn't understand why I no longer wished to handle his business, after all these years of doing so, of being his personal consultant on stones." Stevie leaned back in her chair, and she did not take her eyes off her son.

Despite his arrogance and bravado, Nigel found himself flushing under her fixed scrutiny, and this mortified him. He loathed the idea that he had to answer to anyone, and most especially to her. He remained silent, for once in his life at a loss.

"Don't you have *anything* to say to me?" Stevie demanded softly, all of her attention focused on him.

"No, I don't, Mother."

"How *amazing* that you don't. After all, you're the one who created the situation with the sultan by telling Gareth James you were now handling my clients."

"You weren't in London when Gareth James phoned to set

up an appointment," he snapped at her. "I was only trying to help."

"A very lame excuse!" she shot back icily, her anger rising to the surface. "It just so happens that I know what you've been doing, Nigel. You've been courting my personal clients in an effort to take them over yourself. But it won't work. As long as I'm head of this company, *I* will handle all of our top customers."

When he made no response, she said, "Do you understand me?"

"Yes."

"There's another thing, I think you owe me an apology."

"For what?" he asked in an insolent tone.

"For lying to me."

"I've never lied to you!"

"Oh, yes, you have. You did so in New York. On December the ninth, to be exact, when you told me that Bruce had told *you* that I'd paid too much for the White Empress."

"You did."

"Maybe you mistakenly think so, but Bruce doesn't. Nor did he ever say to you that I had *always* paid too much for diamonds. That was pure invention on your part, and your grandfather is as angry about this as I am."

"Oh, who cares what he thinks? You said yourself he's retired now."

"I care what he thinks, and so should you. You haven't taken over from me yet, and as long as I'm here, you'll respect Bruce. He's still chairman."

"In name only," he sneered.

Ignoring this, she said, "Why did you lie, Nigel? You must have known you'd be found out."

"It wasn't a lie. Bruce might not have said it *exactly*, but he implied it. He's very forgetful now, he doesn't remember a thing from one day to the next," Nigel lied. "Anyway, it's true, you did overpay. You always overpay. You've no judgment." He walked farther into the room, drew closer to her desk, stood glowering at her.

How unpleasant he can be, and he's such a lovely-looking young man, she thought, gazing up at him, filled with sadness and regret. She knew now that he was indeed her enemy; he had just declared open warfare.

Quietly, Stevie said, "I don't like your tone of voice, Nigel, and you will not speak to me in this way. Furthermore, I don't appreciate your arrogant attitude either. Quite aside from being your mother, and therefore due some respect from you, I'm also your boss. Let's not forget that. You'd better adopt a different manner and tone immediately."

"The whole point is, you shouldn't be my boss!" he cried, suddenly losing all sense of caution. "*I* should be running this company, not *you*. By rights it's mine. Firstly you're a woman, and secondly you're not even a Jardine. This company has always been run by Jardines."

His last statement brought her to her feet. "I *am* a Jardine, and don't you dare say otherwise! I've been a Jardine for over thirty years, since the day I married your father. Don't you *ever* forget that, Nigel."

"I meant you're not a Jardine by blood," he cried, "and you know that's what I meant." He flushed, fighting a losing battle with his growing rage. "I hear you're leaving for the States on Monday. Stay there and do yourself and everyone else a favor. You're not wanted or needed here. And I'm perfectly capable of running Jardine's."

"No, you're not. Furthermore, you're not even going to get a chance to run it. You're fired."

Thunderstruck, he gaped at her. "You can't fire me!" he shouted.

"Oh, but I can. And I shall repeat it. You're fired."

He drew himself up to his full height and said in a cold, superior voice, "I'm a director of this company. Or had you forgotten that, Mother?"

"No, I hadn't, and you will remain a director. I can't take that away from you. However, I can fire you. And I just have."

"I'm going to see Grandfather about this," he spluttered, his face turning bright red. "He won't stand for this, he'll reinstate me."

"No, he won't, Nigel, you're quite wrong about that. Very frankly, I doubt that he'd want to, even if he could. And actually he can't. You see, as managing director of Jardine's, I have the last word."

"We'll see about that," he blustered.

"Hear me, Nigel. *You are fired.* Please vacate your office by the end of the day."

He stood looking at her stupidly for a split second, hating her more than ever, and then he shouted, "You're going to live to regret this!" And so saying, he stomped out.

Alone, Stevie poured herself a glass of water; her hand shook uncontrollably, and this annoyed her. She endeavored to calm herself, but it took her almost an hour to do so. Finally, just when she was settling down to do some work, there was a knock on the door.

As she glanced up and said "Come in," the door opened to admit Miles. Hovering on the threshold, he said, "Hello, Ma, am I intruding? Do you have a couple of minutes to spare?"

"Yes, darling," she said, smiling at him in relief, discovering that she was rather happy to see her favorite son. "Come in and shut the door. Do you want a cup of tea or anything?"

He shook his head and came into the room after closing the

door carefully behind him. "I came in to see Gid, and I couldn't leave the store without popping by." Seating himself in the chair at the other side of her desk, he peered at her intently, and then said, "You look as white as a sheet. Are you all right?"

She nodded, for a moment unable to explain. Finally, taking a deep breath, she said, "I fired Nigel."

"Good God! When?"

"An hour ago."

"Why?" He suddenly laughed. "Do I need to ask!"

Stevie took another deep breath, slowly explained what happened, told him everything, not leaving out any details. When she had finished, she shook her head sadly. "I'm sorry it's come to this, but there was nothing else I could do. He was so terribly rude to me, on top of everything else. He said I had no right to be running Jardine's because I was a woman, and also because I was not a Jardine."

"What a bloody nerve he's got, Ma. Talk about an ingrate, and after all you've done for him over the years. I'm glad you fired him, he deserves it. He's a bigger fool than I thought." Miles held her eyes for a moment. "Imagine how stupid it was of him to go courting *your* customers. They all want to deal with you, because you're the head of Jardine's. They view Nigel as a junior, your *underling*, albeit the heir apparent. Imagine if they'd taken offense, thought you were palming them off on Nigel. They'd be taking their millions elsewhere, like Cartier's, for instance. That would please Old Bruce no end, now wouldn't it?"

She half smiled. "Nigel certainly jeopardized an important area of our business, no two ways about that." She shook her head. "Anyway, that's that. Let's move on . . . Why did you come in to see Gideon?"

"I owed him some money." He laughed wryly. "For your ear-rings."

"You were both very extravagant. And you didn't have to buy me something so expensive, you know."

"We wanted to, Ma, and they came with a lot of love from us both. Gideon did spend a lot of time on the design of them with Peter. He wanted them to be perfect for you, and so did I." Stretching out his long legs, Miles went on. "Miss Chloe's all sweetness and light, and very happy today. She says you're letting her come to London for the Easter break, after all."

"It seemed rather mean not to, she wanted it so much."

"What about you? Will you be spending Easter here?"

"I don't think so, Miles. But she'll be all right, she can stay with my mother and Derek."

"I'm planning to come over around that time, so I'll bring her with me."

"Oh, Miles, that's wonderful, you'll be company for each other on the plane."

He nodded. "Gideon tells me he's confided in you . . . about Lenore."

"Yes. To tell you the truth, I was only startled for about half a minute. I always expected them to marry, you know."

"But without her having to drag herself through the divorce courts, right?" Miles grinned at her. "They really must love each other a hell of a lot. I wouldn't want to tackle that tough old bugger Malcolm Armstrong."

"He is tough, Miles, and I gather you don't like him any more than I do."

"I can't stand him, Mother. He's a phony. I'm actually surprised he's not come a cropper before now. He's another one, just like Julian Saunders, Margot's brother, always skating on thin ice in the City."

"Really," she exclaimed, sounding surprised. "I didn't know. But he was always sneaky even when he was younger."

"I don't know what Lenore ever saw in him," Miles muttered.

"Do you think Gideon and Lenore are going to make it work? The presumption being that they will marry once she is free."

"They will, Ma. You know they've always loved each other, and I for one never understood why she married Armstrong in the first place. After all, she'd had a crush on Gideon for years."

"What do you mean?" Stevie asked, raising a brow.

"Well, Gideon was about eleven, so she was thirteen. For all I know, it may have started even earlier. They were always messing around with each other, undressing each other when we played in the attics at Lindenhill. It began when Gid and I were about seven. They used to make me leave, so they could be alone, to play doctors and nurses."

"Miles, I never knew!"

"Well, I wasn't going to come and tell you then, but there's no harm you knowing now." He couldn't help chuckling. "Oh, Mother, if only you could see your face . . . you look so shocked."

"But they were just children."

"So they started their sex life when they were in kindergarten. What can I say?"

"Nothing."

"Do you know something, Ma, I've been thinking a lot about Nigel lately, and I believe he really changed when he was a teenager. The time you had that awful blow-up with Alfreda, when he took her side. What a lousy desertion that was. Gid and I have never really forgiven him for that. Choosing the old battle-ax Grandmother Jardine over you. Little sod, he was."

"I know. But I forgave him long ago. I put it down to extreme youth." Her private phone rang and she picked it up. "Hello?" As she pressed it to her ear, she went on, "Yes, Bruce, I did talk to him. And I had no alternative but to fire him."

She listened again, and then murmured, "Well, I could come over for a light lunch, but Miles is with me." She looked at her son questioningly.

Miles nodded, mouthed, "Okay."

"Bruce, Miles says yes. So we'll both come over to Wilton Crescent. See you at twelve-thirty." After she had hung up she said to Miles, "You don't have to come if you don't want to, you know."

"I do, Ma. I'm leaving tomorrow, and I would like to say good-bye to Grandfather."

PART THREE

Easter

21

CHLOE HAD BEEN VISITING THE BOND STREET SHOP SINCE SHE WAS A small girl, and she loved the marvelous old building which was a famous landmark in London. It was the epitome of elegance, its huge plate-glass windows filled with magnificent jewels and the finest of merchandise. "The best that money can buy," Bruce Jardine always said, and he was correct.

For as long as she could remember, everyone who worked at the store had made her feel special, from the uniformed doormen who smiled and touched their caps when they saw her, to the sales staff who never failed to have pleasant words for her.

She thought the interiors of the shop were the most impressive she had ever seen; these were a series of showrooms with soaring ceilings, crystal chandeliers, white marble staircases, and plush, dark blue carpeting stretching everywhere.

To her, the store was grand and stately, and perhaps this was what she loved the most about it. Jardine and Company had always been there, and always would be, and it was a symbol of prestige, dependability, and continuity.

She had been raised on family lore; she knew that Jardine's

had held the royal warrant to be Crown Jewellers since 1843, and that it was Queen Victoria who had given them the warrant. Years ago Bruce had explained to her that Jardine's had served six monarchs; he had also told her that the staff at Jardine's had one purpose, one aim—to do the best that could be done anywhere in the world.

It was her mother who had enumerated more about the royal warrants, explaining that they were granted to individuals, not companies. Gideon was the present holder and had the title of Crown Jeweller. This meant, among other things, that he had to take care of the Crown Jewels, which reposed most of the time in the Tower of London, in the new Jewel House which had been built.

As the Crown Jeweller, Gideon was the only person allowed to touch the jewels, and he was personally responsible to the queen for the upkeep of the great Crown of England, the Orbs, and the Sceptre, which Elizabeth II used on state occasions. As her mother put it, "Gideon is responsible for the symbols of the nation."

The size of Jardine's was surprising. It was much larger than most people realized, with many different workshops on the higher floors above the showrooms. It was there that some of the world's great master craftsmen labored on their extraordinary creations, producing objects of stunning beauty in silver and precious metals like gold and platinum. Lapidaries cut and polished diamonds and colored gemstones such as emeralds, sapphires, and rubies; designers created jewelry, the designs fulfilled by other craftsmen.

Last week, when she had come to work at the store, she had walked around the entire building with Gideon. "So that you can familiarize yourself with it, get the feel of it," he had said.

She had been impressed all over again as he led her through

workshops filled with these items, as well as antique clocks and watches, modern clocks and watches, and all manner of decorative objects.

Jardine's was an elegant store and it had an enormous variety of merchandise of the finest quality. Her mother took great pride in everything that was sold, as did her grandfather.

Chloe liked the store her mother had opened on Fifth Avenue in New York, but it was Jardine's in London that she really loved. She had grown up with the London shop from the time she was born until she was ten. It was to this store she had gravitated when she had decided she wanted to work in the family business.

A week ago, when Gideon had asked her what she actually wanted to do, she had been honest with him and told him she wasn't sure. For this reason, he had put her in the jewelry showroom, where some of the store's most magnificent pieces were sold. "Let's try selling first, see how you like that, see how you like dealing with people."

Today it was the Monday of Easter week. On Thursday she and Gideon were going to spend the long weekend in Yorkshire with Nigel and Tamara at Aysgarth End. For the next three days, she would work beside Gideon at his bench; he was going to show her in much more detail what he did as a lapidary.

She was waiting for him now, sitting on a stool next to his, wearing a white cotton coat, just the way he did. After a moment's absence, he returned, carrying a small packet. Putting it on the bench, opening the paper, he said, "This is a diamond I'm going to cut and polish." He glanced at her, adding, "You can cut a diamond only with another diamond."

She nodded. "But you don't use an *actual* diamond. You told me that a long time ago. You use diamond dust."

"Good girl, you remembered. And that's true, we use industrial diamonds crushed to a fine powder." As Gideon spoke, he reached for a glass jar and showed it to her. "This is it. Gray powder, but it *is* ground-down diamonds despite the way it looks. I'm going to mix some of it with linseed oil to make a black paste. You see, the diamond dust cuts the diamond, but it's the linseed oil that makes the dust adhere to the wheel."

Gideon focused his attention on the flat cast-iron wheel on his bench. "This wheel spins 3,200 rpm once it's turned on. If I simply put diamond dust on it, the dust would fly all over. That's why we need linseed oil—to make the dust stick to the wheel."

"I understand."

"I'm going to put the diamond in this tong, Chloe. Watch me now. As you can see, the tong itself is held in position by the arm, which is screwed onto the bench. That keeps it very steady. There, the diamond is now held in place by the tong, which I can move any way I want as I'm cutting the diamond."

After placing a ten-power loupe in his eye, Gideon moved the tong gently, held it over the wheel, and began to cut and facet the diamond.

She watched him, fascinated, not daring to say a word because he was so concentrated.

"So you're going to Yorkshire for Easter," Bruce said, looking across the luncheon table at Chloe. "Gideon tells me you're driving up on Thursday morning and coming back on Monday."

"That's right, Grandfather, but Mom knows all about it," she answered swiftly. "She said it was all right, she said that I could go."

A faint smile touched his mouth. "Of course it is. There's no reason why you shouldn't go to Yorkshire. Nigel behaved very badly, and he could have created quite serious problems in the business. But he's still a member of the family . . . still your brother."

Chloe nodded, her face suddenly very solemn. "Mom told me all about it. She was really upset, and angry, at first, but she's calmed down a bit now. Miles said Nigel's behavior was suicidal, and Gideon says he has a tendency to self-destruct."

"Quite," Bruce murmured, picked up his glass of water, and took a sip. "I must say, the twins have a rather dramatic way of describing events."

Leaning forward slightly, Chloe lowered her voice and said in a confiding tone, "Tamara's been very upset, you know, Grandfather. I mean about Nigel's foolishness. She loves Mom, and she told me she was ashamed of Nigel and the way he's behaved. She thinks he ought to apologize to my mother and ask to come back to work. I bet if he did so, Mom would have him back, don't you?"

"Perhaps," Bruce said cautiously, wondering if Stevie *would* let Nigel return to Jardine's. Would *he* if he were still running the company? He was not sure. Nigel's behavior had been extremely willful, and, as far as he was concerned, rashness was not a laudable trait to have, especially in business. Suddenly realizing that Chloe was staring at him, he cleared his throat and added, "Aside from being brilliant at what she does, your mother's a very compassionate woman, Chloe, and she still loves Nigel, despite the fact that he's behaved very badly toward her. So perhaps she will rehabilitate him. One day. Very much in the future, of course. But that's enough of that unpleasantness for the moment, my dear. Let's talk about *your* future at Jardine's. Do you really want to work in the family business one day?"

"Oh, yes, I do, Grandfather!" she responded enthusiastically. "And I've been fascinated by everything I've seen so far."

"And do you know what area of the business you would like to work in, Chloe?"

Chloe exhaled, then smiled at him, holding her head on one

side. "I know I don't have the talent to design jewelry, and I don't want to be a lapidary like Gideon. But I love stones, Grandfather. Especially diamonds. I'd like to be involved in buying diamonds, and other precious stones too. That's what appeals to me."

Bruce gave her the benefit of a huge smile. "That was always my area of expertise, and your mother's, Chloe. So, you're following in *our* footsteps. When you come back after Brearley's graduation, I shall ask Gilbert Drexel to take you under his wing. You can spend the summer in his department. You'll enjoy it and learn a lot."

"Oh, thank you, that's wonderful! Oh, here's lunch, Grandfather." She sat back in her chair and took a sip of water as the waiter placed the first course in front of them. They had both ordered the same lunch: Morecombe Bay potted shrimps first, to be followed by chicken pot pie, one of the specialities at Claridge's.

As she slowly ate the potted shrimps and the thin slices of buttered brown bread, Chloe did not say much, and neither did Bruce. When she had finished, she leaned across the table once more and said in a conspiratorial voice, "Nigel *resents* Mom working at Jardine's. He's not only a male chauvinist pig but totally out of date."

Looking at her alertly, Bruce agreed. "Yes, I think he is too. Women are involved in every type of business all over the world these days." A tiny amused smile flickered as he continued, "Why, even *I* have been properly educated to accept women as businessmen. You see, your mother always chided me about being old-fashioned, and years ago she decided to really straighten me out. However, it strikes me that she didn't do so well with her son, now, did she?"

"Nigel just slipped through the cracks," Chloe murmured, then added as an afterthought, "Or maybe it's yet another attitude he has developed for himself."

"What do you mean?" Bruce asked, frowning slightly, pinning her with his eyes.

"Well, he would always take a particular stance, when we were growing up, adopt a certain attitude. That's just the way he is ... *attitudinal.* And his attitudes change very quickly. Personally, I think he's mad at Mom."

Again Bruce looked at her with enormous interest, his eyes narrowing a fraction. "Why on earth would he be angry with your mother?" he probed, curious to hear what she had to say.

Chloe shrugged. "I don't know, Grandfather, maybe something from the past. He can be so touchy about things, *that* I'm really aware of."

Bruce merely nodded, thinking that she had turned out to be a very bright young woman. He himself had often thought Nigel was harboring a grudge as far as Stevie was concerned. As for Chloe, he felt a sudden rush of pride in her. She was such a beautiful girl with her glossy hair, shining dark eyes, and her faultless complexion. And she had a lovely, warm, outgoing personality that was very beguiling. *Sparkling* was the word that best described her, and her appearance as well. He suddenly wished he weren't so old, eighty-three next birthday, because he wanted to be around to watch her become a grown woman. She was so very special to him, and he loved her dearly. That was the trouble with dying, you missed so much of the future.

"What's the matter, Grandfather?" Chloe reached out, put her hand over his.

"Nothing, my dear. Why do you ask?"

"You looked so sad just then," she replied, sounding worried.

He smiled again and placed his hand over hers. "I was wishing I were younger, so that I'd be here to watch you growing up a little bit more, see you getting married, having children. Not to mention succeeding at Jardine's."

"But you *will* be here, Grandfather!" she exclaimed.

"I'm an old man now, Chloe."

"You're not to me."

"But you call me *Old* Bruce behind my back," he teased.

Her eyes opened wider and she flushed, then explained quickly, "But it's an affectionate nickname, it's not meant to be unkind."

He nodded and smiled, looking into her earnest young face, and his heart clenched. She was so very dear to him, this lovely young woman who had come into his life far too late. She touched the deepest part of him, brought out a tenderness in him no one else ever had. And it had been like that since the day she was born, since she had been a baby in her mother's arms.

22

It was a blustery day.

There was a high wind that blew the trees, bending them backward and shaking free many of the new green leaves that were sprouting on the branches. These swirled around her feet as she walked along the narrow path across the moors, heading back toward the farmhouse.

It was a chilly morning, but the sky was a clear cerulean blue, filled with bright sunlight and puffy white clouds that raced across the great arc of the sky.

Chloe loved it up on these wild untenanted moors that rolled away toward the distant horizon. The awesome vastness had always appealed to her, held her in its thrall, and she loved coming back to this place where she had spent so much time as a child.

Aysgarth End dated back to the turn of the century; the rambling old farmhouse was built of local gray stone, and it stood on top of the moors in Coverdale, above the picturesque village of West Scrafton, near Coverham.

When she arrived at the gate leading onto the farm property,

Chloe paused, turned, and stood looking out at the panoramic vistas stretching in front of her. They were breathtaking in their austere beauty. Thrusting higher into the soaring blue sky were the great Whernside fells, massive formations that had an aloof majesty to them, and looked as if they had been sculpted by some almighty hand.

The farm itself was surrounded by green fields divided and defined by old dry stone walls built by the crofters long ago. These fields sloped down into the valley below, where the River Nidd was a shining silver thread against the green in the far, far distance.

Chloe squinted in the sunlight and shaded her eyes with her hand, staring down toward the river. After a moment, she swung around, opened the gate, and went along the dirt road. As she approached the farm, she realized how hungry she was. She took a quick look at her watch and saw that it was almost eight. Time for breakfast. She increased her pace. And a few seconds later she was pushing open the oak door that led into the small front porch.

Mingled aromas of coffee, warm bread, and bacon cooking assailed her as she took off her Barbour and red wool scarf and hung them up. Opening the front door, her nose twitched and her mouth watered as she stepped into the kitchen.

Tamara was standing at the big Aga stove, turning bacon in the frying pan.

Looking up, smiling warmly, Tamara said, "Did you have a good walk, Chloe?"

"It was great, thanks." Chloe laughed. "It blew the cobwebs away, that's for sure. And it's given me an appetite."

"*Good.* Is it cold today?" Tamara asked, turning more bacon with a spatula, glancing over her shoulder as she spoke.

"Brisk. But I think it'll warm up if the wind drops. It's lovely and sunny though, a nice day to be outside as long as you're well wrapped up."

Chloe walked across the large kitchen, which her mother had decorated so effectively years before. Nothing had been changed, and it always pleased her to see it looking the same. Standing at the counter near the refrigerator, she poured herself a mug of coffee, added milk and sugar, and carried the mug back to the big wooden table in the center of the room. This was covered with a green-and-white-checked cloth that matched the curtains at the windows; she remembered the day her mother had brought them up to Yorkshire and hung them at the windows herself.

Sitting down, Chloe asked, "Who's the bacon for, Tam? It smells so delicious, I can hardly bear it."

"Anyone who wants it. There're also some other grilled things . . . tomatoes, mushrooms, sausages, and scrambled eggs. And I've got a bread cake warming in the Aga. Would you like me to prepare you a plate, darling? Give you a bit of everything?"

"That sounds good, really yummy. Thanks, Tam. And where is everyone?"

"Nigel went upstairs to look for his wallet. He and the children have already had their breakfast. He's going to take them to Ripon with Agnes. To do some shopping for me. I need a few things. And Gideon's in the back parlor, phoning Lenore. He's driving over to Lindenhill later, to bring her back here for lunch."

"Oh, good, I've always liked Lenore. I'm so glad she's going to marry Gid, aren't you?"

"Absolutely. It's the best thing that's happened to him . . . I mean, that she came back to him. But that awful Malcolm Armstrong is throwing spanners in the works all the time as far as the divorce is concerned."

"Oh, I know. Mom says it's ridiculous."

"Somebody's going to have to pay him off, I think."

"I agree. Mom says everyone has a price, and it's not always money."

Tamara laughed at this pithy comment as she turned her attention to fixing Chloe's plate, enjoying mothering the eighteen-year-old.

Chloe sipped her coffee, glancing around the spacious kitchen. She had always loved this room; it was her favorite in the old farmhouse and very special to her, from its beamed ceiling to terra-cotta-tiled floor. There was a warmth and a homeliness about it that was most appealing and reassuring. Her mother had filled it to overflowing with comfort over the years, placing a big sofa and two armchairs covered in rose-colored linen at one end, near the big picture window facing the moors. She had included two pine chests within the seating arrangement, and these held charming old lamps; the large table in the center of the room was surrounded by eight wooden chairs with rose linen cushions, and it was there that they ate most of their meals, unless they had guests.

The huge stone hearth, where a fire burned brightly, was another addition her mother had made, and it was the focal point of the room. The many copper pots and pans that hung on the hearth gleamed and winked in the firelight, which gave the room a lovely glow on this cold March morning. Logs were piled on one end of the hearth; on the other there was a big copper bucket filled with dried flowers. Facing the fire were two old grandfather chairs with high wooden backs and rose linen cushions, the chairs linked by a colorful rag rug. At the other side of the room, the big Aga stove gave off additional warmth, making the kitchen the coziest of places, one where everyone loved to gather at all hours of the day. In a sense, it was the core of the house.

"Good morning, Chloe," Gideon said, striding into the kitchen, bending down and kissing his sister. Straightening, he added, "And don't you look bonny. Your walk on the moors has brought some color to your cheeks. Do you want to come with me later? I'm going to Lindenhill to fetch Lenore."

"Yes, I'd love to, thanks, Gid." Chloe rose, walked over to the oven, and took the plate from Tamara. "This is awesome, Tam. And so yummy-looking. Thanks."

Gideon went and got a mug of coffee and joined Chloe at the kitchen table.

Tamara asked, "Do you want something to eat, Gid?"

"A bacon butty, if you don't mind making it."

"A pleasure," Tamara answered, and flashed him a bright smile.

Chloe asked, "Is Lenore bringing her children to lunch?"

"God forbid, I'll never cope. Not with hers as well as mine!" Tamara cried, and made a face of mock dismay.

Gideon laughed. "Of course you would, you always cope with everything, Tam. But actually she's not bringing her brood. They've already gone riding with their Brindsley cousins, over near Middleham. Lenore said they wanted to go up on the gallops with the stable boys who exercise the race horses from the racing stables in Middleham. Apparently they really enjoy it, and have a lot of fun competing with the boys."

"It's the best place to ride," Tamara remarked, putting the thick bacon sandwich on a plate and bringing it to him.

"Thank you, Tam. Aren't you having anything to eat?"

"The same as you, Gid."

After serving herself a bacon butty, Tamara finally sat down and went on. "I'm sorry to bring up lunch when we haven't even finished breakfast yet, but I thought I ought to cook fish, since it's Good Friday. However, Nigel's not very fond of fish, so I'm going to make a shepherd's pie as well. I also have a baked ham which I brought up from London. I'll do vegetables and a big salad. What do you think?"

"Sounds fine to me," Gideon murmured. "But I'd prefer the shepherd's pie too, like Nigel."

"Fish for me, with a salad," Chloe said, glancing at Tamara. Then she asked, "Is Mrs. Entwhistle coming up from the village to help today?"

"No, I told her she didn't have to come. You see, her grandson's arriving from Portsmouth for twenty-four hours' leave. He's in the Royal Navy, you know. Well, anyway, I didn't want to spoil it for her, encroach on that special time. I can manage."

Chloe turned to Gideon. "I think I'd better stay and help Tamara make lunch."

"All right. And I'll come back from Lindenhill quickly, and Lenore and I will both pitch in."

Nigel said from the doorway, "We're all set to go, Tamsy darling." He walked over to his wife, kissed the top of her shining silver-gilt hair, and said to Chloe, "Good morning to you, miss. What's the weather like?"

"Morning, Nigel, and it's windy, chilly, but very sunny. A pretty day."

Agnes, the young nanny, followed him into the kitchen, holding Natalie and Arnaud by the hands. She greeted Chloe and Gideon; the children broke free and bounded toward Chloe, threw themselves against her legs.

"Hello, little ones," she said, and bending over, Chloe hugged them to her.

"Come with us, Auntie Chloe," Arnaud said. "*Please.*"

"I'd love to, darling, but I can't. I'm going to stay here and help your mummy make lunch for us all. But I'll play hide-and-seek with you this afternoon. How does that sound?"

He nodded, beaming at her.

Natalie said, "Me too hide seek."

Chloe rumpled her hair, thinking how adorable they looked in their dark green loden jackets and matching pants worn with red sweaters and red Wellington boots.

"Let's go, Pumpkins." Nigel made for the door.

Tamara caught up with him, linked her arm through his, and accompanied him out to the Jeep parked in front of the farmhouse. "Try and find the hot cross buns if you can, Nigel, it's such a bother to have to make them."

"I will, darling, don't worry," Nigel answered, drawing her closer to him. "If they don't have any in Ripon, I'll pop over to Harrogate and stop in at Betty's Cafe. They're bound to have loads of them there." He looked into her eyes, his own full of love, and then he kissed her on the mouth.

"See you later, angel," he said as he strode over to the Jeep, opened the doors, bundled the children and Agnes onto the backseat.

"Good-bye, Pumpkins," Tamara called, blowing kisses.

They blew kisses to her in return, their small faces glowing with health and full of laughter.

"Drive carefully, Nigel," Tamara cautioned.

"Don't worry, I will. See you later, Tamsy."

23

Left to their own devices, Tamara and Chloe had another cup of coffee and chatted to each other in front of the fire for a short while. Mostly they spoke about Gideon again, and his involvement with Lenore. Both women welcomed her entry into the family, and they couldn't help speculating about the wedding.

Once they had exhausted this subject, they wondered out loud about Miles and *his* romantic entanglements. "Has he taken anyone to Paris with him for Easter?" Tamara asked at one point, eyeing Chloe, knowing how close she was to Miles.

Chloe shook her head. "I don't know, he didn't tell me on the way over from New York. But there was just the two of us on the plane. What I mean is, Allison wasn't with us, and he didn't make any reference to her. Actually, I have a feeling that's over now." Chloe shrugged and grinned. "Maybe he has a rendezvous in Paris. What do you think?"

"Could be," Tamara agreed, also chuckling.

It was Chloe who finished her coffee and jumped up first, exclaiming, "This isn't going to get anything done. I'm going to put the breakfast things away, then I'll set the table for lunch. Where are we going to have it?"

"Oh, in the kitchen as usual, don't you think? It's so cozy in here. Besides, without Mrs. Entwhistle to help, it's such a chore to carry things in and out of the dining room."

"I agree." Chloe set to work, moving swiftly around the kitchen.

For her part, Tamara put the leftover food in plastic containers, stacked them in the refrigerator, then filled the dishwasher. When she had finished, she took off her apron, replaced it with a clean one, shaking her head as she did. She turned to Chloe and muttered, "I get more mess on myself when I'm cooking than the children do when they're painting."

Chloe grinned. "I know what you mean, so do I. And I think I'd better have one of your aprons myself. This is a new track suit, and I don't want to get it dirty."

The two women, who were used to working together at the farm, soon had the kitchen shipshape and ready for lunch. Once they had cleaned up and set the table, Tamara took all of the salad ingredients out of the pantry and asked Chloe to wash the lettuce and the watercress, then slice the tomatoes. She herself set about cooking the ground lamb for the shepherd's pie.

"So, do you think you're pregnant yet?" Chloe asked at one moment, giving her sister-in-law a questioning look.

"I don't know, Chloe." She laughed and her eyes sparkled as she added, "Maybe it's happened this weekend. Certainly Nigel's romantic enough."

"He was certainly very sweet and loving with you last night, and in a good mood in general," Chloe commented. "I wish he hadn't done that awful thing to Mom, it's caused such a rift in the family."

"Yes, I know. But time heals everything, at least that's what my mother always says. I think she's right—" Tamara cut herself off, shook her head sadly. "I agree with the rest of you that it was foolish. I don't understand him sometimes, Chloe. I've no idea what gets into him. It's as if there's a demon inside him telling him what to do. And he can be so cantankerous, almost like an old man."

"On the plane coming over Miles told me that Nigel came under Grandmother Jardine's influence too much when he was about twelve or thirteen. Perhaps it's all to do with that. That's what Gideon thinks as well."

"Yes, perhaps they're correct about that." Tamara took a wooden spoon, pressed the meat into the pan, added a little water, and lowered the flame. Then she went into the walk-in pantry, looking for the condiments.

Chloe, who was washing the lettuce at the sink, smiled to herself as she heard Tamara whistling. *She* couldn't whistle at all, even though her brothers had tried to teach her many times when she was growing up.

Suddenly Chloe jumped, startled by the sound of someone moving around in the front porch. She swung around to face the front door just as it opened. A man walked into the kitchen, a man she had never seen before.

"Can I help you?" she asked, frowning, wondering who he was. Certainly he was not one of the locals from the village. She could tell that from his appearance, and from the clothes he wore. He could be French.

The man, who appeared to be in his early thirties, was good-looking in a dark, swarthy way, and extremely well dressed, very much in the continental manner. If he wasn't French, perhaps he was Spanish. He stared at Chloe without speaking.

Again Chloe asked, "How can I help you? Who are you?"

The man remained silent.

Tamara, hearing Chloe's voice, hurried out of the pantry holding the pepper mill, and stopped in her tracks. She gaped at the man speechlessly. Finally recovering herself, she exclaimed shrilly, "My God! *Alexis!* What are you doing here?"

The man called Alexis still did not speak. He continued to stand there as if frozen to the spot.

Tamara asked again: "Alexis, why are you here?"

"I've come for *you*," he said, finding his voice at last. "I've been looking all over for you, my Tamara. I've come to get you."

Chloe detected a distinct accent, and her startled eyes flew from Tamara to the man, and back again to Tamara. Her sister-in-law's face had turned sheet white, and there was a terrified look in her eyes. It was obvious to her that Tamara, usually so cool, contained, and fearless, was actually frightened of this man. Oh, my God, it's her ex-husband, Alexis Dumachev, Chloe thought, and immediately stepped forward protectively.

Moving closer to him, not in the least afraid, Chloe said in the firmest voice she could summon, "I think you'd better go. My brother's going to be angry if he finds you here. Please leave."

Ignoring her, rudely pushing past her, Alexis Dumachev walked across the kitchen and grabbed hold of Tamara's arm. Instantly, she dropped the wooden pepper mill.

He exclaimed angrily, "You're *mine*. You belong to *me*. And you're coming with *me*. Now."

Tamara tried to shake off his hand, struggling with him. But his grip was tenacious; his fingers bit into her arm, and she winced in pain. Swinging her head to face him, she said as evenly as possible, "Please let go of me, Alexis. This is silly, you're being silly. I'm—"

"*Silly,*" he yelled, his eyes bulging as he cut her short. "*Silly* because I *worship* you. My God, you are my life." He began to scream at her in Russian; Tamara shrank back, whilst still trying to break free of his hold.

Chloe ran across the floor and tugged at his coat, then his arm. "Leave her alone."

"Get away from me, you stupid little girl!" he yelled, turning to Chloe, pushing her violently.

Chloe staggered, but instantly steadied herself against the kitchen table. She lunged at him once more, tearing at his body, wanting to free her sister-in-law.

In an effort to fight Chloe off, Dumachev loosened his grip on Tamara. It was the opportunity she had been waiting for, and she struggled free at last. She leapt away from him, running to the far end of the kitchen.

Chloe dropped back, ducked him, and ran to join Tamara; shaking and scared, the two women huddled together behind one of the armchairs. "What are we going to do?" Chloe whispered, trying to catch her breath. "I wish Gideon would get here."

"I'll try to reason with him," Tamara muttered grimly, and took a few steps forward. In a conciliatory voice, she said, "Alexis, please be reasonable. You know I've been married to Nigel for five years, almost six. You and I were divorced so long ago. It's over between us, and it *was* over years ago, long before I met Nigel."

"You're mine! You'll always be *mine*," he cried, his handsome face contorting into an ugly mask. "And I am yours. You know you don't love *him*. I am the only man you love."

"No, no, that's not so," Tamara exclaimed. "You're wrong, Alexis. Please, leave me alone. Go back to Paris. Please, Alexis."

"If you will come with me, yes, I will go," he said in a most reasonable voice, suddenly, irrationally smiling at her.

"No, I can't. It's Nigel I love, and I belong here with him."

"No, no, you don't. I won't let you stay here. He's keeping you from me. Where is he? I'll kill him. I'll kill his children."

Tamara began to shake uncontrollably, and the fear rushed through her; it was more potent than before. Filling with dread, she gripped Chloe's hand and whispered, "He's not himself. I think he's gone crazy. We've got to get away from him, get out of here. Or we've got to get to the phone. Whichever's easier. Come on."

Chloe nodded, and the two of them slowly edged their way in the direction of the long countertop where the telephone sat.

Alexis was watching the two women like a hawk. He said finally, in a quieter tone, "You don't understand, do you, my Tamara? There is nothing for me without you. I have no life. No reason to live. I am going to kill myself." As he spoke, he pulled a gun out of his jacket pocket and waved it in the air. "Look, I have a gun! I will shoot myself."

"Please, Alexis, calm down," Tamara said softly, placatingly, even though terror was rampant in her now. "And put that gun away before someone gets hurt. This is not necessary."

"I love you" was his only response.

After a second, he did as she asked, and put the gun back in his pocket.

Tamara let out a breath of relief, inched her way toward the phone; Chloe stayed close to her. As Tamara picked up the receiver, Alexis jumped her, throwing both his arms around her in a bear hug, pulling her down to the floor with him. They struggled, grappling with each other, but he was the stronger.

Chloe flew across the room to help Tamara. As her sister-in-law strove to fight off her ex-husband, Chloe grabbed at Dumachev, pulled and pummeled him. Finally, Tamara was able to struggle free of his hold. But he was tenacious, and he still gripped the end of her apron. Then, unexpectedly, he let go of it and slumped, breathing hard.

Tamara stumbled, as she pulled herself upright, and hit the leg of the table. She regained her balance immediately and fled with Chloe, circling the table, trying to escape.

Dumachev was instantly on his feet, and he made it to the front door before they did. "If I can't have you, neither can he!" Dumachev screamed. The gun was in his hand and he pulled the trigger, firing wildly, then aiming at the women. He was a good marksman. He did not miss.

Tamara and Chloe were both struck by bullets. They fell instantly. Blood spurted from Tamara's chest and from Chloe's head. They sprawled near the sofa, only inches from the door.

Dumachev looked down at them, frowning, his glazed eyes suddenly registered puzzlement, as if he did not understand what he had done. Kneeling down, bending over Tamara's body, he began to sob, the tears pouring down his face. After only a moment he lay down next to her, put the revolver in his mouth, and pulled the trigger one last time.

He blew off the back of his head, his blood splashing onto the white kitchen walls and countertop, spilling onto Tamara, to mingle with her own blood.

Now all was quiet in the kitchen.

The only sounds were the sizzling of meat in the pan, the running of water in the sink, the crackling of logs in the fireplace.

In the background, the radio played softly . . . a love song.

24

As they drove through the pretty Dales village of West Scrafton, Gideon glanced at Lenore through the corner of his eye, and said, "After we're married, I'd like us to have our own house in Yorkshire. I don't really want to share Aysgarth End with Tamara and Nigel."

Lenore nodded, understanding how he felt. "We could use Lindenhill at weekends. Tony wouldn't mind. After all, the place is so big. Anyway, he's never up here much these days."

"I know, but—" Gideon paused momentarily, and then finished, "Let's think about it. I still might want to have our own place for the weekends, darling."

Lenore smiled and said, "By the way, talking of my darling brother, he wants to give the wedding. And he'd like us to be married in the church in Lindenhill, and have the reception at the house."

"How very nice of him, and it's a great idea." He laughed wickedly. "That's where I fell in love with you, after all."

"Me too, you, dearest one." Lenore also laughed, murmured

in her sexiest voice, "And it's there that you taught me all sorts of naughty things, you bad little boy."

"*You* taught *me*, you beautiful wretch," he shot back.

Still chuckling, Gideon drove on through the village, past the tiny village green and the huddle of ancient gray stone houses, pushing up toward the moors, and the road that would take them to Aysgarth End.

At one moment he said, "By the way, Chloe would love to be bridesmaid. When we were driving up from London yesterday she asked me to ask you if she could be."

"What a lovely idea, Gid, and I'd like that. However, I don't think we should have too grand a wedding, under the circumstances. That wouldn't be appropriate, because of my divorce." She sighed. "Whenever I get it, that is."

Glancing at her swiftly, bringing his eyes back to the road, he murmured, "Everything's going to be all right, Lenore." Suddenly coming to a stop, he waited as several sheep meandered across the road and went into a field; he then drove on up the hill.

"Do try not to worry. Malcolm's going to come around eventually," he reassured her.

"I hope so."

"As for the wedding, I agree it can't be grand. On the other hand, there's nothing very grand about one bridesmaid, is there?"

"No, of course not. And I *want* Chloe to be my bridesmaid. I also think we should invite Tamara to be matron of honor."

"She'd adore that, Lenore."

The two of them fell silent as they continued along the moorland road, lost in thoughts of their marriage which they both prayed would be soon. Just before they reached the side lane that branched off to the farm, Lenore said, "Oh, do let's stop for a moment near the big rocks. The view from there is spectacular. It's as if I'm standing on the roof of the world when I'm up here on the moors. I feel as if I have only to stand on my tiptoes to touch the sky, and grab a handful of cloud."

"I know." Gideon slowed down, then braked and turned off the ignition; the two of them alighted, linked arms, and walked over to the rocks. It was a sheltered spot, and they sat down on a flat rock, stared out toward the great Whernside fells soaring above the valley below. The view of the Dales from this vantage point *was* magnificent, and particularly so on this clear, sunny day. It was picture perfect and breathtaking.

"Look how the Nidd wends its way along the valley floor," Gideon said. "I remember the first time my mother pointed it out to me. It is so special here, just as you said. I feel as if we can see forever, don't you?"

Lenore nodded, pulled her Barbour closer to her body, shivering in the wind. "I'm so glad your mother found the farmhouse when she did, Gideon, and that you came to live here when you were little. Just imagine if you hadn't. We would never have met."

"Oh, yes, we would. I know that for a certainty. We were meant to be, you and I, Lenore. Fate would have found a way to bring us together."

Putting his arm around her, Gideon turned her to face him. Lenore was the most beautiful woman in the world to him. That morning her blonde hair was pulled back from her heart-shaped face and fell down her back in a plait, but there were fronds of hair and little wispy curls around her forehead and cheeks, and these softened the rather severe hairdo. Her fine complexion was scrubbed clean; she wore no makeup on her face today, and she looked like a young girl.

Gideon leaned closer, kissed her lightly on the lips, and then pulled away again, gazing into her misty gray eyes. They were large, luminous, and filled with intelligence. "You do believe it, don't you?"

"What?"

"That we were meant to be."

"Absolutely." She paused, glanced at him, said softly, "You are more myself than I am. Whatever our souls are made of, yours and mine are the same."

"Stolen from *Wuthering Heights*!"

"Just paraphrasing Emily Brontë's words. I'd never steal from *her*, Gid. One of the great geniuses of English literature."

He smiled at her.

She smiled back.

And they drew closer together under the rocks, their arms wrapped around each other.

After a short while, he loosened his grip on her and jumped up, exclaiming, "Come on, darling, we can't sit here daydreaming forever. We'd better go. I told Tamara and Chloe that we'd be at the farm in plenty of time to help them prepare lunch."

Within minutes, Gideon was guiding the Land-Rover down the narrow road to Aysgarth End, and as they went through the gate, he said, "There's a car here, we must have a visitor. But I can't imagine who that would be on Good Friday."

"Maybe it's someone from the village."

"I doubt it, and I know Mrs. Entwhistle isn't coming today. Something about her grandson arriving from Portsmouth."

Gideon parked the Land-Rover in front of the house and the two of them went into the porch.

As Lenore struggled out of her Barbour and hung it up, she said, "Something's burning. I think Tamara must have left a pot on the stove."

Shaking her head and laughing, thinking that Tamara was as careless as she was when it came to cooking, Lenore pushed open the front door and stepped into the kitchen.

Instantly, she gasped, and the laughter fled her face when she saw Tamara and Chloe sprawled on the floor covered in blood.

She cried out in shock and fear. "Oh, my God! Oh, God, Gideon, there's blood everywhere! They've been hurt. Oh, my God! We've got to get help. They've been shot. Look, there's a gun over there next to that man." Shuddering violently, Lenore turned away.

Gideon was standing immediately behind Lenore, and he caught hold of her in an effort to support her as she swayed on her feet. He held her close, staring down at his sister and sister-in-law; he was horror-struck.

His face was ashen. All of his strength ebbed away; he thought his legs were going to buckle under him. There *was* blood everywhere. It was ghastly, horrendous. Surely they were dead. Oh, God, he hoped not. His heart was thundering in his chest, and he could hardly breathe. "Can you stand up on your own, Lenore?" he managed at last.

"My legs are a bit wobbly, I'll be okay. It's the shock. . . . "

"I know, I know. Lean against the door." Swallowing hard, Gideon moved nearer Chloe, knelt down, and took hold of his sister's wrist. "There's a pulse. Thank God she's alive," he gasped in a choked voice. "She has a head wound. All this blood. It looks bad."

"Don't move her," Lenore exclaimed, staring across at him. "That's the worst thing you could do . . . I just know you shouldn't move either of them, in case you injure them further." Lenore closed her eyes and gripped the door frame. Tears leaked out from under her lids. Then, pulling herself together instantly, knowing there was no time to waste, she snapped her eyes open and went to the stove. She turned off the flame and stopped the tap running in the sink.

Gideon was shaking inside as he knelt down and felt Tamara's wrist, seeking her pulse. "She's also alive. Thank God for that. I must phone for an ambulance, get help at once, Lenore. Time's of the essence."

Moving a bit unsteadily across the floor, but also getting a proper grip on himself, Gideon leaned against the counter, reached for the phone, and dialed 999. Endeavoring to control his voice, he swiftly gave the emergency service operator all the necessary details, and then hung up.

"Ambulances, paramedics, and the police will be here as quickly as possible," he said, looking at Lenore. Her face was drained of all color, but she seemed steadier now. "I'm going to call my mother," he added.

Joining him at the counter, Lenore took hold of his arm. "Don't you want to wait until help gets here? Hear what they have to say?"

He shook his head. "I think I'd better call Ma in New York immediately. We need her here, and she should be here for Chloe and Tamara."

"Yes, you're right." Lenore bit her lip, glanced quickly at the two injured women on the floor, and said to Gideon softly, "Who would do this . . . this terrible thing, Gid?" Before he could answer, she murmured, "It was obviously that man. Who is he?"

"I've no idea. But he's dead, that I *can* tell you."

"Can I get you anything?" Lenore asked, touching his arm again, aware of the strain and tension in him.

"No, thanks." He pulled a chair up to the counter and sat down. He glanced at his watch. "It's almost eleven, nearly six in New York. Yes, I am going to call my mother now." As he spoke, he lifted the receiver, then put it back in the cradle. "Lenore, please keep an eye open for Nigel. He should be back any minute now, and I don't want him walking in on this . . . especially with the children."

"God, you're right!" She moved to the window overlooking

the circular drive. "When he does get here, I'd better take the children and Agnes over to Lindenhill, get them out of the way."

"Yes, that would be best," he agreed, and lifted the phone once more. He dialed his mother in New York, steeling himself to break the news to her.

When she answered, he said in the steadiest voice he could muster, "Hello, Ma, it's Gideon."

"Yes, I know it's you, darling. And it's nice to hear your voice," Stevie replied. "You must be up at the farm. How're things?"

He did not answer this question; instead, he asked, "I didn't wake you, did I?"

"No, I've been up since five," she laughed. "I'm just having a cup of coffee."

"Ma . . . I've . . ." He stopped abruptly. Words failed him. He swallowed. There was a silence.

"Are you there, Gideon?"

"Yes, Ma, there's something I must tell you. There's—"

"What is it?" she asked, interrupting, her tone rising an octave. "Something's wrong. I can tell from your voice. What is it, Gideon?"

"Ma, you've got to come here today. To Yorkshire. When we hang up, you must call British Airways and book a seat on this morning's Concorde. The eight forty-five. I'll arrange for a private plane to meet you at Heathrow to bring you up here."

"Gideon, for God's sake, what is it? Tell me, please! Stop delaying the bad news. Because it *is* bad, I know that."

He cleared his throat. "Yes, I'm afraid it is. . . . There's been a shooting here at the farm. But they're alive . . . Chloe and Tamara are alive, Ma. I'm waiting for the ambulance."

"Oh, my God! What happened?" she demanded.

"Ma, I don't know. I wasn't here."

"Let me speak to Nigel."

"He's not here, Mother. He took the children and Agnes to Ripon. Shopping. Lenore and I just walked in on this, only a few minutes ago. *We* found Chloe and Tamara ... Nigel doesn't know yet."

"They *are* alive, aren't they, Gideon? You wouldn't lie to me, would you? Just to keep me calmer?" she asked, her voice shaking.

He could hear the tears in her voice, and he exclaimed, "Honestly, Mother, they are alive. They are, yes."

"Who did it?"

"I'm not sure," he hedged, "but the police are coming. They'll be here any minute. And Chloe and Tamara *are* going to make it, I just know they are."

"Oh, God, I hope so, Gideon! Oh, my little girl. My little Chloe. And Tamara, sweet Tamara ... They've got to make it." Stevie took a deep breath and tried to steady her voice as she finished, "I think I'd better hang up and get moving, unless there's anything else you want to tell me."

"No, Ma."

"All right. Phone your grandmother and Derek, Gideon, please. Tell them what has happened, and ask Derek to charter a private plane for me, for this evening. I'll be on that Concorde no matter what I have to do to get on it. And please stay in touch with Derek and my mother, let them know what hospital Chloe and Tamara are in, so that I know where to come. I'll be in touch with my mother—" Stevie's voice broke. She was unable to say anymore.

"They'll make it, Mother," Gideon reassured her again, praying that they would.

"Yes" was all she could say before she hung up.

Gideon's heart went out to his mother as he replaced the

receiver. He knew how much she loved Chloe, knew what Tamara meant to her.

From her stance at the window, Lenore said, "Your mother's a very strong woman, Gid, she'll be able to handle this, and better than most."

"I know. I'd better phone my grandmother in London."

"That might have to wait," Lenore told him. "I can see Nigel's car coming down the driveway. I think we ought to go outside to meet him, Gideon."

Together, Lenore and Gideon walked forward to meet the Jeep as it circled the urn in the middle of the drive and came to a stop.

Alighting, Nigel glanced at the parked car and said to them, "Do we have a visitor? Who's here?"

Gideon took hold of his brother's arm and drew him to one side, and Lenore ran to the Jeep. She stood talking to the children through the window, preventing them from alighting.

"Nigel, something's happened . . . there's been a shooting—" Gideon began.

"Oh, my God! Not Tamara? Not Chloe?" Nigel tried to pull away, to go into the farmhouse, his eyes flaring with fear. Holding on to him tightly, Gideon said, "They're alive. I've phoned for an ambulance. You must stay calm for the sake of the children."

"Let go of me, Gideon! I want to see Tamara!" he gasped, still trying to pull away, to move toward the house.

"No! Wait a minute. Listen to me. I think Lenore should drive the children and Agnes to Lindenhill, get them out of the way for the time being. Lenore will give them lunch, keep them busy. They can stay there with Agnes for as long as you want. There's staff over at the house."

Nigel stared at his brother, then his eyes flew to his children in the Jeep. Swallowing hard, he nodded. Summoning as much control as he could, he ran to them and said, "Auntie Lenore's going to take you back to her house with Agnes, Pumpkins. For lunch. I've something to do . . . with Mummy. Okay?"

"I want to see Mummy, show her my new ball," Arnaud said.

"See Mummy," Natalie repeated.

"Later. Be good, both of you." Nigel kissed them quickly, trying not to break down. He looked at the nanny, saw her bafflement. "Lady Armstrong will explain everything, Agnes. Take care of the children."

"Yes, Mr. Jardine. You can count on me," Agnes answered quietly, sensing trouble.

Nigel swung around and ran back toward the house.

Gideon ran after him.

Lenore called, "Phone me later, Gid."

"I will, darling," he shouted back without turning around.

As Nigel hurtled into the porch, Gideon caught up with him and grabbed his arm, restraining him. "Be prepared, Nigel, there's a lot of . . . a lot of blood."

Nigel nodded; his face was strained. "What the hell happened here?" he asked in a trembling voice, opened the front door, and went into the kitchen. Horror and shock at what he saw brought him to a momentary standstill, and a strangled cry escaped his throat. Then he hurried to kneel next to Tamara, taking hold of her hand. "Tamara, I'm here, darling. It's me, Nigel. I'm here."

Tamara was motionless. There was no response. He held her wrist, found her pulse. Lifting his eyes to Gideon, he nodded, and bringing his face close to hers, he strained to listen; he could hear her breathing. But it was shallow, faint. "She's alive."

Gideon was now checking on Chloe, and he also nodded. "Chloe's holding on too. There's a nasty wound on her forehead. She's been shot in the head, Nigel. It looks serious."

"Oh, God! What *happened* here?" Nigel asked, noticing the dead man. He looked Tamara's body over again, his eyes stricken. "I think Tam has a chest wound, but it's hard to tell with all this blood." Leaning forward, he moved a strand of silver-gilt hair away from her face. "Tam, oh, Tam, darling, please hang on, don't die. Please fight . . ." His eyes filled with tears; he struggled hard to keep his composure, and all the time he clung to her hand, kneeling next to her, praying silently, praying that she would live.

"Don't touch her, don't move her, Nigel," Gideon warned. "You don't want to hurt her, and you could without knowing it."

Nigel nodded. "What the bloody hell's going on? Where's that ambulance, Gideon?" he asked in a low, intense mutter, sudden anger and frustration rising to the surface.

"It should be here any minute." Gideon looked at his watch. "It's now eleven-thirty. I phoned emergency as soon as I got here. They said it would take about thirty-five to forty minutes. The nearest big hospital is in Harrogate."

Gently Nigel laid Tamara's hand on the floor and stood up. His face was white and taut, his vivid blue eyes dark with worry. He said to Gideon, "The chap next to her . . . I'm pretty sure that's Dumachev, her ex-husband."

Gideon nodded quickly. "I wondered if it was . . . I guess you can't be really sure . . . not even you can be."

"Why?" Nigel said hoarsely, staring at his brother, the tears springing into his eyes once more. "*Why*, Gideon? Why did he do it?"

Gideon shook his head. "I don't know. . . . " His voice trailed off and he thought of Margot Saunders and the potential for violence he had detected in her. He shuddered. Moving away from Chloe, he went to Nigel and drew him to the other side of the kitchen table. "Sit down, Nigel, the ambulance will be here any minute." He pressed his brother into the chair.

"I wonder what time they were . . . when do you think this happened, Gid?"

"I left here just after nine, a little bit after you, and I got back here with Lenore around ten-thirty, at the latest ten-forty. It must have been just before we arrived."

"Isn't it getting riskier by the minute?" Nigel worried aloud. "For them. They need help desperately." He got up and went over to Tamara.

"Yes, they do. And they're about to get it, Nigel. I can hear noises in the drive. Cars." Gideon hurried to the front door and ran outside.

Three ambulances and three police cars were tearing down the drive. They all slowed to a stop; police jumped out of the cars at the same moment paramedics leapt out of the ambulances.

"Are the injured people inside?" one of the paramedics shouted to Gideon as he and his partner hoisted a stretcher.

"That's right. My sister has a gunshot wound on her forehead, my sister-in-law looks as if she has chest wounds. There's a lot of blood on her—" Gideon stopped. The paramedics had already run inside the house.

One of the policemen came up to Gideon. "Mr. Jardine?" he asked, looking him over carefully.

Gideon nodded, thrust out his hand. "Gideon Jardine. My brother Nigel is inside with his injured wife and our sister, Sergeant." Gideon nodded to the parked car. "I think that must belong to the man who did the shooting."

"I see. Let's go inside, Mr. Jardine, and try to sort all this out," the police sergeant answered. "After you, Mr. Jardine."

25

THE BRITISH AIRWAYS CONCORDE FLIGHT FROM NEW YORK WAS A few minutes late when it landed at Heathrow just before six on Good Friday afternoon.

Stevie Jardine was the first person off the plane, the first in and out of Immigration. Since she had no luggage, only her briefcase, she went straight to the Customs Hall. Once again, because she was the first to enter, she was hurrying out into the terminal within a couple of seconds. As she emerged, her eyes scanned the crowd swiftly.

She saw her mother immediately. Blair was standing by the barrier, waiting for her, and she raised her hand in greeting. A moment later the two women were embracing.

As they pulled apart, Stevie stared at her mother worriedly, her eyes apprehensive and filled with questions.

Blair said, "She's alive, darling, they're both alive."

Stevie let out a sigh of relief. "Thank God for that. I'm sure I don't have to tell you that the flight over has been *torturous*. I'm exhausted from worry."

"I can well imagine," Blair murmured.

"Where's Derek, Mother?"

"Waiting for us on the private plane. You know how it is when he's seen in public, he tends to get mobbed. We thought it better for him to board. But let's hurry, Stevie, the plane's on the tarmac, ready to take us to Yorkshire. We can talk then."

Fifteen minutes later, Derek was greeting them as they came up the steps of the plane. After hugging Stevie and telling her not to worry, he showed them their seats. They all fastened their safety belts, and once the Gulfstream IV jet was airborne, the stewardess served hot lemon tea to Stevie and Blair, and a scotch on the rocks to Derek.

"How is Chloe *actually*?" Stevie asked anxiously, looking from her mother to Derek when they were alone. "I'm crazy with worry."

He said very quietly, "She's in a coma, Stevie, and she has been since she was shot. The bullet entered her brain, you see."

"Oh, *no*! Oh, my God," Stevie cried, and brought her hand to her mouth, stifling a cry of anguish. "What are they going to do?"

"They've already done it," Derek answered, putting a hand on her arm, trying to reassure her. "She had an operation on her brain this afternoon. To remove the bullet. And—"

"Were they able to take it out?" Stevie interrupted shakily. She felt as though all the strength had left her body.

"Yes, they did. It took almost three hours to do the operation. She was operated on by one of the best neurosurgeons in the country, in the world actually, Mr. Valentin Longdon. She's in the Brotherton Wing of Leeds General Infirmary. The private wing. In the intensive care unit. And so is Tamara. She was shot in the chest. Several times. They've managed to remove the bullets, but she's still unconscious, Stevie. Very weak. She lost a lot of blood."

Stevie swallowed hard, and her voice was a whisper when she asked, "Are they going to make it, Derek? Are they going to live?"

"We hope so, darling, we're praying they will."

Blair took hold of her daughter's hand and squeezed it. "It's going to be all right, I know it is. Try and have faith."

Stevie nodded, unable to speak for a few minutes. Then she murmured, "So they didn't take them to Harrogate District Hospital." She bit her lip. "It's closer . . . but then, Leeds is such a big medical center . . . "

Derek nodded. "True. And in fact, they *were* taken to Harrogate. But the doctors there wanted Chloe to be sent to Leeds Infirmary, where there's that crack neurosurgical unit. They wanted her to have the very best. From what I understand from Gideon, they decided to send Tamara to Leeds as well, because of the seriousness of her wounds. They were helicoptered from Harrogate to Leeds, and were in the operating theaters by two o'clock this afternoon. It was all handled very speedily, Stevie."

"I know Leeds General Infirmary is a good hospital," she acknowledged.

"And don't forget, it's one of the finest teaching hospitals in Europe, in the world. Bar none. So is St. James's hospital nearby. The Leeds medical complex is world renowned, so rest easy about their care, darling. They're getting the best, and every facility is available."

"I will try, Derek, but it's hard. I just can't help worrying—" She stopped, her voice breaking. Fumbling for her handkerchief, she blew her nose, tried to stem the tears that suddenly blinded her.

There was a small silence among them.

Eventually, clearing her throat several times, Stevie went on. "What about Tamara's parents? Did someone manage to contact them? I know they were supposed to go on a cruise this Easter. To the Far East and China, I think."

"They did go," Blair said. "Gideon had Bruce send a fax to the ship. Fortunately, Nigel remembered his father-in-law telling him they would be arriving in Hong Kong on Good Friday and staying there for the Easter weekend."

"How is Bruce holding up?" Stevie asked, glancing at Derek.

"Not bad under the circumstances. It's shaken him, of course, and he wanted to fly up with us today, but I told him it would be better if he came tomorrow. We've booked him a room at the Queen's. That's where we're all staying."

"Gideon found Miles in Paris. At the Plaza Athénée. He left immediately, and he's probably already in Leeds by now," Blair explained.

"Nigel must be distraught!" Stevie exclaimed, shaking her head. "He loves Tamara so much, worships her, really. He must be out of his mind . . . where are the children, Mother?" Stevie turned to Blair, her face taut with anxiety.

"Lenore took them to Lindenhill the moment they returned from their shopping trip this morning. They're there with Agnes. Apparently Agnes went over to Aysgarth End this afternoon, to get some of their things, and a few bits and pieces of her own. They're going to stay at Lindenhill indefinitely. Until we all go back to London, that is."

"Yes, that's the best solution," Stevie agreed.

"I spoke to Lenore at five o'clock," Derek said. "When your mother and I arrived at the airport. She's the one who told me about Chloe's condition and the operation, and about Tamara. Gideon asked her to stay next to the phone at Lindenhill. She's our base—the person we all call to get information and to whom we give it. That way she can keep everyone informed."

Stevie nodded. She moved slightly in her seat, crossing her

legs, then uncrossing them nervously. After a moment or two, she said to Derek in a low voice, "I guess nobody knows exactly what happened, why the shooting occurred. Or who did it?"

"Since the girls have remained unconscious, they haven't been able to tell Nigel and Gideon—or the police—anything. However, the man who shot them was Tamara's ex-husband, Alexis Dumachev. He's been identified."

"Oh, my God, no! But *why*? Why did he do a horrendous thing like this? I know Tamara hasn't heard from him for years. He went off to work in . . . Japan, I think."

"Yes, that's what Nigel said to Gideon, and it's true, they haven't heard from him for years." Derek sighed. "It seems as if he went berserk. *Why* we'll never know, I suppose."

Stevie inclined her head, and then she leaned back in her seat, closing her eyes. Chloe and Tamara might not make it, she knew that. Although her mother and Derek were being cheerful, she realized they were putting up a front. Derek made a good job of it; why wouldn't he? After all, he was a great actor. But her mother couldn't act, and it was Blair who gave it all away. Things weren't quite as rosy as they wanted her to believe, of that she was absolutely convinced.

The stewardess came and told them they were about to land at the Leeds-Bradford Airport in Yeadon. Opening her eyes, Stevie looked at her watch. It was twenty minutes past seven o'clock.

Miles was waiting for them in the Brotherton Wing of Leeds General Infirmary when they arrived at eight o'clock. As Stevie walked into the small private waiting room, accompanied by Blair and Derek, he leapt to his feet and hurried to his mother. Concern ringed his face.

"Hello, Ma," he said, wrapping his arms around her protectively, holding her close. Stevie clung to her son for a second, taking comfort from his reassuring presence before pulling away.

Looking into his eyes, she asked, "Tell me the truth, Miles, is Chloe going to live?"

"Yes, I think she is. From what I understand, the operation to remove the bullet from her brain was a success. But it's better that you talk to the neurosurgeon. He was just checking on Chloe a short while ago, and he's waiting in his office for you."

"Then let's go."

"Right away, Ma." Turning to his grandparents, he embraced them both before opening the door and leading them out of the private waiting room.

As Miles hurried them down the corridor, Stevie grasped her son's arm, asked urgently, "How's Tamara? Is *she* going to be all right?"

"They're hoping so. She's also in intensive care, and holding her own right now, Ma. Tam's in another part of the Brotherton Wing and Nigel's in a waiting room over there, to be near her. Gideon's with him, giving him support. Once you've talked to Mr. Longdon and seen Chloe, I'll take you to Nigel. The surgeon who operated on her wants to see you."

Stevie nodded. A moment later Miles was ushering them into the neurosurgeon's office.

"Valentin Longdon," the neurosurgeon said, rising, coming forward to greet them, his hand outstretched. "Mrs. Jardine, Sir Derek and Lady Rayner. Pleased to meet you." After shaking hands with them, he added, "However, I'm so sorry we're not meeting under different circumstances. Please, do sit down."

They did so, and Stevie said, "Thank you for taking care of my daughter, Mr. Longdon. I appreciate everything you've done to save her life."

The neurosurgeon inclined his head. "I would like to explain everything, so that you understand fully what has happened."

"Yes, that would be very helpful," Derek murmured, leaning forward slightly, pinning his eyes on the renowned surgeon.

"First let me tell you about the wound. The bullet entered the left side of Miss Jardine's forehead at a forty-five-degree angle, going in at the edge of the eyebrow. It hit the frontal lobe actually, and broke a bone in her skull. It remained in her brain." He paused and looked at Stevie questioningly, a brow raised.

She nodded. "Yes, I'm following you, Mr. Longdon."

Giving her a faint smile, the neurosurgeon continued. "I operated on your daughter immediately after she arrived here from Harrogate, in order to reduce the risk of infection. There was a large area of bruising, bleeding, and swelling. Great trauma in the brain. I operated down the track of the bullet, that is, I followed the track the bullet made as it went through her skull. I first removed the indriven bone, then the damaged brain tissue, then the blood clot, and finally the bullet. It was a three-hour operation, Mrs. Jardine, but she came through it well."

"Thank you for explaining, Mr. Longdon, but I'm not sure I quite understand why Chloe is still in a coma."

"Because of the great trauma suffered to the brain. We must wait for the swelling to go down. She is in an altered state of consciousness right now, as she has been since she was shot. She will come out of the coma slowly, over a ten-day period, or thereabouts."

"But she *will* come out of the coma, won't she, Mr. Longdon?" Derek interjected.

There was only a fractional hesitation on the neurosurgeon's part before he said, "She should, Sir Derek. I am very hopeful for her. And as I just said, she will emerge from the coma rather slowly, come into a lighter consciousness, a more stable state of being gradually."

"How long will she have to be in intensive care?" Stevie said.

"For the next forty-eight hours, at least, Mrs. Jardine. Perhaps longer."

"Is there the possibility that my daughter might not come out of the coma, Mr. Longdon?"

"Well, of course, there is always that possibility with every patient. I don't think this is the case with Miss Jardine, however."

"Could she be left with any brain damage?" Stevie stared at the neurosurgeon, biting her lip nervously now that she had expressed one of her worst fears.

"That is doubtful," he replied quietly.

Stevie continued to stare at him, detecting something in his manner she could not quite put her finger on. She wondered if he was making Chloe's condition sound less serious than it really was. She opened her mouth to ask him this, then changed her mind. Instead, she said, "Can we see Chloe, Mr. Longdon?"

"Of course you can, Mrs. Jardine. I will take you to the ICU now. Please, come with me."

The four of them trooped out after Valentin Longdon, and within several seconds they were entering the intensive care unit in the Brotherton Wing. "It would be preferable if you saw Miss Jardine one at a time," the neurosurgeon murmured. Opening the door to Chloe's room, he stood to one side, allowing Stevie to enter first. He followed her in and closed the door.

Stevie glided across the floor toward the hospital bed as quietly as she could, full of anxiety and apprehension. Her throat closed when she saw Chloe, and she had to fight hard to stem the tears that suddenly filled her eyes. It was with a sense of dread and a sinking heart that she came to a standstill next to the bed and looked down at her daughter.

Chloe was white-faced and motionless, her eyes closed. Bandages swathed her head and IVs were attached to her body.

There was one in her arm, another in her nose. A piece of equipment covered her mouth, and she looked so helpless, so vulnerable, Stevie's eyes welled; she fumbled in her jacket pocket for a handkerchief. After a moment, she composed herself and swung her head to look at the neurosurgeon. She was mute, unable to say anything, so choked up was she. She shook her head.

Understanding her state of mind, observing her anxiousness and worry, Valentin Longdon said quietly, "I'm pleased with her progress since the operation this afternoon. I feel optimistic she's going to be all right, Mrs. Jardine."

"Is she out of danger, Mr. Longdon?"

"I wouldn't go so far as to say that, but she's doing well. Let me explain something. Those are intravenous drips, as I'm sure you know. They give easy access to the bloodstream, just in case of any infection. And as you can see, I have her on a ventilator. Your daughter is being monitored for the blood gases and also for intracranial pressure. And so far so good."

"I know you're doing everything for her, and that she's getting the best of care."

Stevie gazed down at Chloe, the child of her heart, and took hold of her hand. Then she bent down and kissed it. Straightening, turning once more to the neurosurgeon, she murmured, "She doesn't know I'm here, does she?"

"She might, Mrs. Jardine, we don't know for sure." His eyes were full of compassion for her.

After a moment longer, Stevie tiptoed out of the private room; Blair went in to see her granddaughter. When she emerged, Derek entered, but he, too, stayed only for a few seconds.

Not long after this, Stevie walked into the private waiting room where Nigel was sitting with Gideon. Derek and Blair followed her. Both of Stevie's sons jumped up when they saw their mother and their grandparents.

Stevie went straight to Nigel, opening her arms to him. There was only the merest hesitation on his part as he searched her face, and then he stepped forward to take hold of his mother. Stevie put her arms around him and held him very close to her, the love she felt for him far outweighing her anger and disappointment of the last few months. "I'm here for you, Nigel, I'll do anything I can to help you, darling."

He clung to her, and unexpectedly his self-control shattered. He broke down and began to sob. "Oh, Mother, Mother, I don't know what to do for Tamara. She's lying there . . . so helpless. I love her so much, Ma. She's my life. I don't want her to die."

"I know, I know, darling. We must all be strong for her, pray that she pulls through this. I love her too, you know that, Nigel. Take me to see her now."

Finding his handkerchief, blowing his nose, and then pushing his hair back with his hands, Nigel pulled himself together as best he could. After greeting his grandparents, he took hold of Stevie's arm and led her out of the room. They all went to the surgical ward in the Brotherton Wing, where a nurse took them to the ICU and showed Nigel and Stevie into Tamara's room. Gideon waited outside with Blair and Derek.

Stevie's heart sank when she saw her daughter-in-law lying unconscious in the hospital bed, hooked up to so much equipment. She was so still. Stevie couldn't help thinking that Tamara looked ghastly, in a way, worse than Chloe did. The thought struck her that Tamara was at death's door, and she shivered involuntarily. Something inside her told her that it would be a miracle if Tam lived. She thought her heart would break as she leaned over her daughter-in-law, squeezed her hand, and lightly touched the lovely silver-gilt hair. There was a frailty about Tamara that frightened

Stevie, and she knew why Nigel was so distraught. He had detected this too, and it had alerted him to the worst.

Now Stevie turned to Nigel, took his arm, and led him out of the private room. Once again Derek, and then Blair, went in to see Tamara.

Stepping up to his mother, Gideon said, "Are you all right, Ma? Are you holding up okay?" He put his arm around her solicitously. Kissed her cheek.

"I'm fine, Gideon, and I'm glad you and Miles are here to help Nigel and me through this. Where's Lenore? Is she still at Lindenhill?"

"She's driving over to Leeds now. Natalie and Arnaud are just having their supper and then Agnes is going to put them to bed. I spoke to Lenore a few minutes ago. Don't worry about the kids, Ma, they're doing fine."

Nigel said in a hoarse voice, "She's not going to pull through, is she, Mother? Tamara's not going to make it, is she? I could see it written all over your face when we were in the room with her."

"No, you couldn't, Nigel, because I don't believe that at all. I'm just worried about Tam, obviously. That's what you're seeing, my anxiety and concern. And let's be positive, Nigel. Tamara's a strong woman, she's going to fight to live, I just know it. Now, take me to see the surgeon who operated on her."

"All right."

Gideon said, "I'll wait here for Grandma and Gramps."

Nigel and Stevie walked rapidly down the corridor, making for the surgeon's office, but as they turned the corner they ran into him.

"Mr. Jardine," he exclaimed, "I was just coming to see your wife, to check on her."

"This is my mother, Stephanie Jardine," Nigel said. "And, Mother, this is Mr. William Tilden, Tam's surgeon."

After they had shaken hands, Stevie said, "Thank you for everything you've done for my daughter-in-law, Mr. Tilden. From what I understand, her wounds were very bad."

He nodded. "Yes, very serious, Mrs. Jardine. She sustained bullet wounds in her chest and stomach. Unfortunately, there was a lot of internal bleeding, and she has lost a lot of blood. We've given her transfusions, naturally, and now we must wait to see how she improves in the next few hours."

"Is my wife going to die?' Nigel asked in a strangled voice.

"We don't know, Mr. Jardine. I personally think she has a reasonable chance of pulling through. She's a very healthy woman, and she's young."

"But she is in critical condition, isn't she?" Nigel said.

"Yes," the surgeon answered very softly.

26

It was a subdued, sad little group that sat around a table in the lounge of the Queen's Hotel in City Square, having a late night drink and snack: Stevie, Derek, and Gideon.

Exhausted from travel and the strain of the day, Blair had gone to bed. So had Nigel and Miles, who were equally worn out. Lenore had been with them until ten minutes before, but she, too, had now left to drive back to Lindenhill.

Stevie played with a chicken sandwich, not eating it; in fact, it was taking all her energy to force down a cup of tea. Finally, after a long silence, she looked at Gideon and said, "What in God's name made Dumachev shoot them?"

Gideon shook his head and let out a weary sigh. "We'll never know the answer to that, Ma. And I'm sure the girls won't be able to enlighten us either when they regain consciousness. All they'll be able to do is tell us what happened when he arrived at the farm this morning, tell us what he actually said, how he behaved."

"Personally, I think he was deranged," Derek interjected. "No one in their right mind walks into a house and shoots two women in cold blood. And, more than likely, he was obsessed with Tamara."

"Obsessional people can be extremely dangerous," Gideon announced, giving his mother a pointed look.

Stevie frowned, sat back in the chair, a reflective expression settling on her face. After a moment, she said, "Why would Alexis Dumachev be obsessed with Tamara? After all, they were married only a couple of months when they were very young. She was only eighteen, and she was divorced from him by the time she was nineteen. Anyway, Tamara hadn't seen him for years. Nigel told me that at the hospital." Stevie shook her head, bafflement edging onto her face. "Why would he suddenly come back into her life after all this time?"

"Who knows, Ma, and anyway, you don't have to *see* someone constantly in order to be obsessed by them. That is usually in the mind, and in a sick mind at that."

Derek nodded. "Gideon's right, Stevie." There was a little pause; he took a sip of coffee, then went on. "When I was speaking to Nigel earlier this evening, he said that Dumachev became engaged to a Japanese woman when he was living in Tokyo. Seemingly, over the years, Dumachev was in touch with Tamara's parents occasionally. They had passed this news on to her about two years ago."

"Perhaps something happened between him and the woman, something which triggered this," Gideon said, thinking out loud.

"We're speculating," Derek pointed out. "And that can be both dangerous and fruitless."

"You're right, Derek," Stevie agreed. "I'm glad Tam's parents received Bruce's fax and that they're flying to London tomorrow. It makes me feel better knowing they'll be here soon. Not that they can do anything either, but having them close to her will help Tam, I think."

Gideon remarked, "I believe that something made Dumachev snap, and then he fixated on Tamara in a very sick way. That's why he came looking for her. Incidentally, the police told me that he was in England only a couple of days before he came up to Yorkshire. The police found his airline ticket and passport, as well as the car rental papers, in the glove compartment of the car."

"So there's absolutely no doubt that it *was* Alexis Dumachev, Gideon?"

"None whatsoever, Ma." Gideon glanced at his watch. "It's ten-thirty, Mother, aren't you tired?" he asked in concern.

"Not in the way you mean. I'm on New York time, remember, and it's only five-thirty in the afternoon for me. But I must admit, I am a little worn out emotionally."

"That's not surprising." Gideon pushed himself up out of the chair; bending over Stevie, he kissed her on the cheek, squeezed Derek's shoulder, and finished, "I'm going to bed."

"Good night, darling." Stevie tried to smile at him. "Better news tomorrow, I'm sure."

"Good night, Gideon, and thanks for looking after us." Derek stood up as he spoke, and embraced his grandson.

Once they were alone, Derek looked at Stevie and shook his head. "You're not eating that sandwich, just toying with it. Shall I try to get you something else? Something more appetizing?"

"Thanks, Derek, it's thoughtful of you, but I'm really not hungry. I will have a drink though. A cognac. I feel a bit queasy. It might settle my stomach."

"I'll join you." Derek motioned to a waiter, who was hovering nearby, and ordered their drinks. Several moments later the waiter reappeared with a bottle of Courvoisier and two brandy balloons.

Stevie sat back in her chair, sipped her brandy, endeavoring to relax, but without much success. Eventually, she said softly, "Do you believe in premonitions, Derek? You know, of disaster, of trouble . . . "

"You ask *me* that? A Welshman, a true Celt through and through, and right to the very marrow of his bones. Of course I do. I'm very superstitious. I believe in presentiments of doom, and portents and signs. In spirits and ghosts and the supernatural . . . in Merlin's magic at Camelot . . . if it could happen then, it can happen now. It's atavistic, of course, it's in my Celtic blood. But why do you ask?"

"On the Wednesday afternoon before Thanksgiving, I went for a walk through the meadows adjoining Romany Hall. Quite suddenly the weather changed, a fog came down unexpectedly, and I kept thinking of Aysgarth End and the Yorkshire moors. In fact, for a second I thought I'd been transported back there, the two places were so similar. Anyway, I was cold, shivering, and I had such a terrible sense of foreboding, of impending trouble, I was actually frightened. And that's not like me."

"No, it's not."

"Later, back at the house, I experienced that same coldness, that sense of doom at one moment. I pushed the feeling away again, thought of it as being irrational. I even laughed at myself—" She broke off, staring at him.

He nodded. "Go on."

She could see he was taking her seriously, and so she explained further. "Ever since that day I've had nothing but trouble, one way or another. I wish I'd paid attention, done something about it."

Derek frowned at her. "There was *nothing* you could do, Stevie. You can't tamper with fate. What will be will be. You know I've always told you that."

"Yes, you have, and I suppose you're right."

Derek was thoughtful for a moment or two. He took several sips of brandy before he said slowly, "There are so many strange things in this world, so many things we don't understand, and which we cannot properly explain. . . . "

Earlier that day, Blair had gone to Stevie's flat in Eaton Square and packed a suitcase of clothes for her. Now, much later that evening, Stevie began to take her things out of the case, hanging them up in the bedroom of her suite at the Queen's Hotel.

Once she had put everything away, she telephoned Bruce in London, as she had promised she would.

"I'm sorry I'm phoning you so late, it's almost midnight, I know," she said when he answered. "I was hoping to have more news by now, but I don't."

"It's not a problem, Stevie, you can phone whenever you wish. I doubt I'll sleep tonight anyway. Since you've nothing to report, I'm assuming Chloe is still in a coma?"

"Yes, I'm afraid so."

"How is Tamara?"

"The same. In critical condition."

"I see. Well, at least they haven't deteriorated. Or have they?"

"No, they're holding their own, Bruce, and perhaps by tomorrow there will be some improvement, better news. I'll call you—"

"No, no, Stevie, you don't have to, I'm coming up there. I'm taking the Intercity train from King's Cross tomorrow morning. There's one around eight. I'll arrive in Leeds in two hours. And it's the fastest way to get there."

"All right. I'll be at the hospital, of course. Take a taxi from the railway station to Leeds General Infirmary. It's only a few minutes, maybe eight at the most."

"I've arranged for a car and driver. I thought it was the best. Also, a car's useful to have on call. And a room has been booked for me at the Queen's."

"I see everything's taken care of, then."

"Yes, it is."

"What about Tamara's parents? They're flying in to Heathrow tomorrow night. Have—"

"Again, all that's been handled," he explained, cutting in. "There will be a car and driver waiting for them at Heathrow, and they've been booked into a suite at Claridge's."

"Thanks for doing that, Bruce, I know they must be devastated, and worried out of their minds. And they'll be tired after their long flight. Well, good night."

"Good night, Stevie my dear. I will see you tomorrow morning."

After she had hung up, Stevie took a bath before going to bed. Realizing she wouldn't fall asleep immediately, she went to the desk where she had placed her briefcase earlier.

Sitting down, opening it, she took out her journal, which went everywhere with her. She sat for a moment, staring at the page she had written last night in New York. How swiftly and drastically her life had changed since she had made that entry. It was about the trip she was planning to make to Paris next week. Now she made a mental note to cancel it, and to phone André tomorrow. He was her closest friend, had been through so many things with her, and he would want to know. He adored Chloe, who was his godchild, and he had a very soft spot for Tamara as well. Yes, he would want to know what had happened.

As she always did, Stevie wrote in the day and the place at the top of the page.

Good Friday, 1997
Leeds

Today has been the worst day of my life, a nightmare. I've been through many things in the past: Ralph's terrible, untimely death; giving birth to an illegitimate child alone, without her father. But nothing has been as difficult to handle as this.

My beautiful sweet Chloe is lying there in a coma which she may never come out of, and there is nothing I can do to help her. And lovely Tamara is in critical condition, also fighting for her life.

I am suddenly helpless. Me of all people, who is always in control of every situation. I'm usually so good at taking care of things, but I can't take care of this. I'm not a doctor. I need a miracle. An Easter miracle from God. I've never been deeply religious, but I do believe in God and I've always tried to be a good woman, to do good whenever I could, and I think I've succeeded in many ways.

I've prayed a lot today. I hope God hears my prayers. Perhaps He has already. Sometimes God needs a man to work His miracles for Him ... Valentin Longdon ... William Tilden. Good men, good doctors. God's surgeons. I hope they've managed to repair my two girls. My two lovely, and loving, daughters. I have always thought of Tamara as a daughter, ever since Nigel married her. And I've loved her from the start. Such a sweet, unassuming young woman, the perfect wife for Nigel, and the most wonderful mother. I have been blessed, having Tamara as a daughter-in-law.

All of our lives have been changed today ... and in less than a day. By a madman wielding a gun. It's unbelievable when I think about it. I always thought I was in control of my life, but I'm not. No one is, actually. We are all vulnerable, defenseless. We are targets. Anything can happen to us and we cannot stop it happening. We are victims of this violent age we live in, with guns available on street corners, and violence run amok. It's quite terrifying. I've never really thought about it before, but perfect strangers can destroy our lives through their own irrational acts against us. . . .

I must be strong. For everyone. Especially for my mother and Bruce, and for Tamara's parents when they arrive. And Nigel.

Stevie closed her journal, put it back in the briefcase, and locked it. And then she went to bed.

The phone rang shrilly.

Stevie picked it up immediately. "Hello?"

"It's Miles, Mother."

"What is it, Miles? And where are you?"

"I'm here in my room. Gideon just phoned me from the infirmary. Tamara's regained consciousness."

"Oh, that's wonderful!" Stevie exclaimed, feeling a surge of relief.

"But she's not great, Ma. I think she's still in critical condition."

"We'd better go over there, then."

"Yes, Gid wants us to come. He went to the LGI with Nigel at five-thirty this morning. Neither of them slept. Nor did I."

"I didn't either. Are you dressed, Miles?"

"Yes."

"I'll meet you in the lobby. I'm leaving the room now."

"All right."

Stevie hung up. She snatched a burgundy paisley shawl that matched her pants suit off the chair and threw it around her shoulders. Picking up the pen on the desk, she scribbled a note for her mother and Derek, put it in an envelope, and addressed it quickly.

She met Miles in the lobby. Her son greeted her affectionately and kissed her. After she had given the note to the front desk, he led her outside to the waiting taxi.

Nigel stood next to Tamara's bed, holding her hand tightly. He spoke to her softly, telling her how much he loved her, and he was positive she understood him. Earlier, she had opened her eyes and looked at him; he thought he had seen recognition in them, but he wasn't sure of that.

Suddenly, her eyes opened again and she stared up at him. He felt her fingers tightening slightly on his, and it was then he noticed she was trying to speak.

Bringing his face down to hers, he whispered, "What is it, darling? Tell me, Tamsy."

"Ni . . . gel . . . l . . . ove . . . y . . . ou . . ." Her eyes held his.

"I love you too, Tam, so very much."

Slowly, her eyes closed. A moment later her hand went slack in his.

Mr. Tilden, the surgeon, who was standing at the back of the room, glanced at the monitor. The lines had gone flat. He stepped forward, put his hand on Nigel's shoulder. "I'm very sorry, Mr. Jardine."

An anguished cry escaped Nigel's lips. "No!" he shouted. "No!" He clung to his wife. "Don't leave me, Tam!"

"She's gone, Mr. Jardine," William Tilden said gently.

"Leave me alone with her," Nigel mumbled.

The surgeon nodded to the nurse, and the two of them stepped into the corridor.

Stevie, who was waiting near the door with Gideon and Miles, looked at him intently. "Tamara has died . . ." she began, and stopped. Her throat choked up and tears rushed into her eyes.

"I'm very sorry, Mrs. Jardine," he murmured.

"Can I go in, Mr. Tilden?" Stevie asked in a shaking voice. "My son needs me."

"Of course," he answered, and opened the door for her.

Stevie went over to the bed. She gazed down at Tamara, bent over her and kissed her, touched the silver-gilt hair. My lovely girl, good-bye, she said silently. I'll never forget you, Tam, and I'll always love you. Her heart was full of sorrow; she thought it was going to burst. After a moment, endeavoring to marshal her swimming senses, her own grief, Stevie put her arm around Nigel and said quietly, "I'm here, Nigel. I'm here, lovey."

He turned his face to hers. It was wet with tears. "Why, Mam? Why, Mam?" he asked, reverting to his childhood name for her.

"I don't know, Nigel, I really don't. Sweet Tam . . ." She tried to comfort him, but he was inconsolable. His sorrow was unendurable.

A few minutes later Mr. Tilden and the nurse returned to the room. The nurse encouraged Nigel to leave, but he would not. He persisted in clinging to Tamara's hand, tenaciously. When Mr. Tilden attempted to escort him out, he became hysterical, his grief overwhelming him.

"I'll stay with him for a while," Stevie said to the surgeon. "Until he's a little calmer."

27

A WEEK AFTER THE SHOOTING HAD OCCURRED, CHLOE WAS STILL IN a coma. She had been taken out of the intensive care unit and put in a private room in the Brotherton Wing. There was no noticeable change in her state of consciousness.

Now that Chloe was out of the ICU, Stevie was allowed to stay in the room with her daughter, and for as long as she wanted until the early evening. At eight o'clock she usually went back to the Queen's Hotel, since there were no facilities for her to sleep at the Brotherton Wing.

Stevie had been keeping a steadfast vigil by her daughter's side, touching her constantly, holding her hands, talking to her, endeavoring to stimulate her, hoping and praying for a reaction from her. Any kind of reaction, even the slightest, would have been welcome. There was none. Chloe lay in the hospital bed pale and inert, as if she were in a deep, untroubled sleep.

Stevie was never alone with Chloe for very long. Members of the family were constantly in and out of the hospital room, underscoring Stevie's own efforts to stimulate Chloe, to communicate with her. Bruce, Derek, and Blair had been regular visitors, as had Miles and Gideon.

Nigel had gone to London on Monday, accompanying Tamara's body in the private ambulance. Lenore had driven the children and Agnes back to town the same day, and Gideon had followed in his own car on Tuesday morning. His main purpose for going was to help Nigel make all the arrangements for Tamara's funeral. This had taken place yesterday, and every member of the family had attended, except for Stevie and Derek.

Loving Tamara as she had, Stevie wanted to be present when her daughter-in-law was laid to rest. But she had been afraid to leave Chloe alone in case she came out of the coma. She wanted to be there for her daughter, to comfort and reassure her. Stevie's decision to stay in Leeds had been accepted, indeed endorsed, by everyone, Nigel included. Derek had insisted on staying with Stevie, in order to give her moral support, and also because he was so close to Chloe, like a father to her in so many ways.

Now, on this Friday morning at the beginning of April, Derek sat with Stevie in Chloe's room. Thinking out loud, he said, "It occurred to me that I might try reciting to her again. Bits and pieces from some of my roles, especially my Shakespearean roles. You know she loves Shakespeare."

"That's a wonderful idea, Derek. Her favorite role of yours is Hamlet. Why don't you recite the soliloquy?" Stevie suggested.

Derek thought for a moment, then he said, "I don't think it's appropriate, Stevie. There's something rather sad about it . . . Hamlet is talking about dying. The other day I recited some of the sonnets, but I know she likes Byron. We spoke about him at Christmas." Derek rose, walked over to the window, stood looking out for a few moments, composing himself, running the lines of various poems through his head. One of his great talents was his extraordinary ability to commit long speeches and reams of poetry to memory; in fact, he was renowned for this remarkable accomplishment. And like Richard Burton before him, he was able to recite Shakespeare and other writers virtually on request, so well versed was he in their works.

Turning around, he looked across at Stevie holding Chloe's hand, and nodded, smiled at her encouragingly.

Stevie proffered him a faint smile, sat back in the chair, ready to listen to him. But her eyes automatically swung to Chloe, and she gave her daughter all her attention, watching her closely and with enormous intensity.

Derek began to speak softly, his mellifluous voice carrying around the hospital room:

> "She walks in beauty, like the night
> Of cloudless climes and starry skies;
> And all that's best of dark and bright
> Meet in her aspect and her eyes:
> Thus mellow'd to that tender light
> Which heaven to gaudy day denies.
>
> One shade the more, one ray the less,
> Had half impair'd the nameless grace
> Which waves in every raven tress,
> Or softly lightens o'er her face;
> Where thoughts serenely sweet express,
> How pure, how dear their dwelling-place.
>
> And on that cheek, and o'er that brow,
> So soft, so calm, yet eloquent,
> The smiles that win, the tints that glow,
> But tell of days in goodness spent,
> A mind at peace with all below,
> A heart whose love is innocent!"

Derek finished speaking and walked over to Stevie, returning her smile. "My favorite poem by Byron."

"It was beautiful," she said.

"I thought of our lovely Chloe as I was speaking, and it fits her well, doesn't it?"

"Why, yes, it does." Stevie turned back to her daughter and examined her face intently; unexpectedly, she stiffened.

Noticing this, Derek exclaimed, "What is it?"

"I might be imagining it, but I thought I saw a slight movement under her eyelids." Stevie sighed. "But I was wrong. There's nothing, no reaction. She's just lying there motionless."

"Do you want me to recite something else, perhaps—" He cut himself off and glanced over his shoulder as Bruce Jardine walked into the room.

"Good morning," Bruce said. "I just arrived from London and came straight here from the railway station." He shook hands with Derek, and then went to kiss Stevie on the cheek.

Bruce stood looking down at Chloe, studying her carefully as they all did from time to time, frowning to himself. "No change, I suppose?" he said at last, addressing Stevie.

"No change. Although a moment ago I thought I saw an eyelid move. But it was just wishful thinking, I'm afraid."

"She's going to make it, Stevie," Bruce replied quickly. "I feel it in my bones. Remember, it has been only a week since she was shot. The fact that she's been out of intensive care since Sunday is very reassuring to me. What does Mr. Longdon say?"

"That she's basically doing all right, holding her own. He's optimistic."

Derek remarked, "Valentin Longdon has said right from the beginning that it might take ten days, perhaps even two weeks, for Chloe to come out of the coma." Derek walked to the radio and turned it on. "Let's have some music. Hopefully, that might stimulate her. Sounds *are* important. She needs sounds all around her. At least, that's what I've been told by some of my doctor friends."

"It's the swelling in the brain," Stevie murmured, glancing at Bruce. "That has to go down completely."

"Yes, so you told me before." Bending over the bed, he touched Chloe's shoulder, then sat down in a chair near her. Addressing Derek, he said, "How about a little Shakespeare, old chap? You're always so thrilling to listen to . . . it's that marvelous voice of yours. You could read the London telephone directory to me and hold me spellbound."

Derek chuckled. "Thanks for those kind words, Bruce. I just spouted a bit of Byron, so let me put my thinking cap on and come up with something else. Do you have any favorites?"

Bruce nodded. "Many. But mostly the Shakespearean tragedies, and I'm not sure they would be appropriate."

"Why not recite another sonnet," Stevie murmured. "They're gentle enough. Anyway, it's the sound of *your voice* that matters, not what you're saying. You know she's your biggest fan."

Later that afternoon, Gideon and Miles arrived at the hospital, eager to take over from their mother, Derek, and Bruce. They wanted to give their mother a respite from her vigil; they were also concerned about their sister, wished to be close to her.

The twins had just driven up from London, where they had been attending Tamara's funeral on the afternoon before. Taking Stevie to one side, Miles gave his mother a few details about the funeral, reassured her that Nigel was holding up despite the strain and his deep sorrow, and that her grandchildren were all right.

Stevie suddenly found herself weeping again for Tamara. Her death was a waste, senseless. She quickly took control of her emotions; her sole aim at the moment was to try and help Chloe, and she had to be very strong. She dare not give in to her feelings about anything.

It was Miles who said finally, "Come on, Ma, go out for a walk, take a break. You need some air, I'm sure of that. It'll do you good, even if you just walk around the city."

"And you ought to eat something," Derek pointed out.

"Let us go to the Queen's for tea," Bruce suggested, looking at Derek. "It'll do *you* good, old chap. You've been cooped up here all day too."

"That's kind of you, Bruce, but I can't join you for tea, I'm afraid. I'm aiming to catch the five o'clock Pullman back to London. I have a meeting tomorrow with the producers who are doing the revival of *The Lion in Winter,* and I must be there." Turning to Stevie, he explained, "Your mother's going to come up here tomorrow to be with you, love."

"Oh, why don't you spend the weekend in London together!" Stevie exclaimed. "I'm all right, really I am, Derek. Bruce is here, and the twins, I'll be fine. Certainly I'm well looked after."

"And Lenore's coming up tonight," Gideon announced.

"That's a nice thought, Stevie," Derek murmured. "But I don't think Blair will agree to it. She wants to be here with you and Chloe. But then, you know that. Shall we go? Shall we head back to the Queen's? I've got to finish packing my overnight bag."

Stevie became conscious of Bruce's eyes resting on her, and she put down her teacup and said, "You're staring at me, Bruce. Do I have a smudge on my face? Is there something wrong with my appearance?"

He shook his head, but continued to look at her thoughtfully, frowning slightly. At last he said, "Stevie . . . there's something I want to talk to you about—" He came to a stop, glanced away for a moment, and there was hesitation, even a kind of diffidence, in his manner.

"Bruce, tell me what's wrong."

"Almost nineteen years ago, something happened . . ." He coughed behind his hand. "I've never had the courage to talk to you about it before, although sometimes I've wanted to do so. I felt it was better to leave certain things unsaid. . . . But lately I've had the need to broach it to you."

Stevie stiffened, sat rigidly in the chair without saying a word.

Bruce cleared his throat, bent closer to her, and said in a low tone, "She *is* my daughter, isn't she? Chloe is mine?"

Not a muscle moved on Stevie's face, and her eyes were unblinking. She simply stared at Bruce. And she did not answer him.

Bruce went on swiftly, in the same low, intense voice. "What I did was unthinkable, Stevie, so very, very wrong. I don't know what came over me that time we were in Amsterdam, buying diamonds. I've never been able to forgive myself. Or forget it. I've been haunted and troubled for years. I behaved in the most unconscionable manner, and there's no excuse for my behavior. To take advantage of your . . . situation . . . vulnerability . . . to force myself on you that night . . . "

You mean rape me, don't you, Bruce, Stevie thought. Because that's what you did, you raped me. She did not say this. In fact, she did not speak at all.

Puzzled by her silence, Bruce said in a whisper, "I've loved her so much. Always. My Chloe. My lovely daughter."

"She is not your daughter, Bruce," Stevie said in a clear, firm voice.

Bruce gaped at her, his eyes suddenly filling with shock and disbelief. "But she is. She must be! I figured it all out. The timing, the dates. I thought she was probably born a little premature."

"No, Bruce, she wasn't. I was already pregnant by about eight weeks when you forced me to . . . forced your attentions on me. And Chloe was actually born late. *She was late by two weeks.* I conceived Chloe in October of 1977, and she was born in July of 1978. My doctor confirmed my pregnancy of two months at the beginning of December. You and I were in Amsterdam a month later, in January of 1978. She's not yours. There's not even a question about it."

"I am not Chloe's father?" he said in a faltering voice that sounded unexpectedly anguished.

"No, you're not. It never occurred to me that you believed you were. I thought you were nice to Chloe and treated her so beautifully because you were grateful to me for running the business."

Bruce shook his head wonderingly. "I've hardly been able to live with myself all these years. There were even times when I thought I couldn't look you in the eye. I've been so dreadfully ashamed of myself. To do that to you . . . my son's widow . . ." His voice finally broke and he averted his head, stared off into the distance. His aristocratic face was bereft, etched with dismay and a terrible regret.

Stevie did not know what to say to him. Certainly she was not prepared to comfort him. She had never really forgotten that dreadful night at the hotel in Amsterdam. Or her anger and fear when Bruce had forced himself on her. Why mince words? she thought suddenly. He *raped* me; that is the only word for it.

Growing aware that her father-in-law was emotionally upset, and looked as if he were about to break down at any moment, she touched his arm, let her hand rest on it.

He covered her hand with his and brought his gaze back to

meet hers. "I've loved you for years, Stevie. I could not say anything to you about that either. I did not dare."

"Is that why you allowed me such freedom with the business? Gave me such leeway? Let me open the Fifth Avenue store? Because you thought you were Chloe's father?"

"No. Not at all. I gave you power in the company because you deserved it. I trusted you, and I had immense belief in you and in your enormous ability." He sighed heavily. "But I also cared for you." There was another momentary pause, then Bruce continued in a low voice. "When I first met you I disliked you most fervently, thought you were so wrong for my son and for this family. How mistaken I was, Stevie. You have been so *right* for this family, after all. You've become more of a Jardine than even I am, if the truth be known. As the years have gone by, you have truly earned my respect and my devotion. And my love. I care about you and your well-being." He looked at her intently, and his eyes narrowed. "I don't believe you know what a remarkable woman you are. Formidable, in so many ways."

Stevie sat back in the chair. She was startled by the things he had just said, and at a loss for words. She really did not know how to respond.

At long last, Bruce broke the silence. "Who *is* Chloe's father?" he asked, searching her face, longing to know the truth.

"I'm not going to tell you that." She stared him down, her gray-green eyes cool, unflinching.

Bruce took a deep breath. "You never forgave me for Amsterdam, did you?" Before she could answer, he exclaimed, "Why do I ask you that? It's a foolish question. How *could* you forgive me?"

"I didn't, not in the beginning," she responded. "But later on I did forgive you, although I've never *really* forgotten what happened. But, somehow, I managed to bury it so deep, it's never surfaced again. At least, not properly. I suppose I didn't want to deal with it. Or with you either. We had to work together. My sons are your grandchildren, your heirs. I had to find a way to operate around you. *Self-preservation,* Bruce, that was it really. Everybody is driven by self-interest, and I'm sure I'm no different. I think I deep-sixed the memory of Amsterdam in order to function in the family, and at Jardine's."

"I'm so very sorry, Stevie. Will you accept my apology now, after all these years?"

"Yes, I will. I do." She attempted a smile without much success. In a quiet voice, she continued. "You've been wonderful to Chloe, and I do want to thank you for that."

"I believed her to be my daughter. I made her mine in my head and my heart. And in many ways, she *is* mine, actually. I've loved her far too much, do love her very much, so that it would be impossible for me to stop loving her now. She is a part of my life, part of me, part of my soul."

Stevie couldn't help being touched by his words. After a moment, she acknowledged, "I know what she means to you, Bruce."

"I thought she was a Jardine by blood, and so I treated her as a Jardine," he said. "And she became one. A Jardine she will always be, Stevie. Nothing can alter that now."

Stevie sat alone in Chloe's hospital room, holding her hand, staring at her daughter's face, studying it closely. She knew she had done a most terrible thing.

She had denied two people the knowledge of each other. Chloe's father. And, more important, Chloe herself.

How Chloe had longed to know who he was. Only a few months ago, at Thanksgiving, she had been fussing about it, discussing it with Derek and Blair, and anyone else who would listen. How badly her daughter had *needed* to know who John Lane was.

I should have told her the truth then, Stevie thought. She has every right to know about him. Everything there is to know. I have been so wrong. How could I have done such an awful thing? Suddenly, she was awash with guilt, and she knew she would have to live with that for many months to come, perhaps longer.

She sat there for a long time, holding her daughter's hand, willing her to come out of the coma, willing her to live, willing her to flutter an eyelash or move a finger. *Anything* . . . just so long as there was a sign, however tiny, that Chloe's condition was changing, improving.

Imperceptibly, Stevie felt a sudden twitching of Chloe's fingers in hers. She looked down at her daughter's hand swiftly, but it lay there inert and still. She had only imagined that it moved.

Leaning back against the chair, Stevie closed her eyes. Silently she prayed: *Oh, God, please let her get better. Please let my beloved child come out of this. Let her be whole and well again.*

Stevie prayed for a long time. And then she made a silent promise to Chloe. She vowed to her daughter that she would tell her the truth about the man who had given her life. She owed her that. Yes, she would finally tell her who her father really was.

The following morning when Stevie returned to the Brotherton Wing with Miles, the neurosurgeon, Valentin Longdon, was waiting for them. The moment she saw the smile on his face, Stevie knew that the news was good.

"Chloe's come out of the coma!" she exclaimed, her eyes riveted on his face.

"Not exactly," Valentin Longdon answered. "But the nurses tell me there's been some movement. In fact, she's had a restless hour, moving around in the bed, and she has also moved the fingers of her left hand."

"I thought she did yesterday," Stevie told him, "but when I looked at her hand, it was still *lifeless*. I thought I'd imagined it."

"I'm sure you didn't, Mrs. Jardine. I was just about to tell you that when I went in to see her a few minutes ago, she opened her eyes."

"Oh, thank God for that! And thank you, Mr. Longdon, for all that you've done for my daughter."

"Let's go in and see her." The neurosurgeon opened the door, showed Stevie inside.

When Stevie reached the bed she immediately swung around and stared at the doctor. "Is she sleeping? Or has she fallen into the coma again?" she asked anxiously.

"Dozing probably. It's not likely that she'll fall into the coma again. She's now coming out of it."

Stevie touched Chloe's face, and slowly her daughter's eyes opened. They were still her beautiful dark eyes, but they looked glazed and unfocused.

"Chloe, darling, it's me, Mommy," Stevie said, squeezing her hand, holding on to it very tightly.

She loved this child so much, she wanted to weep with relief. But she took firm control of herself, said again, in a stronger tone, "It's me, Chloe, Mommy. I'm here for you. Everything's going to be all right, darling. I'm going to look after you, help you to get better."

Chloe's dark eyes stared back at Stevie. They remained blank and unfocused, and then, quite suddenly, she blinked. She did this several times.

Mr. Longdon moved closer to the bed himself, scrutinizing his patient. Looking up, he nodded, and said to Stevie, "I'm fairly certain she knows it's you, Mrs. Jardine. I believe she is coming back to her normal consciousness."

Miles said, "Once she comes out of the coma, what's the next step?"

"I told your mother a few days ago that your sister will have to go to another hospital for rehabilitation. Once she is no longer in an altered state of consciousness, she can be taken to London by private ambulance. I would like her to go to Northwick Park Hospital in Harrow for several weeks. Maybe even five or six weeks. She will be given physiotherapy, speech therapy, and occupational therapy, which will help her to get her strength back."

"Are you saying that she might be paralyzed? Or perhaps have a problem with her speech? An impediment?" Miles asked.

"That is a possibility, Mr. Jardine. But let us look on the optimistic side, shall we?"

28

"CAN YOU TAKE US ON A TRIP, GRAN?" ARNAUD ASKED, HIS SMALL, eager face upturned to hers. He leaned against her knee, his head on one side. "Please, Gran."

"Well, darling, that all depends on where you want to go," Stevie answered, smiling at him, touching his cheek gently with one finger.

"To heaven. To see Mummy."

Stevie's chest tightened, and she reached out for the child's hands, took them in hers. Softly, she explained, "I don't think we can go this week, Arnaud, you see—"

"I want to see Mummy," he wailed, cutting in. "Daddy says she's staying there. *Forever.*"

"Go to heaven. See Mummy," Natalie said, and patted Stevie's knee. She had been eating a chocolate biscuit and now the chocolate had been transferred from Natalie's sticky fingers to Stevie's pale blue skirt. Glancing down, Stevie stared at it absently for a second, and then turned her attention to her small grandchildren.

"Let's go see Mummy." Arnaud gave Stevie an imploring look. "I want to hug her."

"Me kiss Mummy," Natalie whispered.

Stevie swallowed hard, blinking. "Mummy couldn't see us if we went this week. She's very busy."

"What's she doing in heaven?" Arnaud asked, his delicate blond brows drawing together in a frown.

"Making angels' wings," Stevie improvised, not knowing how to answer them.

"*Oh.*" He looked at her through his big, round eyes. "Do angels fly, then, Gran?"

"Oh, yes, they do. They have lovely white wings and halos and they glide around the sky. I have a picture book of angels at home. Would you like it, darling?"

"Yes, please."

"Me a book, Granma?"

"Yes, you can have one too, Natalie."

Natalie stared at her and suddenly the three-year-old's eyes flooded with tears and she began to cry. "I want Mummy. Get her back, Gran!" she exclaimed hotly.

"Yes, get her back," Arnaud shouted, and his eyes welled. Tears ran down his cheeks.

Leaning forward, Stevie pulled them both to her, put her arms around them and held them close. "Why did Mummy leave us?" Arnaud asked through his sobs. "Doesn't Mummy like us now?"

"Oh, Arnaud, of course she does. And she loves you both very much, sweetheart," Stevie said. "Mummy didn't want to go away and leave you. But, you see, she got hurt and no one could make her better. God was very worried about her, so He decided she should come and live with Him. So that He could make her well again. But no matter what, Mummy's always going to love you both. You're her dearest children."

"Will she always love Daddy?" Arnaud gasped, the tears rolling down his cheeks, spilling onto his lips unchecked.

Wiping his cheeks with her fingertips, Stevie said, "Yes, Mummy will always love Daddy." She stopped, unable to continue, so choked was she. Taking the small tea napkin the housekeeper had given her, she wiped his face and then Natalie's.

Taking a deep breath, Stevie went on, "You must be brave and strong for Daddy. Mummy would want that, and she would want you to look after him."

There was a slight noise. Stevie glanced toward the arched entranceway of the living room in Nigel's Kensington flat. She saw her son standing there watching them, his face shattered, the pain in his eyes unbearable.

"Nigel!" Stevie exclaimed, trying to sound cheerful. "There you are, darling."

When they saw their father, the children pulled away from Stevie, ran across the floor to him, and flung themselves against his legs.

Nigel hunkered down next to them, put his arms around the two of them. "Hello, Pumpkins," he said, forcing a smile onto his ravaged face. "I hope you've been good for Gran."

"Yes. Gran says Mummy's making angels' wings in heaven, Daddy," Arnaud confided. "Angels can fly, Daddy."

"Oh, really, I never knew that," Nigel murmured, trying to hold his emotions in check. He looked over their blond heads at Stevie, and she gave him a faint smile.

Straightening, Nigel walked into the living room, holding each child by the hand.

Stevie rose to greet him, and he kissed her on the cheek, glanced at her skirt, and said, "A little person's ruined that."

"It doesn't matter. There are more important things in this

world than a skirt. Do you want a cup of tea?' she asked as she sat down again.

"A nice cup of tea," Natalie said, mimicking Melanie, the housekeeper.

"I'll go and ask Mel to make me one. Is Agnes back from the dentist?"

"She returned about five minutes ago," Stevie said.

He nodded and disappeared into the foyer, heading in the direction of the kitchen.

Agnes appeared a moment later. "Come on, children, let's go back to the nursery. Kiss Grandma good-bye."

"Can we watch *The Lion King*?" Arnaud asked.

"And why not," Agnes responded. She smiled across at Stevie. "Thanks for being here, for baby-sitting this afternoon, Mrs. Jardine."

"Anytime, Agnes."

Natalie ran and climbed onto Stevie's knee and put her small plump arms around her neck. She gave her grandmother a large, noisy kiss and whispered in her ear, "Gran stay. No go to heaven."

"Yes, Gran will stay with Natalie and Arnaud, darling. Don't worry."

The little girl scrambled off her knee; Arnaud came up to her, leaned against her knees, and kissed her cheek as Stevie bent forward. "Can I have a dog, Gran?"

"If it's all right with Daddy, yes. I'll get you a lovely little Bichon Frise puppy."

"What's that?"

"Like Lenore's two little dogs, Chammi and Beaji."

"Funny names. I'll call my dog Angel," he announced. "And Mummy will make it wings."

Stevie smiled but her heart was aching. She didn't answer her grandson. She couldn't find the right words.

After they had gone off to the nursery with Agnes, Stevie got up and put another log on the fire. Although it was the middle of May, it was a damp afternoon. The big living room seemed awfully cold to her, and dismal.

A few minutes later Nigel came back into the living room, carrying a cup of tea. "Mel wants to know if you would like another one, Mother."

"No thanks. I'm surprised I haven't floated away, all the tea I've drunk these last few weeks."

Stevie walked over to the sofa and seated herself on it. Staring at Nigel, she couldn't help thinking how ill he looked. He had lost weight, his clothes hung on him loosely, and his face was gaunt, drawn. His vivid blue eyes, always one of his best features, were pale today, and bloodshot. There was a cloak of sorrow and despair about him, and Stevie's heart went out to her son. Tamara had been dead and buried for just over six weeks, and it was obvious to Stevie—and everyone else—that Nigel was falling apart.

"You don't look at all well," Stevie began slowly, groping her way, wondering how to skillfully bring the conversation around to what she really wanted to say.

"I feel much worse than I look, Mother." He coughed behind his hand and turned away. When he suddenly brought his gaze to hers, he asked in a tight voice, "How did you manage to go on after my father died?"

"I don't really know, Nigel. I found the strength somewhere. But it was so hard. Extremely difficult. But I had you and the twins, my mother and Derek, and I just knew I had to find the will to continue living somehow. When I look back now, I honestly don't know how I did it, I really don't. I operated strictly by rote, like an automaton, for a very long time. I just got through the days."

Nigel nodded. "I know what you mean—" He paused and shook his head, his face crumpling up with emotion. "I loved her so much, Mam." Finally, his voice broke, but he recovered himself and went on. "Tam was so special, there was just no one like her. She was so sweet, so humorous, and she was such a loving human being."

"She *was* all these things, Nigel, everyone adored Tamara."

"I heard what you were saying to the children when I came in. Thanks for that."

"I didn't know what to say . . . they're so young. And children can ask the most terrible questions. It's hard for them to understand." Stevie let out a long sigh, wishing she knew of a way to help her son. But he could only help himself. That was the problem with grief, it was a heavy burden to carry, and also a lonely burden, in a sense. They were all grieving for Tam; obviously they would recover sooner than Nigel would. She must try to console him, give him what comfort she could.

Stevie spoke softly. "You know, Nigel, it does get a little easier as time goes by. I know that's cold comfort right now, just words, and words don't necessarily help when you're longing for the loved one you've lost. They seem so empty."

He stared at her, said nothing.

"I didn't believe it either, Nigel. But it's the truth. And then there's *work*. That helped me. Once your grandfather had agreed to let me work at Jardine's, my whole life changed. For the better. I found it took my mind off my pain and my longing for your father."

Without thinking twice, or weighing the odds, and speaking from the heart, Stevie went on. "And that's exactly what you need, Nigel. *Work*. There's not much to your life these days, hanging around the flat, seeing the odd friend for lunch. I think you'd better go back to Jardine's tomorrow."

Astonishment crossed his face, displacing the grief. For a second he was not sure he had heard her correctly. He frowned, his brows knitting together in the same way his little son's did. He was at a loss, hardly knew what to say. And so he said nothing.

It was Stevie who spoke again. "You need something to keep you occupied, busy. Work took my mind off my sorrow and the loss I felt. It will do the same for you. Do as I say. Go back to Jardine's tomorrow, Nigel."

"You're giving me my old job back, Mother?" he asked, his voice echoing with disbelief and surprise.

"Yes, I am."

"You would do that, after the way I behaved?"

"Of course I would, Nigel. I fired you for your insubordination, not because you were incapable of doing your job. As a matter of fact, you're wonderful at your job. Brilliant. And I've always said so. Anyway, the company's yours actually. When I step down in a couple of years, which I now plan to do, you'll be running Jardine's on both sides of the Atlantic. I just want you to get a bit more experience under your belt before I retire."

"I'm flabbergasted, I really am," Nigel murmured, looking at her intently. "Very few people would do that, take me back into the business."

"I'm not *people*, Nigel darling, I'm your mother. You're my eldest son, my firstborn child, and I love you very much. I've never stopped loving you, even when I thought you were working against me."

"Some people would hold a grudge."

"I hope I'm far too big a woman to do that. Grudges are petty. They're the tools of the weak and the small-minded in this world. But speaking of grudges, your Jardine grandmother had a grudge against me when she was alive. And lately I've been wondering if she implanted seeds of doubt and hatred of me in your head when you were much younger."

Nigel sat back on the love seat and closed his eyes. Finally, when he opened them, he said, "Grandmother Alfreda was ... she was an old bitch, Mother. But I didn't know it then, when I was a teenager. And yes, you're right, she talked a lot about you ... brainwashed me actually, now that I look back. Her poisonous stories about you, her innuendos and her accusations were all meant to kill my love for you."

"Accusations?" Stevie shook her head, looking puzzled for a moment.

"She said it was your fault that Dad died."

Stevie was taken aback. This was the last thing she had expected. "*What next?* But that's not true. And *you* know better than that. Your father died of peritonitis. A bungled operation by an incompetent doctor. Of her choosing, I might add. If anyone was responsible for your father's death, it was Alfreda, his own mother."

"She really chose the doctor?"

"Yes. He was the son of a friend."

"I didn't know."

"And what else did she say?"

"She questioned your morals ... especially when you got pregnant with Chloe."

"That's typical of her." Stevie got up, went and sat on the love seat next to him. "*Did* she kill your love for me, Nigel?"

"Not entirely, no, Mother. But she did damage it, I've got to admit that. You see, she made me believe you wanted the business for yourself, for your own devious ends. She said that you'd kick me out one day. Take Jardine's away from me."

"And you believed her?"

"I was very young, just a kid."

"I know you were. And impressionable. She was wicked, Nigel, a really wicked woman."

"I'm so sorry, Mother."

"I know. And remember, my love for you has never changed, or altered in any way. I hope you realize that, realize how much I *do* love you, Nigel."

"I'm beginning to understand, Mam."

Stevie smiled hugely, and it was her first real smile in weeks.

"What is it?' he asked, frowning again.

"You probably don't realize it, but you keep calling me Mam, as you used to when you were a little boy."

He did not respond. Unexpectedly, he reached out for her, took hold of her, held her tightly in his arms.

"How will you ever be able to forgive me for what I did to you?" he asked against her hair.

"Oh, I already have, Nigel. Weeks ago."

"How can I make it up to you?"

"By going back to Jardine's tomorrow."

"I don't know how to redeem myself in your eyes," he said, drawing away, searching her face.

"By doing a good job at the store. By looking after your children and loving them well. By loving your brothers and sister. By loving Derek, Blair, and Bruce. By standing tall, Nigel, and being the man I know you can be."

"I will try. No, I *will* do it. I *will*."

She smiled at him, her gray-green eyes spilling her love for her eldest son. She touched his cheek gently. "Love is so important in all of our lives . . . and I mean all kinds of love, Nigel, not just the romantic kind. Love has such tremendous healing powers."

"Yes, I know it does. I've witnessed it with you and Chloe. What progress she's made, and it's all because of you."

"And the rehabilitation hospital. And Bruce and Derek and Blair. And Miles and Gideon and Lenore. And you too, Nigel, and the children. The entire family has been part of her healing, as they will also be part of yours."

29

On Wednesday morning of the following week, Stevie drove to Heathrow and took a plane to Italy. The flight was relatively short, only an hour and forty minutes from London to Milan.

Now, as the British Airways jet approached the Linate Airport runway, Stevie moved her watch one hour ahead, in order to conform with European time. It was exactly ten-forty.

After leaving the plane, everything went very quickly; within twenty minutes she was sitting in the limousine she had picked up at the airport, heading into Milan.

She leaned back against the car seat, feeling relaxed, and much calmer than she had been for some time. Since the shooting, in fact.

Nigel had gone back to Jardine's the day after she had had her heart-to-heart talk with him, almost a week ago now, and already he seemed much better in spirits. Work had been important to him all his life, and just as she had predicted, being at the store again was helping him to adjust to the tragedy that had befallen him. It would take him a long time to recover from Tamara's death, but she knew now that he had a good chance of getting back on his feet. Work was a great antidote to sorrow; she had discovered that for herself. And he had his children. They, too, would help to sustain him, and, because of their need for him, give meaning to his existence, a reason to live.

As for Chloe, she was improving daily, growing stronger and healthier after her five-week stay at Northwick Park Hospital. The therapy had been necessary, had helped to bring her back to normal, and Valentin Longdon was pleased with her progress. He had seen Chloe only last week and pronounced her fit and well, but he had recommended to Stevie that they stay in England for another month. After that, he had said, they could travel back to the States. Or anywhere else they wanted.

I've been lucky, Stevie thought, staring out of the car window, her mind focused on her daughter. Chloe could have died, or remained in a coma, or been left totally paralyzed. God *did* give me an Easter miracle. For Chloe, at least, but not for Tamara. Whenever she thought of her daughter-in-law, her heart ached and she filled with sadness. She would miss Tam for as long as she lived; there would always be a hole in her heart now that her son's wife was gone.

Within twenty minutes of leaving Linate Airport, the car was entering Milan's Centro, the city center, where the hotel she had selected was located. As usual, the city center was busy with traffic, but within seconds the car was pulling up outside the Four Seasons on Via Gesù, near Via Montenapoleone. Once a cloister, the old monastery had been tastefully renovated, the fifteenth-century building updated to become a beautiful hotel, filled with sunlight streaming in through the large windows.

As she walked through the lobby to the registration desk, Stevie glanced around, liking the ambiance, the airiness, the sense of spaciousness that prevailed.

Once she was settled in her suite, she unpacked the suitcase she had brought and hung up her clothes. Seating herself at the desk, she called Jardine's. After speaking to her secretary, she then talked to Nigel and Gideon respectively before phoning the flat in Eaton Square to check on Chloe, make sure she was all right.

Her phone calls finally out of the way, Stevie refreshed her makeup and changed out of the black pants suit she had traveled in. For her appointment that afternoon she chose a dark gray flannel suit and a white silk shirt. Her only jewelry was her double strand of pearls, pearl earrings, and a watch. After glancing at herself quickly in the mirror, she picked up her handbag and left the suite.

Stevie walked to the Caracelli offices located on the Via della Spiga, enjoying being outside on this lovely May afternoon. It was sunny, the sky was blue and cloudless, and the weather was balmy, a nice bonus after the dampness of London.

As she walked she did a little window shopping, looking at the beautiful clothes and accessories in the chic boutiques. Milan was the fashion center of the world, and she decided she would do some shopping later if she had time. Perhaps she would find some pretty things here for Chloe as well as for herself.

When she finally reached the large Caracelli building, Stevie looked at her watch. It was a few minutes before two; she was exactly on time for her meeting.

As she sat waiting in the elegant reception area, Stevie leafed through a couple of fashion magazines to pass the time. Eventually, a pretty, young woman came to get her, made some pleasant remarks in English, and led her down a corridor. A moment later she was being shown into Signore Caracelli's office.

He was sitting behind his desk angled across a corner, facing the door. He rose at once and came around the desk to greet her, smiling broadly.

Stevie felt her stomach tightening. The calmness of earlier, which had so bolstered her self-confidence, instantly disappeared. She was suddenly tense and nervous, shaking inside as she stood in the center of his office.

Striding across the floor, the smile intact, he came to a stop in front of her, took her hand in his, and held it for a moment. Looking down at her, he said finally, in his slightly accented English, "Stephanie. How nice to see you again. Such a pleasant surprise when you telephoned me on Monday."

"It's nice to see you too," she replied, and she was surprised that her voice sounded so normal. "I'm glad you weren't away, that you were able to give me this appointment at such short notice."

He nodded, and, still holding her hand, he led her over to the seating arrangement near the window. "May I offer you some refreshment? Coffee? A drink? Tea, perhaps?"

She shook her head. "Thank you, no. I'm fine."

He smiled again, showing his perfect teeth, very white against his tanned complexion. Seating himself opposite her, he crossed his long legs and leaned back against the sofa, staring at her intently. His undisguised curiosity and interest in her was very apparent. Suddenly he made a sharp gesture with his hand, a chopping motion, and exclaimed, "Forgive me! I am being thoughtless. I should have asked you about your son. How is he?"

"He's doing better," Stevie responded.

"I read in the London *Times* that your daughter-in-law was fatally shot. Such a tragedy."

"It's been very difficult," Stevie admitted. "A painful time for him, for all of us. But he's . . . well, he's holding his own. He has two small children and they keep him . . . sane."

"Yes. I understand. . . ." There was a short pause before he continued. "To lose someone you love when they are so young . . . it is a terrible thing. And in such ghastly circumstances for you. Tragic, so tragic. I am very sorry, Stephanie."

"Thank you." Stevie bit her lip, hesitating, and then she said quickly, in a rush of words, "My daughter was injured in the shooting. I'm lucky she's alive."

A puzzled expression crossed his face. "Daughter?"

Stevie nodded. "She was with Tamara when the shooting occurred . . . at our house on the Yorkshire moors. A bullet lodged in her brain. She was in a coma for a week."

"Good God! She is all right?" He sat back, his expression sympathetic.

"Yes. She had a brain operation to remove the bullet. Thankfully, she recovered."

"I am glad." He had been riddled with curiosity about her since the moment she had arrived in his office, and now it got the better of him. He gave her an odd look and said, "I did not know you had a daughter." His eyes went to her left hand, then swung to her face. "How old is she, Stephanie?"

"Eighteen. She'll be nineteen in July."

"Eighteen . . . "

Stevie nodded.

"What is her name?"

"Chloe."

"*Chloe*." He repeated the name so vehemently Stevie almost jumped out of her skin.

His eyes impaled hers and he said in a gentler tone, "She is eighteen, almost nineteen. Her name is Chloe. Is she . . . she is mine, isn't she? She is my daughter, Stephanie."

"Yes, Gianni, she is."

Stunned, momentarily floundering, he sat staring at her

speechlessly. Then he said at last, "Why didn't you tell me then, when we were together, all those years ago?"

"You were married . . . a married man with a family. And you were so well-known, a big industrialist. I also knew that as a Catholic, you could not divorce. I thought it better that I just end it."

"Oh, Stephanie." The look he gave her was reproachful, full of dismay, and he experienced a rush of sadness so acute, he was startled.

Stevie saw that he was emotionally affected, and this took her aback. She exclaimed, "I ended it, yes, but you accepted it—"

Interrupting her, he said somewhat heatedly, "Because I knew that to continue our relationship would cause you problems. I did not wish to make further trouble for you. With the Jardines. I knew what Bruce was like. And Alfreda. Tough. Hard. Difficult people. Without heart. I accepted your decision because . . ." He did not finish his sentence, but his eyes did not leave her face.

"Because *what?*"

Softening his tone, he replied, "Because I loved you very much, Stephanie. I could not bear your unhappiness. Your pain because we could not be together was like a knife in my heart. I was caught in a trap. A bad marriage. A dying father. A huge company to run. Two children dependent on me. I wanted you. But I could not have you. And so I let you go." A shadow crossed his face; pain lodged in his dark eyes.

Stevie could not fail to notice this, and she knew he was sincere in everything he said. He had always been a sincere and genuine man, and he had not changed. She moved slightly on the sofa, crossed her legs, but made no comment.

Again Gianni said, "It was wrong of you to keep it from me."

"I had to, Gianni."

"You did my thinking for me. That was a mistake, Stephanie. I can think for myself."

"I know you can. It was the best thing for me to do. Or so I thought then."

"How did you explain your child, *our* child?"

"I never did. I refused to name the father."

"The Jardines . . . did they accept this?"

"Yes. In fact, everyone did. I simply refused to budge from my stance."

"Amazing."

"There was nothing anyone could do, or say, Gianni. Besides, the Jardines had no choice. They needed me. At least, Bruce needed me to run the company."

"You've done a remarkable job with Jardine's. I've been proud of you as I've watched it grow." Leaning forward, his manner intense, he asked, "Why have you come to tell me about . . . our daughter? About Chloe? Now, after all this time. Because of the shooting?"

"Absolutely. When Chloe was in a coma, I made a vow. A vow that I would tell her the truth about her father if she recovered. I want to do that, Gianni, I want to tell her about you. And I want you to come to London to see her. It's very important to me that you do. Long before the shooting, she was desperate to know about the man who had fathered her. That's only natural now that she's reached young womanhood."

"It is. Of course it is. I understand that. You have still not told her about me?"

"No, not yet. I know it's a problem for you, and I don't want to intrude on your life and on your family. Look, I don't want to cause you problems of any kind, or—"

"I am a widower," Gianni said, cutting in peremptorily.

"Oh, I'm sorry . . ." Her voice faltered under his stern gaze.

He shook his head. "I am not going to be a hypocrite, Stephanie. You know what a terrible marriage I had. And we were separated when she died. Renata left me twelve years ago. For another man. When she died four years ago, she was still with him."

"I see. How are Carlo and Francesco?"

A sorrowful expression crept into his eyes. "Francesco is dead, Stephanie. My son was killed in a car crash five years ago. But Carlo is well."

"I am so very sorry, Gianni, truly. I know how you loved him." She shook her head. "You too have had your tragedies, your share of pain."

"That is so. But life is hard for everyone. In different ways." There was a brief silence between them, until he asked, "And tell me, who does Chloe think her father is? You must have put some name . . . on her birth certificate. What is the name?"

"John Lane." A smile stole onto Stevie's face. "I do believe you know him."

Gianni laughed, his passionate dark eyes so like Chloe's suddenly full of merriment. "I do. John for Gianni—Giovanni. And Lane because I always stayed at the Dorchester on Park *Lane*. My code name when I telephoned you at Jardine's."

She nodded.

"What is she like, this daughter of mine?"

Stevie reached for her handbag, opened it. As she pulled out a photograph of Chloe, the telephone rang.

"Excuse me, I must take this." He jumped up, hurried across the room to his desk, where he picked up the receiver and spoke into it quietly.

Stevie's eyes followed him. He had not changed much in eighteen years. He was fifty-four, seven years older than she was, but he did not show his age. He had thickened slightly, and appeared more muscular, but his face was relatively unlined, and tan as it always had been. He was a sportsman, loved tennis and skiing and sailing; he was a man who spent time outdoors. His thick dark hair had grayed slightly at the temples, but it was hardly noticeable. And he was still a very handsome man. Probably the most handsome man she had ever known. Tall and vital, he was full of energy, and it had been that energy that had appealed to her years earlier. No, he had not changed, not on the surface at least. But life had got at him, as it got at everyone, and in more ways than he had already mentioned. She could tell; there was a deep sadness in him, a sorrowfulness.

He had become, in the intervening years, Italy's greatest industrialist; he was known as the silk king, but he also owned fashion houses, manufacturing plants, shopping centers, real estate, and hotels. She knew all this because she had read about him over the years; he was frequently mentioned in the *Financial Times* and the *Wall Street Journal.*

As Gianni hung up and walked back to the seating arrangement, she could not help thinking how impeccable he looked in his beige gabardine suit, blue shirt, and yellow-and-blue-patterned silk tie. He had never been anything but beautifully dressed, from the top of his well-groomed head to the tips of his highly polished dark brown loafers.

"Is that photograph for me?" he asked, sitting down again.

Stevie handed it to him, explaining, "It was taken last summer in Connecticut."

Gianni stared at it for a long time. "She looks like me."

"Very much so. Especially the eyes and the forehead, and she has your strong jaw, Gianni."

"May I keep this?"

"Yes. But won't you come and see her for yourself?"

"You could not stop me. No one could." Gianni rose, came

and sat next to Stevie on the sofa. Looking deeply into her face, he took hold of her hands and said very softly, "If only you had told me then, Stephanie, perhaps I could have found a way." That sadness she had noticed before was reflected in his dark eyes once more. It made her catch her breath, so acute was it.

"Perhaps," Stevie murmured, returning his long, intense look. "All I want now is to introduce the two of you. I did a very wrong thing, keeping you apart. I want to make amends."

In the past Gianni had always driven his cars very fast. He had become a much more careful driver, Stevie noticed. As he drove his Ferrari out of Milan, heading in the direction of Lake Como, his speed was moderate.

Gianni chatted to her nonstop, or, rather, he continued to ply her with questions about Chloe, keeping up the continuing conversation, but he never took his eyes off the road.

At one moment he said, "I'm no longer a speed freak, as I used to be when I was younger. When I knew you years ago, Stephanie. Francesco's death cured me of that addiction. He was driving fast and talking to his girlfriend and he didn't see the truck coming. It was a head-on collision. Francesco and Liliane were killed instantaneously."

"I'm so very sorry," Stevie murmured softly. "I remember how much you . . . how much you loved him."

"Yes."

For the remainder of the drive to his house on Lake Como, Gianni was silent. Stevie sank down into herself, thinking about him. During their meeting at his office he had suddenly asked her if she would have dinner with him, and she had accepted. Now, here they were, driving along as if their eighteen-year separation had never happened. They had always been compatible with each other in the past, and incredibly that easiness, that sense of comfort, still existed between them. We're not much different now than we were then, she thought suddenly. Not deep down. Yes, we're older, and life has changed us both in certain ways; but essentially we are still the same people inside. Despite the ease which she felt existed between them, Stevie was tense inside. That acute feeling of nervousness she had first experienced in his office had persisted. And she was also very conscious of him as a man, conscious of his masculinity, his vitality, and his power. She had found him mesmeric when she had been younger; he had not lost his charismatic appeal for her. If anything, it was more potent than ever.

How she had longed for him over the years, longed to see his face, to hear his voice. She had never forgotten his voice. It was deep and resonant. Because he had been educated in England and America, his command of English was flawless.

She had given him up all those many years ago, and she was nothing if not disciplined. Once she had made the decision to cut him out of her life, she had not wavered in her determination. She had never again seen him, but the yearning had always been there.

She stole a look at him out of the corner of her eye, saw the strong set of his jaw, the well-defined nose, the shapely head. Chloe had his head, his eyebrows, his eyes.

Stevie could not help wondering about his life, about the women in his life over the years. And there must have been many, well, some . . . he was too sexual a man not to have been involved romantically. And he had told her he had been separated from Renata for twelve years. She clamped down on these thoughts, clamped down on other more dangerous thoughts of him that had been creeping into her mind for hours. She had come to Milan to see him because of Chloe, their daughter, wanting to bring them together at last. And that was her only purpose for being with him tonight.

When they arrived at the house on the shores of Lake Como, where many of the Milanese lived, Stevie was not in the least surprised at its size or its beauty. After he had parked in the courtyard, he led her inside to the large white entrance hall. It was elegant but somewhat austere, relying on its proportions and simplicity for its intrinsic beauty. Scanning it quickly, her eyes caught sight of a beautiful tapestry on one wall, a large gilt mirror on another. There was a huge crystal chandelier hanging from the high ceiling, a wide staircase flowing upward, and flowers everywhere.

A white-coated houseman greeted them, and Gianni spoke to him rapidly in Italian before taking her through a large living room. They came out onto a long terrace overlooking the lake.

"It's a beautiful house, Gianni," she said after a moment, glancing out at the water, then turning to him.

"Too big for one man, I think."

"Doesn't Carlo live here with you?"

"No."

"Is he married?"

"No, he's not. He lives in Rome. He has a flat there. Carlo runs my Rome office. He and I——" He broke off, shrugged lightly. "Carlo . . . was always his mother's son, hers more than mine. It is odd, is it not, the way one child will gravitate to one parent more than the other? And we never mean to make favorites, do we?" He smiled at her a little regretfully. A brow lifted. "You are a mother, Stephanie, you know how it is."

"I do, Gianni. Of my sons, Miles has always been a child of my heart, as Chloe is too."

"Francesco was the child of *my* heart, but now he's gone. Ah, life. It is difficult sometimes." He gestured to a chair. "Please."

The houseman returned with a bottle of champagne and two glasses on a tray, went to a small table behind them and opened the bottle.

Gianni smiled at her. "Veuve Clicquot for you, Steffie. You see, I have not forgotten."

A moment later they were clinking glasses. "Now. Tell me more about her. Tell me about Chloe." He began to chuckle unexpectedly. "If my grandmother were alive, she would be pleased to know my daughter was named for her. Thank you for that."

She spoke about Chloe for a while, telling him about her childhood, her relationships with her brothers and the rest of the family.

At one moment, when she paused to take a sip of the icy champagne, he asked, "When are you returning to London?"

"Tomorrow."

"Thursday. Mmmm." He regarded her over the rim of his glass, his eyes speculative. "I think I shall go with you. I want to see her."

"But it's too soon!" Stevie exclaimed. "I must prepare her. Explain everything." Stevie stopped when she saw the disappointment flashing across his face.

"How long is that going to take you? Fifteen minutes at the most. If that, Steffie."

There he was again, calling her by the name only he had ever used. Stevie looked across at him, found him suddenly irresistible. She glanced away, biting her lip. She said nothing.

There was a silence between them.

Gianni did not let it lengthen. He said, "That is true, isn't it? It won't take you very long to tell her about me . . . about her father."

"I suppose you're right," she acknowledged without looking at him.

Gianni Caracelli sat back, studying her as she gazed out toward the lake. She had not changed at all. She was exactly the same as she had been twenty years before, when he had first met her in London. At a jewelry exhibition. He had taken one look at her and fallen head over heels in love. And so had she with him. It had been a *coup de foudre,* as the French called it, struck by lightning. It had been the most important and passionate relationship he had had with a woman in his entire life. His eyes narrowed slightly in the dimming light. Not a wrinkle on that lovely face, not a line. He smiled inwardly at himself. Of course there were tiny lines around her eyes and mouth; he had noticed them in his office earlier. But they had disappeared in an instant because he saw her as she had been then, not as she was now. In his mind she had never aged.

Clearing his throat, he said, "Let us go to London together, Stephanie. Tomorrow. On my plane."

Still, Stevie remained silent. She was afraid, if the truth be known. Afraid of him, of his power as a man, and of the appeal he had for her.

"I want to see Chloe," he insisted, although his voice was light. "And as soon as possible. Why wait?"

She turned to look at him.

His dark eyes were intense as they held hers. "So many years wasted, Steffie. Let us not waste any more."

30

"How do I look, Mom?" Chloe asked, coming into Stevie's bedroom. She stood in front of her mother, then turned around slowly. "Do you like this pants suit? Like the color?"

"Yes, I do," Stevie answered, the expression on her face approving. "The burgundy is wonderful on you. It's odd, but dark colors have always suited you, even when you were little."

"It's my olive complexion; I just look better in muted shades."

"I suppose so."

Holding her head on one side, studying Stevie, Chloe exclaimed, "You're very dressed up, Mom! Who did you say we're meeting for lunch?"

"Do I look too dressed up?" Stevie asked worriedly, and went to the mirrored closets that ran along one wall of the blue-and-white bedroom. She regarded herself thoughtfully for a second, then said, "I don't know what you mean. I'm not dressed up at all. I'm not even wearing much jewelry, just a brooch and earrings."

"I know, but that's your new suit. You told me you were saving it for a special occasion. And I've never seen that pin and those earrings before. They're wonderful sapphires, Mom. Are they new?"

"No." Stevie swung around, gave her daughter a careful look, and plunged in. "Your father gave them to me."

"My father! *When?*"

"Nineteen years ago." Walking across the floor to Chloe, Stevie took hold of her arm. "I want to talk to you. Let's go into the study for a minute."

"Okay. But what do you want to talk about? And why have you never worn those sapphires before?" Chloe eyed her mother curiously, wondering what this was all about.

"Come and sit with me" was the only answer Stevie gave her daughter as she hurried out.

Chloe followed her mother, sat down in a chair near the window, and focused all her attention on Stevie.

"When I was sitting at your bedside at the infirmary in Leeds, praying for you to come out of your coma, I made a promise to you in my heart and in my mind," Stevie explained. "I vowed that I would tell you the truth about your father. I am keeping that promise, Chloe, I want to tell you about him now."

Chloe nodded eagerly. She was on the edge of her seat in anticipation. Then before Stevie could say anything, Chloe exclaimed, "He's not dead, is he?"

Momentarily startled, Stevie gaped at her. Finally, she shook her head. "No, but how did you know that?"

"I didn't actually *know*, not for sure anyway. I just . . . well, I sensed it, Mom, I somehow *felt* that as a child. I always thought he was going to show up one day, just walk in and say, 'Hi, Chloe, I'm your dad.' I used to fantasize about it when I was little. I had an image of this tall, dark, handsome man walking toward me. My father. I thought he'd come looking for me, find me one day."

Stevie was speechless. After a moment she recouped and said, "Well, you're right. He's alive. And he *is* tall, dark, and handsome. Although I'll never understand how you knew that."

Chloe leaned forward. "And I bet his name's not John Lane either."

"No, it's not. That's not quite correct . . . part of it is."

"Why, Mom? Why did you hide the truth? Why didn't you tell me anything before?" Chloe asked in a small, puzzled voice, a hurt expression flickering in her brown eyes.

"I couldn't tell you the truth when you were old enough to understand, tell you who he really was, because of the circumstances of his life, his position in the world, his family. He was married, you see, and a very prominent man when we . . . when we were together—"

"Why didn't he divorce?" Chloe asked with a flash of vehemence. "Why didn't he get a divorce and marry you when you got pregnant with me? Didn't he want me?"

"He didn't even know about you. I never told him."

"Mom! Why not?" Chloe demanded, her voice rising.

"Because he was married. And he's a Catholic. I knew there would never be a divorce. There was no way he could get one. And he had children. I just made that decision not to tell him, and rightly or wrongly, I broke up with him before you were born." Stevie shook her head. "Perhaps I was wrong, but that's water under the bridge now. I never saw him again, once I had decided to end it."

"Didn't he try to keep it going? Pester you?"

"No, not when I said it must end because I couldn't live with the pain of it any longer. He respected my wishes, knowing how difficult everything had become for me. A love affair with a married man does become untenable. It's impossible, heartbreaking, Chloe."

A sympathetic note crept into Chloe's voice when she said, "It must have been hard for you, Mommy, not seeing him. I mean, if you loved him so much."

"I did. And it was. Very hard. But he lived in another country, which helped to some extent. He still lives there."

"Where does he live?"

"Italy."

"He's an Italian?"

"Yes."

"Wow! My father's Italian. *Awesome.* What's his real name, then?"

"Gianni . . . short for Giovanni, which means John in English, you know."

"Gianni *what*, Mom?"

"Caracelli. Your father's Gianni Caracelli."

There was a small silence. Chloe eyed her mother in surprise, and said slowly, "Not the Italian industrialist? My father is *him*?"

"Yes."

Chloe stared at Stevie and then she got up and went and peered in the mirror above the mantel. "Do I look Italian, Mom?" She moved closer to the mirror. "My eyes do, I guess. But everyone's always said I look like your mother."

"You do. However, you also look like Gianni. You have his eyes, his brows, and forehead. And his strong jaw. And the shape of your head is the same as his."

"So I look like my daddy?"

Stevie nodded.

"That's why you went to Italy on Wednesday?"

"It is."

"Did you see him, Mom? Have you told him about me?"

"Yes, I have, Chloe."

"What did he say? I bet he was shocked," Chloe asserted.

"Stunned is a better word. I think a man like Gianni Caracelli is unshockable. And he was pleased."

"Was he really?" Chloe suddenly sounded anxious.

"Oh, yes. Thrilled really, and thrilled that I named you for his grandmother. Her name was also Chloe."

"*Oh.*"

"He wants to meet you, Chloe. In fact, he can't wait."

Chloe was suddenly feeling scared inside, yet excited and curious at the same time.

"He's here in London," Stevie announced.

"Is that who we're meeting for lunch?"

Stevie smiled. "It is. At the Dorchester. That's where he's staying. He always stayed there in the past, and I think that's where you were conceived, actually."

"Oh, Mom." Chloe stared at herself in the mirror again. "Are you sure I look all right? Maybe I should change. Oh, God, I look awful, Mom. I wish you'd told me about this before I got ready."

"You don't look awful. You're a lovely young woman."

All sorts of questions were suddenly jostling for prominence in Chloe's mind, and she exclaimed, "What happened to the wife? I mean, suddenly she doesn't matter?"

"Gianni's wife's dead, Chloe. She died a few years ago, but they were separated, and had been for a number of years."

"You said he had a family . . . "

"Yes, Gianni had two sons. Carlo and Francesco. Sadly, Francesco was killed in a car crash. Carlo lives in Rome, he runs the Rome office of Caracelli Industries."

"Does he . . . have a daughter?"

"You're his only daughter, Chloe."

Chloe was silent, digesting this, and then she asked, "Where did the name Lane come from, Mom?"

Stevie couldn't help smiling. "I told you a moment ago, your father always stayed at the Dorchester when he came to see me in London. He used the name Lane, as in Park Lane, when he phoned me. It seemed the obvious name to use on your birth certificate." Stevie rose, walked over to Chloe, and put her arm around her daughter. "I'm sorry I kept the two of you apart all these years, truly sorry. Can you ever forgive me?"

Chloe looked at her mother and unexpectedly tears filled her eyes. "*Forgive you?* Mom, for God's sake, there's nothing to forgive. You're the best mother anybody could ever have. You did what you had to do all those years ago, did what you thought was best for me. And I'm sure it was. I love you, Mommy, there's nobody like you in this whole wide world."

Stevie swallowed her incipient tears, and replied, "I think we ought to be going. To meet your father. He's waiting for us."

"Did he just arrive?"

"No, he came with me yesterday afternoon. Or, rather, I should say I came with him. I flew to London with him on his plane."

"He has a plane. Wow! Neat! Does he fly it himself?"

"No, he has a pilot. Mind you, he's quite the sportsman. You'll like him, Chloe, and you'll grow to love him very quickly."

Chloe hesitated before asking very quietly, "But will he like me, Mom? Will he love me?"

"He already does."

Gianni Caracelli stood up when he saw Stevie appear in the doorway of the Grill Room in the Dorchester Hotel. To his utter amazement, his heart began to thunder in his chest. And his throat tightened with emotion as he watched Stevie and Chloe walk toward the table. What a beautiful girl she was. She not only resembled him, she had a strong look of Francesco. For a split second he was so moved, he thought he would disgrace himself by weeping in a public place. His feelings were very strong; for his dead son, so beloved by him, for this young woman whom he did not know, and who was about to enter his life.

And then they were standing there in front of him.

His beautiful Steffie, the love of his heart, and his daughter. His only daughter. *Chloe.* He was unable to tear his eyes away from her face. They took in every detail of her appearance. She smiled at him, and without any hesitation stepped nearer to him, touched his arm, looked up at him. Her dark brown eyes were twin reflections of his own.

Automatically, Gianni drew closer himself. He embraced her, held her tightly against him. Flesh of my flesh, he thought. My child. He was thankful she was here.

Chloe clung to him for a second. He could not help thinking that he might never have known this extraordinary moment if she had not come out of the coma. She could have died without his ever meeting her.

His heart was suddenly full to overflowing. He thought: God takes so much away from us, but He gives back. And then he looked toward Stevie, filled with gratitude that she had come to see him in Milan. That action in itself had taken courage, for she had no knowledge of the circumstances of his life. Nor had she known how he would react. He was wrong there; of course she had known. No one in the world had ever understood him the way she had. What a fool he had been, never to have gone looking for her years ago.

Quite unexpectedly, Gianni experienced a feeling of peace flowing through him as he held Chloe in his arms. Oh, the blessed peace of it, to have this child. *His daughter.* It was the first peace he had known since Francesco had been killed.

Releasing Chloe, he turned to Stevie, took hold of her arm, kissed her on the cheek, then pulled out the chair for her.

The waiter saw Chloe into her seat and disappeared.

"I see that introductions are not necessary," Stevie murmured, and she smiled at him.

"No, they are not, Steffie." He smiled in return.

Chloe was as fascinated by Gianni as he had been by her. She stared at him quite unselfconsciously. "You look like I thought you would."

He glanced over at Stevie quizzically. And then his eyes swung back to his daughter. He frowned. "I thought you did not know of my existence."

"I didn't. But as I just told Mom this morning, I always *felt* my father was alive. I can't explain why. And I pictured him as being tall, dark, and handsome. And you are."

He laughed, amused by her forthrightness. "Thank you for the compliment. Unfortunately, I knew nothing about your existence, so you have the advantage. But you are lovely, Chloe. And a Caracelli. So like your half brother, Francesco. As he was at your age."

"Mom told me." She touched his arm. "I'm sorry."

He nodded. To Stevie he went on. "I ordered champagne. I hope that is all right. After all, this is a celebration. It's not every day that a man finds a beautiful daughter he did not know he had."

The waiter materialized with the champagne, and within minutes they were toasting each other. Gianni lifted his glass, beamed at them both. "To the two of you. I am so glad we are here together today. It's a happy occasion for me."

"And for us . . . to you, Gianni," Stevie said.

"To you . . . Father." Chloe said this hesitantly. "May I call you Father? Or should I call you Gianni?"

"No, not Gianni. I prefer Father. That is who I am."

"Yes, *Father*." Chloe looked at him closely, her head held on one side, her face reflective. "I've never called anyone that before . . . I never had a father. Only grandfathers."

Stevie stifled a gasp, and she looked stricken. "Oh, Chloe, I didn't—"

"No, Mommy. No," Chloe interrupted swiftly. "Don't be upset. I didn't mean it the way it came out. You know how much I love you."

Stevie realized Chloe was becoming agitated, and she said calmly, softly, "I know, darling, it's all right."

Turning to Gianni, Chloe confided, "She was a father to me as well as a mother. And she's always been wonderful. She saved my life, you know. She stayed with me night and day when I was in Leeds Infirmary. She never left me until I came out of the coma. I might not have lived if it hadn't been for Mommy. She's the best mother in the world."

"Yes, I know that," he answered. "I remember what a good mother she was to your brothers when they were small." Gianni laughed. "You do not have to tell me anything about Steffie. But I would like to know more about you. I understand you have been attending Brearley. Do you like it there?"

"Yes, I do," Chloe exclaimed, and in the same natural way she had greeted him, she began talking to him about school, regaling him with anecdotes.

Stevie interrupted her only once so that they could all order lunch. After they had done so, Chloe went on talking to Gianni nonstop. He nodded and listened, so obviously delighted with her.

Making up for lost time, Stevie thought as she listened to Chloe, surreptitiously studying Gianni Caracelli at the same time. There was no question in her mind that she felt the same way about him as she had eighteen years before. She could not help wondering how he felt about her. Did he, too, have a stomach full of butterflies when he was close to her, did he feel the electricity when they were together, as she did?

"I had a wonderful idea last night, Steffie," Gianni said, cutting into her thoughts.

"Oh, what was that?"

"I would like to invite Chloe and you to come to Lake Como. To stay with me at the villa. It would help her to fully recuperate, do you not think?"

Chloe's eyes widened. "It *is* a wonderful idea . . . Father. Oh, say yes, Mom. *Please*. I'd love to go."

"I'll have to speak to Mr. Longdon," Stevie replied, and explained to Gianni, "That's the neurosurgeon who operated on Chloe to remove the bullet. He did say she couldn't fly back to the States just yet."

"But this is such a short trip. Less than two hours to Milan. And she would be flying in a private plane. When can you speak with him?" Gianni asked.

"After lunch," Stevie responded.

"Oh, thank you, Mommy." Chloe pushed her chair away from the table and picked up her shoulder bag. "Would you please excuse me for a minute."

After she had gone, Gianni looked at Stevie intently, and said in a quiet voice, "My congratulations, you've done a wonderful job with her, brought her up so well. She is a credit to you, Steffie. Bright, self-confident, very natural, and not in the least precocious." He paused and shook his head sadly. "And you did it all alone. . . . "

"Not really, I had my mother and Derek, and her brothers. And thank you for the things you said . . . I'm so glad you like her."

"How could I not? She's lovely, so vivacious. I see you in her."

"And I see you, Gianni. I always did."

"Steffie?"

"Yes, Gianni?"

"There's something I wish to ask you." He hesitated, staring at her.

"What is it?"

"I wondered if we could . . . do you think we can be friends again?"

Stevie stared back at him, not sure what he meant, and she stiffened slightly in the chair.

He noticed this and exclaimed, "Please don't misunderstand me. I'm not proposing . . . that we . . . pick up where we left off eighteen years ago. What I meant was, could we be friends, platonic friends? We do have Chloe. I want to get to know her better." And I want to get to know you again, he thought. But you have not changed. You are still my Steffie, still the same inside. And a love like ours never dies. It only lies dormant when the two people involved are separated. *I need you both.*

Stevie had been watching him closely, and suddenly she understood. She knew with absolute certainty that he still loved her, and just as much as she loved him. Leaning across the table, she said softly, "Of course we can be friends, Gianni, I want that too."

He nodded. She was the only woman he had ever truly loved and, miraculously, she had come back into his life again. He was afraid to speak for a moment, so touched was he.

Stevie saw his love for her spilling out of his eyes, and she felt a surge of happiness like she had not known since she had left him. She touched his hand, which rested on the table. "Let's not waste any more years, Gianni. Let's be the *best* of friends." Her misty gray-green eyes held his.

Returning her steadfast gaze, he took hold of her hand. Bringing it to his lips, he kissed it lightly, and then he smiled at her. "Oh, yes, the *very* best of friends, my Steffie. My heart."

A Sudden Change of Heart

For Bob, with my love

AUTHOR NOTE

Two paintings described in this novel do not exist in real life. *Tahitian Dreams*, by Paul Gauguin, is part of the imaginary collection of Sigmund and Ursula Westheim, fictional characters from my novel *The Women in his Life*, who were victims of the Holocaust in that novel. Sir Maximilian West, their son and heir, and claimant of the invented painting, is another fictional character from the same book. *Moroccan Girl in a Red Caftan Holding A Mandolin*, by Henri Matisse, is part of the imaginary collection of Maurice Duval, a fictional character in this novel. I took literary licence and invented the two paintings for the dramatic purpose of the story, and because I did not want to name real paintings by Gauguin and Matisse. I have no wish to make it appear that actual paintings by Paul Gauguin and Henri Matisse are under any kind of dispute, or in jeopardy.

Barbara Taylor Bradford
New York 1998

CONTENTS

PROLOGUE

Summer

1972

PROLOGUE

The girl was tall for seven, dark haired, with vivid blue eyes in an alert, intelligent face. Thin, almost wiry, there was a tomboy look about her, perhaps because of her slimness, short hair, restless energy and the clothes she wore. They were her favourite pieces of clothing; her uniform, her grandmother said, but she loved her blue jeans, white T shirt and white sneakers. The sneakers and T shirt were her two vanities. They must always be pristine, whiter than white, and so they were constantly in the washing machine or being replaced.

The seven-year-old's name was Laura Valiant, and she was dressed thus this morning as she slipped out of the white clapboard colonial house on the hill, raced across the lawns and down to the river flowing through her grandparents' property. This was a long wide green valley surrounded by soaring hills near Kent, a small rural town in the northwestern corner of Connecticut. Her grandparents had come to America from Wales many years ago, in the 1920s, and after they had bought this wonderful verdant valley they had given it the Welsh name of Rhondda Fach ... the little Rhondda, it meant.

Once she reached the river Laura slowed her pace as she usually did, meandering along the edge, walking under the branches of the weeping willows that dripped down over the water. She paused for a moment to watch the wildlife here. There were ducks circling around on the surface of the water; it was a whole family, with a mother duck nosing her ducklings along; and there were several Canada geese searching around for food on the edge of the lawn nearby. Laura scanned the river, her hand over her eyes shading the sun, as she sought out the blue heron. It was not here today, but it often came and strutted along the far bank, a proud bird. She couldn't help laughing out loud as she watched the mother duck tending her babies. What a fuss the mother was making.

Moving on, Laura hoisted the string bag slung across her body, and made for the drystone wall and the copse where giant oaks and maples grew in abundance. Years before when *he* was a boy, her father and his siblings had built a tree house in one of the giant oaks. It had remained intact, and it was Laura's favourite spot, just as it had been for other young Valiants before her.

Laura was a strong girl for her age, athletic, agile and full of boundless energy. Within seconds she had scrambled up the rope ladder which dropped down from the fork in the branches where the tree house was built.

Scrambling inside the little house, she made herself comfortable in her leafy lair, sat cross-legged, gazing out at the early morning sky. It was six o'clock on this bright and sunny July day and no one else was up, at least not in the house. Tom, the caretaker who ran the farm, was outside one of the red barns near his cottage cleaning a piece of farm machinery. She had seen him out of the corner of her eye as she had run across the lawns a few minutes earlier.

Laura sniffed. Tom had cut the lawns yesterday, and she loved the smell of the newly-mown grass and of new-mown hay. She loved *everything* about Rhondda Fach, much preferred it to New York, where she lived with her parents and her brother Dylan.

Imperceptibly, Laura's young face changed as she thought of her parents. Richard, her father, was a well-known composer and conductor; he was usually travelling somewhere to conduct a symphony orchestra and her mother invariably went along with him. 'Those two are inseparable,' her grandmother would say, but she said it in such a way it sounded like a criticism; Laura understood that it was. And it was also true that they were hardly ever around. When her mother Maggie wasn't travelling, she was painting her famous flower pictures in her studio on the West Side. 'She gets good money for them,' Grandfather Owen kept saying, making excuses for her mother because he was always kind to everyone.

And so it was that Laura and her brother Dylan, three years younger than she, were frequently left in the care of their grand-parents. She loved being with them, they were her favourites, really; she loved her parents, and she was quite close to her father, when he was around to be close to, but most of the time her mother was distant, remote.

Laura thought of the rope ladder which dangled down to the ground, and she moved towards it, intending to pull it up the way her father had shown her, then changed her mind. Nobody was going to invade her private lair. Dylan was too young at four to get much farther than the first few rope rungs, and her friend Claire was afraid to climb up in case she fell. It was true that the ladder was a bit precarious, Laura knew that. She had often offered to help Claire climb up into the tree house, where Claire longed to be, but her friend never had the courage to go beyond the first few steps at the bottom.

Claire was scared of other things even though she was twelve and much more grown up than Laura. She was small, dainty, fragile, and very pretty, with deep green eyes and red hair. 'A Dresden doll,' Grandma Megan called her, and it *was* the most perfect description.

Laura loved Claire. They were the best of best friends even though they were so different. 'Chalk and cheese,' Grandpa Owen said about them; Laura didn't know if she was the chalk or the cheese. Her grandfather encouraged her to be athletic and adventurous; he had taught her to ride a horse, taken her climbing in the hills, given her swimming lessons and instilled in her a confidence in herself. And he had taught her to be unafraid. 'You must always be brave, Laura, strong of heart and courageous, and you must stand tall.'

The problem for Claire was that *she* wasn't at all athletic and she shrank from most physical activity. She couldn't swim and she was unable to ride, being afraid of water, afraid of horses. And yet they were best friends because they shared so many other things, and Claire, despite her physical fragility, had strong mothering instincts. She was warm and loving with Laura and Dylan, and this was especially meaningful to Laura.

Claire was a master storyteller, inventive and imaginative, always weaving yarns, telling them ghost stories and other fantastical tales. They played charades, wrote plays and acted in them, and they shared a love of films and music and clothes. In certain ways, Laura was in awe of Claire. After all, she *was* five years older and knew so much more than they did. Dylan, being only four, didn't know much of anything, and he was very spoilt, in Laura's opinion.

Pulling the strap of the string bag over her head, Laura fished inside for the plastic bottle of orange juice which Fenice, the housekeeper, left for her in the kitchen every morning. After taking a gulp or two, she put the bottle on a small ledge, took her diary from its secret hiding place and began to write her private thoughts, which she did every day.

Soon it began to grow warmer inside the tree house and several times Laura found her eyelids drooping; finally she put down her diary and pen, rested her head against the wall. And although she tried hard to stay awake, she began to doze.

Laura was not sure how long she had been asleep, but quite suddenly she opened her eyes and sat up with a start. Just now she had heard screams coming from somewhere in the distance. Had she been dreaming?

Then she heard it again, a faint scream, and an even fainter voice calling, 'Help! Help!'

It had not been a dream; someone was in trouble. Crawling as fast as she could, Laura backed out of the tree house, bottom first, dangled over the edge until she found her footing on the ladder and climbed down swiftly. She was well practised in this descent and soon reached the ground.

The cries were increasingly fainter, and then they stopped altogether. But Laura knew they had emanated from that part of the river which was wide and deep, beyond the drystone wall, near the meadow where all kinds of wild flowers grew. Sensing it was Claire calling for help, Laura ran at breakneck speed, her long legs flying over the grass. It had to be Claire who was in trouble in the river, Laura was certain. Who else would be in the valley?

Coming to a stop when she saw the flower basket, Laura quickly pulled off her sneakers and jeans, and scrambled down the muddy bank just as Claire's pale face bobbed up above the surface of the water.

'I'm here, Claire!' Laura shouted, dived in and swam towards her friend.

Claire's head went under again, and Laura took several gulps of air and dived once more. At once, she spotted Claire floating underwater.

Swimming to her, Laura grabbed her under the arms and swam them both up to the surface as best she could. She was tall and strong for her age, and she managed somehow. But then when she started swimming them both towards the bank Laura was pulled back along with Claire who was clinging to her.

'It's my foot,' Claire managed to splutter. 'It's caught on something.' Terror etched her stark white face and her eyes were wide with panic.

Laura could only nod. The girl glanced around frantically, wondering what to do. She had to get Claire's foot free from whatever was holding it underwater. Yet she could not let go of Claire, who would sink if she released her. Laura spotted the branch of a tree a short distance away from them. It was a large limb, half on the bank, half in the water, and she was smart enough to know it was probably too heavy for her to lift. But she decided she must attempt to swivel the part which was in the water towards them. If she was successful, Claire could hang onto it, use it as a raft.

Staring at Claire she said, 'I've got to let go of you, Claire, so that –'

'No, no, don't! I'm scared!' Claire gasped.

'I've got to. I'm going to get that branch over there, so that you can hang onto it. Then I'll get your foot loose. When I let go of you, start flapping your arms in the water and keep moving your free leg. You'll stay afloat, you'll be okay.'

Claire was unable to speak. She was terrified.

Laura let go of her, shouted, 'Flap your arms! Move your leg!' Once Claire started to do this, Laura swam upstream in the direction of the branch. It rested on top of the water, and after a bit of tugging and pulling it began to move; unexpectedly, the other end came away from the bank. It flopped into the river with a splash. Grasping the leafy part of the branch, Laura tugged and tugged for a bit longer until it began to float alongside her. Dragging it with her with one hand, she struck out, heading for Claire.

Although she had gone under several times, Claire had kept on moving her arms and leg in the water and had managed to hold her own. As soon as Laura pulled the branch nearer to her, Claire grabbed for it and hung on tightly.

So did Laura, who needed to catch her breath and rest for a few minutes. When she had recouped, she dived underwater, went down to the bottom of the river bed and slowly came up, swam closer to Claire to see what had happened.

Laura was frightened when she saw that Claire's foot was caught in a roll of wire netting, part of which had unravelled. Claire's sneaker was wedged in, entangled with the loose part of the netting. Laura attempted to free her foot, but she could not; nor could she get the sneaker off, try though she did. She floated up to the surface, took several big gulps of air and rested her arms on the branch.

Peering into Claire's worried face, she said, 'I'll have to go and get Tom to help me.'

'Don't leave me,' Claire whispered tremulously, sounding more nervous than ever.

'I have to. Just don't let go of that branch,' Laura instructed and swam across to the river bank.

After hauling herself up out of the water, the girl pulled on her jeans and sneakers, and set off across the meadow. She ran at a good speed, heading for the farm's compound of buildings in search of Tom. When he was nowhere to be found, and knowing there was no time to waste, Laura dashed into his tool shed, found a pair of garden scissors and headed back to the river. After undressing once more, Laura dived into the river, and swam over to Claire who still clung to the tree branch, looking scared.

Showing Claire the garden scissors, Laura explained, 'I can't find Tom. I'm going down, I'm going to cut your sneaker off.'

Claire nodded. She was shaking uncontrollably and goose bumps had sprung up all over her body from being too long in the cold water. Laura dived down into the river, but it was hard for her to reach Claire's foot at first, and she had to try from various angles. Finally, she managed to manoeuvre her right hand and the garden scissors underneath the wire netting. Her first attempt to release the trapped foot was to cut up the front of the laces. She succeeded, but Claire's foot would not come out of the sneaker; after struggling for a few seconds longer Laura had to rise to the surface to breathe in air.

Within minutes she dived down again. This time she cut each side of the sneaker, tugged at Claire's ankle and finally freed her foot. Filled with relief, Laura swam up, flopped against the tree branch, holding onto it and resting, breathing in large gulps of air.

'I'm sorry,' Claire whispered. 'Are you all right, Laura?'

Nodding, Laura continued to rest for a minute or two. Then reaching for Claire, she towed her back to the bank and dragged her up onto the grassy slope.

Both girls were dripping wet and shaking with cold. Although Laura was exhausted, she wasted no time, pulling on her jeans and sneakers swiftly. Supporting each other they made their way back to the house.

Once they reached the back door which led into the kitchen, Laura stopped, and stared at Claire intently. 'Before we go in tell me what happened. How did you get in the river?'

Claire nodded and pushed back her wet hair. Her freckles stood out like dark blotches on her ashen face. 'I was picking wild flowers and got too near the edge of the river, Laura. I suddenly slipped and rolled down the bank into the water. I was scared and I panicked, floundered. I just don't know how I drifted into the middle of the river.'

'Gran says that part of the river is dangerous because there's some sort of current out there. But come on, you're shaking.'

'So are you,' Claire said, her teeth chattering.

Fenice was the first person they saw as they stepped into the big family kitchen.

The housekeeper, tall, red-haired and colourful in her white Austrian blouse and floral dirndl skirt, swung around from the stove as they entered. She gasped out loud at the sight of them.

'Good Lord! What happened to you two?' she cried rushing towards them. 'A couple of drowned rats, that's how you both look!' She saw they were cold and shaking, most especially Claire, and drew her closer to the big kitchen stove where she was cooking breakfast. Glancing at Laura, Fenice added, 'Get some big towels out of the linen press in the back hall, please, Laura. I'm afraid Claire's a bit worse off than you.'

'Yes, I know she is,' Laura said and ran and did as Fenice asked. She returned with an armful of large towels.

'Come on, Claire, wrap yourself in this and let's get you

upstairs. You too, Laura. What you both need is a hot shower immediately.'

'What happened? What's going on?' Megan Valiant asked from the doorway of the dining room which led directly into the kitchen.

'Claire was picking flowers and she fell into the deep part of the river near the meadow,' Laura explained quickly.

'I would have drowned if Laura hadn't fished me out,' Claire interjected. 'I'm sorry, Grandma Megan, for making trouble.'

Megan Morgan Valiant held herself very still, remembering ... remembering another child, her grandson ... Mervyn, who had drowned in the lake in Connecticut. She felt a chill run through her. But at once she pushed aside her memories, and stared at Claire. She was puzzled by the girl's apology and by the way in which she seemed to cower next to Laura, as if seeking protection.

Hurrying across to the two girls huddled together near the big range, Megan looked them over quickly and said in a brisk tone, 'Neither of you seem to be too much the worse for wear, but you'd better go upstairs and have a shower, as Fenice suggested. And Fenice, please put the kettle on, I think the girls need something hot to drink. Grandpa Owen's miner's tea, that'll do the trick.'

'No sooner said than done, Mrs V.' Fenice went to get the kettle, filled it with water at the sink and put it on the stove.

'Come on, Claire,' Laura said, shepherding her friend out of the kitchen.

Megan followed the two young girls, still pondering Claire's demeanour. No wonder she seems frightened, Megan thought, she's had a terrible scare. Falling into the river must have terrified her, since she can't swim. It struck Megan that Claire might well be suffering from shock, and she wondered whether to call the doctor. Perhaps Claire ought to be taken over there to see him. Laura also looked pale, and she was shivering, but otherwise there didn't seem to be too much wrong with her granddaughter.

Climbing the stairs behind them, Megan remarked, 'I see you lost a sneaker, Claire.'

'It's in the river, Gran,' Laura said, glancing over her shoulder.

'I see. Never mind, we'll drive over to Kent later and buy you another pair, Claire.'

'It doesn't matter,' Claire answered rapidly. 'I have my sandals with me.'

'Sneakers are useful in the country, comfortable, and they'll be a gift from me,' Megan told her as they reached the landing at the top of the stairs. 'Now, girls, into the shower both of you.'

Claire hurried off to the blue-and-white bedroom where she always stayed, and Laura went into hers.

Megan followed her granddaughter, and once she had closed the door behind them she said, 'Out of those wet clothes at once and into the shower, Laura. Later you can tell me exactly what happened.'

'But I *have* told you, Gran.'

'Claire could be suffering from shock,' Megan said. 'I think I ought to drive you *both* over to Dr Tomkins.'

'We're both okay, Gran,' Laura protested.

'I'm going to pop along to Claire's room, I want to see how she's feeling.'

'Yes, Gran,' Laura said and went into the bathroom.

Megan knocked on the door of Claire's room and when there was no answer she went in. From the bathroom she could hear the sound of water running in the shower. Turning, she caught sight of herself in the mirror hanging on the wall above the antique French chest.

Pausing for a moment, Megan smoothed her hand over her dark chestnut hair and then straightened the collar of her pale blue shirt. Leaning closer, she stared at herself. How white her face was. But that was no surprise. Claire's misadventure had upset her greatly, even though she had not let the girls see this. Laura had not yet given her the details of the accident, but obviously they had been in a precarious situation. And Laura had put herself at risk because she had run to Claire's rescue.

The wide part of the river was dangerous, and the outcome might have been very different. Megan shivered and goose bumps flew up her arms as she realized how terrible the consequences might have been. Little Mervyn . . . he hadn't been so lucky when he had fallen into the lake . . .

She walked across the floor, stood gazing out of the window for a moment, waiting for Claire to emerge. At sixty-seven, Megan Morgan Valiant was a beautiful woman. Tall and slender, she held herself erect, and in her carriage and deportment she was very much the great Broadway musical star. Although the colour of her rich chestnut hair needed help from her hairdresser these days, it was, nevertheless, thick and luxuriant; her face was relatively free of wrinkles and had remained youthful. Her eyes were her most arresting feature. They were a deep vivid blue, large and set wide apart. Her granddaughter had inherited them, as well as her height and colouring. Lithe and full of energy, Megan was a woman who had remained young in spirit. Her career in the theatre was somewhat curtailed these days, through choice, but her popularity as a star had never waned.

'Oh, it's you, Grandma Megan,' Claire said, sounding surprised as she stepped into the bedroom wrapped in a towel. 'I'm feeling better after my shower. And *warmer*.'

Megan nodded. 'But perhaps we *should* go and see the doctor in Kent –'

'No, no, I don't need a doctor,' Claire interrupted. 'I'm fine, honestly I am.'

'What happened? Why did you venture into the river when you can't swim, Claire dear?'

'I didn't. I fell in. I was picking flowers and slipped. I rolled down the bank. And I somehow got swept into the middle, into the deep part of the river.'

'There's some sort of strange current there,' Megan explained. 'And it *is* very dangerous. We've been aware of it for years. You're very lucky Laura was with you.'

'Oh but she wasn't! I was alone. She must've heard me shouting for help. She dived in, but at first she couldn't get me out of the water. My foot was caught in a roll of wire netting. She had to cut my sneaker off.'

'My God, it's worse than I thought! You were very lucky indeed!'

'Yes, I was. I'd better go and dry my hair.' Swinging around, Claire headed back into the bathroom. As she did the towel slipped down at one side, revealing part of her body.

'Claire, whatever happened to your back?' Megan exclaimed, staring at the yellow bruises under her shoulder blade.

'I must have hurt myself when I fell into the river,' Claire muttered, pulling the towel around herself swiftly.

'Claire, those are old bruises,' Megan answered, her voice gentle but concerned.

'I fell off my bicycle in Central Park,' Claire replied, and disappeared into the bathroom.

A few minutes later Megan found her husband in the dining room, where he was breakfasting on boiled eggs, thin buttered toast and his famous miner's tea, which was very strong and sweet.

'I heard all about it,' Owen said as Megan hurried into the room. 'Fenice told me, and from what she said they're both all right, aren't they, Megan?'

She nodded. 'They are, but it could have been fatal for Claire,' she replied, and then went on to explain what had happened to her.

'Laura's a plucky one, and strong for her age,' Owen exclaimed. 'And thank God she had the presence of mind to jump in and help Claire, rather than running back here for me or Tom. You say Claire's foot got caught in a roll of wire netting. God knows how that came to be in the river. I'll talk to Tom later, and he can lift it out.' Owen gave Megan a pointed look and added, 'But I'm afraid I'm going to insist Claire learns to swim. Laura and I will give her lessons in the swimming pool.'

'That's a good idea . . .' Megan paused, leaned back in her chair and looked off into the distance.

Owen, watching her closely, said slowly, 'I know, I know, my darling, this mishap has brought back bad memories for you . . . you've been thinking of poor little Mervyn.'

'Yes, I have,' Megan answered, her voice as quiet as his. Sitting up straighter, finding a smile, Megan went on, 'I think I'll have a cup of tea. I need it after all this.' As she spoke she reached for the teapot and poured herself a cup.

Owen said, 'I'm glad I helped Laura to become an athlete. It's served her well, and will in the future.'

'Laura's always been brave, Owen, even when she was a small child. And quick thinking, as well.'

'She idolizes Claire,' Owen remarked, thinking out loud. 'She'll always rush to her rescue whatever the circumstances.'

'I know.' Megan sighed and looked across at Owen.

'What is it?' he asked, frowning. 'You look troubled.'

'Claire's back is covered with old bruises.'

'What?' He sounded startled.

'I saw them when she came out of the shower. She said she'd fallen off her bicycle in the park,' Megan explained.

'But you don't believe her?'

'I don't know whether I do or not.'

'I've always thought the Bensons were a bit odd,' Owen said, bringing his hand up to his generous mouth. He rubbed it thoughtfully, his dark eyes narrowing. 'She *could* have fallen, you know.'

'Yes . . .' Megan was silent, but eventually she said, 'I hope you and I live a long time, Owen, so that we can look after Laura and Claire, be there for them.'

Reaching out, he put his hand over hers and smiled at her lovingly. 'So do I. But remember this . . . those two will always be there for each other.'

PART ONE

Winter

1996

1

Whenever she was in Paris on business and had an hour or two to spare, Laura Valiant inevitably headed for the Musée d'Orsay in the seventh arrondissement on the Left Bank.

Today was such a day. The moment her lunch with two prominent art-dealers from the Galerie Theoni was over, she thanked them, promised to be in touch about the Matisse, and said her goodbyes.

Leaving the Relais Plaza, she crossed the lobby of the Plaza Athénée Hotel and stepped out onto the avenue Montaigne.

There were no cabs on the rank in front of the hotel and none in sight, so she decided to walk. It was a cold December day with a hint of rain in the air. She shivered and shrugged further into her black overcoat.

Laura was dressed entirely in black, from the topcoat to her smart woollen suit underneath and soft leather boots that stopped just short of the knee. Her jet-black hair, styled in a short, sleek cut, accentuated both her pale face and her eyes of a blue so brilliant they seemed supernatural. A slender tall young woman, she looked much younger than her thirty-one years.

Laura was a striking figure as she hurried along; many a male head turned. But she did not notice those admiring glances, so intent was she in her purpose.

She lifted her head and looked up at the sky. It was leaden and grey this afternoon; a watery sun was trying to push through the clouds without much success. But the weather was irrelevant here. To Laura, Paris was a city full of nostalgia and memories, memories happy and sad ... so much had happened to her here.

First love – oh, how she had loved him and willingly lost her virginity at eighteen – and first heartbreak, when he had said it was over and had left her with such sudden abruptness that she had been stunned. And oh, the terrible jealousy when she had gone to see him a few days later and found him in bed with another girl. But there was more self-love than love in jealousy, de la Rochefoucauld had written long ago; she had taken those wise words to heart on that awful day and made them her own personal motto over the years. And she *had* fallen in love again, more than once, even though she had believed she never would. Miraculously, or so it had seemed to her at the time, she had eventually recovered from her broken heart to discover that there were other attractive young men in the world, and many were available.

It was her mother who had first brought her to Paris when she was twelve, and she had been captivated. At the age of eighteen she had returned to study art history and literature at the Sorbonne. In the two years she had lived in Paris as a student she had come to know it as well as she knew New York, where she had been born and raised. Whether shrouded in spring rain, wrapped in the airless heat of summer or coated with winter snow, Paris was the most beautiful of cities.

City of Light, City of Lovers, City of Gaiety, City of Artists ... it had so many names. But no matter what people chose to call it, Paris was a truly magical place. She had never lost her fascination with it, and whenever she came back she immediately fell under its spell once again.

Mostly, Laura thought of Paris as the City of Artists, for had they not all worked and lived here at one time or another, those great painters of the nineteenth and twentieth centuries? Whatever their origins and from wherever they sprang, they had eventually come here, armed with their palettes and brushes and paints, and their soaring talent. Gauguin, Van Gogh, Renoir, Manet, Monet, Matisse, Cézanne, Vuillard, Degas, Sisley and Seurat. The Impressionist and Post-Impressionist painters she most admired, and in whose work she was an expert, had all converged on Paris to make it their home, if only for a short while.

The world of art was *her* world, and it had been for as long as she could remember. She had inherited her love of art from her mother Maggie Valiant, a well-known American painter who had studied at the Royal College of Art in London and the École des Beaux Arts in Paris.

But Laura was the first to admit she lacked her mother's talent and vision as a painter, and when she was in her early teens painting became an avocation rather than her vocation. Nonetheless, she had decided she wanted to work with art once she had finished her studies, and after her graduation from the Sorbonne she did stints with several galleries in Paris before returning home to the States. Once back in New York, she did gallery work again, and then completed a rewarding four years at the Metropolitan Museum of Art.

One of her superiors at the museum, impressed by her unerring eye, superb taste, and knowledge of art, encouraged her to become an art-adviser. And so three years ago, at the age of twenty-eight, she and Alison Maynard, a colleague at the Metropolitan, had started their own company. The two of them had made a great success of this venture, which they had named Art Acquisitions. She and Alison bought art for a number of wealthy clients, and helped them to create collections of some significance. Laura loved her career; it was the most important thing in her life, except for her husband Doug, and the Valiants.

A few days ago she had flown to Paris from New York, hoping to find paintings for one of their important clients, a Canadian newspaper magnate. Unfortunately, she had not found anything of importance so far, and she and Alison had agreed on the phone that she would stay on a bit longer to continue her search. She had a number of appointments, and she was hopeful she would find something of interest and value in the coming week.

Increasing her pace, Laura soon found herself turning onto the rue de Bellechasse, where the Musée d'Orsay was located not far from the Eiffel Tower and Les Invalides. She had made it from the hotel faster than she had expected, and as she went into the museum she experienced a little spurt of excitement. Inside were some of her favourite works of art.

The museum was deserted and this pleased Laura; she disliked crowds when she was looking at paintings. It was really dead this afternoon, so quiet you could hear a pin drop. The only sound was the click of her heels on the floor; her footsteps echoed loudly as she walked towards the hall where the Renoirs hung.

She stood for a long time in front of *Nude in Sunlight*. Renoir had painted it in 1875, and yet it looked so fresh, as if he had created it only yesterday. How beautiful it was; she never tired of looking at it. The pearly tints and pink-blush tones of the model's skin were incomparable, set off by the pale, faintly blue shadows on her shoulders which seemed to emanate from the foliage surrounding her.

What a master Renoir had been. The painting was suffused with light – shimmering light. But then to her, Renoir's canvases always looked as though his brush had been dipped in sunlight. Lover of life, lover of women, Renoir had been the most sensual of painters, and his paintings reflected this, were full of vivid, pulsating life.

Laura moved on, stopped to gaze at a much larger painting, *Dancing at the Moulin de la Galette*. It represented gaiety and young love, and there was so much to see in it – the faces of the dancers, merry, sparkling with happiness, the handsome young men, their arms encircling the beautiful girls; how perfectly Renoir had captured their *joie de vivre*. His use of colour was superb: the blues and greens in the trees, the blues and creams and pinks in the girls' dresses, the soft, clear yellow of the men's straw boaters, and the . . .

'Hello, Laura.'

Believing herself to be alone with the Renoirs, Laura jumped when she heard her name. Startled, she swung around. Surprise registered on her face, and she froze.

The man who stood a few feet away from her, went on, 'It's Philippe, Laura. Philippe Lavillard.' He smiled, took a step towards her.

Laura recoiled imperceptibly. Dislike and a flick of anger curdled inside her.

The man was thrusting out his hand, still smiling warmly.

Reluctantly, Laura took it, touching her fingers quickly to his and then pulling them away. This man had always spelled disaster and trouble. She could hardly believe he had run into her like this.

'I thought you were in Zaire,' she managed to say at last, wondering how to get rid of him. There was a slight pause before she added, 'Claire told me you were . . . living in Africa.'

'I am. I arrived in Paris a couple of days ago. Actually, I'm en route to the States. I'm going to see the head of the CDC.'

'The CDC?' she repeated, sounding puzzled.

'The Center for Disease Control. In Atlanta. I have some meetings there.'

'Claire mentioned you were working on Ebola in Zaire.'

'And other hot viruses.'

Laura nodded, tried to edge away.

He said, 'Are you staying in Paris long, Laura?'

'No.'

'How's the famous Doug?'

'He's well, thanks.'

'This is one of my favourites,' Philippe Lavillard began, looking intently at *Dancing at the Moulin de la Galette*, then gesturing towards it. 'I think I favour it because it's so positive. There's so much life in it, such happiness, don't you think, such hope and expectation in their faces, and a sort of quiet exuberance, even innocence –' Abruptly he cut himself off, and glanced to his right.

Laura followed his gaze, saw a woman approaching. As she drew closer, Laura realized, with a sudden flash of recognition, that it was Philippe's mother: a dumpy middle-aged woman in a maroon wool dress, with a black coat flung over her shoulders. She was carrying a handbag on one arm and holding a Galeries Lafayette shopping bag in her hand. She moved at a measured pace.

A second later, Rosa Lavillard was standing next to her son, staring at Laura with undisguised curiosity.

Philippe said, 'You remember Laura Valiant, don't you, Mother?'

'Oh yes, of course,' Rosa Lavillard responded in a cool tone. 'Good afternoon.' Rosa's lined face was impassive, impenetrable; her pale eyes were frosty, and there was a degree of hostility in her manner.

'Hello, Mrs Lavillard, it's been a long time,' Laura answered, recalling the last time she had seen her. At the wedding. Trying to be polite, she added, 'I hope you're well.'

'I am, thanks. Are you here on vacation?' Rosa asked.

'No, this is a business trip.'

'Laura's an art-adviser, Mother,' Philippe explained, glancing down at Rosa and then across at Laura. 'She helps people to select and buy paintings.'

'I see. You like Renoir, do you?' Rosa murmured.

'Very much. He's a great favourite, and I try to come here whenever I'm in Paris,' Laura replied.

'Such beauty,' Rosa remarked, looking about her. 'All these Renoirs . . . they nourish the soul, calm the heart. And they are reassuring . . . these paintings tell us there is something else besides ugliness out there. Yes, such beauty . . . it helps to baffle the clamour of cruelty.' She waved a hand in the air almost absently, peered at Laura and asked, 'Do you like Van Gogh?'

'Oh yes, and Degas and Cézanne, and Gauguin, he's another favourite.'

'His primitives are deceptive. They appear simple yet they are not, they are complex. Like people.' Rosa nodded her head. 'It's obvious the Impressionists appeal to you.'

'Yes, that's my area of expertise. The Post Impressionists, as well.'

'I like them myself. If I had a lot of money that's what I would do, how I would spend my life. I would collect paintings from the Impressionist school. But I am just a poor woman, and so I must make do with going to museums.'

'Like most other people, Mother,' Philippe pointed out gently.

'That's true,' Rosa agreed, and turning, she began to walk away, saying over her shoulder, 'Enjoy the Renoirs.'

'I will,' Laura said. 'Goodbye, Mrs Lavillard.'

Rosa made no response.

Philippe inclined his head, gave her a faint half-smile, as if he were embarrassed. 'Nice to see you again, Laura. So long.'

Laura nodded, but said nothing.

He stared at her for a moment, then he swung on his heels and followed his mother out of the hall.

Laura stood watching the Lavillards depart, and finally went back to her contemplation of the Renoirs. But the Lavillards had ruined her mood. Their intrusion on her privacy had brought too many memories rushing back, and most of them bad memories. Suddenly she felt nervous, unsettled, unable to concentrate on the paintings. But she didn't want to leave the museum just yet; she might not have another chance to come back during this trip to Paris.

Glancing around, Laura spotted a small bench placed against the far wall, and she went and sat down, still thinking about the Lavillards. What a strange woman Rosa Lavillard was. She remembered a few things Claire had told her years ago, mainly that Rosa was unpredictable, a sick woman who had been hospitalized for long periods. Hadn't Claire said she had once been in a mental institution?

From what Laura now remembered hearing, Rosa had led a troubled life . . . there had been a painful childhood in France, growing up during the war, the loss of her family in the Allied bombing raids, later a volatile marriage to Pierre Lavillard, then emigration to the States in the 1950s, where Philippe was born. Their only child. The doctor. The prize-winning virologist whom the medical world called a genius.

Claire had once said in a moment of anger that Rosa was a crazy woman, and should have been kept in the mental hospital. She had been very vehement about it at the time.

Laura closed her eyes, her thoughts settling on Claire Benson: her best friend and confidante, the elder sister she had never had, her role model. Claire had been living in Paris for a number of years, which was one of the reasons she liked to come here, to spend time with Claire.

Opening her eyes, Laura stood up. She began to stroll down the long gallery, determinedly pushing aside all thoughts of the Lavillards, mother and son. Within seconds she had forgotten them, once more enjoying the Renoirs hanging there. Soon she was lost in the paintings, soothed by their beauty.

And then once again she was no longer alone. Unexpectedly, there was Claire standing by her side, taking hold of her arm.

'What are you doing here?' Laura exclaimed, startled to see her friend, filling with a rush of anxiety. Oh God, had Claire run into the Lavillards? She hoped not; they usually upset her. She searched Claire's face, looking for signs.

Claire explained, 'You told me you were coming to the museum after your lunch, so I thought I'd join you.' She peered at Laura. 'What's wrong? You look odd.'

'Nothing, I'm fine,' Laura answered. 'You took me by surprise, that's all.' She was relieved to see that Claire was calm;

obviously she *had* missed the Lavillards. But probably only by a few moments. Forcing a smile, she went on, 'So, come on then, let's walk around together.'

Claire tucked her arm through Laura's. 'I like seeing paintings through your eyes. Somehow I get much more pleasure from them when I'm with you.'

Laura nodded, and they moved on, gazing at the masterpieces on the walls, not speaking for a short while. At one moment, Laura lingered in front of a painting of a mother and child, frowning slightly.

Claire, always tuned into her best friend, said, 'Why are you looking so puzzled?'

Shaking her head, Laura replied, 'I've often wondered lately if any of these paintings are stolen –'

'Stolen! What do you mean?' Claire asked.

'Thousands and thousands of paintings were stolen by the Nazis during the war, and that art, looted by them, hangs on museum walls all over the world. It's from some of the world's greatest collectors, such as the Rothschilds, the Kanns, and Paul Rosenberg, who once owned one of the most prestigious galleries in Paris, to name only a few.'

'I read something about that recently. I guess it's hard for the heirs of the original owners to get their paintings back if they don't have proof of ownership.'

'That's it exactly. And so many records were lost during the war. Or were purposely destroyed by the Nazis in order to blur provenance.' Laura grimaced, and said, 'A lot of museums are fully aware of the real owners, because many of the paintings are coded on the back of the canvases. It all stinks. It's morally wrong, but try and get a museum to give a painting up, give it back. They just won't . . . At least, most of them won't . . . Some are starting to get nervous, though.'

'Can't any of the original owners sue the museums?' Claire asked.

'I suppose they could,' Laura answered. 'But only if they have proof a painting is theirs. And even then it's dubious that they'd ever get it.'

Claire nodded, 'I remember now, Hercule knows something about this ... He mentioned it only recently. I believe he has a client who is the heir to art stolen by the Nazis from his family in 1938.'

'Oh, who is it?'

'I don't know ... He didn't say.'

'A great deal of the looted art is in private hands, and try and get *them* to give it back. They never will, not when they've paid millions for it. There's going to be a lot of trouble in the next few years, now that it's all coming to light. You'll see.'

Claire said, 'You're repeating what Hercule was telling me not long ago. Maybe you should talk to him about it.'

'I'd like that.'

'Maybe we can get together with him this weekend. Anyway, do you represent someone with a claim to stolen art?' Claire asked curiously.

'Not at the moment, but I may well do so in the not too distant future.'

They fell silent as they continued to stroll around the museum, at ease with each other. Laura, forever worried about Claire, stole a quick look at her. In her years of living in Paris Claire had acquired a certain kind of chic that was uniquely French. This afternoon she wore a dark purple wool coat, calf length and tightly belted, over matching pants and a turtleneck sweater. The purple enhanced Claire's large green eyes and auburn halo of curls. Big gold hoop earrings and a dark red shoulder bag were her only accessories, and she looked stylish, well put together. Laura admired Claire's style, which seemed so natural and uncontrived.

Glancing at Laura, Claire came to a halt and said, 'I'm glad you're in Paris for a while, Laura, I miss you.'

'I miss you too,' Laura answered swiftly.

Looking at her watch, Claire went on, 'I think I'd better be getting back to the photographic studio. I'm doing a shoot for the magazine, as you know, and Hercule's coming over later. I need his advice about one of my sets.'

'He's turned out to be a good friend,' Laura said. 'Hasn't he?'

'Yes. But not my *best* friend. That's you, Laura Valiant. Nobody could take your place.'

Laura squeezed Claire's arm. 'Or yours,' she said.

Laura heard the phone ringing above the sound of the water pouring into the bath, and she reached for the receiver on the wall.

'Hello?'

'Hi, sweetie.'

'Doug! Hello, darling.' She sat down on the small bathroom stool near the make-up table, and glanced at her watch. It was six here. Noon in New York.

Her husband said, 'I called you earlier but you weren't there. I'm off to lunch with a client in a few minutes, and I wanted to catch you before you went out again.'

'It's such a clear line, you sound as if you're around the corner!' she exclaimed warmly, happy to hear his voice.

'I wish I were.'

'So do I. Listen, I've got a great idea! Why don't you come in for the weekend? Tomorrow's Friday, couldn't you take it off and fly over? It *would* be lovely, Doug.'

'Wish I could, but I can't,' he answered, his voice changing slightly, growing suddenly brisk, businesslike. 'That's another reason I'm calling you, I have to fly to the coast tomorrow. Meetings with the Aaronson lawyers. The merger's on, after all.'

'*Oh.* It's unexpected, isn't it?'

'Yep, it sure is. But what can I do, I'm needed out there.'

'Never mind. But it would have been nice to have you in Paris if only for a couple of days.'

'Sorry, darling, it can't be helped. When do you think you'll be back?'

'I have appointments set up for the early part of next week, Doug, so I'll probably leave for New York on Thursday or Friday.'

'Great! You'll be here next weekend, and so will I. This is probably going to be a quick trip to LA. In and out.'

'Where are you staying?'

'Er, the Peninsula, in Beverly Hills, as usual.'

'Doug?'

'Yes?'

'I've really missed you this week.'

'I've missed you too, darling. But we'll make up for it, and you know what they say, absence makes the heart grow fonder.'

She laughed. 'I guess it does ... the way I'm feeling right now, I wish you were here ...' She laughed again, a light, infectious laugh.

He laughed with her. 'Got to go, sweetie.'

'When are you leaving tomorrow?'

'My flight's at nine in the morning, and I'm going straight into meetings once I've dropped my luggage off. I'll call you.'

''Bye, darling.'

''Bye, Laura. And a big kiss,' he said, before hanging up.

Laura sat soaking in the bath longer than usual. There had been no cabs on the street when she and Claire had left the museum earlier; they had walked all the way back to the hotel where Claire had finally found a cab.

The water was helping Laura to thaw out and to relax, and she luxuriated in the hot bubble bath for a while, thinking of Doug. She had married Douglas Casson when she was twenty-five and he was twenty-seven. They were a perfect fit, compatible, attuned to each other in the best of ways. But lately he worked too hard. She smiled at this thought. Didn't he say the same thing about her?

To his way of thinking, they were both workaholics, and he seemed to relish announcing this. It was true, of course, but she didn't like that particular word. It smacked of obsessiveness, and she was quite sure neither of them was that. Not exactly.

Anyway, Claire had always said that the ability to work hard for long hours was the most important thing of all, and that this was what separated the women from the girls.

But Laura thought that love was important, too. Hadn't Colette, her favourite writer, once written that love and work were the only things of consequence in life. Certainly she believed this to be so. But Claire didn't – at least not the love part, not anymore. Claire had been burnt. 'And they were third-degree burns, at that,' Claire had said. Those burns had taken a long time to heal. 'Now I have built a carapace around me, and I'll never get burnt again. Or hurt in any way. My shell protects me. Nothing, no one, can ever inflict pain on me.'

Laura loved Claire. She also had enormous compassion for her, because of all the bad things that had happened to her. Laura was well aware that Claire was raw inside; still, she couldn't help wishing her friend would open herself up to love again instead of retreating into her shell the way she did. There was something oddly sterile about a woman's life, if she did not have love in it, if she didn't have a man to cherish and to love.

These days, whenever she broached this subject, Claire only laughed hollowly, and responded swiftly, 'I have Natasha, and she's all that matters. She's my life now, I don't need a man around.'

But a fourteen-year-old daughter wasn't enough, was it? Laura wondered. Surely not for a loving, passionate, intelligent woman like Claire.

Claire. The dearest friend she had ever had. And still her *best* friend, the one she loved the most, even though they lived so far away from each other now. Claire and she went back a long way. Almost all of their lives, really.

She had been five years old when Claire and her parents, Jack and Nancy Benson, had come to live in the apartment opposite theirs in the lovely old building on Park Avenue at Eighty-Sixth

Street. She had instantly fallen in love with her in the way a little girl of five falls in love with a very grown-up ten-year-old. She had worshipped Claire from the start, had emulated her. Once their two families had become acquainted, Claire had taken Laura and Dylan under her wing, had been baby-sitter, pal, and confidante.

Cissy, the Valiant nanny, had had her hands full with Dylan, who was then only two and very naughty. So Claire had been a welcome addition to the Valiant household. An only child, Claire had loved being part of this extended family, especially since Laura's grandparents, Owen and Megan Valiant, were very much in evidence. They all helped to make Claire feel like a very special member of their family.

Because Claire attended Miss Hewitt's School, Laura went there as well. And there came a time when the five years difference in their ages suddenly seemed negligible. As teenagers and young women they were as inseparable as they had been as children, bonded together as sisters in soul and spirit, if not blood.

Claire had married young, at twenty-one, and her daughter Natasha had been born a year later. Two years after that she had moved to Paris with her husband and child. But nothing, not distance, husband or child, had ever come between them or changed the nature of their friendship. Very simply, they loved each other, and, as Claire was wont to say, they would always be sisters under the skin, no matter what.

The sad part was that Claire's life had gone horribly wrong seven years ago. Her marriage had foundered and she had divorced; her parents had died within a few weeks of each other, not long after this, and then Natasha had been in a car crash and had suffered serious injuries. But thanks to Claire's nursing, the girl had made an amazing recovery.

Laura roused herself, pushing herself up in the bath. Here she was daydreaming about the past when she should be getting dressed.

No time to dawdle now.

2

'Don't you like the room, Hercule?' Claire Benson asked, pausing near the grouping of Louis XVth chairs, resting a hand on the back of one of them. 'Is it the chairs? Do you think they're inappropriate? Don't they work?' She shot these questions at him as she glanced down at the silver-leafed wood frame under her hand, and then at the silver-grey upholstery. 'Yes, it *is* the chairs, isn't it?' she asserted. 'Maybe they're totally wrong for the setting.' She looked across at him questioningly.

The Frenchman chuckled. 'Ah, Claire, so many questions you fire, rat-a-tat, and you make the jest, *n'est-ce pas?*'

'No, I'm being serious.'

'The room is superb. *Formidable, oui.* You have the wonderful taste. The furniture, the fabrics you have chosen, this Aubusson rug, everything is perfection. But –'

'But what?' she cut in before he could complete his sentence.

'The room is incomplete, my dear. A room is never finished until it has –'

'Art,' she supplied, and then immediately laughed when she saw the amusement in his face, the twinkle in his eye. 'I need paintings on these walls, Hercule, I know *that*. But what kind of paintings? That's one of the reasons I wanted you to see the setting, to help me make some decisions about art. Shall I use a

Picasso? Or a Gauguin? Or go for a modern work, such as Larry Rivers? A Van Gogh? A Renoir, maybe? On the other hand, I could look for something really old, like a pair of Canalettos.'

'A Van Gogh or a Gauguin would give the room strength, but I do not think it is a strength you require here, Claire. And Canalettos would be wrong. A soft painting would be the ideal choice, something in the pastel tones. It would underscore the stillness, the sense of ... quietude you have created. Also, this space has a light look. Airy. A Renoir, most definitely. *Oui. Parfait.*'

'Perfect, yes, I agree. But where am I going to find one? And who would lend me one for the photography? People don't normally let their Renoirs out of their sight.'

Hercule Junot smiled. 'There is a possibility that I might be able to find one for you. A few months ago, I was shown a Renoir which was for sale –' He paused, shrugged lightly, raised his hands. 'Well, I do not know, *chérie*, perhaps it has been sold.'

'If it hasn't, do you think the owner would agree to lend it to me?' she asked, her face eager.

'*Mais oui*. The owner is a friend, a former client ... I am happy to speak with her. If she still has it, she will allow me to borrow it. For a few hours. If that is enough time for you, Claire. Because of its great value, she would not want to leave the painting here in the studio overnight.'

'And *I* wouldn't want it to be here overnight! Not unless I slept with it. I wouldn't want the responsibility, although we will insure it, of course, even if it's here for only a few hours. Too risky not to.' Claire stepped out of the set, went to join Hercule Junot, who was standing on the studio floor. 'When can you speak to your friend?'

'I shall be happy to telephone her this evening.'

Claire said, 'My lead time is three to four months, as you know, and I'm shooting this for the March issue. It's going to be the cover shot.'

'If she has not sold it, that might be an inducement for her to lend the Renoir. Having the exposure in the magazine could serve a purpose.'

Claire nodded. 'Good thought. What's the painting like?' She grinned. 'Although who needs to know that, a Renoir's a Renoir.'

Hercule's face had lit up at the thought of the painting, and he beamed at her. 'It is beautiful, *bien sûr,* a semi-nude, a bather sitting on a rock. But this is not a large painting, Claire. It would only be suitable to hang over the fireplace or above the console. You will need a larger one . . . for the wall where the sofa is placed.'

'I'm pretty sure I have one already. My assistant found a Seurat at one of the galleries, and they're prepared to lend it to us.'

'That is good. A Seurat will be compatible. It will sit well with the Renoir. I shall telephone you tomorrow, after I've spoken with my friend.' He picked up his dark overcoat, which was thrown over the back of a wooden chair. 'I must return to my *bureau,* Claire. Will you come with me? Can I take you to the magazine? Or are you staying here at the studio?'

'No, I'm not, Hercule. I've finished for today. I'll just have a word with my staff who are still working on another set, and then I'll come with you. I'd love a lift to the Plaza Athénée, if that's not out of your way.'

'*Ce n'est pas un problème,* Claire.'

Claire had known Hercule Junot for twelve years, having met him when she first came to live in Paris as a young bride. They had been seated next to one another at a posh dinner party, and the renowned older man and the unimportant young woman had taken to each other at once. He had found her irreverent, saucy, provocative, and challenging, and her knowledge of art and antiques, coupled with her journalistic flair for telling a good story, had been impressive. She had been the most interesting and entertaining dinner companion he had had in many a year, a sheer delight to be with.

Hercule Junot, who was now seventy-six years old, was one of the most famous interior designers in the world, on a par with his peers Stéphane Boudin, a fellow Parisian, and the Italian, Renzo Mongiardino. Renowned for his elegant and glamorous formal interiors, he had great taste, immense flair, a discerning and critical eye, and was considered to be one of the foremost experts on Fine French Furniture. Another area of his formidable expertise was Impressionism, most especially the paintings of Van Gogh and Gauguin, the latter a great personal favourite.

Rather than lessening as he grew older, his business seemed to be flourishing even more than ever, and he was in constant demand by those who appreciated his extraordinary gift for creating tasteful but eyecatching interiors full of style, wit and comfort; those who had the vast amounts of money required to pay for the antiques and art of the highest pedigree and quality which he favoured in his designs.

Claire had been at a crossroads in her career when they had met. She wanted to continue working as a journalist, but she felt more drawn than ever to the world of visual and decorative arts.

At that first meeting over dinner she had found herself confiding her concerns about her career and the route it should take, and Hercule had made up his mind that he must somehow help her.

The following morning he had talked to a number of influential people, pulled a few strings, and in the process had contrived to get her a job on *Decorative Arts and Design*, a glossy magazine devoted to art, antiques, and interior design which was popular with the French and with the international public. It was owned by a friend of his who had long owed him a favour.

Claire had started out in a most lowly position, that of caption writer, but such was her creative talent and energy that within eight years she had risen to the top of the hierarchy of the magazine.

Four years ago she had been named publisher and editor-in-chief, answerable to no one but the owner. Hercule Junot, not unnaturally, was proud of her success and the name she had made for herself.

In the ensuing years since that first meeting, most propitious for her, these two had remained staunch friends, and Hercule had become her mentor. Claire trusted his judgement about everything in the world of design, and whenever she was doubtful about a project she ran to him for his opinion and advice.

Such had been the case today; a sudden lack of confidence about the set, an unprecedented occurrence for her, had induced her to invite him to the photographic studio to give his opinion.

The set had been painstakingly designed and skilfully installed with the utmost care; nonetheless, she had been unusually critical of her own work when she had seen the finished result. She had also been suddenly hesitant and indecisive about the art she should choose to complete the room.

Hercule had been impressed by the beauty and quality of the formal salon and the splendid choices she had made, and more so than he had actually said. Now he wondered if this had been an error on his part. Perhaps he should have expressed himself more volubly. She was certainly quiet, preoccupied, a silent companion in the Mercedes, and this was most unlike her.

Hercule sighed under his breath, leaned back against the leather upholstery and glanced out of the window. It had snowed earlier, but the light flakes had melted, leaving the dark streets wet and glistening. Under the bright lights of the boulevard du Montparnasse the road looked slick as a mirror, as his chauffeur manoeuvred the car carefully through the busy traffic of the Left Bank.

If he had any regrets about Claire professionally, it was only that he had not brought her to work for him as his assistant all those years ago. She would have been a godsend to him today, the perfect right hand. She had flair and taste, and her skills as a designer were wasted at the magazine; they only came into play when she created a room to shoot for one of the magazine's covers. The rest of the time she was plying her trade as a journalist. *C'est dommage,* he thought. My mistake.

Hercule had one other regret about her, and this was intensely personal. He never ceased to wish he had courted Claire when she and her husband had separated seven years ago. He had wanted to do so, but he had been ... afraid. Yes, afraid of looking foolish ... of being rejected ... of spoiling the friendship. Better to have her in his life as a friend, than not there at all.

There was his age to consider: he was forty years older than Claire. What could she possibly want from him? he had asked himself innumerable times. His late wife Veronica had always said he did not look his age, and he had believed her. He was fit and trim, mercifully not as lined and ancient-looking as some of the men he knew who were his age. Admittedly his hair was white, but it was a full head of hair. And sex was not a problem, not at all.

Initially, he had not pursued Claire or pressed his suit because she had been so distraught at the time of the divorce, a state he had found most odd since she purported to detest her husband. And so time had slipped by, other things had intervened, and the opportunity had been missed. They had fallen into a pattern of loving friendship, and he did not know how to change this without upsetting her unduly.

Veronica had been dead for fifteen years. There was not a day he did not miss his wife; yet he had known, when Claire had separated, that this young American woman could so easily fill the void created by his wife's death. Veronica had been an American too; they had that in common. There any resemblance between them stopped. Veronica had been tall, long-legged, an all-American beauty, blonde, blue-eyed and wafer-thin, one of the great post-war models in Paris, on Christian Dior's runway showing his New Look and on the cover of every fashion magazine in the world. When he had met her it had been love at first sight, a *coup de foudre*, and a most happy union until the day she died.

Hercule stole a look at Claire, surreptitiously, out of the corner of his eye, and for the second time today he thought she did not look well. She had faintly bluish smudges under her eyes, and the short, curly auburn hair, the bright burnished halo he found so attractive, did not have its usual glossy lustre.

What struck him with such force when he had arrived at the studio this afternoon was her weight, or rather loss of it. Always slender, she appeared thinner than ever. *Maigre*. A waif, that was how she appeared to him. An appealing gamin in looks and style, somehow she had become bony. Had she looked like this last week when he had lunched with her at Taillevent? No, she could not have; he would have noticed. He wondered if she were ill? But no, he did not think this was so; she had been full of her usual energy at the studio.

Worries of another nature? Money? If this were the problem then there was no problem. He would readily give her as much as she needed. Instantly, Hercule dismissed the thought that Claire lacked money. The mere idea of it was ludicrous. Her husband provided for Natasha, and she was well paid by the magazine. Could it be that Natasha was causing problems for her? No, no, he did not think this possible either. The girl was unusual, very steady and practical, older than her age in a number of ways. Whenever she had been concerned about her daughter in the past, Claire had discussed it with him and he had given the best advice he could. Since he had never been a father, he felt somewhat inadequate in doing so, and yet how kind she had been, always so appreciative of his interest in Natasha.

He began to formulate an opening sentence in his mind. He wanted to pose certain questions. How he longed to make whatever it was that ailed her go away. He knew he could do that. If she would let him. He loved her. He had loved her for a long time now. He would always love her, and because of this he had the need to ease the burdens of her life, if he could. And if she would permit him to do so. Women, ah, they were so contrary. He was a Frenchman, and he knew about their natures only too well.

Claire had always felt exceptionally comfortable with Hercule Junot, and there was a great sense of ease in their relationship. And so she did not think twice about drifting along with her thoughts, as his car eased its way through the early evening traffic, heading in the direction of the avenue Montaigne.

She considered the older man to be her dearest friend in Paris; and they never stood on ceremony with each other. To Claire, the silence between them was perfectly normal, acceptable; she never felt the need to talk to him, to entertain him. And she knew he felt exactly the same way about her.

She was thinking about Laura; she was looking forward to having dinner with her tonight. Laura was the only family she had, except for Natasha. Her parents were dead; Aunt Fleur was dead; her husband was ostensibly dead since they were long divorced. Momentarily, his face danced before her eyes, but she pushed it away. She did not want to think about him now; it would spoil her evening.

On their walk from the museum she and Laura had planned the weekend. It was going to be fun. Natasha was as excited as she was about Laura's unexpected sojourn in Paris, and without Doug in tow for a change. Not that she minded Doug, he was fine. But having Laura to themselves was a very special bonus.

'Is there something troubling you, Claire?' Hercule asked, cutting into her thoughts.

Turning to look at him, Claire exclaimed, 'No, of course not, Hercule! Why do you think there is?'

'You've been very quiet on our drive across Paris,' he remarked, touching her arm. 'And I have to confess to you, I was most forcibly struck by your appearance this afternoon. You've lost weight, Claire. You're like a . . . a waif.'

'No, wafer-thin!' she shot back, laughing, pleased with her

play on words. 'Remember what the Duchess of Windsor said: "You can never be too rich or too thin."'

'But *you* are *too* thin.'

'I'll confess, Hercule, I've been on a diet. I want to be slender and chic for your New Year's Eve party.'

'You are a lovely young woman; all this dieting is not necessary. Starving, starving, starving, and all for a size four dress. *Mon Dieu*, you could slip through the eye of a needle.'

'It is easier for a camel to go through the eye of a needle than for a rich man to enter into the kingdom of God,' she murmured, smiling at him, grasping one of his hands. 'I first heard those lines from the Bible in that old Tyrone Power movie with Gene Tierney, Anne Baxter and Clifton Webb.'

'*The Razor's Edge*,' he said. 'How could I forget it? Ever. I have seen it a hundred times with you.'

'Not quite a hundred,' she laughed. 'But we're getting there, and I'm fine, Hercule, really I am. Actually, I'm as fit as a fiddle. A bit overworked, that's all. But listen, I want to talk to you about the Renoir. If it's not been sold, Laura might well be interested. For one of her clients. I know she has her heart set on a Matisse and a Bonnard, if she can find them, but why not a Renoir as well? She has several big collectors as clients.'

'I know she does, and that is an excellent idea, Claire. I have a feeling that the painting is still hanging in my friend's house. I am sure she would have told me if she had sold it.' He gave her the benefit of a wide smile, and nodded his head, looking pleased. 'I shall tell the countess there is the possibility of a sale.'

3

'It's going to be like old times this weekend,' Laura said. 'The way it was when I was studying at the Sorbonne, and you'd just arrived here with a husband and a baby. We really had a ball in those days, didn't we?'

Claire laughed. 'Yes, we did. And some baby she is today! Fourteen going on forty, taller than both of us and into make-up, clothes and boys. You'll get a shock when you see her, Laura, she's really sprung up in the last couple of months.'

Laura nodded, settled back against the chair and took a sip of her champagne.

The two women were sitting in Laura's room at the hotel, lingering over their drinks before dinner. In the half hour they had spent greeting each other effusively and discussing the Renoir, the weather had turned nasty. By the time they had been ready to go to Benoît, one of their favourite bistros, it was snowing hard and, according to the door-man, an icy wind had blown up. And so they had agreed it would be much wiser to stay at the hotel and have room service.

'What do you feel like eating?' Laura now asked, picking up the menu on the coffee table. 'I'm going to have *anything* with their *pommes frites*. They make the best, as you well know.' She grinned. 'If I eat too many meals here I'm going to start putting on weight. I just can't resist them.'

'I know what you mean. I'm going to have grilled sole and *pommes frites*, too.'

'That's what I'll have. Want anything first, Claire?'

'Just a green salad. Hercule thinks I look like a waif, far too thin. What do you think? I don't, do I?'

'You're a bit thinner than you usually are, but you look great, Claire, honestly, and very chic. I love you in deep purple. It sets off your red hair.'

'Thanks. I must admit, I have been dieting a bit more strenuously to fit into my dress for Hercule's New Year's Eve party.' She shrugged. 'He gave me a bit of a lecture on the way from the studio. About my weight, I mean.'

'He fusses about you, I know that. But then, he loves you.'

Claire looked at her. 'Like a father, yes, I realize that.'

'Not like a father, *no*. Like a lover, or rather, a potential lover, potential husband.'

'You've got to be kidding!' Claire exclaimed, looking askance. 'Hercule and me. Don't be so silly.'

'I'm not being silly. I've always known he has ... well ... a thing about you, Claire. It's written all over his face. Even Doug has mentioned it to me and more than once.'

'So I'm the last to know, huh?' Claire shook her head vehemently. 'I love him, as a person. He's been wonderful to me always, my best friend in Paris ... but I'm not interested in him ... *romantically*.'

'Because he's too old, you mean?' Laura probed.

'No, age doesn't matter, and in any case he's much younger than a lot of people I know in their thirties, even though he's seventy-six. I'm just not interested in men anymore. I've told you that for years now. Shall we order dinner?'

'Yes, let's, and I'm going to have another champagne. What about you? Another martini?'

'God, no! I'll be drunk. One's enough for me.'

Laura went to the phone, dialled room service, and gave their order. Then she went on carefully, 'Look, just because you had one bad experience doesn't mean you've got to close up shop, close your heart to another man. Okay, so you're not interested in Hercule, but maybe there's somebody else out there who's just right for you, Claire, if only you'd give yourself half a chance –'

'No!' Claire cried softly but emphatically. 'I'm not interested. Marriage is a battlefield, and I have the scars to prove it. I won the war by leaving the battlefield, and I've no intention of putting myself in the line of fire ever again.' She laughed hollowly. 'Being in harm's way is being no place . . . no place at all.'

'Marriage doesn't have to be a battleground,' Laura argued. 'Mine isn't.'

'You've been luckier than most, Laura. You met Doug and fell in love, and somehow, for you, it all went smoothly. No arguments and fights, no big differences of opinion. The two of you perfectly in sync, leading nice, orderly, happy lives together.'

'You make it sound awfully dull!' Laura exclaimed. 'Doug's not all that easy to live with, you know he isn't. He's pernickety, a perfectionist, and he can be very opinionated. And he's a nag! God, he never stops nagging about my having a baby –' Laura broke off and pursed her lips, shook her head. 'That sounds disloyal,' she finished lamely, looking chagrined. She sat back against the sofa.

'I know he nags you about having a child, but it could be his fault you don't get pregnant. Why does he blame you?'

'I don't know, but he does. At least, that's the way it seems to me. We've both been tested again, and there's nothing wrong with either of us, seemingly. But pregnant I'm not.'

'Do you *want* a baby?' Claire asked, looking at Laura intently.

'Yes, I do, I've always wanted a child. But I'm only thirty-one, so there's time. It's not as if I'm ancient, on my last legs.'

'Perhaps Doug's just too uptight about this, Laura,' Claire suggested quietly, her face reflective. 'That often happens. A couple don't make a baby, and they get overanxious and that works against them.'

'I'm not overanxious.'

'No, but perhaps Doug is, darling.'

'Maybe he is. He's certainly highly strung these days.'

'He's going to have to learn to relax.'

Laura laughed. 'Tell that to the marines. *Relax.* My God, he's a bundle of nerves, and always on the go, rushing hither and yon, as Grandma Megan says. She told me recently that Doug doesn't stay still long enough to make a baby.'

Claire burst out laughing. 'Good old Grandma Megan! I must admit, I do miss her pithiness, and her forthrightness. She comes out with some marvellous lines.'

'She told me the other day that her great age gives her licence to say anything she wants. And to anybody, too.'

'Old people are a bit like that. I guess they get to the stage where they don't care anymore. And their bluntness can be amusing.' She punched Laura's arm lightly. 'Hey, do you remember what we used to say when we were growing up? That when we were old ladies and had finished with men and all that nonsense, we'd live together on the French Riviera and sit on the beach wearing large picture hats and caftans, having our toenails painted purple by beautiful young gigolos.'

Laura nodded, her face lighting up. 'Sure I do. We were a fanciful pair in those days.'

'We might still do it, you know,' Claire said, grinning. 'When we're old enough.' She took a sip of her gin martini and said, 'I can't wait for you to see Natasha. I told you, she's sprouted lately, and since you saw her in the summer her face has changed. She's sleeker looking, has lost some of the puppy fat, and it helps. She's just become very, very pretty.'

'Like mother like daughter.'

Claire merely smiled. 'She's a very special child, Laura, even though she's mine and I shouldn't say it. Nonetheless, she *is* special, sort of . . . well, *magical*.'

'You may have lived on a battlefield, but you got something out of it, after all, didn't you now?'

'Yes, I certainly did. Natasha has made it all worthwhile . . . the spoils of war are veritable spoils indeed. She's a jewel, and I love her dearly.' Claire's voice changed, became extremely tender, as she continued, 'I don't know what it's all about, this world we live in, this life of mine, but whatever it's about, my child has given my life whatever meaning it has. And she's the best part of me. I thank God every day that I had her, and that I have her with me. She's very caring of me, in a funny sort of way. Sometimes she behaves like the mother, treats me as if I'm the child.'

'I've always thought she was an old soul,' Laura murmured, and then ventured softly, 'Does her father ever see her?'

'No.' Claire shook her head and grimaced. 'Well, not very often. She doesn't care anymore. She used to, of course, but she's adjusted now.' A small sigh escaped, and Claire added, 'But I can't fault him on the money. His cheques come every month, and he's never missed a payment.'

'I always thought he loved her,' Laura murmured, and stopped abruptly when she saw Claire's expression.

'Mmmm.' Claire twisted her martini glass by its delicate stem, the reflective look in place in her green eyes again. She gazed into her drink.

Laura decided not to say anything else about Natasha's father and his feelings for their child. It had always been a sore subject with Claire.

A moment later, the room-service waiter materialized at the door. Laura went to let him in, and clearing her throat, remarked, 'Here's our dinner, Claire. Oh, should I order some wine?'

Claire said, 'I'll have a glass of white wine with the fish, that'll be nice, Laura, thanks.'

After ordering the wine, Laura sat down at the table and turned her attention to the salad. The two friends ate in silence for a moment or two, until Laura said, 'Did Hercule give you any idea about the price of his friend's Renoir? Or rather, what she wanted?'

'No, he didn't, and to be truthful I'm not sure that he even knows.'

'It won't be cheap,' Laura muttered, raising her eyes from her plate, staring at Claire. 'A Renoir is a Renoir is a Renoir, to paraphrase Gertrude Stein.'

'Well put. Listen, Hercule could be a good source for you. Many of his clients are art-collectors, and they might well have something they want to sell: that's of interest to you, I mean, such as a Matisse or a Bonnard. You said your client craves these two artists.'

'That's right, and I have another who always says he'd give his right arm for a Gauguin, at least that's the way he put it to me.'

'Well, you know Hercule's the great expert on Gauguin, so if there's anything knocking around, he'd know. We should talk to him about it. Over the weekend. I'll invite him to dinner one night.'

'I like Hercule, and I enjoy talking to him about art. About anything for that matter. He's very interesting.'

'Great, I'll ask him to come to dinner on Saturday.' Claire put her fork down and leaned back. 'I forgot to tell you, I saw Dylan a couple of weeks ago.'

'Oh, and how is my baby brother?' Laura asked, sounding surprised.

'Recalcitrant, as usual, even a bit contentious, to be honest. He took me to dinner at Espadon. He was staying at the Ritz, and he seemed determined to pick a fight with one of the waiters. I felt a bit uncomfortable at first, but then he finally calmed down after I'd kicked him on the shin under the table, *and* punched his arm. I hate it when he picks on people who can't answer back.'

'What a pity he hasn't outgrown that nasty little habit yet. Anyway, how's he doing? *Really?* Mom constantly says he's behaving himself at last, and that things are working out for him, but he's always managed to pull the wool over *her* eyes, as you know.'

'I think he *is* doing well, Laura, as surprising as that might sound to you. In a funny way, living in England has ... what's the phrase I'm looking for? It's settled him down, yes, that's it, and it's sorted him out. I think he's come into his own. He says he loves working on *Time*, and I believe him.'

'That's good to hear. But I bet his personal life's a mess.'

Claire grinned. 'He says it's a full-blown calamity, and I'm using his words. He told me his girlfriend Minerva has split, and he's worried that she might be pregnant and is depriving him of his child. And his former girlfriend Nina is stalking him, he insists. He's just met a new young woman, Inga, a Swede, and he was thinking of having her move in with him. Oh, and he's bought a farm in Wales.'

'Par for the course, all this,' Laura said, and she couldn't help laughing. 'We were right, you and I, when we gave up on Dylan years ago. He's just a bad boy, as Gran's forever announcing. And you *know* the way he feels about *us*. He resents us and our friendship, yours and mine. He's never forgiven us for sending him away when he was a little boy, cutting him out of our fun and games. Don't forget that, and his tantrums. He's all mixed up, that brother of mine.'

'Aren't we all?' Claire eyed Laura carefully.

'I guess so. The Valiants are probably as dysfunctional as any other family.'

'Better not let Grandma Megan hear you say that, or she'll have –'

'My guts for garters, to quote dear old Gran,' Laura said.

'I'm glad you let me be part of it, though.'

Laura gazed at Claire, her eyes quizzical. 'What do you mean?'

'Part of that dysfunctional, crazy, wonderful family of yours. Without the Valiants I might have turned out to be quite different.'

'Sane for one thing.'

'No, ordinary and dull.'

'You ordinary and dull, never! You were born special, Claire, take my word for it. And I'm glad you were part of it, *are* part of it, part of us. You've brought a lot of wonderful stuff to the Valiants. And to me especially.'

Laura awakened with a start.

She was bathed in a cold sweat, and her nightgown was clinging to her body. Struggling up into a sitting position, she threw back the bedclothes and swung her feet to the floor, turning on the bedside lamp as she did.

She could not help wondering, as she made her way to the bathroom, if she were coming down with something. To be perspiring like this was not normal; she hoped she was not in for a bout of the flu, or at the least a bad cold. She couldn't afford to get sick; she had far too much work to do, and Christmas was only a few weeks away.

After taking off her nightgown and drying herself, Laura put on a terrycloth robe and padded back to the bedroom. Wide awake, she punched up the pillows and got onto the bed.

Zapping on the television, she found CNN, and sat drinking the glass of carbonated water which she had put on the bedside table earlier but had not touched until now. Leaning back against the pillows, she stared at the set, grateful for the continuing stream of news out of Atlanta. At least it gave her something decent to watch in the early hours of the morning.

Laura put the glass down with a clatter, and sat up a bit straighter, suddenly remembering her weird dream ... She had dreamed about Rosa Lavillard. The dream had been frightening, oppressive. She had been with Rosa in a vast building in some unknown city, and they had been lost within its maze-like corridors which seemed to lead nowhere. The corridors were endless, and there were many, many doors. Every time they opened one a startled occupant would look up, stare at them, and tell them, in answer to their question, that the way out was at the far end of the corridor. But it never was. Another door led only to another corridor. Nervous and distraught, she had begun to panic, but Rosa Lavillard had not. The older woman had remained calm.

'There is always a way out,' Rosa kept repeating, and yet they could not find the door that would lead them to the outside . . . and freedom.

It had become hotter and hotter in the windowless corridors, and she had grown overheated, tired. But Rosa was stalwart, stoical, forever promising she would get them out of this maze, no matter what. The final door opened onto a slide; Rosa had pushed her onto it, and she had slid farther and farther down into terrifying blackness. And as she had slipped into this bottomless pit she could hear Rosa singing in French, but she couldn't make out the words exactly . . . Suddenly Rosa herself was on the slide, hurtling down behind her, singing for all she was worth.

And then she had woken up. Bathed in sweat, and with good reason. She had been afraid in the dream.

Laura was baffled by the nightmare. What could it possibly mean? And why had she dreamed about Rosa Lavillard, a woman she hardly knew? The answer to the latter was relatively simple. She had run into the Lavillards earlier in the day, and obviously they had remained in the back of her mind.

When they were having coffee after dinner, Laura had been about to tell Claire she had bumped into them in the museum, and then the moment had been lost. Claire had started to talk about the Renoir, and Hercule, and the weekend plans. But I should have told her, Laura admonished herself, and she felt suddenly guilty that she had not done so. It's lying by omission, she thought.

Her mind lingered on the Lavillards for a second or two, and then it leapt to her brother Dylan.

She knew she should call him in London, just to say hello, but she was afraid to do so and had kept putting it off for the last few days. And for a simple reason. Invariably, they always managed to quarrel. Her brother was contentious by nature, and she wasn't a bit surprised when Claire had told her he had tried to pick a fight with the waiter the night they'd had dinner at Espadon. He loved picking fights with everyone. He was troubled, filled with demons. But weren't they all? Their lovely Welsh grandparents had always claimed, no, boasted, that they were *different* because they were Celts, and Laura had believed this, at least part of her had.

But she was smart enough to know that she and her sibling *were* odd, troubled, dysfunctional to a certain extent, in part because of a fey, neglectful, if loving mother, who was bound up in her husband and her painting at the expense of her children, an overcompensating father who smothered them with love, and a famous actress for a grandmother who surrounded them with her own theatricality and extravagances and mythic tales of ancient Wales.

Laura smiled. Whatever it was they had made her, she was very sure of *who* she was. A Valiant. And proud of it.

4

'I am happy you were available to meet with me, Laura,' Hercule Junot said, bestowing his warm smile on her. 'My friend is leaving tonight for her château in the Loire, and this afternoon at three was the only time she had free to receive us.'

'No problem, Hercule, I'm looking forward to meeting her, and really excited about seeing the Renoir. I'm thrilled she still owns it.'

'It was lucky for you, and for Claire. But come, let us not waste another moment.' Taking hold of her elbow, he ushered her across the lobby of the Plaza Athénée, continuing, 'My car is waiting outside. My friend lives on the Faubourg Saint-Germain in the *Septième*, not too far for us to go.'

'It's one of my favourite areas of Paris,' Laura confided as they went out into the street and made for the car. Once they were comfortably settled on the back seat and driving off, Hercule remarked, 'Yes, I know what you mean about the seventh. I myself have always found it very special, perhaps because of its diversity as well as its beauty . . . an enclave for aristocrats in their beautiful houses, and yet an area where students, artists and writers abound.'

'I used to haunt the seventh when I was at the Sorbonne, Hercule,' Laura told him. 'When I wasn't trotting around the

Rodin Museum I was at the Café de Flore or the Deux Magots, or heading in the direction of the Hôtel des Invalides to visit Napoleon's tomb.'

'Ah yes, he is a favourite of yours,' Hercule said. 'Claire has told me how much you admire our famous Emperor.'

Laura smiled. 'Napoleon and Winston Churchill are my two great heroes.'

'Not Lincoln or George Washington?'

'Well yes, but in a different way. Churchill comes first with me, then Napoleon. I was tremendously influenced by my Welsh grandfather, who believed that Churchill saved Western civilization from extinction, quite aside from pulling the whole of Europe through evil times in the Second World War. Until the day he died my grandfather Owen Valiant said that Churchill was the greatest man of the twentieth century. And I believe that, too.'

'And Napoleon, the great dictator, how did you come to him?'

'Is that how you think of him . . . as a dictator?'

'Not I. Neither do most of the French, for that matter. The rest of Europe?' Hercule gave a small shrug and lifted his hands. '*They* think of him as a monster, but I do not believe he was.'

'I agree. And I came to him when I was living here as a student. I'm a Francophile, as you know, and I fell upon a wonderful biography of him, by Vincent Cronin, and I was just captivated. He was a genius, in my opinion.'

Hercule nodded. 'There is no half measure when it comes to Napoleon. He is either loved or loathed. Now, to move on, Laura, I must tell you about my friend, who you will be meeting in a few moments. Her name is Jacqueline de Antoine-St Lucien. I have known her for many years. Her late husband Charles was a dear friend, and he indulged Jacqueline in her grand passion . . . collecting art. She has the great taste . . .' He paused, kissed his fingertips. 'Superb taste . . . *formidable*. Her collection is enthralling. You will be seeing some of the greatest paintings in the world in a few minutes.'

'Why does she want to sell the Renoir?' Laura asked, filled with curiosity.

'She has not really confided the reason to me, but I do know the family château near Loches is expensive to run. Last year she sold a Van Gogh.'

'I wish I'd known about that!'

'And I, too, wish I had known, Laura. Certainly I would have informed you. *Immediately*. From what Jacqueline told me later, she did not even have it on the market. Someone saw the Van Gogh and made an offer, and so it was sold – just like that.' He snapped his thumb and finger together. 'From what I understand she had not thought of selling it, but the offer was so tremendous she found she could not refuse.'

'My favourite of all the Van Gogh paintings is *White Roses*.'

'Ah, *mais oui*, the most beautiful. And now it is hanging in France again, at least for the time being.'

'In France, but in the American Embassy.'

'And therefore on American soil, at least technically speaking,' he answered. 'Actually, it is at the Ambassador's residence.'

'I'd give anything to see it.'

'Perhaps that can be arranged. I know the Ambassador, Pamela Harriman.'

'That'd be wonderful, Hercule. By the way, how much does your friend want for the Renoir? Or don't you know?'

'When I spoke with her last night she mentioned that she was thinking of somewhere in the region of four million, or thereabouts.'

'Dollars?'

'Yes, US dollars. Ah, here we are, Laura. This is the house where Jacqueline lives. It has been in the family for many, many years.'

The private house, known as an *hôtel particulier*, was one of a number of similar residences standing on this famous street, hidden behind high walls built of pale stone. Immense wooden doors, studded with huge nails and painted dark green, were opened by a man in a striped uniform a moment after the chauffeur had rung the bell.

As the Mercedes rolled into the cobbled courtyard Laura saw that there was a concierge's cottage to the right, a fountain in the centre of the yard, and two wonderful old white chestnut trees growing against the ivy-clad walls. The trees had shed many of their leaves and so looked somewhat bereft on this cold December afternoon.

Hercule helped Laura out of the car and together they walked up the wide front steps. These led to double doors made of thick glass encased in wrought iron, which had been worked into a scroll design. Before he had even rung the bell the doors were opened by a manservant dressed in a dark suit and a bow tie.

Nodding, Hercule said, '*Bonjour*, Pierre.'

The butler inclined his head. '*Monsieur, madame. Entrez, s'il vous plaît.*' As he spoke he opened the door wider to give them access to the foyer, which was like a long gallery in its architecture. French windows on the wall facing the front door where they had just entered led outside. Laura glanced through them quickly as they were taken down the gallery by Pierre; she could see gardens, a lawn surrounded by trees, and in the centre a fountain that echoed the one in the front courtyard.

'*Madame la comtesse* attends you in the *salon vert, monsieur,*' the butler murmured.

Laura could not help smiling warmly when she saw Jacqueline, Comtesse de Antoine-St Lucien. She was the daintiest, prettiest little woman Laura had ever set eyes on. She could not have been more than four feet ten or eleven inches, and she was slender, with widely-set, bright green eyes, blonde hair, stylishly cut, and an almost cherubic face, hardly lined at all. There was something very girlish and pretty about her, even though Laura guessed she must be in her early seventies, or thereabouts.

Jacqueline was standing in front of the fire in the *salon vert*, pale green in colour, and she smiled back at Laura and hurried forward.

'Hercule!' she exclaimed. 'So nice of you to come, and to bring your friend.'

Hercule kissed her on both cheeks and said, 'I am so happy to see you, Jacqueline. And may I present Laura Valiant. Laura, this is the *Comtesse* de Antoine-St Lucien.'

'I am delighted to meet you, Mademoiselle,' Jacqueline said, shaking Laura's hand.

'And I you, Countess,' Laura responded, smiling at this perfectly groomed and elegantly-dressed diminutive woman.

'May I offer you something? Coffee, tea, a drink perhaps?'

'No, thank you,' Laura said.

Hercule shook his head. 'Nothing for me either, Jacqueline. But thank you.'

'Then do let us sit down,' the countess replied, smiling graciously and leading them across the room to a grouping of comfortable chairs near the fireplace.

Almost at once, Hercule began speaking to her about the château near Loches in the Loire Valley, where she was having some repair work done to the roof. This gave Laura a chance to look around.

Her eyes scanned the room quickly, took in the eau-de-nil walls, the pale green silk upholstery on the chairs and sofas, and the matching taffeta draperies. The pale green walls made a soft and beguiling backdrop for the paintings in the room, which included a Bonnard, a Degas and a Cézanne. And of course the Renoir, which was hanging above a *bombé*-fronted chest set against a small side wall.

Laura was itching to get up, to go and look at it, but her natural good manners forbade this.

It was Hercule who suddenly rose and said, 'Ah, the Renoir, Jacqueline, I must look at it again, if I may.'

'But of course, Hercule,' she answered. 'Please do, and you also Mademoiselle Valiant. Please, go and see it.'

'Come, Laura,' he said, turning to her. 'I know you are anxious to look at all of the countess's works of art.'

'Yes, I am,' she admitted.

They walked over to the Renoir and stood gazing at it, both of them entranced by its beauty and grace.

Hercule said, 'I have seen this many times over the years, Laura, and I must admit I never tire of it. But then Renoir was the great master, as we both know.'

'And this is just gorgeous,' Laura murmured, sounding slightly awed. Nonetheless, she could not help wondering if her Canadian client would find the painting too small. In her dealings with him in the past, he had usually favoured larger canvases. On the other hand, the painting was a little jewel; the skin tone of the model glowed like luminescent pearl under the picture light, and the woman truly came alive, as did the landscape and the pool near the rock she was seated on. Laura hoped that her client *would* buy it.

After another moment or two lingering in front of the Renoir, Hercule took hold of Laura's arm and drew her across the room, first to look at the Degas, then the Bonnard and finally the Cézanne. All three paintings were, like the Renoir, total perfection, prime examples of the artists' work. Laura couldn't help wondering if any of these were for sale, especially the large Cézanne.

Eventually they went and joined the countess in front of the fire, and Laura turned to her and said, 'The Renoir is exquisite, and so are your other paintings, Countess. It is quite an experience to be in a room which contains four such masterpieces. A room in a private home, I mean.'

'*Merci*, Mademoiselle Valiant. You are very kind, and I must say, they are all paintings which make me feel happy when I look at them. But then I have never liked anything that makes me sad or depressed. I have the need to be uplifted by art.'

'Absolutely!' Hercule exclaimed. 'I agree with you, Jacqueline. Now, I would like to take Laura to the dining room, to show her the Gauguins. He is one of her favourite painters. Is he not, Laura?'

She nodded.

Jacqueline stood up. 'I shall accompany you,' and so saying she glided across the Aubusson rug and led them down the gallery to the dining room at the far end.

Its walls had been sponge-glazed in a cloudy, dusty-pink colour, and this shade also made a wonderfully soft background for the paintings. In this instance they were breathtaking primitives by Paul Gauguin, three altogether, each one hanging alone. There was one on the long central wall, and the others had been placed on two end walls. The fourth wall in the room was intersected by windows which filled it with natural northern light, perfect for these particular works of art.

All three paintings were of dark-skinned Tahitian women, either by the sea or in it, or sitting in the natural exotic landscape of the Polynesian islands. The dark skin tones were highlighted by the vivid *pareos* the women wore around their loins, the colourful vegetation and the unusual pinkish-coral colour Gauguin had so frequently used to depict the earth and the sandy beaches of Tahiti. The dusty-pink walls of the dining room echoed this warm coral, and helped to throw the dark-skinned beauties into relief.

Laura was mesmerized. She had never seen Gauguins like these outside a museum, and they were impressive. All three paintings were large, dominant, just the type of art her other important client Mark Tabbart would give his right arm for, as he so frequently proclaimed to her. 'They are magnificent,' she exclaimed, glancing at the countess, and before she could stop herself, she rushed on, 'I would buy any one of these, or all of them, if you would consider selling.'

'They *are* the most fabulous Gauguins,' Jacqueline murmured. 'Gauguin painted all three in the same year, 1892, and what extraordinary examples of his work they are. I could never sell them, I love them far too much. But even if I had the desire or the need to auction them to the highest bidder, I am afraid, Mademoiselle Valiant, that I could not. The paintings belonged to my husband, and he left them to our son Arnaud and his wife Natalie. I have them to enjoy for my lifetime, but I do not own them.'

'I envy you living with them,' Laura said. 'They are so beautiful they are . . . blinding.'

'Perhaps we should talk about the Renoir,' Hercule interjected. 'As you know, Jacqueline, Laura has a client who may well be interested in it, and, of course, there is Claire Benson, who wishes to photograph it on Monday.'

Jacqueline said, 'Let us go back to the *salon vert*, where we can sit and discuss everything in comfort.'

Later that afternoon when Hercule dropped Laura off at the hotel, she thanked him profusely, then said, 'I will phone my client in Toronto, and hopefully I will be able to give the countess an answer by Monday, perhaps even sooner.'

Hercule nodded. 'That will be perfectly all right, Laura.' After helping her out of the Mercedes and walking her to the door of the hotel, he said, 'I shall come in with you for a moment, if I may. I want to talk to you about two things: about paintings. And about Claire.'

Taken aback, Laura stared at him. 'What about Claire? Is there something wrong? You sound odd.'

'I think perhaps I sound worried, Laura, but let us not stand here. Please, let us have a cup of tea, or something else if you wish.'

'Yes,' she said swiftly, 'yes, of course, Hercule,' and she was unable to keep the sudden concern out of her voice as she spoke. 'I don't think I want tea. I'd prefer a drink. Can we go to the bar, please, Hercule?'

'*Mais oui*, let us do that,' Hercule replied, and they walked on quietly without saying another word, and went downstairs to the bar. It was only when they were finally settled at one of the small tables in the dimly-lit, rather clubby-looking Bar Anglais that Laura spoke.

'Why are you worried about Claire? Please tell me, Hercule.'

'I will, in due course. First, let us order. What would you like?'

'A glass of white wine, please.'

Hercule beckoned to the waiter, ordered for Laura, and asked for a Scotch and soda for himself. Then he sat back in the black leather chair and said, 'I'll get to Claire in a moment. First, I want to talk to you about paintings.' He paused and added, 'Something serious about paintings.'

Looking at him alertly, she nodded. 'Please tell me, Hercule.'

'It is about Gauguin's paintings. It is very important that you let me know whenever one comes onto the market in the States. Providing you know this, of course, and if you are interested in it for a client. I am asking you to do this for your own protection.'

'Of course I'll tell you. What's this all about?'

'There are several Gauguin paintings that are, well . . . *questionable*. I know your great interest in him as an artist, and how much you love his work, and I do not want you to make any mistakes. I do not want you to make a commitment without talking to me.'

'You mean there are some fakes around?'

'I am going to tell you a story about a Gauguin, and you will find it interesting, I believe.' He paused, stared at her intently. 'Laura, this is confidential. What I am about to tell you is for your ears only, it must remain between us. At least for the moment.'

'I would never discuss it with anyone,' she reassured him. Her eyes were eager, the expression on her face expectant.

'Many years ago, there was a collector,' he began. And slowly, carefully, he recounted a story to her.

She was rapt, hung onto his every word.

When he had finished, he said, 'Now to Claire. I don't think that she is well. In fact, I would go so far as to say that she is ill.'

Laura gaped at him, then said, 'She told me you'd given her a lecture about her weight.'

He nodded. 'She has lost much weight. She says she has been on a regime. However, it is not so much the weight loss that troubles me. It is ... the *look* of her, Laura.'

Frowning, shaking her head, Laura murmured, 'I don't understand what you mean.'

'Yesterday, at the studio, there was a moment when she was talking to me from the set, and she had ...' He stopped, looked off into space, as if trying to remember something, and then he said, 'She looked very peaked, no, that is not it. What is the word I am looking for ... she looked pinched ... drawn ... as if the skin of her face were stretched very tightly over her bones.' He took a deep breath, and added, very quietly, 'Her face was like a death mask; it frightened me, Laura.'

'Hercule! That's awful! An awful thing to say,' she exclaimed, and shuddered.

The waiter brought their drinks, and they were silent until he disappeared behind the bar again. Then Hercule continued, 'I have the most terrible apprehension for her. I cannot explain it. You see, I love her –' He cut himself off, and stared at Laura, suddenly at a loss.

She said swiftly, 'I know you love her, Hercule, I've known it for a long time. You don't have to be embarrassed or feel shy with me. I do understand. And I'm glad you love her, glad you care so much about Claire.'

Looking relieved, he answered, with a slight nod, 'I am pleased I have told you this, and I thank you, my dear, for your understanding.' He lifted his glass and took a sip of his Scotch.

Laura, also sipping her drink, asked, a moment later, 'What do you mean when you say you feel apprehensive?'

'As I told you, I do not think she is well, but I cannot explain why I feel this, not in a rational way. I thought she looked tired, worn out, yesterday, with the black smudges underneath her eyes, and so very thin. At one moment, when she turned to speak to me, the light fell upon her and she looked . . . like a skeleton, and so *ill*. I was frightened.'

'Perhaps it was just the way the lights on the set hit her face; you know that can happen.'

'Yes, that is true. I tried to tell myself this last night. I reviewed the time I had spent with her at the studio, and certainly she had been energetic, as she always is. But –' He cut himself off again, sat back drinking his Scotch and soda; his eyes were troubled, his shoulders taut with anxiety.

Laura could see how upset he was, and she waited until he had collected himself before she said slowly, 'What do you think is wrong with Claire? You say you think she's ill, but with what?'

He lifted his hands in that typical gesture of his and shook his head. 'Alas, I do not know, Laura.' He sighed and continued, 'I push the worry away, as I did when we were at Jacqueline's earlier. Yet it creeps back into my mind. Has she . . . has she confided anything in you?'

'Nothing, Hercule, and I'm sure she would if she were sick, or worried about herself. She did mention you'd chastised her about the weight loss, and she *is* thinner, I agree with you. But I didn't think she looked ill last night over dinner.'

'The cosmetics, they help,' he said pointedly.

'That's true. She's very . . .' Laura paused and did not continue, changing her mind all of a sudden.

Hercule, looking at her intently, asked, 'She's *what?*'

Laura shook her head and answered softly, 'She's still very angry. About her bad marriage, about men, or perhaps one man. It seems to eat her up at times, consume her. Perhaps it's just that, the anger, the disappointment. Plus working hard, being tired occasionally.' Leaning forward, Laura put one hand on his arm. 'Try not to worry so much. I don't think she's sick, Hercule, I really don't.'

Her words seemed to help him to relax, and the tight lines around his eyes eased slightly. 'I hope you are correct. When you love a woman as I love her, it *is* worrying if she seems ... well, not herself.'

Taking the plunge, Laura said, 'Why don't you tell her how you feel, Hercule? Tell her you love her?'

'Oh but I could not do that, Laura. Never, never. Claire does not feel the same way about me as I feel about her. *I am afraid.* Yes, I admit that to you, Laura, I am afraid to tell her. I do not want to lose her, you see, and I might, if she ... knew how I truly felt. Being her friend, and part of her life is so important to me.'

'You ought to tell her. You might be surprised how she reacts.'

'Laura, how can you of all people in the world, say that to me? *Mon Dieu!* You have just told me that she is angry about her failed marriage, about *him*. No, there is no room for me in her life, as much as I want there to be.'

His gently-spoken words seemed to strike at Laura, and she flinched inside. She sat back in her chair, thinking how sad it was that Claire was being so cruel to herself, and was, in a way, punishing herself without reason. *No room for me in her life.* She replayed his words of a moment ago in her mind, and she knew it was true, and that this was indeed a tragedy. Hercule was much older, but he was a good-looking man, well-built, tall, and strong as an ox, and he was a kind and loving human being. He would have looked after Claire, protected her, given her so much.

He said, 'Maybe I worry about nothing. Is that what you are thinking?'

She shook her head. 'No, I was thinking how sad it is that Claire has this attitude about ... life.'

'You do not think she is ill?'

'No, I do not. In fact, I'm positive she isn't, at least not in the way you mean. Not physically.'

'Mentally?' he asked, his voice growing slightly sharper; he stared at her intently.

'No. I don't mean that either. She's very sane, our Claire. But she is a *tormented* woman, Hercule, and I don't know how to help her. I have tried for years.'

'Do you think . . . she still loves her ex-husband?'

'No. I think she is filled with hatred for him.'

Hercule was silent for a moment, sat nursing his drink. Eventually he lifted his head and looked into Laura's eyes, and his own were moist with tears. 'What a terrible waste. How tragic that is . . . to cut yourself off . . . to deny yourself the possibility of love in that way.'

'Yes,' Laura said, her voice a whisper.

Later that evening, after a light supper in her room, Laura worked on her papers for a while. But for once in her life her concentration was fleeting. Finally, she put down her pen and sat back in her chair.

She was troubled about Claire.

Not in the way that Hercule was, not about her physical health, but about her mental state. Claire had harboured a dislike of Philippe ever since their break-up, perhaps even before that. But now it had turned to hatred and Laura couldn't understand why.

Claire had changed in the last six months. In the summer, when she and Doug had been in Paris, Claire had been much more relaxed, more at ease with herself. Now Laura realized that Claire was taut, full of tension, and at times she could be quite volatile.

Laura could not help asking herself why there had been this change. She's alone and lonely, Laura thought, rising, walking across the room to the window. Parting the curtains, she looked down into the courtyard below. In spring and summer it was a garden restaurant; now it was devoid of flowers and furniture, a simple paved yard flooded with light from the windows of the rooms that looked down onto it. Empty, cold, uninviting. Like Claire's life. If only she could meet someone. A nice man of the right age with whom she could fall in love, perhaps settle down with. But Laura knew instinctively that this would not happen because Claire would not permit it. She's her own worst enemy, Laura muttered under her breath, loving her friend but at the same time feeling suddenly somewhat disturbed and critical about her behaviour. I want to help her and I don't know how to do that, Laura said to herself, remembering how difficult that had always been, even when they were children. Claire had tried to be so independent and brave, but Laura had always sensed, even then, that she was afraid. Claire had been . . . timid. That was a good word to use to describe her. Her grandmother had once said that: 'Claire's a scared little thing, isn't she? So *timid* and reluctant.' She had often wondered what Claire was frightened of when they were little, and once or twice she had asked her, but Claire denied her fear. There was one thing, and it came rushing back to Laura. Her grandmother had never really liked Claire's parents. She had said her mother was ineffectual and her father a womanizer. But those were not reasons for Claire to be *frightened*, were they?

Sighing under her breath, Laura turned away from the window, got undressed and went to bed. Feeling wide awake she zapped on CNN and lay watching it for an hour. She had just turned it and the light off when the phone rang; reaching for it she said, 'Hello?'

'Hi, darling,' Doug answered.

'I wish you were here,' Laura grumbled.

'I can be there if you want.'

'But not fast enough for me.'

'How's three seconds?'

'Three seconds? What are you talking about?'

'I'll be right up,' he replied, and laughed. 'I'm in the lobby.'

5

'What are you doing in Paris?' Laura asked, smiling at Doug as he came through the door. 'You're supposed to be in Los Angeles.'

'I was never going there. I lied. I wanted to surprise you, darling.'

'You succeeded,' she said, and came into his arms.

Pushing the door closed with his foot, Doug held her close to him for a moment then bent down and kissed her on the mouth. Finally pulling away, he said, 'I thought a weekend in Paris would be great for both of us. So here I am.'

'I'm thrilled, it's just wonderful, that's all I have to say.'

He walked across the room, his arm around her shoulders, and said, 'So whatever you have planned I think you should cancel it. I want you all to myself.'

'I'm glad you do, and I feel the same way. There's no problem about cancelling things. All I have are two appointments with galleries, but they don't matter all that much. Oh but Doug, I told Claire I'd have dinner at the apartment tomorrow night. I can't really cancel that.'

'I don't want you to, and you know I love Claire. It'll be good to see her and the Shrimp.'

Laura laughed. 'I'd forgotten that you call Natasha that. She's not much of a shrimp anymore, though. More like a . . . golden salamander.'

'Mmmm. So she's growing up gorgeous, is she?'

'Absolutely.'

'There's the bell. It's my bag,' Doug said and went to open the door. The porter placed his suitcase, briefcase and overcoat in the room, thanked him for the tip, and left.

Laura said: 'Are you hungry? I'm sure the Relais Plaza is still open. I'll get dressed and we can go down for a bite.'

'No, don't bother, darling. I ate dinner on the plane. But I would like a drink. White wine would be great.' Leaning into her he kissed her on the cheek, took off his jacket and tie. 'I'm going to have a shower and then I'll be right with you. Order a bottle of Pouilly Fumé, sweetheart.' He continued to undress and Laura went to call room service.

She was propped up against the pillows on the bed sipping a glass of carbonated water when Doug came out of the bathroom swathed in a bath towel which he had wrapped around him toga style.

'The wine's over there on the chest,' she said. 'I had the waiter open it.'

'Thanks. Do you want a glass with me?'

'But of course.'

Doug poured two glasses and carried them over to the bed. After giving one to Laura, he strolled around to the other side, climbed onto it, sat propped up next to her. Turning to look at her, he lifted his glass and touched it to hers. 'Here's to our weekend together, darling,' he said and smiled.

Laura smiled back at him over the rim of the glass. 'To the weekend. And to you, darling. You're a crazy fool, flying all this way just for two days, but I love it.'

After a few sips of the white wine, Doug placed his glass on the bedside table; drawing closer to Laura, he kissed her cheek, then her neck.

Immediately putting her wine on the nightstand next to her,

Laura shifted her body around to face him, and a moment later he was pulling her into his arms. Doug renewed his kisses, showering them on her neck, her shoulders, her bare arms; reaching inside her nightgown he began to caress one of her breasts sensually, drawing small sighs from her.

Moving closer to him, Laura loosened the towel wrapped around him, let her hand trail down over his flat stomach, making gentle circular movements; her fingers fluttered down, and she began to stroke him.

Doug lay very still, his eyes tightly closed; he luxuriated in her touch, drifted with his sensual thoughts. He felt a slight movement against his legs as Laura slithered down the bed and crouched over his thighs. She was still stroking him and then unexpectedly her moist lips encircled him and he let out a long sigh as she took him fully in her mouth. Suddenly he was aroused. After a second or two, she stopped, lifted her head, kissed his stomach, and then pushing herself up the bed she brought her mouth to his.

Doug's excitement was mounting. He returned her fervent kisses and with suddenness, almost abruptness, he rolled them over so that he was on top of her. Their mouths stayed locked together. Her tongue grazed his and they shared a moment of intense intimacy before Doug pushed his hands under Laura's buttocks, fitted her long, lean body into the curve of his. And at last he was hard enough to slip inside her, easily and expertly, and within moments they had a rhythm, were rising and falling together, their movements swifter, almost frenzied. Her legs went high around his back and he shafted deeper into her, sinking deeply into the warmth.

Soon Doug felt as though he were falling through dark blue water, falling down, falling further and further down into a bottomless dark blue sea. The waves washed over him, beat against him. He squeezed his eyes tighter shut. Images danced behind his lids. Oh yes, he thought, oh yes, and as he began the long slide down into total ecstasy he saw that face, trapped as it was in his mind . . .

'Doug, oh Doug!' Laura cried. 'Now. Please. Oh please don't stop, darling.'

Her voice came to him from far away. And yet it was clear, sharp, the voice he knew so well. And it brought him down. Instantly he lost his erection. His fantasy shattered. Falling against her, Doug lay still, breathing heavily. He was flaccid, drained of energy all of a sudden. And he was mortified.

After a long moment, Laura whispered, 'Why did you stop? What happened?'

'I don't know,' he whispered back. 'I'll be all right in a minute.' But he wasn't, and after a short while he slid off her, and lay on his back, still breathing deeply.

'Are you all right, Doug?' she asked, concern giving her voice an edge.

'I'm fine,' he replied in a low voice. He felt vitiated, sapped of his strength.

Laura's hand reached for him; she began to stroke him, endeavouring to arouse him once more. But a moment later when her lips encircled him, he knew her efforts would be in vain. This happened a lot with her these days, this loss of strength and vitality at the crucial moment. Doug got off the bed, hurried into the bathroom.

Snapping on the light and locking the door, he went and looked at himself in the mirror. What in God's name was wrong with him? Why couldn't he bring the act of love to its true culmination for them both? He had always been proud of his prowess as a lover, his staying power.

It was odd how he fell apart, though, somehow never reached fulfilment these days. Panic struck him. Was it always going to be like this? For the rest of his life? Was he always going to be an ineffectual lover, a man incapable of satisfying a woman, satisfying his wife? Suddenly, Doug was hit by a rush of embarrassment. He had flown all this way to make love to her and he had failed her, failed himself.

And then he thought: It's all in the mind, of course. That's where all this begins. And ends.

6

Laura had always thought of herself as an observer. She would sit back and watch, saying very little but hearing everything. And there had been a great deal to see and hear, whether she was observing her brother Dylan, the rebel, her father, the composer and conductor; or her mother, the artist.

Then there was her grandmother Megan, the once-great musical star, and her grandfather Owen, theatrical manager and professional Welshman. And Claire Benson – her heroine, role model, and best friend.

Each one of them was highly individualistic, a complex personality, and therefore a fascinating study.

The two people she most enjoyed observing were her grandparents, Owen and Megan Valiant. They were the greatest influence in her life, especially her grandmother; and, because she loved them so much, she saw them through eyes that were not in the least critical. So many of her values had come from them, and it was on her grandparents that she had based her own notions of romantic love.

Grandfather Owen would boast, 'Ours is one of the greatest love stories that ever happened. I fell in love with Megan when I first heard her singing in the Chapel at Port Talbot, and I've loved her truly ever since.'

And whenever he said this, which was very frequently, her grandmother would blush prettily and smile at Owen with adoration. 'It's true, Laura. The day I set eyes on your grandfather I was kissed by the angels. It was the luckiest day of my life, meeting him.'

When she was young she was well aware that her parents loved each other, too. But unlike Owen and Megan, who never quarrelled, Richard and Margaret were often engaged in roaring battles.

'It's a feast or a famine with your parents,' her grandmother would say. 'They're either in each other's arms or at each other's throats. Goodness me, I've never before seen such goings on in my life.'

Her parents' way of making up after one of their regular tempestuous falling outs was to go off on a trip for a week or two. 'Another honeymoon,' Claire would say, and she would become a kind of surrogate mother to the two of them, aided and abetted by Mae, the housekeeper, Dylan's nanny, Cissy, and Grandma Megan, who would swoop down in full force to take charge of the household.

Claire had been the other important influence in her life, and she had observed her dearest friend through loving eyes and hardly ever found fault.

'Always the observer, Laura,' her lovely gran had often said in those days, laughing lightly, and then Megan would go on to predict that her favourite grandchild would become a writer. She hadn't, of course; nonetheless, she continued to be the observer, forever watching everyone, and assessing.

She was doing exactly that tonight as she sat on the stool in Claire's kitchen, where Claire and Natasha were preparing dinner. As she looked from mother to daughter she saw the enormous love and friendship flowing between them. It was so potent, such a palpable thing, Laura felt as though she could reach out and touch it. To see them in such harmony made Laura happy. Neither she nor Claire had been close to their own mothers, a situation which had often saddened Laura. But then she'd had Grandma Megan, and so had Claire, for that matter. And they still had her, in fact.

Everything that Claire had said about Natasha earlier in the week was true. Laura had not seen her goddaughter for almost five months, and in that time she had lost her puppy fat and grown even taller. Like her mother she had bright auburn hair, although hers was full and flowing, unlike Claire's which was cut short. Her resplendent locks gave her the look of a girl who had stepped out of a Renaissance painting. Her large eyes were a peculiar golden brown, a sort of amber colour, which Laura had always found unusual, and there was a faint dusting of freckles across the bridge of her slender nose. Otherwise, her creamy skin was without blemish.

Natasha had a short torso and long legs, and, as Claire had pointed out, although she was only fourteen, she dwarfed them both these days. She's growing up to be a real beauty, Laura thought, then turned her attention to Claire.

Contrary to what Hercule believed, Laura was quite convinced there was nothing wrong with her friend. Tonight she was full of her usual bountiful energy; her face was flushed, her eyes shining brightly, and her short auburn curls were like a burnished halo around her pretty face. No, there was nothing wrong with her, Laura decided, filled with a sudden sense of relief. Her dearest friend was the picture of good health.

Claire was wearing a red wool tunic over matching leggings, and she was full of laughter and gaiety as she skilfully prepared Navarin of lamb, her famous lamb stew with vegetables. Simultaneously, she was putting finishing touches to another speciality of hers, Strawberries Romanoff.

Claire had always been a marvellous cook. This was the one thing Laura envied, since she herself had little talent in that direction. Although Claire had been an enormous influence on her in other ways, she had never been able to teach her the simplest rudiments of gourmet cooking.

On the other hand, Claire had shown her such important things as how to put on make-up, pluck her eyebrows and paint her toenails; it was also from Claire that she had learned how to walk properly in high heels when still too young to wear them, and most importantly, how to flirt with boys.

Flirt with boys. Laura smiled, thinking that before long Natasha would be doing that. She almost laughed out loud; in all probability, Natasha was flirting already.

Shifting slightly on the stool, Laura said, 'Please let me do something to help.' As she spoke she glanced across at Claire and Natasha, and added, 'I feel like a spare wheel.'

Claire laughed. 'Everything's under control, I promise you, so just relax and keep us company until Hercule gets here, then you can entertain him while we finish up.'

'All right, that's a deal. But let me know if you need me to peel a potato, chop something, or whatever.'

'I've done all the whatevers for Mom,' Natasha said, laughing as she looked up. Then she returned to the task of dropping dollops of chocolate-chip-cookie mixture on a metal cookie sheet.

'It certainly smells delicious, Claire,' Laura remarked. 'I like your lamb stew better than Dina Zuckerberg's famous specialities.'

Claire burst out laughing on hearing this, and Laura started to laugh with her; their peals of laughter rang out, echoed around the kitchen.

Puzzled by their sudden and unexpected hilarity, not understanding it at all, Natasha asked, 'Who's Zina Duckerberg?'

'It's not Zina Duckerberg, it's Dina Zuckerberg,' Laura corrected. 'She used to live in the same building in New York when we were growing up, and she was always inviting us to dinner when her mother was out or away travelling.'

'And she always "cooked" the same thing, pizza from Ray's Pizza Parlor and Dayvilles vanilla ice cream,' interjected Claire, who began laughing again, as did Laura.

Natasha shook her head wonderingly, smiled indulgently at the two women, whom she thought were suddenly slightly crazy, and immediately changed the subject. 'You could do one thing to help, Laura. Would you go and ask Doug if we need more ice?'

'Good idea,' Laura replied, and slid off the stool. She found Doug on a sofa in front of the fire, nursing a drink.

'Do we need more ice, Doug?'

'No, darling, there's plenty in the bucket.'

Laura glanced around, once more admiring the room. Claire had decorated it with a great deal of style and flair, and a little help from Hercule. It was easy for Laura to spot his touches here and there, such as the bouffant taffeta curtains at the windows. 'Dance dresses,' he called them, because they were narrow at the top and flared out like a skirt before they reached the floor. And the large silk lamp shades, the urns of twigs and leaves were also Hercule's well-known imprints.

The room was old-fashioned, traditional, with spacious, rather grand proportions. A highly-polished wood floor met crisp white walls, with bookshelves soaring up to the ceiling on the long wall facing the fireplace.

On the other walls were hung oversized framed prints, all of them colourful reproductions of Toulouse-Lautrec's Moulin Rouge Can-Can girls. A cream Savonnerie rug, patterned with red, black and green, covered part of the dark floor, and there were two large cream velvet sofas and several chairs arranged in an airy seating arrangement.

Claire had been collecting French country antiques for a number of years and their ripe woods gleamed in the lambent light, adding a touch of elegance and warmth to the room. She had arranged lovely old pieces of porcelain on some of the antique chests and tables, and grouped together a large collection of silver-framed photographs on a Provençal sideboard. Laura gazed back at all of the Valiants, as well as herself. And Natasha, Claire and her parents were also captured in different poses on celluloid.

The air was fragrant with the scent of fresh flowers, bowls of potpourri and Rigaud candles, all of which were trademarks of Claire's. It was a lovely room at any time, but especially so at night, with the candles burning, the silk-shaded lamps glowing and the fire blazing in the hearth. There was a welcoming warmth here, and a great deal of love.

Walking across to one of the tall windows, Laura stood looking down at the place de Fürstemberg, which she considered to be one of the most picturesque little squares in Paris. It was a cold night. The inky sky was clear, without cloud, and the stars were few. But a curving crescent moon was bright as it cast its silvery light across the shadowy square.

Directly below the apartment windows was the solitary, old-fashioned lamppost with its five globes which gave off the only other illumination, except for the light streaming out from the windows of the adjacent apartments. Laura had always thought of the lamppost as a charming little sentinel standing next to the ancient Paulownia trees which were much treasured by every inhabitant of the square.

Laura knew the Sixième, the sixth arrondissement, very well and especially this quaint square with its great charm and old-world atmosphere. It was she who had found the apartment for Claire seven years ago, just after she had separated from her husband. It had belonged to Madame Solange Puy, grandmother of her old friend Marie-Louise Puy, who dated from her Sorbonne student days.

Marie-Louise had inherited the apartment from her grandmother and had just put it up for sale. Fortuitously for Claire, as it turned out, Laura had been in Paris at this particular time, and the moment she heard about the apartment going on the market she had told Marie-Louise that Claire might well be interested in buying it.

The three of them had met at the apartment and Claire had instantly fallen in love with it. Within a couple of months the sale was complete with all the documents signed, and the place finally belonged to Claire. As soon as the deed was in her hands she began to decorate. Hercule, as always, was the chief adviser and initiator of ideas, and together they had created what Claire called, 'My first real home as a grown-up.' And it *was* beautiful, Laura was the first to acknowledge.

It had pleased Laura to see Claire so happy on the day her friend had shown her the finished apartment. Claire's excitement about her new home had wiped the anger and pain off her face, for a little while at least.

'Laura.'

At the sound of Natasha's voice Laura swung around. 'Yes?'

'Your lipstick . . . well, it's not right . . . not the right colour. I've brought you this . . . one of mine. It's much better for you.' Natasha hurried forward and handed the tube of lipstick to Laura.

Laura automatically took it, startled as usual by Natasha's candour. The girl was breathtakingly honest, blunt even, but then weren't most fourteen-year-olds today? 'What's wrong with the colour I'm wearing?' Laura asked, after a moment.

'It's too red for you. Anyway, bright red's *out*. Old-fashioned. Look at the one I've given you. It's sort of brownish with a hint of pink, and it's much more *in*. Just ask Mom. She uses one of my browns now. Red is definitely gross.'

'Thanks for your beauty advice, darling. It used to be your mother passing on tips, now it's you.'

'You're not mad at me, are you, Laura?'

'No, of course not,' she answered with a light laugh, amused by the girl's seriousness and look of concern about the lipstick.

The doorbell rang, and Natasha exclaimed, 'That's Hercule, he's always on time!' She glanced at the clock on the mantelpiece. 'Just two minutes past seven,' she added as she ran across the floor to the entrance hall.

Laura followed at a slower pace.

Doug jumped up and straightened his jacket.

Natasha wrenched open the door and cried, 'Hercule, we

were –' Her sentence was bitten off abruptly. Natasha stood stock still, gaping at Hercule's companion. It was Philippe Lavillard.

Laura stared at Philippe, as speechless as Natasha.

Philippe looked from Natasha to Laura, and then took a step forward, drawing a bit closer to the threshold. It was obvious that he was about to say something; he opened his mouth then immediately closed it. The words remained unsaid.

The kitchen door had flown open with a clatter at this moment and Claire now rushed into the living room; she was laughing. 'There you are, Hercule, as punc –' She, too, instantly cut off her sentence midway, when she saw Philippe Lavillard; she was flabbergasted at the sight of him. 'What the hell are you doing here?' she exclaimed, but the words sounded more like a snarl than anything else.

'We met, he and I, on the doorstep,' Hercule began, already sensing trouble, wishing to keep things at least civilized; he knew they would never be amicable. That was an impossibility between these two antagonists. 'We came up the stairs together,' he finished somewhat lamely, and shrugged.

Claire stared at her old friend without uttering a word, blinking rapidly, as if suddenly afflicted with a nervous tic. Then her eyes swung to Philippe. 'What do *you* want?' she demanded, her voice shrill.

It struck Laura that Claire was spoiling for a fight with Philippe, and she wondered how best to diffuse the situation before it spiralled out of hand, became a full-blown row. She glanced at Doug; he stared at her pointedly.

In answer to Claire, Philippe said quietly, 'You know what I want.'

'What you want and what you'll get are two entirely different things. You can't just come here without warning and make demands on me. And you know that,' she snapped, her eyes icy.

'I'm entitled to see Natasha.'

'Huh! *You*! You don't give a damn about Natasha. If you did you wouldn't bury yourself in darkest Africa, tending to the natives and their Bubonic Plagues and Black Deaths or whatever other horrendous diseases it is they have. You'd be here, living in Paris, and *available* to be with your daughter whenever she needs you. Instead, you're thousands of miles away, half the time incommunicado because of your deadly viruses, and of no use to her or me when we might need you urgently.'

'You know if there were an emergency I'd be here as quickly as possible, if you asked me to come. And I do have a right to see my daughter,' he answered, cool and reasonable in his tone.

'You gave those rights up when you ran off!'

'I didn't run off, as you put it, Claire, and you know it. And don't forget, I do have visitation rights.'

'If *I* say so. And don't *you* forget that I have sole custody, and that I control your visitation rights. They're at my discretion. The judge said so. And you accepted that stipulation without a murmur.'

'I don't wish to fight with you, Claire,' he replied, sighing imperceptibly, holding his temper in check, knowing it was futile to squabble with her. Invariably her rage turned into a terrible verbal violence that frightened him because he never knew where it was going to lead. Again, he said, 'Look, I just want to see Natasha for a while.'

'But she doesn't want to see you, do you, Natasha?' Claire turned to their daughter.

At first Natasha did not answer, then she said softly, 'No, Mom.'

'You see!' Claire cried triumphantly, and threw him a smug smile. 'You've even antagonized your own daughter, not that she really knows you as a father. Basically, she never had a father. You were always away, far too often, ever to be one of any consequence. In fact, you're a stranger to her.'

'That is not true,' Philippe shot back swiftly. He shook his head and shifted slightly on his feet, wanting to be gone from her. 'And let us not dredge up the past,' he went on, his control still tightly held, his voice steady. 'I just thought we could spend a bit of time together, she and I. I'm only here for a few days.'

'*Now?* At this hour? Why *did* you come at this particular time? I'm not going to ask you to stay to dinner, if that was your intention.'

'I don't want to stay to dinner. I want to see my daughter.'

'You can't. Not now. You should have phoned me. That would have been the proper thing to do.'

'I knew you'd say no, or slam the phone down if I called you.'

'I'm slamming the phone down now. You're not welcome here. Please leave.'

'Claire, be reasonable,' he begged, his tone now becoming even more conciliatory. 'Please agree to –'

'No way,' she cut in swiftly. Her hatred for him flooded her eyes, washed over her face. He saw it and flinched.

He said, 'Tomorrow, Claire. For a short while. For lunch?'

'*No.*'

'For coffee, then? In the morning. Here at the apartment. Or at a café. Whatever you say.'

'Please go, I don't want you in my home,' Claire almost shouted and she stamped her foot.

Laura was not only appalled but troubled. She had never seen Claire behave like this before.

Hercule said, 'Perhaps it would be more appropriate to have this discussion inside the apartment, rather than out here in the hallway.' He took a long stride into the foyer, and carefully closed the front door of the apartment behind him. At the same time, he managed to give Philippe a gentle push into the room. Then he struggled out of his overcoat, which he hung in the cloakroom.

Philippe spoke in a coaxing tone, making a last ditch effort as he said, 'Let me spend an hour with Natasha tomorrow. That's all I ask.' Growing bolder suddenly, he took another step towards his former wife.

Claire backed away.

They glared at each other.

There was a rush of immense dislike flowing between them like waves. It filled the room.

Hatred, Laura thought. They have only hatred for each other. How terrible that they should end up like this. Once they so loved each other, shared all their hopes and dreams, planned a future, a whole life together. Now they are embattled.

Natasha also felt the hostility flowing between her parents, and as always it dismayed and troubled her. But she managed to diffuse it to some extent by saying, 'It's okay, Mom. Coffee tomorrow is fine.'

'No!' Claire exclaimed. 'I don't want you to do this, Natasha, just to placate him.'

Natasha went and put her arm around her mother, who was so much smaller than she, and held her close to her, as if somehow protecting her. She couldn't stand her mother's pain. It broke her heart. 'Mom, I don't mind, honestly I don't, and it's better this way.'

Claire did not respond, simply leaned into her daughter, taking sudden comfort from her close proximity, her warmth and the love she exuded.

Looking across at her father, Natasha continued, '*Ten o'clock.* I'll be ready. We can go to the café on the corner.'

Philippe nodded, and an unexpected smile struck his sombre mouth. 'Yes, that's perfect, and thank you, Natasha. Thank you.' He cast a glance at Claire. 'Is that all right with you? You're not going to throw a spanner in the works, are you?'

'Everything will be all right,' Natasha answered swiftly, suddenly in command here, in charge of this volatile situation. 'I promise. No problems.'

Relieved, reassured by the oddly grown-up girl who was his daughter, Philippe relaxed a little. For a moment he gave his attention to Laura. 'Nice seeing you the other day,' he murmured, and then nodded to Hercule: knowing it was wise to disappear before Claire did indeed find a way to object to the date their daughter had made with him, he let himself out without further ado.

The moment he was gone, Claire pulled away from Natasha, and swung her head to look at Laura. She frowned and said in a puzzled tone, 'You *saw* him the other day?'

'I ran into him at the d'Orsay, just before you arrived. He was looking at the Renoirs.'

'And you never told me when *I* got there . . . never told me he was in Paris. Why not?'

'I was going to, Claire darling, but then I decided against it. I realized you didn't know Philippe was here, passing through, as he'd told me, otherwise you would have mentioned it to me. And to be honest, I didn't want to upset you. Mentioning his name is like a red rag to a bull, you know that, and I was just . . . Well, I was waiting for you to tell me you'd had a phone call from him. But when you didn't, I decided not to say anything. Obviously he hadn't been in touch with you. Why open a can of worms?'

'Lying by omission,' Claire pronounced, her mouth drooping. 'I can't believe it,' she added in a low mutter.

'Oh, Claire, come on, don't take exception like this,' Laura exclaimed. 'It wasn't lying by omission.' She cleared her throat. 'Well, not really,' she now thought to say, remembering that she herself had thought the same thing two nights ago, when they were having dinner at the Relais Plaza. 'Surely you understand, Claire?'

But Claire remained silent.

Laura continued, 'Look, I didn't want to bring up Philippe's name, to say I'd run into him accidentally. What good would it have done? You'd only have been as mad as hell that he was in Paris and not calling you, not asking to see Natasha.'

'I'm mad now.'

'Mom, don't take it out on Laura. She hasn't done anything,' Natasha said gently, a worried expression clouding her eyes.

'Never a truer word spoken, my dear,' Hercule agreed. 'I don't know about anyone else, but I'd like a drink.' He moved further into the room, and glanced at Laura. 'Actually, I *need* one, don't *you?*'

'Absolutely, Hercule. Go and sit down, I'll fix them,' Laura answered, walking across to the drinks table. 'Scotch and soda, as usual?'

'*Oui. Merci.*'

'What about you, Claire?' Laura asked, as she dropped ice into two glasses. 'I'm fixing myself a vodka, for a change.'

'I won't have anything thanks,' Claire responded, her voice suddenly back to normal. 'I think I'd better go and look at the dinner.'

'I'll come with you,' Natasha cried, rushing into the kitchen after her mother.

'What about you, Doug? Do you want something?' Laura asked.

'I'll have a glass of white wine, please.'

Laura carried the drinks over to the sofa in front of the fire, handed the Scotch to Hercule, and the wine to Doug, then sat down on a chair opposite them. 'Cheers,' she said, lifting her glass. Doug lifted his, and smiled at her.

'*Santé,*' Hercule replied and took a sip. Leaning back against the cream velvet sofa, he stared at the fire for a brief moment, a look of abstraction on his face.

Laura sat observing him, giving him a few minutes to collect himself, to relax.

Eventually, she said in a low, concerned tone, 'I've never seen Claire act in that way before, not in all the years I've known her.'

'A dreadful scene,' Hercule replied, shaking his great leonine white head. Turning to look at her, he went on, 'I've not witnessed anything like it, either. However, I must tell you, Laura, she now harbours the most terrible hatred for Philippe.'

'I've never been able to get to the bottom of *that*, Hercule. I mean, after all, a lot of marriages fail and people get divorced. But there isn't always this hideous acrimony.'

'That is true, yes. I am rarely if ever with Claire and Philippe when they meet, but Natasha has told me that it is always stormy, and that Claire rages on and on at Philippe.' He shook his head; there was a hint of bafflement on his face. 'It seems to me she has grown to hate him more and more as the years have passed. Extraordinary, I think.'

Laura made no comment; she was at a loss for words. But she knew deep down within herself that Hercule was correct. A sense of dismay suddenly lodged in her stomach, and she said slowly, 'I hope this hasn't ruined the evening. Claire was so lighthearted in the kitchen before Philippe showed up. But then –' She cut herself off, sipped the vodka.

'But then?' Hercule's eyes rested on her quizzically. '*What?*'

'Philippe Lavillard has always spelled trouble. And I've never really liked him.'

'Oh, I don't think he's such a bad fellow, Laura,' Doug interjected.

Hercule smiled at her, and said, 'Perhaps you see him through Claire's eyes, and not your own, my dear.'

'Perhaps,' Laura had the good grace to admit.

Hercule chuckled softly to himself and glanced into the fire, his face grown contemplative again.

'What is it? Why are you chuckling?'

'We can control so much in our own lives ... except what other people say and do. And their actions and their words affect us tremendously. Therefore we do not have as much control as we think we do, Laura.'

'No, we don't,' Laura agreed.

'You can say that again,' Doug said.

7

Natasha could see her father standing on the far corner of the place de Fürstemberg, and she ran across the square to join him.

'Hello, Natasha,' he said, when she drew to a standstill in front of him, and hugged her to him.

'Hi, Dad,' she responded, hugging him back, and when they drew away, she went on, 'Let's go somewhere else for coffee, not the café on the corner, and then maybe we can go for a walk.'

'But your mother . . .' he began and then stopped, peering at his daughter, his dark eyes suddenly worried. 'Won't she expect you home soon? Within the hour?'

'Oh no, it's okay, Dad, honestly,' Natasha reassured him. 'I told Mom I wanted to have a longer visit with you today, and she said it was all right.'

Philippe Lavillard continued to regard his daughter for a moment, assessing what she had just said. Although he did not know her as well as he wished he did, he was, nevertheless, quite sure she would not say anything to him which was untrue. Claire had brought her up well.

'All right,' he said at last. 'Since you say your mother's agreed, let's walk for a bit and find a place for breakfast. I haven't had any yet, have you, darling?'

Natasha shook her head, smiling up at him. She tucked her arm in his and they set off at a brisk pace. Natasha loved her father, and she did not think he was the ogre her mother constantly made him out to be. And she was baffled by her mother's perpetual anger, who would never discuss her past relationship with Philippe. But then she was often baffled by adults, whom she considered to be very strange at times, to say the least, and most especially when it came to relationships.

'I'm planning to leave Africa,' Philippe announced out of the blue.

Taken by surprise, and startled by this statement, Natasha exclaimed, 'Why Dad? I thought you enjoyed working there.'

'I have enjoyed it and I've done some good work there, but I want to get out now. I'm tired, Nattie. Anyway, I want to be near you, able to see you more frequently. Would you like that?' he asked, and was suddenly trepiditious. He had always believed she felt the same way he did, that she loved him in return, and now he hoped he had been right in this assumption.

When she did not immediately respond, he asked, 'Well, how *would* you feel if I were around more?'

'I'd like it, I really would,' Natasha said, meaning this. 'And I think Mom would let me see you more often, wouldn't she?'

'I'm sure of it, Natasha. Your mother is angry with me, not you and if *you* ask her then I know she'll agree.'

'Why is she angry with you, Dad?' Natasha asked, voicing a question that had nagged at the back of her mind for the last couple of years.

'She thinks I let her down, I suppose that's it.'

'Did you?' the fourteen-year-old asked, gazing at him, her eyes questioning.

Philippe sighed. 'We let each other down in so many ways, and you suffered as a result.' He glanced at her, smiled ruefully. 'It's children who always suffer in a divorce.'

'I guess.' Natasha hesitated, and then blurted out, 'Is it true what she says? About other women?'

'No, of course not. But Claire was always suspicious of me, especially when I went away to do research.'

'But why, Dad? I don't understand why she didn't trust you.'

He shook his head and a sigh escaped again. 'I don't know, Nattie. But she believed it, she truly did, and she wasn't pretending to be angry. It was genuine, is genuine.' They walked on in silence for a few minutes, and then Philippe volunteered, 'I have a feeling . . .' He paused, wondering if he should continue.

'Go on, Dad, what feeling do you have?'

'I have a feeling your mother has an enormous and deep-rooted distrust of men for some reason. It seems to me that it's very well ingrained in her, and I think I fell victim to this in some way. I'm not saying I wasn't also at fault in the disintegration of our marriage, but I was often accused unfairly of things I didn't do.'

Natasha nodded quickly. 'I know you're not the villain Mom makes you out to be. Actually –' She stopped abruptly, looked up at him and suddenly grinned. 'I think Mom's still in love with you, Dad.'

Momentarily Philippe was startled, and he exclaimed, 'I doubt it, Nattie! That's your romantic imagination running away with you.'

'No, it isn't, Dad. I just feel she is.' Natasha shrugged, and made a *moue*. '*You* think it's wishful thinking on my part, but I don't think it is.'

He was silent, and she hurried on, '*That's* why Mom's so angry with you . . . that you're not *here*, living with us. I know she still loves you, Dad.'

'Well, in a way, I still love her.'

'That's already something. Don't you think you should try to get back together?'

Philippe came to a sudden standstill, took hold of his daughter's arm and turned her to face him. Very gently, he said, 'I wish it *were* possible, Nattie, for your sake, but I can't. And in all truthfulness, I don't think your mother wants me back. I said

I still loved her in a certain way, but it isn't the kind of love that would support a marriage. Perhaps I should correct that and say I'm very fond of your mother, because of our early relationship and because of you. There's a big difference.'

'I know.'

They began walking again.

Natasha slipped her arm through his, clinging to him as they fell into step. They were very much alike in looks, and Natasha was almost as tall as he was. And to passers-by there was no doubt that they were father and daughter. Philippe was slim, elegant in appearance, and handsome in a quiet way, his lean face sensitive, his dark brown eyes compassionate and kind. Natasha now realized that her mother and father would never get back together, something she had often dreamed about. But she hoped they would be more amicable with each other in the future. Perhaps if her father did come back to work in Paris her mother would see him in a better light, and relent.

'Would you work at the Pasteur Institute again, Dad?' she now asked.

'I'd like to, yes, Nattie, but I'm not sure that this would be possible. However, they're interested in talking to me. Actually, I'm seeing the director tomorrow.'

'You're such a brilliant virologist, they'll want you, Dad. I just know they will.'

He laughed. 'Thank you for that vote of confidence, Natasha. I'm glad I have you on my side.'

'I *am*, Dad.'

'How about going in here?' he suggested, stopping in front of a café. 'I remember it well. They have wonderful croissants and do the best fried eggs. Come on, let's try it.'

Once they were inside the café, Natasha shrugged out of her green quilted-down coat, and Philippe hung it up for her, along with his brown suede jacket lined with sheepskin. After they had been seated and had ordered, he said, 'I'm going to New York later next week with your grandmother.'

Natasha looked across the table at him alertly. 'How is she?'

'Quite well, thanks, Nattie. Longing to see you again.' He pursed his lips. 'Perhaps you and she can get to know each other one day.'

'It could happen if you were living in Paris,' Natasha said, unable to keep the eagerness out of her voice. 'I mean she could come here to see you. And me. Don't you think?'

Philippe nodded. He was glad he had made the effort and had gone to see Claire and Natasha last night. The outcome had been better than he had expected, despite Claire's outburst. And he knew now that he *did* have his daughter's love, and that perhaps his mother would also have it one day. And that pleased him greatly.

'I'm sorry to intrude, Laura,' Philippe said, speaking to her from a phone in the lobby of the hotel. 'But I had hoped we might get together, if only for a few minutes. I need to speak to you about Natasha. And Claire.'

'Just a moment please, Philippe,' Laura said.

Although she had covered the receiver with her hand, he could vaguely hear her speaking to Doug, and then she came back to him. 'Yes, all right. I'll be down in a few minutes. Why don't you go and wait for me in the long gallery where they serve tea.'

'That's fine. Thanks,' he said, and hung up.

Walking across the lobby, Philippe Lavillard headed into the gallery where tea and drinks were served, and found himself a table. He took off his suede coat, put it on a chair and settled in the other one to wait for Laura Valiant.

He had always liked her, and considered her to be a truly good friend to Claire. Many times he had often wanted to ask her if she knew anything about Claire's past that would shed light on her distrust of men, himself in particular. But he had always lost his nerve at the last moment.

Suddenly Laura was there, standing in front of him, looking elegant in a dark red jacket and black trousers. Beautiful as always, he said to himself as he jumped up and stretched out his hand.

After shaking it, Laura sat down and asked, 'Did you have a nice morning with Natasha?'

'Yes, it's always great to be with her, she's a very special girl, very grown-up for her age. We walked, had breakfast and then took another walk through the Luxembourg Gardens. We enjoyed being together.'

Laura said, 'I'm glad. And you're correct, Philippe, she's a terrific girl. Claire's done a good job.'

'Yes, she has, Laura. I'm the first to say it.'

Laura looked at him and asked politely, 'Would you like a cup of tea? Or a drink? It's about that time.'

He shook his head. 'Thanks but I don't really want anything. Except to talk to you for a few minutes about Claire.'

'What about her?' Laura asked cautiously.

Leaning forward, Philippe said in a quiet, confiding tone, 'Look, Laura, I want to spend more time with Natasha, and she'd like that too. But you know how fierce Claire is, and she's determined to keep us apart.'

A thoughtful look crossed Laura's face and she replied, 'I have a feeling Claire thinks you're the one who has created the situation. I mean because you work in Zaire.'

'I know she does. And I'm planning to leave there. It may take me some time to extricate myself and to find a new job, but I've made up my mind to be in the same city as my daughter. If that's at all possible.'

'I see,' Laura said, and added, 'Last night was really awful. I must admit, I was a bit startled by Claire's anger. I've never seen her like that.'

'Neither have I, to be honest, Laura. She's been furious with me for a long time now. And I admit there's been quite a lot of acrimony between us, but last night she was worse than ever. Claire didn't seem like herself. I even wondered if there was something else upsetting her. Was there? Is there?'

'Not that I know of,' Laura answered, and instantly thought of Hercule's concern that Claire was ill. But she refrained from mentioning it. After all, Claire's life had nothing to do with Philippe anymore.

He said, 'Once I'm back in Paris I'm hoping I can establish a better relationship with Claire. Do you think that's possible?'

For a moment Laura was silent, pondering this, and finally she said, 'Perhaps.'

'Only perhaps? You don't sound very certain.'

'I guess I'm not. On the other hand, her complaint is that you're so far away in Zaire. So, once you're back maybe she'll understand how serious you are about Natasha, serious about helping to bring her up. Because that's what you'd be doing, wouldn't you?'

'Absolutely. And I want her to get to know my mother better. She's hardly seen her grandmother in the last few years, and that's not right, Laura. You more than anyone else should understand that.'

Laura merely nodded, but deep down she agreed with him. And she was coming to understand how sincere he was about changing his life in order to accommodate his daughter in it. How obvious it was he wanted to be with her, share time with her. She loved Claire, but like all people, Claire was not infallible. Last night, Hercule had suggested that she had always seen Philippe through Claire's eyes and not her own. Even Doug had pointed out that he was not such a bad fellow. Perhaps they were right. She suddenly adjusted her thinking about Philippe Lavillard.

Now Laura said, 'Yes, I do think it's important Natasha gets to know her grandmother. After all, we all need family. But I thought your mother lived in New York?'

'She does, but she often comes to Paris. She was born here, you know. Anyway, if I were living here she'd probably come more often.' He paused, and looked at Laura intently. 'I know how close you are to Claire, and I almost hesitate to ask this, but do you think you can put in a good word for me? I'm very serious about getting closer to Natasha, being with her in these important years of her life.'

'I know that. Still, Claire might wonder why I'm suddenly intervening.'

'You could tell her I'd been to see you.'

'I suppose I could.'

'You still sound very hesitant, Laura, and I don't want to put you in an awkward situation with Claire. Look, why don't you think about this ... once I've moved here maybe you could talk to Claire and then get her to come around to my way of thinking.'

'Yes, I could do that, Philippe. I realize how important this is to you, and I think it's important to Natasha, as well. She *should* know her father.' Laura nodded. 'Okay. I'll talk to Claire, but not until you're settled in Paris and ready to participate in Natasha's life.'

He smiled at her and his dark eyes lit up. 'Thank you, Laura. Thank you very much.'

8

It seemed to Laura that the rest of the week in Paris flew by. Suddenly, before she knew it, Friday morning was upon her, and she was scurrying around doing last minute things.

By the time she finally arrived at the Bar des Théâtres across the street from the Plaza Athénée, it was one-fifteen and she was late for her lunch date with Claire.

But Claire merely smiled as she began to apologize, and said mildly, 'It doesn't matter, I know what it's like when you're pushed for time. Come on, Laura darling, take off your coat and sit down.'

Laura did this, agreed to the glass of champagne Claire suggested, and then sat back. After taking a deep breath, she grinned and said, 'Everything just piled in on me, all of a sudden, but it was all good stuff! A lot of things came to fruition, *finally*, this morning.'

'So it's been a successful trip?' Claire asked.

'Very much so. Our Canadian client has committed to the Matisse and the Cézanne, and then this morning a private dealer I know came up with a Bonnard that's simply beautiful. I'm sure the same Canadian client will buy that, too. And I think another client in New York is going to buy the Renoir ... the countess's Renoir.'

'That's great! Hercule will be pleased, and so will the countess. Apparently she needs the money for repairs to the château in the Loire,' Claire said. 'Although I'm not sure why she feels the need to maintain that place. Hercule says it's enormous. She ought to sell it, in my opinion.'

'Hercule said something to me, too ... about it being in the family for hundreds of years, and there's the countess's son, who inherited the title and the lands. I'm sure the house is ... well, part of them. It's their heritage, his heritage, actually.'

'I guess so,' Claire agreed. She chuckled suddenly. 'My mother used to say that a house is a thief. It steals all your money. Don't ever forget that.'

'As if I could! When Grandma Megan gave me her house in Connecticut I was thrilled, until I realized that it's a money pit. And that's with Doug doing a lot of repairs and other things himself. You know how handy he is.'

'Give the famous Doug my love. It was lovely to see him last weekend.'

'I will.' Laura took a sip of the champagne, which had just arrived, saying cheers as she did so. With a frown, she then asked, 'Why does everyone call him *the famous Doug* in that way?'

'I didn't know everyone did; I thought it was only me,' Claire replied, looking at Laura curiously, her head on one side.

'Well, actually Philippe said the same thing the other day –' Laura stopped, wondering if she had made a faux pas by mentioning Philippe's name.

'Philippe said, *give the famous Doug my love,* when you saw him in the museum? Is that what you mean?' Claire murmured, her puzzlement reflected on her face.

'No, not that. He said, "*How's the famous Doug?*" And what *I'm* getting at now is why you and he call Doug *famous?*'

'I think I was the one who started it, because when you first met him you talked about him so much, raved about his looks and his brains and ... his brawn.' Claire laughed as she finished, 'You were so crazy about him, you made him seem like a movie star, and therefore famous. And he *is* so good looking, the proverbial tall, dark and handsome hero, right?'

Laura laughed with her old friend. She said, 'I guess I was pretty bowled over at the time. He was the most gorgeous thing on two legs that I'd ever seen. Still is, really.'

'So, give him my love.'

'I will. And I know he reciprocates. You've always been his favourite.'

Claire looked pleased on hearing this, but she made no comment. Then she asked, 'What do you want to eat? I think I'll have the omelette *fines herbes*, and a green salad.'

'I'll have the same, Claire, I'm not very hungry.'

Once Claire had ordered lunch for them, she confided, 'It's been wonderful having you here, Laura. I'm going to miss you, and so is Natasha. You're the only person she has in this world, you know. After me, of course.'

'And her –' Laura began to cough, covered her mouth with her hand. Once she calmed herself, she finished. 'She has Hercule,' knowing how stupid it would be to say she has her father, which she had just been about to do.

'You started to say her father, didn't you?' Claire said.

Laura felt herself flushing. After a moment, she nodded.

Claire went on quickly, 'But she doesn't have him, you see. She never had him. He's never been a good father to her. Nor was he a good husband, for that matter. His work and his women invariably came first. He was extremely independent, and did what he wanted. And very selfishly so. He was neglectful of me, and of Natasha.'

Suddenly they were right in the middle of something Laura had not intended, had, in fact, wanted to avoid at all cost. She wondered how to respond, was afraid of upsetting Claire by saying the wrong thing. And so she said nothing at all.

Suddenly, Claire leaned across the table, staring into Laura's troubled face. 'I'm so sorry about last Saturday night. I wish it hadn't happened. It was ugly and unnecessary. But Philippe shouldn't have arrived like that, *unannounced.* He knows it upsets me when he does. Somehow he always manages to create problems.'

'I know how hurt and angry you've been, and still are, Claire,' Laura acknowledged in a sympathetic voice. 'But I do wish you could put all that on one side, turn away from it. Philippe is no longer a part of your life, except for seeing Natasha from time to time. It's so ... *enervating* to hang on to anger the way you do, darling.'

Claire sighed. 'I wish I *could* turn away, Laura, but I can't forget all the terrible things he did to me. I suppose I'm bitter.'

The waiter arrived with their food, which saved Laura the trouble of replying. She was greatly relieved, since she did not know how to answer Claire. At least, not in a way that would please her friend. Laura was aware that to harbour bitterness was deadly: it only bred more pain and hurt in the long run. However, getting Claire to accept this was another matter altogether. Even to attempt it would be a futile exercise on her part.

Deeming it wiser, Laura still did not respond; she picked up her fork and began eating the salad, then took a forkful of omelette.

They ate in silence for a while. It was Claire who eventually broke it, when she said, 'It's funny, I'm very ambivalent about Philippe in certain ways. I want him to see Natasha, to be a father to her, and yet another part of me wishes he would just stay away from Paris altogether, never attempt to see her. That way we would all know where we stand. Perhaps I should say that to him. What do you think?'

'Is he still here?' Laura asked quietly.

'I don't know. He never reveals much to Natasha when he sees her. What did he say to you, when you ran into him at the museum?'

'Just that he was passing through, en route to Atlanta to see the head of the Center for Disease Control.'

Claire nodded. 'That figures. First and foremost, always the great scientist.'

Laura wanted to remind Claire that Philippe Lavillard had done some remarkable work and made some extraordinary discoveries in his field, but she decided to hold her tongue. Instead she said, 'Listen, Claire, I've been thinking about something for the last few days, and I want to pass it by you now. How about coming to New York for Christmas? Or rather, to Connecticut. You and Natasha, and even Hercule, if he'd enjoy it. We'd have a wonderful time . . .' She paused and laughed, added, 'It would be like old times, you know. Mom's coming up, and she's going to bring Grandma Megan. And Doug's friend Robin Knox is bringing his fiancée, Karen. There'll be a houseful, and it'll be warm and happy and fun. What do you say?'

Claire's face had lit up, and Laura could see that she loved the idea. But then she shook her head. 'I just can't get away right now, and anyway, I promised Hercule I would host his New Year's Eve party with him.'

'But you could go back in time for that. It's only the thirteenth of December today.'

'Friday the thirteenth,' Claire cut in, and grimaced.

'Oh, I know, so what!' Laura exclaimed dismissively, and hurried on, 'If you came next weekend, that's Saturday the twenty-first, or Sunday the twenty-second, you could easily stay for a week, even eight days, and then fly back for Hercule's party on the thirty-first. Oh *do* try, Claire! Just think how much Natasha would love it. And *I* would too. All of us would.'

'I'll think about it,' Claire said, and took a mouthful of salad. 'There is something *I* wanted to ask *you*, Laura.' Claire hesitated before saying, 'Could Natasha and I come and stay in the country with you in the summer? I never really know what to do with her then, they have such long school holidays in France. Hercule usually takes us to Brittany, to stay with him there, but normally we only go for a couple of weeks. What do you think?'

'It's a fabulous idea! And of course you can come. But I don't want you to substitute the summer for Christmas. Promise you'll try your damnedest, and that you'll ask Hercule?'

'All right, I'll see what I can do, and of course I'll extend your invitation to him.' She shook her head. 'It's just that I have so much work,' she finished worriedly.

'I understand, I'm sort of snowed under myself. Even though I'm supposed to go to Palm Beach, to see a client's house, to recommend the kind of art she should use, I don't think I'll make it before Christmas,' Laura explained. 'I'll have to go in January.'

'I suppose Grandma Megan still has that pretty little cottage on Island Drive in Palm Beach?'

Laura nodded. 'Mom likes to spend time there in January and February, she says she paints well at Bedelia Cottage. But Grandma doesn't go there anymore, she hasn't been for years. Don't ask me why. Personally, I think the warm weather would do her good.'

'Yes, it would. But you know what she's like. Nobody can tell Grandma Megan what to do.'

Laura smiled, thinking of her grandmother. 'She's just wonderful, that's all I know.'

They fell into a discussion about Megan Valiant, whom they both loved, and who had been such a force in their lives when they were young. Then they reminisced about their girlhood spent together in New York and at the house in Connecticut, and they remembered those days with love and warmth and a great deal of nostalgia.

They were loath to say goodbye to each other, so closely bonded were they, and so they drank another cup of coffee, wanting to be together for as long as possible. Finally, it was Claire who brought their farewell lunch to an end, pointing out that she must return to her office.

The two women walked across the avenue Montaigne, and stood in front of the hotel for a few more moments, still talking, clinging to each other verbally. And then they were doing that physically, as they hugged and said their goodbyes.

'Please try for Christmas,' Laura said, squeezing Claire's arm.

'I will, Laura, I promise,' Claire answered, and then she smiled a bit wanly and hurried off down the street without looking back.

I really will miss her terribly, Laura thought, staring after Claire's retreating figure. Turning, she went into the hotel, and took the lift up to her room. It was time to pack and conclude the remainder of her business.

9

Douglas Casson was well pleased with his handiwork. He had swept the leaves into the centre of the terrace, and all he had to do now was shovel them into the wheelbarrow. He had just begun to do this when a sudden, gusting wind began to blow. The leaves ended up swirling around his feet. He cursed mildly under his breath, accepting that his sweeping had been in vain. And then he chuckled to himself, threw down the shovel and went and sat on the wall.

Oh what the hell, he muttered, I can't compete with the wind. He would have to deal with the leaves later. And what did they matter anyway? Not at all.

He continued to sit on the low wall that encircled the terrace, for a moment enjoying the winter sunshine and fresh air. It was a cold day, bracing, but the sky was very blue, and although there was no warmth in the sun it enhanced the day.

Douglas didn't sit long on the drystone wall. Very quickly he was beginning to feel the cold through his sheepskin-lined suede jacket, and he stood up, put the shovel in the wheelbarrow and trundled it over to the garden shed.

Within minutes he was back in the house, standing in front of the fire in the great hall, warming himself. The weather was deceptive. From the windows the bright sparkling day beckoned beguilingly, but once outside the raw cold bit into the bones. It was a freezing day, as Laura had warned earlier. Not a day to be outside very long, she had said.

He should have listened to her; she was always right about the weather in Connecticut. After all, she had grown up in this old colonial house in Kent, spending many weekends here with her grandparents, as well as Christmas, Easter, and summer vacations.

Dumped on Megan and Owen, he thought now, while her parents went off, doing their own thing. He had never seen a couple as engrossed with each other as her mother and father had been. It seemed to him that they hardly knew that Laura and Dylan existed, although when he had once said that to Laura she had pooh-poohed this idea. 'Dad was always there for us when we needed him. Admittedly he was more involved with us than Mom, but she loved us as much as he did.'

Douglas had never been really sure about that. He thought that Margaret Valiant was a self-involved and selfish woman, although he had never dared to voice this opinion to Laura. She always defended her mother, whatever he said. But then that was human nature, wasn't it? A child could criticize its parents and family, but God forbid if a stranger did. Holy hell usually broke loose.

But he knew he was correct in his assessment of Laura's mother. Her painting and her husband had been the only things of any real consequence to her. Not that he had been around when Laura was growing up, but Maggie had practically told him that herself once in a moment of weakness, when they were sharing confidences of sorts. He was aware that she regretted it later; he saw the regret reflected in her dark soulful eyes.

He wondered what it was like to love someone in this way? He never had. Of course he loved Laura, but not to the exclusion of all else in his life.

Walking over to a wing chair, he sat down heavily, leaned his head against the dark red velvet and closed his eyes.

His marriage was in trouble.

He knew it and had known it for a long time now. But he wasn't sure if Laura was aware they had problems. He didn't know how to tell her, had not the slightest idea how to even broach the subject.

The problems had nothing to do with their inability to produce a child together. This did not even worry him much anymore. Rather, it had to do with *them*, with their relationship, and their future together. Of late they had spent a lot of time apart, travelling because of their careers. And were they not growing apart? Emotionally and physically. *He* believed they were, but he was quite certain Laura had no conception of this. None at all. Not because she wasn't smart, she was one of the savviest people he knew. But because he was different now; he had changed.

'Doug, can you come and help me?'

Laura's voice echoed down from the staircase at the far end of the great hall, and he snapped open his eyes and instantly jumped up.

'Of course, what do you want me to do?' he asked.

'I need you to get a window blind back into its notches, or whatever they're called. It's slipped out and fallen down.'

'Be right there, sweetie.'

Laura watched him walking towards her, thinking how well he looked this morning, very young in his cream fisherman's knit sweater and dark blue corduroys. The time spent outside had brought a rosiness to his cheeks, which enhanced his boyish good looks. Black hair, green eyes, six-foot-two and all athletic muscle. Tall, dark and handsome, as Claire had said in Paris just over a week ago. There was no doubt about it, Doug was an exceptionally attractive man, and looked much younger than his thirty-three years. More like twenty-five, she decided, as he strode down the hall purposefully.

'Sorry to disturb you when you were relaxing,' she said as he bounded up the stairs two at a time. 'But I must get everything finished before Robin and Karen arrive later this afternoon.'

'No problem, I was only whiling away the time, and getting warm after my abortive efforts with the leaves.' He smiled lopsidedly and explained, 'They're hard to handle when there's a strong wind.' He leaned against the bannister at the top of the stairs.

Laura laughed, her blue eyes crinkling up at the corners. 'The leaves can wait.'

'I know. Anyway, isn't it time I started throwing some lunch together, while you do your bit of last minute decorating for Christmas? Your mother and Grandma Megan will be here tomorrow, and before you know it, you'll have your hands full.'

'I'll be finished today. And don't make anything complicated for lunch, Doug. A sandwich is all I'm interested in.'

'That's good enough for me too, but how about a cup of soup? Chicken noodle from a packet, courtesy of the Knorr kitchen?'

'Sounds delicious,' she said, and hurried down the long corridor to one of the four guest rooms situated at the far end.

'It's at this window,' Laura said, entering the yellow room with its four-poster bed, colourful antique quilt and framed flower-prints hanging on the sunny walls.

It took Doug only a few minutes to roll the blind properly, and then slot it back into the notches on the reveals on either side of the window. 'There you go, all done! Now, what else can I fix for you?'

'Nothing. We're in pretty good shape here. But I would like you to decide which room you want Robin and Karen to stay in.'

'Who's sleeping in here?' he asked, glancing around. He had always liked this particular room because it was so cheerful, full of bright yellows and pinks.

'I'd thought of giving it to Mom, but if you want I can put them in here.'

'No, no, let your mother have it. I suppose you're giving your grandmother her old room, as usual.'

'It's hers for as long as she lives, you know that. Listen, she slept in it for almost sixty years, so I'm sure she'd feel disoriented anywhere else.'

'I agree.'

Laura walked out of the yellow bedroom, and said over her shoulder, 'I had thought of putting Robin and Karen in the blue-and-white room, it's so crisp and fresh. But they could have the little suite upstairs under the eaves. What do you think?'

'The suite upstairs! It's cosy, charming, and Robin's going to love it. It has a French feeling to it, and he likes anything French, he's quite the Francophile. Let's go up and have a look.'

Together they climbed the narrow, twisting staircase that led to the top of the house. Doug wandered through the set of four rooms, which were actually the old attics. There was a bedroom, a tiny sitting room, a small den-dressing room and a bathroom. Laura had decorated the suite in red and white, using a *toile de Jouy* in these colours on the walls throughout, and a matching fabric for the headboard. A red-and-white checked fabric appeared on several armchairs, and there was a big red velvet sofa that matched the bright red carpet.

'Yes, Robin will definitely like this,' Doug said, scanning everything. 'So will Karen,' he thought to add. 'Also, they've got privacy up here.'

'Are they definitely staying through Christmas Day?' Laura asked.

Doug nodded. 'Yes. Robin's taken a few days off from the bank, and Karen's closed the shop until January. It makes a nice break for them both.'

'I'll bring some books up,' Laura said, as they went downstairs. 'And the latest magazines along with a bowl of fruit.'

'Let's do it after lunch,' Doug suggested. 'I'll help you finish up once we've eaten.'

In the end lunch became a long, rather drawn-out affair, since Doug decided to make something more substantial than a packet of soup and canned tuna fish sandwiches. Instead he prepared

Eggs Benedict with toasted muffins and Canadian bacon, followed by one of his specialities, caramelized grapefruit and vanilla ice cream.

'That wasn't too bad, was it?' he asked, at the end of lunch, clinking his glass of white wine to Laura's.

'Hardly, it was delicious. You can cook for me any time,' she said, her eyes dancing as she peered at him over the rim of the glass.

'That's what I've always done, or so it seems to me,' he shot back, laughing with her. It was an old story, a family joke really, the fact that she couldn't cook at all and he loved nothing better than to hover over the stove in the big country kitchen.

'I suppose we ought to go upstairs and put finishing touches to the little suite under the eaves,' Laura murmured, lifting her glass to her mouth again.

'I'll help you, but we might as well finish this wine, there's only a drop left. A shame to waste Pouilly Fumé,' Doug said, topping up both of their glasses. 'That's a dead soldier,' he added as he picked up the empty wine bottle and carried it over to the recycling bin.

Returning to the kitchen table, where they were eating, he went on, 'I guess we're going to be ten for Christmas lunch, after all, Laura. My parents now say they'd like to come, and Malcolm and Gloria Mason finally accepted the invitation. Yesterday. I forgot to tell you.'

'Oh good, it'll be fun, and I know the Masons like Robin and Karen.' Swallowing the last of her wine, Laura now pushed back her chair and stood up. 'I suppose you'll do your fabulous goose with all the trimmings, and I'll help you the best I can. But we'll plan the menu later, shall we?'

'Plenty of time,' he replied. 'We don't have to do the shopping until early next week.'

Laura began taking things out of the cupboard, arranging them on a large wooden tray. After putting glasses, small plates, napkins, dessert knives and forks on it, she reached for pieces of fruit in a big wooden bowl on the table, filled a glass dish with apples, bananas, and grapes. 'This should do it, don't you think?' She eyed Doug, who nodded his agreement.

He said, 'I'll go to my den and get a few magazines, some of the books you picked up last week. Do you want me to carry that tray up for you? Or can you manage?'

'I'm fine, darling.' Laura hoisted the wooden tray as she spoke. 'We can take the bottled water later.'

'I'll be there in a minute,' Doug announced before heading in the direction of his den.

Laura was a little out of breath when she reached the suite under the eaves, and after placing the tray on top of a chest of drawers, she flopped down on the large red sofa, endeavouring to catch her breath.

A moment later Doug came in with his pile of magazines and popular books. He burst out laughing when he saw Laura leaning back against the sofa, her breathing still laboured.

'It was a long climb,' she gasped, by way of explanation. 'Three flights. They winded me a bit.'

He smiled at her, shaking his head. And quite suddenly he was captivated by the way she looked at this moment. The last remnants of the afternoon sun were washing over her high cheekbones and delicately-articulated face; she was bathed in a crystalline light. What a truly beautiful woman she was, his wife. He wanted her; he wanted to make love to her.

Doug dropped the books and magazines onto a nearby chair, and went and sat next to her on the sofa. Putting his arms around her, he pulled her closer to him, brought his lips to hers, kissing her gently at first. And then as she responded, and stroked his face, the kisses became more forceful. They clung to each other, their passion accelerating. Doug now kissed her more fervently than ever, his tongue seeking hers in a moment of profound intimacy. It seemed to them both that they were melting into each other.

Doug went on kissing his wife's face, her eyelids, her brow, her neck; his hands went deftly to her breasts and he delighted that her nipples were erect under her cotton blouse.

Pausing, he whispered against her neck. 'Come on, let's go and find a bed.' Taking hold of both her hands, Doug pulled her to her feet; with their arms wrapped around each other they went into the adjoining bedroom.

Within a few seconds they were both naked, lying on top of the antique quilt. 'You're not cold are you?' he asked softly.

'No. This room's always been warm. Actually, I'm hot,' she whispered.

So am I, he thought, but he said nothing, simply buried his head between her breasts. Throwing one leg over her, he pressed his body alongside hers, slowly caressing her arm, and then her thigh. It was true, she *was* hot; he could feel the heat rising from her body.

Encircling her with his arms, he rolled them over on the bed, so that he was on his back and she lay on top of him. Automatically, she went to kneel in front of him, loving him the way he liked her to do.

But a moment or two later he was pulling her up so that she was on top of him. When he entered her he did so with such suddenness, and so swiftly, she let out a little cry. Then they began to move together in the old familiar rhythm that was theirs.

Both of them were carried along by their mutual passion. Rising upward together, they felt as if they were floating ... higher and higher ... soaring ... soaring ...

Far away, as if from a long distance, Doug heard a faint noise. He snapped his eyes open, stared across at the doorway.

Robin Knox was standing there, watching them, his blue eyes startled, his face pale. And then he was gone. In an instant he had disappeared.

Doug blinked, wondering if he'd imagined Robin's unexpected presence. He knew he had not.

Laura fell against him, asking in an almost inaudible voice, 'Why did you stop? What happened? Is something wrong?'

'Nothing,' he said. 'Nothing.' But there was.

There was a long silence. He cleared his throat. 'I guess the wine at lunch got to me,' he lied, hoping she believed him.

PART TWO

Winter and Spring

1997

10

Laura left her office on Sixty-Eighth Street and hurried down Madison Avenue, walking in the direction of Sixtieth. One of Laura's greatest assets was her power of concentration; yet another her ability to compartmentalize matters in order to deal with the single most important problem of the moment. This ability to truly focus on something to the exclusion of all else – she called it her tunnel vision – was one of her strong suits. As she hurried to her appointment her mind was geared to the difficult situation she was certain she was about to encounter.

Laura was thinking about Mark Tabbart, one of America's cleverest, shrewdest and most successful financiers, one of the new mega-rich buccaneers of big business with a lavish lifestyle, money to burn and a high profile. He had been a client of hers for the past two years, and although he was tough, brash, opinionated and dictatorial they had, until this moment, enjoyed a good relationship based on an easy rapport and mutual respect of each other's abilities. For the most part he took her advice and bowed to her better judgement, but she had an uneasy feeling that this was about to change.

Laura and Alison were considered to be two of the best in the business, self-assured, confident in their knowledge of Impressionist art and the international market. They had helped to build fine collections for high-powered business executives and celebrities with newly-made fortunes who wanted to invest in art. All paid strict attention to what she and Alison said and took their recommendations, relying on their professional judgement, knowledge and experience. Their credentials and reputation were impeccable in the art market of the late 1990s, which was enjoying another high.

When she had first been introduced to Mark Tabbart by one of her other clients, he had asked Laura why anyone would feel the need to use her services, or those of any other expert. 'I've got eyes in my head, I know whether I like a painting or not, and I can read the name of the artist on the canvas. So why do I need an art expert?'

Laura had responded with a question of her own. 'Would you sign a binding legal document involving millions of dollars without first seeking the advice of a lawyer? I very much doubt it.'

'You're right, I wouldn't,' he had answered, and encouraged by his straightforwardness Laura had gone on to pose another question.

'Surely then, you would agree that it's foolish to buy an expensive painting without asking advice from someone with a great deal of knowledge about art and the market.'

'Agreed,' Tabbart had concurred and that same day he had become a client.

In the ensuing two years Laura had helped the entrepreneur build a fine collection. She had acquired for him some of the great French Impressionist and Post-Impressionist paintings, including works by Cézanne and Matisse, and such American painters as John Singer Sargent and Frank Benson; and she had picked up two paintings by Dame Laura Knight, the British Post-Impressionist painter.

But the one thing she had not been able to do thus far was to fulfil his desire to acquire a Gauguin. Suddenly, out of the blue, he had discovered one for himself, one that was actually for sale.

Laura had learned about this development four days ago, when Tabbart had phoned her from Aspen, chortling with glee about his extraordinary luck. They had arranged to meet today and she realized as she turned into the lobby of Tabbart's office building that she might have to do battle with him. Taking a deep breath, Laura braced herself as she entered the lift and rode up to the fortieth floor.

Mark Tabbart had kept her waiting twenty minutes already, but Laura was well aware that this did not signify anything special or untoward. Certainly it had nothing to do with her. He was an exceptionally busy man, with endless demands on his time, and this was not the first occasion she had hung around in the reception area until he had finished whatever bit of business he was transacting.

At the exact moment she pulled out her mobile phone to call Doug at his office, Mark's assistant Alec Fulham suddenly appeared at the private entrance to Mark's inner sanctum. She put the phone back in her handbag and stood up swiftly, realizing she would have to call Doug later.

Alec hurried forward, sounding apologetic as he said, 'Sorry about this. Mark's been on a complicated call. He just finished.'

'No problem,' Laura replied. She followed him along the corridor to Mark's office in silence.

When they entered the room Mark Tabbart was standing looking out of the window. He was short, thin and wiry, a baby-faced, balding man who was not particularly prepossessing physically; but he was brilliant in business and considered by his peers to be a financial genius. He was in his shirt sleeves, as he usually was when he was working at his desk, his dark jacket slung across the back of the chair.

He turned around, moved lithely across the thickly-carpeted floor to greet her effusively. His face instantly changed, became genial, although his warm smile was not reflected in his pale grey eyes which, as always, were cold, appraising.

After kissing her on both cheeks and exchanging a few pleas-antries Mark went to his desk, picked up several photographs, and began, 'I want you to see these pictures of –'

'*Tahitian Dreams*,' Laura finished for him, swiftly cutting in, wanting to gain the advantage by proving a point to him. 'Painted by Paul Gauguin in 1896. It's the portrait of a Tahitian woman on a starry night, inky-blue sky, brilliant white stars. The woman is reclining under a tree, there's a bowl of fruit by her side, the faint outline of a horse under a tree, and off to the right a Tahitian man gazing at her. Gauguin's wonderfully vivid colours are much in evidence, a lovely deep red in the fan she's holding, the warm coral he often used for his earth tones, a mingling of dark greens in the trees behind her, with pavonine blues in the sky. The woman's nude, except for a strip of yellow silk thrown across her thighs, and she bears a strong resemblance to the woman in Gauguin's painting called *Vairumati* which is in the Musée d'Orsay in Paris, but the actual setting is similar to the one Gauguin used in his painting called *Te Arii Vahine* which is hanging in the Pushkin Museum in Moscow. And, by the way, Gauguin painted *Tahitian Dreams* on his second trip to Tahiti.'

Mark Tabbart made no response whatsoever. He simply sat staring at her.

Laura returned his hard stare unflinchingly; she knew she had the upper hand because, for the moment, he was impressed by her knowledge. When he chose not to make any com-ment, Laura asked, 'I have described the painting correctly, haven't I?'

His nod was almost curt. 'It seems that you know this painting intimately,' he finally remarked with acerbity, his pale, pellucid eyes still fixed on her intently.

'Yes, that's true, I do.'

'Therefore you must be acquainted with the owner.'

'I am. Norman Grant owns *Tahitian Dreams*.'

'Norman told me the painting has been on the market for

about three months. Did you know *Tahitian Dreams* was for sale?'

'I did. Many people in the art world knew of its availability, Mark.'

'Then why didn't you tell me about it? Recommend it?' he asked, sounding puzzled.

Laura said, very quietly, 'I thought the painting was not right for you.'

'Why not? You know how much I've wanted a Gauguin, been salivating about owning one for years.'

'This is a problem painting. I wouldn't recommend it to anyone.'

Mark frowned. 'What do you mean by *problem*? It's not a fake, is it?'

'No,' she said quickly, shaking her head. 'I didn't mean to imply anything like that. The painting is one of Gauguin's best, in my opinion, and I'd give anything to be able to recommend it to you. But I can't. Please forget this painting, it's not for you.'

Mark Tabbart's fixed scrutiny of her lasted for the longest moment before he finally lowered his eyes and stared at the photographs he was holding. He disliked being thwarted, and suddenly he exclaimed in a cold voice, 'I want it, Laura! I've every intention of making an offer to Norman Grant.'

'I really don't think you should. Please don't go near that painting, it's only going to create problems for you.'

Mark threw the two photographs on his desk and walked around it, sat down heavily in the chair, glaring at her.

When Laura remained standing in the middle of the room, he motioned to her. 'Sit down, Laura, in the chair opposite me, and let's get to the bottom of this.'

She nodded, did as he said.

'Now, please explain. Tell me why I shouldn't make an offer.' Unexpectedly, a grin surfaced and spread across his face. 'It's not stolen is it?'

Laura hesitated, then answered with firmness, 'Yes, it is.'

The grin slid off his face; he sat up straighter in his chair and leaned forward. 'You can't be serious.'

'I'm afraid I am.'

'But Norman Grant is reputable, a man of some standing. He's not going to offer me a painting which has been stolen, for God's sake.'

'But he just did, Mark. Four days ago, to be exact.'

'This is preposterous, and I –'

Laura interrupted him, said, 'Let me explain, so that you fully understand. May I?'

Mark Tabbart settled back in his chair, but his expression was impatient. 'Please do,' he snapped.

'*Tahitian Dreams* is in jeopardy, and it could very easily become the object of a dispute in the not too distant future, that's why I'm trying to steer you away from it.'

'Who was it stolen from?' Mark demanded. 'And how do you know this?'

'I'm a professional art-adviser, Mark, it's my business to know these things. A great deal of information comes across my desk every day, and from all over the world. Very recently, the painting was brought to my attention. *Tahitian Dreams* has a strange history, and incidentally it has changed hands quite a few times, but without much fanfare.'

'I know that. I have the provenance of the painting from Norman Grant,' he pointed out in an irritable voice.

'I would *expect* you to have it. Norman Grant bought the painting from a woman called Anthea Margolis of Boston, about five years ago. She, in turn, had purchased it fifteen years before that from someone called Joshua Lester of New York, or rather, Mr Lester's widow. The Lesters had owned the painting for about eighteen years before selling it to Mrs Margolis. Mr Lester bought the painting from an Arthur Marriott who lived in London and he had owned it since –'

'1950!' Mark spluttered, annoyed with her. 'Look here, I know all that.' He glanced at the paper he was holding, waved it at her. 'I *have* all the relevant dates here.'

'Then read on, Mark, please, and tell me who Arthur Marriott bought it from in 1950,' Laura responded, shifting slightly in the chair, crossing her long elegant legs, looking at him pointedly.

'It doesn't say, only that he had owned it since that particular year. And why does it matter? It's now January of 1997. Forty-seven years are accounted for. What more do you want?'

'Forty-seven years don't mean very much, you know, when you consider that the painting was executed by Gauguin in 1896. That's one-hundred-and-one years ago. Where do you think it was for fifty-four years before that? Before this gentleman called Arthur Marriott bought it?'

'I've no idea,' Mark replied coldly. 'And do we *care*?'

'*You* ought to care, since you've considered buying it.'

'The provenance Norman Grant has provided is good enough for me,' he shot back, glaring at her once more.

'Let me give you a little more information,' Laura murmured, returning his cold stare steadily. He had not been able to intimidate her yet. 'Arthur Marriott was an art-dealer in London, and he bought the painting from the Herman Seltzer Gallery in Vienna, Austria,' Laura went on, then paused, took a deep breath and plunged in. 'The gallery had acquired it about a year earlier, in 1949, from one Josef Schiller. He had been a general in the SS, a Nazi, one of Hitler's top echelon. The painting was, in fact, confiscated by Schiller's lieutenants from the art collection of Sigmund and Ursula Westheim, a wealthy Jewish banking family in Berlin. The Westheim Bank, a private merchant bank, was famous; so was the Westheim Art Collection, which was started by Sigmund's grandfather, Friedrich, in the late nineteenth century. This was immediately following the historic first Impressionist showing in Paris in 1874. Friedrich Westheim was an avid collector, and over the years he acquired some extraordinary art. He bought the paintings of Renoir, Matisse, Manet, Vuillard, Van Gogh, Sisley, Seurat, Monet and Degas, and sculptures by Degas and Rodin, as well. He was also a big collector of Gauguin's primitives, and it was Friedrich Westheim who purchased *Tahitian Dreams,* just after it was first exhibited in Paris in 1897, or thereabouts. In any case, not very long after Paul Gauguin had shipped it to France from Tahiti, along with other paintings he had recently completed. Friedrich happened to be a close friend of Claude Monet's and used to frequently visit the artist at Giverny, and he acquired some remarkable paintings by him. You may not have heard of it, but in art circles the Westheim Collection is well known. It was the greatest Impressionist and Post-Impressionist collection ever put together, in fact. There's never been one like it since, either in private hands or in a museum. And it disappeared in *its entirety* in 1938–9.'

Laura paused, gave Mark a careful look, and finished, 'It was confiscated by the Nazis. *Confiscated* being another word for *stolen,* of course.'

'I see.' Tabbart nodded his understanding, then added, 'And that is why the Gauguin which Norman Grant owns is in jeopardy.'

'Exactly. I'm not sure whether you are aware of this or not, but the World Jewish Congress's Commission for Art Recovery is hellbent on retrieving art which was stolen by the Nazis from the Jews of Europe . . . whenever it turns up somewhere, whatever the circumstances, and *if* there is a claimant.'

'And there's a claimant for *Tahitian Dreams!*' Mark said. 'Of course! That's it. There's a Westheim heir who can prove that the painting belonged to the Westheim family. I'm right, aren't I?'

'Yes. Some new documentation has come to light that leaves no doubt.'

'And where does this development put Norman Grant?'

'With a problem. He could lose the painting.'

'It seems to me he's an innocent bystander.'

'Perhaps. On the other hand, the painting was stolen, and it therefore belongs to its original owner, the person from whom it was stolen originally.'

'Come on, Laura,' Mark said, his tone irate. 'The painting was apparently lost in 1938–9, and that is some fifty-nine years ago now. *Really!*'

Laura shook her head vehemently. 'It can't be reasoned that way. No, no. Listen to me. If I go into your house and steal something, be it a painting or a small object of some kind, and then I go and sell it to someone else, it's still your property. It's not mine. You haven't sold it. *I* have sold it . . . a *thief* has sold it. Am I correct?'

'Yes. But that doesn't wash, in this instance, does it? There are some extenuating circumstances here, Laura.'

'I don't think there are. That painting was seized illegally by the Nazis, and therefore it rightly belongs to the heir of the Westheim family. As does the rest of the Westheim Art Collection, actually. As I just told you, that vanished without a trace.'

'I don't know . . .' Mark's voice trailed off, and his expression was one of uncertainty all of a sudden. He seemed less sure of himself than he had been a moment ago. 'Half the art world's going to be up in arms about this, if the Westheim heir sues,' he muttered. 'It's opening a can of worms, isn't it?'

'Maybe it is. On the other hand, I truly believe it is wrong to shield the provenance of stolen goods from proper scrutiny, which is what happened all those years ago. This problem goes back to Arthur Marriott, who should have asked for, no *demanded*, the proper provenance when he bought *Tahitian Dreams* from the Herman Seltzer Gallery in 1950.'

'And would the owner of the gallery have given it to him, do you think?' Mark asked, a hint of scepticism in his tone.

'I don't know, although I think General Josef Schiller would have had plenty of phoney documentation to make it appear that he had come by the painting legally. The gallery is probably an innocent party to this also. Well, there's one thing I'm absolutely certain of, and it's this. The heir of Sigmund and Ursula Westheim is the rightful owner of the Gauguin, and it should go back to that family, no matter who possesses the painting at this moment.'

Mark was thoughtful for a split second, rubbing his chin with one hand. Then he glanced across at her, his eyes narrowing as he said, 'I suppose you see a string of lawsuits ahead. You do, don't you?'

'Look, I don't know what's going to happen. The situation could get volatile, yes.'

'I can hazard a guess, make a prediction even,' he volunteered. 'Norman Grant will have to sue the woman he bought it from, and she'll have to do the same thing, and so on and so on, right down the line. I can now understand why you don't want me to go anywhere near the painting.'

'I'm glad you do, Mark.'

'Does Norman Grant know anything about the Westheim heir?'

'I have no idea. But the story has begun to make the rounds – at least, it has in the art world. A few people I know are aware of it. But I don't think any legal steps have been taken yet. By the Westheim heir, I mean. I did hear the heir has been doing a lot of digging, investigating, trying to trace the painting's long journey over the years, and so I'm certain that by now he knows Norman Grant owns it.'

'How come *you* know so much about this situation anyway?'

'I explained before, a great deal of material comes to my office, and it's my business to sift through it all. And then a friend in the art world told me something about it, quite a lot actually, and what a story it was. You see, my friend knew how much I love Gauguin's work. He wanted to alert me.'

'I doubt Norman Grant knows anything. Shouldn't he be told?'

'Not by me. Or you, for that matter. Stay out of it, Mark.'

'You know what, Laura, this is all wrong.' Mark settled back in his chair. 'The painting was lost all those years ago, and the Westheim heir should accept that, not expect to receive reparation or to get the painting back. Not only that, let's not forget that Norman Grant paid good money for it, *in good faith*, and now he could be sued for it, could lose a painting which cost him millions. And he's done nothing wrong.'

'*Tahitian Dreams* was stolen by a Nazi general, a member of the SS. It is morally wrong to say that Grant owns it. What he bought is a stolen painting, and now the rightful owner wants it back.'

'But Grant didn't know – and doesn't know – it was stolen,' Mark protested, his impatience with her flaring again.

'As far as we know he doesn't,' she snapped back acidly.

'I bet Norman won't give it up so easily,' he announced and laughed dryly. 'I don't know him, but he looks like a tough son of a bi – son of a gun, and the heir *will* have to sue if he wants to get his hands on that Gauguin. I sort of sympathize with Norman, I must admit. Nobody wants to be out millions of dollars.'

Laura said slowly, 'A moment ago I thought you saw this my way, but obviously not.' She bent forward, drew closer to him, frowning. 'Don't you think that acquiring art from those condemned to die in the death camps, and not paying them or their families for that art, is an unacceptable way to build an art collection?'

'Put that way, yes, I have to agree with you. But look here, this situation had its genesis in 1950, at that gallery in Vienna. The gallery sold the painting to an innocent person who had no knowledge of the provenance.'

'We don't know that, Mark. In those days, people in the art world knew of the Westheim Collection and what was in it before the war. We're talking about only twelve years here, from 1938 to 1950, and remember, the fellow who bought it from the Seltzer Gallery was an art-dealer.'

'Point well taken, but we're dealing with the present, the here and now. Incidentally, just out of curiosity, who is the Westheim heir?'

'Sir Maximilian West.'

'The British industrialist?'

'Yes.'

'He changed his name,' Mark asserted.

'No, he anglicized it. From what I've heard about him, he went to England as a child, grew up there and became a British citizen after the Second World War.'

'I see.'

They both fell silent for a moment or two, and it was Mark Tabbart who broke it when he asked, 'How come he hasn't done anything about the painting before now?'

'According to my information, he only recently found out who owns *Tahitian Dreams*. Also, he apparently just came across some old documents which absolutely support his claim of ownership.'

'I see.'

Laura said, 'Shall I call Norman Grant and tell him you're going to pass on the Gauguin?'

Mark gave her an odd look out of the corner of his eye, glanced down at the photographs, and answered without looking up, 'No, no, I'll talk to him myself.'

'But I don't mind making that call, as your art-adviser.'

'I said I'd handle it myself,' Tabbart snapped and rose. He looked at his watch pointedly. 'I'm afraid I have another meeting, Laura, if you'll excuse me now.'

11

Laura was angry.

She walked back to her office at a rapid pace, seething inside. There was no question about it, Mark Tabbart had literally pushed her out of his inner sanctum, so unceremoniously that his behaviour had verged on the point of rudeness.

Maybe he did have another appointment; on the other hand, he had never propelled her out into the reception area so quickly and in quite the same way before. All of a sudden he had wanted to get rid of her. In order to make a phone call to Norman Grant? she wondered. Obviously she could not be certain about that, but it was a strong possibility.

It struck her that Mark was not going to take her advice. He was convinced he was infallible. Perhaps he was in business, but not in this particular matter. He knew very little about the art world. What to do? How to get him to see it her way?

Then abruptly she stopped in her tracks, as it suddenly struck her that she must get rid of her anger. And immediately. Being angry with Mark for not heeding her was ridiculous. In the end he would do what he wanted, because that was the nature of the man, and it was his money after all. I must be calm, she reminded herself, continuing up Madison, shivering in the cold evening air. Anger blocks all rational thought, and I must think rationally. Yes, that's what I must do now. And I must try to protect Mark Tabbart from himself. If he'll let me, that is.

As Laura let herself into the office and slammed the front door behind her, Alison Maynard, her partner, came out into the reception area to greet her; Alison's pretty face was full of expectancy, and her eyes were questioning.

Slender and petite, with short blonde hair, Alison Maynard gave the appearance of being delicate, even breakable, but there was nothing fragile about her. She was tough, a woman of some force, with strong opinions, good values and, like Laura, she prided herself on her integrity. Also, she too could strike a hard bargain when necessary, and she knew her own mind, her own strengths and weaknesses. The two women made a good team, balancing each other well.

Alison asked: 'How did it go? Uh, uh, need I ask? I can tell from the expression on your face that Mark was difficult.'

Taking off her coat and hanging it in the closet, Laura answered, 'I don't think difficult is the right word. He was quite adversarial at one point. And he asked a lot of questions . . . in the most challenging way. And, of course, he took the attitude that Norman Grant was an innocent bystander.'

'He *is*, in actuality, Laura,' Alison reminded her.

'I know, *he* didn't steal the painting from the Westheim Collection – a Nazi general did – and I wasn't pointing a finger at Grant. We're trying to *protect* Mark, if he'll allow us to do so.'

'From himself!' Alison exclaimed. 'Look, we both know he's a tyrant, and that he thinks he's the greatest. But surely he understands that if he goes anywhere near that painting he'll find himself entangled in the biggest mess?'

'I made that crystal clear.'

'As his art-advisers, how would we extract him, Laura? If, in fact, that happened?'

Laura shook her head, and followed Alison into the latter's office, her expression thoughtful, worried.

It was a large, square room with two windows overlooking a small garden in the back, and a high, coffered ceiling. The antique furniture was handsome, predominantly mahogany, almost masculine in feeling, and the walls were covered with old art prints from the 1920s and 1930s, beautifully framed.

Alison walked around her antique Georgian partners' desk, and sat down in the wing chair upholstered in old tapestry. She stared across the polished mahogany expanse, waiting.

Laura flopped down in the leather chair placed at the other side of the desk; she leaned forward intently, and explained, 'I had a strong feeling that Mark was going to call Norman Grant the moment I left. He practically *hustled* me out of his office. In fact, he couldn't wait to get rid of me.'

'Do you mean he wanted to call Grant to make an offer for *Tahitian Dreams*? Or to alert him that he was about to become enmeshed in enormous problems?'

'I'm not sure,' Laura admitted honestly, and sat back, biting her lip, pondering for a split second. Then she said swiftly, 'I don't think Mark would be foolish enough to make an offer for the painting now. He's a financial genius, and smart as hell, and as a businessman he has great respect for money. So he's not going to spend it casually. He knows the painting has a bad history. I'm sure he's no longer interested in it. But he might feel obliged to tell Norman Grant what I said, explain about Maximilian West and the provenance of the Gauguin.'

'It's possible. No, *very probable*. But according to Hercule Junot, Sir Maximilian is about to put Norman Grant on notice that as the Westheim heir he is the rightful owner of *Tahitian Dreams*, and that he's seeking its return. Isn't that so, Laura?'

'Any moment. Perhaps it's already happened, for all we know. When I spoke to Hercule in Paris yesterday, he said there was no reason why I couldn't explain the situation to Mark, tell him everything. Otherwise I couldn't have done so, since I'd given my word of confidentiality to Hercule.'

'It's a peculiar situation, when you think about it,' Alison murmured, leaning forward, putting her elbows on the desk, propping her chin in her hands. 'Norman Grant *did* buy the painting in the most legitimate way, and in good faith. Now the poor guy's about to find himself in the middle of a major scandal.'

'I feel a bit sorry for him, but our main concern must be our client,' Laura said.

Alison nodded.

Laura went on, 'Mark won't do anything foolish. Having calmed down, I now realize that. But I was furious when I left his office. He can be so superior, such a know-all.'

'That's Mark's personality.'

Laura laughed. 'But knowing that, understanding his quirks, doesn't make him any easier to bear,' she shot back. 'Still, I'd better keep reminding myself he's an important client . . . I guess I'll just have to bite the bullet where he's concerned, and so will you. Of course, we might get lead poisoning in the process.'

'What we must do is distract him,' Alison announced, smiling beatifically at her partner. 'And I have just the right thing for that.'

'*Oh.* What?'

'A small bronze. A ballet dancer.'

'*Not a Degas?*' Laura said, sounding suddenly awed.

'A Degas, yes indeed.'

'Oh my God! Where is it?' Laura's excitement was evident on her face.

'En route to New York from Beverly Hills, as we speak. It's being shipped to us in care of Hélène Ravenel. She agreed to accept it on our behalf and keep it for us at her gallery.'

'That's fantastic! What a *coup*. And aren't you the secretive one. Why didn't you tell me?'

'First of all, I wanted to be sure we could get it. This particular Degas has changed hands several times in the last few years, and there was a question about whether it would go on sale at all. Then again, I wanted it to be a surprise for you. I thought, when

I first heard about it, that we could offer it to John Wells, Laura, but don't you agree it's the ideal thing to distract Mark?'

'You're absolutely right. What a clever girl you are. Go to the top of the class.'

Alison laughed, and so did Laura.

Laura now said, 'I can just picture Mark salivating over the Degas.'

'Instead of the Gauguin.' Alison pushed her chair back and rose. 'I'm afraid I have to go. I promised to meet my sister at the Carlyle for a drink, and I'm already running late.'

Laura also got up and walked towards the door of Alison's office. 'And I'm going to see my grandmother. I must go over some of the papers on my desk, and then I'll be leaving myself in half an hour. So I'll lock up.' Turning, she blew her partner a kiss. 'See you tomorrow.'

Alison said, 'Give my love to Grandma Megan, and tell her she's a fantastic example for all of us.'

Laura nodded. 'I will indeed. It's the truth.'

Laura smiled to herself as her thoughts stayed with her grandmother. What a remarkable woman she still was, formidable really. She had always been proud to be descended from her.

Megan Morgan. The beautiful, feisty gifted girl from the Rhondda Valley of South Wales, who had come to America in 1922, at the age of eighteen, to marry her childhood sweetheart from Port Talbot, Wales. Owen Tudor Valiant. Named for Owen Tudor, legendary Welshman and progenitor of the three great English Tudor monarchs – Henry VII, Henry VIII and Elizabeth I – because nothing less than an heroic name would do for *him*, his doting parents had announced, for wasn't their son going to be a king amongst men.

From the steel mills of Port Talbot to the steel mills of Pittsburgh Owen Tudor Valiant had gone, seeking his fortune and a better life. But it was in New York that he ultimately found it, where the streets were not paved with gold after all, but with opportunity. Those with guts seized it immediately.

Leaving the steel mills behind forever, Owen had cheerfully, and very optimistically, migrated to Manhattan, filled with belief in himself and his darling wife, the incredible Megan.

Loving music as she did – had she not sung three times a day every Sunday in the chapel in Port Talbot since she was a little girl – and being enterprising by nature, the young Megan had used the world of music to make friends and further their fortunes in Pittsburgh. She had entered local singing competitions, appeared in amateur theatrical productions, given renditions of her favourite songs at recitals, many of them Welsh in origin, and had won superlative reviews for her efforts. Everyone loved Megan, taken by her dark good looks and presence, awed and moved by the purity of her voice.

And so it was that one day in 1923, Owen Valiant, twenty-three years old and full of piss and vinegar, drive and burning ambition, made a momentous decision. It was the third most important and decisive step of his life; the first had been proposing to Megan before he left the Rhondda, the second had been emigrating to America. Now came the third: they would go to New York and take their chance in that gleaming metropolis of skyscrapers and seething humanity, the Great White Way and dreams of glory, the centre of the world, as far as Owen Valiant was concerned.

In his mind Owen had no doubt that they would succeed, that Megan would conquer Broadway, soon have her name glowing in lights on a marquee. As it turned out, his faith in her was more than justified. She made a name for herself after only two years of playing small roles and acting as understudy to various leading ladies. Her great chance, the break of a lifetime, came when she was just twenty-one-years old, in May of 1925. The actress she was understudying at the time fell seriously ill; she stepped into her shoes forthwith and never looked back. Megan Morgan had become a star overnight.

'Because she has a bell in every tooth,' the proud young Owen was wont to pronounce about his wife's thrilling voice, one that excited and captivated all those who heard it.

Musically talented himself, he and Megan had decided that he must become her agent and manager. Together they made a wonderful combination, were a great team; they built a happy and successful life for themselves, and raised four children, each one born in between Megan's long runs in a string of Broadway hits.

One of those four children was Richard, Laura's father, and it was from him, as well as from their grandparents, that Laura and her brother heard so many fascinating stories about the Valiants of Port Talbot and their early years in America. They were also regaled with marvellously entertaining stories about Wales, these tales told with relish, amazing flourishes and a great deal of hyperbole. Always heroic, mythic, these were grand tales that glorified the Welsh above all else. 'Nobody like us,' Owen would boast, meaning not only the Welsh race but the Valiants. And so Laura and Dylan grew up on Welsh legend and myth and were made to feel proud of their Celtic heritage. It was this heritage which made them different, Grandfather Owen was swift to point out; by *different* he meant better, special.

Her father had been a composer and conductor, successful, well-known, well-thought of and sought after, but never as celebrated or as popular as his very famous mother, who was *the* great musical stage star of the 1930s, 1940s, 1950s, and even well into the 1960s. Her popularity with the public never waned; the people loved her, and they had for half a century.

If Owen persisted in boasting about Megan, she played down everything about herself, always saying she was, 'Just a little girl from the Welsh valleys who was lucky to be born with something of a voice.'

Amazingly, their grandmother was still alive, a sprightly ninety-two-year-old, going on ninety-three, remarkably clear-headed and healthy, who still went out and about socially in Manhattan, as well groomed and as chicly dressed as ever. Owen had died in 1989, at the age of eighty-nine, but Megan was still going strong, defying the years, much to the joy of her family.

Their grandparents had been dominant forces in their lives, involved and caring and exercising enormous influence over them. But it was their father who had always been there for them until the day he died in 1994, aged sixty-four. Unexpectedly stricken by a fatal heart attack – and he a man with no previous heart troubles – he had been far too young to die.

12

It was cold outside, a very cold night, and windy, she could tell that from the frost coating the edge of her windows, and the look of the East River – turbulent, choppy with waves. Above the ink-dark river the sky was black, without cloud. Stars shone brightly; there was a full moon. It was one of those sharp, clear winter nights when everything appeared pristine, the kind of January night she had always loved.

Her eyes, once a vivid cornflower blue but faded now to a softer, paler hue, settled on the helicopter zooming closer. It looked like a flying saucer, and it was coming towards her unerringly, as if this old landmark building where she lived was its target.

At the last moment, or so it seemed to her, the helicopter veered away, no doubt heading for the heliport, a few blocks up the river in the East Sixties.

The sky was suddenly empty again except for the cold white stars and the Pepsi-Cola sign rising up like a bright red neon sentinel at the edge of Queens. The sign had been part of her life for so many years, she knew she would miss it if it were suddenly no longer there. My bit of pop art, she called it.

Megan Morgan Valiant turned away from the bay window of her library and walked towards the fireplace at the other end of the room. She was a tall, slender woman, regal in bearing; her dark brown hair, lightly streaked with silver, was fashionably styled, and the great beauty of her youth still lingered in her face.

She could not help thinking how good it was to be alive. So many people she had known were dead now. She was ninety-two and still going strong, defying time and the odds. She was luckier than most and in so many ways: well off enough to live as she'd always lived, to do what she wanted. She was also fortunate in that there was nothing much wrong with her, other than a few aches and pains, a bit of arthritis in her feet and a slight deafness in one ear. Nonetheless, she could still hear very well when she wanted to, even when they whispered.

There was no sign of osteoporosis, the curse of so many older women, no senility, no Alzheimer's. She was lucky indeed.

She had outlived her beloved husband Owen, dead almost eight years, and her two eldest children, her sons Emlyn and Richard. Only her daughters left, Rhianon and Cara, and her grandchildren, the children of Richard and Maggie. *Richard.* Her favourite. You shouldn't have favourites, but you always did. It was human nature to favour one above all the others, but you must never let them know. No reason to hurt any of them. Her special child had been her second son. It was curious, she often thought, that his brother Emlyn and sister Rhianon had never had any children. Cara had had two, Mervyn and Lydia, but Mervyn had died in a drowning accident in the lake in Connecticut, Lake Waramaug it was called, and he only twelve. A tragedy. It had haunted the family for years. The loss of a child was always hard to bear. His sister Lydia had never seemed to recover. She had married young and gone to live in Australia, as if she wanted to put great distance between herself and her family, and the memories.

Megan paused at the console table and its silver-framed photographs of her family. The Valiants ... Owen and her, Rhianon and Cara, Richard and Emlyn, so many pictures taken at different ages ... their children. The children when they were small, in their teens and grown. Funny, she thought, how you could identify each one from the baby pictures. None of them had changed much. The faces were the same in adulthood.

Reaching for a photograph of herself when she was twenty-one, she studied it carefully for a moment. It had been taken the year she had become a star overnight. And thankfully she still had that same face – underneath the wrinkles. Not *that* many wrinkles, though. She had worn well, even if she said so herself. It was easy to see they were all from the same family. Black hair, blue or green eyes; dark Celtic Welsh, the Valiants, yes, the lot of them.

Fey, mystical, sometimes otherworldly, and touched by the magic, that was what Merlin of Camelot had said about the Welsh, whom others called the lost tribe of Israel. Part of that magic was in the throat, in the tongue, in the love of song, the love of language, both the spoken and the written word. Actors and writers and singers, the Welsh were. Special, Owen had said.

Her voice had been *her* magic, a gift from God, was the way she thought of it. She had always played down her success, but it was her voice which had given them their fortune – and seen to their future. In a sense, every Valiant owed almost everything they had to her gift, and to Owen's brilliance as a manager and to his business acumen. He had spun gold for them.

She missed Owen. She would miss him until the day she shed this mortal coil and went to join him.

But not just yet, she added under her breath. Too much still to do here on earth. She knew he'd understand.

Megan placed the photograph on the console, leaned forward, peered at her grandson Dylan. A little sigh escaped her. Dylan had been spoiled by Richard and Margaret, and by Owen and even by Laura, sometimes. But not by me. I've never spoiled him, and I never will.

Next to Dylan stood the silver-framed picture of Laura, taken when she was just twenty-two. A smile touched Megan's mouth, lit up her eyes, brought a sudden radiance to her face. She's the one, she's the best. Strong, reliable, loyal, and steady as a rock. She's the racehorse with the breeding *and* the stamina. I'll put my money on her any day. Megan drew closer to the picture, loving Laura so much, and then glanced at the one of herself taken in 1925. Spitting image, she murmured: Laura looks just like me when I was that age.

Straightening, Megan moved to the fireplace, warming her hands against the flames. Lily, her housekeeper, had kept the fire going since teatime, knowing how much she liked a fire, especially in winter. It cheered up a room. Sitting down, leaning her head against the blue silk brocade of the chair, her eyes fixed on the painting on the opposite wall.

It was a springtime scene of a New York square, painted by Childe Hassam in 1896, one of her better paintings. I'll give it to Laura for her birthday in May, or perhaps she would prefer to choose one for herself. I'll let her decide. Yes, that's what I'll do. That was the best thing.

Now Megan's eyes shifted to the portrait, hanging above the fireplace . . . she had been thirty-one when it was painted. In her prime. The same age as Laura was now.

Closing her eyes, Megan let herself sink down into herself. Remembering, remembering . . . so much to remember, so many memories. They filled her heart. It was still young. Sometimes she thought she was only eighteen in her heart. It was her mind that was old and wise – full of knowledge, too much knowledge, she often thought, of people and their strange ways, of human nature with all its frailties and weaknesses, as well as its strengths . . . She drifted with her thoughts and her memories . . . and she dozed.

'Hello, Megan,' Laura said, gliding into the library.

Megan sat up with a little start and blinked, then she smiled when she saw her granddaughter.

Vivid eyes, vivid hair, vivid personality. Full of vivid life. Her favourite grandchild. Laura bent over, kissed her on the cheek, squeezed her shoulder. She loved her grandmother very much; after all, they had been extremely close ever since she was a child. She had always felt closer to her grandmother than she had to her mother, or anyone else.

'I can smell the cold on you, Laura,' Megan said. 'I hope you didn't walk here.'

Laura laughed, touching her grandmother's cheek gently with one finger. 'All that way, Gran, from Sixty-Eighth and Madison to Fifty-Second and First, and on an icy night like this. You must be joking. I took a cab.'

'Good. Much warmer. Much safer, too. The sherry decanter's over there, darling, in its usual place. Pour for us and let us get cosy for a while. You know how much I enjoy our chats.'

'Sherry coming up, Gran,' Laura murmured over her shoulder as she walked to the round table standing in a corner of the room.

A moment later she came back, carrying two glasses. After giving one to Megan, she sat down in the chair opposite, reached forward to clink her glass against her grandmother's and said, 'Here's to you, Grandma Megan, and another new year. May there be many more.'

'Well, I hope so, Laura dear, I don't want to leave this earth just yet. I've more damage to do, you know. Much more,' she laughed.

Laura laughed with her.

After taking a sip of sherry, Megan continued, 'Is your mother feeling better? I thought she seemed a bit glum at times over Christmas.'

'Yes, I agree, she *was* in a strange state of mind, but she's all right now. I think she cheered up once she got down to Florida, and she's apparently felt much better, is in good spirits.'

'How is that little cottage of mine?'

'As charming as ever, Gran.'

'Your grandfather and I bought it over thirty-five years ago, before you were born, and it was always a pretty place, my beach cottage where I could potter around and relax, be myself.'

'Why don't you go down there for a week or two, Gran? The weather's warm, much warmer than New York. It would do you good. And Mom would love your company. Please think about going, I'll take you there, if you want.'

'I can take myself, thank you very much, my dear girl! But I don't want to go, I don't want to be there, Laura, not without your grandfather. It was always our place, a very *special* place, and it brings back too many memories, makes me feel sad.'

Laura stared at her in surprise. 'But Grandpa Owen lived here, in this apartment with you as well, and surely –'

'The cottage was our very special place, our holiday home. We loved to escape there, it was always just the two of us . . .' Megan lifted her shoulders in a tiny shrug. 'I don't know how to explain it, darling, but I have no desire to go there anymore. As much as I loved it then, now I don't care about it at all. And it'll be yours one day, yours and your brother's, after I'm gone.'

'I hate it when you talk that way, Gran.'

'I know. But we must face reality. I *will* die.'

'Yes, I know,' Laura mumbled.

Megan glanced into the fire reflectively, and after a moment of silence, she remarked, 'Your father's been dead three years now. Don't you think your mother ought to start a new life? She's only sixty, after all.'

'She's trying hard, Grandma. She's gone out and got herself a lot of work.'

'She ought to go out and find herself a new man.'

'Grandma, you're something else!' Laura exclaimed.

'But it's the truth, and sixty is *young*. It certainly looks awfully good to me, from where I'm sitting, and considering *my* age. Anyway, what about this fellow in the Bahamas? The one whose ceiling she's gone to paint.'

'Forget about him, Gran, he's too old. He's eighty-two.'

'The father is, yes. I mean *Harry* Lightfoot, the son. I've met him, and he's very nice. Your mother could do worse.'

'And how old is he?'

'Oh about fifty-five, fifty-six, something like that. Just right for Margaret.'

'Mom'll say he's too young.'

Megan shook her head, took a swallow of sherry, pondered for a second, then announced, 'A younger man keeps a woman young.'

'Speaking from experience, Grandmother?'

Megan had the good grace to laugh. 'No, but I can imagine. Anyway, I'm quite serious, I think your mother should have another man in her life — boyfriend, husband, it doesn't really matter.' Megan leaned forward slightly, pinning her wise old eyes on Laura. 'Margaret's healthy, vital, full of energy, a good-looking woman. Fun, too. Any man would be lucky to have her on his arm, and in his life.'

'I agree, Gran, but try telling that to Mom.' Laura paused, then nodded her head, said with sudden enthusiasm, 'I'm going to encourage her.'

'Good girl,' Megan said.

Laura nodded, sipped her sherry, said nothing.

After a moment Megan remarked, 'But your mother is not the reason why I asked you to come to see me, darling girl. I want to talk to you again about the art collection, such as it is. I've been wondering if we should put it up for auction.'

Laura frowned and her eyes filled with sudden alarm. 'Do you need money, Grandma? Do you have problems? I thought the trusts Grandpa set up were –'

'No, no, there's not a problem about money!' Megan cried, interrupting her granddaughter. 'I just thought it might be more practical to sell the art now. I've been reading about auctions lately: paintings seem to be fetching good prices. The economy's good. If you think we should do it, why not?'

'I don't want to make a snap decision, Gran, not just like that.

I think I ought to evaluate every painting you have and then talk to Jason. You remember him, he gave us evaluations on the small Cézanne and the Sisley.'

'I do remember him. Very well. He was a nice young man. So, you make the decision, and do what you have to do.'

'All right, I will.'

Megan smiled at her granddaughter, loving her so much, full of pride in her. 'In the meantime, let's have another sherry, darling,' she said.

Laura did as she was asked, went and poured more sherry for them both, and carried the glasses back to the fireside. After handing one to her grandmother, she returned to her seat, and said, 'Claire's very excited about coming to spend August in Connecticut, Gran, and naturally she's thrilled that you've agreed to visit for a few days.'

'It'll be nice to be there with you. And Claire and Natasha. I was so very sorry when they didn't come for Christmas. I'd sort of set my heart on it, and when she cancelled I felt sad, quite sad indeed, Laura. After all, I might not be here next Christmas.'

'Don't say things like that, Gran!'

'But it's true, darling, we must face the inevitable.'

'Dylan didn't come either. He's a stinker at times.'

'Oh pooh. Dylan's just a silly boy. He's never grown up. Your parents' fault, too. They spoiled him, especially your mother. I've said it before, and I'll say it again . . . the breeding's there, but no stamina. No backbone.'

'Perhaps if he got married and settled down, he'd grow up a bit,' Laura muttered, eyeing her grandmother over the rim of her sherry glass. 'What I mean is, I think he needs a bit of responsibility to make him pull his socks up.'

'Bah! Don't be a foolish girl, Laura. Responsibility won't change your brother. He'd probably run away from it the first chance he got. As for getting married, I pity the poor girl who takes such a foolhardy step.'

'You sound cross with him.'

'I am in certain ways. But I still love him. He's one of mine, even though he is very silly at times. I haven't quite recovered from his recent venture into real estate. Fancy buying that farm in Wales.' Megan shook her head and grimaced. 'He needs his brains washing.'

'I know. He should have put the money in the bank, as you said at Christmas. But that's Dylan, going back to his roots he calls it. Mythical Wales and the world of legend, Grandmother. He always talked about having a home in Wales.'

'I know, I know, you blame me for filling his head full of fanciful stories and ideas, and your grandfather did it too ...' Megan looked into the fire for a moment, then lifted her eyes to Laura's, and added, 'But *you* heard the same stories, and you're as sane and practical as I am. I think it's something to do with character, darling girl. And talking of marriage, I'm surprised Claire is still single after all these years. I suppose she hasn't met anyone?'

'She doesn't give herself a chance,' Laura said, and stopped. She shook her head. 'That sounds a bit mean which is the last thing I'd be about Claire.'

'I know how much you care for her. So she's still bitter is she?'

Laura looked at Megan in surprise. 'How did you know? You haven't seen her for a couple of years.'

'She was bitter then and I merely assumed she still was, if she hasn't given herself a chance, as you put it. What a pity really, such a loving girl at heart. And Philippe and she were so very much in love. I thought it would last forever.'

'Didn't we all.'

'I wonder how his mother Rosa is doing these days?'

'Goodness, Gran, imagine you remembering her name.'

'I've always had a good memory. How do you think I learned all my lines when I was an actress, for heaven's sake, child? And I still have a good memory I want you to know, better than most people half my age. I'm not senile yet, Laura.'

'I know, Gran, I know. Don't get excited.'

'I'm not excited,' Megan said, lowering her voice; she took a sip of sherry and settled back in her chair.

Laura said: 'It's odd you should ask about Rosa Lavillard, because I ran into her when I was in Paris.'

'Oh. Was she visiting Claire?'

Laura shook her head. 'Oh no, that would never happen. Claire doesn't like her much.'

'Why not?

'Claire thinks she's . . .' Laura sought around in her mind for the right word, then said, '*Peculiar*. Yes that's it. Claire thinks Rosa is odd, weird.'

'She'd be weird too if she'd had Rosa Lavillard's life, her childhood. Poor woman. Most people would have been in a mental home if they'd gone through what she did. Rosa's a very brave woman. Courageous.'

Laura stared at her grandmother, and asked, 'How do you know about Rosa Lavillard's childhood?'

'She told me.'

'When?'

'Before Claire and Philippe were married. Don't you remember, I gave a small dinner party for them here. It was after dinner. She and I sat in this very room talking for a long time. The rest of you were in the drawing room having coffee and liqueurs.'

'Yes of course I remember the dinner. What did she tell you, Grandma?'

'About the war years in France, what it was like growing up during the Nazi occupation. I was able to sympathize with her, and I also understood because I'd been over there to entertain the troops. That was in 1944 and 1945. Your grandfather hadn't wanted me to go but I really felt I must do something, anything that might help. Those poor boys were over there fighting and risking their lives for us, fighting for the cause of freedom. And so I went. Your grandfather came too in the end. He wouldn't let me go alone because he was afraid something might happen to me.'

'Yes, you've told me stories about when you went to entertain the troops in the Second World War. It must've been exciting, Gran.'

'In some ways. But also heartbreaking . . . it was so dreadful to see the dead and the dying. But I know we helped those who were wounded. We entertainers did manage to cheer them up, show them that we cared, give them a feeling of home. But they were just boys. Soldiers are always so *young*, it's heartrending.'

'I know. At least, I can imagine. How old were you, Grandma?'

'Still in my prime, still good-looking, still able to kick up my legs and sing my heart out.'

'You haven't changed much,' Laura said, leaning over, squeezing her grandmother's hand. 'And you've always been the best.'

'That's nice, darling, thank you. But getting back to Rosa, she suffered greatly when she was a child. She saw too much brutality and evil. In France in those days it was terrible – no food, constant bombings, the Gestapo around every corner. France was under siege then, and it was especially hard for Rosa.'

'She told you all this that night?'

'Some of it she told me, when it applied to her life. But I know what France was like in those days, darling.'

'Why do you say it was especially hard for Rosa?'

'Because she had lost her parents. She was on her own.'

'How old was she?'

'I'm not exactly sure now. Young, Laura, perhaps nine, but no more than ten or eleven. There was no self-pity in her. She told me in a very matter-of-fact way, and then only because I had asked her about her life. I knew she was French by birth and that she and her husband had emigrated here after the war.'

'I see. How sad.'

Megan gave her granddaughter a hard stare. 'You say that in a strange voice. Almost as if you don't believe Rosa's story. I can assure you it's quite true.'

'I do believe you, Gran. I was just thinking it's a pity Claire doesn't understand about Rosa's childhood. Perhaps if she knew more about it she would be more . . . sympathetic.'

'Surely Philippe must have told Claire about his mother and all that she went through?'

'He did tell her certain things, I know that, because Claire once told me. But somehow I don't think she has the full picture.'

'Perhaps not.' Megan was on the verge of telling Laura the whole story about Rosa Lavillard, and then she changed her mind. It was such a harrowing tale, and she suddenly felt that she didn't have the strength this evening. Instead she said, 'If you see Rosa again give her my very best wishes. I liked her.'

'Yes I will. Claire never got on with Rosa. Do you think that's strange in view of your opinion of Rosa?'

'Show me a woman who genuinely gets on with her mother-in-law, and I'll eat my hat.'

Laura had to laugh at this expression, which sounded so odd coming from her grandmother, and then she remarked, 'My mother gets on with you.'

'I'm the exception to the rule, didn't you know that, darling girl?'

'I suppose I did.'

Megan chuckled. 'I'm teasing you, Laura. It was like this . . . your mother and father were so completely besotted with each other they never noticed anyone else. Not her mother, or me or your grandfather, not even you and Dylan. Not really. And when you don't know someone exists, that person can't very well be an irritant to you, can she? And I knew that if I ever voiced one word of criticism or disapproval of your mother, your father would not have spoken to me ever again. Richard meant the world to me, and I couldn't have borne that. All I wanted was his happiness. And your mother made him happy.'

'I understand.' Laura leaned back against the chair, and stared out of the window, seeing very little except the dark night sky, the dark waters of the East River. She was thinking of Rosa

Lavillard and Philippe, wondering about them. Suddenly surprising herself, she confided: 'Claire harbours a dreadful hatred for Philippe these days, it's quite upsetting to witness. He stopped by unannounced when I was there for dinner and there was a terrible scene.'

'That's such a pity, and particularly distressing for Natasha. But children always suffer in divorce, and of course Claire has always been so extreme as well as independent of nature.'

'*Extreme*. What do you mean?'

'Funny word to use, isn't it? But I suppose I do mean *extreme*. Claire is right or left, never in the middle. With her, things are black or white, never grey. She was like that when she was growing up, and I don't suppose she's changed much.' Megan let out a sigh. 'Claire lacks the ability to compromise. Surely you of all people know that, Laura.'

'I do, but I sort of ignore it. Nobody's perfect, least of all me.'

'Oh I don't know about that,' Megan replied in a teasing voice.

Laura smiled at her grandmother and sipped her sherry.

A silence fell between them for a short while. But it was a companionable silence. Laura and her grandmother had been on the same wavelength since Laura had been a child, and they understood each other very well. Grandfather Owen often said that Laura was more like her grandmother than Megan's own daughters, and this was the truth. The two of them were very similar and in so many ways.

Megan suddenly said, 'Is everything all right between you and Doug?'

Taken by surprise, Laura gaped at her grandmother.

'Is your marriage all right? Or is it in trouble?' Megan asked.

Finding her voice, Laura said, 'I don't know, Gran.' Laura had always told her the truth and she was being scrupulously honest now. 'I think there's something wrong, but I'm not sure what it is. Anyway, it's not *right*. Not anymore.'

'I thought as much.'

'You did?' Laura gave her grandmother a puzzled look. 'Did you notice something over Christmas?'

'Doug was preoccupied, abstracted. To me he seemed faraway a great deal of the time, not *with* us.'

'And yet he was very sweet to me, to you, to my mother.'

'That is absolutely true. But there were moments when he thought he was unobserved that he let his guard down, and he looked quite miserable to me. As if he didn't want to be there at all.'

'Oh Gran . . .'

'You must talk to him, Laura. That's the problem with most people, they never communicate their feelings. And they make silent demands.'

'I'll have to pick the right moment.'

'Certainly you will. But don't leave it too long. Don't let whatever it is that's troubling him fester inside.'

'I won't, Gran, I promise.'

13

Laura said, 'So I didn't misunderstand you.'

Turning to look at Alison, she continued, 'When you said a bronze of a ballet dancer, I immediately thought of *The Little Fourteen-Year-Old Dancer* by Degas and I was right. This is from the unnumbered edition of at least twenty-five examples cast in the 1920s. The Shelburne Museum owned one, and if I remember correctly it was auctioned for just over eleven million by Sotheby's last year.'

'Correct. And who owns it now still remains largely a mystery,' Alison remarked, adding, 'and any serious collector would grab this one, don't you think?' She continued to study the Degas Bronze she'd had shipped in from California; it stood on a plinth in the centre of Hélène Ravenel's Madison Avenue art gallery, highlighted by a ceiling spotlight.

'A posthumous, second-generation cast of the original wax sculpture by Degas, done at the Hébrard foundry by the great caster Albino Palazzolo, supervised by Degas's friend, the sculptor Albert Bartholomé,' Laura said, speaking from memory.

'That's absolutely right. The provenance arrived in this morning's mail and I put it on your desk. You can look at it later. So, what do you think?'

'It's an incredible piece, Alison, perfectly beautiful. God, look how dirty and tattered the net tutu is. Mark will want it, I'm sure of that. And even though we have no real reason to distract him now, I think we must show it to him.'

Alison laughed, her eyes filling with merriment. 'Aren't we a couple of idiots, thinking that he would go after a Gauguin against our wishes, and one that was shrouded in problems. He's much too smart a man for that.'

Laura said, 'It was my fault. I was the one who made the judgement about Mark. Flawed, as it turned out.'

'We know he didn't make an offer for the painting, but do you think he told Norman Grant about Maximilian West?'

'It's more than likely, yes, I'm sure he did. But it's of no consequence, since Sir Maximilian put Norman Grant on notice the day after my meeting with Mark. In other words, it wasn't a secret.'

'What do you think will happen about the Gauguin?'

Laura lifted her shoulders in a small shrug. 'I don't know. It's probably going to be a Mexican stand off, an impasse. Both men claim they own *Tahitian Dreams*.'

'It's a terrible situation, it could drag on for years,' Alison murmured and then focused her attention on the Degas again. 'What about John Wells? Do you think he would like this if Mark doesn't want it?'

'Yes I do. John would jump at it, and don't forget our new client Olivia Gardener in Palm Beach. This piece would be perfect for the entrance foyer of her new house on South Ocean Boulevard. I can just see it on a beautiful antique circular table in the middle of the foyer. In any case, Hélène told me she would be interested in buying this herself if we don't place it with one of our clients.'

'I am certainly interested,' Hélène Ravenel exclaimed, coming to join them. 'Very much so.'

The three women stood talking about the sculpture for a few moments and then Laura looked at her watch and said, 'I'm late for my lunch with Hercule. It's a good thing I'm meeting him at the Carlyle.'

'Give him my best,' Alison said, as Laura hurried through the gallery, heading for the front door.

'I will. See you back at the office, Alison, and thanks Hélène, thanks for everything.'

The Ravenel Gallery was only a couple of blocks away from the Carlyle Hotel and Laura set out at a brisk pace; she was soon turning onto East Seventy-Sixth Street, where the front entrance to the famous hotel was located.

After checking her coat she went into the restaurant, where Didier, the maître d', greeted her pleasantly and led her over to Hercule Junot's table.

Hercule was on his feet in an instant, kissing her on both cheeks, beaming at her, pressing her down onto the banquette next to him.

'I am very happy to see you, Laura,' he said, still smiling, 'and delighted that you were able to have lunch with me today, and such short notice.'

Laura returned his smile. 'So am I. It was a lovely surprise to hear from you yesterday. How long are you staying?'

'For about a week. I came to see one of my clients. She has asked me to redecorate her house in Southampton, and so I am going to drive out there on Saturday. To spend the day reviewing the house. Now, Laura, what would you like? A glass of champagne?'

'No, thanks, Hercule. Normally I'd say yes, but I have a mountain of paperwork on my desk and I have to get through it today. I'll have a grapefruit juice, please.'

After ordering their drinks, he continued, 'My client mentioned that she wishes to buy some new paintings, and that she is looking to hire an art-adviser. I immediately thought of you, Laura.'

'That's nice of you, Hercule. Thank you very much.'

'Whilst I was sitting here waiting for you I had this idea . . . that you would drive out to Long Island with me on Saturday morning. We could leave the city early, around eight o'clock, meet Mrs Newsam, my client, and speak with her about her art preferences, and you could do a tour of the house with me as well.'

Laura hesitated.

Hercule immediately noticed and said quickly, 'Is it a problem for you on Saturday, my dear?'

'Not really. It's just that Doug and I only get to see each other at the weekends, we're so busy during the week, and –'

'But that is not a problem,' Hercule cut in. 'He could come along with us. My client's house is situated on the dunes, and Doug could take a walk on the beach if the weather is good, whilst we look over the house and chat with Mrs Newsam. And there is no question about it, I know she would love us all to join her for lunch. No problem, my dear, none at all.'

Laura still hesitated and then finally she nodded, gave Hercule a bright smile. 'I'm sure he'll want to come, and thanks for thinking of me. As you know, I'm always interested in meeting prospective clients.'

'Would Alison like to drive out there with us?'

'No, she wouldn't. I'm *positive* of that. She always spends the weekends with the twins, her two little girls, and she never lets anything interfere with her time with them and her husband Tony.'

'I do understand. Ah, here are the drinks,' he said as the waiter placed the glasses in front of them. Lifting his flute of champagne, he toasted, 'Your health, Laura.'

'And yours, Hercule.'

They talked for a few moments about the Southampton house of the client he had flown to New York to see, and then Hercule suggested they order lunch. 'Since it's a working day for you, Laura, I'm sure you don't wish to linger too long.'

Laura smiled at him, picked up the menu and glanced at it. 'I'd like to have the cold asparagus vinaigrette and then afterward the grilled sole.'

'I will join you in the fish, but I will start with *des huîtres.*

To me there are no better oysters than the ones I have in New York, not even in *la belle France.*'

Much later, when the meal was more or less over, Hercule suddenly said in a low, confiding tone, 'I would like to propose a project which would be very profitable for you, if you were to take it on.'

'You know I'm always interested in doing business, Hercule. What's the project?'

'Sir Maxim West.' Hercule smiled, and lifted his hands in his typical Gallic way. 'What I mean is, I want you to meet him. He will be in New York on Monday, and I wish to take you to see him at his office. He would like to totally revamp his art collection – revamp is the word he uses – Laura, and I think you are the perfect person to help him. I have known him a long time, many years, he is a client of mine, and I understand him. He is very low-key these days and doesn't like fuss. I believe the two of you will be . . . compatible. Very compatible.'

Although somewhat taken by surprise at Hercule's suggestion, Laura was excited and she exclaimed, 'Hercule, I would love to meet him! How wonderful of you to do this. Alison will be thrilled when I tell her that we might be acquiring *two* new clients.'

'I am delighted to be of help to you, my dear, and your expertise can only reflect well on me,' he answered, his eyes twinkling. 'Now that we have settled this, tell me your news, Laura.' He gave her the benefit of a warm, avuncular smile and sat back.

'There's not much to tell,' she replied, taking a last forkful of fish, then placing her fork on the plate, also leaning back against the banquette. 'Business is quite good, as I told you last night on the phone, and I've no other news.'

'As I told you, Sir Maxim has informed Mr Grant about the long history of *Tahitian Dreams*, or rather, I should say his lawyers have done so. And now we can only wait and see what is going to happen. However, in my opinion, such as it is, I do believe this is not going to be easy. I doubt very much that Mr Grant will relinquish the painting, hand it over to Sir Maximilian without a protest. Why should he?'

Laura nodded. 'Morally he should, of course, but I tend to agree with you, it's not going to be quite so simple. I'm totally on the side of the original owner, because the work of art was stolen from him. No matter what anyone says to me, or the arguments they make, I believe it's wrong to shield the provenance of stolen goods from proper scrutiny. And by rights *Tahitian Dreams* should go back to the owner, or, if he's dead, the heirs.' Laura paused, then finished, 'But it's going to be a battle. Still, there's a solution to everything, Hercule, although I can't quite envision a solution to this dilemma. At least not at the moment.'

He gave her a long, thoughtful look. 'If you come up with a solution please let me know immediately, I am certain Sir Maxim would want to hear it.'

'Doug's been calling you,' Alison said, walking out of her office into the reception area of Art Acquisitions as Laura came in. 'He tried reaching you during lunch but your mobile was switched off. He called back here to tell me he's now on his way to Teterboro Airport. He'll phone again from the car.'

'Why is he going out there?' Laura stared at her partner, puzzlement flashing across her face.

'He's being sent to the coast. There's an –'

'Just like that, on a minute's notice,' Laura interrupted, walking into her own office, throwing her coat and handbag on a chair. 'Did he say anything else?' she asked over her shoulder, sounding angry.

'Only that there's been an emergency apparently. He told me he rushed home, put a few things in a bag, and now he's heading out to New Jersey. Aaronson International are flying him to LA on their private jet.'

'I see.' Laura sat down behind her desk and looked across at Alison who was leaning against the door frame. 'Did he say how long he's going for?'

Alison shook her head.

The phone rang at this moment, and Laura pounced on it. 'Art Acquisitions.'

'Hi, Laura, it's me. I've been trying to reach you,' Doug said.

'Alison just told me. Why are they sending you to the coast at a moment's notice, Doug? What's the sudden emergency?'

'Will Laxton was out there dealing with the merger for Aaronson, and he had a heart attack. That's why I'm being sent.'

'Oh God, how awful. Poor Will, he's not . . .' Laura paused, took a deep breath, and before she could continue, Doug supplied the end of her sentence.

'No, he's not dead, thank God. He's in intensive care at the hospital. He'll be okay. Out of action for a while, but they say he'll make a good recovery.'

'I'm glad to hear it. How long will you be gone? Will you be back at the weekend?'

'I doubt it, Laura. Today's Thursday, so I'll only have tomorrow as a working day. I'll have to pick up on Monday and keep going for the rest of next week, I'm sure. There's still rather a lot of legal work to be done.'

'Why did they have to send *you*? Couldn't Peter Pickering have stepped in for Will?'

'Pete's there, sweetie, you know what a big deal this is for the firm. We've got half a dozen lawyers on it already. They need *me* to replace Will, to *lead* the team.'

'I understand, I'm sorry, I don't mean to be difficult. It's just . . .' She let her sentence remain unfinished.

'Just *what*?'

'We don't seem to spend much time together these days, Doug.'

'We're both working hard, that's why. But come on, Laura, be happy for me. It's a big boost for me within the firm to be sent out to the coast on this deal. The Aaronson merger runs into billions of dollars.'

'I am glad for you, Doug,' she responded swiftly, suddenly feeling guilty; she realized she had sounded churlish, perhaps even childish.

'I'll call you tonight. I'll be at the Peninsula, as usual,' he told her in his carefree, breezy voice.

'Fly safely, darling, and do a good job. Show 'em what you're made of, Doug.'

'I will. 'Bye, sweetie,' he answered and hung up before she could say anything else.

Laura stared at the phone, frowning, and then she rose and went to find Alison who had returned to the other office during her conversation with Doug.

From the doorway, she said to her partner, 'I think we might have two new clients. Courtesy of Hercule Junot.'

'Come in, come in, and tell me everything!' Alison exclaimed.

Because there was no urgent reason why she should rush home, Laura worked late. After Alison and the two secretaries, Lynne and Joni, had left for the day, she settled in to tackle the paperwork which had piled up on her desk.

At eight o'clock she finally stopped, put down her pen wearily and sat back in her chair, glancing around the room as she did. Like Alison's office, hers also faced out onto the small back garden, and it was similar in size, with the same dimensions and high-flung, coffered ceiling. Laura too had used English antiques and a collection of old art prints exceptionally well framed. But whereas Alison's walls were white she had had hers painted a lovely primrose yellow, a colour that was sunny and cheerful.

Ever since they had leased the ground floor of the town house on East Sixty-Eighth Street Laura had found her office pleasant to work in, but tonight she discovered she'd suddenly had enough of it. On the other hand, the thought of going home to the empty apartment appalled her; it was too late to make a supper date with a girlfriend or to go over to see her grandmother.

A sandwich and a glass of wine, that's my lot tonight, she muttered to herself as she turned off the lights in her office and went out into the reception to get her coat.

As she was taking it off the hanger Laura was unexpectedly filled with a sense of dismay, and for a split second she did not understand why she was experiencing such feelings.

And then she thought: It's Doug. It's because of Doug. Somehow he's drawing further and further away from me and I don't know the reason why.

14

It was windy, bitterly cold. But there was a bright sun in the flawless sky, and so Laura, tempted by the glittering day, had donned her bright red, quilted-down coat and gone out into the garden.

Now, as she walked along the paved path that led to the stone wall fronting onto the dunes, she noticed how lifeless the garden looked. The trees were leafless, dark, skeletal etchings against the azure sky and the lawn was dun-coloured, patched here and there with old snow that had frozen over. Desolate gardens in winter, wherever they were, depressed her, made her feel ineffably sad, and Mrs Newsam's garden in Southampton, Long Island was no exception.

Increasing her speed, Laura hurried, wanting to leave the forlorn landscape behind, and within seconds she was pushing open the gate in the wall and stepping onto the dunes. Shrugging deeper into her coat, her hands thrust in her pockets, she trudged across the dunes and went down an incline onto the beach near the sea.

Icy though it was on this February morning, Laura enjoyed being by the ocean; she was intoxicated by the tangy smell of salt and seaweed, and the fresh, breezy air was a wonderful tonic after being cooped up in her office all week.

This morning the Atlantic was rough and choppy, topped with whitecaps, but as beautiful to her now as it was in the summer months when it was usually much calmer. Being close to the sea had a calming and restorative effect on her, and within minutes she was beginning to feel more at ease with herself. Some of the tension she had been holding for days began to slip away, much to her profound relief. Sunny by nature, she hated being down in the dumps.

There was no real reason for her to be here in Southampton with Hercule, even though Sandra Newsam had just become a client, after the meeting they'd had here last Saturday. But when Hercule had invited her to come along again, if only for the ride out to the beach, he had said, she had accepted without hesitation. She had nothing better to do, and she did not relish the notion of spending the entire weekend alone. And in any case it gave her a chance to look around Mrs Newsam's lovely old grey-shingled house for a second time.

Sandra Newsam had been impressed with her credentials, and had hired Art Acquisitions to buy art for her, after visiting them at their New York office the previous Wednesday. 'I won't be your biggest client,' she had said to her and Alison. 'I don't have millions in loose change to spend. But I do want to start collecting some really good paintings, and your advice is going to be invaluable to me. Once we've found things for the beach house, I'd like to start looking for art for my New York apartment. The whole idea is exciting to me. We might even discover some great new talent between us.'

She and Alison had liked Sandra Newsam, who, they quickly discovered, was straightforward, down to earth and totally lacking in pretence. 'Thank God she's not like Mrs Joyce,' Alison had said after Sandra Newsam had left the office, referring to a client they had felt compelled to drop because she was the total opposite of Mrs Newsam. Laura had grimaced, remembering the dreaded Mrs Joyce and her pretensions of grandeur, bitchy demeanour and acerbic tongue.

As she walked along the edge of the sea Laura continued to think about her work. She and Alison were doing exceptionally well, better than they had ever expected, and their business was in the black, growing more successful every day. They were both aware they might have to hire another art expert to work with them, if only on a part-time basis. They now had more clients than they had dreamed possible; handling them all effectively, *and* finding the right art, could easily become a problem.

'Let's hold off hiring somebody for a few more months,' Laura had said to Alison last night. 'I can handle the extra workload, so you don't have to worry about staying late or travelling. I'm quite happy to do that.'

Alison had been grateful because she liked to be with the twins as much as possible, especially at weekends. Also, she didn't really want to hop on and off planes anymore, or rush around the world seeing clients and scouting works of art. Tony grumbled so much when she went away, that Alison always travelled with a worried and overburdened mind, which Laura thought could affect their business adversely. To balance the workload, Alison had volunteered to handle all of the basics in the office, and do most of the paperwork, which, as she explained to Laura, she could do at home on the weekends if that was necessary.

Laura wasn't sure what Doug would say when he discovered she had agreed to do all of the travelling for Art Acquisitions. As her thoughts automatically swung to her husband she felt a terrible heaviness descending on her, weighing her down. She tried to shrug it off but to no avail.

He had been in Los Angeles for ten days already, and he would be staying there for another week at least. She felt a sudden rush of depression at the thought of this. A few days ago he had asked her to pack a suitcase with extra clothes for him, since he had taken so little when he had left in January. This she had done, and the suitcase had been picked up from the doorman of their apartment building by a lawyer from his firm; the young man was flying to join the legal team working on the Aaronson merger and had been pressed into service by Doug.

Doug called her every day but he did not have much to say; he was even uncommunicative about his work, which was unusual for him. It seemed to her now that all he ever said was, 'Hi, sweetie! How are you? Got to go. Goodbye.'

It's odd, Laura now thought, but he's changed radically in the last few months. So much so, it's even become noticeable on the phone. He used to have so many amusing little things to tell me, odd titbits to share, confidences to make, and now he offers nothing except banalities. And, of course, he usually gets off the phone as fast as he can.

With a rush of clarity, Laura realized that this was *it* exactly, and it brought her to a standstill momentarily. He was only making the phone calls every day out of a sense of duty, of wanting to keep the peace between them, at least for the time being.

On several occasions since he had been in Los Angeles she had tried to speak to him about their life together, the route it was taking, and their problems. But he had brushed her words to one side, told her there was nothing to discuss, that everything was *fine* between them. And then he would hang up before she could argue with him. But it wasn't *fine*. Even if he didn't know it, she certainly did.

Once he came home she was going to sit him down and make him listen to her, make him reveal his thoughts and his feelings. Perhaps then he would share with her whatever it was that troubled him so much. Whatever it was, it was driving a wedge between them.

Doug *was* troubled. Even her grandmother had spotted it at Christmas, although Laura recognized that it hadn't started in December, but dated back to last year, to sometime in the spring, in fact.

Grandma Megan had noticed it, not only because she was a wise old bird who missed nothing, but also because Doug was normally such an untroubled, carefree person, a man who made light of any burdens he might carry. He simply shrugged them off with a cheery laugh, and got on with his life. 'Got to live life to the fullest, enjoy every moment. Because none of us know how long we're going to grace this world,' he would say, and he repeated the words so often they had become his motto. That was his nature, and he had been like that since the first day they had met.

Laura sighed as she swung around and began to walk back along the beach in the direction of the Newsam house. Even though she didn't want to admit it, Doug had become an enigma to her. Here was a man she had believed she knew inside out, but it wasn't true. She didn't know him at all. But how well do we ever really know another person? she wondered, and acknowledged that one never did. Most people were mysteries to others and frequently to themselves.

When she returned to the house ten minutes later, she found Hercule in the library, talking on the telephone. Wanting to give him privacy she started to leave, but he swiftly motioned to her, indicating he wished her to stay. Laura smiled, nodded, and went and sat down on the large overstuffed sofa in front of the fire. She picked up a magazine and flipped through it absently.

After only a second or two, Hercule hung up and came to join her by the fireside. Lowering himself into a nearby chair, he explained, 'I telephoned the Carlyle for my messages and found one from Sir Maximilian West. I have just spoken to him. He has finally arrived in New York after those unexpected delays. He wishes us to join him for lunch tomorrow. Is that possible, Laura? Or are you busy, my dear?'

'No, I'm not, and as you know I've really been looking forward to meeting him.'

'He's going to telephone me tomorrow morning at nine, and he will do so exactly at that time. He is very precise. Once I have heard from him I will let you know where we are to meet.'

'That's fine, Hercule. You told me you'd known him a long time, but you didn't say how long. Is it many years?'

'Ah yes, it is indeed. I first met Maxim well over thirty years ago. I was introduced to him by a friend and client, Margot Derevenko. Her daughter Anastasia was married to him, although sadly they were later divorced. When they remarried in 1990 we all rejoiced.'

'Everyone loves a happy ending,' Laura murmured and glanced into the fire, a shadow of pain crossing her face as she did so.

Hercule noticed the look of anguish, fleeting though it was, and he wondered about her. He thought Laura had seemed both sad and distracted on the few occasions he had seen her in the past ten days. Because he had had to stay longer than first anticipated, to confer with Sandra Newsam about the various decorating schemes for her house, Laura had taken him under her wing. They had dined with her grandmother, seen a movie together, and lunched several times.

It was impossible not to detect her loneliness due to her husband's delay in Los Angeles. Now he asked himself if it were more than that? Could something else be troubling her? He hoped not. She was such a lovely young woman, so good looking and bright, and extremely clever when it came to business. She was also one of the most knowledgeable art-advisers he had ever met. Although he thought of himself as a connoisseur of Impressionist and Post-Impressionist paintings, he realized that this was a small vanity on his part. Although he outstripped her in his knowledge and understanding of Gauguin's work, she knew much more than he did about many other artists from these periods, and her memory was prodigious. She could reel off facts and figures without hardly giving them a thought, or so it appeared to him. Apart from this, she had an extraordinary eye and fine taste in paintings. Perfect taste.

Hercule knew that Laura and her partner were becoming more and more successful, and therefore were accruing power in the world of art. What was it Claire had said to him recently? Ah yes, she had told him that Laura had 'a lot of clout'. Funny expression, but he rather liked it.

Now, as he sat back in the chair studying her surreptitiously, he sincerely hoped that her marriage was in the same good shape as her business. Sadly, women with successful careers were not always so lucky in their personal lives he had noticed over the years.

Sitting up straighter on the sofa, and turning to face Hercule, Laura immediately saw the look of concern in his eyes. She gave him a dazzling smile. 'I'm looking forward to Claire's visit next month,' she said. 'In fact, I'm trying to talk her into staying for a week, after she finishes her shoot for the magazine.'

'Yes, a vacation *would* be good for her,' Hercule agreed. 'She works very hard and she's so intense about it. But then, that is the way she is made. It is her nature, yes. Whatever Claire is doing she gives it everything she has. Her heart and her soul.'

'She's not changed, Hercule, she was like that when we were girls. Ferociously focused.'

He smiled at her, shook his head, looking unexpectedly amused. 'You both are that, Laura my dear.'

'If you're not focused, you don't get anything done, so *I've* discovered.' Laura stood, glanced around the room. 'By the way, what's happened to Yves?' she asked, referring to Hercule's assistant, who had flown in from Paris to help the designer earlier in the week.

'He's upstairs, measuring the windows, and Sandra has gone out to lunch. And I think that is what we should do, once Yves has completed his task. Are you not hungry, Laura?'

'I am, yes. That walk on the beach has given me an appetite.'

At this moment, Yves Pannone walked into the library carrying a yellow pad attached to a clipboard. He addressed Hercule in his careful English: 'The cook wishes to know if we would like to have the lunch, *Monsieur*.'

'It would be simpler if we went into the town. Come, Yves, put on your coat, and you too, Laura, and let us go at once. I myself am ravenous. I will have a word with the cook on the way out so that she will not be offended.'

15

Hercule had insisted that Maximilian West be his guest for lunch on Sunday, and now Hercule sat with Laura in the dining room of the Carlyle Hotel, waiting for him to arrive.

As they waited Hercule told her a few things about Maxim, wanting her to have an inkling of the kind of man she was about to meet, and for whom she might possibly do some work. 'He was knighted by the Queen a few years ago for his contribution to British industry,' Hercule explained. 'It was well deserved. But he wears this honour lightly, almost casually, and like most other truly great people, he has humility and compassion. And he is also down-to-earth, unpretentious.'

'You told me the other day he had remarried his first wife. He had several others in between, didn't he?' Laura said.

'Several. Camilla Galland, the English actress, who died tragically in an accident. Later Maxim married Adriana Macklin, the well-known American businesswoman, but they were subsequently divorced. I always believed that Anastasia was the love of his life. Everyone was stunned when she left him and he was sick at heart about it, very distressed. None of us understood her behaviour at the time, but then we do not know what goes on between two people in their private lives.' Hercule took a sip of champagne, and continued, 'When Anastasia and Maxim remarried in 1990 we were all relieved, especially their children Alix and Michael. Anyway, my dear, you will find Maxim relaxed, pleasant to be with. He has a knack of putting everyone at their ease, making them feel comfortable. Ah, here he is now.'

As Maximilian West walked towards their table Laura could not help thinking what a handsome and distinguished-looking man he was. She had seen photographs of him in newspapers and magazines, but they hardly did him justice. He was tall, lean, with black hair touched by silver at his temples, and his black eyes were brilliant in his tanned face. He wore an impeccably tailored brown-and-beige houndstooth-check sports jacket, pale blue shirt, darker blue tie and grey slacks. She thought: My God, he's gorgeous, no wonder women fall all over him.

After greetings had been exchanged, introductions made, Maxim turned to Laura and started talking about art, and just as Hercule had predicted, she was instantly comfortable with him. Within minutes she was chatting to him as if he were an old friend. Between the first and second courses they covered quite a lot of ground, mostly talking about his art collection in London.

At one moment, after glancing at the dessert menu and then putting it down, Hercule turned to Maxim and said, 'When you told me you had stumbled on new information regarding the Gauguin, you never explained it further, Maxim. You merely said it was old documentation. I must admit, I am very curious to know more.'

'I'll be happy to tell you about it,' Maxim replied. 'I didn't actually stumble on it myself though, to be honest, Hercule. Rather, Aunt Irina did.'

Maxim paused, glanced at Laura and, as though he felt it was necessary to explain, said, 'She's not really my aunt. Irina and my parents were inseparable for many years, and I've known her since I was a small child. Her name is Princess Irina Troubetzkoy.'

Laura, intrigued by this fascinating man, nodded, but before she could say anything, Hercule exclaimed, 'I have met Irina. A most unusual woman. We became acquainted through the Derevenkos, *naturellement*, years ago. She is well, I hope, in good health?'

'Yes, thank you, she is, Hercule. Still going strong at eighty-five, and quite a wonder. And I remember now, you met her quite a few times if I'm not mistaken.'

'That is correct. But please continue with your story, Maxim. I'm afraid I interrupted you.'

Maxim nodded. 'All right. As you know, Irina lives in Berlin, but several months ago she came to stay with me in Paris for a week. One afternoon, wanting to buy a gift for me, she took herself off to the Left Bank. There are, as you're well aware, Hercule, many wonderful bookshops in that area. She spent most of her time browsing in one of them on the Quai Saint-Michel, mostly because the shop has a rather grand collection of art books, art catalogues, and French classics beautifully bound in leather and hand-tooled in gold. She knows I collect old first editions, other rarities, as well as art books, and it was whilst she was browsing amongst the art books and art catalogues that she noticed the name Westheim on the spine of a particular book. The gold lettering was somewhat worn and she couldn't make out what else it said, but because the name was so meaningful to her she naturally pulled it out. And she was stunned when she saw the cover. Inscribed in gold across the front was the title *The Westheim Collection*. The author was my grandfather Ernst Westheim. When she opened it and turned to the frontispiece, her heart leapt, she told me later. The book had been updated by my father Sigmund, but what really took her breath away was the following page. Written on it was my mother's name Ursula Westheim, and even more remarkably, the signature was in my mother's own handwriting. Irina recognized it immediately although the ink was a little faded. She was thrilled, excited, as you can imagine. She bought the book and returned at once to my apartment – in fact she could hardly wait to give it to me. Aunt Irina was in tears. "Such a treasure, Maxim. Ursula's own book," she said as I leafed through it. "Who would have thought I would come across this in Paris, *her personal* copy of a book about your family's great art collection." I couldn't believe it myself, that it had turned up in Paris in this way.'

'What a marvellous find indeed, and how fortuitous for you,' Hercule exclaimed.

'Wasn't it just,' Maxim responded, his eyes lighting up. 'Extraordinary when you think about it. Anyway, the book had been privately printed and only given to friends, and incidentally the signature *is* my mother's. I've compared it with letters I have from her.'

'And when was it printed?' Hercule asked.

'In the mid 1920s originally, and seemingly my father had it reprinted in 1936, and then there was a new edition in 1938. That is the edition in my possession now.'

Laura was amazed at this story. The chances of finding the book were one in a million. Leaning forward, she asked, 'Did you recognize it, Sir Maxim?'

'No, I didn't,' he answered. 'I'd never seen it before. At least, I don't recall seeing it when I was little. I was only four when my father had the book reprinted. However, Aunt Irina began to recollect a few things later that same evening. Vague memories came back to her ... mostly about my father working on papers to do with the art collection, in 1935 or thereabouts. It was around this same period of time that he told her he had almost finished writing about the art collection.'

'And that's all she could remember?' Laura asked.

'Unfortunately. Those were very bad times, Laura,' Maxim explained. 'Germany was in the hands of the greatest criminals the world has ever known, and death, upheaval and fear permeated everyone's lives. My father was trying to get us out of Nazi Germany to safety. That was his priority, his main concern in those days, and Irina was helping him with the aid of the

German underground, the Resistance movement, of which she was a member.'

'I understand,' Laura replied. 'It sounds as if your grandfather and father created a *catalogue raisonné* about the collection.'

'They did. But it's also a picture book, in a sense, since it has hundreds of photographs of paintings and sculpture from the collection.'

'And *Tahitian Dreams* by Paul Gauguin is one of those photographs,' Hercule asserted, a pleased smile tugging at the corner of his mouth. 'How wonderful, Maxim.'

'It is, yes. And since that painting and the entire Westheim Collection disappeared not long after the book was reprinted, I think it proves beyond a shadow of a doubt that the Gauguin hadn't been sold, that it was still in the possession of the Westheim family.'

'What a pity the book wasn't discovered before,' Laura murmured. 'But never mind, now you have proof of the provenance of the entire collection, should any of it suddenly turn up on the art market.'

'That's true.' Maxim shook his head. 'It's amazing when you think about it . . . that this book survived. It's probably the only one in existence today. I'm quite sure there were a number of them at my parents' home, but they couldn't have escaped destruction. Our house on the Tiergartenstrasse was heavily bombed. Then when Marshal Zhukov marched into Berlin at the end of the war he turned twenty-two thousand guns on a Berlin already battered by the Allies, reduced what was left standing to rubble and dust. The city was flattened. Nobody's possessions could have withstood that kind of bombardment.'

'I wonder how the book found its way to Paris?' Hercule mused. 'That in itself must be an interesting story.'

'Perhaps your mother gave it to someone as a gift, Sir Maxim,' Laura suggested. 'Do you think that's the answer?'

'It's possible, of course. Personally, I think she took it with her when we went to Paris in 1939.' Maxim paused, his dark eyes suddenly intense and reflective. After a moment, he explained, 'My mother had brought Teddy with us, a family friend who acted as my nanny, and in March of 1939 my mother sent us both to England, to safety. And, most fatefully, she returned to Berlin.'

Laura nodded and glanced across at Hercule.

He signalled her with his eyes to be careful, to be still. Laura understood that this was dangerous emotional ground they were suddenly treading on, and so she did not speak. Maximilian West had sounded extremely tense and he seemed stressed.

Abruptly, he sat back in his chair and looked off into the distance, his jaw clenched. But eventually he continued quietly, 'I have my own theory, and Irina is in agreement with me. I believe my father planned to bring some of our paintings out. *Somehow.* He had remained in Berlin after we left, waiting for visas. He finally received them and was about to leave with my grandmother, aunts and uncle, when my mother went back to help him with my grandmother, who was frail and ailing. But I just can't believe that he wouldn't have tried to smuggle a few of the canvases out. He was apparently very resourceful. Rolled-up canvases are not too difficult to transport and he would have certainly had the assistance of Admiral Canaris. The admiral was head of the Abwehr, German military intelligence, but by birth, upbringing, tradition and conviction he detested Hitler and all that he stood for, as did many of the men under him. Canaris and his men were working against Hitler from within, and one of the things the admiral was doing was helping to save people who were in danger from the Nazis, by getting them out of Germany. He helped Teddy and me escape. Subsequently, he paid with his life for his beliefs. He was hanged at Flossenburg concentration camp in 1945,' Maxim finished and sat back; he fell silent once more.

Laura made no comment and neither did Hercule. Both of them were aware that strong memories were assailing Maximilian West and they wanted to give him a moment to recoup himself.

Then suddenly, in a brisker tone, Maxim resumed: 'I am positive my mother took the book to Paris to show it to art-dealers. What better way to present the Westheim Collection to them, just in case my father managed to bring out a canvas or two. She must have left it with an art gallery.'

'That is a perfectly acceptable theory, Maxim,' Hercule agreed. 'Very viable.'

Maxim nodded, lifted his glass and took a sip of Montrachet. 'It seems to be the most probable explanation of how the book got to Paris, although we'll never really know. And it's perfectly amazing to me that it survived at all. The Nazis were not only looting art owned by Jews in Germany, but in France and other European countries as well. They also stole *catalogues raisonnés*, records, and other forms of documentation. Much of the art and its documentation was shipped to Göring and Hitler in Germany. However, from what I understand, a great deal of the documentation was destroyed by the Nazis on the spot in France, and in Germany in the same way. And so the provenance of much of the art became blurred.'

'How terrible that such an awful thing happened, that so much art has been lost, has disappeared into oblivion as a consequence. And if only *you* knew where your paintings are, whose hands they are in today, you could make moves to get them back, since you now have this book,' Laura said.

'That's true, but I doubt that I'd ever be able to track them all down. That's a mammoth task; I would think virtually impossible. The only reason I found out that Norman Grant owned *Tahitian Dreams* was because he put it up for sale. When it came onto the market my daughter knew at once.'

'Is she an art-dealer?' Laura asked.

Maxim shook his head. 'Not exactly. She's an art and antiques broker working primarily with English and European dealers, and she lives here in New York. So she knows what's going on, in the same way, I'm sure, that you do. Naturally, she was aware that we were the real owners of the Gauguin, that it was once part of the

Westheim Collection, because I had told her about it. And these days we do know quite a lot more about the collection. I myself don't remember anything, I was so young when I left Germany. However, Aunt Irina and Teddy have recalled many things, and they've been making notes for years now. They both knew my parents' houses in Berlin and Wannsee, and my grandmother's house in the Grunewald, and they've helped to spark each other's memory. But obviously there was no way I could claim *Tahitian Dreams*, even though I suddenly knew who had it, because I had no proof that I owned it. At least, not until Irina came upon the book by chance.'

'How did you trace the Gauguin back to General Schiller? Through the Herman Seltzer Gallery in Vienna, I suppose,' Laura said.

'Yes, that's right. Alix went to see the painting, and naturally, as a potential buyer she was shown the provenance. She then telephoned the details to me later, and since I happened to be in Paris I flew to Vienna and paid a visit to the Herman Seltzer Gallery. He is long dead, but his grandson Paul was happy to show me all of the records they had in regard to the Gauguin. He bent over backwards to help me, in fact. The provenance stopped with General Schiller. There was no reference to any previous owner before him. Paul Seltzer told me that art stolen by the Nazis was usually stamped on the back of the canvas with a small Swastika, and next to this was written the first two letters of the surname of the owner, and then there was a number. But not all of the art was stamped in this fashion, most especially paintings looted by individuals for their own purposes, such as Schiller. He obviously hung onto it until the end of the war. He then sold it to the Viennese gallery, apparently not an unusual occurrence. According to Paul Seltzer that was happening a great deal in Paris and Switzerland in those days.'

'Yes, it was very systematic, the looting and selling of art, both in France and Germany,' Hercule interjected. 'And why would it not be? It was big business for the Nazis.'

'Of course it was,' Maxim said, and reached for the menu. 'I think perhaps we should order dessert. We've spent the last half hour talking without giving it a thought. What would you like, Laura?'

'I'm not sure,' she answered, smiling at him. 'Everything sounds fattening.'

'*You* don't have to worry,' Maxim said, returning her smile.

'I think I shall indulge myself for once,' Hercule murmured. 'I will have the chocolate mousse. It is delicious.'

'I'll join you,' Maxim said.

'And I think I'll have the fruit salad, please.' Pushing back her chair, Laura rose. 'If you'll excuse me, I won't be a moment.' She hurried off to the powder room.

Once they were alone, Hercule leaned closer to Maxim and confided, 'Laura has an assured taste in art, which I believe springs from her great knowledge of it. In fact, she has a deeper knowledge than anyone else I know. I find that astonishing since she is so young.'

'How old is she?' Maxim said.

'Thirty-one.'

'Really, she looks much younger. Mind you, she seems very intelligent, and she certainly makes sense about revamping my art collection.' Maxim suddenly chuckled. 'Actually, she didn't appear to be impressed when I told her whose work I owned. I think if I hired her she'd then tell me to sell most of it.'

Hercule also laughed. 'She was outspoken, yes, I must agree.'

'Well, she's correct, Hercule, old chap, I do think I should unload most of it, except for the Laura Knights. I do love those, and incidentally, I think your friend can be of help to me in more ways than one.'

'What do you mean?'

'As you know, I'm about to file suit against Norman Grant for the return of the Gauguin. Before I get into any costly litigation, it has occurred to me that I ought to try a different route.'

'Such as?'

'Laura. Earlier, when we were talking, it struck me that she might be better equipped to negotiate with Grant than my lawyers, less intimidating, don't you think?'

Hercule smiled and gave him a knowing look. 'I have the distinct feeling that Laura could be as intimidating as any tough lawyer.'

Maxim laughed again. 'Perhaps so. It wouldn't surprise me at all. But you know, a woman's always got such an advantage, she can be so much softer than a man, most especially when she turns on the charm.'

'That is true, Maxim.'

'I'm seriously thinking of hiring her to handle the matter of the Gauguin, Hercule, quite aside from revamping my art collection in London. She is a personable young woman, obviously very bright, and from what you tell me her knowledge of art is formidable.'

'That is so, and she is well educated and diplomatic. I cannot recommend her highly enough.'

16

Doug came home from Los Angeles the following weekend, and from the moment he walked into the apartment Laura knew instinctively, deep within herself, that their marriage was over.

He was as affable and as charming as he always was, but part of him was simply not there. He seemed more detached and remote than he had ever been before, and it struck her that his interest obviously lay elsewhere. Not for the first time in the past few months, she wondered yet again if there was another woman in his life. It was a distinct possibility and it would certainly explain the changes which had been wrought in him.

Even though she had contemplated this idea before, the thought of it now nonetheless shook her up; she excused herself and left Doug in their bedroom where he was unpacking. Retreating to the kitchen, she stood leaning against a worktop, looking out of the window at the backyard of the brownstone opposite, waiting for the sick feeling inside to go away.

It was a cold grey Saturday night in late February, and the only reason she could see the garden was because light flooded out from the brownstone's windows, illuminating the bare branches of a tree and the garden wall. The scene was bereft, isolated, lonely, and it echoed the way she felt. She shivered slightly, and then an immense feeling of sadness enveloped her like a shroud, and she felt her throat tightening. For a moment she struggled with her emotions and squeezed her eyes tightly shut, pushing back the incipient tears. I won't cry, I just won't, she told herself. I'm going to be mature about this.

For the entire month Doug had been in Los Angeles she had been mindful of his vagueness on the phone, his lack of interest in her and what she was doing, and his ill-concealed impatience, his need to say goodbye and hang up. She was far too smart not to suspect that he might well be having an affair. She wondered whether to come right out and ask him, but instantly changed her mind. Eventually he would open up to her, she felt sure of that, and for the moment she wanted to give him a bit of space.

Opening the refrigerator door, she took out a bottle of carbonated water and drank a glass of it, before returning to the bedroom. Sitting down on a chair, she made idle conversation with Doug as he finished unpacking.

Once he had put his suitcase away, he told her he had a few urgent business calls to make. Excusing himself with a faint smile, he went into his small study at the back of the apartment.

After an hour on and off the phone he finally left the study and found her in the living room where she was working at her desk. She glanced up as he appeared in the doorway and stood leaning against the door frame, looking carefree and nonchalant, as if he didn't have a worry in the world.

'I've booked a table at Le Refuge,' he said, giving her his lopsided smile. 'For nine o'clock. I'm going to shower and put on some fresh clothes. Okay, sweetie?'

She smiled back and nodded. 'I'm surprised you got a table, especially on a Saturday night,' she replied. 'But that's great. And I'm more or less ready. I just have to put on some lipstick and brush my hair.'

'You look great, Laura,' he said, swung around and walked down the hall.

Laura watched him go, thinking how great *he* looked. He was trim and fit, and his face was tanned, as if he had been out in the sun a lot. Well, he had been in sunny California, hadn't he? And apparently not always anchored to his desk, as he had frequently implied. Tall, dark and handsome . . . that was the way Claire had described him in Paris in December, and he was . . . this was the very phrase which had popped into her mind the first time she had met him.

They walked to the restaurant. It was on East Eighty-Second Street, just off Lexington Avenue, not far from their apartment on Eightieth Street and Park Avenue. The evening was pleasant, not too cold, with a bright silver orb of a moon riding high in the black sky.

'Just look at that moon, Laura,' Doug said, glancing up. 'It's a truly *full* moon, perfect! Well, all the loonies will be out tonight, you can bet on that.'

Laura did not respond. Instead, she tucked her arm through his, trying to stay in step with him; he always took such long strides. She was about to tell him she was glad he was home, but instantly she choked back the words. It was too late. In the way that a woman senses these things, she felt she had lost Doug, at least a large part of him. He had started to change last spring, almost a year ago now; and he was a much different man from the one she had married six years ago. This year would be their seventh anniversary, but somehow she didn't think they would be celebrating it. One thing she was certain of, though. Whatever happened between them from this day on, they would always be good friends, and she would always love Doug.

Le Refuge was a charming little French bistro, a favourite of theirs; Laura was pleased Doug had chosen it. As he pushed open the door and escorted her inside, they were greeted by a rush of warm air and the fragrant smells of delicious food cooking, the low-key chatter of the other diners, the bustle of the busy waiters as they hurried about.

After they had shed their overcoats and been shown to a cosy corner table, Doug sat back in his chair and looked at her. 'Champagne? Kir Royale? White wine? What would you like?'

'I think a glass of white wine, please, Doug,' Laura answered, glancing around the restaurant before settling into the chair.

'I'll have the same, I guess,' he murmured and motioned to the waiter. Once he had ordered, Doug went on, 'So tell me more about your new clients. You're getting to be a regular tycoon in the art world, or so it seems to me.'

'You know all about Olivia Gardener in Palm Beach, since we signed her in November, but now we also have this lovely woman, Sandra Newsam. Hercule's doing her house in Southampton. She's recently widowed, and although she won't be spending millions on art, she's going to be a good, steady client; worthwhile, I can tell that. And certainly she'll be nice to work with. But the plum of course is Sir Maximilian West.'

Doug nodded. 'I know. I was impressed when you told me he was considering you. So he took you on, did he?'

'We signed the contract yesterday,' Laura answered, realizing he'd paid far more attention to her on the phone than she'd thought. 'I'm going to reorganize his art collection in London. I'll be weeding out a lot of paintings, getting rid of some, buying new ones. It'll be exciting.'

'It sounds like it. Alison must be really thrilled.'

'She is, and we've agreed that she'll run the office and do most of the paperwork with Joni and Lynne. I'll be on the outside more, seeing clients, tracking down appropriate art, and travelling whenever it's necessary.'

'That'll please Tony. He never did want her to move around much. He likes her joined to his hip.'

'That's true. But it suits *me* this way, Doug. I much prefer to deal directly with the clients, as you well know. The main thing is, Alison's happy with the way we've worked it out and so am I.'

'I understand. And Hercule's turned out to be a really wonderful business contact for you, hasn't he? Quite aside from being a good friend.'

'Very much so, and he's such a lovely person, thoughtful and caring.'

The waiter placed their drinks before them; after clinking glasses they both took a sip and Laura continued, 'I was bowled over when Hercule told me he'd recommended me to Sir Maxim. Having him as a client is a real feather in my cap, and it's good for Art Acquisitions.'

'I should say.' Doug glanced at her quickly and remarked, 'His fame precedes him. What's he like? Really like, I mean?'

'Down-to-earth, pleasant, practical. But charismatic, a genuine presence. And he's suave, charming, extremely good looking. Tall, dark and handsome too, just like you, although he's much older, somewhere in his early sixties, I would think. And he happens to be the best-dressed man I've ever met. *Impeccable.*'

'That's quite a profile you've given him,' Doug said and laughed. 'He's got a helluva reputation as a businessman ... tough negotiator, inspired deal maker, and all that. He used to be a fierce corporate raider in the seventies and eighties, and a very successful one. But I think his son is running the company these days, isn't he?'

'Not exactly. Hercule told me Michael does have a great deal of power, but Sir Maxim hasn't retired yet. They're running the business empire together, I believe.'

'Some team that is,' Doug murmured, and took a swallow of wine. They both accepted menus from the waiter, and Doug asked, 'Do you know what you want?'

Laura shrugged and studied the menu carefully.

Doug studied her, an amused expression suddenly lighting up his green eyes. 'I bet I can guess. You're going to order country pâté with cornichons, lots of extra ones on the side, and then grilled sole to be followed by crème caramel. Your usual.'

'That's right,' she replied, and grinned at his expression. 'I guess I'm very predictable.'

'When it comes to the restaurants you know well.' Stifling his laughter, Doug motioned to the waiter and ordered their food, then asked for a wine list. Once he had perused this for a moment or two, he summoned the waiter, told him which wine he preferred, then turned to Laura once again. 'Robin and Karen have broken up, broken off their engagement,' he said.

Laura was startled, and she sat up straighter in the chair, staring at him. Her surprise showed on her face as she exclaimed, 'My God! When did that happen?'

'About a week ago, but I was so harassed with the Aaronson merger I forgot to tell you. It had slipped my mind.'

'What happened, Doug? I thought they were very much in love, and happy together. Certainly they were well suited. Or so it seemed to me.'

'What happened?' Doug shrugged, shook his head. 'I don't exactly know, Laura. Robin called me in Los Angeles and told me it was off, that Karen had ditched him. She apparently announced it was finished one night over dinner, and the next day she sent the engagement ring back, by bonded messenger. Can you believe it, she didn't even give it to him personally.'

Laura was still somewhat flabbergasted at his announcement of the break-up, and she took a few moments to absorb his words. At last she remarked, 'I suppose she didn't want to face Robin a second time. At least she *did* return the ring, which is more than some women would have done.'

'That's true,' he responded, and shook his head. 'I have to admit, Laura, I was as taken aback as you're looking right now.'

Laura was silent for a moment or two, her expression thoughtful. Then she said slowly, 'If Karen thinks it's not right, then it's better they break it off now. At least this way they won't have to go through a divorce later.'

Doug gave her an odd look, opened his mouth to say something. But at this precise moment the waiter arrived with their first course. He let the moment pass.

Back at the apartment several hours later, Doug went into the living room, poured two brandies and held one of the crystal balloons out to Laura. 'Come on, let's have a nightcap.'

Although Laura was not a big drinker, she did not even hesitate as she might have in the past. 'All right,' she said, walking into the room, taking the glass of cognac from him. 'Why not? We haven't seen each other for a month, we've a lot to catch up on.'

'Mmmm,' was his only comment before he let his eyes wander around their living room. 'You know, you really did a wonderful job with this room, Laura. It still looks great. I'm impressed all over again when I come back after being away.'

Laura followed his gaze, her own eyes scanning everything more objectively than usual. They took in the pale cream walls and cream silk draperies, the matching cream sofas and chairs, the Art Deco wood pieces with their touches of black, the old Aubusson rug on the floor. It was a restful ambience, and her only regret was that their art was not better. The paintings were good, and she liked them, but they were not her favourite French Impressionists; only her clients could afford *those*, which ran into the millions.

Finally Laura said, 'Yes, the room did hold up well, Doug. The scheme is so classic I guess it'll never date.' She lowered herself onto the cream sofa and placed her glass on the Art Deco coffee table, being careful to place it on top of a book and not on the wood.

Leaning back into the cushions, she thought: This is as good a time as any to talk to him. She felt very determined to bring their problems out into the open. Very simply, she knew she had to clear the air; she must know where she stood with him. She couldn't go on any longer in this way. It was far too nerve-wracking, upsetting.

Doug took the chair near the fireplace, and almost as if he had read her mind he said carefully, 'There're a few things I'd like to talk to you about, Laura. I should have mentioned them before, but it's always difficult on the phone, and anyway I *have* been so pushed with work.'

'I know. And we should talk, Doug. I feel you've been very distant, and certainly not too forthcoming.' She shook her head, and made a *moue* with her mouth, finishing, 'I had the feeling you were only calling me out of a sense of duty.'

'Oh come on, Laura, you know better than that!'

'I'm not stupid, Doug. Whenever you've phoned in the last few weeks, you couldn't wait to say goodbye and get off.'

'Mostly because of pressure. The Aaronson merger has been, and still is, very complicated. And it's still not finished.'

'So you've got to go back to LA? Is that what you're telling me?'

'Yes, I do have to go back. To finish the merger.' Lifting his brandy balloon, he sniffed the Courvoisier, took a small swallow, then sat nursing the glass between both hands, staring down into the amber liquid. When he lifted his head, he focused his eyes on her, and said, 'I've had an offer, a very big offer. To go to another law firm.'

Although Laura was surprised, she smiled and exclaimed, 'But that's wonderful, Doug! I'm so pleased for you. Which law firm?'

He hesitated fractionally before saying, 'It's a Los Angeles firm, Laura.'

'*Oh.*' She sat back, staring at him. So it's not an affair after all, she thought. It's business that's been preoccupying him. Frowning, she asked swiftly, 'Does that mean you have to move to Los Angeles? Or would you be at their New York office? If they have one, that is.'

'They do have one, yes, but they want me in Los Angeles.'

'I see. Which law firm is it?'

'Arnold, Matthews and McCall: they're very prestigious. And they've offered me a partnership. It's really a big deal, big for me, I mean.'

She was silent for several seconds, her eyes on him, and then she said, 'You've accepted it, haven't you?'

Doug did not at first answer. He returned her penetrating stare and cleared his throat several times. At last he murmured, 'Not exactly. I've indicated I want to take it, but I haven't actually accepted it. Not formally.'

'Oh Doug . . .' Laura began and then let her voice trail off. She took a sip of the cognac and stared at a painting on the far wall. Finally, with a heavy sigh, she went on, 'You're splitting hairs. You know you want the job and that you're going to take it. Come on, it's me you're talking to.'

Doug bit his lip, looking slightly shame-faced, and then he leaned closer to her, reached out, took hold of her hand. 'I guess you do know me better than anyone, Laura.'

She nodded. '*I* think so. Well, as much as we can ever know another person.' There was a slight hesitation on her part, and then she said softly, 'But I haven't known you at all lately, Doug. You're almost like a stranger to me, in some ways.'

He nodded. 'I haven't known myself at times, Laura, I must admit. I think I've changed a great deal in the last few months.'

'The past year,' she corrected. 'It all started last spring.'

Letting go of her hand, he sat back in the chair, then leaned forward jerkily and picked up the glass of brandy. After a deep swallow, that made him cough for a moment, he said, 'Did it really start then? The change in me, I mean?'

'I believe so, Doug. Look, I've given a great deal of thought to it whilst you've been in Los Angeles, and it *was* then. It became more pronounced around Christmas, even Grandma Megan noticed and mentioned it to me.'

'She did?' He sounded startled; concern flooded his face.

'Oh yes, she doesn't miss a trick, you should know that by now. Anyway, she said you didn't seem to be there, that you were distracted; she even said she thought you wished you were somewhere else.' Laura leaned closer and stared into her husband's face. Very pointedly, she added, 'Did you wish you were in another place? With another person perhaps? With another woman?'

He shook his head vehemently. 'No, I certainly didn't want

to be anywhere else. Or with anyone else. But I wasn't the same anymore. I felt . . . ill at ease with myself over Christmas. And I have ever since. The feeling doesn't go away. Except that I've been too busy working to dwell on it much.'

'I knew it,' she said quietly. 'I just knew you were . . . *different* . . . another person, not *you.*'

Laura flopped back against the cushions and closed her eyes. When she opened them a split-second later she said, 'The marriage isn't right these days, is it, Doug?'

Staring at her, staring into those vivid blue eyes, so blue they were almost blinding, Doug felt himself choking up. His throat tightened to such an extent he couldn't, for a moment, speak at all. He loved her, he would miss her, but it had to be, this end to their marriage.

He got up and went to sit on the sofa, reached for her blindly, tears dimming his vision. Clinging onto her tightly, he tried to regain his composure. He was shaken, much more than he had expected to be. Doug had accepted days ago that this kind of discussion would take place with Laura once he was home, and he hadn't relished it. But he had not realized how upset he would be.

Eventually, when he had full control, Doug pulled away from her slightly, and looked deeply into her eyes once more. 'I love you, but it doesn't work anymore, our marriage.'

'I know. I think I've known that since Christmas,' Laura answered. 'I just haven't really wanted to admit it, I suppose.'

Doug pulled her into his arms again and she clung to him. Against his cheek she said softly, 'You can be honest with me, Doug. Are you having an affair? Is there another woman?'

'No, there isn't, absolutely *not.* I'm telling you the truth. There is no other woman in my life.'

'Then what happened to us, to our marriage?'

'I'm not sure.'

'Is it because . . . we haven't had children?'

'Good God, no! Of course not.'

'Then why?'

'I just don't know. I love you, Laura, I really do, but something's gone.'

'The spark's not there,' she whispered, suddenly understanding, and she sighed. 'You love me, but you're not *in love* with me, that's it, isn't it?'

'I don't know.'

'But I do. Admit it, I won't be angry, Doug, these things happen. You've changed, that's all, and people do change, I realize that.'

'Perhaps you're right,' he finally agreed. 'Maybe the spark *isn't* there any longer.'

Laura made no response. The old familiar heaviness descended on her; it was like a dead weight on her shoulders. And inside she felt cold and empty. Bereft; she thought, I've been bereft for a long time. Like a widow, I've been grieving for him because I've known for months he was gone from me forever.

Doug sighed, aware of her pain. He did not know how to comfort her, there was no way really. And so he did not speak.

Now a long silence fell between them. Neither of them dared say another word, for fear of hurting the other too deeply.

But at last Laura found the strength to mouth the words that had rolled around in her head for weeks. 'I think we should get a divorce, Doug.' There, the dreaded words were out at last. They seemed to hang in the air between them.

After a moment of utter stillness, he answered in a quiet voice, 'No, a trial separation.'

'That's only putting off the inevitable. Look, maybe I've changed too.'

'I don't think you have. Not you. Not Laura, ever true blue.' He drew away, looking at her closely. His heart ached; he was full of regrets, but he could not alter things, not now. It was too late. The die was cast. In a sense it had been cast long ago. He touched her face gently with one finger, running it down her cheek, as he had done so frequently in the past, and then attempted to smile at her, but the smile faltered.

This old familiar gesture undid her. She stared at him and gasped, and fell against him.

As he held her in the circle of his arms she began to cry inconsolably, as though her heart were breaking; and, in a way, it was. She wept for the end of their marriage, for the children they had wanted and would never have, for the future together now lost to them. Suddenly overcome, Laura pushed herself away from Doug and rushed out of the room, her eyes streaming. Running into their bedroom, she closed the door and leaned against it, pressing her hands against her eyes, wanting to stem her tears. She found a box of tissues by the side of the bed, took one and blew her nose. And once she felt in control of herself again, she returned to the living room.

As she walked in she passed the skirted table in the corner, and she paused, glanced at the many photographs of family and friends arranged on it. Prominent amongst them was a picture of Doug, herself, Karen and Robin which had been taken the previous summer in Martha's Vineyard, when the four of them had been on vacation together.

Laura had always thought that Robin and Karen were ideally suited, two intellectuals at heart, sharing a love of the theatre, music and art. In her mind they had always been The Beautiful Couple in capital letters, both blond, blue-eyed and good-looking. Karen, so slender and willowy, stylish and chic, dress designer *par excellence* with her own boutique in Soho. Robin, lean and handsome and somewhat dapper, well-groomed to the point of old-fashioned perfection. He was the cool, precise banker by day, a man who rarely cracked a smile; at night he became the laughing, fun-loving bohemian.

Well, they hadn't been the perfect couple after all, since the engagement was now off. When Doug had told her earlier she had been momentarily taken aback; but she wasn't so surprised after all, now that she thought about it carefully. The pieces had all fallen into place. Suddenly she understood what all of this was about, understood who it was that had come between them.

Doug was sitting on the sofa, his elbows on his knees, his head in his hands. 'Are you all right, Laura?' he asked as she moved into the room, but he did not look up at her.

Ignoring the question, she said, 'It's Robin, isn't it? That's what all this is about. It's Robin who's come between us. You're leaving me for him.'

Doug was silent.

Laura went and stood in front of him, her back to the fireplace. When he did not respond, she exclaimed, 'We've been married almost seven years, and I think you should tell me the truth. You owe me that, at least.'

He still did not respond and his silence infuriated her. She cried, 'I know things have been strained between us; I know we've drifted apart, but at the root of it stands Robin. Don't pretend otherwise, Doug.'

'I wasn't going to pretend otherwise,' Doug said, lifting his head at last. 'I *was* going to tell you,' he went on, and then faltered.

'Tell me *when* exactly,' she demanded. 'Next month, next year?'

'No, of course not, don't be silly. I was going to tell you . . .' He shook his head, his expression chagrined. 'Okay, I lost my nerve a short while ago. But I would have told you before I went back to LA.'

'Would you?' she asked quietly, sounding sceptical.

'Laura, I still love you, and I respect you, and I was going to explain.'

'Then why don't you tell me now?'

He nodded. 'I've always known . . . known I was . . . bisexual. There was another man once, when I was in college, as well as various girlfriends. I wanted very badly to get married and have children; but I never met a woman I wanted to marry. Until I met you. I was totally bowled over by you, and when I fell in love with you I thought everything was going to work out. It seemed to be the perfect marriage. And then I met Robin when I went to that retreat two years ago. I discovered I was very . . . stirred by him, touched by him emotionally and physically. But nothing happened. I thought at the time it was something inside me and only in me. He and I became good friends, and *we* made a great foursome, and that was that. I tried to block out my feelings, Laura, I really did. I tried to concentrate on you, on us, on our marriage; but other things were going on inside me. My attraction for Robin was growing steadily. It simply wouldn't go away. And then last summer, when we were in Martha's Vineyard, Robin and I were alone on the boat one day, and everything exploded around us. It just happened . . . we were together.'

'I see.' Laura sat down on the nearest chair, stunned by what he had told her, and then she asked quickly, 'Were there any other infidelities during our marriage?'

'Absolutely not!' Doug exclaimed, staring at her. 'And that's the truth.'

She nodded. 'Robin's also moving to Los Angeles, isn't he?'

It was Doug's turn to nod.

Laura said, 'What would have happened if we'd had a child? Children? Would you have stayed in the marriage?'

Taken aback by this question, Doug sat back on the sofa and wondered how to answer it. What would he have done? Would he have left a wife and children for his lover? Other men had. But he wasn't sure, and he said quickly, 'I don't know, Laura, honestly I don't.'

'Thinking about it, our marriage was very passionate in the beginning, but the passion . . . sort of dwindled, didn't it, Doug?'

'Yes.'

She was silent, looked off into space. She felt, suddenly, a terrible sense of defeat. Her marriage had started off so well and then it had gone awry, and he had fallen in love with someone else. Man or woman, it really didn't matter because the outcome was the same. He had chosen someone else over her. Sadness trickled through her, and she discovered she had nothing else to say.

Doug said, 'I'm sorry, Laura.'

She looked at him helplessly. She was wordless.

'I didn't mean it to happen, but it did. I can't help it, Laura . . . it's just . . . the way it is.'

17

'It was all handled nicely, Gran,' Laura said, looking across at Megan, then she laughed somewhat hollowly, and added, 'If you can use that word when talking about a divorce. What I meant is we were civilized, grown-up about it, and Doug was thoughtful, very nice really.'

'Doug's always been a nice young man, and in my experience a leopard doesn't change its spots, even when there's a divorce in the offing,' Megan responded. 'So he's gone back to Los Angeles has he?'

'Yes. To finish the Aaronson merger. He's told them at Cohen, Travis and Norris that he's leaving the law firm once the deal has been completed, or rather this particular stage of it. He said he's going to start looking for an apartment, but for the moment he'll be at the Peninsula.'

Laura rose and walked across the solarium, her high heels resounding loudly on the terracotta tile floor. Leaning against the French windows, she gazed out across the lawns; these sloped down to a band of willow trees that dipped their flowing branches into a slow-moving stream which sliced through the property in Kent, Connecticut. In the fading, misty light of the afternoon the grey-green landscape looked ethereal, a Turner painting.

After a moment, almost to herself, she muttered, 'And he's taken all of his clothes with him.'

Megan heard this, and she said quietly, 'Then there's no question about it, Laura, he's gone for good. Is that what you're saying, my darling?'

Laura swung around to face her grandmother; her expression was woebegone. 'Yes. And I feel as isolated and alone as if I'd been abandoned on the Patagonian Ice Cap and left to fend for myself.'

Megan couldn't resist laughing despite the moroseness echoing in Laura's voice. 'You do have such colourful phrases at times. I always did tell you to become a writer. So he's gone, and you're sad, and sorrowing, but that's only natural. Doug has been there by your side, and there *for* you, for almost seven years. You're bound to feel the wrench, especially since I'm quite aware you still love him.'

'I do, Grandma, and I always will. But I've realized for a while now that I've changed in certain ways myself. He's not *in love* with me anymore, and neither am I with him.' At least I don't think I am, she said to herself, as she came back and sat down next to Megan. Staring at her grandmother intently, she continued, 'In the same way that we fell in love, we've . . . grown out of it. And as strange as this might sound to you, Gran, I honestly think we might have killed it off ourselves, working so hard trying to have a baby.'

Megan nodded. 'I can well imagine. Sex became too clinical, too mechanical perhaps, it wasn't romantic sex anymore, is that what you're trying to say?'

'More or less. Anyway, we're friends, and we'll stay friends for the rest of our lives, I feel sure of that. We were both in tears when he went back to Los Angeles last week. All that luggage he took made it seem so . . . *final.* Suddenly Doug didn't want to go. We just clung to each other for ages, until the doorman buzzed again to say that the driver was worried Doug would miss the plane. In the end I had to virtually push him out of the apartment.'

'It must have been difficult for you both. On the other hand, Doug hasn't dropped off the edge of the world. He's only gone to Los Angeles.'

'I know. But there's something quite awful about the end of a marriage, or any relationship for that matter.'

'Oh yes, I know that only too well. However, it's not as if he died. And Doug will always be *there* for you, should you ever need him. I feel that in my bones. That's the kind of man he is.'

'Yes, that's what *he* said, that if I ever needed him I only had to call. He offered to give me alimony, but I turned it down. Why should I do that to him, hamstring him in that way, when I earn a decent living myself?'

'Some women wouldn't be quite so selfless,' Megan responded with her usual pithiness.

'But I'm not some women. I'm *me*.'

'Thank God for that, and I wasn't being critical, I was merely commenting.'

'Yes, Gran. Doug says he wants me to have the apartment. As you know, we bought it together, but he told me he doesn't need his share of the money back. All he wants are his books, the paintings he bought, and his grandfather's Georgian desk and chair.'

'It sounds to me as if the two of you don't have any problems with each other when it comes to the financial side of your marriage, and that is truly quite remarkable.'

'He's bending over backwards to be decent, and so am I.'

'You're a good girl, and I'm proud of the way you're handling this situation.' Megan paused, shifted slightly in her chair, and gave Laura a penetrating glance. 'Forgive me, but I feel I must ask you this. Do you think there's another woman in his life? Has he fallen in love with someone else? Is that what this is all about?'

'Doug denies it. I asked him, Gran. He says there isn't another woman, and I believe him.'

'I trust your judgement. However, he's being so obliging it made me wonder, that's all. Anyway, because your marriage has seemingly gone awry I think it's a good thing you're getting divorced immediately, rather than clinging to it. You're still young enough to start all over again, and the same applies to Doug.'

'I know, but it's a bit hard at times,' Laura whispered, and pushed down the tears which had sprung into her throat. Much to her mortification, her eyes were unexpectedly moist; she brushed her hand across them and blinked rapidly, then cleared her throat.

Megan, ever eagle-eyed, noticed this rush of sudden emotion, but observing how well her granddaughter was handling herself she decided to ignore it. Instead she said, '*Of course* it's hard, but then life *is* hard, and it always has been. And don't let anyone tell you otherwise. It's never been easy, not for anyone. The important thing is how you handle life and all of its hardships and pain. I've always believed you've got to deal with life's troubles standing up, fists raised, fighting hard. It's vital to battle through and come out triumphant. You're a winner, darling, of that I'm absolutely sure.' Megan nodded and her wise old eyes were gentle, full of love, as she finished, 'I have no fears about you, Laura. You'll do fine.'

'Oh Gran, I hope so.'

'You will, because you're a true Valiant. That's the way I brought you up. As your grandfather would have said, a chip off the old block.'

Laura smiled, filled with love for this wonderful old woman who had given her so much love and understanding every day of her life. Whatever would I have done without her, she suddenly wondered; my mother was never around.

Megan said, 'Don't let things drift, start the divorce proceedings as soon as you can. It's better to make a swift, clean cut. Prolonging things gets messy. Anyway, you seem to have worked everything out with Doug in the most amicable way, in a mature manner, and that augurs well for you.'

'We've tried to make it easy on each other, and Doug says he'll recommend a divorce lawyer. He's going to call me regarding one sometime next week.'

Megan nodded and pushed herself up out of her chair. 'I think I'll go and have a rest now, Laura dear. And by the way, lunch was delicious, thank you for making it.'

Laughing, Laura exclaimed, 'You know very well all I did was unpack it and unwrap it. But the smoked salmon *was* lovely, wasn't it?'

Megan nodded. 'Petrossian, I've no doubt. That's another trait you inherited from me. *Extravagance.*' Winking at her granddaughter, she murmured, 'And now I'm going up to my room to daydream about the past. That's what old women do, you know. Live their lives all over again . . . in their dreams. It's a beautiful way to spend an afternoon when you've nothing better to do.'

Laura put her arms around her grandmother and held her close for a moment or two. Then she said, 'Do you want me to help you upstairs, Gran?'

'Get along with you, you silly girl!' Megan exclaimed, sounding irritated as she moved away from Laura. 'I'm not decrepit yet, as I keep telling you. I can manage very well on my own, ninety-two or not. I'm very sprightly, I'll have you know.'

Laura smiled lovingly. 'I've got to come upstairs anyway, to check Claire's room. I know Fenice came in to do a thorough clean during the week, but I want to make sure Claire has everything she might need for the weekend.'

'I'm glad she's coming to stay for a few days, and don't forget to put flowers in her room. Now, come along, Laura, don't dawdle, let's go upstairs.'

A little later Laura put on her Barbour and green Wellington boots, and walked down towards the river. The sky had changed; it was a strange mottled green along the rim, and it looked cold and remote. The dimming light, combined with the mist rising from the river, gave the garden a strange mysterious feeling.

Only a short while ago it had seemed ethereal as she had viewed it through the French windows of the solarium. Now, suddenly, it was distinctly eerie.

Although it was not cold, Laura shivered. Goose bumps speckled the back of her neck. Somebody walked over my grave, she thought, remembering a saying of Megan's, and she shivered again, pushed that dolorous thought out of her head.

Moving away from the river's bank and the dripping willows, she headed towards a small copse where mostly maples and oaks grew, and she caught her breath in surprise and pleasure as she moved forward into the bosky glade. The hundreds of daffodils, which her grandmother had planted over the years, were already shooting up near an old drystone wall that bordered this end of their land. They were early this year, the tender green shoots pushing up out of the rich dark earth. Their yellow bonnets had not yet opened, but she felt sure they would burst into bloom next week, if the weather remained mild.

Years ago her grandfather had placed a green-painted wooden Adirondack bench at the edge of the glade, near the stone wall, and Laura sat down on it, brought her feet to the seat and hunched in a corner, her arms wrapped around her knees. Her thoughts turned to Doug and the end of their marriage, and she sighed to herself.

She had given her grandmother a carefully edited version of everything that had happened. She had not wanted to rehash their parting, or relive it, and so she had shortened the story and smoothed it out and made it sound amicable. Not that it had been a rancorous parting.

Doug had stayed in New York for ten days, working things out with his law firm, and packing; in the evenings there had been any number of discussions, soul searching and endless tears. But finally they had both agreed that everything was truly over between them. There was no way to salvage their marriage; deep within herself Laura knew she didn't even want to try. Perhaps their relationship would work for a while, but Doug would pull away again. Eventually. He would always pull away because he had no wish to be married. Not to anyone. She closed her eyes for a brief moment. She knew he wanted to be with Robin.

She was glad now he was gone: having him around her had been extremely painful; she had felt as if she were living on an emotional rollercoaster whilst he was still ensconced in the apartment. It had exhausted her.

Tears came into her eyes and for a moment she wondered if it was her fault. Had she failed him? She shrugged off this idea. Of course it wasn't her fault. She wished Doug well. She hoped he would be happy. Everybody deserved to be happy. But so few people were.

Groping around in her jacket pocket she found a tissue, wiped her eyes, and then she stood up and walked slowly back to the old white clapboard house on the hill. Claire was coming tomorrow, to stay for a long weekend, and there was so much to do before her arrival.

18

What a blessed relief it is to be here, Claire thought, glancing around the bedroom again, just as she had earlier in the day. She had always loved this room, for as long as she could remember.

When she had first arrived at Rhondda Fach just before lunch she had felt debilitated, terribly worn down after finishing the major photographic shoot in New York for her magazine. It had been a tough assignment, and everything that could go wrong had, but somehow she had managed to pull them all through it, and get the two apartments on film. She was certain they would make good spreads for the magazine. But at what cost, she asked herself, as she wrapped her cashmere cardigan more tightly around her body and went to stand near the fire.

Still, after spending several hours here with Megan and Laura, whom she loved, in this house which she loved, she had begun to feel so much better. Just being in this marvellous old house was such a powerful restorative. She had been coming here to stay since she was ten years old, and this bedroom was known as 'Claire's room'. She did consider it to be hers; she had been its main occupant for all those years, even if other people did stay in it from time to time.

Throwing off her shoes, Claire walked over to the four-poster bed hung with blue-and-white striped cotton, and got onto it, slipping her legs underneath the soft down duvet. Settling back against the mound of pillows in their snow white antique pillow-cases, she let her eyes roam around the room, taking pleasure from everything in it.

There was nothing new in her room; each item was familiar and well-loved, and it was just like coming home. Her eyes rested briefly on the lovely old cherrywood armoire, the pretty carved chest from France where Fenice had put her sweaters and underwear earlier, just as she had been doing for twenty-six years. Then her gaze moved on to the collection of paintings on glass. All of them were Chinese scenes; they were very old, Grandma Megan had told her once, painted by Russians, and bought in Shepherd's Market in London's Mayfair over forty years ago by Grandpa Owen.

Her own contribution to the room had been the blue-and-white wallpaper, which Megan had allowed her to choose when she had been redecorating some of the bedrooms at least twenty years ago now. It was an eyecatching pattern composed of Chinese ginger jars, sprays of orange blossoms, men pulling rickshaws and Chinese ladies dressed in cheongsams and holding lutes. All of these images were coloured bright blue on a pristine white background.

When she had first seen the sample, Grandma Megan had said it looked far too busy, and had ordered the rolls reluctantly; once it was up on the walls she had agreed it was as enchanting and as effective as Claire had said it would be. And she had thanked her for choosing it, told her she had a good eye.

Despite the coolness of the blue-and-white colour combination there was a cosiness to the room; earlier, Fenice had switched on the white-silk-shaded blue porcelain lamps and lit the logs and paper in the fireplace. The fire was still burning brightly in the hearth and it brought a golden glow to the room.

Just looking at the logs hissing and spurting and flaring in the grate made her feel drowsy, and Claire closed her eyes, relaxing her tired limbs, drawing comfort from the warmth in these very dear and well-loved surroundings.

As she drifted, her thoughts turned to Doug. Laura had told her only moments after her arrival about their break-up. On first hearing this Claire had been startled, and had found it not only distressing but very puzzling. Now she wondered why she had ever considered it to be puzzling. Nothing that happened between a man and a woman should surprise her, of all people. A small sigh escaped. If men were stupid then women were surely fools. So how could they possibly get anything right?

Nonetheless, Claire couldn't help feeling somewhat saddened because theirs was a marriage she had believed would work. Laura had said she had no explanation for its collapse; did Doug perhaps? Doug would be the loser in the long run, of this Claire was convinced. Laura was such a winner, such a positive and optimistic person she was always going to come out on top. In her opinion, Laura had a much better chance at finding happiness with someone else than Doug did, although she wasn't exactly sure why she felt this. She just did. Doug was far too . . . pernickety. Yes, that was the word that truly applied to him.

Shifting under the duvet, Claire tried to find a little ease. Her bones ached today; she felt as though she were coming down with the flu, but she knew she wasn't. Being on her feet for days on end without a break had been a punishing ordeal, and she was glad there were no more photographic shoots like this in the offing. At least shoots which she had to direct. The next two would be overseen by Giselle Cravenne, she would see to that.

For the next five days she would be here at Rhondda Fach; she knew she would have a wonderful rest . . . doing nothing except reading, listening to music, and basking in the warmth and love of Laura's company, and Grandma Megan's, too. This little vacation was going to be much more than a treat; it would be a great luxury for her.

She wondered when to give Laura her news. Should she tell her later this afternoon, when they had tea, which was something of a ritual with Grandma Megan? Or should she wait until later? After a moment's consideration Claire thought: I'll play it by ear, that's the best way.

Claire couldn't help thinking about the next few weeks ahead of her, all that she had to do, and she began to make lists in her head. It was an old, compulsive habit of hers, especially when she was overburdened, which she was at this moment. She had so much to do before the summer. She wasn't sure how she was going to accomplish it all. But she would. She had to. She had no choice.

Sliding further down under the duvet, Claire turned on her side and stopped fighting the feeling of drowsiness which had slowly crept over her. Within minutes she had fallen off. She slept a dreamless sleep.

The long green valley was surrounded by verdant hills that swept up towards the sky, half of them layered with Scottish pines, oaks and ash. The entire valley and its rolling hills covered over five hundred acres which Owen Valiant had bought some sixty years before, in the middle of the 1930s.

He and Megan had fallen in love with this beautiful fertile valley in Kent, at the heart of the northwestern highlands of Connecticut. They had called it Rhondda Fach, which in Welsh meant the little Rhondda, and it was named for the Rhondda Valley, that most beautiful and famous of all the Welsh valleys from which they came.

The house itself was named Rhondda Fach Farm, although few people ever called it a farm. And it had not been a proper working farm since the day Grandpa Owen had bought it. He had usually referred to himself as a gentleman farmer, and he did so smiling proudly.

Gentleman farmer, though, he had been; he had cultivated apple and pear orchards, herb gardens, and vegetable plots where everything from marrows to potatoes, parsnips and carrots grew; he had also developed fields of corn, and there were large cutting gardens for fresh flowers in the spring and summer. All still flourished, gave bountiful harvests of vegetables and fruit and fragrant blooms. The caretaker Tom Flynn kept chickens for them, and tended to Grandma Megan's greenhouses, where she grew tomatoes, and, most successfully, orchids of all kinds. 'Tom's good with the chickens; we certainly get a lot of eggs,' Grandma Megan would say, adding swiftly, 'but he's a genius when it comes to my orchids. He's got a green thumb. Or perhaps I should say green fingers.'

The old clapboard house, painted white with black shutters and a black roof, had been a small structure when it was first built in 1790; over the many decades it had acquired numerous wings and additions, and these sprawled out at each end. But the house had a lovely symmetry to it and a certain gracefulness which added to its charm.

It stood nestled against the green foothills which rose up behind it in a great swathe like a giant-sized Elizabethan ruff, and it was backed by a copse of dark green firs that threw it into bold relief.

In front of the back terrace, smooth, manicured lawns sloped away to the gardens and a stream which meandered through the property. Beyond were rolling meadows filled with wild flowers in summer, and further beyond there were woods where bluebells, primroses and daisies grew alongside mushrooms under moss-covered trees.

Standing together to the right of the house was a small compound of buildings, including Tom's cottage, the stables and several barns. Nearby was a large pond, which Grandpa Owen had built when he had purchased the valley so long ago, and for years it had been home to all manner of wildlife. To it came Canada geese, ducks and other fowl, and occasionally a blue heron sauntered along its banks. A family of owls nested in a stand of trees not far from the pond, which in summer was filled with pale pink water lilies floating on its surface.

To Claire the valley was a haven of tranquillity and beauty, wide open land with wide open skies and nothing in sight. Lonely perhaps to some, but to her it was a refuge.

As a child she had fallen in love with it, and that love had never wavered. Now, as she walked down towards the river and the weeping willow trees, she hoped that when they came to stay in August Natasha would fall under its spell as she herself had done so long ago. This was such a special place; for her it was also full of memories . . . memories of her childhood and youth, her difficult teen years, of Laura and Megan, and the family who had given her so much love. They had miraculously made her part of them, made her feel so special, so wanted, and a Valiant herself, in a sense. She wanted this for her Natasha . . . a family of Valiants for her daughter.

Claire glanced up at the afternoon sky. It was a clear, bright blue, filled with soft white clouds and the sun was still shining brilliantly. What a glorious March day it had been, more like May, unusually warm for this time of year, a soft day. But Laura had told her over lunch that the weather was going to change radically tomorrow. 'It'll be cold,' she had warned. 'There'll be a frost. Tom's already mentioned that he's worried about the daffodils and the other early bloomers.' Laura, like Tom, was something of a weathervane.

Circling the lawn, Claire began to walk towards the house, but stopped when she came to the group of trees at the edge of the glade where the old drystone wall ran down towards the river, where she had once almost drowned.

Spotting Owen's old Adirondack bench, she went over to it, sat down and found herself watching a squirrel racing up a tree. It disappeared instantly into the upper branches; she smiled to herself, thinking of the chipmunks that used to play around the back porch years ago. They had always sped away under the foundations at the sight of a human being. Now there was one that was fearless, and it came out and waited for nuts and other titbits – so Megan had told her over lunch.

After a moment or two Claire rose and walked to the drystone wall, where she stood looking downstream, her busy mind soothed at last, at least for a few moments anyway.

'Coo-ee! Coo-ee!'

Smiling, knowing it was Laura, Claire swung around and waved to her, and then she sat down on the wall, waiting for her dearest friend.

A second or two later Laura came bounding up, flushed and out of breath. 'I've been looking all over for you, Clarabelle,' she exclaimed, using a cherished childhood name. 'You've been the elusive one. Fenice told me she saw you set off towards the barns, and then Megan told me you were heading towards the hills. And now I find you in our favourite glade.' She shook her head, still laughing.

'I started out that way, heading for the pond actually. But in the end I decided to linger here for a while. I find it so peaceful, and calming.' She paused, shook her head, and there was a hint of a smile on her face as she went on, 'Old habits die hard. Don't you remember, we always came here to think when we were younger; it was a place to struggle through our problems.'

'How could I forget? You've found me here weeping many a time in the past.'

'And so have you, found me I mean. The last time you were so comforting, a rock, Laura. You gave me such a lot of strength.'

'It was when you'd come back from Paris, just after you'd separated from Philippe.' Laura sat down on the wall next to Claire. 'You were distraught.'

'I know. Aren't women foolish?'

'Sometimes.' Laura looked deeply into Claire's face and added, 'We haven't been so lucky, you and I, have we? I mean with men. We've both failed at marriage, but at least you've got Natasha to show for it.'

'Yes.' Claire returned Laura's long stare, and touched her arm.

'You've been such a wonderful friend to me all these years. I don't know what I would have done without you, or how to thank you.'

'Thanks aren't necessary, Claire.' Laura smiled at her lovingly, then glancing up at the sky, she added, 'I'm so glad you came out to Kent today, instead of waiting until tomorrow. It's such a gorgeous afternoon.'

'A beautiful day,' Claire agreed, looking up at the sky herself, her eyes misted. It took her a moment to regain her composure, and she was thankful Laura hadn't seemed to notice. Bringing her gaze back to Laura's, she stared into those startlingly blue eyes, and said in a low but even tone, 'There's something I have to tell you.'

Laura frowned, gazed at Claire more intently. Her expression was quizzical as she asked, 'What is it? You sound funny, *odd*.'

'The other day you complained you hadn't seen me since I'd been in New York, that I'd been far too busy with the photo shoot, and that I should have been able to find time for a cup of coffee with you, at least. You remember saying that, don't you?'

Laura nodded.

'If only you'd told me about Doug on the phone, I would have somehow found a moment to run over, to be with you, Laura. But you didn't, and I was caught up with something vitally important to me. Other than the shoot, I mean.'

'What were you caught up with?' Laura asked, still frowning, looking even more perplexed.

'I was having tests.'

'What's wrong with you?' Laura demanded, her eyes opening wider. 'You're not ill, are you, Claire?'

'I'm afraid so.' There was a momentary pause before Claire said quietly, 'I'm dying.'

Laura recoiled slightly and sat up straighter, blinking. Shock assaulted her and she felt a terrible icy-cold feeling creeping over her body. The sun was still shining and the sky was that marvellous clear blue, but the brightness of the day had dimmed.

Laura leaned closer to Claire and took hold of her hand. 'I don't understand . . . How can you be dying? What's wrong with you?' she asked, her voice breaking.

'I have breast cancer.' Claire answered as softly and as evenly as she possibly could. She was trying not to become hysterical, as she had been several times in the privacy of her hotel room in the last couple of days.

Laura gaped at her. She was disbelieving, unable to properly absorb Claire's frightening words. She exclaimed, 'Oh God, Claire, not you! Not you, darling . . .' Laura stopped mid-sentence, choked-up and unable to continue. Her face had turned ashen and her blue eyes were filling with fear.

Claire nodded. 'But it's true. I've spent the last few days having tests at Memorial Sloan-Kettering Cancer Center.'

'And they told you that you were dying?' Laura whispered, trying hard not to cry, hanging onto her control as best she could. She was shaking inside.

'Not in so many words, no,' Claire answered. 'They never do of course. Doctors don't want to diminish the hope a patient might have, or take hope away. But I know I won't make it beyond this summer. Certainly I won't be alive when . . .' She looked around her, and finished in a voice that had begun to falter, 'When the leaves start changing here.'

'Oh Claire.' Laura shook her head. Her eyes filled with tears. 'I can't believe this is happening.'

'You must. I'm going to need you to be strong, Laura. For all of us.'

'I will be, you can count on me,' Laura replied, the tears trickling down her cheeks. Drawing closer to Claire, she put her arms around her friend and held her close.

Finally, despair got the better of Claire and her control slipped. She began to weep, clinging to Laura, needing her love and friendship more than she ever had in all the years they had known each other.

19

'When did you find out you were ill?' Laura asked, her voice low, echoing with concern. 'Was it in December when I was in Paris? You know Hercule thought you didn't look well, and he was worried about you.'

'It wasn't then, I was fine then. I didn't feel sick at all . . . but obviously I was,' Claire responded, and leaned back in the chair. She closed her eyes for a brief moment, wishing the pain in her back and hips would go away; it had nagged at her constantly for the last hour or two. Making a supreme effort, she sat up, leaned forward and reached for the mug of tea Laura had just brought her, sipped it gratefully. The tea was scalding hot, strong and sweet, and it reminded her of her childhood days spent here. Grandpa Owen had always made tea like this. 'Coalminer's tea', he had called it, and it was addictive.

The two women had not remained in the garden for very long, once Claire had broken her distressing news to Laura. After wiping each other's tears and calming each other as best they could, they had made their way back to the house, had settled themselves in the solarium. The moment Claire had complained of feeling ill, of the general achiness in her bones, Laura had immediately hurried off to the kitchen; a short while later she had returned with Tylenol and the mugs of tea.

Now Laura asked somewhat tentatively, 'Do you feel like talking yet?'

'Yes, it's fine now, Laura, ask me anything you want.'

'I was wondering how you discovered it? Did you find a lump in your breast?'

Claire shook her head. 'No. It was under my arm, and I only found it last week.' Claire grimaced. 'The strange thing is, I had a very small lump under the same arm last month, but it went away. I thought it was caused by clogged pores, you know, from using the wrong anti-perspirant. I didn't give it a second thought, especially since it disappeared almost overnight.'

'And when it came back a few weeks later, you immediately went to Memorial Sloan-Kettering,' Laura stated.

'No, I didn't, I first called my friend Nancy Brinker. You remember her, don't you, Laura? That lovely Texan you met with me in Paris a couple of years ago.'

Laura nodded. 'Of course I remember Nancy. We had lunch at the Ritz Hotel together. Her sister died of breast cancer, and she started a foundation to help fight the disease.'

'That's right, the Susan G Komen Breast Cancer Foundation. Nancy invented Race for the Cure, and she's raised millions and millions. Anyway, since she is the one person I know who has a mountain of knowledge in her head and at her fingertips, I phoned her in Dallas within minutes of finding the lump under my arm again. It was Nancy who made arrangements for me to go to Memorial Sloan-Kettering.'

'And they did tests immediately?'

'Oh yes, a lot of them. The doctor was very thorough. When he discovered the lump was hard and did not move, he tried to put a needle into it, to aspirate it. You see, he thought it might be a cyst. When that didn't work, he sent me for a whole series of other tests.' Suddenly, abruptly, Claire stopped; she shook her head. 'You don't need to hear all this, it's very depressing.'

'I do, Claire! I want to know everything. That way I will

understand, and I will be able to help you, help you to get through this.'

Claire took a deep breath and plunged on: 'When he couldn't aspirate the lump, the doctor sent me for a high-definition mammogram and a sonogram. These were followed by a needle biopsy, bone scans, blood tests and liver scans. The day after these tests had been completed I was diagnosed . . .' Claire came to a halt, before finishing, 'I was diagnosed as having highly aggressive metastic breast cancer. I'm what they call a Stage 4 patient.'

'What does that mean?'

'That I have a very small chance of surviving. A five percent chance, actually.'

'*Claire* . . .' Laura was stunned, and she found it impossible to say another word. Her throat tightened, and she could feel the tears gathering behind her eyes. But in the face of Claire's enormous courage, she took steely control of herself. She said quickly, 'But many women do *survive* breast cancer.'

'That's true, yes, and I'm going to be having very aggressive treatment, but there's no guarantee it will work. The outcome may not be good.'

'Does the doctor want you to have a mastectomy?'

'No. Chemotherapy. The doctors at Sloan-Kettering wanted me to stay in New York, to have several courses of high-dose chemo, but I'm going back to Paris next week, as planned. I can have the same treatments at the American Hospital there. And look, I can't stay here, Laura, I have to get back to Paris because of Natasha, and anyway, there's my job at the magazine.'

'But perhaps it would be better if you stayed in New York, had your treatment at Sloan-Kettering. There's plenty of room at my apartment, and anyway, there's this house. You could stay here if you want, it's only a couple of hours to New York. We could send for Natasha. She could go to school in Manhattan and come here at weekends. Or she could go to school up here.'

Claire shook her head. 'I have to go back, but thank you, Laura, thank you for being so supportive.'

'Please think about it, though. About coming back to New York. *Permanently.*'

'I will, I promise.'

'Do you ... have any other pain, Claire?'

'No, just the general achiness I've told you about, like you feel when you have flu. My bones ache.'

'Didn't they give you anything for that?'

'Only Tylenol.'

Both women now fell silent, absorbed in their own thoughts.

Claire wondered whether or not to continue, to tell Laura how very bad her condition really was, much worse than she had indicated so far. And then she decided against it. She had said enough for the moment. She did not want to burden Laura any further. Later, before she returned to France, she would confide the rest of it.

For her part, Laura's thoughts were on the future. Her main priority was how to help Claire get through this. She stubbornly clung to the hope that chemotherapy would arrest the cancer. Alison's older sister Diane had battled it through and won; *her* cancer had been chemically destroyed and she was living proof that it worked, wasn't she? Laura shivered, despite the warmth in the solarium. Only now was the shock beginning to recede and even so only very slightly; the surprise, the unexpectedness of Claire's news, and the enormity of it had stunned her, left her feeling helpless and undone. But she knew she must be strong and brave if she were to be of help.

Finally Claire broke the silence when she murmured, 'Obviously, I haven't said anything to Natasha yet, not over the phone. I need to be there with her when I tell her, so that I can reassure her, give her comfort.'

'Yes, that's best,' Laura replied, thinking how devastating this was going to be for Natasha. Then before she could stop herself, she asked, 'What about Philippe? When are you going to tell him that you're sick?'

'I'm not. At least, not for the moment.'

Laura simply nodded, although she wondered about Claire's answer. After a moment's thought, she asked quietly, 'May I tell Grandma Megan? I think she ought to know.'

Hesitating, looking uncertain, Claire bit her lip, shook her head. 'It might be too much of a shock to her, too upsetting, don't you think?'

'She's pretty tough, you know that. And she's bound to guess something's wrong, just from the expression on my face. Concern and worry are difficult to hide, Claire.'

'Then you should tell her. Yes, I agree that it's better that she knows.'·

Later, when she was back in her own room, Laura gave vent to her feelings. She sat down on the sofa near the window and wept inconsolably for Claire. Her own shock and heartache were enormous, so she could hazard a guess how Claire must be feeling. She also knew how much suffering her friend was facing, so much so that she found it unbearable to contemplate. Her heart squeezed and squeezed at the thought of it. But, on the other hand, she knew she would have to come to grips with her own emotions in order to help Claire. Already Laura was experiencing a terrible sense of loss; deep within herself she realized that Claire might not win this battle. As she had said herself, there were no guarantees the treatment would work.

Her thoughts swung to Hercule. How right he had been in December. He had noticed something wrong in Claire she had not seen; and neither had Claire, for that matter. He had told Laura that, when he had looked at Claire in the photographic studio at one moment, her face had been like a death mask. At the time she had shuddered. Now she wished she had hauled Claire off to a doctor. Laura sighed and wiped her eyes, and took herself firmly in hand. Weeping wasn't going to get her anywhere, or Claire either. She must be a rock, full of strength, as Claire needed her to be.

My best friend, my dearest friend, Laura thought, and I'm

going to lose her. It didn't seem possible that one day she would not be here, that they would not live out their lives together, grow old together, as they had always said they would. Although they lived in different countries they had remained as close as they were when they were girls, sisters under the skin.

Taking a few deep breaths, Laura rose and went into the bathroom. She splashed cold water on her tear-stained face, brushed her hair, put on a touch of lipstick, then sprayed herself with scent.

A few minutes later she made her way down the corridor, heading in the direction of Grandma Megan's room.

Laura paused when she came to the end of the corridor and stood looking out of the huge Palladian window, her eyes trained towards the distant hills. They rose up in a magnificent sweep to touch the sky, its colour fading now in the late afternoon light, a crystalline light that seemed to emanate from behind the hills, rimming them with silver. Such beauty in this world, she thought. And such pain and heartbreak. Laura felt that icy chill settle over her again and involuntarily she shivered.

Turning, she tapped on her grandmother's door, and then put her ear against it, listening. She was about to tap again, when Megan called, 'Come in, Fenice.'

'It's me, Gran,' Laura said as she opened the door and walked inside. 'Do you need Fenice for something?'

'No, darling girl, I don't. But she said she'd bring me up the *New York Times*. I never finished reading it this morning,' Megan answered and leaned back on the pillows.

'I'll go and get it for you in a moment. Fenice has probably forgotten, or she may be preparing afternoon tea. You know what a production she makes of it when you're here.'

'That's true.' Megan peered at Laura and then patted the edge of the bed. 'You look as if you've come to tell me something serious, Laura, or something important.'

'How do you know that, Grandma?'

'I can tell. That expression. You look as if you've lost a pound and found a sixpence. You're troubled, Laura. Come along, tell me. It can't be all that bad.'

'I'm afraid it is,' Laura said, sitting down on the bed, taking hold of Megan's wrinkled old hand mottled with liver spots.

Her grandmother stared at her, her eyes narrowing. 'Give it to me straight. That's the only way to break bad news.'

'It's going to be a shock. I want you to be prepared.'

'I'm used to shocks, Laura, I've had them all of my life, and somehow I've managed to survive. Come along, get it out.'

'It's Claire, Grandma Megan. She's very ill, she has breast cancer. She doesn't think she'll make it through the autumn.'

Megan gasped, her face draining, and then she fell back against the pillows and snapped her eyes shut, almost convulsively. When she opened them a moment later they were pooled with tears. 'Oh my God, that poor child! And she's so young, only thirty-six.'

Laura nodded. 'It's heartbreaking, Gran.'

'Tell me everything,' Megan instructed tensely, fixing her eyes on Laura.

Once she had finished giving her grandmother all of the pertinent details of Claire's illness, Laura said, 'I tried to get her to move back to New York, but she won't. Apparently she can have the chemotherapy treatment in Paris. At the American Hospital there.'

'I've heard it's a good hospital,' Megan murmured, and frowned. 'But I agree with you, I think it would be far better if she came home. She doesn't really have anyone in Paris, does she?'

'There's Hercule.'

'Oh yes, of course. Such a lovely man, and I'm sure he'll try to help her the best way he can, but she has *us* here. After all, we're the only family Claire's really ever had.'

'I'll try to persuade her, Gran.'

'Yes, do that, darling. I suppose she's going to tell Philippe Lavillard. And Rosa.'

'I don't think so. At least, she said she can't, *not yet.*'

'But she must tell them!' Megan exclaimed. 'They have to know because of Natasha. Perhaps you should tell them.'

'Gran! Don't be silly. I can't do that, go against Claire's wishes. Anyway, it's like playing God with someone else's life. She has to tell Philippe herself.'

'Yes, you're right.' Pushing herself up, making motions to get out of bed, Megan went on, 'Is Claire going to come down to tea?'

'I think so. We agreed I should tell you about her illness first. Do you want me to help you out of bed, Grandma?'

'Yes, for once I do need your help, child.'

'How did she take it?' Claire asked, staring across the room at Laura. She, too, was in bed, or rather lying on top of it under the duvet.

'With her usual stoicism,' Laura answered, and smiled faintly. 'Gran's like an old battleship, I suppose. She's used to knocks and shocks and traumatic bumps, but she manages to stay on a relatively even keel. Naturally, she was upset, and she's very, very concerned about you, Claire. And for you. She agrees with me . . . she thinks you ought to come home. To be with your family, that's the way she put it.'

Claire was touched, and her eyes filled with tears. She passed her hand over them, blinked several times, and said, 'Oh Laura, it's such a blessing having you and Grandma Megan. So comforting, reassuring. But for the moment I think I'll go back and see how it goes in Paris.'

'Okay, but don't forget, you promised to think about moving back home. Listen, Gran wanted to know about Philippe, I mean when you'll be telling him about your illness.'

'I don't know . . . I told you that.' Claire threw off the duvet and got out of bed; she went and sat in front of the fire, staring into the flames. After a moment, she looked up and said, 'Come and sit with me for a minute. I want to talk to you about something else.'

Laura did as Claire requested; she took the other chair near the fire and asked, 'What is it? You sound more anxious than ever, Claire.'

'It's true, I am very anxious, Laura. About Natasha. About her future. She'll be fifteen in the summer, that's so young, even though she is grown-up in such a lot of ways.' Claire brought her gaze to Laura's, and asked, 'When I die will you take Natasha for me? Will you look after my daughter for me? Until she's a bit older.'

Laura was momentarily startled, and she stared back at Claire, and exclaimed, 'Of course I will. You know I love Natasha.'

'She's a good girl, Laura, she won't be any trouble to you, I promise . . .' Claire was unable to say another word. She blinked a bit and cleared her throat and looked away for a moment or two.

Laura, who was also moved, swallowed hard, took hold of Claire's hand and squeezed it. Then she went and knelt in front of Claire, gently turned her face so that they were looking at each other. 'Did you think I would refuse?'

'No, not you, my true blue Laura.' Claire let out a small sigh. 'It's hard . . . knowing I'm not going to be around for her . . . I won't see her growing up, graduating, getting married . . . I'll never see my grandchildren . . .' Her voice broke.

'Oh, Claire darling, please don't give in. We must fight this. I told you, so many women do make it through cancer.'

'I won't.' Claire's voice quavered and once again she had to pause, trying to steady herself. After a moment's respite, and a few deep breaths, she was able to say, 'The cancer has metastasized through the lymph nodes under my arm. I've got twenty-three positive lymph nodes. It's metastasized to my bones, gone through my skeletal structure. It'll spread to my liver soon . . . I told you, Laura, I won't live to see the leaves turn here at the farm . . .' Now facing the reality of her illness, the tears spilled unchecked from Claire's eyes, slid down her cheeks.

Shocked and despairing, and frightened for her dearest friend, Laura also began to weep.

Claire reached out her arms to Laura, and, just as they had in the garden, they clung to each other, trying to give comfort, the one to the other. They stayed like this for a long time, weeping quietly, and it was then that Laura accepted finally that Claire was doomed.

Eventually she went and found a box of tissues in the bathroom; she dried her eyes and her face, and took the box out to Claire, who had remained seated by the fire.

After a while, Claire managed to regain her composure, and she said, 'Sit with me again for a second, Laura, won't you, please?'

Laura nodded and dropped into the chair. 'Now tell me what else is on your mind, darling.'

'Next week, when we get back to New York, can we go and see your lawyer, or a lawyer, and draw up the papers that will make you Natasha's legal guardian?'

'If that's what you want, yes, of course.'

'I do want it.'

'But what about her father?'

'He's never been a father to her, and he won't want her. Trust me on that.'

'But wouldn't you need his permission to make me her legal guardian?'

'No. I have sole custody of Natasha, and his visits are at my discretion. In any case, he wouldn't put up a fight. That's not his way. And how could he manage to look after a daughter in Zaire, when he's in quarantine part of the time? And then there are his women. Natasha would cramp his style.'

Laura was silent.

Claire went on, 'You will take care of her for me, won't you, Laura? It will be an uneasy grave I lie in if you don't.'

'Claire, please don't talk like that. You know there's no question about it. I promise you I will look after Natasha as long as she needs me – all of her life, in fact. She'll be like my own child.'

'It's settled then?' Claire pinned her green eyes on her friend.

'It's settled,' Laura answered, her voice strong.

Claire smiled for the first time in days.

PART THREE

Summer

1997

20

Work, which had always been a pleasure for Laura, now became her salvation. It helped her to keep worry and concern for Claire at bay. And she was so busy and on the move she did not have a single moment to dwell on problems she knew she could not solve. And that was the way she wanted it.

'I've just got to keep going, I can't stop,' she kept telling Alison, who was constantly advising her to slow down. 'This is my way of dealing with Claire's cancer and my divorce from Doug. If I stop for breath I'll become hysterical, and I'll fall apart,' she explained.

Wisely, her partner left her alone after this last conversation; Alison managed to refrain from making any further comments, even when Laura appeared to be overly stressed and worn out.

During the months of April and May, Laura made four trips to London to see Maximilian West, whose art collection she was editing, refining and organizing. Each time she returned to New York she flew back via Paris, so that she could stop off for a day or two to be with Claire and Natasha.

Claire was in the middle of high-dose chemotherapy treatments and trying to keep up a brave front; Laura never stopped praying that the treatments would work and that the cancer would go into remission.

The sojourns in Paris, short as they were, enabled Laura to spend cherished time with Claire and with Natasha as well. Every visit filled Laura with amazement, and her admiration of the fourteen-year-old girl grew. Natasha was handling the heartbreaking situation of her mother's deadly illness in the most extraordinary way; she had become a tower of strength for Claire, a loving and caring companion, always there for her night and day. But the thing which startled Laura the most was Natasha's practicality. She had developed a very down-to-earth way of taking charge and dealing with matters.

'In fact, I'd even go so far as to say she is extremely business-like,' Laura said to Doug one evening in early June. He had come to New York on business, had phoned her at her office and asked her to have dinner with him before he left for Los Angeles. They made their date for his last night in New York.

Now, as they had supper at Felida, their favourite Italian restaurant, Laura was telling him about Natasha and singing her praises.

'*Businesslike* is a curious word to use,' Doug remarked, peering at Laura across the table. 'I'm not sure I know exactly what you mean, especially when you're applying it to a teenager.'

'She's got her feet on the ground, Doug, she's very practical. Efficient. I find it quite remarkable. She takes care of everything, the bills, Claire's banking, all of her mother's paperwork, and she pays the housekeeper, gives her instructions.' Laura smiled. 'She's like a little mother, organizing their lives. Mind you, she's always been mature, as you know, much older than her years. I guess that comes from being with adults a lot of the time, and being an only child. Claire brought her up to be self-sufficient and independent, of course, and it shows.'

'What's Claire . . .' Doug broke off abruptly, looked carefully at Laura, and when he went on, his voice was warm and loving, 'What are Claire's chances of getting better, Laura?'

'Not good, I'm afraid,' Laura responded, her expression suddenly turning sad. There was the faintest hint of resignation in her voice as she added, 'I pray she'll go into remission, but we just don't know yet.'

Doug could not fail to miss her tone and he put his hand on top of Laura's, wanting to comfort her, as he said, 'I'm sorry, so sorry she's ill like this. You two have always been so close. I know how worried you are.'

'Yes, I am, but I'm also very proud of Claire, Doug. You would be, too, if you could see her. She's the bravest person I've ever known, and she's just remarkable the way she's handling the treatments. They're very harsh, extremely strong, and there are so many unpleasant side effects.'

'They're horrendous, from what I've heard.'

'Claire has suffered a lot with nausea and vomiting, and she's lost all of her hair.'

'Oh no, not her beautiful red hair! It was her pride and joy. She always loved it when I called her Red.'

'I know she did. But Natasha and Hercule went out and bought her a wig, a fabulous auburn wig. It's short and curly, made of real hair. It suits her, too. In fact, it's hard to tell it's a wig. They got it at the best place in Paris, a theatrical hair company which actresses use. Claire makes such a big effort. She's trying to lead as normal a life as she can.'

'She's not working at the magazine is she?' Doug asked.

'Sort of. The owner has given her leave of absence, but she does go in when she feels she can make it through the day, or even half a day. She gives instructions and directions from home, and she edits at home. And the staff come for meetings at the apartment. The owner wants her back full time, as soon as she's feeling better, but in the meantime he's being very understanding. And he's still paying her salary, thank God.'

'How's Hercule bearing up?' Doug eyed her over the glass of red wine he was holding.

'Oh God, Doug, don't ask. He was devastated at first. He loves her, as you know. Then again, his wife Veronica died of cancer. Lymphoma, I believe. He was truly wiped out when Claire told him. And then he got angry with himself. He'd spotted something odd about Claire in December, and, as I told you at the time, he suspected she was ill. How right he was. Hercule was so mad at himself for not doing something, pushing her to see a doctor in December, and I know how he feels. I was angry that I hadn't done that either. Got her to a doctor, I mean, since he'd confided his worries in me. He's being the most wonderful friend to Claire. Caring, loving and generous. He can't do enough for her. It's been a comfort to me knowing he's around.'

'He's a good person. A good guy. And what about Philippe? Has she told him how ill she is yet?'

'Yes, she has. I talked Claire into it, with Natasha's help. He has a right to know, and we persuaded her to call him in Atlanta. It was last month actually. In May. I was staying in Paris with them for a long weekend.'

'What was Philippe doing in Atlanta? Visiting the Center for Disease Control again?' Doug's expression was quizzical.

'No, he's actually working there now. Since the end of April. The reason he flew over to see the head of the Center last December was apparently for an interview. He's now got a very big position with the Center.'

'That's a far cry from being a virologist in Zaire,' Doug remarked.

'It is, yes. But being in Atlanta is a relief to him, I think. That's what he conveyed to me over the phone, anyway. He'd apparently grown very weary, he said he was burnt out.'

'I can understand that. But what about the guardianship? Does he know you've become Natasha's legal guardian, Laura?'

'Oh yes. Again, I insisted that Claire tell him. It's only right that he knows, and Grandma Megan was on our backs about it anyway. After all, he is Natasha's father.'

'How did he take it?' Doug probed.

'Very well really. Look, I wasn't face to face with him ... he was on the phone. But he sounded all right. He seemed understanding. He said a girl of Natasha's age needs a woman around. And naturally Claire told him he could see Natasha whenever he wants.'

'I'm glad she did that . . .' Doug took another sip of the wine, then put the glass down and leaned over the table. 'Listen to me, Laura, this is one hell of a responsibility you've taken on. If Claire . . . if Claire doesn't make it through this, then you're going to be bringing up a teenager. Not the easiest task in the world, especially in this day and age.'

'I know. But I can do it. I just know I can, Doug. And she's a good girl.'

'If it happens, it'll change your life.'

'A lot of things change lives, Doug darling. That's the way life is.' Laura gave him a pointed look. 'Like divorce. That changes lives. It's certainly changed mine.'

He took her hand in his. 'I'm sorry, Laura, so sorry we didn't make it.'

'I know you are. So am I.'

'I worry about you and about this situation, should it develop.'

'Don't, Doug. I'll be okay, really I will. Even if I have to bring up Natasha, I'll be okay. I'll make it, Doug.'

'Yes, you will.' He gave her an appraising look, and continued, 'You're strong and courageous. I've always admired your strength. There aren't many like you, you know.'

She smiled at him. 'Thanks, but I think there are a lot of strong women in this world, women who are brave and dependable, loyal and indomitable. Take Grandma Megan, she's indomitable.'

'That she is. But you're still an original. I spotted that about you right away. In the very beginning.'

'I know. You told me that. Anyway, Claire wants Natasha to be part of a family – well, part of the Valiant family.'

Doug stared at her and a look of disbelief crossed his face. 'But there's only you, Laura.'

She stared back at him without responding, lifted her coffee cup and took a long swallow. Then she sat back in the chair; her gaze was unwavering. 'No, there's my mother and Grandma Megan and Dylan. Not to mention my two aunts Rhianon and Cara.'

Doug shook his head in wonderment. 'Dylan's in London working for *Time Magazine* and wrestling with all of his women. And responsibility is hardly his strong suit. Your mother, never a very reliable family member, is off painting murals in exotic places. Your two aunts you never see, since they're both decrepit and reclusive. And your grandmother's about to be ninety-three. There *is* only you, Laura.'

'But I don't feel that way, I don't feel alone. I just don't, Doug.'

Doug shook his head, sighed. 'Listen, I love you and I'm there for always, if you need me. But let's not forget I'm now living in Los Angeles. It's not as if I'll be around much to help you bring up Natasha.'

'But perhaps *I* won't have to do that either. I'm hoping I won't. I'm rooting for Claire . . . rooting for her to beat this.'

It was two weeks later that Laura found herself having a very similar conversation with Philippe Lavillard. Since she thought nothing of working at weekends, she had gone to the office on a Saturday afternoon to sift through the European art catalogues stacked on her desk.

She was halfway through the pile when the shrilling of the phone startled her. Reaching for it, she said, 'Art Acquisitions.'

'That is you, isn't it, Laura? It's Philippe Lavillard here.'

'Oh hello,' she exclaimed, surprised, for a moment, to hear his voice.

'I'm in New York,' he explained, and as usual got straight to the point. 'I wondered if you could spare me a few minutes to see me? I realize you must be working, so I hope I'm not an intrusion.'

There was no hesitation in her voice as she said, 'No, no, it's okay. Come on over to the office.' After giving him the address, she hung up, went on reading one of the art catalogues.

Ten minutes later she was opening the door to Philippe. 'Hello,' she said, and stepped to one side to let him enter the small reception area.

'Hello, Laura,' he answered, following her through into her office. 'Thanks for seeing me at such short notice.'

She nodded, indicated a chair. 'Please sit down.' Walking around the desk she lowered herself into her chair, asked, 'Are you in New York for the weekend?'

'Just today. Well, actually I'll be here this evening, I'm going back to Atlanta tomorrow. I had a business lunch today with a colleague. I wasn't sure how long it would take, that's why I didn't call you before now.'

'That's all right,' she said. 'I guess you want to talk to me about Claire and Natasha.'

He nodded. 'Mostly Natasha.'

Laura stiffened, staring at him. 'What about her?'

'I think certain things need to be said.' Leaning back in the chair, he crossed his long legs, looking thoughtful.

Regarding him carefully, wondering what he had on his mind, Laura couldn't help thinking that he seemed comfortable, at ease with himself, and with her. She relaxed a little, and sat back herself, waiting for him to continue.

'You and I have only spoken on the phone since . . . Claire . . . became ill, and I wanted to make a few things clear. Face to face, Laura.'

'What things?' she asked, wary again, her eyes narrowing slightly.

'I want you to know that I won't give you any trouble about the guardianship, if Claire doesn't make it, that is.'

'I'm praying she goes into remission.'

'So am I. But she *is* a Stage 4 patient, and that doesn't bode well for her. As a doctor I have to face reality, Laura. Anyway, to continue, Natasha is at that age when she needs a woman in her life. I know you love her, and that you will do the right thing by her. I trust you, Laura, but I felt I had to say that to you. Also, my life is at sixes and sevens at the moment. I'm not really settled in Atlanta, and I don't know where my work is going to take me in the future.'

'I never thought you would create problems,' Laura responded, leaning forward slightly. 'I realize how much you care about Natasha, how much you love her, and I would like to reassure *you* that you will always have as much access to her as you want. After all you are her father, and she loves you. She's made that very clear to me.'

'Thanks for saying that, Laura,' he said, smiling faintly. 'I like the idea of Nattie being in New York, of continuing her education here. After all, she is an American.'

'Yes,' Laura replied, thinking that he made it all sound like a foregone conclusion. But then, as he had just said, he was a doctor and he was not blinded by hope; he looked at the facts and made a judgement. Clearing her throat, Laura continued, 'If I end up taking care of Natasha, I'd like you to be involved in every part of her life, and especially her education.'

'I would be, and that brings me to another point. *Money.* I would take care of her financially, I wouldn't want her upbringing to be a burden to you. And I'll take care of the cost of her education as well. I hope all that goes without saying.'

'Yes, anyway, you more or less indicated that when we spoke on the phone.'

'I also want you to feel you can phone me whenever you need to, Laura, if there's anything to discuss about Natasha and her wellbeing.'

She nodded. 'I think we understand each other, Philippe. But I'm glad we've had a chance to talk face to face, as you said. How's your mother? I suppose you're staying with her?'

'She's good, and yes, I am at her apartment. How's Doug?'

Laura stared at him, wondering how to answer this question. She suddenly felt awkward, and she wasn't sure why. She said,

'He and I, well, actually, we've separated, Philippe. We're getting a divorce.'

'Oh, I'm sorry,' was all he could think of to say, taken by surprise as he was. What a fool Doug Casson must be, to let a fabulous woman like Laura Valiant go. He had always thought her to be exceptional, so intelligent yet a compassionate woman with an understanding heart. Deep down it had always troubled him that she appeared to dislike him, when he had felt just the opposite. But then he knew she had been influenced by Claire's turbulent emotional view of him.

As he continued to regard Laura steadily across her desk, Philippe was struck again by the vividness of her eyes. She was a beautiful woman.

Before he could stop himself, he said, 'Are you going to be working here much longer, Laura?' He glanced at his watch. 'It's almost four o'clock. Do you feel like having a cup of tea?'

For a split second Laura hesitated, and then she said, 'All right, why not? I'd like that, Philippe.' I might as well be cordial with him, she thought as she stood up. After all, Natasha is going to be a common bond between us.

21

Laura was used to being kept waiting by tycoons and Norman Grant was no exception to this rule.

She sat in the grandiose, cold-looking reception area of his humongous offices on Fifth Avenue wondering why he had allowed the architect to use so much white marble. It was the most unflattering material, unless it was gracing a villa in a hot climate, and it made the reception area look like a mausoleum. Or a giant-sized toilet, perhaps.

As she idly flicked through a beauty magazine, she wondered how long she would have to wait this time. On the last occasion she had been here it had taken Grant almost half an hour to admit her into his presence.

Glancing away from the blonde receptionist, who sat at a glass-and-steel desk facing her, Laura smiled to herself. The only one who never kept her waiting for longer than a few minutes was Maximilian West. But then he was quite different from all of the other businessmen she dealt with. He was unique, and a gentleman.

Glancing at her watch, Laura saw that she had been sitting on this sofa for half an hour. Under different circumstances she would now have risen and departed without wasting another moment of her valuable time. But she could not do that today.

Keep your cool, she told herself. You've got to win this. And today's your last chance to pull it off, to succeed.

As she placed the magazine on the coffee table in front of her, Norman Grant's secretary finally came to fetch her. There was no apology, greeting or smile of recognition, and she had been here before. The grim-faced woman simply said, 'He'll see you now,' and led the way down the corridor to his suite of private offices situated at the end.

Norman Grant, sixtyish, silver-haired, red-faced and portly in his dark blue suit, rose from behind his huge modern desk as she entered.

He nodded to her as she was ushered in, and indicated the chair facing his desk. 'Good morning, Miss Valiant. Please sit down.'

'Good morning, Mr Grant, and thank you,' she replied politely, then lowered herself into the chair.

'I don't know why I've agreed to see you a second time, since I've said everything I have to say about *Tahitian Dreams*,' he announced, getting straight to the point at once, without preamble.

'I think I can answer that for you, Mr Grant. You agreed to meet with me today because you want to avoid a lawsuit at all cost.'

Norman Grant glared at her. 'I bought the Gauguin in the most legitimate way. There won't be a lawsuit,' he said.

'Oh but there will be, Mr Grant. Sir Maximilian West plans to file suit at the end of this week. His lawyers are poised to do so, and they have been for months.'

'The case will be thrown out of court because it's not a legitimate case,' Norman Grant shot back.

'Yes, it is. Similar situations regarding Nazi-looted art are coming to light, and a number of cases have already been filed. Not only in Europe but in the United States. Also, an American museum which is in possession of a painting, a Matisse, looted by the Nazis from a Jewish family in France, is prepared to give it back to the family it was stolen from. If the family's ownership of it can be proven. As I told you when I came to see you a few weeks ago, Sir Maximilian West can prove that the Westheim family owned the Gauguin. He can prove provenance because he has the *catalogue raisonné*, which you have been shown.'

'I'm not a museum. Furthermore, I'm not going to *give* him the painting. I bought and paid for it. It belongs to me, Miss Valiant. Any reasonable person would agree with that.'

'Would you really want to embark on a long and tedious litigation? You're a businessman, Mr Grant, these things can become very costly. And time-consuming.'

'I know. But as I just said, the case will be thrown out of court. Because it's not a legitimate case.'

'I think it is, and so do Sir Maxim's lawyers, not to mention a number of museum curators and art experts.' Laura leaned back in the chair and crossed her long legs, outstaring Norman Grant.

He blinked finally, and wondered how to get rid of this unusually beautiful woman in her severe black suit who made him so uncomfortable. He felt uneasy in her presence, and yes, he had to admit it, inferior. 'We're just wasting each other's time,' he snapped. 'I made a mistake agreeing to see you again. I've nothing further to say. I won't change my mind. So don't threaten me.'

'Sir Maximilian and I have discussed this matter at great length and he's given me the authority to deal on his behalf. I'm prepared to make you an offer. And I'm not threatening you, by the way. I was merely pointing out that he will start litigation if we, that is you and I, do not resolve the problem today.'

'What's the offer?'

'We will pay you what you paid when you bought the painting from Anthea Margolis five years ago. We'll pay you the six-point-four-million dollars.'

'I paid more than that!'

'Not according to Mrs Margolis. I went to see her in Boston, and she showed me all the relevant documentation.'

Caught out in a foolish lie, Norman Grant flushed. 'I won't take six-point-four,' he said, and leaned back in his swivel chair, his face set.

'I know you want to triple what you paid, that you want to get nineteen or twenty million dollars. Mark Tabbart told me. But we're not going to pay that.' Laura gave him a long, hard stare and finished, 'And you won't get it anywhere else. I don't think there's a market for this painting anymore. It's tainted.'

Ignoring her last point, he said confidently, 'Sure there's a market.'

'If there is, which I doubt, it will rapidly diminish. The painting will lose its value after my press conference next week.'

'Press conference? What press conference?'

'I am going to hold one next week, on behalf of Sir Maximilian West,' Laura explained softly. 'As his art-adviser, I am going to tell the world about the Westheim Collection, how it was started, how it was illegally confiscated, stolen by the Nazis in 1939. I'm going to tell them all about *Tahitian Dreams*, show them the sequence of ownership, take the press on the journey of the Gauguin, from Friedrich Westheim's purchase of it in 1897, to its looting and illegal sale by General Josef Schiller of the SS to the Herman Seltzer Gallery in Vienna.' She smiled. 'It will make fascinating reading. I am also going to show them the *catalogue raisonné*, tell them the story of how Princess Irina Troubetzkoy found it only very recently in a bookshop in Paris. It's all wonderful stuff, the press will love it.'

'For what reason would you have a press conference? It sounds ridiculous to me,' Norman Grant muttered, giving her a baleful look.

'I don't agree. The story will get the public interested, and certainly there's going to be a lot of sympathy for Sir Maxim, not to mention all kinds of opinions. The Gauguin will become famous. But nobody will buy it.'

'Who cares about the Gauguin except us and other collectors?' He laughed at her. 'The general public don't care about art.'

'Oh really. Is that why museums are filled? Lack of interest on the public's part?' Laura moved slightly, leaned forward and continued, 'From a moral point of view, the painting does not belong to you, Mr Grant. And so this must be a moral decision on your part, not a legal or financial one. I did point out to Sir Maxim that you, too, are a victim in a way, and that is why he is willing to pay for the painting. But you cannot in good conscience make a profit on this art stolen from his parents. Both of them were Holocaust victims who perished because they were Jews. His mother was tortured and beaten to death in Ravensbruck, and his father was shot in cold blood in Auschwitz.' Laura paused, and finished, 'No, no, no, you're not going to make a profit on the dead, Mr Grant.'

'No deal,' he said coldly.

'You're being very unwise. The press will have a field day, especially when they know you're Jewish.'

Grant turned bright red. 'What are you saying?' he spluttered.

'That you're Jewish, Mr Grant. You may go to the Unitarian Church on Lexington Avenue and you may have changed your name . . . and why not? There's no reason why you shouldn't do either. But you *were* born Norman Gratowski and you grew up on the Lower East Side, a nice Jewish boy, of Jewish parents who luckily escaped the Warsaw Ghetto before it was too late.'

Laura gave him a pointed look and sat back.

Grant was silent. He appeared to be floored.

'How will it look to the world if you, a Jew, tries to make a profit on art stolen by the Nazis from a couple who lost their lives in the death camps of the Holocaust? I don't know if it would affect your business, probably not.' She shrugged lightly. 'But you never know.'

Norman Grant said nothing. He sat there in his black leather swivel chair looking sick.

Laura stood up. 'You bought a stolen painting. The rightful

owner wants it back. He's prepared to pay you what you paid . . . isn't that eminently fair?'

'No deal,' Norman Grant said again.

The moment Alison heard the front door slam, she shot out of her office and dashed to the reception area.

'What happened? Did it work?' she cried, her eyes on Laura. Laura shook her head. 'Not yet.'

'Damn,' Alison said, and motioned for Laura to follow her into her office. Once they were both seated, Alison continued, 'I thought your strategy was brilliant; I was positive it would do the trick. So was Sir Maxim. All that hard work you did investigating Norman Grant's background . . . down the drain.'

'I wouldn't say that,' Laura murmured, shifting in the chair. 'I think we're going to win this. Let's give it time to sink in. Norman Grant's going to wrestle with it for a while, but I have a feeling he's going to come around in the end.'

'I'm not so sure about that. He's a tough guy, and he's not about to budge, in my opinion. He wants a lot of money for the Gauguin. He's going to sit it out,' Alison muttered, her expression suddenly dour.

'No, he won't,' Laura answered swiftly. 'Trust me on this, Alison. First of all, he knows the painting's tainted already. If he didn't before he does now, because I made that clear. Mark Tabbart turned it down because he didn't want problems, and Grant understands that. Nobody's going to buy *Tahitian Dreams* for twenty million dollars or indeed for six-point-four million, not after my press conference next week. It's a painting that's about to be jeopardized. Then again, Norman Grant doesn't want to be embarrassed, he doesn't want the world to think he's a Jew who's insensitive . . . to the Holocaust victims whose art was stolen by the Nazis.'

Alison shook her head. 'I don't agree with you, Laura. He's one tough son of a gun, and I don't believe he gives a hoot in hell what people think of him.'

'Let's see what happens, Alison, let's stay cool and wait.'
'Aren't you going to call Sir Maxim?'
'Yes I will. In a minute. From my own office.'

22

It was Megan who opened the front door of her apartment to admit Laura, who stared at her in surprise and asked, 'Where's Lily?' as she walked into the foyer and hugged her grandmother.

'It's her day off,' Megan replied and then with a sweet smile she added, 'that's why I'm going to take you out to dinner.'

'Oh,' Laura said, sounding surprised, eyeing her grandmother curiously. 'But you told me Lily was making my favourite dinner.'

'That's true, I did, but no fish cakes and parsley sauce tonight for you, darling girl.' Giving Laura the benefit of another sweet smile, Megan walked slowly into the sitting room, remarking, 'Now, let's have a sherry before we go. It's a bit early to leave.'

'All right,' Laura answered, followed her through the sitting room and into the adjoining library, asking herself why she was feeling suddenly suspicious of Megan. Her grandmother was really dressed up tonight, wearing a black silk-shantung dress and jacket, a three-strand pearl necklace and pearl earrings. But this did not really signify anything special; Megan Morgan Valiant was always beautifully turned out whenever she sallied forth to fulfil her social obligations. Like that other nonagenarian Brooke Astor, she was well known in New York for her style and chic.

After filling two glasses with dry sherry, Laura carried them over to her grandmother, handed her one, and sat down on the sofa next to her. 'Cheers, Gran,' Laura murmured, touching her crystal glass to Megan's.

'Cheers, darling girl.' Megan glanced at Laura as she spoke, and then followed her granddaughter's gaze, which was resting on a painting, 'Ah, yes, the Childe Hassam. I gave it to you for your birthday, but you never took it. Do you want it?'

'Oh, yes, I do, Gran, and thank you again, it was so generous of you to give it to me. It's a lovely gift, but I can't take it down until I find something for you to hang in its place. You can't have a blank spot on the wall, over the other sofa.'

'Oh, don't worry your head about it, anything will do, a print of some kind.'

'I'll find a beautiful lithograph for you, Gran. I know the kind of thing you like. By the way, I should have the appraisal for you next week. Jason's put a specific figure on each individual painting, so you can sell one, or all of them, whichever you prefer. Or you don't have to sell any at all. It's up to you.'

'I'll think about it, and thank you for getting him to come over. Such a nice young man.' She peered at Laura. 'Is he married?'

'No, he's not, Grandma Megan, and don't try to be a matchmaker. I'm not interested in him.'

'More's the pity,' Megan said, and went on, 'by the by, what's happened to your mother? You haven't mentioned her in ages.'

'Oh, she's still in the islands. Painting away.'

'*Murals*, I've no doubt. Maggie's such a fine artist, she should be painting pictures not walls.'

'She needs the money, Grandma.'

'I know. Your father didn't leave her a great deal. Talking of leaving things . . . do you want that portrait of me over the mantelpiece? I have left it to you in my will, you know.'

'I'd love it, Grandma, thank you. But for the time being I'd like to hang on to the living thing, the flesh-and-blood you.'

'Oh, I'm not planning to go yet, child. But later, when I'm

dead, if you don't want the painting you can always give it to the charity shop.'

'Megan Valiant, I'd never do anything so awful!'

Megan smiled, and muttered, 'I don't know anybody else who'd want it but you.' Then she asked, 'How's Doug? What's happening with the divorce? You haven't said anything about him or it lately.'

'Doug's fine, I spoke to him yesterday. The divorce will be through any time. And as far as his work's concerned, he's doing well at the law firm in LA. He's found an apartment he likes in Century City and he's thinking of buying it. I guess he's enjoying his new life.'

'Well, I certainly hope so, considering that he divorced you to get it!'

'It wasn't quite like that, Gran.'

Ignoring Laura's comment, Megan announced, 'I think we'd better be going to dinner. I don't want to be late.'

'Shall I phone for a taxi?'

'No, I ordered a car for the evening. From the limousine service.'

'Oh.' Laura frowned. 'Where is it that we're going, Gran? What restaurant?'

'It's a surprise.' Putting the empty sherry glass down on the antique side-table, Megan stood up. 'I'll just get my handbag, and then we can leave.'

Laura nodded, watched her grandmother walk out of the library, so erect, so elegant, a miracle of a woman, really. And she couldn't help wondering what she had up her sleeve. Something was afoot, Laura was quite certain of that.

Rising herself, she walked over to the bay window and stood looking out at the view of the East River. It was a beautiful evening in the middle of June; there were several boats on the river, sailing down towards the end of Manhattan Island. What a pretty sight they were, a hint of the summer months ahead.

'I'm ready, Laura,' Megan called from the foyer, and Laura swung around and hurried through the sitting room.

As they went down in the lift, Laura looked at Megan and said, 'Come on, Gran, out with it. Where are we going?'

'I told you before, it's a surprise.'

Laura sighed. 'All right, it's a surprise, but I'm not sure I trust you. There's a certain look about you tonight, one I can't quite fathom. It's a look that tells me you know something I don't.'

'Good Lord, my girl, I certainly hope I *do* know more than you. I'm three times your age, and I've been around the block a few times more than you have.'

Laura laughed, and held her elbow as they went through the hallway to the car waiting outside. Laura had never seen the driver before, but her grandmother seemed to know him.

'Good evening, Peter,' Megan said, adding, 'this is my granddaughter, Miss Laura Valiant.'

'Evening, ma'am,' the driver said, inclining his head politely; he helped her grandmother into the limo solicitously.

Laura decided not to ask any more questions; she sat back against the car seat, glancing out of the window, only half listening to her grandmother who was talking to Peter about his family, asking how they were. But she did notice they were heading uptown on First Avenue, and was somewhat surprised when the driver turned down East Fifty-Seventh Street and then continued up York Avenue. She couldn't imagine where they were heading. As they drove on towards the East Eighties and East End Avenue Laura began to suspect they were going to someone's apartment.

Laura's heart sank as a sudden thought struck her. She hoped her grandmother wasn't trying to be a matchmaker again, as she had several weeks ago. God forbid, Laura thought.

The limo finally came to a standstill in front of one of the grand old pre-war buildings on East End Avenue near East Eighty-Sixth Street. Peter, the driver, parked; helped Megan out of the car, and then Laura took hold of her arm and escorted her into the building.

As they entered the hallway, Laura asked curiously, 'So, who are we going to have dinner with, Grandma?'

'Rosa Lavillard.'

For a moment Laura was speechless, then she exclaimed, 'Why have you done this, Gran? I can't have dinner with her.'

'Why not?'

'Claire wouldn't like it, and you know I can't upset her right now. She's fighting for her life.'

Megan nodded, her face grave. 'I realize that, and she's very courageous. But how is she going to know you've had dinner here unless you tell her?'

'I'll know, and it'll make me feel I'm being disloyal.'

'I know all about your integrity, Laura dear, but this *is* just a dinner, you know. Now don't let us stand here in the lobby making a spectacle of ourselves.'

'Gran, I really don't –'

'Laura,' Megan interrupted in a stern voice, 'please be sensible, and just listen to me for a moment. You may well be bringing up Natasha and very soon. Actually, I'd say it's more than likely, and you're going to need help, whatever you might think. Rosa's help, and yes, perhaps even Philippe's. After all, I won't be much use to you, even if I'm still around. You're a divorced woman on your own, and you're going to need a support system.'

'But Rosa Lavillard . . . Oh Gran, I don't know . . .'

'I do. She's a very decent woman, kind, warm-hearted, and her great wish is to get to know her granddaughter. You adore Claire, and so do I, but I'm afraid Claire has given you the wrong impression of Rosa. She's not the enemy, you know. Come along, we're late.' So saying, Megan walked on towards the lift, her head held high, her step firm.

Laura had no alternative but to follow her grandmother. They rode up in silence to the sixth floor, and a few seconds later they were standing outside Rosa's apartment. It was she who opened the door to them.

'Good evening, Megan . . . Miss Valiant,' Rosa said, and opening the door wider, she added, 'please come in.'

'I'm sorry we're a little late. My fault,' Megan murmured, walking into the hallway and offering her hand to Rosa.

'Good evening, Mrs Lavillard,' Laura said, also shaking the woman's hand.

'Please call me Rosa. I prefer it.'

'And I prefer to be called Laura.'

Rosa led them into a spacious living room overlooking East End Avenue and the East River. Its high-flung ceiling, many windows and a fireplace gave the room a traditional feeling as did all of the furnishings. Laura, glancing around quickly as she followed Rosa and her grandmother, noticed that the antiques were mostly French. It was a really lovely room, decorated primarily in white and light pastel colours. Handsome porcelain lamps with white silk shades, a glass-fronted china cabinet filled with antique porcelain and two French gilt mirrors denoted fine taste. The overall look, she decided, was definitely old Europe. There were some interesting lithographs on the walls, as well as several good paintings.

'What would you like?' Rosa asked, glancing at them and then at the tray of drinks on a dark mahogany chest.

'Sherry please, Rosa,' Megan said.

'The same, thank you.' Laura went and sat down in a chair next to the large cream sofa on which her grandmother was now seated comfortably, relaxing against a pile of needlepoint cushions.

Rosa gave them each a dry sherry and joined Megan on the sofa. After murmuring a toast, Megan started to recommend a play she had just seen, and it soon became apparent to Laura that the two women had been seeing each other recently, and perhaps even frequently. There was a familiarity between them, a certain ease, the kind of rapport that springs up between women who like each other and have become friends.

When there was a lapse in their conversation, Laura jumped in, saying, 'Have you been seeing a lot of each other lately?' She directed her question at Rosa.

'A little. Megan and I have certain things in common, especially the theatre.' Rosa pushed herself up off the sofa. 'Excuse me a moment...' She hurried off in the direction of the kitchen, saying over her shoulder, 'I must check on something in the oven.'

'Keeping secrets from me, eh, Gran?' Laura whispered, leaning closer to Megan when they were alone.

Megan gave her granddaughter a long look through her perceptive, faded blue eyes and merely smiled.

Laura knew better than to press Megan or say anything else, but she realized that the two women were fond of each other. And she was quite certain that it was her grandmother who had made the first move, who had contacted Rosa after all these years. It was just the sort of thing Megan would do.

Laura got up and walked across the room, stood looking at an oil painting which hung on a wall between two windows. 'What a charming Marie Laurencin,' she said to Megan.

'Yes, it is,' Rosa answered as she walked back into the living room. 'I bought it many, many years ago in Paris, and I've always loved it.'

Turning around, Laura looked at her and said, 'You prefer Renoir, though.'

'Ah yes, but Renoir I cannot afford. Only the prints of his work. Now, if you will come to the dining room, dinner is ready.'

The dining room had been decorated in different shades of blue, running from the pale blue of a summer sky to the aquamarine and turquoise of a tropical sea. Laura felt as though she were surrounded by the waters of a Caribbean island, submerged in seawater so clear you could see below the surface of the waves.

The effect was magical, and after Rosa had hurried away

to bring the first course, Laura mentioned it to her grandmother.

Megan nodded in agreement. 'Yes, I know what you mean. It *is* like being in the sea. Perhaps that's because the ceiling is mirrored and the colours on the walls flow up into it, then flow down. They reflect in the glass top of the table.'

Laura had been looking at the Renoir prints gracing the far wall, and she had not noticed the mirror work in the room. She glanced up at the ceiling and nodded. 'The mirror is reflecting all the different blues ... what a clever device it is, Gran.'

'She's a clever woman, self-supporting and self-sufficient. She runs the antique porcelain shop, you know. I like Rosa. Actually, I admire her.'

'Self-sufficient?' Laura repeated questioningly.

'Yes, yes. Rosa appears to be perfectly happy being alone. She doesn't seem to need anyone.'

'Not even her son?' Laura asked now, sounding puzzled. 'I thought she was rather possessive of him.'

'I don't think so,' Megan replied, giving Laura a strange look. 'Whatever gave you that idea? Oh, I know. I should have said *who*. It was Claire, wasn't it?'

'Well, yes, but she didn't actually use the word possessive, she just implied it.'

Megan nodded, shifted slightly in her seat, and was about to respond when the door was pushed open and Rosa came in from the kitchen.

'Rosa, the soup smells delicious!' Megan exclaimed, looking up at her hostess and smiling as the steaming bowl of fragrant liquid was placed in front of her. 'Thank you.'

Laura could tell that Rosa was flattered to receive her grandmother's compliment. Although she didn't reply or smile, or make any kind of acknowledgement, her eyes seemed to brighten as she inclined her head, and then she quickly disappeared again.

'I've had this soup before,' Megan said to Laura. 'It's crystal clear, and delicious. You're going to love it.'

A moment later Rosa was back once more, putting a bowl of the chicken soup on the table for Laura. 'Thank you,' Laura murmured.

'I'll be right back,' Rosa said. 'Please . . . start.'

Laura stared into the soup. It *was* very clear, but a pure golden colour with a few slices of carrot floating in it along with a small matzo ball. Her grandmother was right, it did smell delicious and Laura found her mouth watering.

'Please, let us eat, Megan . . . Laura,' Rosa cried as she finally sat down at the table. '*Bon appetit*,' she added, picked up her spoon and dipped it into her bowl.

Out of the blue, Megan announced, 'It takes twelve chickens to make a soup like this,' and then she looked at Rosa and asked, 'am I not right, Rosa?'

'You are, Megan.'

'How did you know that, Grandma?'

'Oh, I know a lot of things you don't know I know,' Megan answered somewhat enigmatically, and then observing the bafflement on Laura's face, she explained, 'your grandfather and I had a wonderful partner at one point in our theatrical careers. He co-produced a lot of my musicals with your grandfather. His name was Herbert Lipson – Herb we called him – and his mother made the best chicken soup in the whole world. She used to call it Jewish penicillin, and whenever we were in Philadelphia she invited us to dinner and she always served us her soup.'

'Yes, that's what it is, Laura, Jewish penicillin because it does seem to cure everything,' Rosa explained.

The two older women immediately embarked on a discussion about the healing properties of ethnic foods, and Laura spooned up the soup and listened, lifting her head from time to time to scrutinize Rosa.

Laura had been very much aware of Rosa's pleasant and welcoming demeanour from the moment they had walked into the apartment. The last time she had seen her had been at the museum in Paris looking at Renoirs, and Rosa had appeared cold, hostile, wary, and slightly odd. Tonight she was a different person entirely. It was true she had a curious reserve about her, but Laura now decided this must just be her natural manner, perhaps a reflection of her personality. On the other hand, when she had hovered over Megan earlier a lovely warmth had emanated from Rosa, and Laura found this touching; it pleased her that Rosa apparently cared about her grandmother.

Rosa even *looked* different, better, not as old as she had appeared in the d'Orsay, and much less dumpy. Perhaps this was because she was wearing a well-cut, tailored suit of deep purple silk, gold earrings and a matching gold pin. This evening Rosa's dark hair was stylishly coiffed, and the grey streaks she had noticed in Paris were no longer there. They had been carefully tinted out.

Studying her surreptitiously for a moment, Laura decided that Rosa's face was much more attractive than she'd realized; but what she needed was a bit of make-up to define her good bone structure, bring out the luminosity of her large, pellucid grey eyes, the richness of her thick chestnut hair. But perhaps she can't be bothered or doesn't care, Laura thought. Some women didn't, they were content to be as they were, without artifice.

Two things about Rosa were most distinctive, and Laura had noticed them particularly tonight: her beautiful, shapely legs and her voice. The latter was husky, even sexy, and her French accent added a special flavour.

Suddenly she wished she knew a little more about Rosa Lavillard than she did. Unexpectedly, Laura was riddled with curiosity about her. What she did know was that she was Jewish, French born, and had grown up in France during the war. After marrying she had come to America, where her son Philippe had been born. And she had lived here ever since. Laura remembered that Philippe was about forty-one or two, and so Rosa was probably in her mid sixties, even late sixties, perhaps.

Her husband Pierre Lavillard had died some years ago; Laura, with her prodigious memory, had an instant recollection of him.

She had met him at Claire's wedding, and in her mind's eye she saw a tall, distinguished man with a great deal of Continental charm. His expertise was in French antiques and porcelain from all over the world, she remembered. He dealt in the great marks such as Meissen, Dresden, Herend, Limoges, and the important porcelains of England from Royal Worcester to Royal Crown Derby. He had owned a shop on Lexington Avenue when Claire and Philippe had married, and it was there that he had sold French antiques and antique porcelains.

Laura was roused from her reverie with a small start when Rosa announced, 'I will bring the next course.' As she spoke Rosa pushed back her chair and stood, picked up Megan's plate and her own.

Laura attempted to rise. 'Let me help you,' she said, getting to her feet.

'No, no, I can manage. It is better I do this alone, I am well organized,' Rosa insisted, and was gone before Laura could protest further.

The next course was steamed carp served with home-made horseradish sauce and freshly-baked challah, followed by a chicken which came out of the oven a crisp golden brown and was succulent and moist inside as Rosa carved it at the table. This was served with mashed potatoes, gravy, and peas and carrots.

Finally, Rosa brought in the dessert. It was the most extraordinary apple strudel Laura had ever tasted, topped with whipped cream and cherry sauce. Always a picky eater, Laura realized at the end of the meal that she had demolished everything, and with relish.

Essentially, it had been a simple dinner, but every dish had been meticulously prepared and beautifully cooked, and that was the secret of its perfection. Laura said this to Rosa, adding, 'It's the best dinner I've had in a very long time. Thank you. I really enjoyed it.'

'Yes, it was superb,' Megan murmured, and added her own thanks.

Rosa looked gratified. 'Thank you,' she said. 'I enjoy cooking. And now I shall serve coffee.'

At one moment, over coffee in the living room, Rosa said, 'Congratulations, Laura.'

Laura glanced at her quickly. 'Thank you. I assume you're referring to the return of the Gauguin painting to Sir Maximilian West?'

'Exactly. I read about your press conference in the *New York Times*, and I thought it was wonderful you had negotiated a deal with Mr Grant.'

Rosa Lavillard smiled for the first time that evening, and went on, 'It was a triumph for you, and it gave me great hope that other people will do the decent thing . . . if they *know* they possess art looted by the Nazis. That they will return it to the heirs of those poor souls from whom it was stolen during the war.'

'Some people will. Others won't,' Laura replied. 'I truly believe it's a moral question. Naturally there are those who disagree and think of it in financial terms. They won't want to give up paintings they have paid good money for. That was Norman Grant's attitude at first. He wanted to triple his investment in *Tahitian Dreams*, make a lot of money out of the painting. But I finally convinced him, managed to induce him to accept Sir Maxim's offer of six-point-four million dollars. If you remember the details in the story in the paper, that was exactly what Mr Grant paid for it five years ago.'

Megan volunteered, between sips of her coffee, 'He would not have accepted the money if he'd been really smart. Instead he would have given the painting to Maximilian West. And if he had been wise enough to do that he would have come out a hero. As it is, he looks like a greedy little man.'

'Sir Maximilian must be thrilled to have the painting back after all these years,' Rosa murmured.

'He was,' Laura told her, suddenly smiling. 'And so was I, on his behalf. Actually, looking back, I think I accomplished a miracle.

And you, Rosa, I can see that you love art.' Laura glanced around. 'You love beauty in all its forms – that's apparent from all the lovely things you have gathered here.'

'Yes, beauty is essential to me. There is far too much ugliness and suffering in this world. Such immense cruelty. Beauty does soothe the soul . . .'

Laura did not say anything. She had caught the faint echo of words Rosa had uttered in the d'Orsay on that cold December day last year, and there was such great sorrow in the woman's voice it pierced Laura's heart.

Megan said slowly, 'Rosa's father was a well-known art-dealer in Paris, Laura. She inherited his love of paintings, especially the great Impressionists. You and she have the same taste.'

'A gallery in Paris?' Laura began. 'What was its name? Where was it?'

'It was called *Duval et Fils.* My father was the *fils,* the son. But then my grandfather was also the *fils,* the son. For three generations we were art-dealers. The gallery was on the rue La Boétie in the eighth arrondissement, which was sometimes called the French Florence.'

'I know all about the rue La Boétie from my studies at the Sorbonne. It was very famous because every major dealer had a gallery there,' Laura exclaimed.

'That is true. There were the Bernheim-Jeune brothers, who represented your favourite and mine, Renoir. And also the great Paul Rosenberg. Wildenstein, Cailleux, and Josef Hessel all had galleries on the rue La Boétie as well. It was the centre of art through the 1920s into the 1930s, and of course it became the focal point of Hitler's greed for art during the Occupation.'

Laura nodded. 'Yes, I know that altogether the Nazis looted some twenty thousand paintings, drawings and sculpture from France, and that they were all shipped to Germany during the war.'

'Stamped property of the Third Reich,' Rosa muttered grimly.

'Do you feel like telling Laura something about your life, Rosa?' Megan asked in a low voice. 'Or would it be too exhausting for you? Too draining?'

Rosa shook her head. 'No, Megan, it would not. I will recount a little of my life to Laura ... I think that perhaps, under the circumstances, she should know something about the Rosa Duval I once was.' Rosa looked across at Laura, her eyes on her, and finished, 'If you want to hear about that part of my life?'

'Yes, I would like to,' Laura answered. 'But as my grandmother just said, I wouldn't want you to tire yourself out.'

'Oh no, that is all right, I will be fine. But I think I would like to get myself a glass of water first. Would you like one, Laura? And what about you, Megan?'

'Iced water would be lovely,' Megan said. 'And perhaps a little more of the coffee. Thank you, Rosa dear.'

'I'd like a glass of water too, please,' Laura said. 'But let me come and help you.'

Rosa shook her head. 'I can manage perfectly well. I will only be a moment.'

23

'Now I shall tell you about my life when I was a little girl in France,' Rosa said, her attention on Laura. Leaning back in the comfortable armchair, she took a sip of water and then began:

'I spent my early years growing up in the art gallery on the rue La Boétie. *Duval et Fils* was our home, as well as my father's place of business. My father Maurice Duval had inherited the gallery, which was an entire building, from my grandfather who had died in 1934. On the first and second floors my father showed Impressionist and Post-Impressionist paintings, some modern art, and sculpture. My grandmother Henrietta, my father's mother, lived on the third floor with her daughter, Aunt Sylvie. We were on the fourth and fifth floors, and the domestic help was on the sixth. It was a wonderful arrangement, in the time-honoured tradition of old Europe when the family lived above the store, so to speak.

'Grandmother spent a lot of time with us, and so did Aunt Sylvie, who wasn't married. We were six in our little family. Mama, Papa, my brothers Michel and Jean-Marc, and my sister Marguerite. I was the youngest and the favoured child in a sense, everyone's pet.'

Rosa looked off into the distance, as if seeing something very special in her mind's eye, and a faint smile touched her mouth.

'My father called me *mon petit choux à la crème*, his little cabbage with cream, and he adored me. I was the spoiled girl, I suppose, but I was a good girl. Those years were wonderful. My father was a most gregarious man, outgoing, charming, hospitable and very giving of himself. He entertained both clients and artists at the gallery, gave splendid evenings. Picasso was a favourite visitor, and sometimes Matisse came with his model Lydia Delectorskaïa. They all made a big fuss of me, and I have never forgotten them.

'My father's gallery was considered one of the most elegant in that very elegant neighbourhood; it stood at the corner, near avenue Matignon. It had beautiful exposition rooms filled with extraordinary light from the windows, and a glass ceiling in one of the rooms. It was soft filtered light which was perfect for the paintings. My father believed in providing rich back-drops for art and he had walls covered in red silk-brocade and blue damask. The exposition rooms were like a museum, and clients came just to sit there and admire the art . . . at different times my father represented Cézanne, Renoir, Degas, Marie Laurencin, and, of course, Picasso and Matisse, to name only a few.

'When France and Britain declared war on Germany on September 3rd, 1939, I was nine years old. My father was worried because we were Jewish, but he did not want to flee the country at first. He was a clever man and he believed in studying situations, appraising everything, and he wanted to see what would happen. And so he continued to study and evaluate the situation before making any rash moves. However, because he was afraid Paris might be bombed by the Germans, fearful that the gallery could be damaged if such an event occurred, he decided it would be wiser to move some of the paintings from the gallery. He began to systematically send them down to the Gironde, to a château in the countryside just outside Bordeaux, which belonged to an old friend of his. He had thought of storing the paintings in the cellars of the château, and his friend agreed that this was a prudent move. And so arrangements were made.

'Jacques Pointine was my father's right-hand man, and it was Jacques who transported the paintings down to the château. Pointine was married to an Englishwoman, Phyllis Dixon, who also worked for my father as a personal assistant handling many of his art deals. She was very knowledgeable and intensely loyal. A little later Phyllis and Jacques took another collection of canvases to Bordeaux, where they were stored in a bank vault my father had rented. He was sure the paintings would be safe there, and he suggested to several artists that they take the same precautions with their work.

'My father had all of the paintings registered under the name of Jacques Pointine's married sister, Yvette Citrone, again as a precaution. Then he shipped one-hundred-and-twenty more to a warehouse in Grenoble, this time in Phyllis's name. Altogether he managed to move over five hundred paintings out of Paris, some of them from his own personal collection, the rest part of the gallery's considerable inventory. Other dealers were taking similar steps, especially the Jewish dealers and gallery owners, and a number of painters were doing the same thing . . . Picasso, Braque and Matisse included.

'In November of 1939 my father decided we could no longer stay in Paris and so he took the whole family to Bordeaux, which he knew was safe, and where he rented a large family apartment. He insisted that Phyllis and Jacques come with us, and Papa left the gallery under the management of Alain Brescon, who had worked for him for years and was as loyal and devoted as Phyllis and Jacques.

'Our life in Bordeaux settled into a relatively normal routine, and anyway it was the period known as the phoney war when nothing much was happening. Every day I went to school with my brothers and sister; my mother and grandmother supervised our household; Papa worked with Phyllis and Jacques on the inventories of the art, and stayed in daily contact with the Paris gallery. He also talked with many of the other dealers and artists he was close to and cared about. But in a sense, I suppose, we were all holding our breath.

'But by June of 1940 that phoney war had become a real war. The news was suddenly alarming. On June 3rd Paris was hit by 1,100 bombs from 200 Third Reich planes. The Wehrmacht was on its steady, and relentless, march across France. Its destination: Paris. The French Army was almost at the end of its strength and resolve, and the roads were overrun with hundreds and hundreds of refugees fleeing south. The Germans entered Paris on 14 June and France fell. The French Government in Exile in Bordeaux surrendered, and was replaced by the right-wing Vichy Government, under the leadership of Maréchal Pétain. Almost immediately, Vichy passed anti-Jewish laws, long before the Nazis had demanded that any measures be taken against Jews.

'My father had gone down with bronchitis that same June and it turned into pneumonia, as often happens with this kind of illness when it strikes in summer, it took him a long time to get well. Even then he was left debilitated and listless. Certainly he was not in a frame of mind to move out of Bordeaux. In any case we were in the southwest, which was Unoccupied France, and my parents believed us to be safe.

'It was not until July of 1942 that disaster and tragedy struck my family. I have often wondered if we stayed too long, have asked myself what *I* would have done in the same circumstances. But I have no real answers. The times were difficult, the situations hard to gauge accurately, and in any case we were not being bothered.

'I will never forget the date. It was July 16 and I was almost twelve. My mother had asked Phyllis Dixon to take me to the doctor that afternoon, because I had been complaining of my tonsils. We were walking down the street towards our apartment when she suddenly grabbed hold of me and dragged me into the doorway of a building. 'It's the police,' she whispered. 'There is a French Police truck outside the door of your building, Rosa.

I cannot take you home.' I remember that I started to cry and frantically tried to pull away from her, to escape her clutches. But she was too strong for me. She held onto me tightly and wouldn't let go of me. She kept peering out, and it was when I heard her choke on the words, 'Oh my God,' that I knew the police had come for *my* parents. Finally we heard the truck driving off. I wanted to race home to make sure my parents were safe. I kept telling myself that I had been *wrong*, that they had *not* been arrested. But Phyllis wouldn't let me leave the doorway for a very long time.

'When we did eventually return to my family's apartment there was no one there. Not Papa, or Mama, or Grandmama. Aunt Sylvie was gone, as well. And so were my brothers and sister. They had taken them all ... even the children. Phyllis and I were in a terrible state of shock. Jacques was in Grenoble, checking on the paintings in the warehouse, and we didn't know what to do, since he wasn't coming back until late that night. Phyllis was afraid to leave me alone; anyway, she didn't know who to go and see to find out what had happened. In the end, she grabbed a few of my things, threw them in a suitcase and took me home to their apartment. It was not far away and it was there that we waited for Jacques.

'When he returned home at about nine o'clock in the evening he was as shocked as we had been, and as frightened for my family as we were. He had always been very close to my father. Jacques immediately went to the authorities in Bordeaux. Eventually he discovered that my parents were being held in the prison there, along with other Jews ... men, women and children. It seemed there was nothing he could do.

'I never saw my parents again. Nor the rest of my family. The next day they were shipped to a French concentration camp in Drancy, just north of Paris. It was the first stop on their fearsome journey ... to Auschwitz.'

Rosa stopped, her voice suddenly trembling, and then after a moment she continued more steadily. 'They all perished there ...

Papa, Mama, Grandmama and Aunt Sylvie . . . my brothers Michel and Jean-Marc, and Marguerite. Just like that, in the blink of an eye, everyone I loved was gone, ripped away from me forever. I couldn't believe it, I had seen them only a few hours ago, and been with them. Suddenly I was alone, except for Phyllis and Jacques. I will never forget how stunned and terrified I was. And Phyllis and Jacques were terrified *for* me. They feared the police might come back to get me. Later that night, Jacques sent me with Phyllis to his sister's house at the other side of Bordeaux, until he could work out a plan for me, for all of us. The Pointines were not Jewish and Jacques hoped I would be safe with his sister. For a while.

'Jacques Pointine was sharp, clever. I suppose he was the kind of man we would call streetwise today, and he was beginning to worry about the art. But even so he did not fully grasp exactly what was going on, or the extent of it. But then very few people did. It was only later that information about the massive looting of artworks came out.

'Jacques also worried that he and Phyllis could be in danger, because of their association with my father, and he determined that we should all disappear.'

Rosa paused in her sorrowful tale and drank some water before continuing.

Neither Megan nor Laura spoke.

Megan leaned back against the needlepoint cushions and sighed, looking around this gracious room, her mind awash with thoughts of evil and man's baseness and cruelty and inhumanity. Once again her heart went out to Rosa Lavillard, as it had when she had first heard her story so long ago.

Laura wanted to say something to Rosa, but she did not have the right words. There *were* no right words. Words were meaningless. Anything she could say would sound trite, even ridiculous, in view of the enormity of what had happened to Rosa all those years ago. It was beyond human comprehension. Glancing at her grandmother, she tried to imagine what it would be like to have *her* family taken away and murdered in cold blood in a death camp. She *couldn't* envision it; the mere idea overwhelmed her.

In a low, subdued voice, Laura finally said, 'How . . . how did you manage to go on, Rosa? The horror of it . . .' Laura was unable to finish her sentence and she felt sudden tears pricking behind her eyes.

Rosa said, 'I don't know, I have often asked myself that. And there were times when I wished I had been at home, that I had been with my parents, my family, so that I could have shared their fate, been taken with them to Auschwitz. At least we would have all been together. But I wasn't, I was saved by chance, by luck, and by Phyllis Dixon. There were times afterwards, when I was growing up, that I thought I might have been saved because I had a special purpose in life. But I don't know. It's as I just said, fate played a hand, along with Phyllis.' Rosa looked at Laura. 'You asked how I managed to go on . . . I suppose because I was a child. Children are resilient. I wept a lot, I worried about my family, and sometimes I was almost paralysed by fear for them, but we were on the run, moving around a lot, and Phyllis kept telling me I had to keep my wits about me, in order to survive.

'It was soon very apparent that the Vichy Government was deporting Jews to Germany on a large scale. Jacques and Phyllis found it incomprehensible that the French state was so casually delivering *children* to their murderers. There was complicity everywhere. Perhaps you do not know this, but the French Jews were the most assimilated of any other Jews in Europe, they had become, over the centuries, part of the fabric of French life. It was obvious that ordinary French people were turning Jews in . . . without those dossiers at the prefecture, Jews would not have been found. They could not have been deported. Or killed.

'Jacques was conscious of this, and he became convinced that my father and the family had been turned in by a collaborator, which is why he feared for *my* safety. You see, I was not only another Jew to be exterminated, but I was also the heir to

Maurice Duval's immense and valuable art collection. And so we moved around a lot. We went to stay with relatives of Jacques in Mérignac, then we moved on and stayed in Grenoble for a short while, before going to friends of Phyllis who lived near La Martellière. It was there that we moved into a small house. It was on the outskirts of La Martellière, and belonged to the sister of Phyllis' friends. At first Jacques was relieved that we had a respite, could stay put for a while, that we did not have to move around so much. But then it became a nightmare. Suddenly, Jacques was convinced the police were watching the house, and just when he had finished making arrangements for us to leave, Phyllis broke her shoulder and leg when she fell down a flight of steps leading into the cellar. She was incapacitated, and so Jacques had to cancel our plans to go to Bellegarde, near the Swiss border. He thought it was too long a trip for Phyllis.

'One day, about a week later, Jacques was told by a member of the French Resistance to hide me, that the French police were looking for me, that they were convinced I was being sheltered by Phyllis and Jacques. The information had come out of the Bordeaux prefecture ... the woman from the Resistance told Jacques that they were looking for the Duval girl to deport.

'It wasn't safe to send me to any of their friends, and so Jacques hid me. In a hole in the ground —'

'Oh my God, no!' Laura exclaimed, her voice rising. She stared at Rosa aghast.

Rosa nodded. 'It was the only thing he could do. There was no other place. The hole was actually a small cave in the side of a hillock, at the end of a field. The field abutted the garden of the house, so Jacques felt secure about putting me in the cave. It was dry, and air came in from somewhere higher up, above a ledge in the cave, and so I knew I would not suffocate. But I was always worried something would happen to Jacques and that I would be stuck in the cave forever. You see, in order to properly hide me securely, he had to roll a large stone in front of the opening. I wasn't strong enough to move it myself. Often I panicked, and

I hated being in that dark hole. Jacques would only let me burn candles in the daylight when it didn't matter, because the candle flame couldn't be seen. I wasn't allowed to light them at night. But he always brought me out at night, surreptitiously, cautiously. I was able to go to the house nearby, have a bath, eat, see Phyllis and be comforted by her. But it was an horrendous experience. I've hated dark places ever since.' Again Rosa stopped talking, sipped her glass of water, trying to relax.

'How long were you in the hole?' Laura ventured, her voice strained.

'For a year. Phyllis could not travel, she was ill a long time. Finally we were able to leave the area. Jacques thought we were too close to Mérignac and Dax, where many Jews were still being arrested and deported to Germany. He wanted to get closer to Switzerland, hoping one day to cross the border. But we never did. Anyway, we kept on moving around a lot, until we finally settled in the countryside between Lyons and Bellegarde. Life was hard, we were always afraid of being caught by the police, and food was scarce. And I saw so much killing and ugliness . . . However, I *was* out of the cave, I was no longer living like the troglodytes of Tunisia. But that year was the worst in my life.'

Glancing around the spacious living room awash in pale colours, Rosa added quietly, 'I've surrounded myself with airiness, lightness ever since. Anything dark is forbidding. It reminds me of that hole.'

24

Megan leaned forward and said, 'Are you tired, Rosa? Oh, how silly of me to even ask that! Of course you must be exhausted, telling this story again, reliving your early life. It must be harrowing for you. Perhaps I shouldn't have asked you to do so.'

'No, I'm all right, I'm not tired, Megan.' Rosa glanced at Laura. 'I've tried hard to get past the Holocaust, but it's always there, hidden deep in my heart, because it involves my family, whom I loved, and I can never forget *them*.'

'I understand,' Laura said. 'It must be almost impossible . . . to *ever* forget.'

'Eventually you do bury most of it deep, that's only natural. No one could live with that kind of mental anguish on a daily basis. And once it *is* truly buried it becomes very hard to dredge up. Far too painful. But their memory lives on in my heart . . .' She sighed and shook her head as she continued, 'Anyway, I have never wanted to force all the details of what happened to me on anyone. I've tried not to be bitter, to move forwards always, to look to the future in a positive way. I was spared. I was given a life to live, and I've tried to live it . . . as my parents would have wanted me to, as best I could. The Germans murdered my whole family. But there is no reason why I should allow them to ruin the rest of my life. If I did, then I would be letting them triumph over me.'

'Your spirit is indomitable, Rosa,' Megan murmured. 'I've always admired the way you've managed to cope so well.'

'I've done my best to be . . . *happy*, as I just said. After all, I'm living proof that Hitler didn't succeed, didn't win his genocidal war against the Jews. He lost it, just as he lost the war against the Allies.'

'You've been through so much, Rosa. I don't know what to say to you, how to express my feelings. There are no words to tell you how your story has affected me,' Laura began and hesitated. 'To offer you sympathy, to say I'm sorry, would be . . . banal, in view of the enormity of what you experienced. Your suffering would be diminished, somehow. Well, that's what I think.'

Rosa simply nodded.

Laura hesitated once more, and then she said slowly, in the gentlest of voices, 'You have a brave heart, Rosa, a very brave heart.'

For a few seconds Rosa was silent, her face very still, expressionless; then she reached out, touched Laura's arm. 'That you understand it at all . . . that is enough.' Pushing herself to her feet, Rosa asked, 'Shall I make some fresh coffee? I know I would like some.'

'That'd be great, Rosa,' Laura answered, and this time she did not offer to help, since she knew her offer would be refused.

When they were alone, Laura said, 'It *is* a remarkable story, Grandma Megan, isn't it?'

Megan nodded. 'Yes. But she's left a lot out tonight . . . Perhaps she wasn't up to telling it, or maybe she thought you'd find it too upsetting.'

'Why? What do you mean?'

'Goodness gracious, I can't go into it now, child!'

'I understand. Anyway, what I find strange is that Claire –'

'Not now, Laura dear,' Megan cut in quickly. 'We'll discuss everything when you take me home.'

'Yes, of course.' Laura glanced at her watch. 'You know, it's turned *eleven*, Gran! Perhaps I shouldn't have agreed to have a cup of coffee. Isn't it past your bedtime?'

'No, it's not,' Megan said, sitting up straighter, giving Laura a sharp look. 'And it's not necessary for you to fuss over me, as if I'm an old lady.' Megan laughed. 'Well, I know I am one, but I don't feel old. And in any case, bed is overrated. Furthermore, you die in bed, so I'm quite happy to stay up late. And most nights I do.'

'All right, all right,' Laura said, shaking her head. 'There's no one like you, Grandma.'

'I should hope not,' Megan shot back.

Within a few minutes Rosa returned with a pot of fresh coffee and a selection of biscuits, and as she poured the coffee into the clean cups, Laura said, 'There is something I would like to ask you, Rosa.'

Rosa lifted her head and looked over at Laura. 'Please, you can ask me anything. I will answer if I can.'

'I was just wondering . . . was your family arrested and murdered because they were Jews or were they murdered for the art?'

Rosa did not reply. She passed the cups of coffee to Megan and Laura, and then sat down in the chair again. 'It was for both reasons. That is what I believe,' she said finally.

'What happened to all the paintings your father had shipped out of Paris?' Laura continued.

'They disappeared. When we tried to find them at the end of the war they had vanished into thin air. Stolen, of course, by the Nazis. Jacques and Phyllis were frantic, trying to find out what had transpired, but naturally they met a wall of silence. They did manage to get some information from my father's friend who lived at the Château Le Beauve. Gerard de Castellaine owned the château and he was an old, old friend of my father's. It was he who had stored some of the paintings in his cellars. According to Gerard, one day a truckload of German soldiers came and took the paintings away at gunpoint. That was in the winter of 1942. They had papers which described all of the paintings he was storing, and they knew where to look.'

'But how could that be?'

'We all believed that one of the employees at my father's gallery in Paris had alerted the Nazis about the whereabouts of the paintings which my father had removed. Not everyone was as loyal as Jacques and Phyllis, and Alain Brescon.'

'So it was an act of plunder by the Nazis,' Laura stated.

'It was. Just as they confiscated the Westheim Collection, so they looted the art of Maurice Duval.'

'You read about the Westheim Collection in the *New York Times* when I had the press conference,' Laura remarked.

Rosa inclined her head. 'I did, and I found it fascinating. But at least Sir Maxim has a *catalogue raisonné*. I don't have anything quite so comprehensive, just one record book and a couple of inventories, which Jacques managed to retrieve from my parents' apartment in Bordeaux before we started to move around.'

'And not everything was listed?'

'No. Only about thirty paintings. Jacques couldn't find the other record books and additional inventories,' Rosa explained. 'Maybe my father had hidden them somewhere in the apartment for safety, or maybe they were taken when my family was arrested. It is hard to know exactly what happened to them.'

'But at least you have the details of about thirty paintings. Are they good paintings?'

'A Van Gogh, several Cézannes. Two wonderful canvases by Matisse, and a number of paintings by Picasso, Braque and Marie Laurencin.'

'Oh my God, they're worth a fortune!' Laura exclaimed.

'I am sure of that. But their whereabouts are unknown. I believe they are lost forever, as are all the others. I am certain they were sent to Germany during the war. As you know very well, Göring was looting art for himself and for Hitler. Many private collections similar to the Westheim Collection were taken in Germany, France and other countries. The private collections of the Rothschilds, Paul Rosenberg, the Bernheim-Jeunes and the David-Weills were confiscated in France, as well as the collection of Maurice Duval.'

A small silence descended on the room.

Rosa sat back and looked off into the distance; a sorrowful expression settled on her face. 'My father's great collection is lost to us. I shall never see those paintings again. Who knows on whose walls they are hanging.' There was a small pause, before Rosa ended quietly, 'It would please me to get just one back. It would be like retrieving part of my father, a piece of his soul. And a piece of my family's soul.'

'Are you still annoyed with me?' Megan asked as Laura followed her down the corridor to her bedroom.

'What do you mean, Gran?'

'When we arrived at Rosa's you were put out with me. I don't think you liked my surprise. In fact, I thought you were annoyed.'

'I was startled more than anything else,' Laura replied.

Megan made no comment until they had entered her bedroom, and then she murmured, 'I thought you felt you shouldn't be at Rosa's because of Claire.'

'I guess so, Gran, but I'm glad you arranged the dinner after all. Meeting her was a revelation.'

'I thought it would be.'

'I fully expected her to say something about Claire though.'

'I think she's afraid to, Laura dear. She knows how close you two are, and I believe she was being careful. She didn't want to offend you in any way.'

'I see. But she didn't mention Natasha either,' Laura said.

'For the same reason. She very badly wants to see Natasha, to get to know her better, eventually. And from what she's told me, she wants to see Claire too. But, I happen to know that Rosa is afraid of being rejected,' Megan finished.

Laura was silent as she helped her grandmother to get undressed. It was not until Megan was settled in bed that Laura said, 'There's something I don't understand, Gran.'

'What's that, child?'

'Claire's attitude towards Rosa. In the past I mean. How could anyone feel ill will towards Rosa Lavillard in view of what she's been through?'

Megan shook her head but said nothing.

'Surely Claire must know Rosa's story ... Philippe would have told her, even if Rosa didn't reveal it herself. Oh, I've just remembered something. Years ago, Claire told me that Rosa had grown up alone in France, that her parents had been killed in the bombings, which I now know is wrong. So perhaps she didn't know the truth.'

'I think she did, Laura,' Megan responded. 'But she probably didn't want to discuss it with anyone. I can't imagine why, but there it is.'

'She told me Rosa was crazy, and that she'd been hospitalized.' Laura frowned. 'Do you know if that's true, Gran? The hospital part?'

Megan said: 'It's true, Rosa was in hospital several times. She was treated for depression. But that's understandable, wouldn't you say, in view of her past? Who wouldn't be depressed, knowing your entire family had perished in Auschwitz? But crazy, no, no.' Megan shook her head vehemently. 'Perhaps Claire misunderstood something Philippe confided. Or Pierre. Rosa and Pierre had a good marriage, but volatile at times; and Claire might have misunderstood him, misunderstood a comment Pierre made. In any case, Laura, Rosa wants to see Claire when she comes here later this month.'

'I hope Claire will see her.' Laura frowned, shook her head. 'I don't know ...'

'You must arrange it, darling. It's important to Rosa, and it will be important to Claire. You see, Rosa wants to apologize.'

Laura stared at Megan, looking surprised. 'Apologize for what?'

'For always being cold to her, in the beginning, when Philippe and Claire first met. And then later, after they were married. Rosa confided recently that she never liked Claire, that she thought she was totally wrong for Philippe.'

'I told you she was possessive of him,' Laura interjected.

'Protective is a better word,' Megan answered. 'Rosa knew that Claire would not be able to handle Philippe, because he was the child of a Holocaust survivor. That he had his own problems to contend with because of Rosa's history, and Claire would never understand him. But now she feels she should have been warmer, should have tried to like her, even though she knew the marriage was doomed.'

'How could she know that?'

Megan shrugged. 'She says she did. It would be helpful if you could get Claire to see Rosa. I should tell you that she's devastated Claire is so desperately ill.'

When Laura was silent, Megan pressed, 'Promise me you'll try it, darling. It's important for the future, for Natasha's future. She ought to know her grandmother . . . Rosa's the only grandmother she's got.'

Laura went and sat on the edge of the bed. Leaning forward, she kissed Megan on the cheek and said, 'I promise, Gran. I think you're right, Natasha needs a grandmother just as Rosa needs a granddaughter. And Rosa and Claire should make their peace.'

25

Laura worked quietly at her desk in the solarium at Rhondda Fach. She was perusing letters and catalogues about art for sale in England and Europe, as well as in the United States, and making copious notes on a yellow pad.

From time to time she glanced up and looked across at Claire, who was resting on the big overstuffed sofa and had fallen asleep. Laura stood up and walked across the room, wanting to check on Claire but moving softly so as not to awaken her.

It was a hot morning in the middle of July and brilliant sunlight streaked through the many windows. It highlighted Claire's auburn wig, turning it into a fiery halo of curls around her narrow face. Her cheeks were slightly flushed, and in repose she looked better than she had in days. Underneath that wig there was a stubble of hair growing, spiky and still thin, but new hair nonetheless, and it was her natural red. Another good sign, at least according to Claire.

Being here at the farm had worked wonders for her; she had seemed to acquire more energy, both mentally and physically, and Laura was suddenly hopeful once again. Perhaps her dearest friend would make it after all. Maybe she would be one of the lucky ones, like Alison's sister Diane.

Claire and Natasha had arrived three weeks ago, in plenty of time for the Fourth of July picnic which Megan had traditionally given for years; and how they had enjoyed it.

Megan had wanted Rosa Lavillard to come for the picnic and to spend the weekend at Rhondda Fach. Laura had balked at this suggestion, explaining to her grandmother that it was too soon.

Laura knew that Claire wasn't up to it yet, even though she had been settled in at the farm for over a week. 'Not yet, Gran, let's give her a chance to get on her feet, to acclimatize herself.' Megan had immediately agreed that Laura was right; and so she had come up to Connecticut alone.

Laura was relieved that Claire had finally made the decision to come back to New York to live. She had resigned from her job at the magazine in Paris and put her apartment on the market. Hercule was supervising the crating and shipping of her furniture and all of her other possessions. He was constantly in New York because of his decorating and design assignments, and he had accepted Laura's invitation to come and stay at the farm whenever he wished. 'I can't wait to be with you all, with my darling Claire,' he had said to Laura only the other day, and she was now expecting him this coming weekend. Just like Laura, Hercule was trying to be optimistic about Claire's eventual recovery, and he was encouraged by Laura's reports of the improvement in her.

Laura had told Claire she should have the furniture shipped to the farm where it could be stored in one of the outbuildings; she had also offered her an old barn as a weekend home. 'Convert it into a studio for Natasha and yourself,' Laura had said. Claire had leapt at the idea, and in the moments when she had the strength she was creating designs. 'It'll be a place of your own in the place you've always loved the best,' Laura had said encouragingly, praying that the highly aggressive chemotherapy was working. Claire had been thrilled at the idea of remodelling one of the red barns. She saw it as a project for the future.

Natasha had settled in comfortably and quickly, much to

Laura's relief, and Claire's as well. She would be fifteen in a few weeks. Thankfully, she loved the farm and had adapted with ease to the country environment. Next week she would take the entrance exam for the Chapin School on East End Avenue. Laura was confident she would pass and be accepted at the private high school, considered to be one of the best in Manhattan.

Of course Laura knew deep inside that Claire's health was precarious, and that she might not go into remission, that she could die. But there was the slim chance that the heavy doses of chemo were working. She clung to this hope; they all did.

Unexpectedly Claire opened her eyes and stared at Laura. 'I knew you were standing there looking down at me.'

'Liar!' Laura exclaimed, laughing. 'You didn't know I was here. Not at all.'

'Oh yes I did, I can sniff your presence out even when I'm sleeping.'

Laura smiled and sat down on the low-slung Voltaire chair next to the sofa, pleased that Claire was revitalized after her nap and obviously in a bantering mood. 'Men came and went in our lives, but we were always there for each other,' she said.

Claire grinned. 'Bet your ass we were. We were steadfast when it came to each other ... I'll always be there for you, Laura.'

'As I will for you, darling.'

'You've already proven that. And I know I couldn't have lived through the last few months without you. You've been my rock, my strength, Laura. You and Natasha. She's been so supportive, such a source of help and comfort to me.'

'She's been incredible. Now, what would you like to have for lunch?'

'I'm not really hungry,' Claire murmured, pushed herself up to a sitting position on the sofa and settled against the many cushions.

'There must be something you fancy?'

'Strawberries and cream! I'd love that. And maybe a piece of watermelon for dessert.'

Laura smiled, shook her dark head and sighed. 'My darling Claire, you're not going to build yourself up on a bit of fruit. But all right, it's a deal, providing you'll try and eat a little scrambled egg first.'

Claire nodded. 'Yes, I will, I'd like a taste of scrambled eggs with a slice of bread and butter.'

'That's the spirit. I'll have to go to Balsamos for the fruit. Do you mind if I leave you alone for a while?'

'No, I don't. Anyway, Natasha's somewhere around, isn't she?'

'She's gone riding with Tom's son. Lee has taken her up on the trails through the hills where we used to ride.'

Claire smiled. 'Those trails are so beautiful. Anyway, I'm enjoying resting here, relaxing. Could you lower some of the shades and turn the air conditioning up a bit, please, Laura? The sun's making it very warm in here.'

'Of course,' Laura said, and then bending over Claire she kissed her cheek and hurried out of the solarium, glancing at her watch as she did. It would take her a good half hour, maybe a bit longer, to drive to Balsamos, but the trip was worth it. They had the best produce in the area.

Claire drifted, half dozing, and slowly she tumbled down into herself. Thoughts of the past intruded, memories flooded her mind. Mostly they were happy memories of her younger days, spent here with Laura and the Valiants. At one moment bad memories began to insinuate themselves, but she pushed them away. She wanted to recall only the good times. They filled her with joy . . . remembrances of her childhood and those growing up years . . . spent here at Rhondda Fach . . . All the seasons of the year . . . She had loved them all . . .

Winter days of icy skies and crystal light. Snowflakes blowing in the wind. Icicles dripping from the trees. Cool sunlight on snowdrifts taller than a man. Stalwart horses carrying them up through the trails. Up into the hills high above the valley. The green swathe of spring and summer gone. The splashy red-gold of autumn obliterated. A great spread of white and crystal far below. Stillness. A silent landscape.

The crunch of hooves on powdered snow. The bray of horses. Laura's laughter tinkling in the air. Her own voice echoing back to her. Cooee! Cooee! Calling to the Harrison boys waiting at the top. Geoffrey. Hal. Tall in the saddle astride stallions gleaming dark in the sun. Boyish laughter. Fumbled hugs under the trees. Tender kisses. Shy looks and pounding hearts. Young love blooming under icy skies.

Sultry summer nights. Diamond stars. A sheltering sky like black velvet. Hal's mouth on hers. His gentle hands touching, stroking, learning her. Hands insistent, greedy. Hot breath against her cheek. Strangled cries lodged in her throat . . .

'Mom, Mom, are you all right?' Natasha asked, her voice tight with concern as she peered at Claire on the sofa.

Slowly Claire's eyes opened, focused on her daughter, and on her worried expression. 'I must have dozed off. I was dreaming. Or remembering. Or both.'

'You cried out,' Natasha explained. 'I was studying over there at the desk. Are you sure you don't need anything?'

'I'm fine.' Claire smiled at her daughter. 'I was back here when I was young, when I was your age, darling. Remembering things.'

'What things?' Natasha asked, sitting down in the chair, taking hold of her mother's hand, stroking it.

'I guess I was remembering my first boyfriend, my first love.' Claire shook her head and smiled again. 'So long ago.'

'What was his name?'

'Hal. Harold Harrison. He and his brother Geoffrey lived on the other side of the hills above the valley. They used to ride up to meet us at the top, in the woods up there. His brother Geoffrey was Laura's boyfriend. We often rode up the trails where you've been this morning with Lee.'

'It's so beautiful up there, Mom. *Awesome*. I know why you've always loved Rhondda Fach. I didn't before . . . I guess I was too young to appreciate it, to understand. Now I love it too.'

'I'm glad you do, darling. It's a special place. How's your studying coming along? For the exam?'

'Okay. Laura's been helping me. Do you want me to get you some apple juice?'

Claire shook her head. 'I'll wait until lunch.'

'Mom?'

'Yes, Natasha?'

'I want to ask you something . . . about Dad.'

'What about him?'

'He wants to come and see you, Mom.'

Claire frowned. Her eyes narrowed slightly. 'How do you know that? Stupid question. I guess he's spoken to you on the phone.'

Natasha nodded. 'He's worried about you, Mom. Very concerned. He asked me to call him back at the Center in Atlanta. To tell him if you agree, and let him know when he can come.'

Claire was silent. 'I have to think about it.'

'But he *can* visit us, can't he, Mom?' Natasha asked, biting her lip. 'He wants to so badly.' When Claire was silent, Natasha said, 'And I want him to come, Mom. It's important to me, too.'

'Why?'

'Because I'd like it . . . I'd like you to be friends. You and Dad. You will let him come, won't you?'

'I suppose so, since you seem to wish it so badly. Let me work out a date with Laura. Maybe after your exam next week? How does that sound?'

'It's good, Mom.' Natasha's young face brightened. She would call her father later to tell him her mother had agreed he could visit, but they had yet to settle on a date. She knew he would be pleased. He was extremely troubled about her mother's illness.

Claire said, 'Laura's gone to Balsamos.'

'I know. She left me a note. And then I ran into Fenice in the kitchen. She said I'd have to cook lunch, because Laura can't even boil an egg properly. As if I didn't know.'

Laughing, Claire said, 'Poor Laura, she does get teased about her lack of culinary skills. But why can't Fenice prepare the scrambled eggs?'

'She says she has to go shopping, but actually she did say later that she'd make the eggs if I want.'

'It's up to you, Nattie.'

'Oh, I can do it, Mom, there's nothing much to making a bunch of eggs in a pan.' There was a small silence before Natasha said in a low, tentative voice, 'Do you think the chemotherapy has worked, Mom?'

'I do, my angel. I'm convinced of it; I'm feeling so much better. I want to go into New York next week, to do some shopping. I hanker after Bergdorf Goodman's, it was always my favourite store when I lived here. And I'd like to go to Serendipity too, for a hamburger with French fries, and a banana split. With you and Laura. Grandma Megan says she wants to come too.'

Natasha smiled at her mother. 'I love Grandma Megan. She's . . . *awesome*, Mom.'

'She surely is, darling, and she always was. Later, I'm going to ask Laura to get out Megan's photograph albums and clippings books. From the time Megan was a Broadway star. She was so famous, and totally gorgeous, Nattie. We'll play some of her old records, too. You'll get a kick out of them. Grandpa Owen used to say she had a bell in every tooth.'

Natasha grinned. 'What a funny expression.'

'It's very Welsh. And she did have the most sensational voice.'

'When I start going to school in New York in the autumn, will you be living in the city with Laura as well?' Natasha now asked, her eyes on her mother. 'I want you to be there with us, Momma.'

'I will be, part of the time. I'll be having chemo at Sloan-Kettering. But it's very comfortable for me out here, and Laura thought I might prefer to spend as much time as possible at Rhondda Fach. You'd both come at weekends, to be with me. And Megan would come too.'

'But who'd look after you, Mom?'

'Fenice. She's happy to live here full time, as she used to when Megan came up all year round. In any case, her cottage is only on the other side of the meadow. Fenice'll look after me very well.'

'I certainly will,' Fenice said, gliding into the solarium carrying a large tray. She was a tall, well-built woman, with salt-and-pepper, faded red hair and angular features. Now in her early fifties, Fenice Walton had worked at Rhondda Fach since she was sixteen. She had always idolized Megan, and she loved Laura and Claire like a surrogate mother, had bossed them around for years. Prone to bohemian clothes that often resembled theatrical costumes, Fenice was wearing a colourful cotton skirt that fell almost to her ankles, a fancy white blouse with big puffy sleeves and a huge starched white apron that was obviously Victorian. White ankle socks and red sneakers completed the outfit.

'I've brought iced tea for you, Claire. I know you love it. I found your favourite yesterday at the market. *Honey peach.* And for you, Natasha, I've squeezed fresh grapefruit.' As she spoke, Fenice placed the laden tray on the coffee table in front of the sofa. 'There's some chocolate chip cookies, too. Just out of the oven. And as soon as Laura gets back I'll be fixin' the eggs and the bread. Can't have you starvin', now can we?'

'Oh don't worry, Fenice, you're too busy to do the eggs. I can manage!' Natasha exclaimed. 'I'm a good cook.'

'Get on with you, it's no trouble for me. Stay with your Momma, keep her company.'

'Thank you, Fenice,' Claire said.

Fenice beamed at them both, swung around on her heels and went marching out, looking very much like a woman totally in command of her domain.

Watching her go, Natasha asked, 'Has Fenice ever been married?'

'Oh, no, she's married to Rhondda Fach,' Claire explained. 'At least, that's what Laura and I think. She never got too involved with a man, because she didn't want to leave the valley and this house.'

'And those who live in it, I guess,' Natasha added, sounding much wiser than her years.

Laura was pleased.

She sat opposite Claire in the small dining room watching her eat a plate of scrambled eggs along with a slice of Fenice's freshly-baked bread spread with butter.

'The strawberries look delicious,' Laura volunteered. 'Big and luscious, Claire, and Fenice has whipped up some cream. It's a real treat.'

'I can't wait,' Natasha said, then turning to Laura, she confided, 'Mom says Dad can come and see her. He wants to very much. It's just a question of the right date. Mom said perhaps he could visit after my entrance exam for Chapin. What do you think, Laura?'

'It would be fine,' Laura murmured, and glanced at Claire quizzically. She was suddenly curious about this new development.

'I agreed, Laura.' Claire then explained, 'Natasha told me her father's upset about my illness. And *she* wants him to visit me here as much as *he* wants to come. Whenever you say, Laura. It's your call.'

'Hercule will be here this coming weekend. He could come then.'

'Or during the week,' Claire suggested. 'I don't think Philippe would expect to stay overnight.'

'But maybe –' Natasha began, and stopped when she saw the startled look on her mother's face.

Changing the subject, Claire now said, 'I dozed off when you were out buying the strawberries, Laura. So many memories came rushing back. Do you remember when we painted Dylan gold?'

'Oh my God! How could I ever forget!' Laura cried, shaking her head and laughing. 'Did we get it from Grandma Megan!' Sobering, she added, 'But seriously, we really could have hurt him, you know. I tremble whenever I think about it now.'

'You didn't really paint him gold, did you?' Natasha asked, putting her fork down, looking first at Laura and then at her mother in amazement. 'It's very dangerous. The pores can't breathe through paint, you know.'

'Exactly.' Laura grimaced. 'We were well and truly punished.'

'But why did you paint him gold?' Natasha pressed.

'We were doing a little play, for Grandpa Owen and Grandma Megan. Very short, only two scenes, about Antony and Cleopatra. Dylan was the most beautiful little boy and we decided to make him into a golden idol,' Laura explained. 'And your mother knew enough, even if I didn't, not to paint every part of him. So we fashioned a mask for his face out of cardboard painted gold, and we made him a pair of tiny briefs from a piece of gold lamé Fenice found in the ragbag here at the farm.'

Natasha began to laugh. 'I would have loved to have seen your tiny golden idol. I suppose he was adorable.'

'But sticky. The paint didn't dry very well,' Claire remarked, and then looking across at Laura, she added, 'and it was all your idea.'

'You always blamed me for everything,' Laura complained, grinning at her.

'Only when I thought I could get away with it,' Claire retorted, and began to chuckle.

26

'This is an extraordinary story, Laura,' Hercule Junot said, steepling his fingers, looking at her over the top of them. 'Rosa Lavillard is in the same position as Maxim ... she's the heir to a great art collection she can't find.'

'*Exactly*. But I might find it for her,' Laura answered. 'Or rather, I might come across a painting or two in the course of my work. After all, an enormous amount of material comes across my desk, as you know, every day of the week. All I need is the right information from Rosa, so I know what to keep my eyes open for ... names of artists ... names of paintings.'

'I am quite certain she will be only too happy to give the information to you.'

'She is. She's had the record book and inventories copied, and I'm hoping she's going to give everything to me tomorrow, or on Sunday. You see, Grandma Megan wants her to come up for lunch on one of those days this weekend. And I –'

'But what about Claire, my dear? Won't she object?' he ventured, cutting in. 'You know that Rosa Lavillard is not a favourite of hers.'

'I do. But I'm planning on chatting to Claire about Rosa later today, if she's not too tired.'

'That would be good. Certainly it would be a relief if they

could be on cordial terms. I do loathe dissension of that kind. *Mon Dieu*, Laura! Would it not be wonderful if Natasha got to know her grandmother?'

'Yes, it would. Especially under the circumstances.'

Hercule gave her a worried look and asked swiftly, 'What *are* those circumstances? Please tell me the truth.'

'I would never lie to you, Hercule, surely you know that by now. Claire's about the same. No real improvement, but at least she's not worse. She's finished the course of chemotherapy treatments, and she doesn't have to go back to Memorial Sloan-Kettering Cancer Center for a few months, in the autumn, actually. But what pleases me is that she's been so much better since she's been here at Rhondda Fach.'

'That is good to know, yes,' Hercule murmured.

'I'm praying she's going to beat it, Hercule.'

'So am I.' He sighed and looked away, shading his eyes from the sun with his hand. After a moment, he brought his gaze back to Laura, and went on quietly, 'If I have any regret in my life, it is that I never told Claire how I felt about her, that I didn't ask her to marry me. What a fool I've been. And it has been such a waste of years. Years when I might have been able to make her happy. Perhaps I could have helped her to allay her pain, helped her rid herself of that terrible bitterness. Just to make her mental anguish disappear would have been rewarding.'

'Tell her now,' Laura said, leaning closer to him under the sun umbrella. She touched his arm affectionately, and smiled up into his face. 'Tell her how you've always loved her. You don't have to actually propose, but you could make her understand how much you care. I think it could only be a plus for her. And it may very well make *you* feel better, Hercule. I can guarantee this . . . she won't be angry. Claire's changed. Well, a little bit. Some of her fierce anger has evaporated, at least. *Tell her.*'

'Do you think I really should, Laura?' Hercule exclaimed, his eyes lighting up. 'I will do it, but only if you are certain I will not upset her.'

'Of course you won't. Any woman would be flattered to hear a declaration of love from a man like you, and it's something for her to look forward to . . . getting better, spending time with you.'

'Do you think she would want to do that?'

'It's possible, yes. I do know she cares a lot about you. She's told me so.'

He smiled broadly. 'I could give her a life of ease. We could travel, do anything she wants. I wouldn't expect her to marry me . . . as long as we are together, that is all that matters.'

'Then tell her that.'

Hercule nodded but made no further comment. He sat staring into the distance, his eyes fixed on the willows at the edge of the stream at the bottom of the garden.

He and Laura were sitting on the terrace having an aperitif before lunch on Friday. He had arrived at Rhondda Fach the night before and had been pleased to see Claire looking relaxed, so much more vital and energetic than he had expected.

He thought for a moment or two about Laura's advice, and then putting the matter of Claire to one side, he said: 'It will be a challenge for you . . . seeking Rosa's paintings.'

'Obviously I can't actually go out and look for them, because, like Sir Maxim, I wouldn't know where to even start looking. But if one of them should come onto the market, I'll be poised and at the ready . . . I can go after it.'

Hercule nodded.

Laura said: 'I want to do it for Rosa, but it's for Natasha as well. The art collection is her inheritance.'

'Lunch looks splendid, Fenice,' Megan remarked as she eyed the buffet which had been set up at one end of the dining room. 'You've outdone yourself today.'

'Thanks, Mrs V. But all I did was bake the rolls. Natasha made everything by herself. The salade niçoise, the quiche Lorraine and the caramel custard and raspberries for dessert. The girl's a wonder in the kitchen, a good little chef. My hat's off to her.'

'Thank you, Fenice,' Natasha said as she came into the dining room carrying a bottle of rosé. After putting it in the bucket of ice, she turned to Megan and said, 'Can I sit next to you, Grandma Megan?'

'Well of course you can, Natasha dear,' Megan replied, smiling at her. 'And my congratulations on this wonderful lunch.'

'Mom taught me everything about cooking. She's a much better chef than I am. But I'm striving to reach her level.'

'You will, if you're not there already, and I have a feeling you might be. Where is your mother, Natasha?'

'Hercule's bringing her in from the garden; she sat out there for a while. And Laura went upstairs to change her clothes. Oh, here they are now. At least, here's my mother with Hercule.'

Hercule and Claire came into the dining room together; Claire was well-groomed and looked pretty in a caftan made of amber-and-red printed cotton.

Megan said, 'Where do you wish to sit, dear?'

'Over there, with my back to the window, so the sun's not in my eyes,' Claire answered, and allowed Hercule to shepherd her to a chair solicitously.

Laura finally arrived dressed in a loose, white cotton tunic over narrow black pants and sporting black-rimmed sun glasses. 'It was blistering in the garden, Gran, I'm glad you stayed indoors.'

'Yes, she's right, it was far too hot for me,' Claire interjected.

'You'll soon cool off, Claire,' Megan assured her, and went on, 'you've made a fine little chef out of Natasha. This splendid lunch is all her creation.'

'Not the rolls,' Natasha was quick to point out. 'Fenice made the rolls.'

Everyone laughed at this comment, and then they served themselves the summer fare, except for Claire whose plate was prepared by Natasha. Hercule went around the table pouring the rosé and Laura filled their glasses with iced water.

It was halfway through the lunch that Claire said, 'I'm so happy we're all here together today. The people I love the most in the whole world are with me ...' She paused, smiled at them.

'We all love *you*, Claire,' Megan said, and reached out and touched her hand affectionately.

'I want to thank you ... all of you ... for giving me such support, for helping me to cope with my cancer. For giving me the courage to keep fighting.'

Later that afternoon Claire walked slowly down the corridor to Laura's room, tapped on the door and went inside. 'You said you were going to work, I hope I'm not disturbing you,' Claire said, leaning against the door frame.

'Not at all, I was just looking through some of the art catalogues that came to the office this week. I'm not doing anything very pressing.'

'It's good of you to spend so much time out here with me, Laura. I worry that you're neglecting your work.'

'You know better than that, and in any case July and August are pretty slow months usually. Everyone's on holiday. Don't worry, Alison won't hesitate to give a yell if I'm needed at the office.'

Closing the door, Claire wandered into the room, sat down on the sofa facing Laura, who was perched on a chair behind her big French provincial desk.

Lifting her feet up onto the sofa, Claire gave Laura a penetrating look, and said, 'You advised Hercule to come right out and tell me that he loved me.'

'Yes, I did. Because it was nagging at him, and it has been since last December, probably even before that. I thought it would make him feel better, and you too, Claire. It's nice to know a truly wonderful man cares, isn't it?'

'It is. But there's no future for us.'

'Is that what you told him?'

'No, not in so many words. I sort of fudged it. I didn't want him to become upset.'

'What do you mean?'

'Laura, there is no future for me. So how can there be a future for me with Hercule?'

'But you're so much better!' Laura cried. 'Aren't you? Or are you acting?'

'No, I'm not acting. I do feel stronger than I have for ages, and I don't have much pain. But my days are numbered, whether it's weeks or months or even a year, and therefore I can't offer a man a life with me. *I don't have one to offer.*'

'Doug once said to me that we are all dying, that we die a little bit every day.'

'You're splitting hairs, Laura, and you know it.'

Ignoring this remark, Laura asked, 'Do you love him?'

'Yes, you know very well I do ... as a friend. He's always been perfectly wonderful to me, but I'm not in love with him, not as he is with me. Still, if I weren't so ill I'd probably give it a shot ... I mean I'd live with him, see how it worked out ...'

'Did you tell him this?' Laura asked.

'I told him I loved him, but perhaps in a different way than he loved me. And I said if I were in better health I would be honoured and flattered to be his permanent companion.'

Laura didn't say anything. She sat back in the chair and let her eyes wander around her bedroom. Its pale apple-green walls were gentle, a cool backdrop for the heavy white cotton draperies patterned with red roses, the antique French country furniture, the big bed dressed entirely in white, and the dark green carpet.

'It *is* a charming room,' Claire murmured, following her friend's gaze. 'I've always liked it and for as long as I can remember.'

'Most of your life and mine,' Laura whispered, and pushed down the sudden, incipient tears that threatened to spill.

'Laura?'

'Yes, Claire?'

'There's something ... something I've never told you,' Claire began and then suddenly stopped. She sat staring at Laura, the dearest person in the world to her except for her daughter, and wondered how to go on.

'What is that?'

'I should have told you long ago. Perhaps my life would have been different if I had.'

'You sound very serious,' Laura remarked, returning Claire's intense gaze. 'And what do you mean when you say your life might have been different?'

'Maybe it wouldn't have been so screwed up, and maybe I wouldn't have been so screwed up either, so angry, so bitter and resentful . . .'

Laura seemed baffled. Slowly she said, 'I'm not following you.'

'Do you remember how you sometimes found me here in your room, crying my heart out on that very bed, hugging a pillow?'

Laura nodded. 'You never would tell me what was wrong.'

'I was crying because I was sick at heart. And I was clinging to the pillow as if I were holding onto you. My Laura. You were the only thing I had in my life that was good and decent.'

'Tell me what happened to you, Claire. Tell me what this is all about.'

'It was my father . . .' Claire came to a halt. She stared at Laura. Her face had turned chalk white, and she was unable to continue.

Laura rose from behind the desk and went and sat with Claire on the sofa. Taking hold of her hand, she held it tightly in hers. 'Your father hurt you. Is that what you're trying to tell me?'

Claire could only nod.

'Oh darling, why ever didn't you say anything then? I could have helped you!' Laura exclaimed.

Shaking her head, Claire answered in a whisper, 'How could you have helped me? You were only a little girl, younger than I. My own mother couldn't help me.'

'Did she know?' Laura asked in a horrified voice.

'She tried to stop him!' Claire cried, anger surging through her. She tried to clamp down on it and continued in a calmer tone, 'My mother tried to protect me, to stop him. But he would beat her until she couldn't stand, and then he would turn back to me. He started when I was seven, hitting me, as well as touching me, kissing me. I resisted him as long as I could . . . but he became more and more insistent . . . finally I gave in to him. I had to. It was the only way to stop him from beating my mother. It was easier just to lie there and be silent than to get her involved and see her so badly hurt. Occasionally, I would fight him off. He really had it in for me after that. He would beat me until I couldn't move.'

'Oh God, how terrifying for you! You must have been frightened to death most of the time.'

'I was.

'He was foul, awful. I hated him.' Claire began to weep. Tears trickled down her face as she continued, 'But at least, once I gave in to him, he stopped hurting my mother.'

Laura put her arm around Claire and drew her closer, in an effort to soothe her. 'If only you'd confided in me and Grandma. We could have done something, I know we could.'

'I was afraid to tell you,' Claire gasped between her tears. 'I was embarrassed. Ashamed. It was so sordid. Sometimes I thought it must be my fault. I was torn up. I didn't know what to do. So I just concealed it, pushed it down inside, pretended it had never happened.' Claire began to sob uncontrollably, her body shaking as the dam of suppressed emotion finally burst inside her.

Laura held her closer, stroking her shoulders, saying gentle words of sympathy, giving Claire her love and compassion. Eventually, Claire managed to calm herself; gradually the tears ceased. She sat up, groped for a tissue in the pocket of her caftan, and wiped her eyes, striving for control.

Laura said: 'Your father . . . Well, Grandma Megan once insinuated that your father was a womanizer, and that this was the reason why your mother drank. But she was wrong, wasn't she? He was an abuser.'

'He was both, Laura. Please believe me, he was chasing after women all the time. It broke their marriage. And my mother's heart, I'll admit that. She found escape and solace in the bottle.'

'I'm so sorry,' Laura whispered. 'I'm so terribly sorry you had to go through that alone, Claire, when you were so young. It breaks my heart to think about it.'

'I wasn't alone, in a sense. Because I had you and Grandma Megan. And Grandpa Owen. You were my refuge. Just as this place was. Rhondda Fach was always my safe haven. I always felt secure, safe and loved when I was here with all of you.'

'When did . . . when did he stop?'

'When I was fifteen I told him I was going to tell your grandfather, and ask Grandma Megan to take me to a doctor for an examination. So that she'd know I was speaking the truth. I finally realized I needed words – not fists to stand up to him. He was scared of being exposed to the Valiants. It's a pity I hadn't understood that years ago, because it would have been a weapon I could have used.'

'I think so, and I wish it had been different for you. I can't believe I didn't detect something was truly wrong. I know you cried a great deal, but I thought you were unhappy and worried because your mother drank such a lot of vodka.'

'I was a good little actress, wasn't I?'

'That you were.'

'My father made me hate men, distrust them. He scarred me, and he ruined my life. I know I would have been a very different person if he hadn't abused me. Laura, I was only *seven* when he started . . .' Claire's voice broke, and she had to wait a moment or two before continuing: 'I am sure I would have trusted Philippe, been a better wife, if not for my father's abuse.'

Laura nodded. 'I agree with you.'

Claire now explained, 'Whenever Philippe had to go away

on a trip, to do research, or be in quarantine for his work, I always believed he was really with another woman. Like my father had been. My father was a *genuine* womanizer. Anyway, I was constantly suspicious of Philippe. I was resentful and bitter as well, and I made a lot of mistakes with my husband.' Claire let out a heavy sigh and shook her head sadly. 'I think that in many ways I treated Philippe unfairly. He's not a bad man.'

'Is that why you've agreed to let him come and see you on Sunday? Because you know that you were also at fault in the marriage, and that he never was entirely to blame.'

'Partially. But also because Natasha is so anxious for him to visit me. She longs for us to be friends. Lately I've come to understand that she loves her father.'

'Yes, I know that, Claire. She's conveyed the same to me.' Laura cleared her throat and gave Claire a long careful look. 'Do you still believe Philippe had a lot of women when he was married to you?'

Claire bit her lip, appeared chagrined all of a sudden. 'Perhaps not. I've examined my life a lot in the last couple of weeks, and I realize how very damaged I was as a person. How could I possibly think straight with my history?'

'Your father's behaviour was monstrous! He's responsible for all of the mental anguish you've had to contend with since you were a child.' Laura was angry.

'That's true. And he's responsible for my cancer.' Claire sat up straighter and looked directly into Laura's eyes. 'I mean that.'

'I know you do, and I tend to agree. You believe that your repression of all of this for so many years left you vulnerable to cancer.'

'His acts were reprehensible. The only way I could go on living was to bury them deep inside myself. But nevertheless they still gnawed at me, destroyed me, turned me into an angry, distrustful woman. I was ravaged by a bitterness I couldn't rid myself of. At one point I was really consumed by the memories, but I managed to keep going, somehow. I thought when he died

I'd feel differently, feel better, but I didn't. And the memories just ate at my innards . . . like a cancer.'

'It has been medically proven that mental and emotional stress, plus repression of strong emotional pain can cause all types of illnesses in people. So I'm with you on that, Claire.'

'I feel a sense of relief at last, now that I've confided these things. Perhaps I might start healing . . . and in many ways.'

'I hope so. Didn't you ever tell *anyone* about your father? Not even Philippe?'

Claire shuddered. 'Oh God, no. How could I have told anyone else except you? You're the closest person to me, and look how long it's taken me to speak about it to you.'

'If only you'd unburdened yourself sooner.'

'I should have.'

Laura said, 'You look drained. Would you like a cup of tea?'

'Thanks, that'd be nice,' Claire replied, and forced a smile.

It was true, she did feel very tired, sapped of all energy. And so Claire went and lay down on Laura's bed, nestling herself in amongst the mounds of white pillows. How often she had done this as a child. Waiting for Laura, as she waited for her now, breathing in the smell of her shampoo, the scent of her perfume. Ma Griffe. Laura had worn it for years; a fresh, green smell, that was the way Claire thought of it.

She had always longed to be part of the Valiants, for as long as she could remember, part of that wonderful family and all the love that spilled out of them. Thankfully, they had taken her in, transformed her into one of theirs, and miraculously they had made her forget her father and what he did to her when she was at home. For a short while, when she was with them, she was a different person. And it was Laura who made her feel clean again, just like Laura was herself. Pure. Innocent. Untouched. A good girl.

Claire curled up in a ball in the middle of the bed and closed her eyes for a moment or two. Her thoughts ran amok; but she managed to rein them in, take control of them again. She could not dwell on the past. She had to think of the present and the future. She knew she did not have much longer to live. She was dying.

She kept up the façade, going along with Laura and everyone else, agreeing that she had improved in health. It was true that she had been revitalized here at Rhondda Fach, that she had more energy all of a sudden. But she wasn't getting better. The chemotherapy hadn't worked. The doctors had told her that, confirmed what she already knew herself.

All of the things she had to do had been done. The only outstanding matter was the sale of the apartment in Paris. But Hercule would take care of that and transfer the money to Laura who would put it in the trust account they had opened for Natasha. Her thoughts turned to her daughter. The miracle of her life. Her joy. Claire smiled, feeling warm inside thinking of Natasha. She had gone out for a drive with Megan and Fenice. Actually, they had gone shopping; Natasha was planning a special dinner for tonight.

Claire took a deep breath, feeling unexpectedly dizzy. She closed her eyes once again. After a few minutes she saw her daughter's face in her mind's eye, so fresh, so young, a beautiful girl with her whole future ahead of her. Claire was thankful Natasha had Laura to guide her, to look after her in the years ahead. *I can die in peace because of my true blue Laura.*

Natasha had been very brave and courageous so far. When Claire had told her that she had made Laura her legal guardian there had been no problem. Natasha had said she understood. But later, from the things she had said, Claire realized there was a good rapport between the girl and her father. And so she had finally given in and said Philippe could visit. He was coming to see them the day after tomorrow. Somehow, she would get through it.

Hercule had told her that Rosa Lavillard had asked to see her. To apologize, that was the way he had put it.

Hercule believed it was important for Natasha to get to know her grandmother, and Claire wondered if he was right about that. In the end it would be up to Laura's discretion, though. After all, she was going to be in control. Just the way I wanted it, Claire thought to herself, and she pushed herself up on the bed as Laura came bustling in with the tea tray.

'Two mugs of Grandpa Owen's famous miner's tea!' she cried. 'Hot and strong and sweet. And slices of chocolate cake, courtesy of Natasha. She made it this morning for you.'

'It's my favourite,' Claire said, smiling. 'And so is this tea.' As she spoke she made an effort to get off the bed.

'Stay there, Claire,' Laura instructed and hurried across the floor. She placed the mug of tea on the bedside table, along with a plate of cake, and then arranged the many pillows behind Claire. 'There, that's much more comfortable, isn't it?'

'Yes, thanks, darling.' Claire took a sip of the tea, and continued, 'Hercule told me about Rosa's request. Why does she want to see me?'

'She's devastated about your illness, and she wants to come here and tell you how sorry she is that she wasn't a good mother-in-law to you.'

'So Hercule was right. I tended not to believe him, Laura. So, she's coming to apologize. Is that it?'

'Yes. Hercule was just repeating what I'd told him.'

'Could she come with Philippe this Sunday? I think I'd like to get them out of the way at the same time, if you know what I mean.'

'I do. And all right, I'll arrange it, if you're up to it on Sunday.'

'I am.'

'Then I'll have Grandma Megan phone her later.'

'They should drive up together,' Claire murmured, 'that would be best.'

Laura stared at her. 'You've certainly agreed very readily.'

Claire nodded. 'I've had a sudden change of heart.' She smiled faintly. 'I'm doing it for Natasha. That's what this is all about really. And also for you, Laura. If I don't get through this bout with cancer, you'll appreciate having them around. And so will Natasha, of course. They'll be supportive.'

'That's exactly what Grandma Megan said to me.'

'She's a wise woman, and she knows the way of the world. She's certainly got everybody's number . . . that's why I believe her theory about Doug.'

'I didn't know she had a theory,' Laura exclaimed, looking startled.

'She says she told you.'

'She never did. When did she do *that*? Did she say?'

'Yes, she told me she mentioned it to you when you first broke up. She said she suggested to you that there must be someone else, another woman, and that was the reason he was being so obliging about the apartment, and the other financial matters.'

'It's true, she did say that,' Laura muttered, remembering, and went and sat on the edge of the bed. 'Doug does have someone else, Claire.'

'Did he tell you finally?'

'I'm afraid so.'

'Who is she?'

'Actually, it's Robin Knox.'

Claire was silent for a moment, a thoughtful expression crossing her face, and then she asked, 'Are you sure?'

'I'm positive. And Robin's fiancée broke off her engagement to him . . .' Laura's voice trailed off. 'Doug is Doug, and a law unto himself. In any case, we're not married any longer, so what he does is his business. I gave him my blessing when we split up, and he knows I'm always there for him if he needs me. Just as he's there for me. That's the way we feel about each other, Claire. We're good friends.'

'I know you are,' Claire said. 'And it's better it happened now, that you ended your marriage when you did. You're still young enough to start a new life with another man.'

'I don't know about that,' Laura said softly.

'You will, Laura, trust me, and in the not too distant future.'

Laura threw her an odd look but refrained from answering.

27

Rosa Lavillard sat very still in the chair near the bed, looking at Claire, wishing she were not so ill, wishing *she* could do something about making her feel better. But she knew she couldn't; neither could Philippe, even though he was a brilliant doctor. Such a pity, Rosa thought. So young. *She's so young.* Her heart filled with compassion, and it took all of her self-control not to start weeping for Claire.

Suddenly Claire opened her eyes, and smiled faintly at Rosa. 'I'm sorry, I didn't mean to fade on you a moment ago.'

'Can I get you anything?' Rosa asked in a worried tone.

'No, thanks,' Claire murmured.

Taking a deep breath, Rosa said, 'I was wrong, Claire, all those years ago. Very wrong to behave the way I did towards you. I should have tried to understand you, tried to get to know you better, before I made any judgements about you.'

Claire blinked and shook her head. 'Whatever your judgement was, it was more than likely correct. I was a very troubled young woman in those days.'

'I didn't give you a chance, and that was unfair. I was being protective of Philippe. You see, I thought you wouldn't understand the complexity of his nature, wouldn't understand his background as the child of a Holocaust survivor.'

'I did love him a lot.'

'As he loved you, Claire. However, you were both volatile, just as Pierre and I were, and volatile marriages don't augur well for the future. Not usually. Somehow mine lasted. But your stormy relationship was something else which troubled me. Going back to the beginning of your courtship, I realize that I wasn't nice to you, merely civil and nothing more. I should have known better, as a mature woman. I should have given you the benefit of the doubt.'

'I guess my marriage to Philippe wasn't meant to be. But at least the most glorious child came out of our union. A truly wondrous gift she's been, my darling Natasha.' Claire's green eyes shone brightly.

'From what everyone tells me she's very special, unique,' Rosa murmured. 'And she's a beautiful young woman. She looks older than her age in some ways.'

'They all do these days. You haven't seen much of her, or spent much time with her, but that's partly because you live in New York, Rosa, and she's lived in Paris most of her life. I'm . . . I'm so sorry you don't properly know your only grandchild.'

Rosa inclined her head, but she didn't respond, simply leaned back in the chair and tried to relax a little. She had wanted this meeting, but she had also been apprehensive about it.

'Natasha's going to be living with Laura in the city, going to the Chapin School,' Claire volunteered.

'That's near me!' Rosa exclaimed, unable to conceal her sudden excitement.

'I know. What I was going to say is that I want the two of you to get to know each other. It's about time, too. I've told Laura she must arrange it in the autumn.'

'I would love to spend time with her, Claire, and with you too. I want to repair the damage. Do you think there's a chance we can be friends?'

When Claire didn't reply, Rosa continued, 'I apologize to you, Claire, with all my heart. I did a terrible thing all those years ago, and I've regretted it for the longest time. Can you see it in your heart to forgive me?'

'There's nothing to forgive. We were all wrong in our different ways.' Claire closed her eyes for a moment, settled against the pillows. A second or two later she opened them and looked at Rosa intently. She said, 'What did you mean when you said you thought I wouldn't understand Philippe's problems?'

'He is the child of a Holocaust survivor, as you know, Claire.' Rosa paused, shook her head as if reproving herself, and went on, 'That was another stupid thing on my part, I should have told you about my life during the war. Since you didn't know much, it was virtually impossible for you to understand anything about me. Anyway, Philippe, like many similar children, has had a hard time coming to grips with what happened to me and to my family when I was a child. He thought he was somehow an insignificant part of my life, nothing of any great consequence in view of the *enormity* of the Holocaust. That horrendous catastrophe somehow manages to overshadow and overwhelm our children. Some children of survivors are even oddly jealous of their parents because they know they will never experience anything so immense as the Holocaust.'

Claire was frowning when she said, 'I don't think Philippe is the kind of man to feel that.'

Rosa nodded in agreement. 'He didn't, and doesn't. What was problematical was the absence of a family, of a family past, and of a family history and inheritance. I know he definitely had feelings about all that. You see, the common element that binds together all of the children of survivors is this unnatural disruption of family history . . . because of that catastrophic occurrence which wiped out so many people.'

'I can understand that, and Philippe *was* odd in certain ways, I agree. He was an angry young man in those days.'

'That is the truth, Claire.'

'He did feel he must do something worthwhile, something for humanity like saving lives.'

'That was always the driving force in his life.'

'Is he still troubled, Rosa?'

'I think perhaps he always will be, but he's learned to live with my past as well as his own life. Just as Pierre did. He and his family were in Switzerland when war broke out in France, and they remained there for the duration. So thank God my husband didn't personally suffer, although his family did. They, too, had many losses. Philippe has learned to control the anger and the despair. He's a good man, a worthwhile man, and I think he is at peace with himself.'

'I hope so,' Claire whispered.

'Are you all right?' Rosa asked, leaning forward, a concerned expression ringing her mouth.

'Yes, I'm all right. Just catching my breath.'

They sat in silence for a while, and when Claire finally opened her eyes again and looked at Rosa, the older woman said, 'Claire, please forgive me, won't you?'

'I forgive you, Rosa. I know you want to hear that, but truly, there's nothing to forgive.'

'Oh, but there is,' Rosa insisted.

Claire reached out, groped for Rosa's hand. 'Grandma Megan told me your story recently, she told me about the hole . . . where they hid you . . . she told me about the things that happened to you. However did you survive?'

'I'm not sure. I often ask myself that. Willpower, determination, the desire to conquer, not to be beaten by the Nazis. Just wanting to live, I suppose.'

'Why didn't you tell me years ago? Why didn't Philippe tell me?'

'I don't know . . . except that once a woman I met said she was sick of the professional Jews who were always showing their numbers . . . the numbers tattooed on their arms when they were in the death camps. Her words stunned me, and I never ever spoke of my past to anyone again. Not that I'd discussed it much at all, but that woman had diminished in the most dreadful and derisive way the suffering of so many . . . millions.'

'I understand,' Claire said, shifting her position in the bed and leaning on her side. 'Rosa?'

'Yes, Claire?'

'Will *you* forgive *me* . . . for keeping your granddaughter away from you?'

'Of course, of course,' Rosa said swiftly, and added, 'but as *you* just said, there's nothing to forgive.'

Claire beckoned with one finger for Rosa to come closer. 'Come and sit on the edge of the bed,' she murmured softly.

Rosa did so; her eyes did not leave Claire's face.

Claire whispered, 'I'm not going to make it,' and took hold of Rosa's arm. 'I'm dying.'

'No, don't say that, Claire!' Tears filled Rosa's eyes; she blinked them away. 'I know you're very sick, but Laura said you'd *improved.*'

'Yes, I did for a while, here at Rhondda Fach. But I can't last much longer, I can't fight any more, Rosa, I'm tired.'

'Oh my poor Claire,' Rosa said and the tears fell from her eyes and splashed down onto her hands holding Claire's.

'Don't cry,' Claire murmured. 'I'll be all right where I'm going . . . it's just that I'll miss Natasha and Grandma Megan and my darling Laura.'

Rosa was unable to speak. She sat on the edge of the bed, holding Claire's hand for the longest time. Finally she bent forward, put her arms around Claire and held her close, just as she had held her son when he was a small boy. And they stayed like that for a long time.

Eventually the two women drew apart and Claire said, 'Don't say anything to the others, will you?'

'No, I won't,' Rosa said and thought: Laura knows, even if everyone else is deluded. She knows but she's keeping up a front for Natasha.

Rosa shifted slightly on the bed and started to get up, when

Claire opened her eyes. 'Don't go, please. Stay for a few minutes longer. I need to gather my strength before I see Philippe.'

Rosa nodded. 'All right. Do you want me to get anything for you, Claire? A glass of juice perhaps?'

'No, thanks. I just need you to stay with me, Rosa.'

Philippe Lavillard sat with Laura in the solarium, drinking a tomato juice and chatting to her. They were alone. He and his mother had arrived at Rhondda Fach an hour ago only to find that Natasha was out with Fenice and Hercule Junot.

Now he said to Laura, with a faint smile, 'They must be buying an awful lot of groceries, it's taking them so long.'

Laura explained, 'It's about half an hour to Balsamos, the best produce stand in the area, and half an hour back, and they did have to go into Kent to pick up other stuff. But they'll be here soon. Don't worry.'

Philippe nodded. 'It's just that I'm anxious to see Natasha . . .' He looked at Laura more intently, and said in a warm voice, 'I haven't thanked you, Laura, for all that you've done for Natasha, and *will* be doing. I'm very grateful.'

'She's a wonderful girl. Certainly she makes it easy for us all to love her. She adores Grandma Megan, they've got quite a little thing going between them. Anyway, we're just happy to have her around. Natasha's got such spirit and warmth, a *joie de vivre* that's infectious. She's always willing to pitch in and help, and she has a great sense of responsibility; she's actually very grown up for her age.'

'Yes, she is, but then I think a lot of European children are. They just seem to mature at an early age. Natasha's been brought up in a single-parent family environment, and that's more than likely made her independent and capable. Anyway, you know what Claire's like . . . she's always treated Natasha as an adult, and expected her to behave like one.'

'I know,' Laura said, and laughed. 'Natasha's always had to stand up and be counted on. By the way, I'm glad you agree with us about sending her to Chapin. Claire selected the school, and I just hope Natasha gets in.'

'I'm fairly certain she will,' Philippe answered. 'Natasha likes school, and that makes her a good student. She seems to be diligent and hard-working.'

'She is.' Laura sipped her apple juice, and then went on, 'Do you like living in Atlanta?'

'Yes, I do, although if I had the choice I'd be in New York. There's no place like one's hometown. But aside from that, New York's such a great city, I get a hell of a kick out of it.'

'I guess you don't miss Africa,' Laura remarked looking at him questioningly.

'Not at all.' He grimaced. 'If I lived to be a hundred I won't miss the sickness and disease, the grinding poverty, the cruelty of the politicians, the barbarity of the soldiers. Nor will I miss the droughts, the famine, the violent wars, the wholesale death and destruction on an unimaginable level.'

'I asked a stupid question,' Laura muttered, looking embarrassed. Suddenly, she felt a bit foolish.

'No, you didn't,' Philippe was quick to assure her, smiling warmly. 'Of course, Africa is beautiful, and the game parks are extraordinary, out of this world. In fact, there's something about being out there in the bush that simply takes my breath away. But I've had my fill of Africa . . . I just became burnt out, Laura. Utterly exhausted. I wasn't functioning properly anymore, and as I said to Francine, I'd better get out before I get sloppy and manage to infect myself with some deadly virus like Ebola or Marburg.'

'Who's Francine?' Laura asked, looking at him alertly.

'Francine Gillaume is a French socialite with a conscience. She's given a lot of money to some of my research programmes over the years. Almost all the time I worked under the auspices of the Pasteur Institute. And naturally she agreed with me, even though it meant I was off one of her pet projects.'

'Being a virologist is pretty dangerous. Hazardous work, isn't it?'

Philippe grinned at her. 'Only if you're sloppy, as I just mentioned. Getting burnt out, becoming over-exhausted, can easily be a death warrant.'

'Claire looks quite good. But she isn't, not really,' Laura said, suddenly changing the subject. 'I know she gave you permission to talk to her doctor at Sloan-Kettering. Did you?'

'Yes, I did. He says she's a real fighter, a tough one, and that she –' Philippe stopped as Natasha came rushing into the solarium, her face wreathed in smiles as she flew across the room to greet him.

Jumping up, Philippe met her halfway, enveloping her in his arms, hugging his daughter to him. Natasha clung to her father, her face buried in his shoulder.

He loves her very much, Laura thought. And what's more, she loves him. Laura suddenly asked herself why she had ever thought otherwise, and she had the answer to that immediately. How alike these two were in appearance. There was no doubt at all whose daughter she was. They were both tall, lean, athletic looking; Natasha had long legs like Philippe. And the shape of their faces was the same, as was the slant of their eyes. Natasha's were golden-amber; Philippe's were dark and full of compassion in his angular face.

Laura was seeing him differently. I'm seeing him as he really is today, she thought, not the way he was when he was young and tempestuous. But we were all different then. I've changed. Claire's changed. And so has Doug. People grow and evolve, and if they're lucky they acquire positive, worthwhile characteristics. I hope I have. I know Philippe has, I can tell. He's become a whole person and his own man. And Natasha knows him, and knows him well.

As father and daughter drew apart, Natasha exclaimed, 'We went to the fishman's stand, and he had fresh lobster. So it's lobster salad for lunch. Mom loves lobster!'

'Yes, she does, and I'm glad you've found something to tempt her.' Glancing at Philippe, Laura went on, 'Perhaps we ought to go upstairs, so you can spend a little time with Claire.'

'I'd like that,' Philippe replied.

Philippe sat holding Claire's hand, his heart aching for her. He knew how much she was suffering, the kind of pain she was in, and there was nothing he could do for her. Except assuage her worry about their daughter. He must reassure her that he would not interfere with the arrangement she had made with Laura, and that he would be there to give his support. As would his mother.

Philippe Lavillard had realized when he walked into Claire's bedroom that Claire and his mother had made their peace. Why does understanding always come too late? he wondered to himself. Why does it always have to be a catastrophic event that brings people together? If there had been this healing long ago, his child's life would have been very different; all of their lives would have been better.

Claire lay against the pillows, staring at him. He was still the best-looking man she had ever met, the famous Doug included. Lean, tough, with a body as hard as a rock, that was Philippe Lavillard. Eighteen years ago she had fallen madly in love with him; it had been a *coup de foudre*, and deep down inside she had never stopped loving him. Very simply, they had been unable to live together . . . because of her terrible secret, her history of abuse, and because of his own troubled background as the only child of a Holocaust survivor. The dice were loaded against us right from the start, she thought. We didn't have a chance.

Tough, determined and ambitious, that was the essential man her ex-husband was, but he was also warm, loving, tender – a man of immense compassion. She understood that now. *Too late. Too late for me now*, she thought, but not for someone else. He's ready finally for someone else, for another wife. All these years he's waited . . . yes, perhaps now it's time for him.

Claire said, 'I'm sorry it didn't work for us, Philippe. I'm sorry I caused you such pain . . .' She broke off; her eyes filled with tears.

'Hush, Claire,' he said very gently. 'It was nobody's fault, not yours, not mine, it was . . . circumstances. And we were too young.' He smiled at her. 'We'd be better off if we met today.'

She nodded. 'Except that I'm of no use to you anymore.'

'Hush,' he whispered, lifted her hand to his mouth. He kissed it, and continued, 'You've done a remarkable job with Natasha. She's a great kid, Claire. I love her, she's my only child, and I've always loved her. You thought I didn't care, but I did.'

'I know. And I was wrong to keep you and her apart. I'm sorry for that, Philippe.'

'No recriminations, Claire. We were both at fault in our different ways.'

'You'll keep an eye on Laura for me, won't you? Be there for her if she needs support? She's strong and resourceful, but even so . . .'

'You don't have to worry about Natasha and Laura. I'll be there for them, I promise you, Claire.'

'Rosa and I . . . we've made our peace.'

'I could tell. I saw it written all over her face only a moment or two ago.'

'Can I ask you something?'

'Go ahead.'

'Why did you never get married again?'

'I never found anybody I loved enough to marry.'

'Oh.' Claire sighed. There was a moment or two of silence before Claire said, 'It's funny, but everything is so clear to me now that I'm dying. What a ridiculous time to find the answers I've been seeking all my life. When they're of no use to me.'

Philippe, listening to her attentively and watching her closely, realized that she was growing tired; there was a strained look on her face, a sudden weariness about her. 'Are you in a lot of pain, Claire?'

'No. Well, a little, but the medication helps a bit. I think I'd like to rest for a while.'

Philippe rose, bent over her and kissed her forehead. 'I'll see you later.'

'Philippe?'

'Yes?'

'Why did you want to see me today?'

'I wanted to reassure you, to tell you you don't have to worry about Natasha. Not in any way.'

She smiled at him and closed her eyes.

Philippe moved a strand of hair away from her face and quietly left the room. He ran downstairs in search of Laura.

Laura was waiting for Philippe in the solarium. The moment he strode into the room she knew before he said anything that Claire was waning. She could read it on his face.

'She's not good, is she?'

Philippe shook his head. 'I'm afraid not. I think she's very weak, exhausted. Although she's trying to keep up a front for everyone. And she certainly can't get up for lunch, I wouldn't really like her to do that. I doubt that she wants anything to eat. I know Natasha's making her lobster salad, but –' He cut himself off sharply, and walked over to the window, stood gazing out at the summer garden for a moment or two. Finally, he turned around, and looked directly at Laura. He said gently, 'Perhaps it's best if you both go up and see her, sit with her.'

Laura nodded. Her throat was tight and she found it hard to speak for a moment. Gripping the chair-back, she steadied herself, and stared at Philippe, still unable to say a word.

Philippe said again, 'Go upstairs, Laura. I'll send Natasha to you.'

Laura did as he said, hurrying up the stairs, pushing down the feeling of panic that was rising inside. Her heart felt tight in her chest, almost constricted. She went into the blue-and-white bedroom, quietly closing the door behind her. Gliding over to the bed, she sat down in the chair next to it.

Her eyes rested on Claire, her dearest friend, her sister under the skin. Laura knew it was over. Claire had put up a courageous fight but the intense battle was finally drawing to its close. Soon she would be at peace.

There was a slight noise and Laura glanced over her shoulder, saw Natasha coming into the room. The girl's face was as white as bleached bone, stark against her red hair, and her freckles stood out like dark blotches. She crept up to Laura's chair, knelt down next to her.

'Mom's dying,' she whispered, looking up at Laura, the tears spilling from her eyes. 'Dad didn't say that, but I could tell from his face.'

Laura nodded, put her arms around Natasha, drew her closer to her knee. 'Yes, she is,' she whispered. 'And it's so hard for us to bear. But her pain's been excruciating lately. Soon . . . soon she'll have relief.'

'I know,' Natasha whispered back, and wiped her fingertips across her streaming eyes.

Claire moved slightly and said, 'Are you there . . . Laura? Nattie?' She tried to reach for them but her hand fell away, fell against the duvet.

Laura took hold of it, clasped it, and slipped down onto the floor, knelt by the side of the bed next to Natasha.

'Mom,' Natasha said, stifling a sob. 'We're here, Mom.'

'I'm glad I came back to Rhondda Fach, Laura. It's the only place I've been happy,' Claire murmured and opened her eyes.

'I know that, Claire, and *I'm* glad you came back too,' Laura answered softly.

'What would my life have been like without *you*, Laura?' Claire sighed, looked at her very intently, and then at Natasha. Her eyes were suddenly very green, greener than they'd ever been. Claire smiled at them both . . . it was a valedictory smile, full of radiance. 'Take care of each other,' she said. 'For me.'

'Always, darling, always,' Laura answered, tears streaming down her face.

306 ~ *Barbara Taylor Bradford*

Natasha clambered onto the bed and put her arms around her mother.

Claire lifted her face to her daughter, and smiled that radiant smile once again. 'You're the best part of me, the very best part,' she said.

'Mom, I love you,' Natasha cried, her tears falling onto Claire's face.

There was no response.

Natasha cradled her mother in her arms, and Laura knelt by the side of the bed clinging to Claire's hand. Neither of them could bear to leave her, and they sat with her for a long time.

It was Laura who finally released her grip on Claire's fingers. Letting go of her hand, she stood up and bent over her, kissed her cheek.

And then she let herself out of the room and went downstairs to tell the others that Claire was free at last.

PART FOUR

Spring

1998

28

Megan sat studying Natasha, thinking how lovely she looked tonight, rather grown-up in the hand-embroidered burgundy silk dress Laura had just bought for her in London. Her flowing auburn hair cascaded around her face, accentuated its delicacy, and her large golden-amber eyes seemed more soulful than ever. She'll be sixteen this year, Megan thought, yet she seems much older in so many ways. But perhaps that's not a bad thing.

'You're staring at me, Grandma Megan. Don't you like this dress after all?' Natasha asked.

'I do indeed, and the only reason I was staring is because you look very fetching tonight, really lovely, darling girl.'

Natasha beamed at her. 'Thank you. I love my dress, it's cool, sort of medieval.'

Rosa came bustling in from the kitchen at this moment, carrying a large platter, exclaiming, 'I hope it's all right, I hope I didn't overcook this,' and set the platter down on the sideboard. Picking up a spoon and fork she began to put pieces of meat and vegetables on a plate and then took it to Megan.

'Thank you,' Megan said, went on, 'I don't think you can overcook pot roast, can you, Rosa? Anyway, you're such a good cook nothing ever spoils in your hands.'

Rosa laughed. 'We can all have a bad day in the kitchen.'

'I agree with Grandma Megan,' Natasha said, glancing up at Rosa as she came to the table with her plate. 'Thanks, Gran Rosa. And you're the best cook in the world except for Mom. She was the greatest.'

'Start eating, Nattie, before it gets cold,' Rosa said, and went to serve herself.

It was the first day of May, and Megan and Natasha were having their usual Friday dinner at Rosa Lavillard's apartment on East End Avenue.

Whenever she could, Laura joined them, but tonight she had gone to an art exhibition at Hélène Ravenel's gallery on Madison Avenue. And she was dining with Hélène after the show. 'I'll come and pick you up at Gran Rosa's, so wait for me there,' Laura had told Natasha that morning, as the girl had been leaving for school. She had added, 'And you can wear your new dress if you want.' Natasha had hugged her, said, 'Have a wonderful day,' before hurrying out of the front door.

Claire had been dead for almost a year now. Everyone had made a tremendous effort to help Natasha through this difficult period of grief and mourning. And because of the sympathy, understanding and love she had received from Laura, Megan and Rosa, Natasha had managed to cope better than she had expected. She missed her mother and she thought of her every day, but she was mature enough to understand that she had to get on with her own life without dwelling too much on the past.

It was Laura she turned to mostly when she had a problem, and her father whether he was in New York or Atlanta. Philippe came to visit her frequently, staying with Rosa at her apartment, and they had had some wonderful weekends together. Sometimes they were alone, but often Laura was with them, and they always managed to have a lot of fun when they were all there.

Natasha thought of this now, thought of Laura and her father and their growing friendship, and before she could stop herself, she blurted out, 'My father's stupid, and so is Laura.'

Megan was so startled she put down her knife and fork, and looked across at Natasha, frowning. 'Is that what they're teaching you at Chapin? To be disrespectful? And about your father, no less, who bends over backwards to please you. And Laura, who devotes all her free time to you?'

'Megan's right,' Rosa clucked, shaking her head, her expression reproving. 'Why do you speak like this?'

'I wasn't being disrespectful, Grandmas,' Natasha said, looking from Rosa to Megan. 'I was only trying to say what I think, which is what Laura's always telling me to do.'

'So, tell us why they're stupid,' Rosa said. 'Don't keep us in the dark.'

'Perhaps stupid is the wrong word to use. They're being silly . . .' She let her sentence fade away, wondering if she should continue.

Megan's eyes rested thoughtfully on Natasha, and then she glanced quickly at Rosa. The two older women exchanged knowing looks, and Megan said, 'Come along, out with it, child. What is this all about? What are you getting at?'

'Well, they're in love with each other. I know they are,' Natasha confided, her tone suddenly conspiratorial.

'That's wonderful!' Rosa exclaimed, beaming.

'I'm inclined to agree,' Megan said with a huge smile.

'It *would* be wonderful if they told each other,' Natasha exclaimed. 'But they don't. They just go bumbling along, bumbling around each other, looking sort of . . . glazed when we're all together. Dazed, is a better word. Don't you see, my father's being –' Natasha shook her head impatiently. 'There's only one word for it, Grandmas. He's being *stupid*. So is Laura. She should tell him how she feels. After all, a woman can do that today, you know.'

Rosa bit back a smile, and said, 'Perhaps it's not quite the way you think, Nattie. Are you sure they're in love?'

'I'm positive and so is my friend Katie. We *know*.'

'I'm sure you do, in view of your vast experience in these matters of the heart,' Megan said pithily.

Natasha giggled.

'I think I would have noticed something,' Rosa said, looking suddenly thoughtful. 'But I haven't, I really haven't.'

'Neither have I,' Megan said.

'Perhaps the situation will clarify itself, once Philippe is living in New York,' Rosa murmured, thinking out loud. 'I'm so glad he's accepted the Research Fellowship at Columbia University. That's going to be good for him, and for you, Natasha, having your father in New York at last.'

'And it'll be good for Laura,' Natasha said, and began to giggle again.

'You say you know they're in love, but *how* do you know? I mean, what have they actually done to make you believe this, Natasha?' Megan pressed.

'I've seen the looks my father gives Laura, when she doesn't know he's looking at her. And the way she gazes at him when he's off doing something – like helping me in the kitchen at Rhondda Fach. And they're always laughing at the same things, and if he pays her a compliment she goes all red and looks confused.' Again Natasha glanced from Megan to Rosa, and said firmly, 'Grandmas, you've just got to believe me, my father is in love with Laura, and she's in love with him.'

The two women exchanged pointed looks again, and it was Rosa who said, 'You want this to happen don't you, Natasha?'

The girl nodded, smiling, and her eyes gleamed with happiness. 'Yes, I do, I do. I want them to get married and the three of us can live together.'

Rosa said: 'But maybe you're imagining it, Nattie, because you want it to happen so badly.'

'No, no, Gran Rosa, honestly I'm not imagining anything. My friend Katie's seen it too. I just wish he'd kiss her. I've thought he was going to do it when we were in the country. But he didn't. I think Laura thought he might, too, because she looked disappointed.'

'And when was this?' Megan asked. 'I've been at Rhondda Fach every time you've been up there.'

'Yes, but it was when we were outside down by the river,' Natasha explained. 'They were walking ahead, and Katie and I were trailing behind. And they stood looking out across the river, and then they turned to each other, and they were staring. And Katie grabbed my arm, and she said he's going to do it, but he didn't.'

Megan glanced away, hiding a smile. She finally looked directly at Natasha and asked, 'What are we going to do about this? Do you have any ideas?'

'No.' Natasha shook her head. 'Don't you, Grandma Megan?'

'Not exactly,' Megan answered.

'What about you, Gran Rosa?'

Rosa pursed her lips. 'I can't think of anything, not offhand. I mean what can *we* do . . . we can't very well interfere, they're both adults.'

Suddenly, Natasha exclaimed, 'We've got to put them in the right situation together! That's it. And I think I've got it . . . the perfect situation.'

'And what is that?' Rosa asked.

'It's Laura's birthday later this month. We can have a little dinner for her and invite Dad, and somehow it's going to happen, I just know it is.'

Megan nodded. 'Giving a birthday dinner for Laura is quite a good idea, Natasha, I wish I'd thought of it myself. So, let's start making plans.'

29

Rosa Lavillard started to prepare the afternoon tea early. Far too early, she knew that, but she was anxious and excited, and so she couldn't help herself.

After plugging in the electric kettle, she took the damp cloth off the metal tray of honey cakes and glanced down at them. They looked tempting; she knew Laura would enjoy them. Laura also liked macaroons, and there was a plate of these as well, freshly baked that morning.

Laura had telephoned yesterday and had invited herself to tea today, explaining that she had some exciting news for Rosa, news she preferred to impart in person. Rosa had no idea what it could be . . . news of her and Philippe? Was Natasha right about them? *Perhaps.*

Rosa sighed and began to take the best china out of the kitchen cupboard. Philippe and Laura had been thrown together a lot over the past ten months, ever since Claire's tragic death. Their common bond had been, and was, Natasha. She herself had observed them together, and like Natasha she had noticed them circling each other. In fact, she had often wondered if her son would make some move towards Laura. But it seemed to her that he never had. At least, that was her impression of late. And Natasha had confirmed this only the other evening.

Humming under her breath, Rosa put two rose-patterned cups and saucers and two small plates on her best silver tray. She told herself there was no use speculating. In a short while she would know why Laura had asked to see her.

When the intercom rang a few seconds later and Laura was announced from the lobby, Rosa sallied forth, a broad welcoming smile affixed to her face as she headed for the front door. She opened it just as Laura stepped out of the lift, raised her hand in greeting and came down the hallway.

'Hello, Laura, hello!' Rosa exclaimed, taking her hand, embracing her warmly. 'Come in, come in.'

'Hello, Rosa,' Laura answered, hugging the older woman, then closing the door behind her.

'It's such a treat to see you,' Rosa went on, and standing away she gave Laura an appraising glance, taking in the smart navy suit and accessories. 'And you look lovely, very lovely indeed.'

'Thank you, Rosa. You're looking well yourself.'

Rosa smiled and murmured her thanks, and the two women went into the living room. 'Sit down, do, Laura,' Rosa said. 'The tea is ready. I'll go and get it, I won't be a moment.'

Laura glanced around and sat down on one of the comfortable chairs. She smiled to herself, wondering how Rosa was going to react when she heard her news. She'll be surprised but deliriously happy, Laura decided and sat back, the small smile continuing to play around her mouth. She herself was pleased about the turn of events, and could hardly contain herself, so anxious was she to confide in Rosa.

Hurrying back into the room with the tea tray, Rosa put it down on the coffee table, and took a seat opposite Laura. 'I know you like it with lemon, don't you?'

'Yes please, and a sweetener.'

Rosa nodded as she dropped in a slice of lemon. 'I made honey cakes and macaroons,' she told her. 'Your favourites.'

'You're so nice to me,' Laura said with a light laugh. 'Always spoiling me, Rosa.'

Rosa said nothing, merely smiled at Laura as she handed her the cup of tea.

'Thanks,' Laura murmured and took a macaroon, bit into it. 'Delicious. I love coconut. You'll have to teach Natasha to make these.'

'I certainly will, and she's a good little cook, she'll have no problem with the recipe.' Rosa took a sip of tea, put the cup down and sat back in the chair. Looking intently at Laura, she said, 'Yesterday you told me you had some exciting news for me. I can hardly wait to hear it.'

Placing her own cup on the table, Laura said, 'It's wonderful news. *Thrilling.*'

Rosa leaned forward expectantly, her face beaming. '*Tell me.*'

'I've found one of your paintings.'

'Oh.' Rosa pulled back slightly, gaping at Laura. 'You've found a painting,' she repeated.

Laura, returning Rosa's startled gaze, said swiftly, 'You understand, don't you? Understand that I've managed to trace a painting which belonged to your father? A painting which was looted by the Nazis. It's a Matisse, Rosa. Imagine, a *Matisse.*'

Rosa cried, 'Oh my God, one of Papa's paintings! I can't believe it. How did you find it, Laura? What happened?'

'About five months ago, when I was in London working on Sir Maximilian West's art collection, I came across a catalogue from a small museum in Vienna. As you well know, art seized by the Nazis hangs in museums all over the world. Anyway, in the catalogue there was a photograph of a Matisse. It caught my immediate attention because it bore the same name as one of the paintings in the record book of your father's which you lent me some time ago. I'm sure you'll recognize the name too ... *Moroccan Girl In A Red Caftan Holding A Mandolin.*'

'Oh yes, Laura, yes!' Rosa cried, her hands flying to her mouth. Sudden emotion and memories of long ago brought a rush of tears to her eyes. Blinking them back, she said, 'I remember the name very well. And the painting. It's fabulous, extremely colourful, with a lot of red and violet, deep blue, and a brilliant yellow. A typical Matisse.'

'That's correct. Once I had seen the photograph in the catalogue, I flew to Vienna from London. I went to the museum to view the painting and talk to the curator. I tried to convince him it was your painting. Obviously I had to present clear title to him, the provenance. And so once I got back to New York I sent him a copy of the page in the record book, which listed the Matisse and all details about it. A week later he telephoned me and said he needed more proof. Naturally I was stumped.'

Rosa nodded. 'There is no other proof, not anymore. So what did you do?'

'As I said, I was at a loss, and then an amazing coincidence occurred. I mentioned my experience in Vienna to a client of mine, Sandra Newsam. She instantly recognized the name of the Matisse and said she had recently seen a photograph of it in an old art catalogue. She became very excited when she realized she had come across this at the home of a friend in Switzerland. She phoned her friend, a Mrs Gilda Sacher, and discovered that she had seen the photograph, not in a catalogue, but in an art magazine which had run a story about the Sacher Collection. The Matisse had once been part of that collection.' Laura sat back, pausing for a moment.

Rosa said: 'Oh, don't stop, please, this is so exciting.'

'Obviously I went to Switzerland. To Montreaux, actually, where Mrs Sacher lives. She's a woman in her late sixties, English by birth, and she inherited the Sacher Collection from her late husband, Leon Sacher, a Swiss businessman. During his lifetime Leon Sacher had amassed an amazing collection of art. Naturally, every painting in the collection had its provenance, and listed on the one for the Matisse was the name M Duval, Paris, France.'

'Oh my God! I can't believe it!' Rosa's eyes had widened and she could hardly sit still. 'And so you were able to convince the curator in Vienna finally?' she asked.

'Not exactly. There was a bit more to it than that,' Laura

responded. 'Let me tell you the rest of the story. I asked Mrs Sacher how the Matisse had come to be in the museum, and she told me she had sold it along with a couple of other paintings, to a dealer in Geneva, who in turn had sold it to a client in Vienna. Later it was sold to the museum. She gave me all of the names, just in case I needed them. I asked her if there were any markings on the back of the canvas, and she said there were the letters DU, then a slash and the number 3958. I explained to Mrs Sacher that this was the way the Nazis had catalogued the paintings they had stolen. They used the first two letters of the owner's surname and added a number. She hadn't known this. In any case, she then produced a copy of the provenance. It proved to be quite a remarkable document. According to the provenance, before Mr Sacher bought it, the Matisse had passed from M Duval of Paris to a Madame Wacker-Bondy of Paris, and from her to an H Wendland. Now those two names jumped out at me, meant a lot to *me*, although not to Mrs Sacher.'

'What did they mean to you, Laura?' Rosa asked.

'I will tell you. As I am now very familiar with the fate of Jewish-owned art stolen during the Second World War, those names rang bells immediately. Hans Wendland was notorious. He worked for the Nazis, and he spent most of the war years in Switzerland, where he helped Göring and Hitler exchange "degenerate" art, such as the Impressionists and Post-Impressionists, for the rather pallid old masters the two Nazi leaders preferred. Now it just so happened that almost immediately after my meeting with Mrs Sacher, yet another document came into my hands, almost by chance. It was a British Ministry of Economic Warfare paper, which I got via Sir Maximilian West, and it said that in 1942 one Hans Wendland, working for the Nazis, took delivery in Switzerland of a railway van of art from Paris. And this came from the transport firm of Wacker-Bondy.' Laura stopped and stared hard at Rosa. 'You do see the connection?'

'Yes, I do.'

'What is even more extraordinary, around this time, when I was doing research on your Matisse, Sir Maximilian was given a copy of a memo which had been written in June of 1966, by a woman called Marguerite Gressy, who had been a wartime Resistance heroine in France. She was a curator and she had somehow managed to keep track of many of the paintings which were looted in Paris by the Nazis. Her memo confirms that a painting by Henri Matisse entitled *Moroccan Girl In A Red Caftan Holding A Mandolin* was stored by Maurice Duval of Duval et Fils "chez Madame Wacker-Bondy". Meaning stored in the warehouse belonging to their company.'

Rosa sat looking at Laura speechlessly, trying to absorb everything.

'Mademoiselle Gressy's memo had been sent to Sir Maxim by an old friend in the French art world, a noted dealer, because several Renoirs were listed. However, they were not from the Westheim Collection, as it turned out. But Sir Maxim, very much aware that I was looking for information about the Matisse, passed it on to me.'

'Surely you didn't need more than this?'

'Not really. At least, that's what *I* thought. Armed with a copy of the provenance in Mrs Sacher's possession, a copy of the British Government paper and a copy of the Gressy memo, I returned to the museum in Vienna, and met once again with the curator. This time he was a little less contentious, especially when I showed him the documentation. In fact, I gave him his own set of copies. I also informed him that I would soon start litigation against the museum for the return of the Matisse to you if we couldn't come to an agreement. I also mentioned that I was planning a press conference to announce my findings and my plans on your behalf to the media. He seemed to be quite obdurate, said nothing had changed, and so I left. But I must have scared him because he telephoned me at the hotel that evening. He asked me not to do anything until he had spoken to the board of the museum. After a couple of days, when I didn't get a positive reaction from him or the museum, I left. I flew back to London, then on to New York. Once I was home I started to prepare all of the documentation I knew I would need, and then suddenly three days ago I received a call from the curator. The museum is going to recognize your claim, Rosa. Although they say they bought the painting in good faith, knowing none of its history, they are going to give the painting to you.'

Rosa shook her head. 'Since they bought it legally, why are they giving it to me? Just like that? I don't understand.'

'They're frightened, Rosa. They don't want bad publicity, the kind that Switzerland's had about dormant bank accounts and stolen Jewish gold, and cheating Holocaust victims. All of that's been a world-class scandal. They're trying to avoid this occurring with the museum, and, also, I like to think they might see that it's your moral right to have the Matisse in your hands after all these years.'

Rosa didn't speak. She couldn't, she was so touched. Again she shook her head wonderingly, and then she began to weep, totally overcome by the news.

Laura went and sat next to her on the sofa, took hold of her hand. 'A little bit of justice for you at last, Rosa,' she murmured.

Rosa looked at Laura through her tears. 'I can't believe it . . . that you did all this for me . . . Thank you, thank you. You've restored a piece of my soul, Laura, a little piece of my family's soul. I will be forever grateful, forever in your debt.'

30

'You did something really marvellous for my mother, Laura,' Philippe Lavillard said several days later, when he had driven up to Kent for a visit with Natasha. 'And I thank you for that.'

'Honestly, Philippe, thanks aren't necessary. I did it because I had to, once I'd stumbled on the painting.'

He laughed. 'I know how you feel about Nazi-looted art. You're like a dog with a bone. But very seriously,' he went on, his voice changing slightly, 'I also know you're a very ethical person, Laura. I admire your integrity.' His eyes settled on her intently. 'Well, anyway, it's such a good feeling inside, knowing that the Matisse is there, waiting for my mother at the museum. Certainly it'll be satisfying to have it back in the family. But the most important thing to me is that you've given my mother something ... something ... rare. *Peace of mind.* And it's more than likely the first time she's had that since her parents and siblings were taken off to Auschwitz by those criminals so many years ago.'

'I hope I have done that!' Laura exclaimed quickly, returning his steady look. 'I love Rosa. She's the most remarkable woman, and it truly pleases me to think I've helped to make her feel better. God knows, her life's been hard, harder than most people could ever imagine. So much loss and pain and fear when she was a child. I can't help trembling when I think about it.'

'She's told you most of it, hasn't she?'

Laura nodded. 'Yes she has. But you sound surprised.'

'I was actually when she first intimated that to me. Not because it was you and Grandma Megan, but because she doesn't ever confide anything about her past. At least, she hadn't until she told both of you.'

'Why do you think that is, Philippe?'

He thought for a moment before answering, and then he said, 'Somebody once made a strange remark to her about professional Jews showing the numbers tattooed on their arms, and she said it made her shrivel inside because she couldn't imagine a Holocaust survivor being anything so crass as a *professional* Jew. The woman who said it offended her deeply, and it made her . . . protect her past. She held it to her, allowed no one to share it but my father and me . . . I'm certain you'll understand this . . . in a peculiar way her past became *sacred* to her. She didn't want it sullied by people's sympathy, indifference or scepticism. Those were her very words, and I do understand what she means, don't you?'

'Yes, I do. Her past is very private to her and so many people wouldn't . . .' Laura's voice trailed off. Clearing her throat, she finished, 'Wouldn't have the compassion to recognize the trauma it caused, the sense of dislocation she experienced.'

Philippe sat back, not responding. As she usually did, this woman had managed to touch and startle him yet again. That was her way, he supposed. At least it was the way she affected him. He tried not to dwell on Laura Valiant too much. He knew he was in love with her, but he was afraid to make this known to her because he didn't know where she stood. He supposed he would never know unless he made some kind of move towards her.

Laura remarked, 'Your mother is going to let me know when she can come to Vienna with me to collect the painting. Has she discussed it with you?'

'She has, and I think she's hoping that you'll be able to go at the end of this month.'

'I'm pretty sure we can . . . and to tell you the truth, I'm as excited about the trip as she is.'

'We're all excited. Actually, Laura, what do you think about taking Natasha along with you? It's going to be such a memorable occasion, stupendous really, she shouldn't miss it.'

'You're right, I think she should come, Philippe.'

'I'm glad you agree. You won't mind if I tag along, will you?'

Although she was momentarily startled by his question, she was able to disguise this, and she said cautiously, 'No, of course not. After all, the painting will be yours one day. And I think you *must* be there to share your mother's joy.'

As she spoke Laura shrank inside, worried about travelling with him, staying in the same hotel as him, and having to be in his company for any protracted length of time. In fact, lately it had become an agony to be anywhere near him, feeling the way she did. To her amazement she had fallen in love with him. Once she had recovered from the shock, and regained her equilibrium, she had realized she was in an untenable situation. She had to spend time with him because he was Natasha's father and Natasha was in her care. But to see him was like putting herself on a rack. And so, finally, she had decided to make herself scarce whenever he was coming to visit his daughter. She invented business appointments, ran off to the office to work, and did as many other disappearing acts as she could. But eventually Natasha had become upset with her, and had insisted they all did things together; the girl had contrived to have them spend time together here at Rhondda Fach, and in the city. Oh well, she thought, I'll have to manage in Vienna. But deep down she knew it wouldn't be all that easy.

He said, 'I couldn't help thinking about the coincidences that happened to you, how you got onto the Matisse in the first place, and then all those documents that came your way. Just like that.' He snapped his fingers and smiled. 'You had lots of lucky breaks.'

Laura did not crack a smile. Her face was serious when she responded: 'I must tell you something rather strange, Philippe, there seems to be a lot of coincidence when it comes to tracking the purloined art of the Second World War. The Goodmans, two brothers now living in Los Angeles, just recently encountered *four* major coincidences when they were tracing art which their father had sought for forty years, art which had belonged to their grandparents in Holland. It seems to happen to everyone who is on the track of Nazi loot ... somebody finds an old record book or a document or a deed of title. Then someone stumbles on a painting in an obscure museum, hanging in an exhibition, or coming up for sale. It's quite uncanny really, all the coincidences.'

'Maybe God has a hand in it,' he said softly.

Laura glanced at him swiftly but didn't say anything. Maybe God does, she thought.

Philippe rose, walked across the library floor and stood at the window, thinking how peaceful the scene outside was: a long meadow, two horses grazing, and faintly, in the distance, the plop-plop-plop of tennis balls. Natasha and her friend Katie were enjoying a game on the tennis court. What a reassuring sound that is, he thought, just as the bucolic setting is also reassuring. A far cry from the sound of Nazi jackboots and prison doors clanging, the anguished cries of the victims of the Holocaust. Almost sixty years ago now, but still those terrifying memories haunted his mother. The past *is* immutable, he thought. She never escapes her past. It is with her always.

Laura startled him when she said, 'Your mother never confided much in Claire, I mean about her past, did she?'

He swung around to face Laura, feeling as though she had just tapped into his thoughts. 'No, she didn't. She just wasn't able to, as I told you a moment ago. I did explain a few things to Claire myself, but perhaps I didn't tell her enough. I've often wondered about that. I was nervous, I suppose.'

'What do you mean?'

'I was nervous about upsetting Claire, frightening her with the horror of it, the horror of my mother's tragic past. I mean, Claire led such a quiet sheltered life as a child, and she came from such a privileged and protected world.'

Laura was flabbergasted and before she could stop herself, she exclaimed, 'Privilege, yes! If you're talking about wealth, but protected, no! She wasn't protected.'

Philippe looked at her oddly, realizing he had touched a nerve, caught Laura on the raw. He came back and sat down near her in front of the fire, and said slowly, 'I'm not sure I'm following you.'

Laura shook her head, took a deep breath and said even more quietly than ever, 'There's something I've been meaning to tell you for a while now. Something about Claire that I think she would want you to know. But I was waiting for the right moment. I guess I've already started to blurt it out, so I might as well tell you the rest. Do you remember, you once asked me in Paris if I knew anything that would shed light on the reason Claire so hated men?'

'I remember.'

'Not long before she died, Claire confided in me, told me about her childhood, and what she told me was so horrific I don't know how she managed to live through it.'

Philippe frowned. 'Are you trying to tell me Claire suffered at the hands of her parents?'

'Yes, I am.'

'But why didn't she tell you before? Or me, when we were married?'

'Philippe, she was ashamed, embarrassed. That's what she said to me. You see, she was physically abused by her father. He used to beat her and her mother when he was drunk. Even when he wasn't. He treated her mother abominably. Aside from beating her, he was grossly unfaithful. Jack Benson was a regular dyed-in-the-wool womanizer. And at times he even sexually abused Claire. I suppose you could say she had plenty of reasons to mistrust and hate men.'

A terrible coldness had settled over Philippe as Laura had been speaking, and he could not shake it off. He felt icy inside and his heart ached for Claire. After a moment, he said slowly, 'I'd say she had more than enough reasons, yes. Poor Claire, poor darling. She was such a fragile, dainty little thing, and she must have been more so as a child. How could anyone beat her, hurt her? It's just horrendous, inhuman. Her father must've been a monster. Oh God, I can't bear to think of what she must have suffered.' He brought his hands up to his eyes, closed them for a moment, and when he eventually looked across at her Laura saw the tears glistening on his black lashes.

'She managed to hide it all very well,' Laura told him, speaking softly. 'And she managed to escape her father's hideous brutality when she was here at Rhondda Fach with us. In fact, she dealt with him very well when she was a little older. She threatened to expose him to my grandparents, and that curtailed his violent and disgusting activities.'

'If only she'd told me I would have understood. And perhaps I could have helped her in some way, Laura. How sad that Claire shut me out in the way she did. Perhaps . . . well, to be honest, I think she saw me as the enemy.'

'Oh I'm sure she didn't, not deep down. Not you, you're such a decent man, Philippe –' Laura stopped abruptly, cutting off her sentence, knowing better than to say another word.

Now wanting to change the subject, Philippe asked, 'Shall we walk over to the tennis court and see how the girls are doing out there?'

'Why not?' Laura answered, jumping up and heading for the door, no longer wishing to be alone with him.

Philippe had also risen, and as Laura passed him he caught hold of her arm, stopping her in her tracks. Staring into her bright blue eyes, he said, 'Thanks for telling me about Claire's

childhood, it explains so much. I'm glad you had the trust in
me to confide.'

Laura could only nod, wishing he would let go of her arm.
His touch was like an electric current running through her. She
knew she was vulnerable to him.

'It's been such a rotten year in so many ways, I don't really feel
like having a birthday dinner,' Laura said to Megan, giving her
a faint smile. 'Thanks, but no thanks, Gran.'

'But a birthday means you're actually starting a whole *new*
year in your life, and perhaps it might be a wonderful year for
you,' Megan pointed out, wondering how to make her change
her mind.

Laura did not answer. She got up and walked over to the
window and stood looking down the East River, her thoughts
on Philippe Lavillard. She sometimes wondered if Natasha suspected something, realized how she felt about her father, and
was trying to play the matchmaker. But it wasn't possible to be a
matchmaker if the other person wasn't interested. And certainly
Philippe wasn't interested in her. There was no special woman
in his life, Natasha had announced that only the other day.
Suddenly, Laura wondered why she had felt the need to say
this. Perhaps the girl *had* tuned into the way she felt about her
father. She was certainly bright enough. Thank God I don't have
to spend more than a couple of days in Vienna, Laura thought. I
can dash off to London once Rosa has received the painting.

'You seem very preoccupied with something, Laura,' Megan
said, cutting into her thoughts.

Laura swung around and nodded. 'I am a bit, Gran. Lots
of business is coming through the office these days. I'm really
snowed under.'

'Oh dear, only business. And I was hoping it might be a young
man you were thinking about.'

'Don't be silly.' Laura walked back to join her grandmother on
the sofa. 'What time do I have for a man, young or old? I work like

a dog, I have to travel constantly to London for Sir Maxim, and I'm bringing up a fifteen-year-old. Soon to be sixteen, actually. That's the birthday party we should be planning, Gran. Natasha's Sweet Sixteen bash.'

'We will, later. At the moment, I'm thinking of *your* birthday. And I do want to give this dinner. It'll be small. Just you and me and Natasha, and Rosa of course. Unless you'd like me to invite anyone else. What about Alison and Tony?'

'Alison and Tony won't come, they're not very social these days since Alison's pregnant again. No, there's nobody else I want.'

'Nobody else at all?' Megan pressed hopefully.

'Not really.'

'Definitely no young man.'

'No, Gran,' Laura said, and laughed for the first time in days.

'But you have agreed that I can give a dinner for you, haven't you, darling girl?'

'I guess you sort of trapped me into it, you wily old thing you, and why not? But please, no birthday cake.'

'Absolutely not. And no balloons either,' Megan quipped, keeping a poker face.

'When are you planning on giving this dinner, Gran?'

'That's up to you. Are you going off to see Sir Maximilian West this month?'

'No. He and his wife will be travelling. However, I do have to go to Vienna with Rosa. At the end of this month, so I can fit in with you.'

'Then I shall have your thirty-third birthday *on* your birthday. That's the way it's meant to be, you know.'

31

'Happy birthday, Laura!' everyone cried, lifting their champagne flutes and sipping the Dom Perignon.

Laura smiled and said, 'Thank you. And thank you, Grandma Megan, for my wonderful dinner party. Everything was absolutely beautiful.'

'My pleasure,' Megan said, and pushing back her chair she continued, 'now, let's go into the sitting room. It's time to open your presents, Laura dear.'

'Oh yes, let's do that!' Natasha cried, jumping up. 'Come on, Laura, come on, Dad.'

Not wanting to linger near Philippe, Laura got up quickly and hurried into the sitting room with Natasha. From the moment Philippe arrived at her grandmother's apartment, she had felt queasy inside, shaky. He had been a surprise. She certainly hadn't expected him to fly in from Atlanta for her birthday. In a sense, she was pleased he had made the effort, touched even; but the saner part of her told her not to be. After all, what did it signify? Tonight was Friday, and he frequently came to New York to be with Natasha at the weekend.

Natasha ran to her, caught hold of her hand as she was entering the room and said, 'Sit here, Laura, on the sofa. I'll sit next to you and hand you your gifts.'

'All right,' Laura answered, and did as she was told.

Megan and Rosa followed more slowly, escorted by Philippe. Once they were seated, he went and stood near the fireplace, watching the proceedings from this vantage point. He hoped Laura liked his gift which he had found in an antique shop last weekend when he'd been in New York. At the time he had been quite certain it would please her. Unexpectedly, he was no longer sure. But oh how he wanted it to be exactly right.

Automatically, his eyes were drawn to her, as they always were when she was in the same room. To him she was the most beautiful of women, not only on the outside but inside as well. Laura was a very rare being, a woman of integrity, understanding and compassion. There weren't many like her in this world.

He loved Laura Valiant. He had loved her for many months now, perhaps even longer than that, if he were honest with himself. That cold day in December, almost two years ago now, he had wanted to prolong his contact with her in the d'Orsay Museum. But his mother had arrived, and their conversation had been interrupted. And suddenly he was hurrying after Rosa, wondering when he would see Laura again. Now he wondered how to get their relationship on a different footing. Perhaps he could attempt it this weekend. If not, it would have to wait until he moved permanently to New York. He couldn't wait to be in the same city as Laura ...

'Thank you, Rosa,' Laura exclaimed. 'The Renoir book is marvellous.' She went to kiss Rosa, then returned to her place on the sofa.

'This is from Grandma Megan,' Natasha announced, handing Laura a small package.

Ripping off the paper, Laura found herself holding a worn leather jewellery box. As she peeked inside she saw a narrow ring set with diamond chips, and taking it out she slipped it on her little finger.

'Oh Grandma, it's beautiful. Thank you!' Laura went to hug Megan.

'Your grandfather gave it to me many years ago,' Megan said, 'and I was sure it would fit you.'

'And this is from me.' Natasha presented her with a long slender box. Laura looked up at Natasha, who was sitting on the arm of the sofa, smiled, then tore off the wrapping paper. Out of the long cardboard box she lifted a white chiffon scarf handpainted with pink peonies. 'Why it's lovely,' Laura said, reaching for Natasha.

Natasha bent down and they embraced. 'I painted it myself, and I chose the peonies because they're your favourite flower. And now here's your final gift. From Dad.'

Laura's eyes flew to Philippe standing near the fireplace. He half smiled and nodded. 'I hope you like it,' he muttered, feeling suddenly awkward and a little embarrassed.

'I'm sure I will,' Laura responded, carefully taking off the ribbon and the paper. Again, it was an old leather jewellery box, and with a sudden rush of excitement Laura lifted the lid. She found herself staring at one of the most beautiful cameo brooches she had ever seen. 'Why it's exquisite, Philippe,' she exclaimed and rose, slowly walking across to the fireplace. She gave him a quick peck on the cheek, stepped away from him swiftly, and added, 'Thank you so much.'

Natasha said, 'I knew something was missing. And it's music. I won't be a minute.' She rushed out of the sitting room, humming under her breath.

Megan said, 'She's a whirlwind at times, but then I suppose I was too, when I was her age. Now, Laura, let me look at Philippe's gift.'

Laura took it over to her grandmother and showed it to her, and then to Rosa. They both exclaimed over it, and Laura said again, 'It's very beautiful, Philippe.'

He merely smiled at her.

The strains of music filled the room as Natasha came back and said, 'There, that's better, isn't it, Grandma Megan? You did say you wanted music tonight.'

'I did indeed, child, and it's perfect.'

Natasha, now standing next to her father near the fireplace, whispered, 'You should ask Laura to dance, Dad, it's her birthday after all.'

Philippe looked at Natasha and asked in a low voice, 'But where would we dance?'

'Out there in the front hall. Near the dining room.'

Philippe followed the direction of her gaze, and nodded. But then he hesitated, and did not move until Natasha squeezed his arm and whispered, 'Go on, Dad.'

Crossing the room, Philippe came to a stop at the sofa, looked down at Laura and gave a small half-laugh. 'Since the music's playing just for you, for your birthday, would you come and dance with me, Laura?'

'I'd love to,' she responded. Together they walked through the doorway of the sitting room and out into the front hall.

Taking hold of her hand, Philippe put his arm around her, and brought her closer, then slowly they moved around the marble floor, not saying a word to each other.

Laura was shaking inside. She could hardly breathe.

Philippe was as nervous as she was, but he managed to conceal this as they danced. When the music came to an end he said, 'There, that wasn't so bad, was it?' He dropped her hand, stepped away from her.

'No it wasn't,' Laura replied, also moving away.

They strolled back to the sitting room, only to find it empty. They heard voices and laughter coming from the library and turned to face each other in puzzlement. Just as they did so another disc started to play, and strains of a romantic ballad echoed throughout the apartment.

Philippe, looking down at Laura, said, 'Do you think we're the victims of a conspiracy?'

'I don't feel like a victim,' Laura murmured. 'Do you?'

'Not at all,' Philippe answered, and taking hold of her hand he led her out of the room, back to the front hall where, miraculously, the lights had been dimmed.

They stood in the middle of the marble floor, staring at each other. Their eyes locked. Neither of them could look away. And then before he could stop himself Philippe took a step closer and pulled Laura into his arms. Their mouths met; she clung to him. He kissed her passionately, and she responded ardently. When they finally pulled away, he said quietly, 'Dare I hope you feel the same way I do, Laura Valiant?'

'I think so. But how *do* you feel?' she asked, her eyes on his face.

'I'm crazily, madly, in love with you,' he answered.

'Then we feel the same way,' she said, and moved back into his arms. 'And that's the way I'm going to feel for the rest of my life.'

'The rest of *our* lives,' he murmured against her hair.